Edward Higginson

The Spirit of the Bible

Vol. II

SALZWASSER
VERLAG

Edward Higginson

The Spirit of the Bible

Vol. II

Reprint of the original, first published in 1863.

1st Edition 2022 | ISBN: 978-3-37500-279-4

Verlag (Publisher): Salzwasser Verlag GmbH, Zeilweg 44, 60439 Frankfurt, Deutschland
Vertretungsberechtigt (Authorized to represent): E. Roepke, Zeilweg 44, 60439 Frankfurt, Deutschland
Druck (Print): Books on Demand GmbH, In de Tarpen 42, 22848 Norderstedt, Deutschland

THE

SPIRIT OF THE BIBLE.

VOL. II.

THE

SPIRIT OF THE BIBLE;

OR

THE NATURE AND VALUE

OF THE

JEWISH AND CHRISTIAN SCRIPTURES

DISCRIMINATED,

In an Analysis of their several Books.

BY

EDWARD HIGGINSON.

"THE LETTER KILLETH; THE SPIRIT MAKETH ALIVE."

VOL. II.

CONTAINING THE APOCRYPHA AND THE NEW TESTAMENT.

Second Edition, Revised.

LONDON

1863.

PREFACE TO FIRST EDITION.

I DID not mean to have a Preface to this second volume; nor, indeed, shall I now *write* one. But I find one written for me in the observations of a recent *Quarterly Reviewer*, so admirably maintaining the free and natural principles of thought upon which these volumes proceed in the investigation of Scripture, that I cannot refrain from thus adopting them into my pages.

I do not desire to protect myself, by this means, under a reputed *orthodox* authority, though it may perhaps encourage some of my readers to free thought. To a true man, the terms *orthodox* and *heterodox* are simply indifferent. They ought to be quite unknown in Biblical criticism, because they have no intrinsic meaning, but merely express the partialities and prejudices of those who use them. I cite the *Quarterly Review*, simply in order to express the gratification with which I mark the growing prevalence of that rational and self-evident, but much dissembled, principle: That the Scriptures must be studied just like all other ancient books, with all the aids of literature and science, if we would find what they really contain that distinguishes them from other books. This cannot be more broadly and fearlessly stated than in the *Quarterly Review* of September last, in an article on the well-known book entitled, *The Eclipse of Faith;* to the clever and dashing author of which the Reviewer administers a serious rebuke for his irrational and dangerous assumption of the verbal inspiration of Scripture, while arguing against Mr. Newman's *Phases of Faith.* The *Quarterly Reviewer* says:

"But there is one important topic of the 'Phases' which is less successfully met in the 'Eclipse.' Mr. Newman dwells much upon the historical, geological and exegetical mistakes which he supposes to be found in Scripture, and describes the process by which he was himself led to unbelief through his discovery that, in such points, the Bible was not infallible. He relates how at this period he was stopped in his descent for a time by a conversation with Dr. Arnold, who, while allowing Scripture to be fallible in human science, maintained its infallibility in moral and spiritual truth. Subsequently, however, Mr. Newman found a difficulty in drawing any line which should accurately separate the domain of science from that of religion, and he was thus led to reject the Bible altogether. In the present day this is a very common road to unbelief. The difficulty may be encountered in two ways: either by denying the existence of any mistakes in Scripture, or maintaining, with Neander, Tholuck and Arnold, that the occurrence of such mistakes does not detract from the religious inspiration of the writers. The former is the view taken by Mr. Rogers. He contends, in intire agreement with Mr. Newman, that a distinction between the Divine and human contents of Scripture is impossible,—that historical inaccuracy cannot co-exist with religious infallibility. 'Men will think it strange,' he says, 'that Divine aid should not have gone a little farther, and, since the destined revelation was to be embedded in history, illustrated by imagination, enforced by argument, and expressed in human language, its authors should have been left liable to destroy the substance by perpetual blunders as to the form.' Hence he concludes that, textual and transcriptional errors excepted, the whole of Scripture is infallibly accurate, and that all its writers were miraculously preserved from the possibility of error, whether physiological, geological, astronomical, historical or exegetical.

"The argument relied on, it must be observed, is here intirely *à priori*. 'Men would *expect* that a revelation should be infallible in all respects; it would be *desirable* that it should be so; it would involve us in great perplexities if it were not so.' Yet surely, in a matter of this kind, it is our duty to investigate the facts before we lay down so peremptory a conclusion. Having the most cogent reasons for believing the Bible to be a revelation from God, we should carefully examine what its construction and character actually is, and not permit ourselves to decide dogmatically what it ought to have been. If we find that there are historical discrepancies and scientific inaccuracies in the canonical books, it is vain to say that their occurrence is perplexing, and it is worse than vain to explain them away, as some commentators have done, by subterfuge and evasion. We will not venture dogmatically to assert, in contradiction to the opinion of Mr. Rogers, that the apparent mistakes in Scripture are absolutely incapable of such an explanation as would vindicate them from the charge of error; but it is certain that those who have devoted the most patient investigation to exegetical study, are the most thoroughly convinced that there are some cases which do not admit of such a possibility. This is now so generally admitted, that it is acknowledged even in the standard educational works of orthodox divinity. For example: in the edition of the Greek Testament published for collegiate use by Mr. Alford, whom no one will accuse of want of reverence for the Bible, or the articles of our most holy faith, there occurs the following sentence: 'In the last apology of Stephen, which he spoke being full of the Holy Ghost, and with Divine influence beaming from his countenance, we have, *at least, two demonstrable historical mistakes;* and the occurrence of similar ones in the Gospels does not in any way affect the inspiration or the veracity of the Evangelists.' (*Alford's Testament,* Vol. I., *Prolegomena.*) Nor have Mr. Alford's most orthodox reviewers excepted against this statement. Such being the case, it is surely very dangerous to maintain that *historical* infallibility is essential to the inspiration of the Scriptural writers. This belief, if unfounded, exposes the faith of its votaries to tremble at every German commentary, every scientific treatise, and every fresh discovery of Egyptian hieroglyphics, and it is but too likely to bring them to the conclusion which Mr. Newman draws from the same premises.

"Moreover, the apostles themselves do not lead us to suppose them infallible in matters of *human* knowledge. They speak of themselves as 'earthen vessels,' though employed to contain a heavenly treasure. They call themselves 'ambassadors' charged with a message from God; and in the case of ambassadors from an earthly sovereign, the credentials would not be invalidated, nor the substantial accuracy of the communication rendered doubtful, by mistakes on details irrelevant to the substance of their commission. Even looking at the question *à priori*, we see no reason why men should have expected a revelation of moral and spiritual truth to supersede the researches of history or to anticipate the discoveries of science. Nay, as a fact, the heathen philosopher who most earnestly desired such a revelation, expressly guards against such expectations. He tells his disciples to expect no revelation from heaven concerning matters open to human investigation, while at the same time he encourages them to hope for Divine communications on subjects beyond the scope of man's discovery." (*Quarterly Rev., Sept.* 1854, pp. 473-4.)

It is quite refreshing to read the avowal of such principles of sacred criticism in a book widely circulated and trusted. Their more general adoption is the only source of solid Christian conviction. Tacit unbelief reigns in default of them. The assailants of Revealed Religion never assail these views of it; but, on the contrary (with more policy than honesty), assume the high orthodox views of Scripture as the only ones admitted among Christians, and content themselves with a wretched triumph over the folly and weakness of such false pretensions. The citadel is still untouched by such attacks, as it is undefended by such advocates. Its real strength is ignorantly misunderstood by the latter, and wilfully discredited by the former.

CONTENTS.

THE CHRISTIAN SCRIPTURES, OR BOOKS OF THE NEW COVENANT.

THE APOCRYPHA;

OR,

GREEK JEWISH SCRIPTURES.

THE APOCRYPHA.

This title, which literally means *hidden*, and seems intended to describe these books as of obscure origin or doubtful authorship, does not correctly nor sufficiently intimate their real character. It may be true that the authorship of almost all of them is unknown; but so is that of many books of the Old Testament. Who can tell us the origin or the author of the book of Joshua, or Judges, or Kings, or Chronicles, or Job, or Ruth, or Esther? Yet these books are not "called Apocrypha." Plainly, then, *Apocrypha* is not a good descriptive name for the set of books which now follow. They have, in short, a distinctive character of their own, being (with the exception of one which is in Latin, and probably more recent than the rest) the

GREEK JEWISH SCRIPTURES,

and belonging chiefly to the Alexandrian period of literature. They hold the same kind of relation to the older Hebrew literature, as the Alexandrian Greek writers in general do to the earlier poets and historians of Greece proper; with this specialty in the case of the former authors, that they had acquired a new language with their new country, whereas the Greeks brought their own language thither. This general account of the "books called Apocrypha," has been already in substance given (Vol. I. pp. 11, 12). We have now to enter into the subject a little more fully. The Church of England, quoting Jerome, says that "the Church doth read these books for example of life and instruction of manners; but yet doth it not apply them to establish any doctrine" (Article vi.). And Lessons are read from the books of Wisdom and Ecclesiasticus chiefly, but also from less edifying books, such as *Bel and the Dragon*, *Judith* and *Susanna*.

The conquests of Alexander, and the kingdoms founded by his generals after his death, were the means of diffusing the Greek language (as a written, where it was not also a spoken, language) throughout Egypt, Asia Minor and Syria, and through remoter countries in a less degree. This language thus occupied for several centuries the same position in the world's literature, as a still living language, which was afterwards held (in the middle ages) by the Latin, as a dead tongue studied throughout Europe. It was the literary language of the whole civilized world,—written, of course (like the Latin afterwards), in very different degrees of purity by different nations and individuals, and now presenting to the scholar a rich store of historical facts and national characteristics, as safely imbedded in forms of speech as fossils are in their geological strata.

Egypt was the first consolidated and the soonest and most permanently tranquil of the new kingdoms that arose upon Alexander's death. The first three Ptolemies, through the greater part of a century, devoted their attention to the encouragement of literature. The first and second of the race, Soter and Philadelphus, collected the celebrated Alexandrian libraries; and the third, Euergetes, continued to patronize learned men. In the long unsettled state of the other Greek kingdoms, including the fallen mother country herself, learned men resorted in great numbers to Alexandria, thankful to pursue their philosophical or literary studies under the protection, if not the more active patronage, of the Ptolemies,—the great library giving them hitherto unheard-of facilities as readers, and the papyrus new advantages for writing.

The Jews were already numerous in Egypt, where many had taken refuge in the times of the Assyrian and Babylonian conquests of their own land, and at various times subsequently. In the time of the first Ptolemy (who held Palestine in subjection for some years, and in whose kingdom it was included by treaty after the battle of Ipsus, B.C. 301), many more were added to the number of the Jews in Egypt, some through voluntary and some through forced immigration. Alexandria thus became, during the next few centuries, the place of meeting between the Hebrew and the Greek culture; and the majestic theology and elevated religious spirit of the former were thus made widely known to the civilized world. The Jews, whether simply in order to recommend their own noble literature to the notice of their lively and philosophical Greek neighbours, or also because many of their own nation were becoming better acquainted with the Greek than with the Hebrew language, translated the Scriptures of the Old Covenant into Greek in the reigns of the first and second Ptolemy. And what we have of their additional literature written during this period, is also (with one exception) in the Greek language; though some parts are supposed by some learned men to have been produced at first in Hebrew (probably in Palestine), and then to have been translated into Greek in Alexandria. Whether this may have been the case or not with certain books of the

Apocrypha, the Greek is *to us* their original language, as no Hebrew original now exists.

To an age of literary or artistic eminence, in any country, there generally succeeds an age of imitation. The great poets, orators or historians, like the great artists, of one period have many copyists in the next, if not in their own. And if a national literature, on being transplanted into another country, is able to put forth any second bloom, it is to be expected that this should be but a feeble representation of the first.

It was so with the Greek literature of the Alexandrian period. The characteristic studies of that age were different from those of classical Greece. They were chiefly grammar and criticism, geography, natural history and natural science, which do not furnish the most genial atmosphere for poetry and genius. To the Alexandrian critics the world is indebted for the preservation of a large amount of earlier Greek literature, which would otherwise have been lost. Euclid, the geometrician, is the scientific glory of that age and country. The Alexandrian poets were chiefly of the didactic and altogether of the learned sort; and didactic or learned poetry is anything but poetical. Philosophy (in the Greek sense of abstract, metaphysical speculation) having been derived originally by the Greeks from Egypt, now returned thither from her sojourn in the schools of Socrates, Plato, Epicurus and Zeno, to gain new and strange admixtures with Egyptian superstition, and to force herself into yet more unnatural union with Judaism in the first instance, and afterwards with Christianity.

This Alexandrian period of Greek literature abounded also in fictitious compositions for the purpose of deception (among which the writings of Euhemerus are notorious); and the example of the Alexandrian Greeks in this respect seems not to have been altogether lost upon the Alexandrian Jews. In Greece proper, indeed, as well as in Alexandria, it was the practice of the later rhetoricians to write (by way of exercise, but also by way of experiment upon public discernment) speeches such as might have been spoken by Pericles, Thucydides, or other celebrated men. And among the Jews of the Greek period we find an avowed but anonymous imitator of the "Wisdom," or wise sayings, of Solomon; and another obvious imitator, though in his own name, Jesus the son of Sirach.

The books of the Apocrypha are of very various kinds; some, historical and biographical, or at least in the form of history and biography; others, poetical. The chief part of them profess to belong, in point of subject-matter, to the periods already embraced in the Old Testament, as additions to its histories or to its didactic and devotional poetry. The only exceptions are Ecclesiasticus, or the Wisdom of the Son of Sirach, avowedly belonging to the age of the Ptolemies; and the books of the Maccabees, containing the history of the Jews in Palestine during that most eventful and truly heroic period, their wars with Syria. In briefly describing and analyzing each of these books, there is no clear reason for taking them in any other order than the very miscellaneous one in which they stand in the common Bible.

1 AND 2 ESDRAS.

IN the English Protestant Bible, the two books of Esdras stand at the head of "the Books called Apocrypha."

Esdras is only the Greek and Latin name for the Hebrew *Ezra*. And as the Hebrew book of Nehemiah is called by the Jews, and by the Greek and Romish Churches, 2 *Ezra*, these two Apocryphal books are sometimes reckoned as 3 *and* 4 *Ezra* respectively. (See Vol. I. p. 305.)

This first book of ESDRAS is written in Greek, and is merely a free translation of the latter part of the Chronicles, the chief part of Ezra, and certain portions of Nehemiah, with a few original additions to be presently described. The second book is not to be found in Greek, but only in Latin, and is of considerably later date than the time of Christ.

No section of the Christian church regards the latter of these books as canonical. The Greek Church admits the first among its Scriptures. The Romish Church (which accepts all the other books of the Apocrypha, without any distinction between them and the Hebrew Scriptures of the Old Testament) admits neither of these. Luther did not translate either of them in publishing his German Bible. They are usually passed by with little or no attention by commentators and critics,—the one as being scarcely more than a transcript from other books; the other as a feeble Latin exercise upon Hebrew ideas, proclaiming its own failure and its palpably modern origin. Still they are interesting and instructive in their way; and it is at least desirable that the scriptural student should know what they really are.

That the first book of Esdras is really a *recoction* of certain parts of Chronicles, Ezra and Nehemiah, must strike even the English reader. Let him compare any of the corresponding portions (as arranged below), and he will find the order of thought in almost every sentence identical, and the mere expressions varied just to such a degree as will be explained at once by supposing the original Hebrew, which had been translated carefully into Greek by the Seventy interpreters at Alexandria, to have been used again more freely, or more carelessly, by some book-maker in later times. Our English books of Chronicles, Ezra and Nehemiah, are, in fact, careful translations from the original Hebrew, and our first book of Esdras from the free or careless Greek version; so that the Greek of 1 Esdras may be described as differing from the Greek of the corresponding parts of the Septuagint, in the same degree as the English Esdras does from the English Chronicles, Ezra and Nehemiah.

1 Esdras i. 1—ii. 15 corresponds to 2 Chron. xxxv. xxxvi. and Ezra i.
rest of ii. „ Ezra iv. 7—.
iii. iv. are original.
v. corresponds to Ezra ii.—iv. 5 and Nehem. vii. viii.
(but varies from both in the enumeration of families).
vi.—ix. 36 corresponds to Ezra v. to end of the book.
ix. 38 to end „ Nehem. viii. 1—12.

The third and fourth chapters being the only original part, we naturally suppose that it was for the sake of introducing them that the writer has reproduced the rest. And what are their contents? They exhibit the later Jewish taste for *parables* of the enigmatical kind, laboured and wire-drawn, if not far-fetched and unnatural, such as marks the imitative and declining period of a literature. The legend itself related in these chapters is very improbable, though Josephus, in repeating it and overlaying it with rhetorical ornament after his manner, smooths its introduction somewhat more artistically than the pseudo-Esdras had done. (Joseph. Ant. B. xi. Ch. iii.) It is the story of the Jewish prince-royal, Zerubbabel, contending in wise sayings with two other young men of king Darius's body-guard, and the king deciding in favour of the first and granting him a boon in consequence,—which boon is, that the king will remember his vow to rebuild Jerusalem. The wise sayings, by maintaining which the young men severally pleaded for the royal favour, were these: "The first wrote, Wine is the strongest. The second wrote, The King is the strongest. The third wrote, Women are the strongest; but above all things, Truth beareth away the victory." This third was Zerubbabel. His illustrations of his double topic prevailed. He was proclaimed "the king's cousin," and bidden to ask what he chose besides the promised honour. Such is the legend added by later Jewish taste to the simple fact recorded in Ezra (vi.), that, after the hindering of the building of the temple during the reign of Artaxerxes (Cambyses), it was resumed on the accession of Darius. This book may have been produced any time during the Alexandrian period, before the time of Josephus, who was born A.D. 37. It was meant, doubtless, as an improvement upon the more sober history in the Hebrew and Septuagint Scriptures.

The SECOND book of ESDRAS is a palpable forgery of very late date. The mere English reader is struck with finding in it a number of expressions and ideas which the Jews never could have had till after the Christian era. "My son Jesus," "My son Christ," descriptions never found in Jewish prophecy, are introduced here. The doctrine of the resurrection is repeatedly cited. The entailed curse of Adam, as represented here, is many steps in advance even of Paul's doctrine on that subject, and evidently growing fast towards the ultimate orthodox idea. And there are many expressions which seem taken from passages in the New Testament, as well as those which are evidently founded upon the Old. Some of these expressions recal to us the language of the Gospels, many that of Paul, and some emblematic and visionary thoughts are very like those of John in his Revelation, while yet more are evidently imitations of the book of Daniel. As if conscious of the want of internal evidence, the author studiously begins by intitling his performance, "The Second Book of the Prophet Esdras, the Son of Saraias, the Son of Azarias," &c., with his pedigree traced up to Aaron; whereas no such title is prefixed either to the book of Ezra, or that of Nehemiah, or to the first of Esdras.

But what must we think of a book written originally in *Latin*, yet professing to be the work of Ezra? Did Ezra speak Latin, or the Jews of his day (B.C. 450) understand it? In his day the Jews spoke and wrote Chaldee, a mere dialect of their old Hebrew, not differing more from it than modern Scotch does from English, if so much. From and after about B.C. 300, they spoke and wrote Greek increasingly, till it became almost as common among them as Hebrew,—the Septuagint translation of their Hebrew Scriptures being completed probably about B.C. 280. But a Latin or Roman era of Jewish literature never occurred. The Greek language was only abandoned to resume the Hebrew in the Talmuds and Targums. In all probability, therefore, this Latin Esdras was not written till after the Scriptures of both the Old and New Testament had been translated into Latin, perhaps two or three hundred years after Christ. Its author must, apparently, have been either a Jewish Christian impressed with the expectation of a coming millennium and the reign of Christ in Jerusalem, or else (which is almost the same thing) he must have been a Jew with his Messianic ideas accommodating themselves in part to the past earthly ministry of Jesus Christ, while further compensating themselves by the anticipation of a New Jerusalem yet to be established, and to receive the allegiance of the Gentile world. These hopes he has seen fit, however, to represent in the person of Ezra, as if they had been expressed by him to his fellow-Jews in Babylon 600 years before, when exhorting them to follow him and rebuild Jerusalem. We need not be surprised that a number of anachronisms occur in his allusions to facts, as palpable as those in his theological ideas above mentioned. The writer has indeed shewn but little skill in his fiction; and the whole interest of his performance consists in our taking it as a picture of certain ideas of the early Jewish Christian church, mixed with those of the times of Ezra, to which they are fictitiously and grotesquely referred.

The book scarcely merits minute analysis here. The word of the Lord comes to Esdras, bidding him shew his people their sinful deeds (ch. i.); and a great part of the book is devoted to reproaches of this kind, in imitation of the prophets *before* and *during* the captivity, but quite unlike the tone of those who hailed and led the return. How strange that, when the second Isaiah had been all exultation and hope, and Haggai and Zechariah all encouragement, Esdras should be all reproach and terror again, while still preaching the return! The following passage, in which he claims, Moses-like, to have had his divine commission in Horeb, is a favourable specimen of the style of the book, and contains hints of its peculiar doctrines of the resurrection, the New Jerusalem or millennium (or whatever else we may call it), the reception of the Gentiles, &c.

"I Esdras received a charge of the Lord upon the Mount Horeb, that I should go unto Israel; but when I came unto them they set me at nought, and despised the commandment of the Lord. And therefore I say unto you, O ye heathen, that hear and understand, Look for your Shepherd, he shall give you everlasting rest; for he is nigh at hand, that shall come in the end of the world. Be ready to the reward of the kingdom, for the everlasting light shall shine upon you for evermore. Flee the shadow of this world, receive the joyfulness of your glory: I testify my Saviour openly. O receive the gift that is given you, and be glad, giving thanks unto him that hath called you to the heavenly kingdom. Arise up and stand, behold the number of those that be sealed in the feast of the Lord, which are departed from the shadow of the world, and have received glorious garments of the Lord. Take thy number, O Sion, and shut up those of thine that are clothed in white, which have fulfilled the law of the Lord. The number of thy children whom thou longedst for is fulfilled: beseech the power of the Lord, that thy people which have been called from the beginning may be hallowed. I Esdras saw upon the Mount Sion a great people, whom I could not number, and they all praised the Lord with songs. And in the midst of them there was a young man of a high stature, taller than all the rest, and upon every one of their heads he set crowns, and was more exalted, which I marvelled at greatly. So I asked the angel, and said, Sir, what are these? He answered and said unto me, These be they that have put off the mortal clothing, and put on the immortal, and have confessed the name of God: now are they crowned, and receive palms. Then said I unto the angel, What young person is it that crowneth them, and giveth them palms in their hands? So he answered and said unto me, It is the Son of God, whom they have confessed in the world. Then began I greatly to commend them that stood so stiffly for the name of the Lord. Then the angel said unto me, Go thy way, and tell my people what manner of things, and how great wonders of the Lord thy God thou hast seen" (ii. 33—48).

The third chapter inadvertently exposes the unhistorical character of the book by dating its visions as having happened "in the thirtieth year after the ruin of the city," which was one hundred and eleven years before

Ezra's return to Palestine! The rest of the book is a series of pretended visions, in which Esdras confers with the Lord, or with the angel Uriel (a more modern impersonation not known among the angels of the book of Daniel), in a style of minute and loquacious familiarity such as is never found in the Hebrew Scriptures, running over the customary topics of Jewish history and prophecy, and lamenting the captivity, but without anything specially appropriate to the assumed period. But even here occurs a passage of considerable beauty in reference to Esdras's desire to pry into the secret counsels of the Most High:

"And the angel that was sent unto me, whose name was Uriel, gave me an answer, and said, Thy heart hath gone too far in this world, and thinkest thou to comprehend the way of the Most High? Then said I, Yea, my lord: and he answered me and said, I am sent to shew thee three ways, and to set forth three similitudes before thee: whereof if thou canst declare me one, I will shew thee also the way that thou desirest to see, and I shall shew thee from whence the wicked heart cometh. And I said, Tell on, my lord. Then said he unto me, Go thy way, weigh me the weight of the fire, or measure me the blast of the wind, or call me again the day that is past. Then answered I, and said, What man is able to do that, that thou shouldst ask such things of me? And he said unto me, If I should ask thee how great dwellings are in the midst of the sea, or how many springs are in the beginning of the deep, or how many springs are above the firmament, or which are the out-goings of Paradise: peradventure thou wouldst say unto me, I never went down into the deep, nor as yet into hell, neither did I ever climb up into heaven. Nevertheless, now have I asked thee but only of the fire, and wind, and of the day where-through thou hast passed, and of things from which thou canst not be separated, and yet canst thou give me no answer of them. He said moreover unto me, Thine own things, and such as are grown up with thee, canst thou not know? How should thy vessel then be able to comprehend the way of the Highest, and the world being now outwardly corrupted, to understand the corruption that is evident in my sight? Then said I unto him, It were better that we were not at all, than that we should live still in wickedness, and to suffer, and not to know wherefore. He answered me, and said, I went into a forest into a plain, and the trees took counsel, and said, Come let us go and make war against the sea, that it may depart away before us, and that we may make us more woods. The floods of the sea also in like manner took counsel, and said, Come, let us go up, and subdue the woods of the plain, that there also we may make us another country. The thought of the wood was in vain, for the fire came and consumed it. The thought of the floods of the sea came likewise to nought, for the sand stood up and stopped them. If thou wert judge now betwixt these two, whom wouldst thou begin to justify, or whom wouldst thou condemn? I answered and said, Verily it is a foolish thought that they have both devised, for the ground is given unto the wood, and the sea also hath his place to bear his floods. Then answered he me, and said, Thou hast given a right judgment, but why judgest thou not thyself also? For like as the ground is given unto the wood, and the sea to his floods, even so they that dwell upon the earth may understand nothing but that which is upon the earth: and he that dwelleth above the heavens, may only understand the things that are above the height of the heavens" (iv. 1—21).

The ideas of a resurrection and ensuing millennium come vaguely out in the seventh, eighth and ninth chapters. Then in the tenth, a vision of a woman weeping in a field and suddenly vanishing, and a city appearing on the spot, is meant to denote the restoration from captivity. In the eleventh and twelfth, a vision is attempted in evident imitation and avowed completion of the visions of Daniel. The thirteenth is a vision of the Son of God coming out of the sea, and standing on the top of Mount Zion, to destroy wicked nations and to restore the ten tribes to their own land. The fourteenth chapter presents that absurd and rash fiction by which many modern

Jews are still content to peril the authenticity of their oldest Scriptures. Esdras sits under an oak, and a voice comes to him out of a bush, in express imitation of the commission of Moses, to whose work in the past that of Esdras in the future is compared. He is ordered to go to the people and reprove them; but asks how future generations shall be instructed, now that "the Law is burnt." Then he is bidden to prepare a great number of box-wood writing tablets, and dictate as he shall be inspired, to five scribes mentioned by name; who accordingly, in forty days and nights, during which Esdras never ceased speaking, write two hundred and four books, the last seventy of which are to be kept for "the wise," and the rest to be read by both "worthy and unworthy." The absurdity of this story is only paralleled by the serious damage it inflicts upon the real authenticity of the Hebrew Scriptures, while attempting to give them a fallacious authority. (We have alluded to it in Vol. I. p. 70.) The last two chapters contain vague denunciations against Egypt, Babylon, Asia (Minor) and Syria, and a description of general calamity, many of the images of which seem referable to Christ's prophecy of the destruction of Jerusalem. The book ends thus:

"Hear, O ye my beloved, saith the Lord: behold, the days of trouble are at hand, but I will deliver you from the same. Be ye not afraid, neither doubt, for God is your guide, and the guide of them who keep my commandments and precepts, saith the Lord God: let not your sins weigh you down, and let not your iniquities lift up themselves. Woe be unto them that are bound with their sins, and covered with their iniquities: like as a field is covered over with bushes, and the path thereof covered with thorns, that no man may travel through. It is left undressed, and is cast into the fire to be consumed therewith" (xvi. 74—78).

TOBIT

Is a very interesting family picture of a religious Jewish household in the time of the Assyrian captivity under Shalmanezer (called in this book of Tobit, "Enemessar, king of the Assyrians"). Whether this is essentially a real history, or a pure fiction, or a tale founded on fact, it is impossible to decide. Some things in it are fabulous enough; but the leading events are perfectly credible, and the spirit of the story is unexceptionably good and pure. Tobit in the Apocrypha, like Ruth among the Judges, is sweet and refreshing to read.

The original is in Greek, and may be referred with much probability to 100 or 200 years B.C., though it does not seem to have been known to Josephus. Some critics think the book was originally written in Hebrew; but the only Hebrew version now existing is a translation back again, of quite modern date. And the various other versions in Syriac, Chaldee and Latin, are singularly loose and diverse from each other. The Douay English version of the Roman Catholics differs in the same way from the English received version.

The story is evidently designed to illustrate the blessedness of a faithful adherence to the divine law. Tobit, and his wife Anna, and their son Tobias, are carried to Nineveh by the Assyrians (B.C. 722), where they resolutely observe the faith and practices of pious Jews, though all their kindred "did eat the bread of the Gentiles." Almsgiving is highly commended; a fact to which some minute critics point as shewing that the Pharisaic spirit had taken its rise before the time when this book was *written*, but which is equally appropriate, surely, to the time of its *action*, when so many poor countrymen in exile appealed to the generosity of the more prosperous. There are some beautiful passages on alms in iv. 7—11 and 16, 17, among other admirable precepts of the father to his son when leaving home:

"Give alms of thy substance: and when thou givest alms, let not thine eye be envious, neither turn thy face from any poor, and the face of God shall not be turned away from thee. If thou hast abundance, give alms accordingly: if thou have but a little, be not afraid to give according to that little. For thou layest up a good treasure for thyself against the day of necessity" (iv. 7—9).

This journey of young Tobias from Nineveh on the way to Rages in Media, on business for his father, under the guidance of the angel Raphael *incognito*, and his calling at Ecbatana and there marrying his kinswoman, Sara, forms the staple of the story. And it is full of nature and beauty, in spite of the occasionally perverted supernatural, which is perhaps not meant to be taken quite literally. The parental and filial feelings utter themselves truthfully; and we are charmed to find that "the young man's dog" is not forgotten, but goes with him and his angelic companion on their journey. This touch of nature is greatly admired in Salvator Rosa's representation of it to the sight. But the real artist is the writer of the book of Tobit.

The devotional parts of this book are to be commended for their simplicity and beauty; especially the marriage prayer of Tobias and Sara (viii. 4—8),* and Tobit's "prayer of rejoicing" in ch. xiii.

* "And after that they were both shut in together, Tobias rose out of the bed and said, Sister, arise, and let us pray that God would have pity on us. Then began Tobias to say, Blessed art thou, O God of our fathers, and blessed is thy holy and glorious name for ever: let the heavens bless thee, and all thy creatures. Thou madest Adam, and gavest him Eve his wife for a helper and stay. Of them came mankind. Thou hast said, It is not good that man should be alone; let us make unto him an aid like unto himself. And now, O Lord, I take not this my sister for lust, but uprightly; therefore mercifully ordain that we may become aged together. And she said with him, Amen."

There are various matters of theological interest in this book, exhibiting the growth of opinion which was taking place in the interval between the Hebrew and the Christian Scriptures.

The doctrine of angels is evidently maturing fast. Raphael, not known by name in the Hebrew Scriptures, is the guardian of the youth on his journey. And while seen visibly by men, he is an unsubstantial form: "All these days I did appear unto you, but I did neither eat nor drink; but ye did see a vision" (xii. 19).* And then he vanished, to "go up to him that sent" him. Raphael is "one of the seven holy angels which present the prayers of the saints, and which go in and out before the glory of the Holy One" (xii. 15). He is sent, in answer to prayer, to cure Tobit of blindness, and to bind the evil spirit Asmodeus, who had a strange influence over the destiny of Sara, having destroyed seven bridegrooms in succession on the very nights of their marriage to her.

This evil spirit (δαιμόνιον, demon; not *diabolus*, devil) loves her, and hurts nobody but those who come to her (vi. 14). Tobit, directed by Raphael, drives him away, by the smell of burnt perfumes and of the liver of a certain marvellous fish, into the utmost parts of Egypt, where the angel binds him (viii. 2, 3). Here is the demoniac theory in process of growth, which Josephus afterwards describes, and which the New-Testament writers exhibit in the form of inward *possession*, rather than outward injury as here exhibited.

The fish which Tobias encountered when bathing in the Tigris (vi.), and which "would have devoured him"

* The Douay version has—"I seemed indeed to eat and to drink with you; but I use an invisible meat and drink, which cannot be seen by men." This is translated from the Latin Vulgate; our common version is from the Greek Septuagint; and this instance is an average specimen of the strange diversity between the two.

but that the angel encouraged him to "take the fish," and preserve its heart, liver and gall, for medicinal uses, seems to have been suggested to the writer by associations with Nineveh, as the former scene of Jonah's mission.

Tobit, grown old and about to die, is made to predict to his son the coming desolation of Jerusalem and the Temple, the restoration of the Jewish people, and the conversion of all nations from idolatry. This passage exhibits the Messianic expectation, therefore, as it existed one or two hundred years before Christ. Tobit ascribes to the prophet Jonah predictions which do not appear in the book of Jonah.

"Go into Media, my son, for I surely believe those things which Jonas the prophet spake of Nineveh; that it shall be overthrown, and that for a time peace shall rather be in Media; and that our brethren shall lie scattered in the earth from that good land; and Jerusalem shall be desolate, and the house of God in it shall be burned, and shall be desolate for a time; and that again God will have mercy on them, and bring them again into the land, where they shall build a temple, but not like to the first, until the time of that age be fulfilled; and afterward they shall return from all places of their captivity, and build up Jerusalem gloriously, and the house of God shall be built in it for ever, with a glorious building, as the prophets have spoken thereof. And all nations shall turn, and fear the Lord God truly, and shall bury their idols. So shall all nations praise the Lord, and his people shall confess God, and the Lord shall exalt his people; and all those which love the Lord God in truth and justice shall rejoice, shewing mercy to our brethren. And now, my son, depart out of Nineveh, because that those things which the prophet Jonas spake shall surely come to pass. But keep thou the law and the commandments, and shew thyself merciful and just, that it may go well with thee" (xiv. 4—9).

JUDITH.

THIS book is a transparent fiction, and is written in the worst Jewish taste; commending treachery and bloodshed in the person of a beautiful woman, as an acceptable service to God, when done for the deliverance of his people. Judith is Jael over again (or Debŏrah, who celebrates her deed); but Judith is premeditative instead of impulsive, and wants all the circumstances that give credibility to that story and lend excuse to that deed of the older time. (See Judges iv., v.)

The book dates itself in the twelfth year of Nebuchadnezzar, which was shortly after the destruction of Jerusalem; but the author soon forgets himself, and makes the Jews to be "newly returned from captivity" (iv. 3 and v. 19). Nebuchadnezzar, reigning in Nineveh, is at war with Arphaxad, king of the Medes, reigning in Ecbatane (here are anachronisms in profusion), and sends to all his western dominions, as far as Asia Minor and Egypt, for help; which being refused, he sends his general, Holofernes (quite an unknown personage), to avenge himself upon Cilicia, Damascus and Syria, and to slay all in Moab, Ammon, Judea and Egypt. Holofernes presently besieges Bethulia, in Judea (no such place was ever known); and when the people are about to capitulate, Judith intreats longer delay, and goes, arrayed in rich attire, with her maid-servant, to the camp of Holofernes, where her beauty fascinates the general, and whence she returns after a few days with his head. The besiegers flee away, and the Jews rejoice; Judith sings a thanksgiving in imitation of Deborah; and so the story ends with declaring, "And there was none that made the children of Israel any more afraid in the days of Judith, nor a long time after her death."

Such is the outline of this poor and immoral fiction.

It was probably intended—perhaps piously intended—to inculcate a lesson of national confidence towards the God of Israel. In that case, how mistaken the execution of a pious design! Luther thought it was a fiction, denoting the destiny of the Jewish people to overcome all their enemies. Some refer its origin to the time of Titus and the siege of Jerusalem, as explaining its composition by the too natural wishes that might, in such a time, be fathers to the thoughts.

The book is in Greek, and has one palpably Greek idea in it, namely, the allusion to the "sons of the Titans and the high giants" in Judith's song (xvi. 7). This proves it to be of late origin among the Greek Jewish literature. The "giants" are indeed mentioned also in the books of *Wisdom*, *Ecclesiasticus* and *Baruch*, and may be taken, perhaps, as the later Jewish interpretation of a word of disputed meaning in Genesis vi. 4, used in describing certain men of violence in very remote times. But this interpretation of their own Hebrew scripture may itself have grown in the Jewish mind through their becoming acquainted with the Greek ideas of the "heroic age;" and from that source alone can have come the name, as well as the idea, of the Titans. (See *Wisdom* xiv. 6; *Ecclus.* xvi. 7; *Baruch* iii. 26.)

THE REST OF THE CHAPTERS OF THE BOOK OF ESTHER,

WHICH ARE FOUND NEITHER IN THE HEBREW NOR IN THE CHALDEE.

THESE additions have an honest title, whatever we may think of the purpose of their unknown writer. They seem to have been intended to be inserted in suitable places in the original book of Esther, upon which they are just so many enlargements or paraphrases. Their main point of contrast with the original book of Esther, has been already mentioned in speaking of that book (Vol. I. pp. 306, 307). The directly religious allusions are here as ostentatious, as their absence in the former instance is remarkable. In the Douay version, as in Jerome's Latin Vulgate, these chapters are added to the Hebrew book of Esther, without being incorporated into it in their designed places. They form a clumsy patchwork any how.

As Josephus, in his History, implies some of these passages, they were certainly written before his time; and no doubt at Alexandria, during or after the time of Ptolemy and Cleopatra, as disclosed by the author himself in xi. 1. This would be shortly before the Christian era. It is curious to find this Alexandrian supplementer of Esther, changing Haman the Agagite (that is, we suppose, Amalekite) into a Macedonian (xvi. 10, 14), and making the Persian king fear lest his dominions should pass into the hands of the Macedonians,—a power well known to the writer of these chapters, but not on the stage of history at the time which he professes to describe. But there is a strange unconsciousness of the necessities of time and place in many of these later Jewish legends. They could scarcely be intended to be believed literally.

THE WISDOM OF SOLOMON; OR RATHER, WISDOM, BY SOLOMON.

THIS book is written in imitation of the Hebrew works of Solomon, by an unknown Greek author of the Alexandrian age, probably from one to two hundred years before Christ. Some have ascribed it, but without sufficient reason, to Philo, the learned Alexandrian Jew who flourished about half a century before the Christian era. Many of the philosophical ideas in it are such, indeed, as are found in Philo, but also occur in other philosophical writers of the period, who, like him, had imbibed deeply the peculiar notions of Plato, the most acute at once and most poetical of the Greek sages. Some of these ideas recommended themselves to the more speculative of the Jews by a seeming, though somewhat remote and fanciful, analogy to certain religious ideas already attained by themselves; and Philo presently afterwards matured a kind of Hebrew Platonism. Its fainter traces are all that can be seen in the book of Wisdom; but these cannot be mistaken.

"Thy almighty hand made the world out of *matter without form*" (ἐξ ἀμόρφου ὕλης), (xi. 17), is remarked as the very expression of Plato (ὕλη and τὸ ἄμορφον); and the majority of Christian interpreters would probably regard this doctrine as opposed to that of the first verse of Genesis, which is generally (though perhaps needlessly) considered as implying that the world was created from nothing.

The division of the cardinal virtues, again (viii. 7), is taken from Plato: Temperance, Prudence, Justice and Fortitude;—the names are identical in the Greek.

Further, Wisdom herself, the personified topic of this book, is fast assuming a Platonic appearance, through a process of philosophical thought, vague and mystical enough, but which must now be described.

Plato "held the doctrine of the existence, in the Reason, of certain *innate notions* which form the basis of our conceptions, and precede in the soul the representation of what is individual and peculiar, besides forming the elements of our practical resolutions. These notions have for their object *the Ideas*, the eternal archetypes* or unities, which are the essence of infinite things, and the principles to which we refer the endless multiplicity of things by means of thought. * * * Inasmuch as the manifold objects, whose elements are the great and the little, correspond in part with the eternal Ideas, they must have some principle in common between them and the cognizant soul; that principle is the Divinity, who has formed these external objects after the model of the Ideas." (Tennemann's Hist. of Philosophy, pp. 104, 105. Bohn, 1852.)

The same authority explains the Jew Philo's views as follows: "He assumes that the Divinity and Matter are the two first principles, existing from eternity. Agreeably to the principles of Plato, he characterizes them thus: the Divinity, as a Being, Real, Infinite and Immutable, Incomprehensible to any human understanding (Ὄν, *that which is)*; Matter, as non-existing (μὴ ὄν, *that which is not)*, but having received from the Divinity a form and life. He represents the Deity, by certain oriental figures, as the Primitive Light, as an Infinite Intelligence, from whom are derived, by irradiation, all finite Intelligences. In the soul of the Divinity are concentrated the ideas of all things possible. This λόγος of the Divine Being, the focus of all ideas (λόγος ἐνδιάθετος), is in fact the Ideal World; and called also the Son of God, or the Archangel. He is the image of God, the type after which God by his creative power (λόγος προφορικός)

* The book of Wisdom seems to imagine such an eternal archetype of the Temple of Solomon: "Thou hast commanded me to build a temple upon thy holy mount, and an altar in the city wherein thou dwellest, *a resemblance of the holy tabernacle which thou hast prepared from the beginning*" (ix. 8). This is the Platonic expansion of the older and simpler Jewish doctrine that Moses, on Mount Sinai, was shewn a *pattern* of the tabernacle and utensils which he was required to make (Exod. xxv. 9, 40).

formed the world such as it is presented to our senses. Hence three hypostases in the Divine Being.* We cannot become acquainted with the nature of God, but by his immediate influence on our minds: hence the doctrine of Internal Intuition. We may clearly observe how the views of the Jews were modified by the representations of Platonism, and how this admixture gave birth to new opinions. *Numenius*, of Apamea in Syria, in part admitted this mode of representation, and maintained that reason is the faculty of acquiring a knowledge of the Absolute and Supersensuous. He perfected the notion of the Trinity, by distinguishing, in the Divine Incorporeal Being, first, the Primitive and Supreme God, the immutable, eternal and perfect intelligence; secondly, the Creator of the world or Demiurgos, the νοῦς, having a twofold relation to the Divinity as his Son, and to the World as its Author." (Pp. 170, 171.)

Now the book of Wisdom presents the divine *Wisdom* and the divine *Word* in an intermediate state of progress towards that subordinate deification which they afterwards severally assumed, as just described. The fine personifications of Wisdom in the book of Proverbs, are exaggerated in this book beyond the limits of tasteful personification merely; and Wisdom becomes, as it were, a real being, an angel of the Divine will. The pseudo-Solomon says, "O send her out of thy holy heavens, for she knoweth and understandeth all things, and she shall lead me soberly in my doings and preserve me in her power" (ix. 10, 11). And the Logos, too, the Word of God, becomes vividly personal in this book of Wisdom: "Thine almighty Word leaped down from heaven, out of thy royal throne, as a fierce man of war into the midst of a land of destruction, and brought thine unfeigned

* Namely: (1) the Supreme Deity; (2) the λόγος ἐνδιάθετος, or *Word arranged in thought;* (3) the λόγος προφορικός, or *Word pronounced.*

commandment as a sharp sword" (xviii. 15, 16). This personification of the Logos is a hint in store for the interpretation of St. John's introduction to his Gospel, and the corresponding language in the opening of his first Epistle.

The book of Wisdom seems to be written without any very distinct plan. It contains many powerful and striking passages reminding us of the best parts of the Proverbs, and many also that are diffuse and feeble. Virtue is vindicated, and vice convicted of folly, in the high court of Morals. "Righteousness is immortal." "Wisdom is a loving spirit." The just man calls himself the "Son of God." A future life is opened to the view of the good, connected perhaps with the Messianic hope:

"For God created man to be immortal, and made him to be an image of his own eternity. Nevertheless, through envy of the devil came death into the world, and they that do hold of his side do find it. But the souls of the righteous are in the hand of God, and there shall no torment touch them. In the sight of the unwise they seemed to die; and their departure is taken for misery, and their going from us to be utter destruction; but they are in peace. For though they be punished in the sight of men, yet is their hope full of immortality. And having been a little chastised, they shall be greatly rewarded: for God proved them, and found them worthy for himself. As gold in the furnace hath he tried them, and received them as a burnt-offering. And in the time of their visitation they shall shine, and run to and fro like sparks among the stubble. They shall judge the nations, and have dominion over the people, and their Lord shall reign for ever" (ii. 23—iii. 8).

Again (v. 14—17):

"For the hope of the ungodly is like dust that is blown away with the wind; like a thin froth that is driven away with the storm; like as the smoke which is dispersed here and there with a tempest, and passeth away as the remembrance of a guest that tarrieth but a day. But the righteous live for evermore; their reward also is with the Lord, and the care of them is with the Most High. Therefore shall they receive a glorious kingdom, and a beautiful crown from the Lord's hand: for with his right hand shall he cover them, and with his arm shall he protect them. He shall take to him his jealousy for complete armour, and make the creature his weapon for the revenge of his enemies."

In chaps. vii.—ix., the author, speaking in the person of king Solomon, enlarges upon his acquisitions in wisdom in a style very unsuitable to the first person; and from the tenth chapter to the end of the book, he illustrates the benefits of Wisdom historically, presenting her as the presiding guardian of men from the first of days, and especially as watching over the Jewish people in Egypt and the desert. The last four chapters, on these last-named topics, are feeble and often obscure. But there is a fine chapter (xiii.), truthfully and sympathizingly illustrating the origin of idolatry, as having sprung from the very beauty of the Divine works, and contrasting the elevation of Jewish Theism with the moral degradation of Heathenism; the further description of which (xiv. 21—27) reminds one of Paul's first chapter to the Romans. And here is a sweet song of the Divine mercy:

"For the whole world before thee is as a little grain of the balance, yea, as a drop of the morning dew that falleth down upon the earth. But thou hast mercy upon all, for thou canst do all things; and winkest at the sins of men, because they should amend. For thou lovest all the things that are, and abhorrest nothing which thou hast made: for never wouldst thou have made anything, if thou hadst hated it. And how could anything have endured, if it had not been thy will? or been preserved, if not called by thee? But thou sparest all: for they are thine, O Lord, thou lover of souls. For thine uncorruptible Spirit is in all things. Therefore chastenest thou them, by little and little, that offend, and warnest them by putting them in remembrance wherein they have offended, that leaving their wickedness, they may believe on thee, O Lord" (xi. 22—xii. 2).

Passages like this, amid a class of books betokening whatever degree of intellectual poverty and weakness, shew us how the world is indebted to the old Jewish dispensation for its purest morality and highest devotion. That venerable faith was indeed the salt of the ancient world. The next book is of a yet higher character than this.

THE WISDOM OF JESUS THE SON OF SIRACH, OR ECCLESIASTICUS.

THE prologue to this book states that it was originally written in Hebrew by one Jesus (or Joshua) the Son of Sirach,* grandfather to the Jesus who translates it into Greek and writes this explanatory prologue. The latter says that he himself came into Egypt—from Palestine, it is presumed—"in the thirty-eighth year" (probably of his own age), "when Euergetes was king" (that is, Ptolemy III., who reigned B.C. 247—222); and that, continuing there some time, he found this book,—"a book of no small learning,"—and "thought it most necessary to bestow some diligence and travail to interpret it;" that is, to translate it into Greek. He speaks of the Hebrew Law and Prophets with reverence, and of the subsequent Jewish literature, including this work of his grandfather's, with pride and affection. And, with true critical discrimination as well as modesty, he apologizes for the necessary inferiority of a translation compared with "the same things uttered in Hebrew." There

* See also ch. l. 27, where the writer describes himself as "of Jerusalem."

is no reason to doubt the correctness of this account of the book before us. It is confirmed by internal evidence, particularly where the author carries down his list of Jewish worthies whom he celebrates, to "Simon the high-priest, the son of Onias" (chap. l.). This is Simon "the Just," beyond all reasonable doubt, who lived in the reign of the first Ptolemy, and administered the Jewish affairs in Jerusalem, from the year 300 B.C.* The book may thus have been written in Hebrew, probably in Palestine, about 280 or 290 B.C., by Jesus the Son of Sirach, and translated into Greek in Alexandria by his grandson between B.C. 247 and 222. Learned men think they can trace its Hebrew origin in some of the Greek phrases. The original Hebrew is lost. *Ecclesiasticus* (meaning *Church-book)* is a later name given to this book by the Latin Church. In the Roman Catholic Bible, it is placed, with the book of *Wisdom*, next after the Hebrew writings of Solomon, and "is received as canonical and divine," though confessedly "written after the time of Ezra, and not in the Jewish canon."†

Its contents are similar to those of the book *Wisdom*, but more full and varied; while their not being marked with the same strong tinge of Platonism, supports the Palestinian origin of the book, if not also its earlier date. The personifications of Wisdom are indeed scarcely more bold than in the writings of Solomon himself. The belief in a future state seems not to have been in the writer's mind when he speaks, in various places, of death

* Milman's Hist. of the Jews, II. 32.

† In ch. li. 10, there is an expression that seems to belong to the Christian age—"I called upon the Lord, *the Father of my Lord.*" Perhaps this last phrase has been inserted by a later pen. It seems quite an anachronism, but is not sufficient to discredit the higher antiquity of the whole book. The English *text* of this book, it must be added, is very corrupt; the Latin Vulgate continually differing from the Greek, and the common English version in many places differing from both.

and of the good reputation that survives the wise and pious. (See xiv. 17—19; xxii. 11, 12; xxxviii. 23; xli. 1—13; xliv. 8—15.) Yet there is one passage which seems to contrast with these silent omissions—"Blessed are they that saw thee (Elijah), and slept in [rather, were adorned with] love; for we shall surely live" (xlviii. 11).

The imitation of the book of Proverbs by this writer is quite undisguised. "My son, if thou come to serve the Lord, prepare thy soul for temptation." "Hear me, your father, O children, and do thereafter, that ye may live." "My son, defraud not the poor of his living, and make not the needy eyes to wait long." These sentences are quite in the style of Solomon. So is the description of the blessings of wisdom; or rather, it is his description paraphrased and enlarged:

"Wisdom exalteth her children, and layeth hold of them that seek her. He that loveth her, loveth life; and they that seek to her early, shall be filled with joy. He that holdeth her fast, shall inherit glory; and wheresoever she entereth, the Lord will bless. They that serve her, shall minister to the Holy One; and them that love her, the Lord doth love. Whoso giveth ear unto her, shall judge the nations; and he that attendeth unto her, shall dwell securely. If a man commit himself unto her, he shall inherit her, and his generation shall hold her in possession. For at the first she will walk with him by crooked ways, and bring fear and dread upon him, and torment him with her discipline, until she may trust his soul, and try him by her laws. Then will she return the straight way unto him, and comfort him, and shew him her secrets. But if he go wrong, she will forsake him, and give him over to his own ruin" (iv. 11—19; see also vi. 18—37, and xxiv.).

Like the book of Proverbs, Ecclesiasticus has a multitude of weighty and pithy maxims on all subjects, prudential and moral, secular and religious; many being reproduced from the old Hebrew Scriptures, but some of them being quite new in this collection. Some of these re-appear afterwards in the Christian Scriptures, and some live in our common speech as racy proverbs. Several of the latter are very clever.

"Be not ashamed to confess thy sins; and force not the course of the river." *Rowing against the stream* is commonly said by us for contending against outward circumstances. Here the thought is finely applied to suppressing the spontaneous flow of penitence.

"Let not thine hand be stretched out to receive, and shut when thou shouldst repay," is a maxim of high honour well expressed.

"Do no evil; so shall no harm come unto thee." Here is the negative rule, from which the gospel generously and comprehensively advances to the positive: *All things whatsoever ye would that men should do unto you, do ye even so unto them.*

"Depart from the unjust, and iniquity shall turn away from thee." St. James puts it more strongly: *Resist the devil, and he will flee from you;* and adds the glorious converse, *Draw nigh to God, and he will draw nigh to you.*

"My son, sow not upon the furrows of unrighteousness, and thou shalt not reap them sevenfold." *They have sown the wind, and they shall reap the whirlwind,* says Hosea (viii. 7).

"Strive not with a man that is full of tongue, and heap not wood upon his fire." *The tongue is a fire,* says St. James (iii. 6).

"Rejoice not over thy greatest enemy being dead; but remember that we die all." Washington Irving has beautifully enlarged upon this tender and generous sentiment: *O, the grave! the grave! It buries every error—covers every defect—extinguishes every resentment! From its peaceful bosom spring none but fond regrets and tender recollections. Who can look down upon the grave even of an enemy, and not feel a compunctious throb, that he should ever have warred with the poor handful of earth that lies mouldering before him?* (Sketch Book—Rural Funerals.)

"Pride was not made for men, nor furious anger for them that are born of a woman." The first clause is a very common proverb.

"Commend not a man for his beauty; neither abhor a man for his outward appearance." *Fronti nulla fides,* says the Roman proverb.

"Blame not before thou hast examined the truth; understand first, and then rebuke." *Strike, but hear,* said Themistocles to Eurybiades.

"In the day of prosperity there is a forgetfulness of affliction; and in the day of affliction there is no more remembrance of prosperity."

Donec eris felix, multos numerabis amicos;
Tempora si fuerint nubila, diffugiunt.

"A friend cannot be known in prosperity, and an enemy cannot be hidden in adversity. In the prosperity of a man enemies will be grieved; but in his adversity even a friend will depart." *Summer friends!*

"Judge none blessed before his death; for a man shall be known in his children." Truly characteristic of Jewish thought and feeling is this addition, in the latter clause, to the well-known maxim of Solon in the first.

"He that toucheth pitch shall be defiled therewith; and he that hath fellowship with a proud man shall be like unto him." The first part is often quoted, with more striking applications than to the proud man.

"Riches are good unto him that hath no sin, and poverty is evil in the mouth of the ungodly." *A man's life,* says the Great Teacher, *consisteth not in the abundance of the things that he possesseth.*

"He that contemneth small things, shall fall by little and little." Often quoted and often disregarded; ever true of the growth of *Habit.*

"A man's attire, and laugh, and gait, shew what he is."

"The heart of fools is in their mouth; but the mouth of the wise is in their heart." A proverb used by the prudent; abused by the politic, till a modern diplomatist could dare to describe the use of language as being, "to conceal the thoughts."

"When the ungodly curseth Satan, he curseth his own soul." Often virtually quoted, but inverted in form, when we talk of *Satan reproving sin.*

"As a nail sticketh fast between the joinings of the stones, so doth sin stick close between buying and selling." Here is the keen satire of truth.

"The birds will resort unto their like; so will truth return unto them that practise in her." *Birds of a feather*, is seldom applied by us with equal seriousness to this.

"If thou blow the spark, it shall burn; if thou spit upon it, it shall be quenched; and both these come out of thy mouth." *Blessing and cursing from the same mouth*, says St. James.

"Many, when a thing was lent them, reckoned it to be found, and put them to trouble that helped them." What was there in ancient times (like books in our days of cheap literature, and umbrellas in our climate!) so often borrowed and so remissly returned as to give occasion for this broad hint?

"The chief thing for life is water, and bread, and clothing, and a house to cover shame. Better is the life of a poor man in a mean cottage, than delicate fare in another man's house." True maxims these of contentment and independence!

"Gold hath been the ruin of many, and their destruction was present. It is a stumbling-block unto them that sacrifice unto it, and every fool shall be taken therewith." *I prefer a man without money to money without a man*, said a Roman father once in choosing a son-in-law.

"Do nothing without advice; and when thou hast once done, repent not." *Priusquam incipias benè consulto, ubi consulueris maturè facto, opus est.*

These are a specimen of the practical wisdom that pervades the book. Some of its precepts are, it must be confessed, low and selfish enough; as, for instance, the heartless passage on mourning for the dead (xxxviii. 16—23). It is worthy of the Stoics. So is the advice, "Remove sorrow far from thee" (xxx. 23), which repeats the very doctrine of the Hebrew Ecclesiastes. But there are other things more worthy of the best followers of Moses and the Prophets. Here is, by anticipation, the morality of Christ himself on the subject of oaths:

"Accustom not thy mouth to swearing; neither use thyself to the naming of the Holy One. For as a slave that is continually beaten shall not be without a blue mark, so he that sweareth and nameth God continually shall not be faultless" (xxiii. 9, 10).

And here is a passage that re-appears almost verbally in the Lord's Prayer, and in the moral precepts of Christ and of St. Paul:

"He that revengeth shall find vengeance from the Lord, and he will surely keep his sins in remembrance. Forgive thy neighbour the hurt that he hath done unto thee; so shall thy sins also be forgiven when thou prayest. One man beareth hatred against another; and doth he seek pardon from the Lord? He sheweth no mercy to a man which is like himself; and doth he ask forgiveness of his own sins? If he that is but flesh nourish hatred, who will intreat for pardon of his sins? Remember thy end, and let enmity cease; remember corruption and death, and abide in the commandments" (xxviii. 1—6).

On the whole subject of sin and forgiveness, this Son of Sirach is as sound and moral as the old prophets. Sacrifice and ceremony are no part of the atonement which he recommends. Repentance and duty are the only specifics. High among human duties he places that of almsgiving; but he also says, "Whoso honoureth his father, maketh an atonement for his sins;" and if any critic sees the dawn of Pharisaism in this frequent praise of alms, he will intirely miss the more marked characteristics of formal, ostentatious prayer and scrupulous or superfluous sacrifice. (See, on these subjects, vii. 29—33, xii. 1—7, xxix. 9—12.) The duty of almsgiving is indeed grudgingly confined by this Son of Sirach to "godly" men as its objects: "Give to the godly man, and help not a sinner." Yet the same writer can inculcate true delicacy in the act of giving: "My son, blemish not thy good deeds, neither use uncomfortable words when thou givest anything. Shall not the dew assuage the heat? So is a word better than a gift. Lo, is not a word better than a gift? but both are with a gracious man" (xviii. 15—17). And in his precept, "Lay up thy treasure according to the commandments of the Most High, and it shall bring thee more profit than gold; shut up alms in thy storehouses, and it shall deliver thee from all affliction,"—we meet the spirit of Christ's Sermon on the Mount.

Let us hear the Son of Sirach more expressly on the subject of Sacrifice:

"He that keepeth the law, bringeth offerings enough; he that taketh heed to the commandments offereth a peace-offering. He that requiteth a good turn, offereth fine flour; and he that giveth alms, sacrificeth praise. To depart from wickedness is a thing pleasing to the Lord; and to forsake unrighteousness is a propitiation"

(xxxv. 1—3). The whole chapter (as also that which precedes it) is sound in moral feeling. Repentance and reformation and good deeds are the only atonement known to this thoughtful and pious Jew:

"My son, hast thou sinned? Do so no more, but ask pardon for thy former sins" (xxi. 1, &c.).

"Bind not one sin upon another; for in one thou shalt not be unpunished. Say not, God will look upon the multitude of my oblations; and when I offer to the Most High God, he will accept it" (vii. 8, 9; see also v. 5—7, and xvii. 20—32).

The doctrine of temporal retribution is strongly, though vaguely, laid down; and the Jewish hope of national blessing is devoutly cherished as the great coming vindication of the ways of Providence. In ch. xxxvi. 1—17, the writer prays for the gathering together of all the tribes of Israel, and the manifestation of the Eternal God to all nations through them.

Some of the finest passages in the book are those on Friendship. Such is that in the sixth chapter. True friendship has a religious basis:

"Be in peace with many; nevertheless have but one counsellor of a thousand. If thou wouldst get a friend, prove him first, and be not hasty to credit him. For some man is a friend for his own occasion, and will not abide in the day of thy trouble. And there is a friend, who being turned to enmity and strife, will discover thy reproach. Again, some friend is a companion at the table, and will not continue in the day of thy affliction. But in thy prosperity he will be as thyself, and will be bold over thy servants. If thou be brought low, he will be against thee, and will hide himself from thy face. Separate thyself from thine enemies, and take heed of thy friends. A faithful friend is a strong defence; and he that hath found such an one, hath found a treasure.

Nothing doth countervail a faithful friend, and his excellency is invaluable. A faithful friend is the medicine of life, and they that fear the Lord shall find him. Whoso feareth the Lord shall direct his friendship aright; for as he is, so shall his neighbour be also" (vi. 6—17; see also ix. 10, xix. 13—17, xxvii. 16—21).

There are some terse precepts on the various relationships of life in vii. 23—28, and ix. 1—9. Solomon's own doctrine of the rod, as a salutary instrument of fatherly instruction, severe enough as the royal sage himself left it, is here exaggerated into downright domestic cruelty (xxx. 1—13);—a mere proof, one would hope, of the vicious literary tendency of paraphrasing, rather than a sign of a sterner domestic sway having prevailed in Jewish families in the days of the Son of Sirach.

The writer touches on the deep questions of moral evil and man's free agency and responsibility, and the retribution to follow; but he cannot be said to have thrown much light upon them, except in the way of practical precepts. He strongly maintains the power of man to do right *if he will*, and never loses himself in metaphysical refinements. See xv. 11—20, also the three following chapters, for the most continuous developement of these ideas. There is a fine assertion of the Divine omniscience in xvi. 17—21.

In ch. xliv. begins a studied eulogy on the great men of Jewish history, from Moses down to Simon, the high-priest, the son of Onias. In his mention of the Jewish prophets among these national worthies, we find an incidental confirmation of the late date which we have ascribed to the book of Daniel, together with the clearest attestation to the reception of all the rest of the existing books of the prophets in this writer's time. He mentions by name Esay (Isaiah), Jeremias and Ezekiel, as prominent in the times of the approaching and completed captivity; and then adds, "And of the twelve prophets let the memorial be blessed, for they comforted Jacob" (xlviii. 20—xlix. 10). But he says not a word about Daniel. Three major and twelve minor prophets thus seem to have been all that were known in the days of the Son of Sirach. The book of Daniel cannot surely have been known to him. We have given (Vol. I. p. 510) other reasons for thinking that it was not written till the second century before Christ.

"A prayer of Jesus the Son of Sirach" concludes his book.

It is said that Mr. Burke expressed himself as more indebted to this book for precepts of practical wisdom, than to any other uninspired production. The estimate is essentially true. The book is a noble monument of the obligation which the world owes to Judaism, on the score alike of elevated devotion and of pure morality.

BARUCH, AND THE EPISTLE OF JEREMIAH.

In the book of Jeremiah we read of Baruch (the son of Neriah, and brother to Seraiah, the chief chamberlain of king Zedekiah) as a devoted friend of the prophet, attesting his redemption of his inheritance (Jerem. xxxii. 12), writing down some of his predictions from his dictation (xxxvi.), sharing the odium under which he fell, and accompanying him into Egypt after the overthrow of Jerusalem (xliii. 6).

We also read (ch. xxix.) of Jeremiah writing a letter to the Jews in Babylon who had been carried away with king Jeconiah, exhorting them to quiet submission and trustful hope (which letter is preserved in its place in the history); and of his afterwards sending, by the hands of Seraiah, Baruch's brother (who accompanied Zedekiah on the final overthrow), a copy of his prophecy against Babylon, which he charged him to read to the captives (li. 59).

On this basis of historical fact, the imagination of a later author or authors, in the imitative Greek age of Jewish literature, has ventured to put forth two other letters, in the Apocryphal book intitled as above. The one purports to have been sent by the Jews in Babylon "in the fifth year" (of Jeconiah's captivity?), to their compatriots still in Jerusalem, accompanied with money for sacrificial offerings, and the expression of a desire that they would pray for the life of Nebuchadnezzar and for the restoration of the exiles to their land. Baruch is made the writer of this letter from Babylon, which seems hardly reconcilable with the part he took in Jerusalem during Zedekiah's reign. And the Babylonians are described (Baruch i. 8) as returning "the vessels of the house of the Lord" at the same time,—an arrangement necessary, in the writer's mind, for the due performance of the sacrifices, but a very unlikely act of courtesy on the part of the Babylonians, and quite contrary to the facts of the history, which restores the sacred vessels under Cyrus. This fictitious letter occupies the first five chapters. It is largely founded upon the language of the Jewish Scriptures, confessing the sins of the nation and the righteousness of the doom inflicted in their captivity, but praying for mercy and anticipating restoration.

The remaining chapter, intitled "the Epistle of Jeremy," calls itself "a copy of an epistle which Jeremy sent unto them which *were to be led captives* by the king of the Babylonians." It does not tell us where the writer is supposed to have been when he wrote this letter to those who were to be led captives. While they were at Jerusalem, and he there too, prophesying and writing his prophecies, it seems a poor device to have ascribed this piece of gratuitous letter-writing to him. The letter tells them they shall be in Babylon for "seven generations,"—a most unaccountable variation both from the seventy years of Jeremiah's own words, and from the seventy weeks of the book of Daniel. The chapter is a somewhat ingenious and recondite, but tedious enlargement of the fine satire of the old Hebrew psalmists and prophets against idols and idolaters. The quotations from the Old Testament seem to be taken from the Greek version. Therefore, the book was originally written in Greek. Its date is thought to be about the time of the Maccabees, perhaps the middle of the second century before Christ.

THE SONG OF THE THREE HOLY CHILDREN; THE HISTORY OF SUSANNA; THE DESTRUCTION OF BEL AND OF THE DRAGON.

THESE Greek additions to the book of Daniel have already been briefly alluded to in speaking of that book (Vol. I. p. 512). The history of *Susanna* was evidently designed by its writer to be prefixed to the book of Daniel, and in some manuscripts it is so placed. But it will not piece on neatly. And it is here candidly described as "set apart from the beginning of *Daniel* because it is not in the Hebrew, as neither the narration of *Bel* and the *Dragon*." Its purpose is to illustrate the wisdom of Daniel, when a youth, in preventing the judicial murder of a virtuous Hebrew matron, on the false charge of two elders who were themselves judges among the Jews in Babylon,—that wisdom consisting simply in interrogating two false witnesses separately, and permitting them to contradict each other's evidence. "From that day forth," the legend proceeds, "was Daniel had in great reputation in the sight of the people." Meanwhile, the book of *Daniel* itself traces his conduct at court, and his growing reputation with king Nebuchadnezzar.

The Song of the Three Holy Children was intended (as its heading explains) to be inserted after the 23rd verse of Dan. iii., and it is so inserted in the Romish Bible;* the holy children being the three youths in the fiery furnace, Shadrach, Meshach and Abednego. Azarias (or Abednego) stands up in the flames (which are described, in the usual exaggerative style of the Jewish paraphrasts, as streaming forth forty-nine cubits above the furnace) and utters a prayer, in which he sums up the Hebrew history of divine blessings and national unworthiness and resulting captivity,† and prays for deliverance. Then the angel of the Lord comes down into the furnace and smites the flame aside; and then the three, "as out of one mouth, praised and glorified and blessed God," in a beautiful hymn, which is very much in the style of some of the Psalms, invoking all nature and all creatures to praise God. This hymn is well known. It begins,—

"Blessed art thou, O Lord God of our fathers;
And to be praised and exalted above all for ever.

* The Douay version explains, in a note, that this passage was not in the Hebrew in the time of Jerome, but conjectures that it once was in Hebrew or Chaldee, and declares that the Church receives it as canonical. The same is said of the other additions which are placed at the end of Daniel in that version.

† From his being made to say, "Neither is there, at this time, prince or *prophet* or leader or sacrifice," some would too nicely prove that the book is later than the time of Daniel; as if the writer could forget that he was assuming the time of Daniel. The external evidence and the legendary character of the additions are far more decisive marks.

And blessed is thy glorious and holy name ;
And to be praised and exalted above all for ever," &c.

This alternate response (after the manner of Ps. cxxxvi.) continues, till the song changes into an invocation of the works of the Lord to bless the Lord, when the response is varied accordingly, thus :

"O all ye works of the Lord, bless ye the Lord !
Praise and exalt him above all for ever.
O ye heavens, bless ye the Lord !
Praise and exalt," &c.

The *History of the Destruction of Bel and of the Dragon* is designed as a supplement to the book of Daniel. It dates itself as belonging to the beginning of the reign of Cyrus, in the third year of which the last visions of the book of Daniel are placed (x. 1), when Daniel must have been about eighty-seven years old, and the proclamation for the return from exile had already gladdened the heart of Israel. These additions to the book of Daniel represent the aged prophet as giving a not very dignified *coup de grace* to the stupid idolatry of the Babylonians, to the apparent satisfaction, if not with the connivance, of the king. The detection of the trickery of Bel's priests, and the destruction of themselves and their temple by the king's orders, encourage Daniel further to contrive the self-suffocation of a deified Dragon, to whose voracious appetite he administers pitch and fat and hair boiled up together. The indignation of the Babylonish populace is roused against the king, whom they accuse of having become a Jew : and to pacify them, he casts Daniel into a den of seven lions for six days. The lions do not hurt him ; and a prophet of Judea, named Habbakuk, who was carrying a bowl of pottage to some reapers in a field, is brought by the hair of his head, by the angel of the Lord, from Judea to the lions' den in Babylon, to feed Daniel! A feeble, while exaggerated repetition, indeed, is this of the sufficiently difficult story of the lions' den in the sixth chapter of the original book. And not very credible so far as Cyrus is concerned, whose edict permitting all Jews who desired to return to their country, was princely if it was also politic; but whose alleged interference with Bel and with the Dragon would have been neither the one nor the other. If the book of Daniel was written in the Maccabee period, about B.C. 165, of course these additions are later still; how much later is of little importance to decide.

THE PRAYER OF MANASSES.

It has been mentioned (Vol. I. p. 457) that the book of *Chronicles* makes the idolatrous king Manasseh, son of Hezekiah, to have been carried away captive to Babylon, there to have repented of his idolatry, and to have returned home and restored the temple worship. As the book of *Kings* (by far the more reliable history of the two) gives no hint of this kind, but represents his whole reign of fifty-five years as intirely abominable, without any redeeming period, the alleged incident cannot be received as a clear historical fact. But the incident as alleged, and the statement of the *Chronicler* that the Prayer of Manasseh was written among the sayings of the seers, suggested to some Jew of late date a theme on which to exercise the seductive faculty of writing compositions which *might* be real. The wonder is, that "the words of the seers who spake to him in the name of Jehovah, God of Israel," have not also been reproduced by fancy. "The Prayer of Manasses, king of Judah, when he was holden captive in Babylon," is too rhetorical in style, and is not such a prayer as a repentant King *ought* to have spoken, for he does not allude to his people as involved in his misdeeds; but in religious sentiment, if taken as a private prayer, it is true to the best moral standard of Judaism. The Divine supremacy and goodness; free forgiveness awaiting man's repentance; the king's acknowledgment of deep sin and utter unworthiness; his bowing the "knee of his heart," beseeching grace from God and deliverance, and vowing to praise God for ever all the days of his life, with no allusion even to sacrifice (which it would have been the very sign and symptom of amendment for Manasseh to have promised to offer according to the Law);—such, in outline, are the contents of this Prayer, and such the implied theology and morals of its unknown author. It is not known to have existed before the third century of the Christian era. It is wanting in many copies of the Greek Septuagint. When it was written, the Jewish temple services had ceased, and the writer seems almost to have forgotten that they had ever existed; but he retained the pure sentiments of morality and piety to which the ceremonial law had always been subservient as its end and purpose.

THE MACCABEES

(AND JEWISH HISTORY TO THE TIME OF CHRIST).

THE books of the Maccabees contain the history of the Jews during a most eventful and truly heroic period of forty years, beginning with the accession of Antiochus Epiphanes to the throne of Syria, B.C. 175. This is the only part of the Apocrypha that contributes any historical materials for the long period intervening between the close of the Old-Testament history and the opening of that of the New. This seems, therefore, a convenient place for introducing a brief abstract of the Jewish history prior to the date of the Maccabees, and for carrying it rapidly downward after their time nearly to the birth of Christ. The chief authority for this period is the well-known Jewish historian, Josephus, whose account of the Maccabean wars, however, is no doubt founded upon these books, and whose rhetorical and showy style, when compared with the first at least of these books, betrays a more rapid course of deterioration in the Jewish literature, than these books present when compared with the Hebrew histories. The first book of the Maccabees contrasts advantageously also with the Apocryphal parts of Esdras, and with the various other Greek and Latin additions to the early Hebrew records, contained in the Jewish Apocrypha.

The history of the Jews, from their restoration to the time of Christ, is admirably narrated in Dr. Milman's fascinating book, so often referred to in these pages. (See Hist. of Jews, Vol. II. pp. 1—126.) See also Kitto's History of Palestine; and (for a fuller account) Jahn's "History of the Hebrew Commonwealth from the Earliest Times to the Destruction of Jerusalem, A.D. 72." The merest abstract is all that can be attempted here.

From the time of Ezra and Nehemiah, when the difficulties of the Return had been at length surmounted,—when the temple service was effectively restored, the Law again enforced, and copies of the sacred books multiplied,—the Jews appear to have enjoyed a considerable period of comfort and prosperity. The Persian power appears to have been very much humbled by the Athenians under Cimon, not long before the expedition of Nehemiah; and it seems probable that this circumstance may have had no little influence upon the Persian counsels in suggesting a liberal policy towards the Jews, and especially in recommending the fortification of Jerusalem, as being near the Persian border towards Egypt.* The rival temple of Samaria, on Mount Gerizim, was built by Sanballat, the Horonite, the father-in-law of a priest, Manasseh, whom Nehemiah had expelled for marrying a foreign wife (Neh. xiii. 28). From this period dates the irreconcilable schism between the Jews and the Samaritans.

From this time till the conquest of Alexander the Great (about 120 years, that is), the Jews seem to have been happily unnoticed and unknown to the great world. The head of their civil administration was their High-priest. The silence of history is its most conclusive testimony to their tranquil prosperity and happiness in the main. Had they been either conquering or suffering under conquest, we should have known all about it. From what we see of the national character afterwards, this seems to have been the period during which was matured that inflexible regard to their sacred Law, which ever afterwards characterized the nation in general, and shewed itself especially in their firm endurance of savage persecutions for the sake of their religion.

Alexander the Great, after taking Tyre by siege, summoned Jerusalem to surrender; whereupon the priests and people, with Jaddua the high-priest at their head, solemnly marched out to meet the conqueror; who, through whatever motive (probably that of policy), paid

* Hist. Jews, II. 22. The alleged terms of the peace effected by Cimon, most humiliating as they must have been to Persia, have, however, been disputed—as, indeed, has the fact itself of Cimon's treaty of peace—by more searching recent historians; but still the greater fact remains, that Persia's successive attempts against Greece had been abortive and disastrous to herself. The date of Marathon is 490 B.C.; of Salamis, 480; of Eurymedon, 470; of Cimon's alleged treaty, 449; of Ezra's expedition, 457; and Nehemiah's, 446.

conspicuous respect to the high-priest, and declared that he had seen that very figure, in a vision, encouraging him to the conquest of Persia (B.C. 332). It is said that the conqueror afterwards transplanted a number of Jews to his new city of Alexandria.

On the death of Alexander (323), Palestine soon became a bone of contention among his rival generals and successors. The first Ptolemy, endeavouring to possess himself of Syria, besieged Jerusalem on the sabbath, and met with no resistance. He carried off 100,000 captives to Alexandria and Cyrene, and presently afterwards enrolled Jewish soldiers to garrison the fortresses of Judea for him. Antigonus, one of Alexander's generals ruling in the southern provinces of Asia Minor, contended with him for the possession of Syria and Judea, but was defeated in the battle of Ipsus, and so the spoil fell to Ptolemy (B.C. 301). Under him and his next two successors, Philadelphus and Euergetes (whose reigns reached to B.C. 222), the Jews, both in Palestine and in Egypt, seem to have enjoyed many privileges. It was in the reign of the second Ptolemy (Philadelphus), according to Josephus, that the sacred books of the Jews were translated into Greek in Alexandria, where the noted library of the Ptolemies was founded, and a second culture of Greek literature took place. Then and there it was that the Hebrew Greek Scriptures of the Apocrypha began to be written.

Meanwhile, Seleucus had established the Greek kingdom of Syria, with Antioch for its capital; and this kingdom afterwards came into frequent conflict with that of the Ptolemies, Judea being often the scene, and sometimes the subject, of their disputes. The establishment of the dynasty of the Seleucidæ became a date for historians, and is used as such by the writer of the book of Maccabees, and by Josephus after him. This era of the Seleucidæ is the year B. C. 312; at which time Seleucus, son of Alexander's general Antiochus, became master of Babylon. Both at Seleuceia, which he founded near the site of the modern Bagdad, and at Antioch, which he ultimately made his capital, he gave considerable privileges to the Jews as inducements to settle. The sixth on the Syrian throne, Antiochus III., or the Great (who reigned 223—187), endeavoured to wrest Judea from the hands of Ptolemy IV. (Philopator), but was defeated. In the reign of the next Ptolemy, however, he was more successful, and was received as a deliverer by the Jews, who had experienced a change of treatment under the 4th and 5th Ptolemies. This Antiochus married his daughter to the young king of Egypt (Ptolemy Epiphanes), and made Judea and Cœle-Syria her dower. But they again relapsed to the sway of Syria.

Domestic dissensions now afflicted Judea; and the 4th Antiochus (*Epiphanes* the Illustrious, or *Epimanes* the Madman) brought upon them the crisis of calamity. Voluptuous in character and versatile in talent, he took delight in insulting the Jews by forcing upon them Grecian customs and heathen abominations. He promoted the formation of a gymnasium and the institution of all kinds of Grecian amusements. Among the Jews themselves there were some, indeed, who favoured the adoption of these Greek practices. Jesus, or Joshua, the high-priest's brother, was among this party. He bought his brother's deposition and his own appointment, and *grecised* his own name into Jason. Antiochus, after a successful invasion of Egypt, only checked by Roman interference (see Vol. I. p. 523), returned homewards through Judea, where he pillaged and wantonly desecrated the temple, sacrificing a swine upon the altar, to the unspeakable horror of the Jewish people. He let loose his soldiers upon them, and seemed bent upon their extermination. He dismantled the city, and built a fortress on Mount Zion commanding both city and temple. He set up the statue of Jupiter Olympius in the temple, and other statues and altars all over the land of Judea. This was the "ceasing of the daily offering," and the setting up of "the abomination of desolation," described in the book of Daniel; which is, with great probability, believed to have been written soon after the tyrant's death. These atrocities provoked resistance, and led the way to the heroic acts of the Maccabees.

THE FIRST BOOK OF THE MACCABEES takes up the history from this point.

It opens with a brief general notice of Alexander's conquest of Persia, and of the kingdoms erected by his successors; and, at the tenth verse, comes to Antiochus surnamed Epiphanes, "a wicked root," son of Antiochus the king, who had been an hostage at Rome;* and he reigned in the 137th year of *the kingdom of the Greeks*. In these last words the era of the Seleucidæ † is described, which being B.C. 312, thus gives (312—137=) 175 B.C. as the opening date of this history. The spoiling and profanation of the temple, and the enforcing of idolatrous observances throughout the country by

* This was on the discomfiture of the father, Antiochus III. (the Great), by Cornelius Scipio, near Magnesia, B.C. 190, which terminated his attempts to possess himself of Greece, against the Romans. He had protected Hannibal, and been encouraged by the latter in his designs against the Roman power. His son Epiphanes was sent as hostage for the fulfilment of the terms of the final treaty with Rome.

† "It is made use of all over the East by Jews, Christians and Mahometans. The Jews call it the *era of contracts;* because, when subject to the Syro-Macedonian princes, they were obliged to employ it in all contracts and civil deeds. The Arabians term it the *era of the two-horned;* a denomination taken from the coins or medals of Seleucus, in which he is represented with horns, like those of a ram. In the book of the Maccabees it is called the *era of the kingdom of the Greeks.*" (Tytler's Universal Hist., II. 38—*Murray's Fam. Lib.*)

the reckless king, are painfully described. It is sadly recorded that "many also of the Israelites consented to his religion, and sacrificed unto idols, and profaned the sabbath." The most savage cruelties are described as perpetrated; but it is added, with true Hebrew pride, "Howbeit many in Israel were fully resolved and confirmed in themselves, not to eat any unclean thing. Wherefore they chose rather to die, that they might not be defiled with meats, and that they might not profane the holy covenant: so then they died. And there was very great wrath upon Israel" (i. 62—64).

In the second chapter we are introduced to the fine old priest Mattathias and his five sons, who live in Modin, near the Mediterranean coast, and who become the leaders and nucleus of a brave and romantic revolt against the Syrian power. The watchword of Mattathias was, "Whoever is zealous of the law and maintaineth the covenant, let him follow me." His followers mustered in the mountainous country, where they were pursued by the Syrians; and a considerable body of these refugees were unresistingly massacred on the sabbath-day. From that moment Mattathias and his sons boldly and rightly proclaimed the lawfulness of resistance on the sabbath (ii. 41); and the Jewish practice thenceforth was, to maintain defensive operations in war, but to abstain from aggression, on that day. A great accession is made to their standard, especially by the adhesion of the party of the Assideans, or Chesidim (etymologically, the *righteous*),—those zealous for the Law, from whom the Pharisaic party afterwards degenerately sprang. Old Mattathias died in the 146th year of the Seleucidæ; that is, the 9th of the reign of Epiphanes; and, according to his dying injunctions, the command devolved upon his third son, Judas, surnamed Maccabeus *(Hammer)*, from whom this surname was afterwards extended to the other brothers. Simon is, by the father's parting words, designated as "a man of counsel," to whom he exhorts the brothers always to give ear, as to a father.

Under Judas, the enthusiasm of the Jews rises high. They perform prodigies of valour, regain the temple, cleanse it and restore its worship, and institute, in memory of the occasion, the feast of the Dedication, which we find observed in the time of Christ (iv. 59). In connection with the renewal of the altar of burnt-offering, which had been profaned by Antiochus, it is implied by the historian that there was at this time no prophet in Israel, but that expectation was eagerly fixed upon the advent of some future guide. It is an illustration of the fluctuating but ever-recurring hope of Israel, shewing the state of the "Messianic idea" at this period: "And when they consulted what to do with the altar of burnt-offerings which was profaned, they thought it best to pull it down, lest it should be a reproach to them, because the heathen had defiled it; wherefore they pulled it down, *and laid up the stones in the mountain of the temple in a convenient place, until there should come a prophet to shew what should be done with them.* Then they took whole stones (unhewn ones, that is), according to the Law, and built a new altar according to the former" (iv. 44—47; see also ix. 27, xiv. 41). After this, Judas fortified the temple, and strengthened Bethsura, a fortress to the south, as a defence against Idumæa.

The successful exploits of Judas, accompanied by his brother Jonathan, to the east of the Jordan, and those of Simon in Galilee, occupy the fifth chapter, together with the narrative of a reverse experienced by the troops left by him in Judea under a commander who disobeyed his orders, but whose ill success Judas soon retrieved. The sixth chapter records the death of Antiochus in

Persia, while endeavouring to plunder a temple, in the 149th year (B. C. 163); and with poetical justice, but doubtful historical accuracy, the Jewish historian makes him think with remorse of "the evils he did at Jerusalem," and confess that his death in a strange land is the retribution upon his conduct.

The Syrian throne was now disputed between Antiochus Eupator, son of Epiphanes, and Demetrius, son of Seleucus the elder brother and predecessor of Epiphanes. Antiochus, with his general Lysias, attempts the reduction of Judea from the Idumæan frontier; takes Bethsura, but assaults Jerusalem in vain. Elephants form part of the Syrian army; and Eleazar, one of the brothers of Judas, earns a renowned death by stabbing one of these huge beasts from beneath, by whose fall he is himself crushed.

Chap. vii. shews Demetrius (Soter) victorious over Antiochus and Lysias, and established on the throne of Syria (B. C. 162). He adopted a new policy, that of investing a high-priest in order to make him his tool. The priest so appointed was Alcimus, and with him the general Bacchides was united in the government. Onias, the rightful high-priest, hereupon retired into Egypt, where, under the countenance of Ptolemy VI. (Philometor), he directed the zeal of the Jews in those parts to the building of a temple at On (or Heliontopolis). This seems, indeed, quite in opposition to the great idea of the Jewish Law; yet the Egyptian Jews pleaded in their own justification the prophecy of Isaiah (xix. 19), "In that day there shall be an altar to the LORD in the midst of the land of Egypt." And the Jewish sacrificial worship was actually conducted there, to the great scandal of the Palestinian Jews, till the reign of Vespasian, when it was extinguished together with that of the temple at Jerusalem.

To return, however, to the time of Onias, when the priesthood in the person of Alcimus was upheld by the favour of the Syrian crown,—the Assideans (vii. 13) were at first deluded by the specious appeal to their Jewish reverence; but soon the treacherous murder of a number of them by Alcimus called forth the renewed energy of Judas and his comrades in arms. Nicanor is sent by king Demetrius to uphold Alcimus as high-priest, but is defeated and slain by Judas, who thereupon (chap. viii.) puts himself under the protection of the Romans by a treaty of mutual alliance. The Syrian king sends Bacchides and Alcimus again with new forces, and the heroic Judas is slain in battle (B.C. 161). But Jonathan is chosen in his place; and after a period of desultory warfare, he is enabled to make honourable terms of peace with Bacchides, including the restoration of Jewish prisoners of war. Perhaps the known protection of Rome may have facilitated this treaty.

The tenth chapter brings upon the stage a new claimant for the throne of Syria, in the person of Alexander Balas, an alleged, if not a real, son of Epiphanes. The Romans, for the sake doubtless of strengthening their influence in that part of the world, sanctioned his claim; and both the rival kings of Syria now pay court to Jonathan, who accepts the proposals of Balas, in accordance, if not express compliance, with the conditions of the Roman alliance. He becomes high-priest and prince,—the first of the line of the Asmonean kings of Judea. Balas defeated and slew Demetrius, and married the daughter of the king of Egypt, who, however, afterwards (xi.) favoured the side of young Demetrius and defeated Balas. Demetrius (Nicator) then became king of Syria (B.C. 145). Jonathan, who had been true to the cause of Balas, was now, however, confirmed by Demetrius in "the high-priesthood, and in all the honours that he had before," and obtained remission of tribute (xi. 26—36). He renewed the alliance with the Romans, and civilities are stated to have passed between him and the Spartans.*

But another revolution of Syrian affairs placed the young Antiochus (Theos, son of Alexander Balas, seven years old) on the throne; a mere puppet in the hands of one Tryphon (xi. 39), who at first confirmed Jonathan in the priesthood; but finding the integrity of the latter a hindrance to his own schemes for empire (xii. 40), managed to practise upon his unsuspicious nature, treacherously captured him and presently murdered him, after receiving his stipulated ransom! On his capture, Simon, the only remaining brother, took the command of the Jewish nation. Tryphon having murdered the young Antiochus and obtained the Syrian throne, Deme-

* How the Jews and Spartans claimed kindred, as alleged in the book of Maccabees, seems quite inexplicable. See Whiston's Josephus, Antiq. xiii. 5, 8, *note;* see also 1 Macc. xii. 2; xiv. 16; 2 Macc. v. 9. Jahn (Hebrew Commonwealth, B. ix. sect. 91) has the following note upon this curious subject:

"Under the reign of Seleucus Philopator, Josephus (Ant. xii., iv. 10) places the letter of Arius, or Darius or Onairus, king of the Spartans, to Onias the third, high-priest of the Jews. This letter, together with a reply to it, is preserved in 1 Macc. xii. 5—23. This unknown king is said to have found it written in a book, that the Spartans were the descendants of Abraham, and consequently the brethren of the Jews. This is altogether in the taste of those times, when all nations were curious to ascertain their origin and their relationship to other nations; but among the kings of Sparta, history preserves none of the name of Arius, or Darius or Onairus, and the reply of the Jews is not such as we should expect it would have been, if intended for the Spartans. It is therefore highly probable that the true name of the people referred to was corrupted by some early transcriber, and is now unknown. Michaelis, in Anmerkungen zu dem Ersten Buch der Makk. xii. 5, s. 263 sqq., conjectures that the true reading is *Σπαρδιάται*, *Spardians*, and that the country ספרד, *Sepharad* (Obadiah 20), is meant, the situation of which is now unknown. Jerome supposes ספרד is the Bosphorus, or Crimean Tartary, where it is very probable that there might have been in those times a petty king over a colony of Hebrew exiles."

trius successfully re-asserts his claims, and strengthens Simon in the government of Judea (xiii. 36). Simon's administration was a period of quiet and prosperity, upon which the historian of the Maccabees enlarges with delight and pride: "He made peace in the land, and Israel rejoiced with great joy." The Jews began to use it as a date, and "to write in their instruments and contracts, In the first year of Simon the high-priest, the governor and leader of the Jews." Civilities were renewed between the Jews and "their brethren, the Spartans," on the accession of Simon; and a shield of gold was sent to Rome to confirm the league with that great arbitress of the fate of nations, who not merely returned a gracious answer, but wrote also "unto the kings and countries," including Syria, Egypt, Pergamus, Asia Minor, Sparta, and the islands of the Ægean, "that they should do them no harm, nor fight against them, nor aid their enemies." Antiochus (Sidetes), son of Demetrius Soter and brother of Nicator (who was a prisoner with the Parthians), now takes the field against Tryphon, with Simon's aid, whom he at first confirms in his authority, and to whom he gives permission "to coin money with his own stamp for his own country"* (xiv. xv.). But his policy changed after Tryphon's defeat; and on his demanding possession of the fortresses in Judea held by Simon, war was again renewed between the Jews and the Syrians. Simon being now old, gives the direction of the war to his two elder sons, Judas and John, who defeat Cendebeus, the Syrian general (xvi.). Treachery is again employed against this race of heroes, and Simon and two of his sons are murdered by his own son-in-law, Ptolemy, the son of Abubus, who aimed at obtaining the priesthood through subservience to Syrian interests. John

* Simon's coins are known to collectors. See introductory chapter to "Humphreys's Coins of England," p. xvi.

alone escapes the fate which was intended to include him with his father and brothers. This was John Hyrcanus, so called from his having served under king Demetrius in Hyrcania, and who now succeeded to his father's office as king-priest, and inherited the valour of his family with better fortune than some of them (B.C. 135—106).

But here the first book of the Maccabees abruptly ends, just telling us that the acts and wars and worthy deeds of John "are written in the chronicles of his priesthood," documents quite unknown to us. But, in spite of this vague allusion, one may be tempted to think the book of Maccabees (all but this little addition) was written before the death of John. Otherwise, why was it not carried further? At any rate, Josephus is our authority from this period for such events as do not appear on the pages of general history.

The Second Book of Maccabees is not a continuation of the history, such as one would expect from the title, but contains a number of attempted additions to the incidents in the first, chiefly of the nature of exaggerations and marvels. These may be compared to the additions to the book of Esther, or those made to the book of Daniel; for these are in like manner by a later writer, who seemingly could not be satisfied with the unembellished story of the Maccabees as already written. He does not indeed allude to the first book, but one can hardly doubt that it was known to him, as most of his embellishments are additions or expansions, rather than repetitions. They reach no further down than the time of Judas, terminating abruptly, as if the writer was tired of his task. He professes (ii. 23) that his book is an abridgment of five books by one Jason of Cyrene, and introduces it by a curious preface, purporting to be a letter from the Jews in Judea to those in

Egypt, exhorting them to keep the feast of Dedication. This letter is a curious jumble of chronology. It speaks (i. 7) of the Jews in Judea as having written, "when Demetrius reigned, in the 169th year" (B.C. 143), "in the extremity of trouble" about Jason's defection; and (ver. 10) of another letter in the 188th year (B.C. 124); and then (ver. 13) seems to connect this last date with the death of Antiochus Epiphanes, which happened in 165! The book is plainly later than B.C. 124, and this is all we can say about its origin. Of Jason of Cyrene, nothing is known. The taste for the marvellous is freely indulged in the silly legend of the preservation of the sacred fire during the Babylonian captivity (i. 19—22), and that of Jeremiah's having commanded the tabernacle, ark and altar of incense to go with him to Mount Sinai, where he hid them in a cave for the same period! The prodigies assigned to the time of Judas chiefly consist of aerial horsemen and youths in bright armour, at one time protecting the temple from spoliation, at another encompassing the Jewish hero, and virtually damaging instead of sustaining his renown. The savage cruelties detailed with horrid minuteness as inflicted by Epiphanes, we must hope are exaggerations also. The style of this book is rhetorical and inflated, while in many places vague, and palpably unhistorical throughout, presenting a strange contrast to the grave dignity of the first book.

A THIRD BOOK OF THE MACCABEES (so called), written like the two preceding in Greek, is not admitted even into the Romish Canon, nor found in the Protestant Apocrypha. It refers to an earlier time than that of the Maccabean princes, namely, the year B.C. 217, in the reign of Ptolemy IV. (Philopator) of Egypt, and that of the Syrian Antiochus III. (the Great). Its contents are: a legend about Ptolemy's intrusion into the holy place of the temple, as he returned from an unsuccessful expedition against the Syrians, and his falling down speechless on the spot, his subsequent persecution of the Jews in Alexandria, and their miraculous deliverance. This book is supposed not to have been written till after the time of Christ.

A FOURTH BOOK OF THE MACCABEES, but of unknown contents, is also spoken of in ecclesiastical history.

A book written in Latin and translated into Arabic is given in Walton's Polyglot Bible, bearing the name of *the Second Book of Maccabees,* which is made up chiefly of the contents of the Greek first and second books, but is also continued down to the times of Herod and Pilate, —that is, the time of Jesus Christ. This is not received as canonical in any part of the Christian Church.

We must now resume our brief abstract of the Jewish history.

JOHN HYRCANUS succeeded his father Simon, as priest and king, B.C. 135, as mentioned at the end of the first book of Maccabees. Josephus ascribes to him also the gift of prophecy (which the writer of the Maccabees, however, had evidently no idea of, as he regrets the want of a prophet). The dispute still raging between the brothers Demetrius (Nicator) and Antiochus (Sidetes) for the throne of Syria, Hyrcanus is enabled to regain the independence of Judea, which it retained till brought under the Roman power by Pompey, B.C. 66. He subdued Samaria, and destroyed the rival temple on Gerizim; subjugated Idumæa, and made it henceforth one nation with Judea. He renewed the treaty with the Romans for offence and defence, and restored the reputation of the Jewish kingdom through a reign of thirty years. During his reign, the rival factions of Pharisees and Sadducees become conspicuous; the former representing the Assideans, or Chesidim, of an earlier day, now sadly degenerated into formalism, ostentation and bigotry; the latter being the more philosophical and thoughtful, and sometimes sceptical, order of minds; much as we find them in the gospel history a century and half later. The rivalries of these parties caused serious domestic trouble to the otherwise glorious reign of Hyrcanus; and the king, on receiving personal offence from some of the Pharisees, changed his policy, and conspicuously favoured the Sadducees thenceforth.

ARISTOBULUS, son and successor of Hyrcanus (106 B.C.), reigned only one year, dying, it should appear, of horror for having unintentionally occasioned a brother to be assassinated, while exercising cruelty without compunction towards his mother and his other brothers.

ALEXANDER JANNÆUS, the third son of Hyrcanus, succeeded, and reigned twenty-six years (B.C. 104—78) vigorously and successfully, but cruelly. Syria was now weak and divided. Cyprus was his principal foreign foe; Egypt his ally. The Pharisees were his deadly opponents at home. On his death-bed, he counselled his wife Alexandra to throw herself upon them for support, which she did accordingly.

HYRCANUS II. (B.C. 78—40), a man of weak mind, the eldest son of Jannæus, was raised to the high-priesthood, the queen-mother Alexandra administering secular affairs vigorously during his first nine years, till her death. After her death, Aristobulus, her second son, disputed the throne with Hyrcanus, who quietly retired into private life. Antipater, an Idumean, the prime minister of Hyrcanus and father of Herod, afterwards the Great, now also appears on the stage of Jewish politics, plotting for his own ends, and persuading Hyrcanus to take refuge with Aretas, king of Arabia, in his capital, Petra. Aretas and Hyrcanus enter into a treaty of mutual interest, and march against Aristobulus, who retreats to Jerusalem.

While they press the siege, the Romans interfere in the person of Scaurus, the lieutenant of Pompey, who has taken Damascus, and has his eye upon Petra and the trade of the Red Sea. Scaurus orders that the siege be raised; and the rival brothers present themselves before Pompey at Damascus, who temporizes with both while pursuing his own designs. Aristobulus shuts himself up in Jerusalem, and the Romans take it after a siege of three months, advancing their earth-works and engines every sabbath without opposition from the Jews, whose idea of self-defence, according to their own historian (contrary to the practice established by the Maccabees), did not admit of their opposing such operations on the sabbath! On gaining possession of the temple, Pompey went into the holy of holies, and was astonished to find no statue or symbol of deity there. He respected the furniture and wealth of the temple (which was afterwards, however, plundered by Crassus), and confirmed Hyrcanus in the priesthood, but without the crown. Five courts, or sanhedrims, were soon after instituted in different towns of Judea by the Roman general Gabinius. The Romans sustained this state of things for a while against several attempts on the part of Aristobulus and his sons, till Julius Cæsar restored Hyrcanus to his royal dignity, Antipater being, however, the virtual king under the other's name. He appointed his eldest son, Phasael, to the government of Jerusalem, and Herod, his younger, to that of Galilee, defying the Jewish sanhedrim and trusting to Roman sanction.

After the death of Cæsar, Cassius came into Syria. His exactions were oppressive in Judea, but Herod courted him successfully, as he did afterwards Mark Antony.

One struggle more had Herod to make for the acquisition of sovereignty. Antigonus, the son of Aristobulus, and now the only remains of the Asmonean family besides Hyrcanus, takes advantage of the invasion of Syria by the Parthians to interest them in his quarrel. Hyrcanus is taken prisoner, and mutilated in the ears by order of Antigonus, to disqualify him for the priesthood ever after. And while the Parthians are plundering the country, Herod successfully pays his court to Augustus and Antony at Rome, and is invested with the kingdom of Judea, which, with the assistance of the Romans, he has no very great difficulty in securing against his competitors. Herod's accession to the throne brings us to the year B.C. 37. He is known as

HEROD THE GREAT. The leading facts of Herod's reign may be thus summed up. Having adhered to the cause of Antony, who represented the Roman power in the East, he proceeded, on the death of that Triumvir, to lay his crown at the feet of the victorious Octavius, at Rhodes; and boldly making a merit of his fidelity to his former master, proffered the same service to Octavius, and received his diadem again.

His administration was stern, relentless and cruel. His domestic history (his ten wives and mixed family the sure root of discord) is a series of dark dissensions and intrigues, tragic crimes and avenging woes. His patron, Augustus, is said to have satirically remarked, that "it were better to be one of Herod's swine than one of his sons."

He shocked the zealous Jews by the erection of amphitheatres, and by his patronage of Roman games and customs. His love of magnificence shewed itself in building towns, especially Samaria, which he named Sebaste (Latin, *Augusta),* in compliment to Augustus Cæsar; and Cæsarea, where formerly stood a little fort known as the Tower of Straton. More acceptably to the Jews, though the proposal was received with a natural jealousy on their part at first, he lavished his magnificence also upon the rebuilding of the temple, now 500 years old, and much dilapidated through age as well as injured by repeated wars. He acquired the country to the east of the Lake of Galilée, known as Trachonitis, which had been previously overrun by banditti. His death took place shortly after the birth of Christ, but before the current Christian era (which seems to be placed about four years later than it ought to be). The frenzy of his mind during his last illness, makes it quite credible that he should have issued a very undiscriminating order for the massacre of any number of young children, among whom he might suppose a future king of the Jews to be possibly included.

Herod, by will, divided his kingdom between his two sons by his wife Malthace. To Archelaus, he gave the southern part, including Idumea, Judea and Samaria; to Antipas, the northern and eastern, consisting of Galilee and Peræa ("the country beyond Jordan"). Archelaus went to Rome to have his title ratified before he would put on the crown; and Antipas met him before the court of Augustus to claim the whole government by virtue of an earlier will of Herod's. Meanwhile, Sabinus, the procurator of Syria, took military possession of the country with a view to plunder, and his oppressions drove the Jews to revolt. At length the imperial edict arrived, making Archelaus ethnarch (not king) of the parts bequeathed to him, and Antipas of Galilee and Peræa; while to Herod-Philip (the son of Herod by Mariamne) were assigned the districts of Trachonitis, Auranitis, Paneas and Batanæa, lying north of Peræa. Antipas is the "Herod tetrarch of Galilee" in the gospel history (see Luke iii. 1).

The administration of Archelaus was unjust and cruel. After nine years, he was summoned to Rome to answer

[P. 66]

Parallel Dates from the end of the Old-Testament History to the beginning of the New.

Persia.		Judea.		Egypt.		Rome and the World.	
Cyrus	536	Decree of Cyrus and Zerubbabel's return	536				
Cambyses	529			Conquered by Cambyses	525	Confucius, China, fl.	520
Smerdis	522	Temple finished (?)	515			Zoroaster, Persia	
Darius Hystaspis	521					Hippias expelled Athens	510
Xerxes I.	485					Marathon	490
Artaxerxes I. (Longim.)	465	Ezra's return	458			Thermopylæ and Salamis	480
Xerxes II.	424	Nehemiah's	446			Herodotus fl.	445
Sogdianus	424					Peloponn. War began	431
Darius II. (Nothus)	423	Joiada, high-priest	413			Thucydides fl.	,,
						Socrates died	399
Artaxerxes II.	404	Jonathan or Jehu ,,	373			Plato	428—347
,, III.	358	Jaddua ,,	341			Aristotle	384—322
Arses or Arogus	337					Philip, king of Macedon	360
Darius III. (Codomanus)	335					Alexander ,,	336
Alexander's Conquest	331	Onias ,,	321	Ptolemy I. (Lagi)	323	,, died	323
				Judea subject	320—314		
Syria.							
Seleucus Nicator (Era of the Seleucidæ)	312	Simon the Just ,,	300	Battle of Ipsus gave Judea to Ptolemy	301		
Judea under Syria	311—301	Eleazer ,,	292				
Seleuceia built	291			Ptolemy II. (Philadelphus)	284		
Antiochus Soter	280	Manasses ,,	277			First Punic War	264
,, II. (Theos)	260	Onias II. ,,	250	,, III. (Euergetes)	246		
Seleucus II. (Callinicus)	245	Simon II. ,,	217				
,, III. (Ceraunus)	225						
Antiochus III. (Magnus)	223			,, IV. (Philopator)	221	Second Punic War	218
Seleucus IV. (Philopator)	186	Onias III. ,,	195	,, V. (Epiphanes)	204	(Hannibal took refuge with Antiochus III.)	
Antiochus IV. (Epiphanes)	175	Jason ,,	174	,, VI. (Philometor)	180		

Syria.		Judea.		Egypt.		Rome and the World.	
Antiochus V. (Eupator) (Lysias Guardian)	164	Menelaus, high-priest	172			First Roman army in Asia defeats Antiochus	190
Demetrius Soter	162	Judas Maccabeus	165				
Alexander Balas	150	Alcimus, high-priest	161	Ptolemy Euergetes II. or Physcon	145	Third Punic War begins	149
Demetrius Nicator	145	Jonathan, king	160			Carthage and Corinth destroyed	148
Antiochus VI. Theos	144	,, high-priest	153				
Tryphon	142	Simon, king and priest	143				
Antiochus Sidetes	140	John Hyrcanus ,,	135				
Demetrius Nicator II.	130			,, Soter II. or Lathyrus	116		
Antiochus Grypus	123						
,, Cyzicenus	112	Aristobulus I.	106			Pompey and Cicero born	106
		Alexander Jannæus	104			Julius Cæsar born	100
Seleucus VI.	96						
Tigranes, king of Armenia	83	Alexandra, Queen Mother	78	,, Alexander	80	Sylla Dictator	82
Antiochus Asiaticus	69	Hyrcanus II. and Aristobulus II.	69				
Syria made a Roman province by Pompey	65	Hyrcanus II.	63	,, Auletes	65		
		Gabinius, Rom. Governor	58			First Triumvirate	59
		Crassus	55	Ptolemy and Cleopatra	51	Second ,,	43
		Antigonus	40				
		Herod the Great	37	The Romans	31	Battle of Actium	31
		Archelaus	3			Augustus Emperor	27
		Judea a Rom. province	A.D. 8			Tiberius	A.D. 14
		Pilate, Procurator	26			Caligula	37
		Jesus Christ crucified	30			Claudius	41
						Nero	54
		Paul called to the Apostleship of the Gentiles	36			Galba	68
						Otho, Vitellius, Vespasian	69

the accusations of his brothers and his subjects, and was banished to Vienne, in Gaul. Judea was now made a Roman province (A.D. 8), as we find it in the time of the New Testament. The consequent levying of tribute gave occasion to an insurrection under Judas Gaulonitis, one of the numerous self-instituted prophets, or Christs, who were continually throwing themselves on the popular expectation of a temporal deliverer and king. Pontius Pilate was appointed procurator of Judea, A.D. 26, by the emperor Tiberius, succeeding Valerius Gratus, who had governed eleven years. During this time, Judea was tranquil on the whole. The prætor had resided in Cæsarea, making his winter quarters in Samaria, till Pilate's time, who took up his winter residence at Jerusalem, but found himself obliged to respect the religious scruples of the Jews by withdrawing the emblematic Roman *Eagle* from the city.

A chronological table may be usefully inserted here, presenting the Jewish dates from the end of the Old-Testament history to the beginning of the New, with the parallel dates of Persia, followed by those of Syria on the one side, and Egypt on the other, and the Roman and World dates in a fourth column. (Pp. 64, 65).

[These dates are derived from popular sources, and do not pretend to have been adjusted to any particular chronological system; but they are sufficiently reliable for all ordinary purposes. My authorities are chiefly the following: Milman's History of the Jews, Kitto's History of Palestine, the Penny Cyclopædia, and the chronological tables appended to the Outlines of History in Lardner's Cabinet Cyclopædia. There is frequently a difference of a year or two (seldom more) in the same date as given by these different books. One year's difference of notation is often due to the fact of the years of an ancient era not being *conterminous* with those of the Christian era, into which they have been converted; just as the Old Style and New make the difference of a year to all events in January, February and March, up to the 25th day.]

THE CHRISTIAN SCRIPTURES;

OR,

BOOKS OF THE NEW COVENANT.

THE CHRISTIAN SCRIPTURES.

CHAPTER I.

THE CLAIMS OF CHRISTIANITY AS A DIVINE REVELATION.

CHRISTIANITY claims to be a *Divine Revelation.* By this we understand that it professes to be something beyond the range of Nature,—taking that term *Nature* in its widest meaning, to include both the ordinary phenomena of the outward universe, and the constitutional faculties of the human mind as taught and developed by the ordinary course of phenomena and events around it.

In one sense, indeed, the Religion of Nature might itself be called a divine revelation, inasmuch as God is known in His works. The Scriptures themselves expressly point to the works of Nature as manifestations of the Supreme Being. "The heavens declare the glory of God, and the firmament sheweth his handiwork." "The invisible things of Him from the creation of the world are clearly seen, being understood by the things that are made; even his eternal power and godhead." Christianity, in announcing itself as a supernatural revelation, admits, or rather assumes, all this as its very basis. It assumes that man has a religious *Faculty* to which it may address itself; and that the *Creation* in which he stands and the *Providence* which is over him have already imparted to him some perception of religion. It necessarily assumes all this, when it professes to give him additional religious knowledge and a higher religious culture.

Let no one, then, disparage the Religion of Nature, with the idea of exalting that of Revelation. They do not fully understand either, who think the two can really be at variance, or that the latter can be jealous of the admitted excellence of the former. Natural Religion lies at the basis of Revealed, whether argumentatively, or historically, or in the progress of the individual mind. We assume the belief in a Supreme Being, the moment we begin to inquire whether He has supernaturally revealed His perfections and will. The evidences of revealed religion are offered expressly to Theists, not to Atheists. With the latter (if there really be such persons) we must go a great step further back, and present to them the primary arguments of natural religion in proof of the being of a God.

It is not within the scope of this book systematically to set forth the *Evidences* on which it may be intelligently believed that Christianity is a divine revelation. Those evidences, in their proper time and order, ought, however, to be most rigidly examined by every one who has the leisure, learning and ability requisite for such an investigation. They are partly *external*, partly *internal*. The external proofs of the divine origin of Christianity, being altogether historical, imply a careful inquiry into literary and critical matters of great variety and of no little difficulty. They are the appropriate study of the scholar and the professional divine. The internal are the class of proofs most open to general perception, and most likely reasonably to satisfy the intelligent Christian who possesses ordinary knowledge and cultivation, but who is destitute of technical and professional learning. They are such as impress the mind and heart, in reading the New Testament, with a sense of the reality of the things there related, and of the elevated religiousness of the instructions, precepts, promises and examples there enshrined; suggesting the more or less defined feeling or conviction, that "never man spake like that man;" that "no man could do such miracles as Jesus did except God were with him;" that he is "the way, the truth and the life," "the holy one of God," who has "given us the words which he had himself heard from God."

But in the true logical order of thought and study, the proper preliminary to all these inquiries into either the internal or the external evidences of the truth of Christianity would plainly be, to ascertain first *what its scriptures really are*, and *what the religion itself is* which they offer for our acceptance. Not till we know what Christianity really is, and what are its actual claims on our assent, are we really able rationally to decide whether we can, or cannot, admit its claims and adopt its principles into our hearts and lives. The study of the Scriptures, in short, should, in logical order of study, precede that of books on "the Evidences," and might in part supersede the latter by narrowing the further topics of inquiry.

This preliminary office, then, is attempted in the present pages; while in its pursuit, no doubt, the internal class of evidences, and some of the external also, will be incidentally developed through this very study of the real character and claims of Christianity and of the nature of its Scriptures. I only wish, therefore, in this chapter, devoted to "the Claims of Christianity as a Divine Revelation," to give clear and unequivocal expression to a few of the broadest, if not the most generally admitted, principles of religious philosophy, in opposition to certain abstract or *à-priori* objections which, under ever-varying phraseology, still repeat themselves from age to age, and which, if regarded as valid, must preclude our acceptance of Christianity at all, as supernatural or superhuman.

The principles here avowed in reference to Christianity, are equally true in reference to Judaism also, which, in its time and place, claims likewise to be viewed as of divine authority. But the remoteness of the facts on which Judaism rests, and the serious difficulties attaching to many parts of its very ancient records, remove them from the reach of that minuter criticism which may be satisfactorily applied to the comparatively recent books of the Christian revelation. The thoughtful Christian accepts the divine origin of Judaism chiefly, it may be, as a retrospective inference from his more definite and clear belief in the divinity of the Gospel; and while confessing himself unable to define the precise limits of the natural and the supernatural in all the venerable records of the Old Testament, he may without blame satisfy himself to rest in a general conviction of the revealed origin of its pure theology and high morals, as the only theory that is consistent with the sadly contrasted history of the rest of the ancient world.

But as regards the claims of Christianity, which arose nearly fifteen centuries lower down the stream of time, and in a properly historical and (more than that) an eminently literary period, no such vagueness of general belief ought to satisfy an intelligent mind. And, as we are now about to inquire into the nature and contents, the occasions and the authorship, of the various books of the New Testament, in which the claims of the religion of Jesus Christ to be regarded as a divine revelation set themselves forth, it seems the proper occasion for at least protesting against any such argumentative assumptions as would prejudge, or even preclude, those claims. Having done this briefly, I shall leave the claims of the

Christian Scriptures to speak for themselves, while endeavouring to exhibit the leading characteristics and contents of the respective books of the New Testament.

It is quite right, as it is inevitable, that our advancing knowledge of the works of creation in a scientific age like the present, should impress us more and more with a general presumption in favour of that majestic uniformity as having been unbroken in times past, which we never find to be broken now. If we look at it religiously, we recognize in this uniformity of nature the wisdom and goodness of the Divine Being, whose continued operation we acknowledge in the laws of nature, and whom we can only imagine to have imposed upon Himself this strict regularity of operation *for the sake of His rational and moral creatures*, whose peculiar faculties are continually exercised and trained through their experience and expectation of uniform results from uniform causes, but would have been given in vain if they were placed in a world destitute of law. Such is our religious recognition of the uniformity of nature. We ascribe it to the wisdom and goodness of God. And when we read of any alleged violation of this majestic and beneficent order of things, we are naturally and rightly affected with a feeling of its *primâ facie* improbability. We demand strong evidence for the alleged facts. We scrutinize them carefully, to see whether they may not admit of philosophical solution on natural principles. And we also involuntarily, but tacitly, demand a *moral* reason to justify us in ascribing to the Deity such a departure from the beneficent uniformity which He has Himself ordained. All this is rational and truly religious.

But upon some minds this uniformity of nature produces a further result that is not rational nor religious,—a result merely mechanical and passive in its growth;

and sadly contracting to the mind in its influence. From seeing nature thus uniform, they begin to regard it as *necessarily* uniform, and not as uniform at the pure will of the Deity, and for His wise and kind purposes. They come, in short, to idolize Nature, and tacitly take its Laws to be the supreme Power or Will of the universe. And then, instead of regarding miracle as simply improbable, and *primâ facie* suspicious, and as requiring to be jealously scrutinized, they become so boldly unphilosophical as to undertake to prove that it is *impossible* for the Deity to do sometimes what He does not do always. Hume's celebrated but sophistical argument is simply this feeling put into words; and, in whatever varied phraseology it be reproduced, it is still but the assumption, founded on the general government of the world by certain laws, that the Creator *cannot* relax, control or overbear His own laws if He please. Dr. Channing has described this tendency of mind in his excellent discourse on the "Evidences of Revealed Religion" (preached at the Dudleian Lecture before the University of Cambridge, Mass., 1821). The whole discourse cannot be too highly recommended as an exposition of the gospel evidences:

"These later times are distinguished, as you well know, by successful researches into nature; and the discoveries of science have continually added strength to that great principle, that the phenomena of the universe are regulated by general and permanent laws, or that the Author of the universe exerts his power according to an established order. Nature, the more it is explored, is found to be uniform. We observe an unbroken succession of causes and effects. Many phenomena, once denominated irregular, and ascribed to supernatural agency, are found to be connected with preceding circumstances, as regularly as the most common events. The comet, we learn, observes the same attraction as the sun and planets. When a new phenomenon now occurs, no one thinks it miraculous, but believes that, when better understood, it may be reduced to laws already known, or is an example of a law not yet investigated.

"Now this increasing acquaintance with the uniformity of nature begets a distrust of alleged violations of it, and a rational distrust too; for while many causes of mistake in regard to alleged miracles may be assigned, there is but one adequate cause of real miracles, that is, the power of God; and the regularity of nature forms a strong presumption against the miraculous exertion of this power, except in extraordinary circumstances, and for extraordinary purposes to which the established laws of the creation are not competent. But the observation of the uniformity of nature produces in multitudes, not merely this rational distrust of alleged violations of it, but a secret feeling as if such violations were impossible. That attention to the powers of nature which is implied in scientific research, tends to weaken the practical conviction of a higher power; and the laws of the creation, instead of being regarded as the modes of Divine operation, come insensibly to be considered as fetters on his agency, as too sacred to be suspended even by their Author. This secret feeling, essentially atheistical, and at war with all sound philosophy, is the chief foundation of that scepticism which prevails in regard to miraculous agency, and deserves our particular consideration."

The newest form of *moving the previous question* against the discussion of the supernatural claims of Christianity is, to declare that an "external revelation" is a contradiction in terms. The inward consciousness of the mind, we are told, is the only revelation possible. Yet the upholders of this dogma are accustomed to speak without scruple of the works of nature as "revealing" to them the perfections of the Deity. And whether this be a right or a wrong use of the term "revelation," certainly the source of religious knowledge and impression is, in that case, *external* to the mind. In this often-repeated *dictum of the impossibility of an external revelation*, a strange confusion seems indeed to be made between two things sufficiently distinct and distinguishable, namely, between the necessary *internalness* of the *faculty* which understands and believes, with all its operations in understanding and believing, and the disputed *externalness* of some at least of the *materials* for understanding and belief. It seems strange, indeed, that so loose a fallacy as that of confounding the faculty which believes with the alleged materials which invite or enter into our belief, should beset a highly acute class of writers such as those now alluded to: but how else can we explain the position taken by them against the possibility of an "external revelation" and a "book revelation"? While, however, alluding thus especially to this new phase of the argument against all supernatural revelation, the further statement of the principles on which we vindicate the philosophy of revealed religion, will be made in general terms of the widest applicability.

In considering the grounds of religious belief, whether in reference to natural or revealed religion, we plainly have to examine two distinct matters: first, our own conscious *faculty*, as the believing power; and secondly, the *materials of belief* presented to it. It seems almost superfluous to explain or argue that these two matters are perfectly distinct, though both of them are concerned in the practical acquisition of religious belief and feeling. The one is internal; the other is external, though affecting us inwardly, as we can be no otherwise affected. The one is *of* us,—the other is *out of* us, but works its spiritual results *in* us. We have many other faculties which we never confound with their objects. Sight is a faculty, and visible things are its objects. Hearing is a faculty, and sounds are its objects. The stomach is—a faculty, shall we say? or an organ possessing the faculty of digestion; food is its supply, its object. The conscience is a faculty of higher and more subtle order, and our own and other people's actions are the objects of its attention and judgment. So, the more directly religious sense (perhaps including the conscience) is a faculty: its materials for religious belief and feeling are not themselves the faculty, but matters external to it, while adapted to it and capable of impressing their appropriate qualities upon it. This religious faculty may indeed have (as some maintain, and it matters not to our present purpose to dispute or affirm) certain *intuitive* ideas or perceptions; as the conscience may be believed to have certain *instinctive* judgments, applicable to external occasions, but prior to them. It may be left to the deep metaphysician to decide whether such intuitions or instincts are properly to be called the faculty itself, or its self-developed results; but manifestly there are also large materials, apart from these and quite external to the faculty, which address themselves to it and exercise and develope it continually, and without which the religious faculty can be no more said to be complete in its internal self-action, than the eye can have its vision without access to the external world, or the stomach perform digestion except on the admission of food from without. The faculty, in short, is one thing; its materials are another; and these may be partly self-supplied perhaps, but are chiefly from without, in the first instance at least,—that being true of affection, and of the religious faculty as partaking of both intellect and affection, which was acutely said by Leibnitz of the intellect: *Nihil in intellectu* (affectu) *quod non prius in sensu, nisi ipse intellectus* (affectus). In plain English, All that is in the mind was first in the senses, *except the mind itself.* An important distinction, yet often overlooked!

The religious faculty, then, whatever instincts of feeling or intuitions of thought it may have, is plainly cognizant of *external* sources, occasions or suggestions of feeling and of thought in the world of creation and providence; and there is therefore no childish absurdity, on the face of our argument, in maintaining that it could equally receive (if offered to it) external materials from the miraculous deeds and inspired thoughts of others.

This religious faculty seems as clearly an essential attribute of man as any of his bodily or mental powers; varying in acuteness, like all his other powers, with nations, families and individuals. When it has devoted itself to the investigation of the physical creation, and found order, beauty and kind design in its wonderful arrangements, it ascribes to the unseen Cause of all things the attributes thus betokened. In the course of Providence over human history, if it can trace, though with tremulous thought, the production of good amid evil, and a reigning law of progress amid social complexity and strife, it is proportionately strengthened in the bright and happy convictions of Theism. By acute self-inspection, it further finds that the vague idea of Deity is ultimately developed from germs of Power, Wisdom and Love existing in the human soul itself, and expanding to meet the manifestations of a higher Wisdom, Power and Love in the creation around. And who then shall say it is a thing in itself impossible or incredible, that from yet other sources, just as much external to itself as those works of Nature and ways of Providence,—from a life, for instance, of divinest virtue heralded by radiant miracle, and from instructions inspired by superhuman wisdom,—the same religious faculty should receive yet further developement and aid? This is the question, stated in the abstract, as to the possibility of an external revelation.

And it is difficult indeed to imagine what *à-priori* objection there can be, on *Theistical* principles, to the admission that this is at least possible. Whether actual or not, is a question of fact, to be decided by a careful examination of the alleged case. But our question just now relates simply to its abstract possibility. And I must plainly avow my inability to enter even into the feeling, *as a Theist*, that a miraculous interposition is abstractedly impossible. Its *à-priori improbability* may indeed impress me, *as* a Theist, when I have been devoting myself earnestly to the study of natural phenomena, and have been struck with the majestic uniformity of the Creation's laws, which I find are never relaxed even to save the infliction of grievous pain and suffering, when these result in the course of that grand uniformity;—doubtless because infinitely more pain and suffering are avoided by man's intelligent perception of the uniformity and his self-guidance accordingly. But if, in turn, I devote myself to another study, that of the mental and moral phenomena of my own being, where I find no such laws of mechanical and chemical uniformity existing, but Thought and Will, instead, recognizing the immediate presence of the Divine Spirit in the human soul; the former impression against the probability of supernatural communications from the Deity is apt to give place to the very opposite feeling of expectation, rather, that they may be frequent in my own and all other human souls. And so, while one set of reasoners have, under the all-prevailing idea of mechanical and chemical laws, doubted the possibility of the Deity revealing Himself beyond or above the laws of matter, another set of minds have believed in what they have called *perpetual miracles* within the soul,—that is, in spiritual influences from the Father of our spirits; which *being constant*, they have committed an abuse of language in calling miraculous at all, since they ought rather to have endeavoured reverently to refer them to the supersensuous, but not supernatural, *laws* of the human soul itself. But who shall presume to deny that the Great Ruler of all may, if He sees fit, define for Himself another course of *properly miraculous or supernatural* intervention; and, neither absolutely bounding His operations in the material world by the laws of His general agency when special deviations are warranted, nor, in His ordinary access to the souls of men, influencing them in a manner devoid of appropriate law, may, on rare occasions and for great purposes of blessing, have asserted His supremacy over the general laws both of matter and of mind, for the greater good of His spiritual creature, man?

The theory of the miraculous origin of the gospel maintains that the Heavenly Father *has* thus acted, when He inspired the soul of Jesus Christ with special divine wisdom, and committed to his hands miraculous power over physical nature. Channing, in the admirable discourse already cited, thus powerfully illustrates the true sanctity of the laws of God in nature, and the implied supremacy of Him whose laws they are:

"To a man whose belief in God is strong and practical, a miracle will appear as possible as any other effect, as the most common event in life; and the argument against miracles, drawn from the uniformity of nature, will weigh with him only as far as this uniformity is a pledge and proof of the Creator's disposition to accomplish his purposes by a fixed order or mode of operation. Now it is freely granted, that the Creator's regard or attachment to such an order may be inferred from the steadiness with which he observes it; and a strong presumption lies against any violations of it on slight occasions, or for purposes to which the established laws of nature are adequate. But this is the utmost which the order of nature authorizes us to infer respecting its Author. It forms no presumption against miracles universally, in all imaginable cases, but may even furnish a presumption in their favour.

"We are never to forget that God's adherence to the order

of the universe is not necessary and mechanical, but intelligent and voluntary. He adheres to it, not for his own sake, or because it has a sacredness which compels him to respect it, but because it is most suited to accomplish his purposes. It is a means, and not an end; and like all other means must give way when the end can best be promoted without it. It is the mark of a weak mind, to make an idol of order and method,—to cling to established forms of business, when they clog instead of advancing it. If, then, the great purposes of the universe can best be accomplished by departing from its established laws, these laws will undoubtedly be suspended; and though broken in the letter, they will be observed in their spirit, for the ends for which they were first instituted will be advanced by their violation. Now the question arises, for what purposes were nature and its order appointed? and there is no presumption in saying, that the highest of these is the improvement of intelligent beings. Mind (by which we mean both moral and intellectual powers) is God's first end. The great purpose for which an order of nature is fixed, is plainly the formation of Mind. In a creation without order, where events would follow without any regular succession, it is obvious that mind must be kept in perpetual infancy; for in such a universe there could be no reasoning from effects to causes, no induction to establish general truths, no adaptation of means to ends; that is, no science relating to God, or matter or mind; no action; no virtue. The great purpose of God, then, I repeat it, in establishing the order of nature, is to form and advance the mind; and if the case should occur in which the interests of the mind could best be advanced by departing from this order, or by miraculous agency, then the great purpose of the creation, the great end of its laws and regularity, would demand such departure; and miracles, instead of warring against, would concur with nature.

"Now, we Christians maintain that such a case has existed. We affirm, that when Jesus Christ came into the world, nature had failed to communicate instructions to men, in which, as intelligent beings, they had the deepest concern, and on which the full developement of their highest faculties essentially depended; and we affirm, that there was no prospect of relief from nature; so that an exigence had occurred in which additional communications, supernatural lights, might rationally be expected from the Father of spirits."

It seems evidently impossible to give any definition of what we mean by miracle, except *negatively*. We mean that which the uniform laws of nature are insufficient to produce; but whether it be done immediately by a divine act, or instrumentally through some unknown secondary agent not among the uniform powers of nature, seems useless and absurd to speculate.

If to this definition it be objected (as it often is), that what is a miracle to one age through mere ignorance of its cause, may not be so to another age more advanced in science,—we accept the truth of this very obvious observation; but as an *objection* to the gospel miracles we must say it is quite irrelevant. It shews, indeed, that they necessarily have to be tested by a more perfect science than that of their own day. It is a pledge that they must and shall undergo a continually more and more searching scientific scrutiny; and that those essential and well-attested facts of the gospel history which cannot, with the aid even of our advanced science, be referred to any known law, must have been simply miraculous beyond dispute, if they ensued upon the word of Jesus of Nazareth. This seems the only practical bearing upon the gospel miracles, of an observation which is often very gravely propounded on the general subject, with the implied thought that its application would have the effect of disparaging the Christian miracles; whereas, it does just the contrary. Our modern physical science has not detected any *natural laws* according to which the leper was cleansed, the lame walked, the demoniac was cured and the dead brought to life, at the mere word of Jesus Christ. Nor has the modern science of mind and morals enabled us, when reading history more carefully by its light, to explain the character and pretensions of Jesus as the natural growth of his age and country, or his moral and religious instructions as due to his parentage and education.

I do not attempt to refine or speculate upon the nature of miraculous influences, whether as inspiring the mind of Jesus, or as also ruling outward objects at his inspired word. That which I feel I must accept as miraculous because quite exceptional to the known order of nature in man and around him, I, by so accepting it, confess to be beyond the reach of all further philosophizing as to the *manner* of its causation. I refer it straight to God therefore, without asserting or denying anything respecting the possible means of its production at His sovereign will. Exceptional as it seems, however, in one point of view, from a higher view it is in perfect harmony with the course of the Divine government. The *harmony of design* runs through both the natural and the supernatural alike. With wise and kind design, the Creator has ordained the uniformity of nature; and with the same wise and kind design, He has ordained the specialties of inspiration and miracle.

But in admitting miracles into its belief, just as in accepting any new principles of knowledge, belief or action from unmiraculous sources, the intelligent mind involuntarily requires certain conditions to be strictly fulfilled.

The knowledge, whether professing to come from a natural or a supernatural source, must be *consistent with reason*. New knowledge, like old, may surpass our reasoning powers; but anything that contradicts them is not knowledge. Revelation, like natural science, may wrap us in the veil of mystery, but it cannot mock us with incongruities. Close beside its sublime discoveries may be "the palpable obscure" of vastness or of minuteness, of height or depth; while all around there is always the infinite and the divine. But what is taught must be intelligible. The mystery revealed is, *so far as revealed*, mystery no more. *Mystery* is but the Greek word for *secret*. A secret told, has ceased to be a secret by the telling. And the gospel, revealing mysteries, has communicated knowledge to our reasoning and understanding minds. By just so many the fewer divine secrets are still untold. Yet, O, the depth and height unknown!

So the morality which claims a revealed sanction must approve itself to the purest dictates of *conscience*. A revelation of morals, just as any human speculations on morals, necessarily addresses itself to conscience for its reception. It is absurdity, if not profaneness, to imagine the case of revealed precepts being immoral; though precepts pretending to revelation sometimes have been so. Conscience, duly appreciating its own function, rejects any such claims at once, and requires that whatever it accepts, from nature or from revelation, be accordant with its own purest dictates.

In short, to express this great principle in the most general terms, we expect and demand in any assumed revelation, that its whole influence shall be of an improving and refining kind upon our minds, feelings and characters. To this inward test Jesus Christ himself expressly appeals: "*Why, even of yourselves, judge ye not what is right?*"

It is needless to say, that all these requisites are not only found in Christianity by every one who intelligently accepts it as true and divine, but are confessed to belong to it by many others who find a stumbling-block in its miraculous claims. The want of this harmony with our other knowledge and with the highest and most genuine requirements of our intellectual and moral faculties, is our justification in at once rejecting the divine pretensions of many ancient and modern systems or sects.

Is it then asked, What is the use of miracle, when we submit even its evidence to the test within ourselves? This question bespeaks the continually repeated fallacy, first committed indeed by the highest orthodoxy, and then adopted by the most decided scepticism,—the fallacy of thinking that outward proofs can supersede the inward faculty to which they address themselves. Knowledge implies a knowing faculty. Belief resides not in the things believed, but in the mind believing. So revelation can never supersede reason, any more than the telescope or microscope the eye. The eye sees by means of the lens. The reason knows by means of the revelation. To set them at variance is like saying that revelation is not designed for reasoning man, but for the irrational brute creation. So when, by these primary tests of reason and conscience, we have rejected all palpably unworthy claims upon our acceptance, we have still to scrutinize those remaining claims which do not violate the highest sanctity of the soul. But the very fact of such false claims having been frequently put forth, may fairly be considered as pointing to the reality of some true though rare occasions of miraculous intervention on the part of the benevolent God. As the shadow follows the substance, and no one, from finding the shadow unsubstantial, argues that there was no substance to produce it,—as the counterfeit implies the previous existence of the genuine, and the existence of the genuine alone accounts for the motive or suggestion to imitate it in the spurious,—so the discriminating rejection of false miracles opens the clearer perception of the possibility and the probability of real ones having occurred, when needed by the world for great purposes.

I accept then, fully and frankly, the miraculous in

Christianity as its very basis. I cannot separate its miraculous from its ordinary events without leaving the latter mutilated, unintelligible and unnatural. So far from the miraculous being a difficulty in the way of revelation, the difficulty to me is even to imagine a revelation without miracle. But it is of great importance to clear thought and rational belief, to place the subject of Miracles in its proper *order* in the chain of Christian evidence.

The miracles of the gospel history are of two kinds, *physical* and *spiritual*, or outward and inward;—those wrought in other persons or things at the word of Christ or an apostle, and those wrought upon their own minds by the Divine inspiration. The outward works were those that commanded the largest, or at least the earliest, attention in our Lord's own day; but the great spiritual miracle of his inspired mind and character is that which constitutes the Gospel itself, as a revelation from God to man.

Now it seems obvious to notice the necessarily changed relation in which these two classes of miracle stand to the gospel evidences, through the mere lapse of time and remoteness of place. A physical miracle *seen* must have a very different effect upon the mind from a miracle *reported*, especially one belonging to a distant age and country. The miracle seen, is felt as a proof of something else; but the miracle reported, is felt to want proof itself. When the outward miracles of Christ were done before men's sight, defying explanation from natural causes, carrying with them an evidently benevolent purpose, and, above all, having the warranty of such a character and life as that of the Saviour, his personal disciples saw in them the true signs of a divine mission and conclusive proof of his superhuman qualification to teach and guide them. They argued that "no man could do such miracles unless God were with him." They regarded him as "a man proved to be from God by the miracles and signs which God did by him." They looked to him, therefore, for disclosures of important religious truth, beyond their natural and their hitherto revealed knowledge, but in harmony with all their highest perceptions of truth. Their conscience received with reverence, but without violence to its highest dictates, his expositions of duty, confirming at once and exalting their natural sense of right. Their faith welcomed his promises of spiritual and immortal blessedness, as meeting the most anxious desires and satisfying the highest faculties of their nature.

But it would be a great mistake to attempt to prove the truth of Christianity to an inquirer *now*, by appealing first to the outward miracles of Christ. Those miracles are the very things that *now* chiefly require proving. We do not believe Christianity to be divine *because of its outward miracles;* but we accept its outward miracles as belonging to it and perfectly in accordance with it, *when we believe it to be divine in itself.* Its internal, spiritual miracles are the great proofs by which it now wins assent,—the character of Jesus Christ, the heavenly wisdom of his precepts, the purity and elevation of his morality, the breadth of his philanthropy, the sublimity of his doctrines respecting God and his providence, His will and His designs, and, lastly, the disclosure of human immortality. Because we cannot account for these internal characteristics of the gospel except by admitting its superhuman origin, we accept the INSPIRATION OF CHRIST, the inwardly miraculous part of his mission. Then as to the outward miracles, which we find to be quite inseparable from his history and in strictest harmony with the spirit and objects of his mission,—we accept them as credible in that connection, and as sustaining the unity of impression made by his whole life and teaching,—though, *if* we could look at them as unconnected with the spiritual design and spiritual characteristics of the gospel, we might and ought to feel that almost insuperable philosophical difficulties attached to them.

This is, I believe, the ordinary process of thought by which an intelligent belief of the miraculous in Christianity takes place;—first to accept Christ's character and work as genuine and true in itself, and to feel that inspiration is its true and only solution; and then to feel that the outward array of miracle is not only an inseparable accompaniment in the record, but an appropriate and harmonious one in the idea; that the superhuman in the inspired soul of Christ has its fit expression in benevolent miracle. In this respect, the order of conviction is the very reverse of what we must suppose to have been customary with our Lord's contemporaries, who were first struck with the outward miracle, and afterwards perceived more and more fully the inspiration and holiness of his mind. Yet even with them, the latter became, as it is with us, the fount of Christian principle and hope; the former had but pointed the way to it.

It may be quite impossible further to define the character or the extent of the supernatural illumination which we must ascribe to Jesus Christ. No doubt the estimate of different minds, if they should attempt it, would greatly differ, according to their relative estimates of human nature and of its historical circumstances; and there is room for some variety of comparative estimate among those who maintain the same general conclusion in referring to the supernatural all that is above their highest estimate of the natural.

"It is indeed true" (says Channing in the discourse before quoted) "that human powers are not exactly defined, nor can we state precisely the bounds beyond which they cannot pass; but still, the disproportion between human nature and an effect ascribed to it, may be so vast and palpable, as to satisfy us at once, that the effect is inexplicable by human power. I know not precisely what advances may be made by the intellect of an unassisted savage; but that a savage in the woods could not compose the Principia of Newton, is about as plain as that he could not create the world. I know not the point at which bodily strength must stop; but that a man cannot carry Atlas or Andes on his shoulders, is a safe position. The question, therefore, whether the principles of human nature, under the circumstances in which it was placed at Christ's birth, will explain his religion, is one to which we are competent, and is the great question on which the whole controversy turns."

It is perhaps hardly necessary to add, that in ascribing inspiration of the highest order to the mind of Christ, we do not ascribe it to every word and every act recorded even of him. It would be idle, if not profane rather, so to divest of their natural grace and simplicity his general character and deportment in the common scenes of daily life. It would be doing strange violence to Scripture on every page to attempt it. The supernatural influences, even when most conspicuously exerted, never superseded the use of the natural faculties, but acted through their means; and it is reasonable to suppose they must have left those faculties free to their ordinary workings in all the ordinary scenes of life, in which it would be profane to exaggerate simply human actions and thoughts into miracles. If we imagine the inspired communication of a few surpassingly great truths and purposes to the mind of Jesus Christ, and those truths to have been left to their natural action and reaction within his mind, we may in some degree realize the kind of influence which the supernatural gift might exert upon the natural faculty beyond its immediate suggestions of knowledge and faith.*

* For want of making this distinction, some of the simplest human sayings and doings of Jesus have been stilted and inflated into what is quite unsuitable to the occasion, or (on the same needless assumption of their being superhuman) have been derided as unworthy of miracle. A few instances may be useful.

In the history of the miracle at the marriage-feast at Cana, where the wine failed through the unexpected number of guests (attracted, doubtless, by his presence), there is a brief *aside* conversation of Jesus with his mother, his part of which is given in the Common Version in these words: "Woman, what have I to do with thee? Mine hour is not yet come." Humanized into idiomatic English, it means: "Mother, do not trouble yourself about it, but leave it to me. It is not time for me yet." She understood him and expected the result. How simple and appropriate his few words to her! They are gentle too. "*Woman*, behold thy son!" when spoken by him from the cross, does not sound harsh or disrespectful even to the falsely fastidious English ear, where "woman" and "lady" struggle hopelessly for precedence (John ii. 4).

The cleansing of the temple, mentioned by John (ii. 13) as occurring at the first Passover, and by the other evangelists at the last (and possibly transacted at both), has given occasion for empty ribaldry. But how natural is the scene when we but realize it! In spite of the deadening effect of custom, religiously thoughtful Jews, even at Jerusalem, must have been shocked at this intrusion of traffic upon the place of devotion; and to the fresher Galilean hearts of Jesus and his companions, it must have seemed an abomination that only needed remonstrance to abolish at once. The remonstrance was uttered by him; and was immediately carried into effect by the bystanders aiding him and his apostles, with no more roughness than usually attends the summary course of popular justice. The "plaiting a scourge of small cords," shews no haste, at any rate. The scene is quite natural; and what is natural in the impulses of a pure mind is seldom undignified in the doing.

Many a reader has wondered what Jesus meant by saying to Judas Iscariot at the paschal table, "That thou doest, do quickly" (John xiii. 27). What if he expressed the natural impatience of suspense, that most difficult thing of all to bear, when the mind is nobly strung for endurance, and has no scope left for active effort. "Do at once what I know you are going to do." There is a similar but less urgent expression in the same tone, at an earlier period, about the baptism he was to be baptized with, and his being straitened till it should be accomplished (Luke xii. 50).

And many a reader has failed to find a natural meaning, by seeking a supernatural one, in Christ's words to Mary Magdalene after his resurrection, when in her joy she threw herself at his feet and clung about his knees. "Touch me not, for I am not ascended," &c., surely means, "Cling

The miraculous acts and inspired utterances of Jesus Christ have been put upon record through precisely the same kind of human instrumentality as any of his ordinary actions and utterances contained in the same books, or as those of any ordinary persons in these or any other books. They were just as capable of description and attestation as any other actions or words recorded in history. Their being miraculous or inspired as to their origin, makes not the slightest difference in their capability of being accurately narrated. The narrative, indeed, does not, strictly speaking, give testimony to the miraculous *causation*. *That* is properly the inference of the reader (as it was also that of the writer). The *testimony* goes only to the *facts* of the case. The narrator describes certain phenomena, which, if the reader could reconcile them with his knowledge of nature, would of course not seem to him miraculous. These authors tell us, indeed, that they themselves considered certain actions miraculous; but they describe what those actions were, and we in our turn judge whether they were miraculous or not. They say they considered certain sayings as inspired; but they repeat the sayings to the best of their knowledge and recollection, and we read those sayings in connection with the times and circumstances of the speaker. The records in which these all-important matters are written, are, in short (according to the simple principles already explained and vindicated at the beginning of the first volume *), human records of words, some of which we refer to inspiration, and of deeds, some of which we deem miraculous. These records we must

not to me, hold me not, as though this must be your only sight of me before I ascend. Your affectionate heart shall be gratified. I am not ascending yet. But go to my disciples and tell them I am risen, and that I shall soon ascend to my Father and your Father, to my God and your God" (John xx. 17).

* See Vol. I. p. 25, &c.

use like any other records of any other alleged sayings and doings. It is necessary to repeat this great principle of ordinary justice to the Scriptures,—a principle almost self-evident, yet almost constantly neglected. The Scriptures are the records of revelation, but not themselves the revelation. Inspiration is in the things recorded, though not in the act of recording them. They are histories of miracles, though not miraculously-written histories. Let this distinction never be forgotten or disguised by those who would really understand and wisely vindicate them. Its neglect creates all the absurdities and half the difficulties which beset believers and doubters.

The historical and biographical form in which Christianity is conveyed to us, is peculiarly attractive and impressive. This is an old remark, common to all writers on the internal evidences of the truth of the gospel revelation. Every reader of the gospel feels it, whether distinctly defining it or not. No code of morals, no formal array of precepts, no disquisitions on providence and prayer, on life and immortality, could impress the mind with the same vivid sense of the reality and value of divine disclosures on these subjects, as when we are brought into contact with them through the life and conversations of Jesus Christ. We cannot, even in imagination, detach his gospel from himself. He is the central thought in our religion as Christians. His words have the reality of time, place and circumstance. His life was the essence of the revelation. And the power of the gospel is greatly attributable to this intire identification of the person and character of its Author with all its principles and hopes. We may not be quite sure that we have, in every instance, the very identical words of Christ preserved to us in the gospel histories, any more than we can be quite sure that we have the very identical words of Socrates in Xenophon's *Memorabilia*.

But neither do we need the very words, if we have their sense and their spirit; and practically we have all that we can desire. Under the necessary conditions under which historical sayings and doings of any other kind are transmitted from age to age in other histories, and subject to the common laws of human thought, knowledge and belief throughout every other department, we receive the principles of Christianity in the pages of its memoir-writers. To seek any different or higher certainty than this, is simply to desire exemption from the lot of man. Plenary inspiration (a theory which the Scriptures themselves confront) would not give the absolute certainty desired by its advocates, unless their own minds also could be made infallible in the act of reading. The infallibility of the Church or of the Pope, joined to the plenary inspiration of the Bible, would still be unavailing to procure absolute certainty, unless the individual mind be gifted with infallibility also. All attempts to escape from the necessary conditions of human knowledge and opinion are vain, while they are of course mischievous. The Christian Scriptures are strong indeed in their native strength of evidence, and are only to be weakened by false claims on their behalf. They eminently stand the test of every critical principle that is applied to ancient literature in general. On precisely the same principles of literary criticism on which we receive the histories of Tacitus and Cæsar as the contemporaneous records of certain parts of Roman history, we receive the four Gospels and the book of Acts as the contemporaneous history of the preaching of Christianity. And on the self-same principles of literary criticism on which we accept the letters of Cicero and Pliny as genuine, we accept those of Paul and other letter-writers in the New Testament. The gospel only requires to see its history and its literature fairly treated, like the world's history and literature in general. In the next two chapters we shall endeavour thus to estimate Christianity and the Christian Scriptures. By treating them like all other books, we shall find how they differ from and surpass all others.

CHAPTER II.

THE CHRISTIAN ERA IN ITS CONNECTION WITH GENERAL HISTORY.

THE Christian Scriptures open before us in the full light of the world's history. Unlike those of the Old Testament,—most of which are placed by their venerable antiquity quite above the reach of minute critical inquiry into their origin and authorship, while many of their recorded facts admit of question or confirmation only on abstract and speculative principles, as distinguished from properly historical grounds,—the books of the New Testament belong to a strictly historical, and, more than that, a very conspicuous period, whether as regards the facts recorded and implied in them, or the literary history and characteristics of the books themselves. Unlike the Jewish Apocrypha, which are the feeble repetition, imitation and exaggeration of a venerated past, the Christian Scriptures are the fresh and lively records of a new era, marked with a character of its own. We have now to do with writings which profess to have been composed nearly eighteen centuries ago, and referring to events that were not a generation old at the time when the records were written. It is quite a literary period in which we now find ourselves. The Augustan age of Roman literature is scarcely past. The world abounds in books, authors, readers and critics. Such is the era of the Christian Scriptures.

Christianity was born of Judaism. In the language of the Great Teacher, "Salvation was from the Jews." Unlike as Christianity is to Judaism, as regards the ceremonialism and exclusiveness of the old dispensation, it is the true sequel to the Law and the Prophets, which must have remained incomplete, if not objectless, without it. It bears the unmistakeable signs of its origin in its doctrines, its facts and its writings. The gospel grew up in Jewish soil, in the early part of the Roman empire. It could have originated nowhere else, nor at any great interval of time before or after.

It is impossible to imagine a time when events happening in Palestine could have commanded the same degree of attention from the great world, as in the era of the life of Christ, and when those events, if important in themselves, could have found such ready channels of communication through which to exercise their due influence upon the world at large.

The evident fitness of this period for the developement of a divine religion of unlimited spirit and aims, cannot fail to strike the reflecting Christian's mind, as shewing that the great circle of Providence had plainly embraced and provided for the advent of the gospel.

Rome was now the mistress of the civilized world. The Republic had, through five centuries, developed the energy, the warlike prowess, and the practical and administrative skill of its mighty people; and the Empire was now opening that career of magnificence, which presently began to run into corruption, and thence into gradual decay. The Roman dominion had absorbed all the states of Greece, so long the centre of civilization, literature and art, and still the teacher of these things to her conquerors, whose youth frequented their Greek provinces as a part of the finished education necessary for the statesman, scholar or gentleman. The Roman sway had overrun all the Greek kingdoms of Asia and Egypt which had been founded by the successors of Alexander; it had spread over northern Africa and the middle and west of Europe, including Germany, Gaul, Spain and Britain. Never before had such links of intercommunication been established among such remote parts of the world.

In this vast empire, Judea was by no means the least conspicuous spot. It was, indeed, small in extent, but it was central; and it had been, as we have seen, the theatre of conflict again and again between the greatest powers of the world; first between Assyria or Babylon on the east and the older Egypt on the south-west; and then between the Egypt of the Greek dynasty and the Greek kingdom of the Syrians. And now it had, for some time past, been known to the Romans as a restless dependency of their own, lately constituted a province. It was despised, indeed, by its haughty conquerors for what they were pleased to call its superstitions,—for the peculiarity (that is to say) of its religious observances, and the pertinacity with which its people clung to them in defiance of persecution by their heathen masters; but Judea was at least *notorious* throughout the Roman world for having been thus troublesome and unmanageable ever since it came into their hands. The Christian apostle was right in avowing the publicity of the Christian mission, "This thing was not done in a corner."

Tacitus, the prince of Roman historians, has left us a brief account of the history and manners of the Jews, such as was current in his time among the Romans, written by way of introduction to his notice of the destruction of Jerusalem by Titus. I shall here present a translation of it, as the very best way of shewing, on the most unexceptionable authority, how the Jews stood connected with the Roman world; how far their history was known, and how far perverted or misunderstood by their heathen masters. Many of Tacitus's statements are indeed ridiculous enough, and some, no doubt, quite erroneous; for which the Christian Father, Tertullian, petulantly calls him "that most chattering liar" (mendaciorum loquacissimus); but one may easily explain the sources of some of his amusing mistakes, and his account, subject to such corrections, is very instructive, as shewing the Jews and their country from the Roman point of view. We can easily correct it or complete it from their own national point of view, and from our own Christian retrospect. Tacitus was born at the end of Claudius's, or the beginning of Nero's reign (A.D. 54), and lived till Hadrian's (117). His account is as follows:

"As we are about to narrate the destruction of the notorious city of Jerusalem, it seems a proper occasion to explain its origin. Some say the Jews were fugitives from Crete, who settled on the outskirts of Libya at the time of Saturn's expulsion from heaven by his brother Jupiter; they draw an argument from the name Jews, *Judæi*, being like that of the *Idæi*, the inhabitants of Mount Ida in Crete. Some say that in the reign of Isis in Egypt, an exuberant population relieved itself by spreading to the nearest country, under Jerosolymus and Juda.* Many think they were of Ethiopian blood, and driven out by king Cepheus, either through fear or through dislike of them. Some make them Assyrian immigrants into Egypt in search of territory, afterwards occupying cities of their own, and the Hebrew lands and others nearer to Syria. Some make the Solymi (spoken of in Homer) to have founded the city of Jerusalem *(Hierosolyma)*, and given it their name. Most authors agree that they were driven out of Egypt by king Bocchoris, according to the instructions of the oracle of

* This easy sort of etymologising was very common among the ancients. To account for the name of a place or people, they had only to infer a man, or hero, or demigod as the founder. So a Jerosolymus is imagined as the founder of Jerusalem. *Judæi* and *Idæi* were certainly very temptingly like. But Tacitus does not assent to either of these derivations.

Hammon, as a race offensive to the gods, to cure a filthy disease then prevalent. Thereupon Moses, one of these exiles, when all the rest were inactively bemoaning themselves in the desert, advised them to expect no help from gods or men, as they were deserted by both, but to trust to him as a heavenly leader who would at once rescue them from their distresses. They agreed, and took their journey with him at hazard. Want of water was their chief distress. But, when their destruction seemed imminent, a herd of wild asses, coming from pasture, led the way to a rock covered with wood, where the grassy soil shewed the leader that there was water to be had; and he opened copious streams of it. Thus refreshed, they pursue their journey six days more; and on the seventh (having driven out the inhabitants) they take possession of the territory in which they proceed to build their city and temple. Moses, to confirm his future influence over the nation, instituted new rites, contrary to those of all other people. Among them, all things are held abominable which amongst us are sacred; and, on the other hand, things are allowed to them that are impure with us. In their shrine they consecrated an image of the animal* that had saved them from thirst; sacrificing a ram,† as if in contempt of Hammon. The ox† also, which the Egyptians worship as Apis, is sacrificed by them. They abstain from swine's flesh,† in memory of the mortality once produced among them by the *scabies* to which that animal is liable. They to this day memorialize their long famine of former times by frequent fasts;† and the Jewish bread made without fermentation,† retains the indication of hastily-made food (raptarum frugum argumentum). Some say that they choose to rest on the seventh day† because it put an end to their toils; and afterwards, through the soft encroachment of idleness, that the seventh year† also was

* Was this story a malicious, or an innocent, heathen perversion of the golden calf? or of the Jewish use of the ass in preference to the horse? Could the Messiah's entry into Jerusalem in the simple state prescribed by the Law for Jewish kings, and announced by the prophet as his, have been the origin of this strange assertion of the Roman historian?

† Tacitus here cites many of the characteristic practices of the Jews correctly, but is not always happy in conjecturing their origin or meaning. For

allotted to repose. Others think that this was an honour paid to Saturn; whether that the principles of their worship had been handed down by the Ideans, as the founders of the nation when driven out with Saturn; or that the star of Saturn is reputed to be in the highest sphere and of chief power among the seven stars that govern mankind, and because most of the celestial bodies complete their powers and courses through septenary numbers. These rites, whencesoever adopted, are sustained by their antiquity. Their remaining institutions are sinister, and have prevailed through foul depravity. For every wretch (pessimus quisque) who has despised his country's religion, would carry tribute and offering thither. And so the Jewish state throve.* Among themselves there is obstinate faith and ready compassion; but towards all others a deadly hatred. They separate themselves in eating. They abstain from foreign marriages. Among themselves no license is scrupled. They use circumcision for the sake of being different from other people. Those who join them adopt the same practice; and the first lesson they learn is to despise the gods, to divest themselves of their country, and slight their parents, children and brethren. Yet they take measures for increasing their numbers. For they consider the destruction of children wicked;† and think the souls of those who have

how should a Roman be expected to trouble himself much with Jewish antiquities? Josephus's writings were, no doubt, accessible at Rome; but Tacitus seems not to have been versed in them, any more than in the Jewish Scriptures, which were, at least in their Greek translation, accessible to heathen scholars. He has correctly noticed the opposition (perhaps in some instances a studied opposition, as he suggests) between the Jewish Law and the Egyptian usages. Tacitus did not, at any rate, regard Moses as the copyist of the Egyptian priests, however learned he might be in their wisdom.

* Naturalization among the Jews was not so easy as Tacitus fancies; nor so much coveted by wretches who were tired of their own country and its gods. He writes a cruel burlesque upon their separation from other nations.

† *Necare quenquam ex agnatis, nefas*, is the reading of the text of Tacitus; but Lipsius conjectures *gnatis*, and those who keep the common reading generally force it into the same meaning. The Jewish love of offspring is here truly portrayed, in favourable, though undesigned, contrast with the Roman long-established barbarism of exposing supernumerary

fallen in war or by torture immortal.* Hence their desire of offspring and their contempt of death. They bury, rather than burn, their dead, as is the custom in Egypt; taking the same care of them and having the same conviction about the world beneath.† Their opinion of the heavenly beings is very different. The Egyptians worship many animals and their images: the Jews recognize only one deity, and that one mentally. They consider it profane to represent the likenesses of the gods by perishable material and in human form; the Supreme and Eternal they hold to be neither changeable nor perishable. Accordingly they allow no images in their cities, nor even in their temples. Kings are not to be thus complimented, nor even Cæsars to be honoured by a statue. But, from the custom of their priests singing to the flute and timbrel, crowned with ivy, and from a golden vine being found in the temple,‡ some have thought that Bacchus, the conqueror of the East, was worshiped by them. The rites, however, do not at all correspond; for Bacchus enjoined festive and joyous rites, whereas the way of the Jews is absurd and grovelling.

"The country is bounded towards the east by Arabia; it meets Egypt on the south, Phœnicia and the sea on the west; on the side of Syria it stretches far north. The people are healthy in body and able to bear labour. Rain seldom falls.

infants,—a practice the propriety of which the polite Roman historian never for one moment questions, but merely notes the Jewish scruple as a curious characteristic of this superstitious and despicable nation!

* The Jewish belief in immortality was notorious among their conquerors, though seemingly taken by Tacitus as limited to patriots and martyrs.

† The Jewish burial was widely different from the Egyptian embalming; nor can any trace be found in the Jewish writings of either of the doctrines variously ascribed to the Egyptians respecting the dead; namely, the transmigration of souls, and the continued existence of the soul in the body so long as the latter (embalmed) remains undecayed. On the contrast between Egyptian and Jewish thought, in the next sentence, Tacitus writes truly, but without apparent appreciation of the grandeur of the Jewish thought.

‡ There is plainly no more truth in these reputed facts than in the inference which Tacitus himself rejects as inconsistent with other facts. But the Jewish festivals were not sad and gloomy, as he seems to think; neither were they "bacchanalian;" but cheerful, social and expressive of thanksgiving.

The soil is fertile. Its productions are the same as ours, and it has the balsam and dates besides. The date-palm trees are lofty and graceful. The balsam is a moderate-sized tree. When the branch is swelled, if you cut it with an iron instrument, the veins recoil; but they open if cut with a broken stone or pot. The juice is used by physicians.* The chief mountain is Libanus, remarkable in so hot a climate for being misty and constantly covered with snow (opacum fidumque nivibus). From this ridge the river Jordan rises and is fed. The Jordan does not run into the sea, but, after flowing through first one lake and then a second, is retained in a third. This third lake is of immense circuit, like a sea; more disagreeable in taste, and by its offensive smell pestilential to those who visit it. The wind makes no impression upon it. It harbours neither fish nor water-fowl. Its waters, between solid and fluid, support what is thrown upon them, as if on the ground; swimmers and those who cannot swim are equally borne up by them. At a certain time of the year it throws out bitumen, the mode of collecting which is learnt by practice, like other arts. In its native state, it is a black liquid. On the addition of acid (sparso aceto) it hardens and floats. This is taken in the hand by the collectors and drawn on ship-board. Then, without any further help, it flows in and loads the vessel till you cut it off. But you cannot cut it with a brass or iron instrument. It retreats from blood or a bloody garment.† So the old authors say. But those who know the locality tell us, that masses surging with bitumen are forced along and pulled ashore by hand; and presently, when dried by the evaporation of the earth and the power of the sun, they are cut up with axes and wedges, like logs of wood or stone. Not far off are plains which they say were once fertile and peopled with large cities, till burnt up by lightning; and the traces of such a

* See Harris's Natural History of the Bible (arts. Balm, Balsam-tree) for other accounts of this tree by Strabo, Pliny and others.

† Fugit cruorem vestemque infectam sangine quo fœminæ per menses exsolvuntur. Well might Tacitus distinguish between the stories of the *veteres auctores* and the *gnari locorum*. But he attests the main features of this singular scenery with great correctness, shewing how thoroughly well known Judea was.

catastrophe are said to remain, the land itself being torrid to view and having lost its productiveness. For all plants, whether growing spontaneously or by cultivation, whether grass or flowers, as soon as they have reached their customary form, grow black and hollow, and shrivel, as it were, into ashes. For my part, while I grant that some once famous cities have been burnt by lightning, I also think that the ground is infected by the exhalation of the lake, and that the air above is corrupted, so that grain and fruits decay in a soil and atmosphere alike intolerable. The river Belus* falls into the Jewish sea; at the mouth of which they collect sand to mix with alkali (mixto nitro) and melt into glass. This shore is of moderate extent and unexhausted by what is carried away. A great part of Judea lies in scattered villages; but they have also towns. Jerusalem was the capital of the nation. A temple of immense wealth was there: the city within the outmost walls; then the royal palace; and the temple enclosed within the innermost. None but a Jew had access even to the doors; all but the priests were prohibited from entering. While the East was in the hands of the Assyrians and Medes and Persians, the Jews were the most despised part of the dependent nations (despectissima pars servientium); but when the Macedonians had become ascendant, king Antiochus, endeavouring to take away their superstition and give them Greek manners, was prevented by his war with the Parthians from improving this most foul (teterrimam) nation. (For at that time Arsaces had revolted.†) Then the Jews, as the Macedonians were weak, the Parthians not yet having grown up, and the Romans being far off, set up kings of their own, who, one after another,

* The Belus flows into the Mediterranean by Acre or Ptolemais.

† This parenthesis is, with good reason, suspected of being an interpolation, added by a transcriber who wished to explain the history, but who managed to confuse it, instead, by his own ignorance. Either some such transcriber, or else Tacitus himself (which is not likely), seems to have confounded Antiochus IV. (Epiphanes) with the second (surnamed Theos). It was in the reign of the second Antiochus that Arsaces revolted, about B.C. 250; but Tacitus, in his contemptuous and utterly unsympathising way, evidently describes the times of Epiphanes, who died in an expedition against the Parthians. (See Oberlin's Tacitus, note, *in loc.*)

when expelled by the fickleness of the populace, regained their power by arms; and while committing all the customary atrocities of kings in the expulsion of citizens and the destruction of cities, the murder of brothers, wives and parents, constantly cherished the national superstition, because they were beginning to assume the honour of the Priesthood by way of strengthening their own power.

"Cn. Pompey was the first Roman who subdued the Jews; and he, in right of victory, entered their temple. From that time it was known that the place was empty and its mysteries vain, no image of Deity being in it *(nullâ intus Deûm effigie, vacuam sedem, et inania arcana)*. The walls of Jerusalem were destroyed; the temple remained. Presently, in our civil war, when the provinces had fallen under the sway of Mark Antony, Pacorus, the king of the Parthians, gained possession of Judea and was killed by P. Ventidius; and the Parthians were driven back across the Euphrates. C. Sosius subdued the Jews. Antony gave the kingdom to Herod; and Augustus, on his victory, enlarged it. After the death of Herod, one Simon,* without waiting for imperial permission, had assumed the name of king. He was punished by Quinctilius Varus, who occupied Syria; and the nation, thus put under constraint, was divided into three kingdoms among the sons of Herod. Under Tiberius they were quiet. After that, being ordered by Caius Cæsar† to place his statue in their temple, they took up arms rather than obey. The death of the Cæsar put an end to that movement. Claudius, the Jewish race of kings having died out, or been reduced to insignificance, gave Judea as a province into the hands of Roman knights or freedmen; of whom Antonius Felix,‡ indulging in every kind of cruelty and lust, exercised royal authority with the dispositions of a slave. He married Drusilla, the granddaughter of Cleopatra and Antony; so that Felix was grandson-in-law, and Claudius grandson, of the same Antony. However, the patience of the Jews lasted till Gessius Florus was procurator. Under him war arose; and

* For Simon's attempt, see Josephus (Ant. xvii. 10, 6). Also, for Varus's military career in Judea, the whole chapter 10.

† Caius Caligula.

‡ The Felix in the book of Acts.

various battles, generally adverse, befel Cestius Gallus, the legate of Syria, in his attempts to repress it. When, in the course of fate, or through vexation, he died, Vespasian, commissioned by Nero, aided by fortune and fame in his excellent services, in the course of two summers put his victorious army in possession of all the country districts and all the cities except Jerusalem. The next year, occupied with civil war, passed in quiet as far as concerned the Jews. But when peace was obtained throughout Italy, foreign cares returned. It was an aggravation of angry feeling to think that the Jews were the only people who had not yielded. That Titus should still remain with the armies, seemed the most useful provision for all the chances and issues of a new imperial reign. So, having pitched his camp, as I have mentioned, before the walls of Jerusalem, he shewed his legions in battle array. The Jews drew up their army close under the walls, meaning to venture further if successful, and having provided a refuge if they should be repulsed. Our cavalry was sent against them with some light-armed cohorts, but fought with doubtful success. Presently the enemy retreated, and on the ensuing days joined battle often before the gates, till, after constant losses, they were driven within their walls. The Romans then turned besiegers, for they disdained to wait for famine to weaken the enemy; and they were also longing for perils, some through valour, many through ferocity and the desire of prizes. Titus himself had before his view the wealth and pleasures of Rome, which seemed to be long delayed unless Jerusalem should fall at once. But this city, lofty in position, had been strengthened by works and mounds enough to fortify even a level situation. For two very lofty hills were inclosed by walls artfully sloped, or bowed inwards, so as to expose the flanks of besiegers to blows from the walls. The end of the rock was precipitous; and towers were built 60 feet high where they had the advantage of the hill, and 120 in the hollows, so that they seemed of equal height from a distance, and wonderful indeed to view. There were other walls within, surrounding the palace; and the Antonian tower was of conspicuous height, so called by Herod in honour of Mark Antony. The temple was a sort of citadel, with walls of its own surpassing the others in strength and workmanship. The very porches which surrounded it were an excellent outwork. There was an unfailing fountain of water; the mountains were hollowed underneath, and there were pools and cisterns for preserving the rain-water. The founders had foreseen the probability of frequent wars, from the peculiarity of their customs, and so had planned everything as if with a view to a long siege; and after being stormed by Pompey, fear and practice had taught them many things. Then having purchased leave to fortify their city, through the avarice of the Claudian period, they built walls during peace, as if in preparation for war. Their numbers were increased by the refuse of other cities that had been put to the sword; for all the most intractable had flocked thither, and their proceedings became all the more seditious. There were three leaders among them, and three armies. Simon, called also Bargioras, had garrisoned the outermost and widest wall, John the middle city, and Eleazar the temple. John and Simon were strongest in numbers and arms, Eleazar in position. But they suffered by internal contests, treachery and conflagration, and a large quantity of corn was burnt. Presently John, having sent some men, on the plea of sacrificing, to slay Eleazar and his band, obtains possession of the temple. Thus the city was split into two factions, till, on the approach of the Romans, external war produced union. Prodigies had occurred, which this nation, being addicted to superstition and opposed to religious ceremonies, does not think it lawful to propitiate with victims nor with prayers. Armies had seemed to be rushing to battle in the sky, their weapons gleaming, and the temple illuminated with sudden lightning amid the clouds. The doors of the shrine had been suddenly thrown open, and a superhuman voice had been heard saying, *The Gods are departing;* and at the same time there was a great movement of departure. A few regarded these things as fearful omens; but most persons had a conviction that the ancient books of the priests had foretold that at this very time the East should grow powerful, and that the future possessors of empire should go forth from Judea (profectique Judeâ rerum potirentur). Vespasian and Titus were the persons predicted in those oracles. But the multitude, in the usual course of human wishes, interpreted such a mighty destiny to be awaiting themselves, that not even adversity could turn them to the true conviction. The number of the besieged, of all ages and both sexes, we have understood to have been six hundred thousand. All who could bear arms did so, and they ventured it more than proportionately to their numbers. The women were as obstinately resolute as the men; and life, with a compelled change of abode, was dreaded more than death. Against this city and nation, as its situation defied warlike assault and surprise, the Cæsar Titus determined to contend with the implements of siege. The legions were assigned their respective posts, and there was an end of skirmishing, till all the ancient means of siege and all newer improvements were provided." (Hist. v. 2—13.)

Such is the narrative of Tacitus. He breaks off here, and turns to the history of Roman affairs in Germany and the Low countries, which occupies the rest of this fifth, and last existing, book of his Histories. It is generally supposed, indeed, that he resumed the history of the siege of Jerusalem in another book, which is lost. We can only remark on what is preserved to us. And while the whole passage is of the utmost importance, as shewing the admitted relation of the Jewish history to that of the great world (the heathen conquerors of the Jews being judges),—and while it attests or admits, in its own contemptuous way, a remarkable number of the great facts of the Jewish history and principles of the Jewish religion (as we have continually noted in passing),—our more immediate interest in it, as connected with the opening of the Christian era, arises from the historian's account of prodigies and prophecies near the conclusion.

Tacitus gravely tells us—not as a common report, but as his own express belief—that prodigies had occurred of a warlike kind in the sky (which he describes); and he reproaches the Jews for not propitiating such omens by sacrifice. He evidently hints that their impiety in this respect was unlucky for them in the result. This was Roman "religion," as opposed to Jewish "superstition;" this was the religion of a heathen scholar, philosopher and statesman! Let not the Jews, nor the early Christians, bear all the reproach for superstition. With singular confusedness of religious idea (even when we remember that he was writing for Roman believers in "gods many"), Tacitus makes a supernatural voice declare that "the gods are leaving the Jewish temple," and holds himself responsible for the belief that *they were heard departing;* though he had previously informed us, as something shocking to his religious feelings, that there was no statue there, and that the Jews recognized God mentally alone. Was it "religious," then, to think that the Roman gods had dwelt there and protected the Jews thus far, and that now, on their departure, the Jews were at last given up to the sword of the more devoted worshipers of Jupiter, Mars and Bacchus? We might well call this, indeed, superstition, unless we take it as the mere policy of a Roman historian. He is plainly politic, or at least profoundly courtly, in the next passage, where he ventures to interpret the old Jewish prophecies as alluding to Vespasian and Titus. This is the passage of chief importance in a Christian point of view. Let us consider what it implies.

In this passage, Tacitus declares that the prodigies which, whether real or not, he narrates as real, did not affect the minds of the Jews in general with fear. This he accounts for by stating the general prevalence of a conviction, that at this very period the East was to become powerful, and that from Judea should go forth the future rulers of the world. Now every one acquainted with Jewish history and prophecy, or with the Gospel history, at once perceives that this is an exact picture of the Jewish idea of the Messiah's approaching kingdom,—the very idea set forth in the prophets of the return from Babylon, and continually cherished by the Jews ever since that time, as never having been literally fulfilled, and therefore, as they persistently believed, still to be at some future time accomplished. It is the very idea which is seen filling the minds of the Jewish people when Jesus appeared among them teaching and doing miracles; which, when he did not fulfil it, caused the majority of them to reject him and desire or consent to his death; and which, after his death, kept them still expectant of a temporal Messiah, and exposed them to deception by one enthusiast or impostor after another, till their frequent revolts led the Romans to adopt the decisive policy of destroying the city, as here explained by Tacitus himself. We have here, then, a true picture, as far as it goes, and in Roman colours, of the Jewish Messianic expectation as it existed somewhat less than forty years after the ministry of Jesus Christ; and it is the exact counterpart of the expectation which prevailed for hundreds of years before. That Tacitus really believed Vespasian and Titus to be predicted in the old books of the priests (the prophets, of course he means) as going forth to empire from Jerusalem, is not to be imagined for a moment. But he could adopt even a "superstition," and interpret it into a sanction of the Roman policy. And in doing this, he has become an important witness to the leading facts of Judaism and of Christianity.

Of course, in giving this most strange interpretation to the Jewish prophecy and expectation of the Messianic age, Tacitus was not likely to mention that a certain portion of the Jews considered their scriptures as fulfilled by a very different personage and in a very different manner. For anything in this passage, we might even suppose that Tacitus had heard nothing of the life and actions of Jesus of Nazareth. Nor would it surprise us that those occurrences which filled Judea with intense religious interest, should, if heard of at Rome, have been regarded by a Roman statesman as matters of no interest except to the Jews, and as, in all likelihood, matters of strange and contemptible *superstition*, quite beneath his notice. But Tacitus *had* heard of Jesus Christ; for he mentions him in another connection, when he has occasion to record the fact of Nero's wanton and savage persecution of the Christians in Rome. That passage (in the *Annals)* gives direct testimony to some of the leading facts of the Gospel and early Christian church history, though in our author's usual curt, disdainful and unjust manner when speaking of the Jews, with whom he here pretty evidently confounds the Christians. It is after narrating the event of the great fire at Rome in the reign of Nero, and mentioning the odium under which the emperor lay as the suspected author of the calamity, that Tacitus proceeds thus:

"In order to do away with this report, Nero caused to be accused and subjected to the most exquisite punishments, those who were commonly known as Christians and hateful for their crimes. The originator of this name was one Christus, who was put to death as a criminal, under the procurator Pontius Pilate, in the reign of Tiberius. His destructive superstition, though repressed for a while, broke out again, not only throughout Judea, where the evil had begun, but also through the city of Rome, where all things atrocious or shameful from all quarters meet and publish themselves. Accordingly, some were arrested who confessed themselves Christians; and then, on their information, a great multitude were convicted, not so much on the charge of incendiarism, as of hatred to mankind. And they were put to death with circumstances of wanton derision, being covered with the hides of beasts and worried to death by dogs, or crucified, or burnt to death as the day declined, to serve for lights in the night. Nero had offered his own gardens for these sights, and used to exhibit the games of the circus, habiting himself as a charioteer, and mixing with the populace or himself driving a chariot. Hence, though these people were guilty wretches and deserved extreme punishment, yet compassion began to arise towards them, as being destroyed for no public good, but to gratify one man's cruelty." (Annal. xv. 44.)

Here we find recorded, in the same supercilious style in which the abstract of the Jewish history was given, these great facts :—the origin of a new sect called Christians in Judea, under one Christus as their leader, in the reign of Tiberius; his being put to death by Pontius Pilate; and the spread of his religion throughout Judea and all over the city of Rome to such an extent, that in Nero's reign (A.D. 65, little more than thirty years from the founder's death) a great multitude of his followers were put to death by that tyrant, in the hope of attaching the odium to them which properly belonged to him. We need make no account of what Tacitus says about their being such bad people. It was only his way of expressing himself in all that related to Judea and the Jews.

Other Roman testimonies of a similar kind may be found in Suetonius, and somewhat later in Pliny, which are quoted by Paley in his *Evidences of Christianity* (P. i. chap. ii.) and by most writers on that subject. But Tacitus has served our more comprehensive object of presenting the Gospel times to view, under Roman colouring indeed, but as connected with the great world's history.

I have had another purpose also in view in quoting this long passage from Tacitus, which will explain itself in the next chapter.

CHAPTER III.

THE CHRISTIAN SCRIPTURES IN THEIR PLACE AMONG ANCIENT BOOKS.

It has been already stated, that the age to which the Christian religion and its records belong, was eminently a *literary* period. The true character of the Christian Scriptures, and the evidence of their being the genuine productions of the times to which they profess to belong, will be most clearly seen if we take a brief survey of the great world's literature produced during the same period. And, as it is right (and indeed necessary to every intelligent mind) to ask, how it is known that the books of the New Testament are really the works of those to whom they are ascribed, and how we are justified in believing that they have been preserved free from important or disqualifying corruptions through these nearly eighteen hundred years,—the answer to these important and natural questions is to be found, by asking them also in reference to all the other literature that is generally received as belonging to the same period. The same questions precisely have to be asked respecting all other ancient authors (and corresponding questions respecting some modern ones too); and the same processes precisely must be used in all such cases, in order to obtain correct answers.

The half century before the birth of Christ, and the century after it, embrace the following well-known authors in various classes of literature, whose works we now possess:

Of Latin poets, we have Lucretius, Catullus, Propertius, Virgil, Horace, Phædrus, Ovid, Tibullus, Persius, Lucan, Silius Italicus, Martial.

Of Latin prose writers, we have Julius Cæsar, Hirtius,

Cicero, Cornelius Nepos, Livy, Velleius Paterculus, Seneca, Pliny the naturalist, Pliny the younger, Quinctilian the rhetorician, and Cornelius Tacitus the historian.

Among Greek writers of this period are Diodorus Siculus (or the Sicilian), who wrote a sort of universal history, called the "Historical Library;" Strabo the geographer (a native of Pontus, in Asia Minor); Philo the Alexandrian Jew; and Josephus, descended on his mother's side from the Maccabean princes. The object of the last two writers was, to make known and recommend the Jewish religion and its scriptures to general notice, writing in Greek for the use of the various nations of the Roman world. To this same class of Greek writings belong all the scriptures of the New Testament, written, like the others, in Greek, for diffusion through the Roman empire. The Greek *classical* writers, belonging to a much earlier period, are, of course, not included in our present inquiry; nor those of the later period (such as Plutarch, Arrian, Longinus and Marcus Antoninus), under whom pure Greek literature revived for a while on the decline of the Latin pen. The literature of the period with which we are concerned may be divided into two classes, namely, Roman literature written in Latin, and Cosmopolitan in Greek; the Greek partaking the national peculiarities of the various countries in which it was written, and generally differing considerably from the standard of the days of Pericles. The Greek of the New Testament is, of course, Hebrew or Jewish Greek; that is to say, it abounds in Hebrew idioms expressed in Greek words, which sound strange to a classical ear, but at once proclaim their nationality and also their proximate date.

In the above list of names are contained some of the best known of the classical authors, and many more names of less celebrated writers might be added. The period includes the Augustan or golden age of Roman authorship. Of the writers here enumerated, we do not possess by any means all the works which some of them are known to have published; and many of what we have are imperfect through the ravages of time. Respecting some few of the works generally ascribed to this or that author, there are some doubts, intelligible to the learned, as to the real authorship. The *text* of some of them (that is, the words and expressions as they now stand in the extant copies of these writers) seems to be much more pure than the text of others. In some it is evidently very corrupt. The learned have often great difficulty in imagining what an author can have meant by certain words which are ascribed to him; or they are quite sure that he must have written something very different (which they could pretty confidently restore in some cases by obvious conjecture), and that the ignorance or carelessness of transcribers (like that of an incompetent printer unrevised by a careful corrector of the press) must have been the cause of bringing such obscurity or absurdity into the passage. Sometimes the different printed editions of the same author differ, having been taken in the earlier times of printing from different manuscript copies; and, in such cases, one edition may be often successfully corrected by the aid of another. Where manuscripts older than the days of printing still exist,—as in most if not all these cases they do, in more or less abundance,—a careful comparison (or *collation*, as it is called) of the different printed copies and manuscripts enables a critical scholar to reproduce a *text* (of Cicero, Horace, or any other writer) more true to the original than any of the individual editions or single manuscripts would be, if taken alone. It has therefore been the labour of many learned men,—especially, but not exclusively, in Germany (that nation of scholars),—to produce critical editions of the text of all the great Greek and Latin classics; not only of those whom I have just mentioned as belonging nearly to the same period as the Christian Scriptures, but also of the older Greek writers of the golden period of Athenian literature,—Herodotus, Thucydides and the great Dramatists, Xenophon, Plato and Aristotle, and of the most ancient and venerable Homer himself.

The same work precisely has been done, with yet more zealous care if possible, but purely by the same critical means, for the scriptures of the New Testament. Only, in the latter case, the critical materials have been far more abundant, in proportion to the immensely greater diffusion of the Christian Scriptures and the general reverence for them; and the result has been proportionately more satisfactory, in the production of a Text of the New Testament, which may be deemed practically identical with that originally written by the evangelists and apostles in their respective pages. Such a text is Griesbach's; to which little or nothing of any importance to the meaning of any passsage in the New Testament has been added by all the care of later editors, as Tischendorf, Schultz and Lachmann.

The long quotation, given in the previous chapter, from Tacitus's account of the Jews (Ernesti and Oberlin's edition), will serve to illustrate, to any Latin scholar, the kind of difficulty often presented by the *text* of an old author, and some of the modes of surmounting it. In a certain sentence, the text of all the existing manuscripts has these words, *Necare quenquam ex agnatis, nefas;* but the sagacious editor (though he does not venture to alter the text on conjecture) is confident that Tacitus must have written *gnatis* (children), and not *agnatis* (relations).* Then there is a very strange Latin expression in another place, where, however, the meaning is quite clear, to the effect that there were 600,000 people in Jerusalem, of all ages and *both sexes*. *Virile ac muliebre secus* is considered the true reading; though some copies have *virilis ac muliebris sexus*, and some *virile ac muliebre sexus*, either of which latter would be a much easier expression to the Latin ear. But the critics lay it down as a good rule, to prefer the more difficult reading *(durior preferatur lectio)*, wherever it is possible to get a sense out of it; as it is more likely that a transcriber should have *improved* it by substituting the easier or more customary expression, than that he should have done the reverse. So this text must, on critical principles, remain as it is, *virile ac muliebre secus;* and we must suppose *secus* to be a rare word used by Tacitus with the same meaning as *sexus*.

But let it be mentioned here, that the number of manuscripts of Tacitus now existing is very small. There are only two really ancient ones; or rather only one, as the two contain different parts of his works. This manuscript was discovered in a monastery in Westphalia during the pontificate of Leo X.; that is, early in the sixteenth century. It seems to have been written in the seventh or eighth century, and to have been copied

* Here there can be no practical doubt as to the true reading; and it may seem strange at first that critical editors should, in such a case, deny themselves the pleasure of rectifying a corrupted text. But, if once *conjectural* criticism was to be allowed the power of altering the text without authority from manuscripts, there is no knowing how far it might lead; and the sober decision of learned critics therefore is, to correct the *text* by the best readings of books and manuscripts, and to propose any conjectural alterations that seem further necessary, in the form of *notes*. The New-Testament editors are perfectly unanimous and inflexible in adhering to this rule: and such is, indeed, the abundance of manuscripts in their *critical apparatus*, that there is not a passage in the New Testament which requires a merely conjectural reading in order to make out a good meaning.

from one written in the fourth, the *imprint* of which is copied also in this. All other existing manuscripts of Tacitus were thought by Gronovius to have been copied from this, though they vary in many readings. The *critical apparatus* for the settlement of the text of Tacitus is therefore somewhat scanty;—compared with that of the New Testament (as we shall presently see), very scanty indeed. Yet nobody doubts the practicability of reading the real Tacitus, though here and there we may be obliged to confess ourselves at fault, and believe that the text is hopelessly confused.

While Tacitus is before us, it may be also mentioned, as illustrative of the fate of ancient authors, that his works have come down to us sadly mutilated. His *Histories* are incomplete *at the end;* so it may possibly be doubted whether he ever finished them. But his *Annals* are defective in the midst, wanting most of the 5th book, the 7th, 8th, 9th and 10th, and the beginning of the 11th, as well as the end of the 16th and last book, which breaks off in the middle of a sentence. No doubt the concluding pages were worn away, as we sometimes see in an old book that has lost its back. The loss of the intermediate books we can only charge to the general account of the destroyer, Time.

Another illustration of the curious questions that arise in reference to ancient books, is afforded in the works ascribed to Tacitus. One of these, a *Dialogue on Orators,* is not universally admitted to be his. The style is different from that of his other works, being in fact more like the ordinary phraseology of Latin writers, whereas the characteristic style of Tacitus is very remarkable for its intense condensation of idea, and almost epigrammatic, and often scarcely grammatical, brevity of expression. Hence a doubt has arisen, on internal grounds, as to the authorship of a work not thus characterized. Most probably, however, it is his, but referable to an earlier period of his life; and, thus considered, it will mark the growth of his very peculiar style,—that style itself being more suitable, indeed, to the subjects of his later works than to this on the Orators.

As all these and similar principles of critical judgment are applicable, and must be applied, to the elucidation of ancient literature, whether secular or sacred, it is of the greatest importance to the serious and intelligent, but unlearned, reader of the New Testament, to know something about the history of the preservation of ancient literature in general. A brief popular explanation of the most interesting matters connected with this subject may therefore be introduced here. The reader may further consult Mr. Isaac Taylor's admirable work on the subject, entitled the "History of the Transmission of Ancient Books to Modern Times," which derives its materials avowedly from the learned works of Bernard de Montfaucon, published in the beginning of the last century, and severally entitled, "Palæographia Græca" and "Bibliotheca Coisliniana."

Public inscriptions upon stone, tiles or plates of metal, may have been earlier than books. Wooden tablets covered with wax and written on with a pointed *stylus*, may have been also very early. But no lengthy document could be preserved by such means. Probably the most ancient material used for writing books upon was leather, dyed red or yellow often, and fastened together, skin after skin, in long sheets, on which the document was written in columns downwards from edge to edge; and then the sheet, being rolled up from each end, could be rolled or unrolled in either direction so as to open at any part required by the reader. The synagogue copies of the Jewish law are often of this form. Herodotus (in the middle of the fifth century B.C.) speaks of the use of skins for writing upon, as a very ancient practice. This very curious and instructive passage is as follows (Herodot. v. 58). After speaking of the Greek letters as derived from the Phœnicians, and called Phœnician by the Greeks themselves, he goes on thus: "And the Ionic Greeks from time immemorial have called books *skins* (τὰς βύβλυς διφθέρας καλέουσι ἀπὸ τοῦ παλαιοῦ οἱ Ἴωνες), because formerly, in the want of papyrus sheets (βύβλων again) they used goat and sheep skins. And even in my time, many of the foreign nations continue to write on this sort of skins."

Whether the skins here spoken of were dressed as leather, or as parchment, does not appear. But parchment received its name, Pergamene, among the Romans (whence our word *parchment* is a corruption) from the invention, or more probably the improvement, of the art of preparing it, supposed to have taken place at Pergamus, in Asia Minor, and ascribed to king Eumenes II., who reigned B.C. 197—159. Good parchment is the best and most durable material ever yet used for the preservation of documents, and the best existing ancient manuscripts are written upon it. There is a Virgil in the Vatican Library, believed to be as old as the fourth century; and some other manuscripts of classical writers are about as old. This is the age of the principal New Testament MSS.

But cheaper and more abundant materials were in demand; and the fibre of various trees and plants supplied many such. The Latin name for book, *liber*, originally denoted the inner bark of a tree, used, no doubt, for the purpose of writing; and the Greek word *Biblos* (whence *Bible*), was probably the same as *Byblos*, the name used by Herodotus for the Egyptian papyrus plant, being indeed its name in the old Coptic language. This papyrus (as the Greeks called it, and the Romans after them,—whence our word *paper)* was, for three centuries before Christ and eight after, the customary writing material throughout the known world. Probably the Egyptians had used it from very early times; and every country that became connected with Egypt by trade, successively obtained it. This most valuable material was formed of the inner fibre of a kind of reed that grew abundantly in the marshes and still waters of Lower Egypt, the outer and coarser fibre of which was employed for weaving sail-cloth and making ropes. The inner and softer fibre, being separated into strips, was laid evenly on a flat surface, and crossed with a similar layer in the other direction; and the two layers, being moistened with water, were pressed together and so adhered, seemingly by their own glutinous nature; though Pliny, in his Natural History, describes them as glued with the Nile water. When dry, the sheet of papyrus was rubbed smooth, and a number of such sheets were fastened together to make a roll; or, more commonly, they were cut into leaves to form a book, which would lie flat and escape the friction of constant rolling and unrolling. But even in this latter form the papyrus was found a somewhat brittle and perishable material, and it was not unusual to insert an occasional parchment leaf after every five or six papyri, as a strengthener and preservative of the book. This was an excellent plan. There are books of this sort twelve hundred years old.

Paper, in our sense of the term, meaning a manufacture of fibrous substances into thin sheets by reducing them to a pulp, seems to have been possessed by the Chinese at the end of the first century of the Christian era. And in the seventh century, the Saracens introduced into Europe what was known as the "Charta Bombycina," or *silk paper;* which is now ascertained, however, not to have been composed of silk (unless in a small degree), but chiefly of cotton, the very material which now (in the *cotton waste* of the Lancashire mills) supplies a large part of the manufacture of our most serviceable printing paper, tough, white and fine in texture.

Under the guidance of the known history of writing materials, those who are skilled in ancient manuscripts find, in the material on which any one is written, proximate marks of the age to which it belongs. Other criteria are found in the ink employed; but the most important consist in the character of the handwriting, which varied in different periods, just as the fashion of printing has done since.

"The oldest Greek manuscripts are written in capitals, called uncials, without division of words, and without marks of accentuation or punctuation.* About the seventh century, the custom of affixing the accents and aspirates appears to have been introduced; at the same time a greater degree of precision was observed in the formation of the letters, and in the directness and parallelism of the lines. To these improvements was added a change in the form of those letters which most impeded the rapid movement of the pen. In the eighth and ninth centuries, a mode of writing which had been long before practised by notaries and by the secretaries of public persons, was adopted by the transcribers of books. This was a kind of running hand, those who invented or who most used it being called tachygraphoi, swift writers. To adapt the Greek letters to the purposes of public business and common life, the square forms had been changed for curves, and uprights for slopes; and, while a radical resemblance to the primitive character was preserved, facility and freedom were obtained. The uncial character was not, however, altogether abandoned by the copyists; but modifications were introduced with a view to obtain greater facility: for the unconnected and upright squares formerly used seemed still more operose

* For example, imagine English books printed thus: THEOLDESTGREEKMANUSCRIPTSAREWRITTENINCAPITALSCALLEDUNCIALSWITHOUTDIVISIONOFWORDS, &c.

in execution after the running-hand had been adopted. The copyists of the eighth century introduced the practice of commencing books or chapters with a letter of large size, which they usually distinguished by grotesque decorations, somewhat in the manner seen in the printed books of the sixteenth century. Those who gained their living by copying books, found so great an advantage in the adoption of the tachygraphic character, that they presently sought to improve it by every device that might favour the uninterrupted movement of the pen. Not content with joining the letters of each word, they combined them in forms that often bore little resemblance to the component characters. The books of the tenth and following centuries abound with these contractions and symbols. Many intire words of common occurrence were indicated by single turns of the pen. A great part of these contractions were adopted by the first printers, and many of them continued in use till a very recent date." (Transmission of Ancient Books, pp. 58—60.)

The evident superiority of parchment to all other materials for books, and its comparative scarcity and costliness, gave rise to a practice which has probably deprived us of many valuable works of antiquity,—that of erasing what had been written, and cleaning the skin for a second use. Such manuscripts are called Palimpsests *(scraped again)*. This practice was known in classical Roman times, as Cicero rallies a friend for writing him a palimpsest letter.* But its ravages upon books were chiefly committed in the 12th, 13th and 14th centuries, when (sad to say!) the new writings produced were chiefly monkish legends of little interest and no value; and we know not how many precious ancient classics may have been obliterated to make room for them. In many now existing manuscripts, the marks of an effectual erasure are plain. In many others, the first writing is not wholly erased; and, in some, it has

* Ad Familiares, vii. 18. See also Martial, xiv. 7.

been found practicable, by the aid of chemical skill, to wash off the newer writing, and then bring the old into deeper colour again so as to be legible. A remarkable instance of this kind has occurred in the present century, leading to the recovery of a great part of Cicero's treatise, De Republicâ. A book of this kind was known to have been written by Cicero; and at length Angelo Mai, librarian of the Vatican, found it under a palimpsest commentary of Augustine on the Psalms. It was published in Rome, dedicated to the reigning Pope, Pius VII., and was reprinted in England, by Mawman, in 1823.

To this cursory account of ancient books must be added a few words about the book-makers, or copyists, the precursors of our modern printers. They were generally a distinct class or profession, earning their livelihood by their work. But men of leisure and literary taste were also, to some extent, their own transcribers. The Christian Scriptures were often transcribed by private hand for private use. And from the very origin of the monastic system, the monasteries became great places for both the deposit and the transcription of books. The leisure of the monks in general, and the literary tastes of many, disposed them to this occupation. The Greek and Roman classical authors, not less than the Hebrew and Christian Scriptures, are indeed deeply indebted to the monks of the middle ages for the multiplication and preservation of copies; and while acknowledging their services in these respects, we must hope and trust as well as we can, that no great number of very valuable works were scoured out by them (like Cicero's Republic) for *palimpsest* use. Generally speaking, beyond all doubt, the work of transcribing was done with great care and fidelity; and the diversities in manuscripts are no oftener ascribable to wilful fraud, than the diversities in editions since the days of printing. There may have been justifiable changes in the text in both cases; there may be *errata* in both; there may be occasional fraud in either. But the difference between manuscript and printing causes certain necessary varieties in the *law* according to which, and the limits within which, mistakes would prevail. It is curious to trace these.

There may be different *editions* of a manuscript as well as of a printed book; and the variations in the second edition may have received the avowed authority of the writer, or of some other authorized editor. In this case, manuscripts copied from the one edition or the other will, of course, perpetuate these diversities, just as printed editions do, when new editions are undertaken without sufficient inquiry for the best authorized copies then existing.

In printed books, any mistake of the press of course runs through the whole edition, unless (which is a very rare case) it be discovered and corrected while the book is being *worked off*. In manuscripts this is not exactly the case, but there is something very like it. A mere "slip of the pen" (as of the type),—a "clerical error," which every reader sees to be such and corrects in reading (and probably corrects with a pen in his own copy, whether it be noted in the table of *errata* or not),—would not be perpetuated, but corrected by the next copyist in manuscript, if he were intelligent. If stupid, however, or merely a faithful mechanical writer, he might repeat the error with the same perfect fidelity with which he copied everything else. But various readings of a more important kind, such as the change of a word or phrase, whether materially affecting the sense or not, might go into many copies at once, when (as was often done to facilitate the business of copying) one person *read aloud*, and a number of scribes wrote all at once to his dictation. In this case, of course, any error or carelessness on the part of the reader,—his eye losing the proper place in the manuscript, his omission of a line, or his repetition of something already dictated, his mistaking a word, or mispronouncing it so as to sound like a different word (not to suspect him of *wilfully* varying from his copy),—any of these innocent sources of mistake would cause a various reading to appear in all the copies made at the same moment from his dictation; and in any subsequent copies from these, the same error would be repeated by a faithful transcriber.

Another source of error to which manuscripts were liable at the hands of transcribers, was the insertion of a note, written in the margin of one copy, into the text of the next transcript. A student (or a pedant) might, then as now, make such marginal notes. But a manuscript note in the margin of a printed book tells its own story as such; whereas a manuscript note upon a manuscript page might seem like an omission supplied in the one copy, and requiring to be restored to its place in the next. The passage above quoted from Tacitus supplies an example of a marginal note, apparently, inserted in the text (see p. 102).

On the invention of printing in the 15th century, the books in highest esteem, both sacred and secular, were soon presented to the world *in type*. With the Mass-book and the Latin version of the Scriptures, there also appeared Homer and Virgil, Thucydides and Tacitus, Æschylus and Terence, and all the other Greek and Roman classics. All had been preserved thus far by exactly the same processes;—they were now published in larger editions than ever before, through the multiplying power of type-printing; and through that multiplicity of copies, they might be considered thenceforth safe from all possibility of being lost to the world.

The first printed editions, whether of Homer, Virgil or the New Testament, were usually copies of some *one* manuscript of good repute. The same author, if printed in another place from another manuscript copy, presented, of course, the peculiar readings, whatever they might be, of that second manuscript. But careful editors presently began to correct the earlier printed editions, by comparison with each other and with the best manuscripts accessible; and gradually the science of literary criticism has been so thoroughly matured, and the critical material of manuscripts and early editions so carefully collected together, that all the great surviving works of ancient literature may now be read in the best editions, with a practical confidence that we are reading, to all intents and purposes, the very words of the authors themselves. Of course the *text* of some is more completely satisfactory than that of others; and always the most satisfactory text has been produced where there has been the largest number of manuscripts to compare, and the greatest amount of various readings to choose from.

Now, what I particularly wish to note and impress upon my reader's mind is this: that the preservation of the very words of Matthew and the other evangelists, of Paul and the other letter-writers in the New Testament, has taken place through precisely the same laws of human nature and physical nature, the same qualities of parchment, papyrus and paper, of copyist and pen, of printer and printing-type, of mixed human knowledge and ignorance, care and neglect, through which the Greek and Latin classics have come down to us. How many other valuable writings of the latter have been lost to us, it were vain to conjecture. How many other writings of the age of the Gospels and Epistles may have perished, we know not. Some, no doubt, have; for we know that

Luke speaks of "many" as having, before him, written accounts of the life of Jesus Christ; and Paul speaks of having written a letter to the Laodiceans, which does not appear by that name among the books of our New Testament, and is not now known to exist, unless (as some think) the Epistle to the *Ephesians* be the same. The claims of the particular books of the New Testament will form the subject of the next chapter. But meanwhile, it is desirable to give the reader a practical idea of the kind of variations of reading which prevail among manuscripts of the same book. For when we hear of there being thousands of *various readings* in manuscripts of the New Testament, we may fancy ourselves in danger of serious mistake or doubt as to the contents of the Religion of Jesus Christ, unless it be explained that the chief part of those thousands of readings consist of such minutiæ as the following (representing in English, as nearly as possible, the corresponding varieties in the Greek): *And* is a various reading for *but*, or *but* for *and; but* has been omitted; *and* omitted. Then the Greek having extra particles of this kind, these various readings of the connective particles occur, perhaps, five times as often in Greek as they can in English. If the preposition *in* is in one copy and *at* in another, and a third expresses the idea without either, these are various readings. The pronouns *I, thou, he, we,* &c., expressed in one MS. or understood in another, or their being repeated or omitted with a second verb, form again so many various readings. *Jesus* may stand in one copy, where *Christ* is in another, and *Jesus Christ* in a third. The order of two or more words may vary without change of sense. Thus the great bulk of the various readings is of no importance whatever to the sense, but shews (by their being of this character) the intrinsic faithfulness of the copyists, as well as the minute industry of the modern *collaters* of manuscripts. And the same precisely is the case with the classical writers of Greece and Rome. Sacred and secular writers stand on the same footing of criticism. Tacitus, already quoted, wrote about the same time as most of the New-Testament writers; and his text is perplexed and difficult compared with theirs, for want of sufficiently numerous manuscripts of an early date.

I shall sum up all that need be said on this subject in the clear and forcible words of Dr. Bentley, published in 1713. Six years before that time, Dr. Mill's celebrated critical edition of the New Testament had been published, containing, as was estimated, 30,000 various readings. It was a noble contribution to sacred learning. But it appears that the excellent, but timid and then aged, Dr. Whitby, among others, had weakly expressed himself as afraid of its *unsettling* the text of scripture; and Mr. Collins had used Dr. Whitby's unreasonable fears as a warrant for asserting that the text of scripture was altogether unreliable. Dr. Bentley, probably the first scholar of his age, the editor of Terence and Horace,* in his reply to Collins ("Remarks upon a late Discourse of Free-thinking"), thus clearly and fully explained the critical value of various readings, and shewed that the Scriptures are, in this respect, to be treated exactly like all other books of the same age, and that the result is in their case eminently satisfactory, on account of the abundant manuscripts:†

* Bentley's editions of these classics are remarkable for his freely admitting conjectural readings into the text, while other editors merely place them in notes. Many of his conjectural readings are very happy and tempting; some fanciful; most of them bold. "Slashing Bentley," Pope called him, not without reason. The rule is now held sacred by critical editors, to admit nothing merely conjectural into the text, whatever the intelligent reader may adopt into his own judgment where the text is plainly corrupt.

† This extract, from a book 140 years old, purposely reprinted *verbatim et literatim*, may incidentally illustrate, by its peculiarities of spelling, by its various obsolete contractions and the antiquated use of capital letters,

"The 30000 Various Lections are allow'd then and confess'd: and if more Copies yet are collated, the Sum will still mount higher. And what's the Inference from this? why, one *Gregory*, here quoted, infers, *That no Profane Author whatever has suffer'd so much by the hand of Time, as the New Testament has done.* Now if this should be found utterly false; and if the *Scriptural Text* has no more Variations, than what must necessarily have happen'd from *the nature of Things*, and what are common and in equal proportion in all Classics whatever; I hope this *Panic* will be remov'd, and the Text be thought as firm as before.

"If there had been but one Manuscript of the *Greek* Testament, at the restoration of Learning about Two Centuries ago; then we had had no *Various Readings* at all. And would the Text be in a better condition then, than now we have 30000? So far from That; that in the best single Copy extant we should have had hundreds of Faults, and some Omissions irreparable. Besides that the Suspicions of Fraud and Foul Play would have been increas'd immensly.

"It is good therefore, you'l allow, to have more Authors than One; and another *MS.* to join with the first would give more Authority, as well as Security. Now chuse that Second where you will, there shall be a Thousand Variations from the First; and yet Half or More of the Faults shall still remain in them Both.

"A Third therefore, and so a Fourth, and still on, are desirable; that by a joint and mutual help All the Faults may be mended: some Copy preserving the True Reading in one place, and some in another. And yet the more Copies you call to assistance, the more do the Various Readings multiply upon you: every Copy having its peculiar slips, though in a principal Passage or two it do singular service. And this is Fact, not only in the New Testament, but in all Antient Books whatever.

"'Tis a good Providence and a great Blessing, That so many Manuscripts of the New Testament are still amongst us; some

some of the changes in the style of printing in different periods. The difference of type and paper we cannot reproduce for the purpose.

procur'd from *Egypt*, others from *Asia*, others found in the *Western* Churches, For the very Distances of Places, as well as Numbers of the Books, demonstrate; that there could be no Collusion, no altering nor interpolating One Copy by another, nor All by any of them.

"In Profane Authors (as they are call'd) whereof One Manuscript only had the luck to be preserv'd, as *Velleius Paterculus* among the *Latins*, and *Hesychius* among the *Greeks*; the Faults of the Scribes are found so numerous, and the Defects beyond all redress, that notwithstanding the Pains of the learned'st and acutest Critics for Two whole Centuries, those Books are still and are like to continue a mere Heap of Errors. On the contrary, where the Copies of any Author are numerous, though the *Various Readings* always increase in Proportion; there the Text by an accurate Collation of them made by skilful and judicious Hands is ever the more correct, and comes nearer to the true words of the Author.

"Were the very Originals of Antient Books still in being; those alone would supersede the use of all other Copies: but since That was impossible *from the nature of Things*, since Time and Casualties must consume and devour all; the subsidiary Help is from the various Transcripts convey'd down to us, when compar'd and examin'd together.

"*Terence* is now in one of the best conditions of Any of the Classic Writers; the oldest and best Copy of him is now in the Vatican Library, which comes nearest to the Poet's own hand: but even That has Hundreds of Errors, most of which may be mended out of other Exemplars, that are otherwise more recent and of inferior value. I my self have collated several; and do affirm that I have seen 20000 Various Lections in that little Author, not near so big as the whole *New Testament*: and am morally sure, that if Half the number of Manuscripts were collated for *Terence* with that Niceness and Minuteness which has been used in Twice as many for the *New Testament*, the number of the *Variations* would amount to above 50000.

"In the Manuscripts of the *New Testament* the Variations have been noted with a Religious, not to say Superstitious Exactness. Every difference in Spelling, in the smallest Particle or Article of Speech, in the very Order or Collation of words without real change, has been studiously registred. Nor has the Text only been ransack'd, but all the Antient Versions, the *Latin Vulgate*, *Italic*, *Syriac*, *Aethiopic*, *Arabic*, *Coptic*, *Armenian*, *Gothic* and *Saxon*; nor these only, but all the dispers'd Citations of the *Greek* and *Latin* Fathers in a course of 500 years. What wonder then, if with all this scrupulous search in every hole and corner, the Varieties rise to 30000? when in all Antient Books of the same Bulk, whereof the MSS are numerous, the Variations are as many or more; and yet no Versions to swell the Reckoning.

"The Editors of Profane Authors do not use to trouble their Readers, or risk their own Reputation, by an useless List of every small slip committed by a lazy or ignorant Scribe. What is thought commendable in an Edition of Scripture, and has the name of Fairness and Fidelity, would in Them be deem'd Impertinence and Trifling. Hence the Reader not vers'd in antient MSS is deceiv'd into an Opinion, that there were no more Variations in the Copies, than what the Editor has communicated. Whereas, if the like scrupulousness was observ'd in registring the smallest Changes in Profane Authors, as is allow'd, nay requir'd in Sacred; the now formidable number of 30000 would appear a very Trifle.

"'Tis manifest, that Books in Verse are not near so obnoxious to Variations, as Prose: the Transcriber, if he is not wholly ignorant and stupid, being guided by the Measures; and hindred from such Alterations, as do not fall in with the Laws of Numbers. And yet even in Poets, the Variations are so very many, as can hardly be conceiv'd without use and experience. In the late Edition of *Tibullus*, by the Learned Mr. *Broukhuise*, you have a Register of *Various Lections* in the close of that Book; where you may see at the first view that they are as many as the Lines. The same is visible in *Plautus*, set out by *Pareus*. I my self, during my Travels, have had the opportunity to examin several MSS of the Poet *Manilius*; and can assure you, that the Variations I have met with are twice as many as all the Lines of the Book. Our Discourser here has quoted Nine Verses out of it, p. 151: in which, though one of the easiest Places, I can shew him XIV Various Lections. Add likewise that the MSS here used were Few in comparison:

and then do You imagin, what the Lections would amount to, if Ten times as many (the Case of Dr. *Mill)* were accurately examin'd. And yet in these and all other Books, the Text is not made more *precarious* on that account, but more certain and authentic. So that if I may advise you; when you hear more of this Scarecrow of 30000, be neither astonish'd at the Sum, nor in any pain for the Text.

"'Tis plain to me, that your Learned *Whitbyus*, in his Invective against my Dead Friend, was suddenly surpriz'd with a *Panic;* and under his deep concern for the *Text* did not reflect at all what that Word really means. The present Text was first settled almost 200 years ago out of several MSS by *Robert Stephens* a Printer and Bookseller at *Paris:* whose beautiful and (generally speaking) accurate Edition has been ever since counted the Standard, and follow'd by all the rest. Now this specific *Text* in your Doctor's notion seems taken for the Sacred Original in every Word and Syllable: and if the Conceit is but spread and propagated, within a few Years that *Printer's* Infallibility will be as zealously maintain'd as an *Evangelist's* or *Apostle's*.

"Dr. MILL, were he alive, would confess to Your Doctor, That this *Text* fix'd by a Printer is sometimes by the Various Readings render'd *uncertain*, nay is prov'd certainly wrong. But then he would subjoin, That the Real Text of the Sacred Writers does not now (since the Originals have been so long lost) ly in any single MS or Edition; but is dispers'd in them all. 'Tis competently exact indeed, even in the worst MS now extant: nor is One Article of Faith or Moral Precept either perverted or lost in them; chuse as awkwardly as you can, chuse the worst by design, out of the whole Lump of Readings. But the lesser matters of Diction, and among several synonymous Expressions the Very Words of the Writer, must be found out by the same Industry and Sagacity that is used in other Books; must not be risk'd upon the credit of any particular MS or Edition, but be sought, acknowledg'd, and challeng'd, where-ever they are met with." (Remarks, &c., pp. 64—69, 5th ed., London, 1716.)

CHAPTER IV.

THE CANON OF THE NEW TESTAMENT; OR, WHY ITS BOOKS ARE REGARDED AS AUTHENTIC AND CREDIBLE.

BY the *canon* of Scripture, is meant the list or catalogue of the books that constitute the Scriptures. Etymologically, *canon* is, in Greek, the mechanic's implement called a *rule* or *square;* thence, figuratively, it denotes any rule, or measure, or test, or principle of judgment. Ecclesiastically, a canon of the church is a decree of the church; and in critical theology, the canon of Scripture is the catalogue of books resulting from the real or supposed application of certain tests or rules of selection.

The canon of the Old Testament (in Protestant churches) embraces, as we have before seen (Vol. I. p. 14, &c.), all the remains of Hebrew literature that existed at, and for some time before, the Christian era; the "Books called Apocrypha" being certain Greek Jewish writings of the latter part of the period. The distinction between *canonical* and *apocryphal* is there simply of a literary and chronological kind,—the former class including the native Hebrew and more ancient literature of the Jews; and the latter, their more recent Greek literature, chiefly of Alexandrian growth. The Roman Catholic Church, however, disregards these distinctions, and pronounces all the books of the Old Testament and Apocrypha alike canonical, and all of them alike inspired. That any principle of selection or exclusion was ever adopted in forming the canon of the Jewish Scriptures is, to say the least, very questionable. Time alone appears to have been the discriminator, and not invariably to have been guided by the sacredness of the subject-matter in what he has preserved.

The canon of the New Testament, however, belonging as it does to a much lower antiquity, can be shewn to have been formed upon some kind of principles of selection and rejection. Some books have been, in all periods, regarded by Christians as sacred, and others not. Some have been regarded in a more favourable light by certain churches than by other churches, or by certain Christians than by other Christians. Multitudes of books professing to be holy and apostolical, besides those which we recognize as Christian Scriptures, existed in the early ages of the church. St. Luke, in the first verse of his Gospel, expressly says, that "*Many* have taken in hand to set forth in order a declaration of those things which are most surely believed among us, even as they delivered them unto us, which from the beginning were eye-witnesses and ministers of the word." And, whether he be understood to refer to the labours of his precursors with approval (which seems the obvious meaning of his allusion), or (as some think) with dissatisfaction and with the intention to displace their histories by a more full and accurate one of his own,—the fact is attested by him beyond dispute, that there were already existing many records of the gospel history in part, if not as a whole. That any of these earlier records now exist, we have no reason to believe. The fuller histories by the evangelists may very naturally have thrown the more fragmentary ones into oblivion. But many productions of the first, second and third centuries still exist, and many others now lost are mentioned by ecclesiastical writers, which had assumed the names of various apostles and apostolic men, but were almost with one consent rejected by the early fathers of the Christian church as forgeries, or as not sufficiently important; while the books now forming our New Testament were accepted as canonical, most of them unanimously, and the rest of them with general;

though not universal, consent. These discriminating testimonies will be presently brought forward.

But first, by way of shewing the reader what kind of books falsely pretending to apostolical authorship, were current in the early Christian church, I shall here quote the titles of those which are enumerated in the decree of Gelasius, who was bishop of Rome 492—496. This decree emanated from a council of seventy bishops meeting at Rome. It enumerates the books of the Old Testament, then those of the New, as we have them. Then it mentions certain ecclesiastical writings which, in due subordination to the Scriptures, the Roman Church permits to be used "for our edification." And then follows this curious catalogue of "apocryphal books which are not received." It is alluded to by Dr. Lardner in his "Credibility of the Gospel History" (Works, V. 248), and is quoted by Jones in his "New and Full Method of settling the Canonical Authority of the New Testament" (Vol. I. p. 154), whence I extract it:

"The decree of Pope Gelasius concerning apocryphal books.

1. The Travels under the name of Peter the Apostle, which is also called the Eight Books of St. Clemens, are apocryphal.

2. The Acts under the name of Andrew the Apostle, are apocryphal.

3. The Acts under the name of Philip the Apostle, are apocryphal.

4. The Acts under the name of Peter the Apostle, are apocryphal.

5. The Acts under the name of Thomas the Apostle, are apocryphal.

6. The Gospel under the name of Thaddæus, is apocryphal.

7. The Gospel under the name of Thomas the Apostle, which the Manichees use, is apocryphal.

8. The Gospel under the name of Barnabas, is apocryphal.

9. The Gospel under the name of Bartholomew the Apostle, is apocryphal.

10. The Gospel under the name of Andrew the Apostle, is apocryphal.

11. The Gospels corrupted by Lucianus, are apocryphal.

12. The Gospels corrupted by Hesychius, are apocryphal.

13. The Gospel of the Infancy of our Saviour, is apocryphal.

14. The Book of the Nativity of our Saviour, of St. Mary, and the Midwife of our Saviour, is apocryphal.

15. The book which is called the Shepherd, is apocryphal.

16. All the books which Lentilius, the disciple of the Devil, made, are apocryphal.

17. The book which is called the Acts of Thecla and Paul the Apostle, is apocryphal.

18. The Revelation ascribed to Thomas the Apostle, is apocryphal.

19. The Revelation ascribed to Paul the Apostle, is apocryphal.

20. The Revelation ascribed to Stephen, is apocryphal.

21. The Travels or Acts of St. Mary, are apocryphal.

22. The book called the Lots of the Apostles, is apocryphal.

23. The book called the Praise of the Apostles, is apocryphal.

24. The book of the Canons of the Apostles, is apocryphal.

25. The Letter of Jesus to King Abgarus, is apocryphal."

Many other books with similar titles, and no doubt corresponding pretensions, to those in Gelasius's list, are also mentioned by the writers of the early Christian church. And no small number of such productions are still preserved. They may be read, and all that is known of the others may be learnt, in Dr. Jeremiah Jones's laborious work above quoted. The principal of them were reprinted by Mr. William Hone, in a volume entitled, the Apocryphal New Testament, but without any critical appreciation, on the part of their editor, of their literary or theological characteristics. The perusal of such as now exist amply confirms the judgment of antiquity in setting them aside as apocryphal. Simply to read the books called the *Gospel of the Birth of Mary*, and the *Infancy of Jesus*, excites our pity for the weakness of those who could think they were doing honour to Christ by adopting such wretched fictions into the history of his marvellous life; or else our indignation at the deep designing malice which (one suspects) may have intended by such stories to ridicule the intire belief of Christians. Whether books such as these, ascribing miracles the most paltry, petulant and selfish, to the childhood of him whose holy manhood the gospel history of the New Testament describes as invested with miraculous powers the most sublime, and as using them for purposes of purest benevolence, were written by the weakest-minded of Christian devotees, or by the most artful enemies of the Christian faith, may be a question difficult to decide. But the contrast between the gospel histories of the New Testament and these apocryphal fictions, is indeed most striking. Equally so is the contrast between the simple but dignified history in the book of the Acts of the Apostles, and that addition to the history of Paul which has been offered by some wretched romancer or other of the third or fourth century, under the title of the *Acts of Paul and Thecla*; which, however, exposes its own forgery by the palpable anachronism of making Paul the advocate of celibacy and of the monastic life, while it grievously outrages the New-Testament miracles by its grotesque imitations and ridiculous exaggerations. And just so, the reality and genuineness of the New-Testament Epistles seems almost self-evident, after reading the pretended correspondence of Paul and the philosopher Seneca, in which vapid compliment forms the staple, and none of the real thought of Paul is to be recognized.

That a true discrimination has been exercised in calling such books apocryphal, is plain at once. But it may still not be quite easy to define what should constitute a book canonical, nor to say on what grounds precisely some of our Scriptures have been so regarded.

If those grounds appear to have been the conviction that the books received were *inspired*, and the rejected ones *uninspired*, we have still to ask what were the *tests* or *criteria* of an inspired book. Proved apostolic authorship would probably be admitted, indeed, as proving the inspiration of a book; but what proof, then, was there of the inspiration of the books written by Mark and Luke, who were not apostles? No doubt the intrinsic qualities of those writings, and the harmony of their contents with those of apostolic books, asserted for them a place in the same class of writings, whether under any distinct theory of their being also inspired, or under the natural perception of the general competency and credibility of the writers. And this natural perception of truth was, ultimately, the real test.

On the inspiration of the Scriptures I need say no more than I have already said (Vol. I. p. 25, &c.), in order to keep clear the very necessary distinction between their supposed inspiration *as writings*, and the more evident inspiration of *certain of their contents*. The former is the old doctrine, now in rapid decline among thoughtful Christians,—a doctrine which weakly perils the credibility of the Scriptures themselves, by attempting to lift them above the reach of literary criticism. The latter is the solid basis on which to vindicate the inspiration of the minds of Jesus and his apostles, as manifested through the distinct literary facts of these books, when subjected to the customary tests of competent criticism and philosophy. The books are records of inspired men, but not inspired records of them.

The greater part of the books of the New Testament, then, have been accepted as Christian Scriptures because believed to be, as they profess to be, the works of apostles of Jesus Christ. And a multitude of apocryphal books, bearing (as we have seen) the names of apostles, have been rejected by universal consent, because perceived to be not the works of those whose names they bear; in other words, they have been rejected as forgeries. So far, the rule of judgment has been a perfectly clear one; though in applying it to some particular books of the New Testament there has not been intire unanimity of judgment. Thus the Epistle to the Hebrews has not been universally admitted to be St. Paul's; nor the Revelation to be St. John's; nor have the Epistles known as 2 Peter, 2 and 3 John, and Jude, been universally acknowledged to be the writings of the apostles whose names they bear. In reference to these books, accordingly, the catalogue of Scriptures, as quoted by different ecclesiastical writers, differs. And then there are three of the most important books of the New Testament, namely, the Gospels by Mark and Luke and the Acts of the Apostles (also by Luke), which do not profess to be the writings of apostles, and yet have been acknowledged as scriptures of Christianity in every list or canon that has ever been drawn up. The rule, therefore, for accepting a certain book as scripture or admitting it into the canon, has not been strictly and exclusively that it was believed to be the work of an apostle. A history written by one believed to be competent to his task, was a credible history in the Christian church, as everywhere else. A letter professing to be written by an apostle, was accepted if believed to be his, or rejected if believed to be not his. But a letter (like that to the Hebrews) without a signature, might be accepted for its contents, and its author might perhaps be guessed through his *anonymous*. So the chief part of the New Testament is accepted as of apostolical authorship; the rest as the work of other competent and credible writers. When, therefore, we thus perceive that there is no absolute, hard and dogmatical line of distinction to bound the canon of Scripture and separate its books generically from all others in the world,—when we see that there are a few books in our New Testament generally believed indeed to be of apostolical authorship, but not universally admitted to be so; and that there are certain books universally admitted not to be the work of apostles, but universally accepted into the list of our Scriptures as genuine records of the great facts of our faith,—the conclusion to be rationally and thankfully accepted by us is this:—that these histories and letters referring to the origin of the Christian religion, are to be estimated on the self-same principles by which all other ancient writings stand or fall; that there are varieties in the strength of evidence proving their respective authorship, as there are in the case of other books on other subjects; while, as regards the chief part of them, the evidence for their authorship is the most conclusive that can be offered for any books of equal antiquity. And we thus find existing within the canon of the New Testament, books of various degrees of Christian value and interest according to their respective contents and authorship; while there are many others beyond the canon that are thoroughly authentic and true to their own pretensions as written by known and reputable authors of early Christian antiquity, but not claiming to be regarded as sacred scriptures.

In fact, each book of the New Testament requires to be looked at as a separate book, or volume, or tract (which it originally was); and its enumeration by successive Christian writers as one of a number of writings generally or universally recognized by Christians as containing their religion, is part of the cumulative proof (not quite the same for all the books) of its antiquity and genuineness, of its authorship, and the trustworthiness of its contents. A detected forgery is in every case consigned to contempt or indignation. A book of doubtful authorship and doubtful importance must find rank accordingly, whether admitted into the canon of the church under such avowed doubts or not. These are the general principles of literary criticism, everywhere applicable.

Augustine, Bishop of Hippo in Africa (A.D. 395—430), writing against Faustus the Manichean, thus speaks of the notorious existence of books falsely claiming apostolic authorship; and in this rational and healthy tone (worthy of modern imitation) maintains the identity of sacred and classical principles of criticism:

"What writings can ever claim the weight of authenticity, if not those of the evangelists and apostles? Of what book shall the authorship be considered certain, if it is uncertain whether those letters are the genuine writings of apostles, which are declared and held to be such by the church propagated by the apostles themselves, and proclaimed so clearly through all nations? As if, indeed, there were not also in secular literature well-ascertained authors in whose names many writings have been put forth since their own time, but rejected, either as not harmonizing with their acknowledged works, or because, at the time when the former wrote, these productions earned no such distinction as to be commended to posterity by them or their nearest friends. But as regards those books, on comparison with which we reject others that are produced irregularly, how do we know them to be the works,—of Hippocrates, for instance,—unless for this reason: that from the very time of Hippocrates uninterruptedly till now, a succession of evidence has so constantly attested them, that to doubt it would be the part of a madman? How do men know that the works of Plato, of Aristotle, of Cicero, of Varro, and other such authors, are really theirs, except by the same continuous attestation of successive periods? Many men have compiled many books in ecclesiastical literature, not indeed possessing canonical authority, but with some design of assisting others or of learning themselves. How do we know whose each work is, except because at the very time when each man wrote, he introduced and published his works to all whom he could, and the knowledge of the authorship being from that time forth extended to more and more persons and more widely confirmed to their successors, their works have thus come down to our times; so that when we are asked whose any book is, we do not doubt what we ought to answer." (Cont. Faust. lib. xxxiii. cap. vi., quoted by Lardner, III. 525.*)

This same Augustine gives a full account of the canon of Scripture as received in his day, and enumerates the books of the New Testament *precisely as we have them.* (Lardner, V. 85.) We shall trace the testimonies upwards from this period.

An authoritative decision of the canon of the New Testament is, by some, but without sufficient reason, ascribed to the Council of Nicæa, A.D. 325. Others hold, with better reason, that the Council of Laodicea took the subject in hand, about the middle or latter part of the fourth century. This latter Council enumerated the books of the Old Testament also; and the record is curious as shewing, both in regard to the Old Testament and the New, a general agreement, together with a few diversities of classification. The last two "canons" of this Council are thus cited by Lardner (Vol. IV. 308):

"That private psalms ought not to be read [or said] in the church, nor any books not canonical, but only the canonical books of the Old and New Testament.

"The books of the Old Testament which ought to be read are these: 1. The Genesis [origin] of the World. 2. The Exodus out of Egypt. 3. Leviticus. 4. Numbers. 5. Deuteronomy. 6. Joshua the Son of Nun. 7. Judges, with Ruth. 8. Esther. 9. The first and second book of the Kingdoms.

* The edition of Lardner's Works referred to, is that of Kippis, in eleven vols., 1788.

10. The third and fourth book of the Kingdoms. 11. The first and second book of the Remains [Chronicles or Supplements]. 12. The first and second book of Esdras [Ezra and Nehemiah]. 13. The book of 150 Psalms. 14. The Proverbs of Solomon. 15. The Ecclesiastes. 16. The Song of Songs. 17. Job. 18. The twelve [minor] Prophets. 19. Isaiah. 20. Jeremiah and Baruch, the Lamentations and the Epistle. 21. Ezekiel. 22. Daniel. The books of the New Testament are these: The four Gospels, according to Matthew, according to Mark, according to Luke, according to John; the Acts of the Apostles; the seven Catholic [general] Epistles: of James one, of Peter two, of John three, of Jude one; the fourteen Epistles of Paul: to the Romans one, to the Corinthians two, to the Galatians one, to the Ephesians one, to the Philippians one, to the Colossians one, to the Thessalonians two, to the Hebrews one, to Timothy two, to Titus one, to Philemon one."

In the list here given for the Old Testament, it is to be observed that the Apocryphal books of Baruch and the Epistle of Jeremiah are enumerated with Jeremiah and the Lamentations; and we may perhaps consider the additions to Esther and to Daniel as also implied in the mention of those books; but there is no recognition of the remaining books of the Jewish Apocrypha, including the most valuable of them.

In the list of the New Testament, the book of the Revelation of John is unmentioned; one of the few books respecting which we shall find these ancient catalogues, or canons, continually varying.

It must be added, however, that in some ancient manuscripts these concluding canons of the Council of Laodicea, on the books of Scripture, are wanting. And the opinions of learned men, as to the importance or authority of this Council, are not unanimous. Probably, indeed, its omission of the Apocrypha and the Revelation of John from the list of canonical Scriptures, may have influenced the judgment of some to disparage its competency. Some say it consisted chiefly of Arian bishops; but it is not easy to see how that circumstance, if true, could influence their judgment respecting the Jewish Apocrypha and the Revelation of John.

But it is of little or no real importance to the subject before us, whether the Council of Laodicea really published such a catalogue of canonical Scriptures or not; since our critical means of judging respecting each of the books in question extend far higher up than the time of that Council, and are, in fact, the very materials on which that Council must have chiefly relied for its decision. The testimonies which we have now to adduce are not authoritative decrees of councils fixing a canon of Scripture, but statements of fact as to the general or uniform reception of each particular book. They rest the question of authenticity on precisely the same kind of evidence as in the case of all other books. Le Clerc, quoted by Lardner,* says admirably on this subject:

"We nowhere read of a council of the apostles, or any assembly of the governors of Christian churches, being convened to determine by their authority that such a number of Gospels, neither more nor fewer, should be received. Nor was there any need of it, since it was well known to all, from the concurring testimony of contemporaries, that these four Gospels are the genuine writings of those whose names they bear, and since there is nothing in them unworthy of those to whom they are ascribed, nor anything in any degree contrary to the revelation of the Old Testament nor to right reason, or at all savouring of a later age and more recent hands. There was no need of a synod of grammarians, authoritatively to pronounce that those writings, for instance, of Cicero and Virgil, which we without hesitation ascribe to them, are really the fruits of those gifted minds, and to provide for their reception as such by posterity. Universal assent, not sought or canvassed, but spontaneously signified as occasion offered, and

* History of Apostles and Evangelists. Works, Vol. VI. p. 29.

also the very contents of the books themselves, precluded all doubt on the part of posterity. So also the authority of the Gospels has been rightly established, and has prevailed by perpetual consent, without any decree of the governors of the Church.

"We may say the same of the apostolical Epistles, which owe all their authority, not to the judgment of any ecclesiastical council, but to the concurring testimony of all Christians, and to the matter itself which is contained in them."

Lardner then appeals for similar opinions to Basnage's History of the Church, and Jones on the Canon, quotes Augustine (already quoted a few pages back), and concludes the consideration of the canon of the New Testament in these words:

"Upon the whole, the writings of the apostles and evangelists are received, as the works of other eminent men of antiquity are, upon the ground of general consent and testimony. Nor does the canon of the New Testament owe its establishment to the decisions of councils; but it is the judgment of Christian people in general; and, so far as we are able to perceive, it is a right and reasonable judgment. And it may induce us to believe that if men were encouraged to think freely, in other matters also, and to judge for themselves according to evidence, and proper assistances were afforded them, it would not be at all detrimental to the interests either of truth or virtue." (VI. 31.)

We have now to trace the testimonies to the respective books of the New Testament upwards from the time of Augustine, whose table of contents has been seen to be identical with that of our English New Testament. In doing this, I merely abridge the clear and able Lectures of Bishop Marsh on the Authenticity of the New Testament,* or quote from Lardner's Credibility. Dr. Marsh

* See "A Course of Lectures containing a Description and Systematic Arrangement of the several Branches of Divinity, &c., by Herbert Marsh, D.D., F.R.S. and F.A.S., Lord Bishop of Peterborough and Margaret Professor of Divinity. Part V. On the Authenticity of the New Testament."

begins with the testimony of Jerom, and ascends gradually to the earliest testimonies. Lardner takes the series in its descending order. We get the clearest view by going *upwards* from where we find ourselves with the New Testament in our hands, as now received.

JEROM was the most learned of the Latin Fathers. He was born about the middle of the fourth century, and ordained Presbyter of Antioch A.D. 378. He has given a catalogue of the books of the New Testament, in a letter to Paulinus on the study of the Holy Scriptures, as follows: the four Evangelists, Matthew, Mark, Luke and John; the Acts of the Apostles, also by Luke; Epistles of Paul to seven churches. The Epistle to the Hebrews (he says) most persons did not consider as Paul's (though he himself elsewhere ascribes it to him). Paul wrote also to Timothy, Titus and Philemon. The seven Catholic Epistles he ascribes to James, Peter, John and Jude. The Revelation of John, he says, "has as many mysteries as words."

GREGORY of Nazianzum, in the Greek Church, born about 325, in a poem enumerates "the genuine books of inspired Scripture" as follows: the four Gospels, under the usual names; the Acts of the Apostles; fourteen Epistles of Paul; seven Catholic Epistles, namely, one of James, two of Peter, three of John and one of Jude. He omits the book of Revelation, which he elsewhere, however, speaks of as John's, but which was generally rejected by the Greek Church in the fourth century, as the Epistle to the Hebrews was by the Latin Church.

EPIPHANIUS, contemporary with Jerom, in his third book against heresies, enumerates all the books thus: the four holy Gospels; fourteen Epistles of the holy apostle Paul; the Acts of the Apostles; the Catholic Epistles of James, Peter, John and Jude; and the Revelation of John.

ATHANASIUS, appointed bishop of Alexandria A.D. 326, gives the whole list thus (enumerating the Epistles of Paul individually): the four Gospels, Matthew, Mark, Luke, John; the Acts of the Apostles; the seven Epistles of apostles called Catholic, of James one, Peter two, John three, and Jude one; fourteen Epistles of Paul, Romans, two to the Corinthians, Galatians, Ephesians, Philippians, Colossians, Epistles to the Thessalonians, Epistle to the Hebrews, two to Timothy, to Titus one, the last to Philemon; also the Revelation of John. "These," he adds, "are the fountains of salvation, that he who thirsts may be satisfied with the oracles contained in them. In these alone the doctrine of religion is taught."

EUSEBIUS is perhaps the most important of all our testimonies on this subject. He was born at Cæsarea, A.D. 270, and became bishop of that city. In his Ecclesiastical History, he states the result of his diligent inquiries into the reception of the Scriptures down to his time, in a chapter headed, "Of the Scriptures universally acknowledged, and those which are not so." His careful and candid discrimination as to the universal or partial reception of the different books is so important, that I must quote it more fully in his own words from Lardner (Vol. IV. pp. 227, &c.). In the previous chapter, he has spoken pretty fully of the four Gospels and their authors. He here pursues:

"But it will be proper to enumerate here, in a summary way, the books of the New Testament which have been already mentioned. And in the first place are to be ranked the sacred four Gospels; then the book of the Acts of the Apostles; after that are to be reckoned the Epistles of Paul. In the next place, that called the First Epistle of John and the Epistle of Peter are to be esteemed *authentic*. After these is to be placed, if it be thought fit, the Revelation of St. John, about which we shall observe the different opinions at a proper season. Of the *controverted* books, but yet well known or approved by the most [or many], are that called the Epistle of James, and that of Jude, and the Second of Peter, and the Second and Third of John; whether they are written by the evangelist or another of the same name. Among the *spurious* are to be placed the Acts of Paul, and the book intitled the Shepherd, and the Revelation of Peter; and besides these, that called the Epistle of Barnabas, and the book named the Doctrines of the Apostles. And moreover, as I said, the Revelation of St. John, if it seem meet; which some, as I have said, reject—others reckon among the books universally received. Among these also some have reckoned the Gospel according to the Hebrews,* which the Hebrews who have embraced Christ make use of. All these may be reckoned *controverted.* It was, however, needful that I should put down a catalogue of these also, distinguishing the Scriptures which, according to the ecclesiastical tradition, are *true, genuine* and *universally acknowledged,* from those others which are not placed in the Testament, but are *controverted* and yet appear to have been *known to many:* that by this means we may know these from such as have been *published by heretics under the names of apostles,* as containing the Gospels of Peter, and Thomas, and Matthias, and of some others; and the Acts of Andrew and John and other apostles. Which books none of the ecclesiastical writers in the succession have vouchsafed to make any mention of in their writings. The style also of these books is intirely different from that of the apostles; moreover, the sentiments and doctrine of those pieces are different from the true orthodox Christianity. All which things plainly shew that those books are the *forgeries of heretics.* For all which reasons they are not so much to be reckoned among the *spurious,* but are to be rejected as altogether *absurd and impious.*"

In the next chapter, "On the Epistles of the Apostles," Eusebius says:

* Supposed by some to have been the Hebrew original of Matthew's Gospel. But the question is quite beyond satisfactory solution, and conjecture is useless.

"One Epistle of Peter, called his First, is universally received. This the elders of ancient times have quoted in their writings as undoubtedly genuine. But that called his Second Epistle, we have been informed, has not been received into the Testament. Nevertheless, appearing to many to be useful, it has been carefully studied with the other Scriptures. [*Acts*, *Gospel*, *Preaching* and *Revelation* under his name, are then mentioned as 'not delivered down in the number of Catholic writings.'] Of Paul there are fourteen Epistles manifest and well known. But yet there are some who reject that to the Hebrews, urging for their opinion that it is contradicted by the Church of the Romans as not being Paul's."

Eusebius might certainly have been clearer in his avowed classification. Yet it is plain that the books mentioned by him as *spurious, heretical and impious*, are books not in our New Testament; and of those in our New Testament, he has mentioned the following as *not universally acknowledged:* Hebrews, 2 Peter, 2 and 3 John, James, Jude and Revelation; while all the others he declares to have been *universally acknowledged* by the Christian churches, namely, the four Gospels, the book of Acts, thirteen Epistles of Paul, one of Peter and one of John.

This distribution of the books of the New Testament by Eusebius may fairly be considered as decisive in favour of the authenticity of the "undisputed" books; while, as regards the others, let it be observed, it does not disprove their authenticity by any means. It proves at least that they were in existence, and were well known to Eusebius and many others. The doubt expressed by his classification is as to their *authorship.* And he says, some held them to be the works of Paul, Peter, John, James and Jude respectively, though others doubted. It would be a vain hope for any one in the present age to decide absolutely what Eusebius has thus left doubtful. But it is obvious to remark, that the letters in question ascribed to Peter, John and Jude, are all very brief, and that 2 and 3 John are private letters; both which circumstances would prevent their becoming rapidly or generally known, even if they were written by the apostles themselves. The Epistle ascribed to James is longer, and its matter truly of catholic, or general, use; but, whether from its being addressed pointedly to the Jewish Christians ("the twelve tribes scattered abroad"), or from some other cause, it is conceivable that it may have been his, though not universally received as his. The Epistle to the Hebrews has not Paul's name, nor any other name, appended,—a very evident occasion for different opinions on its authorship. The Revelation calls its author John; yet some, from the earliest times, we are here told, doubted whether it was written by the apostle of that name. We must accept these doubts and uncertainties, from the same sources from which we take the decisive proofs in the other instances.

From Eusebius, we ascend a step higher up the stream of Christian antiquity to Origen.

ORIGEN was born, A.D. 184, in Africa, and lived and taught chiefly in Alexandria. Many of his very voluminous writings are lost; but, from what remain, the following results are clearly brought out by Dr. Lardner, who quotes Origen's own words in each instance:

"Origen received as divine Scripture the four Gospels of Matthew, Mark, Luke and John; the Acts of the Apostles, written by the evangelist Luke; thirteen Epistles of the apostle Paul; and likewise the Epistle to the Hebrews, which he continually quotes as Paul's, though in one place he delivers his opinion that the sentiments only of the Epistle were the apostle's, the phrase and composition of some one else, whose he did not certainly know. He received likewise the First Epistle of Peter and the First of John. We learn from him also that the Epistle of James, the Second of Peter, the Second and Third of John, and the Epistle of Jude, were then well known, but not universally received as genuine; nor is it evident that Origen himself received them as sacred Scripture. He owns the book of the Revelation for the writing of John the apostle and evangelist; he quotes it as his without hesitation; nor does it appear that he had any doubt about its genuineness or authority." (Lardner, II. 543.)

TERTULLIAN, the most ancient of the Latin Fathers, was born at Carthage about the middle of the second century. He does not give any list of the Christian Scriptures; but in various passages of his writings, he mentions or quotes every separate book except Philemon, 2 Peter, 2 and 3 John, and perhaps James. Of the Gospels, he says: "Among the apostles, John and Matthew teach us the faith; among apostolical men, Luke and Mark refresh it." He ascribes the Revelation to John, and says, "the succession of bishops traced up to the beginning will shew it to be his." The Epistle to the Hebrews, he says, is by Barnabas. These are noticeable points of ancient opinion. (See Lardner, II. 256, &c.)

CLEMENT of Alexandria flourished at the end of the second and beginning of the third centuries. He was a teacher of Origen, according to Eusebius. Though many of his works are lost, there are, in what remain of them, quotations from every book except the Epistle to Philemon, the Second of Peter, and the Second and Third of John. He gives one or two noticeable and interesting opinions respecting some of these books. He says the Gospels with the genealogies (Matthew's and Luke's) were first written; and then Mark's, at Rome, on occasion of Peter having preached there attended by Mark, who was intreated by many auditors to write down what Peter had preached. He says the Epistle to the Hebrews was Paul's, and written by him in the Hebrew language for their use, and translated by Luke into its

Greek dress, in which alone we have it. (See Lardner, II. 211.)

Clement brings us very near to the apostolic age. Born in the middle of the second century—say 150—he must have been contemporary, and may perhaps have been acquainted, with some surviving acquaintances of the apostle John, who had died about the year 100. The next and last testimony is that of a disciple of one of John's disciples.

IRENÆUS, bishop or presbyter of Lyons about the middle of the second century, was a disciple of Polycarp, who was a disciple of St. John. He has no list of the Scriptures, but speaks of them casually. He ascribes the four Gospels to the four universally admitted authors, and quotes largely from each. He ascribes the book of Acts to Luke, the companion of St. Paul, and quotes largely from it. He quotes all Paul's Epistles, except the short private letter to Philemon, and ascribes them all to Paul. He says nothing about the Hebrews (which the Latin Church, as before mentioned, rejected). He has quoted all the Catholic Epistles except 3 John and Jude. He has quoted the Revelation, and ascribed it to the apostle John.

And this Irenæus is the disciple of Polycarp, who was the disciple of St. John. We cannot go much higher—at least, not in the same style of testimony—nor need we wish to do. Supposing the Scriptures of the New Testament to have been all written between A.D. 52 and 95 or 96 (the latter date being that generally ascribed to the book of Revelation), they must have been well diffused indeed to be thus known and quoted by the presbyter of Lyons, to whose writings Lardner gives 178 as the proximate date. The editors of classical Latin and Greek authors of the same period would be agreeably surprised to find them quoted with such profuseness up to the same early date. But none of the Greek or Latin classics could ever claim the same ascendancy over the minds and feelings of men as these New-Testament Scriptures; and hence the difference in the amount of testimonies to the one class of writers and to the other.

There are still earlier Christian writers (known as the *Apostolical Fathers*, from their being contemporary, or nearly so, with some of the apostles), who occasionally quote the books of the New Testament, but in a looser style as we rise higher in our dates, till it is more and more doubtful whether they are quoting expressly from a written book before them, or are citing it from imperfect memory, or whether they are only repeating the oral tradition of a sacred event, or the oral record of a sacred saying, which may correspond generally, but not minutely, with the written record. And this is exactly what we ought to expect, if we realize to our minds the nature of the case. The passages in the Apostolical Fathers which are supposed to have reference to certain passages of the New Testament, may be found in Lardner (Vol. II.) ranged side by side with the scriptural passages most like them; and it will be seen that they usually correspond in a certain loose way; just to such an extent, indeed, as would be naturally the case while the Scriptures were rarely to be met with, and some of them perhaps still unwritten. These Apostolical Fathers are Barnabas, Clement of Rome, Hermas, Ignatius and Polycarp.* Their writings demand a brief notice here, as lying close upon the border line of scriptural antiquity, and (some of them, at least) as commanding an interest akin to that which attaches to some of the books

* Cotelerius, a learned French clergyman, published their writings in 1672. Archbishop Wake, of Canterbury, published an English translation in 1693. I quote from the latter, as republished in Hone's Apocryphal New Testament, 1821.

of non-apostolical or doubtful authorship in the volume of the New Testament. These Apostolical Fathers, though highly reverenced by many Christians in all ages, have been rightly refused a place in the canon of Scripture, as their writings do not even pretend to apostolical authorship, nor contribute, like those of Mark and Luke, to the facts of the Gospel history. The authenticity of some of them is very questionable.

The EPISTLE OF BARNABAS is mentioned by Eusebius (in his lists already quoted) as one of the "spurious" books. Clemens Alexandrinus, Origen and Jerom, indeed, quote from it as the genuine work of Barnabas, the companion of Paul. And the moderns in general seem disposed to regard it as his. Archbishop Laud, however, on its first publication, pronounced very strongly against its genuineness; and Dr. Jeremiah Jones is very decided in his opinion that it is the work of a Gentile convert to Christianity, whereas Barnabas was a Jew of the sacred tribe of Levi (Acts iv. 36).

The chief part of the Epistle seems designed to disparage the importance of the Jewish ceremonies. In this respect it may be compared with the Epistles of Paul to the Galatians and Romans, and still more directly with that to the Hebrews. But its inferiority in thought and style to all these is most striking. Barnabas is full of quotations from the Old Testament, including some of the finest anti-ceremonial passages in the prophets; but these are quoted almost without plan or method; while, in point of argument, he is wretchedly feeble, and his allegories (when seeking spiritual meanings for various things in the Old Testament) are far-fetched and fanciful, yet poor in imagination and often low in taste. The Jewish temple had evidently been destroyed when this Epistle was written; and its destruction seems to be alluded to as recent. The passage which suggests this remark, also illustrates the writer's extreme looseness of quotation, if (as it would seem) he had in his memory our Lord's words respecting the *temple of his body:* "Destroy this temple, and in three days I will raise it up" (John ii. 19). Barnabas (if it be really Barnabas) says, "And again he (the Lord) speaketh after this manner: Behold they that destroy this temple, even they shall build it up. And so it came to pass; for *through their wars it is now destroyed by their enemies;* and they shall now, as the servants of their enemies, build it up again" (Barn. Ep. xiii. 14).

From the few things mentioned of Barnabas in the New Testament, we have no means of judging minutely of his mind or character. He was a Levite, and Cyprus was his native country. He sold his land, and brought the proceeds to the apostles (Acts iv. 37). Luke speaks of him as "a good man, and full of the holy spirit and of faith" (xi. 24). He was Paul's companion in his first missions among the Gentiles (xi.—xv.), till they disagreed about taking his nephew Mark as their companion; and Paul speaks of him cordially afterwards in his First Epistle to the Corinthians (ix. 6), as he does of Mark in other Epistles. This is actually all we know of Barnabas. But the puerility of the attempts made by the writer of this Epistle to find spiritual meanings for the simplest things in the Old Testament, as types of Christian doctrines or duties, is quite unworthy of an intellect that could keep company for a single day with Paul. And one of these arguments seems to shew that the writer did not even know Hebrew. From the tradition that Abraham had circumcised 318 men of his house, and the fact that the Greek letters standing for 318 are the first two letters in the name Jesus and a T (which is the same shape in Greek as in English), this writer solemnly argues: "Wherefore by two letters he signified

Jesus, and by the third his cross. He who has put the engrafted gift of his doctrine within us, knows that I never taught to any one a more certain truth; but I trust that ye are worthy of it" (Ep. Barn. viii. 13, 14). The real Barnabas surely would have remembered that Abraham spoke Hebrew, not Greek, and that the Hebrew letters for 318 will not yield the same argument.

Another passage may be quoted, as shewing the utter incompetence of this writer to illustrate the Gospel history. Christ had said to the Pharisees, with well-placed irony, when reviled by them for eating with heathen tax-gatherers ("publicans and sinners"): "I came not to call the righteous, but sinners to repentance." This pseudo-Barnabas tells us: "And when he chose his apostles, which were afterwards to publish his Gospel, *he took men who had been very great sinners;* that thereby he might plainly shew, That he came not to call the righteous, but sinners to repentance" (iv. 12). The writer is far better versed in the Scriptures of the Old Testament than in the facts and sayings of the Gospel history.

These are sufficient specimens of the Epistle of Barnabas, which, in the words of Dr. Jones, "of all the Apostolic Fathers, bids fairest for canonical authority, as pretending to be wrote by one who was expressly set apart and sent forth to the work of an apostle by the order of the Holy Ghost, is called an apostle (Acts xiv. 14), and said to be a good man, full of faith and of the Holy Ghost." The Epistle, it may be observed, does not give itself any name, though a postscript says, "The end of the Epistle of Barnabas the apostle, and fellow-traveller of St. Paul the apostle."

A Gospel under the name of Barnabas was repudiated as apocryphal in Pope Gelasius's list already quoted, and is now lost. But there are portions existing of a later one, in Italian, which appears to have been a Mahometan forgery of a very strange kind, to which the name of Barnabas was attached. (See Jones on the Canon, I. 160—168.)

THE EPISTLES OF CLEMENT. In Paul's letter to the Philippians, written from Rome (ch. iv. 3), he makes affectionate mention of "Clement and other my fellow-labourers, whose names are in the book of life." It is assumed that this is the same Clement who presided over the Christian church at Rome; being the fourth *bishop* of that church according to the Roman Catholics, who reckon Peter as the first, Linus (mentioned 2 Tim. iv. 21) as the second, Anacletus the third, and Clemens or Clement the fourth.

There are two Letters ascribed to him, the first and longer of which has, with general consent, been regarded as genuine; the second is very doubtful, if not decidedly spurious. Irenæus, Eusebius, Clement of Alexandria, Origen and Jerom, vouch for the first as his, but say nothing about a second. Photius, patriarch of Constantinople in the ninth century, considered the first to be spurious. It professes to be addressed by "the church of God which is at Rome, to the church of God which is at Corinth, elect, sanctified by the will of God, through Jesus Christ our Lord;" and to be written in reply to some things which the latter "had inquired." Its subject-matter has reference chiefly to some alleged divisions among the Corinthian church, which, however, are spoken of only under the most vague and general allusions. It mentions St. Paul's letter to them on the same subject, and abounds in expressions taken from that and others of St. Paul's writings, and from the New Testament in general, as well as from the Old, forming a remarkable contrast in this respect to the Epistle of Barnabas. It must have been written by some one well acquainted with St. Paul's writings, and is an evident imitation of them. It was written after the deaths of Peter and Paul (alluded to iii. 12—15), which are believed to have occurred, A.D. 65, under Nero's persecution. But it seems to speak of the Jewish temple as still standing—"The chief-priest has his proper services;" "The daily sacrifices are not offered everywhere, but only at Jerusalem," &c. (xvii. 18, 20);—expressions which some take, however, as meant historically, and date the Epistle about A.D. 96, notwithstanding the destruction of the temple in 70. There is a rich vein of Old-Testament illustration, and a pure moral and devotional feeling, throughout the Epistle of Clement, for which some have been disposed to rank it as inspired; while its claims to this character have, on the other hand, been disputed on the score of its giving currency to the strange story of the Phœnix as a type of the resurrection. The simple Clement propounds the following fable in all good faith (xi. 1—7):

"Let us consider that wonderful type of the resurrection which is seen in the eastern countries; that is to say, in Arabia. There is a certain bird called a Phœnix: of this there is never but one at a time, and that lives 500 years. And when the time of its dissolution draws near, that it must die, it makes itself a nest of frankincense and myrrh and other spices, into which, when its time is fulfilled, it enters and dies. But its flesh putrefying breeds a certain worm, which being nourished with the juice of the dead bird brings forth feathers; and when it is grown to a perfect state, it takes up the nest in which the bones of its parent lie, and carries it from Arabia into Egypt, to a city called Heliopolis; and flying in open day in the sight of all men, lays it upon the altar of the sun, and so returns from whence it came. The priests then search into the records of the time, and find that it returned precisely at the end of 500 years. And shall we then think it to be any very great and strange thing for the Lord of all to raise up those that religiously serve him in the assurance of a good faith, when even by a bird he shews us the greatness of his power to fulfil his promise? For he says in a certain place, Thou shalt raise me up, and I shall confess unto thee, &c."

The Christian feeling of Clement is of a far higher order than his judgment, as the following extract will shew:

"Who is there among you that is generous? Who that is compassionate? Who that has any charity? Let him say, If this sedition, this contention and these schisms be upon my account, I am ready to depart; to go away whithersoever ye please, and do whatsoever ye shall command me: only let the flock of Christ be in peace with the elders that are set over it" (xxi. 14).

There is only one known manuscript of the Epistle of Clement, and it wants some pages. That MS. is remarkable as being appended to the celebrated Alexandrine MS. of the Septuagint and the New Testament, now in the British Museum. Such a collocation shews the estimation in which Clement's Epistle was held by the unknown proprietor or copyist of that ancient MS., the date of which is not later than the sixth century, and perhaps as early as the fourth.

What is called the *Second Epistle of Clement* consists of two fragments; the longer one being much in the style of the First Epistle, and the other being a very absurd, and even irreverent, traditionary saying of the Saviour, expressed in the style of a Delphic oracle or modern enigma, with a ridiculous solution by the supposed Clement.

HERMAS. In Paul's Epistle to the Romans (xvi. 14), he says, "Salute Asyncritus, Phlegon, *Hermas*, Patrobus, Hermes," &c. To this Hermas certain books still extant are ascribed, collectively called the *Shepherd* (because the Angel of Repentance, who appears to him in successive visions, is habited as a shepherd), and subdivided into Four *Visions*, Twelve *Commands* and Ten *Similitudes*.

The *Shepherd* is mentioned slightingly by Eusebius in a passage already quoted (p. 147), and is there called a "spurious" book; but the phraseology of Eusebius is so inexact, that it is not clear whether he means, by *spurious*, to describe it as not written by Hermas, or merely as inadmissible into the list of Scriptures. Elsewhere he says, "Forasmuch as the apostle, in the salutations at the end of his Epistle to the Romans, makes mention among others of Hermas, who it is said wrote the book called the Shepherd, it is to be observed that it is doubted of by some. Wherefore it ought not to be placed among the books of unquestioned authority. By others it is judged to be a most necessary book, especially for those who are to be instructed in the first elements of religion. And we know that it is publicly read in the churches, and that some very ancient writers made use of it." (See Lardner, II. 50.) Hermas is spoken of in a similar way by Jerom.

The book dates itself as belonging to the time of Clement, to whom Hermas is directed (at the end of Vision ii.) to send a copy. Lardner takes A.D. 100 as its proximate date. Only a Latin version now exists, except in the quotations from the Greek made by other ancient writers. Hermas has many evident quotations from all parts of the New Testament, and seems to have imitated the book of Revelation, with the usual bad taste of imitators, as shewn in his wire-drawn *similitudes* and far-fetched explanations. The church is the constant subject of his allegorical visions, being represented as an elderly lady at one time, and at another as a square tower in process of building. The moral tone of the book is mainly excellent, and it has some passages of deep truth and impressiveness. The doctrine of repentance, as taught him by "that Shepherd, the Angel of Repentance," is generous and tender, worthy of the Heavenly Father, and encouraging to his frail human offspring. This is in the Eighth Similitude, of the *willow rods growing green again.* The completion of the church, and a great approaching consummation, not definitely described, but such as was vaguely anticipated by the Christians in general for a century or two after the death of their Lord, is the staple subject of the Similitudes. Martyrdom is especially honoured: "Whosoever have suffered for the name of the Lord, are esteemed honourable by the Lord; and all their offences are blotted out, because they have suffered death for the name of the Son of God" (Simil. ix. 234). Hermas is well worth reading, though rather tiresome towards the end of his Similitudes.

IGNATIUS, bishop or president of the church of Antioch, in Syria, is the next of the Apostolical Fathers. And to him seven Epistles still extant are ascribed, which Lardner dates A.D. 107. He suffered martyrdom at Rome that year. Eusebius says that, as he was marched under guard through Asia Minor on his way to Rome, he confirmed the churches in the cities through which he passed; and that from Smyrna, where Polycarp was bishop, he wrote letters to the churches at Ephesus, Magnesia, Trallium and Rome; and, having reached Troas, that he wrote to the churches at Philadelphia and Smyrna, and also one to Polycarp, the president of the latter. These seven Epistles are generally believed to have been preserved in the compositions now bearing their respective titles. But these compositions exist in two different editions, as it were, the one much more full than the other; and it is supposed that the additional parts are interpolations by later hands. There is great sameness (as might indeed be expected) in these Epistles, each church being exhorted to unity and due subordination to their bishop, and warned against heresies. Among these heresies, the most distinctly named is that of *denying that Jesus Christ had come in the flesh,*—a mystical idea just budding in the New-Testament times, and here full-blown. Says Ignatius, smartly enough, to the Smyrnæans: "If all these things were done only in show by our Lord, then do I also only seem to be bound." And again, more gravely: "He suffered truly, as he also truly raised up himself; and not, as some unbelievers say, that he only seemed to suffer, they themselves only seeming to be. And as they believe, so shall it happen unto them when, being divested of the body, they shall become mere spirits. But I know that even after his resurrection he was in the flesh; and I believe that he is still so."

I believe he is still so! Thus one dogmatic conceit provokes its opposite. The asperity of feeling shewn in the above passage prevails throughout these Epistles. Even the tone in which Ignatius anticipates his martyrdom is hard and defiant, to a degree that seems unnatural, when he begs the Roman Christians not to interfere on his behalf: "I beseech you that you shew not an unseasonable good-will towards me. Suffer me to be food to the wild beasts, by whom I shall attain unto God. For I am the wheat of God; and I shall be ground by the teeth of the wild beasts, that I may be found the pure bread of Christ. Rather encourage the beasts, that they may become my sepulchre, and may leave nothing of my body; that, being dead, I may not be troublesome to any. Then shall I be truly the disciple of Jesus Christ, when the world shall not see so much as my body" (Rom. ii. 2—5). There wants the genuine touch of nature, I think, in these letters. They do not interest one as they ought to do, if really written in the circumstances alleged.

POLYCARP, the last of these Apostolical Fathers, is believed to have written the letter to the Philippians which bears his name, shortly after the death of Ignatius, to whom he alludes as "the blessed Ignatius." There is little doubt, external or internal, about the genuineness of this Epistle. It is genial and interesting to read. It is clearly a letter "that might be real," which one cannot feel in reading those last mentioned. It is full of New-Testament quotations and allusions, all in good taste, while marked by serious earnestness of purpose. Paul and his letter to the Philippian church are most respectfully alluded to, and many expressions from his Epistles are interwoven with the exhortations of Polycarp to the same church. The "Antichrist who does not confess that Jesus Christ is come in the flesh," is firmly denounced, but less fiercely than in the Epistles of Ignatius. This looks more like a genuine letter, free from the interpolations of a later and more controversial age.

Such, then, are the writings of the five "Apostolical Fathers." They are the next in antiquity to the Scriptures of the New Testament, and their non-admission into its canon shews us clearly upon what principles the selection was made. These are not the *writings of apostles;* so far they had no claim to be regarded as Christian Scriptures. Nor are they histories of *Gospel facts* by apostolic men; otherwise Barnabas or Clement might have been admitted, with Mark and Luke, to give his testimony. All the books of the New Testament belong, or have been believed to belong, to one or the other of these classes, and have been accepted more or less confidently as such. All of them, except the histories of Mark and Luke, claim to be, or have been believed to be, the writings of apostles. As regards some, indeed, the authorship has been acknowledged to be less clear than as regards others; and we must therefore look with appropriate discrimination upon the claims of the *disputed* books. This we shall endeavour to do as they come individually under review in the order of the New-Testament Scriptures.

The rejection of all other *apocryphal* books from the New-Testament canon, proceeded upon the perception that they were forgeries so far as they professed to be the works of apostles, and destitute of Christian authority of any kind so far as they called themselves by other names. It is a truly melancholy thing to read the profane legends contained in some of these books, such as the "Gospel of the Birth of Mary," falsely ascribed to Matthew; the "Protevangelion," to James the Less; and those infamous burlesques upon the Saviour's history called the books of his "Infancy," one of which insults the name of Thomas. They are as foolish, in their way, as the weakest fictions of the Jewish Apocrypha. Many of their legends re-appear in the Koran of Mahomet, who professed, indeed, to receive the divine mission both of Moses and of Christ, but whose view of Judaism is as little scriptural as his view of Christianity, the Rabbins of the former and the Fathers of the latter dispensation being confounded by him, in hopeless disorder, with the Scriptures of each. After making all possible allowance for the ignorance and weakness of well-meaning men, converts from Jewish ceremonialism or from Heathen superstition, whose new zeal for Christianity, joined to no small share of self-conceit, may have led them to drive their rash pens in the race of legendary lore,—the perusal of such specimens of early Christian *heathenism* as these books contain (their legends deserve no better name), inclines me to believe that they owe their origin, in many instances, to the artifice of the enemies of Christianity, rather than to the superlative folly of its friends. A clever unbeliever might burlesque the infancy of the Saviour, by ascribing to it miracles of puerile precocity and of boyish mischief and malice; but how any disciple of Christ could think to honour the Gospel or its hero by such wretched fancies, surpasses modern imagination. The result certainly is, what the unbeliever would make his object,—to degrade Christianity.

The canon of the New Testament, then, comes out clearly thus: it contains all books known or widely believed (though not universally believed) to be written by apostles of Christ; together with a Gospel by Mark, and a Gospel and history of the Acts of the Apostles by Luke, both of them companions of apostles, and believed to be competent historians of the origin of Christianity. No other existing books answer either of these descriptions; while, as regards some even of these, the evidence of their belonging to the rank of apostolic writings is less clear than in other cases, and must be taken in each case on its own merits, when we read the respective books.

CHAPTER V.

THE RELATION OF CHRISTIANITY TO JUDAISM, AND OF THE NEW TESTAMENT TO THE OLD.

EVERY Christian feels that there is a close connection between the Scriptures of the New Testament and those of the Old, implying a corresponding relation between the Christian Revelation and the Jewish, of which they are respectively the records.

THE LAW is continually referred to by the first preachers of the Gospel in terms of the highest respect and reverence, even while they vindicate their own freedom and that of their converts from its obligations, as being superseded by the Gospel. The New-Testament Scriptures abound in quotations from the Old, and allusions to its incidents and characters as venerable and sacred. Their facts imply the previous history of the religion of Moses, and their words express an undoubting belief in its divine origin. Thus a belief in the divine origin of Christianity implies the recognition of Judaism as, in a broad and general sense at least, of divine origin also.

But in order intelligently to appreciate the true connection of the Jewish religion and its scriptures with the Christian, it is chiefly of importance, in the first instance, *to keep the two distinct, and look at them apart.* We must first see their respective characteristics, and then judge of their mutual relation. Judaism is not Christianity, nor is Christianity Judaism; and the Scriptures of the two religions are separable, and must be kept separate if their relation to each other is to be faithfully traced. To confound the two, as if they were identical, is not the way to trace their mutual relations. Yet this mistake is often committed. *Scripture,* in the popular way of using it, is made to be all one indivisible book; instead of a multitude of books recording and referring to two different religions, which grew up at an interval of fifteen centuries from each other. Some persons have found, in every individual thing in the Jewish Scriptures, a *type* and prophecy of something in the Christian. Swedenborg imagined a spiritual or mystical sense to belong to the commonest incidents of the patriarchal and Jewish history. The Puritans and Scotch Covenanters applied to themselves, with undoubting faith, all the Old-Testament promises and exhortations to the

Jews as the people of God, and heartily launched against Popery, Prelacy and Monarchy, all the woes of the Hebrew Scriptures against Babylon, Tyre and Edom, the heathen and their idols! The most recent, and perhaps the most extreme, example of this unintelligent confounding of the Jewish and Christian Scriptures, is seen in Mormonism, which again unhesitatingly appropriates all the Jewish promises to its own "Latter-day Saints," and finds its Canaan beyond the Rocky Mountains of North America; while, being unrestrained by the stern morality and high devotional feeling of the old Puritans, it justifies the foul polygamy of its leaders by the patriarchal history and the Mosaic Law, and grossly materializes the Deity by the most stupid literalizing of some of the fine figures of Hebrew poetry.

The first step, therefore, towards seeing the Jewish and Christian Scriptures in their proper connection, is to keep them as distinct from each other as possible, and to notice the respective attributes of the two religions, whether by comparison or by contrast. Their contrasts are indeed very strong in many points of view, while their mutual relation and connection are evident enough, if we will note the progress of Divine Revelation, as from its dawn to its full day.

Judaism was characteristically ceremonial and outward. While the spiritual worship of the One God was plainly its ultimate object, its endless and minute "commandments contained in ordinances" fill the successive pages of its Law. Christianity, on the other hand, is altogether spiritual and inward. It enjoins "no more sacrifice," but "worship in spirit and in truth." Then Judaism, from the very nature of ceremonial worship, and even beyond its inherent necessity, was local;—in one place only might its sacrifices be offered. The Christian worship is unrestricted, requiring neither priest nor temple nor offering, save that of the heart's aspiration to Him who is all-present. Judaism again is, by the palpable facts of nearly eighteen centuries, declared to have been temporary, and to have come to an end. Christianity seems to bear no mark of limited duration, and we believe it to be for all time. Thus distinct and different are the two religions, considered in themselves.

Yet a common basis of revealed truth connects and harmonizes the old dispensation with the new. Their relation is historical, and the developement of divine truth is progressive in their pages.

In connection with the writings of the Jewish prophets, we have traced the growth of a mixed national and religious expectation, which pointed the hearts of the Israelitish people still forward to something unfulfilled. When in captivity in Babylon, they were taught confidently to expect their return to their own land. That return was fulfilled; yet the romantic hopes which had clustered round the vivid descriptions of their prophets, were far from being fulfilled in it. The returning exiles were a feeble band. The nation did not, as with one heart and soul, accept their opportunity. Many lingered and were lost among the heathen nations around. The rebuilding of the temple was a slow and difficult work, and its glory did not equal that of the former house. Happy times returned indeed, but not the glorious times that had been thought of. Judea did not become the pride of the whole world, nor did the Gentiles hasten to learn the Law from Zion. Still the Jewish heart did not droop. Its faith was ever elastic. Its hope looked onward and onward yet, for a better, more complete and permanent fulfilment of the heavenly vision it had caught. And, age after age "disappointed still and still believed," the same Jewish hope is even now patiently anticipating the restoration of Israel from their greatest dispersion to the holy land of their history, and the re-establishment of the Jewish religion, in a purer and more spiritual form perhaps, but still as the model faith and ceremonial of the world. And this same idea of the yet destined restoration of the Jews to their land, is oddly mixed up with the expectation held by many Christians of the millennial reign of Jesus Christ on earth. These very interesting facts in the history of the Jewish mind have fully developed themselves, in the course of our study both of the Jewish prophets and of the later Jewish *Apocrypha*. This kind of expectation is even attested, as we have seen, by the Roman historian, Tacitus, as especially prevailing about the time of the Christian era.

When Jesus of Nazareth began to preach, expectation was on tip-toe in Judea and Galilee, ready to hail him as the inaugurator of the new Judaism. The Messiah was impatiently looked for. Enthusiasm had already welcomed more than one artful claimant of the sacred office, and been sadly disappointed. The functions assigned to this coming personage, in the popular mind, were those of *Prophet* and *King* united. The Jews expected a teacher who should shew the way of God more perfectly; but they also expected a leader who should rescue them from the Roman yoke, "restore the kingdom to Israel," and himself ascend the throne of David his father.

John the Baptist was still preaching and saying: "The kingdom of heaven is at hand. I am the voice of one crying in the desert, Prepare ye the way of the Lord, make his paths straight. I am not the Christ; but there is one standing among you whom ye have not recognized. He it is who, coming after me, is preferred before me; whose shoe's latchet I am not worthy to unloose." John even designated Jesus personally when he baptized him;

and all eyes were fixed upon the latter wherever he taught and wrought his merciful miracles. "The people were astonished at his teaching; for he taught them as one having authority, and not as the scribes," who merely expounded the Law of Moses. When they saw his miracles, "they glorified God, saying, That a great prophet is risen up among us, and that God hath visited his people." Their reasoning comment was: "When Christ cometh, will he shew us more miracles than those which this man hath done?" "Is not this the Christ?" was the great question from mouth to mouth, demanding an answer in the heart and mind of every thoughtfully religious Jew.

Their only grave doubt, as regarded the claims of Jesus of Nazareth to this high office, arose from his intire abstinence from political and military action. One who could have taught as he did, and worked miracles like his, and who would also (if we can conceive the supposition) have raised the standard of national independence, would soon have been at the head of the assembled hosts of Israel. His lowly origin they would not then have scorned, for they believed Jesus to be of the royal house of David, through Joseph his father.* The obscurity of Nazareth they would not then have despised, nor have contemptuously demanded how a prophet could be expected thence, if his prophesyings had touched the keynote of their national prejudices and hopes.

But he raised no standard of revolt. He issued no royal proclamation. And so the national hopes of Israel wavered, and finally (except in a more limited circle of adherents) withdrew themselves from his person and cause. And Jewish vexation and hatred presently procured his destruction at the hands of the Roman gov-

* See Luke iv. 22; John i. 45, vi. 42.

ernor, on the absurd charge of making himself that very king whom they had vainly hoped to find him!

The relation of Christianity to Judaism is seen in a very clear point of view in our Lord's mode of asserting his own claims to the character of the Messiah or Christ. This was such as truth and simplicity required in these most difficult circumstances. He *was* the Christ that *was to come*, but not such a Christ as *was expected*. Jewish expectation did not, in fact, accord with the divine purpose. Though seeming to arise out of Jewish prophecy, it was not destined to be fulfilled even to the letter of the prophets' words. The national hope had not yet been sufficiently purified to understand that the Messiah's kingdom was to be altogether spiritual and inward, not temporal at all. He who came in this popular yet ill-understood character, had therefore a twofold work to do. He had to prove himself the expected Christ, and also to correct the current mistakes respecting the Christ. And how to do this, was the touchstone at once of sincerity and of prudence.

To have said, plainly and publicly on all occasions, "I am the Christ," would have given the most untrue idea of what he really was, because his countrymen would at once have assumed that he was the temporal Christ, the King and Conqueror, whom they looked for. A true word is really false, if used purposely in its true but uncommon sense, without explanation, to those who are sure to take it in the false but popular sense. Jesus, therefore, did not publicly avow himself the Christ till near the end of his ministry. To his disciples, he did indeed so declare himself; but he bade them "tell no man that he was the Christ, till he should be risen from the dead." He most commonly called himself the *Son of Man*, after the manner of the prophet Ezekiel, whose continual use of that beautiful and expressive term we have before noticed.* He constantly appealed to his *works*, in answer to those who inquired about his pretensions. When John the Baptist, being in prison, and possibly thinking himself neglected and forgotten by him whom he had heralded, sent some of his disciples to Jesus to ask, "Art thou he that should come, or look we for another?" the record proceeds: "In that same hour he cured many of their infirmities and plagues, and of evil spirits, and unto many that were blind he gave sight. Then Jesus answering, said unto them, Go your way, and tell John what things ye have seen and heard; how that the blind see and the lame walk, the lepers are cleansed and the deaf hear, the dead are raised, and to the poor the gospel is preached. And blessed is he whosoever shall not be offended in me,"—who shall not be scandalized, shall not stumble, at the contrast between his own expectation and my fulfilment of the office and character of the Messiah (Luke vii. 19—23). When the Jews in Jerusalem, at the feast of the Dedication, came to Jesus and said to him, "How long dost thou make us to doubt? If thou be the Christ, tell us plainly,"—he replied, "I told you, and ye believed not: the works that I do in my Father's name, they bear witness of me" (John x. 24, 25).

In this manner Jesus asserted his Messiahship by his conduct; while, by the same remarkable course of conduct, he set before the minds of his countrymen a purer and more spiritual idea of the Messiah's kingdom than they had attained. His life and actions were intuitively felt to have this bearing. Men "mused in their hearts whether he was the Christ or no;" and if they did not reject his claims for being unlike their own idea, they gradually purified their idea in conformity with what they understood and felt of his character and aims.

* See Vol. I. p. 492.

But the time came when no more reserve on his part was necessary or admissible. Having calmly set forth, in his person and life, the spiritual idea of that Messiahship which he was understood to claim, he avows, towards the close of his ministry, the hitherto ambiguous name of Messiah or Christ. Having fully set forth its true idea, he can truthfully appropriate the word. And he does it in the most decisive and conspicuous way possible,—more plainly than by speech, more widely than by proclamation,—namely, by his triumphal entry (as it is called) into Jerusalem on one of the days of the last Passover. By this act, he avows himself the Messiah, and is understood by every Jew present to express this meaning and no other, while he emblematizes the simple state of the ancient Jewish monarchy, before the horse, forbidden by the Jewish law (Deut. xvii. 16), was known in Jewish usage, and when he accepts the acclamations of the assembled people to the "Son of David who cometh in the name of Jehovah." This was an unequivocal assertion that he claimed to be regarded as the Messiah. And the immediate result of the very act which proclaimed his pretensions thus conspicuously was, to precipitate his death, through the real or affected jealousy of the Roman governor (suggested by the Jewish priests and rulers) towards his alleged claim to be the "King of the Jews." Thus the event itself shews plainly that an earlier avowal of the Messiahship, in the popular ear, could only have led to a fallacious adhesion to his supposed, but not real, claims, and must have precipitated his death before he could have had time to illustrate the real spirit of the Messiah's reign.

Jesus then distinctly claims to have fulfilled the office of the Jewish Messiah, while defining it very differently from the prevalent expectation.

In his character of Messiah, he shews us the connection of the old Judaism with the new Gospel. He fulfils the expectation so far as it is to be fulfilled; he opens new aspects of religious faith and duty that were quite unexpected by the Jewish mind.

Our Lord's personal conduct in reference to Judaism was that of one "born under the Law." He observed its ceremonies. He attended its solemn anniversaries at Jerusalem, apparently with scrupulous regularity. His personal mission was confined to the Jews in Galilee and Judea, and so was that of his apostles during his life, acting under his direction; while various occasions, however, brought him into connection with the hated Samaritan and the despised Gentile, and shewed that his religious ideas and sympathies reached far beyond his countrymen — to the whole world. To the Gentile woman to whom he said, "I am not sent but to the lost sheep of the house of Israel," he gave, with the miracle of mercy, his blessing upon her spirit of religious faith (Matt. xv. 21, &c.). That finest announcement of the spirituality of Christian worship—"God is a Spirit, and they that worship Him must worship Him in spirit and in truth: the Father seeketh such to worship Him"—was made to a Samaritan woman (John iv. 23, 24). And on a Roman centurion he bestowed the memorable blessing—"I have not found so great faith, no, not in Israel" (Matt. viii. 10). In these passages of our Lord's personal ministry, the universality of the Gospel design is manifest, which he also plainly expressed in his discourse recorded in the tenth chapter of John's Gospel, where he speaks of having other sheep "not of this fold," whom he would bring and make "one flock* and one shepherd."

Jesus declared, in his Sermon on the Mount, that he

* *ποίμνη*. The Common Version translates as if αὐλή were repeated, and misses a great beauty in the Saviour's expression (John x. 16).

came, not to destroy the Law or the Prophets, but to *fulfil* them. And how did he fulfil them, except by adding what was deficient as yet, and by giving new prominence to the great principles of essential truth and morality which they contained, so as to throw their local and temporary attributes into the shade, and carry forward the great design, of which they formed the earlier stages, to its full developement?

Jesus Christ, in the very spirit of the old prophets, uniformly disparaged the ceremonial by the side of the moral law. He makes very emphatic the superiority of mercy to sacrifice. Pharisaism, with its self-righteousness and hypocrisy, was the one form of human sin that moved his indignation more than his pity towards the offenders. This Son of Man declares himself "Lord of the Sabbath." The Good Shepherd will bring other sheep into his fold. All this, while the temple is still standing and its service obligatory upon the Jews, is a sufficiently clear preparation for opening the blessings of revealed religion to the Gentiles.

And, besides all this, he most clearly and expressly foretold the coming abolition of the Jewish distinction, the destruction of the city and temple, and the opening of a New Age upon the closing of the Jewish Age, as about to take place before the generation around him should have passed away. In this manner, Judaism was to be *fulfilled* in Christianity; and, being fulfilled, was thenceforth to resign its functions, important and successful as they had been hitherto, in the developement of revealed religion.

The Great Teacher, in his Sermon on the Mount (Matt. v. vi. vii.), passes in review a variety of current maxims and precepts, some belonging to the Jewish Scriptures, others claiming no higher origin than the common thought of mankind; and authoritatively pronounces his judgment upon each, repudiating all that is false in morals, raising what is low in sentiment to a purer atmosphere, deepening what is superficial in motive till it reaches the heart, enlarging what is narrow into worldwide benevolence, and stamping each correction of what "Ye have heard said," by his emphatic "I say unto you."

The Christian Teacher carefully separates the moral from the ceremonial part of Judaism, when he republishes, with the sanction of his express approval, the Ten Commandments of Mount Sinai. He sums these up in two great commandments, in answer to a Jewish scribe who has asked him, "Which is the first commandment of all?"—a precedence variously given by the scribes to the law of Sacrifice, to that of the Sabbath, or to that of Circumcision. "The first of all the commandments is, Hear, O Israel, The Lord our God is one Lord; and thou shalt love the Lord thy God with all thy heart, and with all thy soul, and with all thy mind, and with all thy strength: this is the first commandment. And the second is like, namely this: Thou shalt love thy neighbour as thyself. There is none other commandment greater than these." The scribe understands Judaism well enough to assent to this doctrine, and replies, "Well, Master, thou hast said the truth; for there is one God, and there is none other but He; and to love Him with all the heart, and with all the understanding, and with all the soul, and with all the strength, and to love one's neighbour as oneself, is more than all whole burnt-offerings and sacrifices. And when Jesus saw that he answered discreetly, he said unto him, Thou art not far from the kingdom of God" (Mark xii. 28—34).

Jesus Christ even particularized the six commandments of the second table of the covenant of Sinai, in reply to a young man who asked him, What shall I do that I may inherit eternal life? "Thou knowest the commandments: Do not commit adultery, Do not kill, Do not steal, Do not bear false witness, Defraud not (equivalent to "Covet not"), Honour thy father and mother" (Mark x. 19). The conspicuous place assigned in the Jewish Law to these Ten Commandments, and their subsequent recognition by Christianity, has already been mentioned in connection with their earlier history. (See Vol. I. p. 195, &c.)

Such are the leading traces of the connection of Christianity with Judaism, whether in contrast, comparison or progressive developement, which we see in the life and conduct of Jesus himself. After his death, his apostles were divinely admonished, but with difficulty persuaded (such was the strength of their Jewish prejudice), to preach the Gospel to Gentiles as well as Jews. The vision of Peter, the discussions of the Christian church at Jerusalem, and especially the conversion of Paul and his most vigorous ministry among the Gentiles, are the new features in the progress of the Gospel as detailed in the Acts of the Apostles. Then the Epistles of Paul present to us, in didactic form, the relation of the young Gospel to the old Judaism,—on the one hand as recommending itself to the attention of spiritually-minded Jews, and on the other as asserting its sufficiency for the religious guidance and blessing of the Gentile world. The Epistle to the Hebrews exhibits, in great richness of poetical detail, the process of Jewish thought in accepting Christianity; while those to the Galatians and Romans touch the same subject at various points, in their more immediate purpose of shewing how the new and better covenant of Christianity embraces Jew and Gentile on equal terms of free grace and love, though the first covenant had contemplated the Jews alone.

While Christianity thus recognizes Judaism as its

antecedent, and traces its own origin to the midst of the Jewish history and institutions, thoughts, opinions and feelings, it is very necessary for the Christian student carefully to separate the Gospel as revealed by Christ from certain *Jewish ideas often implied in the record.* The most frequently recurring of these is the Jewish doctrine of demoniacal possession (by which, in our Saviour's time, all disorders affecting the mind and the speech were popularly explained), respecting which notion I have only now to refer to what I have already said on the subject in the preliminary chapter on "the Relation of the Scriptures to Natural Science" (Vol. I. p. 56, &c.). So the Jewish impersonations, Mammon, Beelzebub and Satan, do not necessarily become part of the revealed Christian theology through being found in the record of the origin of Christianity, as the current belief of our Lord's time. If it was no part of his mission to teach or unteach respecting them, they are left to the indirect support or opposition of human science, and of the great principles of the Christian theology as clearly taught by Christ.

There is an idea plainly traceable in the New-Testament writers, and as plainly proved erroneous by the facts of subsequent history, which it is of great importance to keep separate from the revealed principles of Christianity. It is the expectation of a new order of things, outward as well as spiritual,—a physical as well as a moral new creation,—answering the idea of an *end of the world,* rather than the mere *end of the Jewish age* and *the opening of the Christian age.* This idea evidently occupied the minds of the early Christians, and even of the apostles themselves. It appears most plainly (yet not very definitely even there) in the Epistles to the Thessalonians. Perhaps it was the remains of the Jewish Messianic or Millennial expectation. We shall have occasion to speak of it more fully in connection with Christ's prophecy of the destruction of Jerusalem, the coming of the Son of Man, and the end of the age, as recorded in the Gospel histories, where this outward expectation prevailing in the minds of the writers seems to have tinged the records in a way that decisively proves them, at any rate, to be older than the destruction of Jerusalem, when the prophecy was so differently, but so thoroughly, fulfilled. Thus the mistaken idea of the writer may date the antiquity of his record; and the genuineness of the Gospel histories may be seen in the very doubt whether this Gospel prediction has been quite accurately set down.

A very important series of points of contact between Judaism and Christianity are found in the frequent *quotations* from the Scriptures of the former, as being "fulfilled" in the events of the latter. To these we must now give a very careful attention.

We have seen how the Jewish mind, from the days of the Captivity at any rate, was continually looking forward to a brighter, though vaguely defined, future. When Jesus Christ came, those who received his mission as the fulfilment of their Messianic expectations, constantly and very naturally referred to those venerated and poetical Scriptures, the fulfilment of which they had been continually anticipating, as now actually fulfilled in him. And who shall wonder or find fault with them, if they were guided more by feeling and imagination, than by critical exactness and deliberate opinion, in these references? Accordingly, we find it continually said, in the history of our Lord's ministry, "Then was fulfilled that which was spoken by the prophets;" or, "This was done that it might be fulfilled which was spoken." At other times, when an incident is narrated, the narrator introduces a quotation by saying, "As it is written in the prophets," or, "As the Scripture saith," or similar expressions. Often the Scriptures are referred to by the phrase, "According to the Scriptures," where it is difficult to find any passage in the Old Testament distinctly and verbally applicable. The intelligent reader asks, What is the real import of these references from the New Testament to the Old;—whether they are quotations for illustration's sake merely, or whether the passages referred to in the Old Testament can really be regarded as having been written, in every instance, in direct contemplation and prediction of the events to which they are thus applied in the New?

On this question there is room for great difference of opinion. But it is scarcely possible seriously and intelligently to maintain that *all* the passages thus quoted had this original and direct meaning. This will be perfectly obvious from the actual instances which will presently be adduced. The fact is, that many quotations from the Old Testament are applied by the writers of the New in so loose and inexact a manner, that it is impossible to believe either that the New-Testament event recorded was anticipated by the writer of the Old Testament in the words quoted, or that the New-Testament writer believed it to have been intended by those words. Many New-Testament critics therefore regard these quotations from the Old as proceeding simply upon the principle on which we ourselves quote from our own favourite authors, in illustration of the subject in hand, wherever any appropriate and expressive passage occurs to us; and believe that they no more mean by their quotations to say that the old writer had the events of their narrative in view, than we do when we quote Milton, Shakspeare, or one of the old Greek or Roman classics, in illustration of the events we are narrating, or the thought or feeling which we desire to recommend.

Let us hear two high authorities on this very curious and interesting subject. The first is Bishop Chandler:

"Indeed, all the prophecies alleged in the New Testament are not equally clear of Christ, nor were they intended to be equally conclusive. Some are quoted after the *Jewish* manner, in books written for them that already believed, not to convince, but to illustrate and confirm; and among those alleged as proofs, if there be doubt concerning some few of them, *that* doth not affect all the *prophecies* that have been so applied in the New Testament, those especially of which there is no reason to doubt." (Bishop Chandler's *Introduction*, p. xiii.)

The other authority is Dr. Hey, once Professor of Divinity in Cambridge University, who speaks more boldly and in more general terms:

"One thing which has occasioned difficulty is, quotations of prophecies being introduced with '*that it might be fulfilled;*' but this is mere *idiom;* it means no more than *à propos* does in French; or than our saying, 'I dreamt of you last night; now I meet you, the dream is out.'" (Dr. Hey's Lectures in Divinity, Vol. I. p. 259.)

We have already in part anticipated this subject, when noticing some of the most remarkable of those Old-Testament passages, as they occur in their original connection. While pursuing the historical order of investigation (the natural and right order, I should think), I have not disguised my clear and decided conviction (for which I have assigned my reasons as we have proceeded), to the effect that many even of those passages which are most appropriately and strikingly applicable to the mission and times of Jesus Christ, had a much nearer application in view when spoken by the Jewish prophets. I have also endeavoured to develope the very important and interesting fact, that the immediate expectations of the Jews and their prophets were again and again sorely disappointed in the nearer issue, and that the result of such disappointments always was to drive their elastic hope still forward to a more distant future, and progressively to refine their idea of the kind of future to be expected. We have traced this Messianic or Millennial hope through the later prophets of the Old Testament, and in various books of the Greek Apocrypha; and the Gospels next shew us the mixed state of worldly and spiritual expectation with which the Jews of our Saviour's time were more and more eagerly expecting the "Messiah that was to come."

It is indeed very difficult for minds accustomed to the grave literalness of English speech, if not also trained to the confident dogmatism of English theology, to doubt whether it really is meant, when a New-Testament writer says, "Then was fulfilled that which was spoken by the prophet," that the thing had been actually predicted by the prophet with that express and sole application in view. But it is a simple question of idiom, whether such expressions were used with what seems to us so loose a meaning. Those parts of the New Testament in which the quotations occur, must be examined one by one; and it will be found, beyond all rational doubt, that in some instances the prophet appealed to is not a predicter at all, but a teacher, in the larger Jewish sense of *prophet;* and, in some instances at least, it can admit of no doubt that the fulfilment, so called, is brought in merely by way of accommodation, comparison or application. So that this very literal and absolute view of the matter must be quite given up, and the whole question must be approached from a higher point of view, and with a disengaged mind.

I shall now, therefore, bring forward the principal specific instances of alleged fulfilment of the Old Testament in the New; and, by comparing the supposed prediction with the event described, shall supply the materials for my reader to decide for himself, whether these retrospective references from the New Testament to the Old imply strict prediction on the part of the Old, or whether they are (as maintained by the learned men above appealed to) merely quoted as illustrations, accommodations and coincidences.

It is to be observed that, in the original Greek of the New Testament, these quotations for the most part agree with the Septuagint version, thereby shewing that the evangelists and others were accustomed to the use of that version, and did not recall the passages to mind in the original Hebrew. Where the Greek of the Septuagint differs considerably (as in some places it does) from the Hebrew, the New-Testament quotations represent the former, not the latter; and they only differ from the former just as passages quoted from memory might do; for we do not imagine the writer unrolling his MS. of the Greek Old Testament for every quotation he adduces. We are not always more scrupulous in our own practice; but, with a Bible in every room of the house, and a Concordance perhaps also at hand, often quote loosely from memory and apply passages at random.

The quotations from the Old Testament in the New have been very minutely examined by Dr. Palfrey in his *Relation between Judaism and Christianity*, to which book I must refer my reader for a fuller illustration of the subject than there is room for here. But I must here quote his very ample and conclusive instances from other than scriptural writers among the ancients, who, when illustrating their subject-matter by passages from well-known and venerated writers, use expressions exactly equivalent to the New-Testament phrase, "That it might be fulfilled," without ever being suspected of meaning that the older writer had predicted the more recent event. After analyzing the phrase, "That it might be fulfilled," &c., he pursues:

"Let us now pass to the *usus loquendi*, the practice of writers, which is the surest criterion of the meaning of words and combinations of words; and, by a few examples from other sources, enable ourselves to judge what is the received and authorized force of such expressions as that in question.

"Ælian ('Hist. Var.,' Lib. III. cap. 29) says that Diogenes the Cynic used to say, 'that he *fulfilled* (ἐκπληροῖ) and endured in himself all the curses of tragedy, for he was a vagabond,' &c. Olympiodorus, in his Life of Plato, applying to him a line of Homer, says: 'The bees came and filled his mouth with honey-comb, *that it might be true of him*, that 'song sweeter than honey flowed from his tongue.' Cicero, in his Oration for Publius Sextius (§ 57), referring to some lines, which, when recited, had been thought by the audience to be applicable to himself, says: 'Of me the elegant poet wrote.' Again, in his Oration for Cneius Plancius (§ 24), he quotes two lines which he says were addressed to his sons by 'a poet of eminence and talent,' and then proceeds, 'which lines their author *wrote not to stimulate* those royal youth to toil and honor, but to *stimulate* us and our children.' Jerome ('Epist. 103 ad Paulin.') uses this language: '*In us* is that Socratic saying *fulfilled*, 'This little I know, that I know nothing.' ('Opp.,' Tom. IV. Pars II. p. 574, ed. Martianay.) Commenting on the clause, 'and babes shall rule over them' (Is. iii. 4), he applies it to the leaders of the Jews in his own day, and says that in them 'the prophecy is fulfilled.' ('Opp.,' Tom. III. p. 36.) And again, on the words, 'The child shall behave himself proudly against the ancient, and the base against the honorable' (Is. iii. 5), he says ('Opp.,' Tom. III. p. 37) that when this takes place, 'that apostolic saying will be fulfilled, 'They shall bite one another, and be devoured by one another.' (Comp. Gal. v. 15.) Plutarch, quoting a line in which Homer describes Agamemnon, says ('De Fortun. Alexand.,' Tom. VII. p. 310, edit. Reisk.) that 'Homer, in the same verse, set forth the greatness of Agamemnon, and uttered a prophecy of Alexander' (μεμάντευται). Epiphanius ('Opp.,' Tom. I. p. 125, edit. Petav.) says that 'in Ebion is fulfilled what is written, 'I was almost in all evil.' (Comp. Prov. v. 14.) Eusebius ('Hist. Eccles.,' Lib. II. cap. 1), referring to the conversion of the Ethiopian officer by Philip (comp. Acts viii. 27—33), says: 'So that the prophecy obtained its fulfilment in him, 'Ethiopia stretcheth forth her hands to God.' (Comp. Ps. lxviii. 31.) Again (Ibid., cap. 23), in a passage quoted from Hegesippus, relating to the martyrdom of James the Just: 'They fulfilled that which is written in Isaiah (Is. iii. 10), 'Let us take away *the just*, because he is a reproach to us, for they shall eat the fruit of their doings.' In a letter from the churches of Lyons and Vienne to those of Asia, preserved by the same writer (Ibid., Lib. V. cap. 1), after a relation of some persecutions experienced by the former churches, it is said: 'Then was fulfilled the declaration of our Lord, 'The day will come, when every one that slayeth you will think that he doth God service.' (Comp. John xvi. 2.) And again (Ibid.): 'The madness both of the governor and of the people, as of some savage beast, blazed forth so much the more, to show the same wicked hatred to us, *that the Scriptures might be fulfilled*, 'He that is unjust, let him be unjust still; and he that is righteous, let him be righteous still.' (Comp. Apoc. xxii. 11.)" (Relation between Judaism and Christianity, pp. 28—30.)

Dr. Palfrey next adduces similar instances from Syriac and Jewish writers, including the writers of the Apocrypha and the Talmud, who quote the Old Testament in the same simply illustrative way; "though (he adds) what we have been speaking of belongs to a habit, not of the Jewish or the Oriental, but of the human mind; and Ælian, Cicero, Plutarch, Eusebius and Jerom, might serve us sufficiently, without reference to Syriac or Hebrew authorities." (P. 31.)

Dr. Palfrey himself classes the New-Testament quotations from the Old under four heads, as follows:

"1. To the first head belong those passages, which really were supernatural predictions, and really are referred to as such. For instance, when our Lord says that Moses wrote of him (John v. 46), I understand him to refer to the supernaturally conveyed knowledge possessed by Moses of his future advent and character; a knowledge naturally incident to Moses's office as minister of the preparatory dispensation, and expressed by him, for example, in that prophecy appealed to by Peter in an address to his countrymen (Acts iii. 22): 'A prophet shall the Lord your God raise up unto you of your brethren, like unto me; him shall ye hear in all things' (Deut. xviii. 15); as well as in Moses's record of the promise made to the first three Hebrew patriarchs, that in their posterity should 'all the kingdoms of the earth be blessed.' (Gen. xii. 3; xviii. 18; xxii. 18; xxvi. 4.)

"And on this class of references, being to real proof texts,—supernatural predictions fulfilled,—I find occasion for two remarks. The first is, that they present no difficulty whatever in their application. The use of them in the New Testament does not strike the reader as foreign to their original sense. On the contrary, it is the sense which he would naturally put upon them as they stand in their original connection. Secondly, I consider every instance of this class of references to be to the Law, the Pentateuch, the five books of the supernaturally endowed lawgiver Moses; and not to any other part of Old Testament Scripture.

"2. In the second class of these quotations, nothing but a legitimate rhetorical accommodation is designed. They are taken, as from their nature they may well be, indifferently from all parts of the Old Testament collection.

"3. The third class of the texts in question consists of those which are produced as references to, or proof of, the opinions entertained in ancient times concerning the Messiah who was eventually to appear; and, when produced from any other part of the Old Testament except the Pentateuch, they leave it an open question, as far as the mention of the Messiah is concerned, whether the authors of the language quoted possessed any supernatural information concerning him. That a great prophet was to come after himself, could be a fact known to Moses only through a direct divine communication. There was no other source whence he could derive it. They who came after him, however, knew it from his own recorded declaration; and, for a series of ages, every Jew, on Moses's authority, without any new inspiration of his own on the subject, confidently and joyfully recognized the fact. Sometimes this last class of texts, indicative of the opinions of times between Moses and Jesus respecting the coming Messiah, the nature of his office, the extent of his kingdom, and the spirit of his faith, are used by the Apostles in argument with the Jews of their own day. But there is no instance of this kind, where the argument used implies an assertion, on the part of the New Testament writers, of supernatural authority possessed by the authors of the Old Testament language which they quote.

"4. The remaining class of the texts in question, akin to that last mentioned, does not so commonly comprehend particular quotations, but consists rather of references to the general tenor of the Old Testament, showing to the Jews, that, on their own principles of interpretation, without arguing the question whether those principles were correct or not, Old Testament Scripture did not supply them with those objections to the faith of Jesus which they imagined." (Relation, &c., pp. 18—20.)

With these very judicious aids to our inquiry, we proceed to examine the quotations actually made in the New Testament from the Old. If we pursue the subject through the four Gospels, perhaps that will be thought sufficient; and we may safely regard the quotations in the Acts and Epistles as admitting at least equal freedom of interpretation. I shall first take the passages as they occur in the order of St. Matthew's Gospel, with the parallel places in the other three, and then adduce the quotations that are special to each of the others.

1.

Matt. i. 22: "Now *all this was done that it might be fulfilled which was spoken of the Lord by the prophet*, saying, Behold, a virgin shall be with child, and shall bring forth a son, and they shall call his name Emmanuel, which being interpreted is, God with us."

The reference is to Isaiah vii. 14, which goes on thus:

"Milk and honey shall he eat,
When he shall know to refuse the evil and choose the good;
For, before this child shall know to refuse the evil and choose the good,
The land that thou abhorrest shall be forsaken of both her kings."

(See Vol. I. p. 433, &c.) Was this language of Isaiah, then, strictly and literally predictive of the birth of Jesus Christ? What new time of plenty dawned upon Judea, when he began to know how to refuse the evil and choose the good? What opposing country became desolate when he grew into boyhood? And was his name really called Emmanuel? The history tells us he was named Jesus (Saviour). As an application or illustrative quotation, the use made of Isaiah's language is suitable and striking; it may have been vaguely applied by the Jews to their expected prince and deliverer; it is so applied here by the evangelist to Jesus Christ. But as an actual prediction actually fulfilled, the evangelist does not require us to regard it, nor will the connected words of Isaiah allow us to do so.

2.

Matt. ii. 4—6 (see also John vii. 42): "When he (Herod the king) had gathered all the chief priests and scribes of the people together, he demanded of them where Christ should be born. And they said unto him, In Bethlehem of Judea: *for thus it is written by the prophet*, And thou, Bethlehem, in the land of Juda, art not the least among the princes of Juda: for out of thee shall come a Governor, that shall rule my people Israel."

Micah (v. 2) is the prophet quoted. If we read him with the verse preceding and that following, it is plain that Micah was thinking of the Assyrian invasion of his country, and hoping for an earlier and different deliverer:

"Now gather thyself in troops, O daughter of troops:
He hath laid siege against us:
They shall smite the judge of Israel with a rod upon the cheek.
But thou, Bethlehem Ephratah,
Though thou be little among the thousands of Judah,
Yet out of thee shall come forth unto me a ruler in Israel,
Whose goings forth have been from of old, from everlasting.
Therefore will He give them up until the time that she which travaileth hath brought forth:
Then the remnant of their brethren shall return unto the children of Israel."

Referring to Vol. I. (pp. 446-8) for the plain import of Micah's language, we have still a few observations to add here: (1) Micah's words do not seem to imply *birth in* Bethlehem, but *descent* from the family of David which sprang from Bethlehem. (2) The application here made of his words is not by the evangelist, but by the scribes and priests, shewing the current expectation of the Jews to the effect that the Messiah would be born in Bethlehem. (3) The quotation is very loosely made (the comparison of the two passages in English sufficiently represents the variation), and such verbal inexactness, though allowable in quoting for accommodation or illustration's sake, would be inexcusable if literal prediction were believed and literal fulfilment asserted.

3.

Matt. ii. 14, 15: "He (Joseph) took the young child and his mother by night, and departed into Egypt: and was there until the death of Herod: *that it might be fulfilled which was spoken of the Lord by the prophet*, saying, Out of Egypt have I called my son."

Hosea, xi. 1, is the prophet quoted:

"When Israel was a child, then I loved him,
And called my son out of Egypt."

Can any one seriously consider these two passages as prediction and fulfilment? The words of Hosea are not a prediction at all, but a statement of the historical fact, that the Jews had been delivered from Egypt in the days of Moses. To a Jewish evangelist, narrating the flight of the holy family into Egypt and the return thence, it was very natural that the mention of their *coming out of Egypt* should have recalled associations with the long past history of the nation, and the words of Hosea might be very innocently quoted in strict accordance with Jewish scriptural taste. But in this sense alone, of illustrative coincidence, could he mean to say *it was fulfilled.* Even in this sense, indeed, the quotation is somewhat fanciful and far-fetched; and as there are some critical doubts about the absolute genuineness of the first two chapters of Matthew (which will be considered in their proper place), and the journey into Egypt is not mentioned by any other evangelist, these doubts are strengthened rather than diminished by this and a far more flagrant instance (soon after occurring) of inappropriate and whimsical quotation from the Old Testament, such as are thought hardly worthy of St. Matthew's mind.

4.

Matt. ii. 17, 18: "*Then* (in the massacre of the children in Bethlehem by Herod's order) *was fulfilled that which was spoken by Jeremy the prophet*, saying, In Rama was there a voice heard, lamentation, and weeping, and great mourning; Rachel weeping for her children, and would not be comforted, because they are not."

Jeremiah xxxi. 15 corresponds; and the language is irresistibly applicable to the tragedy of Bethlehem, but certainly was not a prediction of it, for these plain reasons: Rama and Bethlehem were not the same place; Rama was in the tribe of Ephraim, Bethlehem in Judah;

Ephraim was descended from Rachel, but Judah was the son of Leah. So it was Leah, and not Rachel, who had cause to weep for her children slaughtered in Bethlehem; as Rachel had done in the time of Jeremiah for the desolation of the kingdom of Israel in war. "All this" (says Dr. Palfrey) "Matthew knew and understood quite as well as we. And it is impossible that he should have intended to say that there was a prediction of Jeremiah, where every intelligent reader sees that there was none; that there was a prediction of weeping in Ramah of Ephraim, which was fulfilled by a weeping in Bethlehem of Judah; and that a prediction of Rachel's sorrow for her children was fulfilled in the death of children not of her blood. We have to trifle very absurdly with words, in the attempt to prove that Matthew trifled with them, if possible, more absurdly still. If we will dismiss such idle and unauthorized refinements, and bring to his Gospel the good sense which we should not refuse to any other book but the Bible, we shall see that the language simply expresses the plain and pertinent meaning:—the sharp and comfortless distress of bereaved mothers at Bethlehem, at this time, might be well described in language used anciently by Jeremiah when he was speaking of the desolation of Ramah and Ephraim." (P. 43.)

5.

Matt. ii. 23: "And he (Joseph) came and dwelt in a city called Nazareth; *that it might be fulfilled which was spoken by the prophets,* He shall be called a Nazarene."

Now it is remarkable that this is nowhere spoken by any of the prophets. There is nothing to be found anywhere in the Old Testament about the Messiah, or any other person, being a citizen of Nazareth. The place is never mentioned in the Jewish Scriptures. Yet we have here the full phrase which English readers so naturally, yet erroneously, consider as pointing to actual prediction and distinct fulfilment—*That it might be fulfilled which was spoken by the prophets.* "Prophets" in the plural number too; thus largely cited, where not one of them has a word on the subject. This passage seems to shew that the habit of referring back to the Old Testament for correspondences with the events of the New, might soon lead to the mechanical use of this phrase, and make those who so constantly used it fancy, or even assume, such correspondences to exist where there are none. It is an idle phrase in this instance truly. The only attempt to find a correspondence in the Old Testament makes matters worse. We are referred to the history of Samson (in Judges xiii. 5), where it is said, "No razor shall come upon his head; for the child shall be a Nazirite* unto God from the womb." If this was the reference in the writer's mind, who claims it as fulfilled by Jesus Christ being the son of a Nazarene family, it shews either a strange confusion of thought in the confusion of two words so like in form, but so different in sense; or else (if deliberately made) it is the perpetration of a mere *pun,* though called the fulfilment of that "which was spoken by the prophets." Dr. Palfrey considers this *conceit* (as he calls it) to have been deliberately adopted by Matthew, and adds: "Could he have anticipated what a race of critics would arise in after times, and what would be the cost of his indulgences, in this way, of a writer's natural taste, it may be presumed that he would have scrupulously abstained from its gratification." Many persons have great difficulty in ascribing either the conceit or the inadvertence to Matthew at all, and (assuming his Gospel to have been originally written in Hebrew) make his Greek trans-

* See Numbers vi. for the "law of the Nazirite" (or, less correctly, *Nazarite*).

lator responsible for this, with the whole of the first two chapters.

6.

Matt. iii. 1—3: "In those days came John the Baptist, preaching in the wilderness of Judea, and saying, Repent ye; for the kingdom of heaven is at hand. *For this is he that was spoken of by the prophet Esaias*, saying, The voice of one crying in the wilderness, Prepare ye the way of the Lord, make his paths straight."

Here John the Baptist seems to apply Isaiah's words to himself, as he also does in the Gospel of John (i. 23). In Mark's Gospel (i. 1—4), the evangelist quotes and applies to him the same words. So does Luke (iii. 2—6), quoting further from Isaiah's animated words:

"Every valley shall be filled, and every mountain and hill shall be brought low; and the crooked shall be made straight, and the rough ways shall be made smooth; and all flesh shall see the salvation of God."

This passage is found in the fortieth chapter of Isaiah, which, whether rightly ascribed to a *second* Isaiah or not (see Vol. I. p. 493, &c.), begins a series of animated promises to the Jews, as captives in Babylon, that they shall be restored to their own land:

"Comfort ye, comfort ye my people, saith your God.
Speak ye comfortably to Jerusalem, and cry unto her,
That her warfare is accomplished, that her iniquity is pardoned;
That she shall receive of the LORD's hand
[Blessings] double to the punishment of all her sins.
The voice of him that crieth in the wilderness," &c.

The original meaning of Isaiah must be quite evident. Whether the Jews of later times had invested the passage with a meaning applicable to their expected Messiah, I know not. But the Baptist and the evangelists very tastefully and appropriately apply it thus.

7.

In the narratives of our Lord's temptation, we have the following citations from the Old Testament:

"He (Jesus) answered and said, *It is written*, Man shall not live by bread alone, but by every word that proceedeth out of the mouth of God."

This is Matt. iv. 4; a little shortened in Luke iv. 4; and quoted from Deut. viii. 3, where it is spoken of the Israelites fed with manna in the wilderness at the word of God.

The tempter then quotes Scripture, saying (Matt. iv. 6),

"If thou be the Son of God, cast thyself down; *for it is written*, He shall give his angels charge concerning thee; and in their hands they shall bear thee up, lest at any time thou dash thy foot against a stone." (Luke iv. 10 corresponds.)

This quotation is from Psalm xci. 11, 12, where the blessedness of him "that dwelleth in the secret place of the Most High" is described.

"*It is written*, Thou shalt not tempt the Lord thy God" (Matt. iv. 7, and Luke iv. 12), is quoted from Deut. vi. 16, where it runs, "YE shall not tempt," &c.

"*It is written*, Thou shalt worship the Lord thy God, and Him only shalt thou serve" (Matt. iv. 10, and Luke iv. 8), is quoted, not with verbal exactness, but in spirit, from Deut. vi. 13, or x. 20:

"Thou shalt fear the LORD thy God, and serve Him, and shalt swear by His name."

"Thou shalt fear the LORD thy God: Him shalt thou serve, and to Him shalt thou cleave, and swear by His name."

All these passages, introduced by the phrase, *It is written*, illustrate the habit of the devout Jew to think in Scripture language, and reason against temptation with Scripture precepts and promises. But no one, I suppose, will maintain that these passages were written in the Law and the Psalms *with a view* to our Lord's use of them, or to the abuse of one of them by another personage.

8.

Matt. iv. 12—16: (Jesus) "leaving Nazareth, came and dwelt in Capernaum, which is upon the sea-coast, in the borders of Zabulon and Nephthalim; *that it might be fulfilled which was spoken by Esaias the prophet*, saying, The land of Zabulon, and the land of Nephthalim, by the way of the sea, beyond Jordan, Galilee of the Gentiles; the people which sat in darkness saw great light; and to them which sat in the region and shadow of death light is sprung up."

This is quoted somewhat loosely (as if by memory only) from Isaiah ix. 1, 2, the meaning of which, in its original connection with the prophecies against the Assyrians and the hopes of the royal house then centering upon prince Hezekiah, may be seen in Vol. I. p. 436. The words were sufficiently appropriate for Matthew to quote in reference to the greater light now rising upon Galilee, though it was not really in Galilee *beyond* Jordan, but on *this side* Jordan, that Jesus dwelt when in Capernaum; for, what would be quite incorrect if seriously quoted as a distinct fulfilment of a distinct prediction, is perfectly true in spirit and meaning when applied as quotations are applied, illustratively and figuratively, by ourselves perpetually. We must learn the meaning of the Jewish expression, *That it might be fulfilled*, by the latitude of these quotations; and not attempt to strain the passages quoted into unnatural meanings because this phrase is used in applying them.

9.

Matt. viii. 16, 17: "When the even was come, they brought unto him (Jesus) many that were possessed with demons: and he cast out the spirits with his word, and healed all that were sick: *that it might be fulfilled which was spoken by Esaias the prophet, saying*, Himself took our infirmities and bare our sicknesses."

The passage referred to is Isaiah liii. 4:

"Surely he hath borne our griefs and carried our sorrows; yet did we esteem him stricken, smitten of God and afflicted," &c.

It is part of the well-known description of the sorrows of the "servant" of Jehovah, and of his expected glory, which goes through chapters lii. to lv. of Isaiah, and the various interpretations of which I have given in its place (Vol. I. pp. 498-9). Matthew here applies his quotation in a manner that must appear to strictly orthodox people merely illustrative and accommodatory, as being quite inconsistent with *their* idea of the meaning of Isaiah. Matthew says: "He took our infirmities and bare our sicknesses," was fulfilled when Christ cured diseases (bare them away, that is). But most Christians would reject Matthew's interpretation, and maintain that it was fulfilled by his suffering the punishment of their sins in their behalf. St. Peter makes what such persons consider a preferable application of the prophet's idea, when he says (1 Pet. ii. 24, 25):

"Who his own self bare our sins in his own body on the tree, that we, being dead to sins, should live unto righteousness: by whose stripes ye were healed. For ye were as sheep going astray, but are now returned unto the Shepherd and Bishop of your souls."

If the latter of these ideas be the original meaning of Isaiah's words, and if they be taken as in that sense a strict prediction of Christ's work and office, the sense ascribed to them by Matthew must be a mistaken one. Yet he introduces his allusion with the usual phrase in its strongest form, *That it might be fulfilled*, &c. Both Matthew and Peter may be correct, however, in using the words as an appropriate and illustrative quotation merely, with varied meanings in view.

10.

Matt. ix. 13 (also xii. 7): "But go ye and learn what that meaneth; I will have mercy, and not sacrifice; for I am not come to call the righteous, but sinners to repentance."

These words, addressed by Christ to the Pharisees who reproached him for eating with Matthew and his fellow "publicans," are quoted from Hosea vi. 6:

"I desired mercy, and not sacrifice,
And the knowledge of God more than burnt-offerings."

There are many similar passages in the Hebrew Psalms, Proverbs and Prophets, which the Pharisees must have strangely overlooked in magnifying the importance of ceremony as they did. But they are not *predictive*.

11.

In Matt. xi. 9—14 (also Luke vii. 27), Jesus, speaking of John the Baptist, says:

"But what went ye out for to see? A prophet? yea, I say unto you, and more than a prophet. *For this is he of whom it is written*, Behold, I send my messenger before thy face, which shall prepare thy way before thee. * * * For all the prophets and the law prophesied (taught—were the recognized sources of instruction) until John. And if ye will receive it, this is Elias which was for to come."

In chap. xvii. 12 (and Mark ix. 12, 13), Jesus again points to John the Baptist under the character of Elias who must first come; and Luke (i. 17) makes the angel predict to Zecharias, that

"He shall go before Him (the Lord God) in the spirit and power of Elias, to turn the hearts of the fathers to the children, and the disobedient to the wisdom of the just; to make ready a people prepared for the Lord."

Malachi iii. 1, and iv. 5, 6, are the Old-Testament Scriptures thus alluded to; and very loosely they are quoted, as will be apparent on comparison, the originals being as follows:

"Behold, I will send my messenger,
And he shall prepare the way before me;
And the Lord whom ye seek shall suddenly come to his temple,
Even the messenger of the covenant whom ye delight in," &c.

"Behold, I will send you Elijah the prophet
Before the coming of the great and dreadful day of the Lord:
And he shall turn the heart of the fathers to the children,
And the heart of the children to their fathers,
Lest I come and smite the earth with a curse."

In the former passage in Malachi, the Messenger of the Covenant seems to be the same person as the Lord who is to come to his temple. In the second, Elijah is mentioned as *preceding* the "day of the Lord." In the Gospel, both the titles *Messenger* and *Elijah* are applied to John the Baptist, though he is not also called *the Lord*, who seems synonymous with *the Messenger* in Malachi. On Jewish principles of quotation, the application is sufficiently illustrative;—on the dogmatic Christian view of prophecy fulfilled, there is endless confusion between the supposed prediction in Malachi and the claimed fulfilment in Matthew. For the original import of Malachi's prophecy, and its progressive meaning in the Jewish mind, I can only refer my reader to the previous volume (pp. 509-10). In the time of Christ, the Jews were expecting the Messiah, and expecting that he would be preceded by some one "in the spirit and power of Elijah," if not by Elijah personally. To the Messiah, or his forerunner, or both, the words of Malachi were irresistibly applicable.

12.

Matt. xii. 17—21. Jesus, knowing the designs of the Pharisees against him, sought privacy, but in vain; and then, continuing his works of healing, charged those who had been benefited "not to make him known:"

"*That it might be fulfilled*" (St. Matthew adds), "*which was spoken by Esaias the prophet*, saying, Behold my servant whom I have chosen; my beloved, in whom my soul is well pleased: I will put my spirit upon him, and he shall shew judgment to the Gentiles. He shall not strive nor cry; neither shall any man hear his voice in the streets. A bruised reed shall he not break, and smoking flax shall he not quench, till he send forth judgment unto victory. And in his name shall the Gentiles trust."

Esaias, here quoted, is he whom we have called the "later Isaiah;" and his theme is quite clear and intelligible in his own pages, through the fortieth and following chapters, which we have lately spoken of as containing the assurance of the return of the captive Jews to their own land. The passage here quoted is Isaiah xliii. 1—4. There are some verbal diversities among the Hebrew, the Septuagint, and Matthew's Gospel. The most instructive of these is the occurrence in the Septuagint of the limiting words, *Jacob* and *Israel* ("Jacob my servant," "Israel mine elect"), which, though not in the Hebrew just here, occur continually before and after in the same prophecy,* and plainly define its original meaning as having reference to the people of Jacob or Israel, and not to Jesus Christ. (See Vol. I. p. 495.) Most appropriately, poetically and tastefully does Matthew quote this passage respecting the meekness of the

* See Is. xl. 27; xli. 8, 9, 14; xlii. 19 and 24; xliii. 1; xliv. 1, &c.

servant of God, in illustration of the deportment of his holy Master. But surely Matthew knew, and would have us know, the difference between original and accommodated descriptions.

13.

Matt. xii. 39, 40 (also xvi. 4, more briefly, and Luke xi. 29—32). In reply to the demand for a sign in the sky, Jesus says:

"There shall no sign be given but the sign of the prophet Jonas. For as Jonas was three days and three nights in the whale's belly, so shall the Son of Man be three days and three nights in the heart of the earth."

Was Jonah's history, then, a type or prediction of the burial and resurrection of Jesus? Our Lord is here predicting his own resurrection, but not quoting Jonah as having foretold it. And he emphasizes the predicted period of *three days* from his own death to his resurrection, by referring to the recorded three days of Jonah's reputed entombment. Without deciding how much of Jonah's story is real and how much fictitious, his name is made to serve as a *memoria technica* to the Jewish mind when Christ's resurrection shall be announced. The sign of Jonah is, *Three days.* The coincidence is remarkable; the suggestion of memory will be completely effectual. When the third day shall be found to have realized the resurrection, three days will be remembered, by the token of "Jonah," as the time predicted.

14.

Matt. xiii. 13—15: "Therefore speak I to them in parables; because they seeing see not; and hearing they hear not; neither do they understand. And in them *is fulfilled the prophecy of Esaias*, which saith, By hearing ye shall hear, and shall not understand; and seeing ye shall see, and shall not perceive;

for this people's heart is waxed gross, and their ears are dull of hearing, and their eyes they have closed; lest at any time they should see with their eyes, and hear with their ears, and should understand with their heart, and should be converted, and I should heal them."

Mark (iv. 12) gives the same quotation more briefly, and Luke (viii. 10) still more so. But they both introduce it rather differently, and in a manner that may seem to require comment. They both represent our Lord as saying, he speaks to the multitude in parables,

"*That, seeing, they may not perceive*, and hearing they may not understand."

This seems, to a literal mind, a very different idea from St. Matthew's, who says, *because they do not see*, &c.

John (xii. 37—41), quoting another passage from Isaiah, puts this by its side in a yet more perplexing way, as if the unbelief reproved as wicked was, after all, no fault of the unbelieving themselves:

"But though he (Jesus) had done so many miracles before them, yet they believed not on him; *That the saying of Esaias the prophet might be fulfilled*, which he spake: Lord, who hath believed our report? and to whom hath the arm of the Lord been revealed? *Therefore they could not believe, because that Esaias said again:* He hath blinded their eyes and hardened their heart; that they should not see with their eyes, nor understand with their heart, and be converted, and I should heal them. These things said Esaias, when he saw his glory and spake of him."

Let us see what Isaiah's own words are, which are so variously quoted and applied. They cannot literally, and as predictions of Christ, bear contradictory meanings. The passage referred to by all the four evangelists is Isaiah vi. 9, 10:

"And he said, Go and tell this people:
Hear ye indeed, but understand not;

And see ye indeed, but perceive not.
Make the heart of this people fat,
And make their ears heavy, and shut their eyes;
Lest they see with their eyes, and hear with their ears,
And understand with their heart, and convert, and be healed."

The passage joined to it by John is Isaiah liii. 1 ("Who hath believed our report?" &c.), and belongs to the series of descriptions of the return from Babylon already alluded to; being quite separate from the other, as found in the book of Isaiah. The one indeed, according to the view we hold, was written by the earlier Isaiah, and the other by the later prophet of the same name. Now what does this *prophecy of Esaias*, quoted by all the evangelists, originally and properly mean?

It is plainly a description of the mental and moral deadness of the Jews of Isaiah's own time, which, it is expressly said (vi. 11, 12), will continue to prevail

"Until the cities be wasted without inhabitant,
And the houses be without man,
And the land be utterly desolate,
And the LORD have removed men far away,
And there be a great forsaking in the midst of the land."

This state of things is announced to Isaiah in vision, at the opening of his prophetic commission, as that to which he is to address himself: it is the state of religious apathy existing in his day, and pointing to the captivity as its end. But this state of things is expressed by him in a remarkable and figurative way. The prophet represents himself as instructed to say to the people, "Hear and understand not." He is told to "*make* their heart gross." Of course we take this to mean, that he was to tell them how unobservant they were, and try to startle their gross minds from such a dangerous insensibility. "*Make* their heart gross" means, *know* how gross it is; *believe* it gross, *suppose* it gross, and *declare* it gross;

for you cannot suppose it, or speak of it as being, more so than is the fact. "Say to them, Hear and understand not." With cutting irony rouse their little thought if possible, by denying that they have any. The meaning is plain enough as it stands in Isaiah. It is a description of his own times; not a prediction of times to come.

But in times long after, it was only too applicable. And Christ and his evangelists variously applied it to the men of their day, and to the stupid insensibility shewn towards the spiritual truths of the Gospel. In Matthew the words vary somewhat from Isaiah; but the variations strip the passage of some of its figurative expressions, and substitute the plain meaning. "By hearing ye will hear and not understand," &c.; "for this people's heart is waxed gross, * * * and their eyes they have closed," &c., is our Lord's exposition, or paraphrase, of the bolder expressions of the prophet, "Make their heart gross;" "Say to them, Hear and understand not."

Then Mark and Luke seem, to the cursory reader, to say, that our Lord "spoke in parables *in order that* they seeing may not perceive," &c. But this is only an abbreviation of the often-recurring phrase, "This was done that it *might* be fulfilled," &c. It does not mean that Jesus so acted to prevent their perceiving; but to fulfil the description of those who do not perceive. And the phrase itself, whether in full or abbreviated, merely describes the *result*, but not the *purpose* of the agent. Perhaps we may say it further bespeaks the habit of mentally referring everything to the inscrutable purposes of Providence. Practically it means, *So this was fulfilled; Thus it came to pass;* while the mind may also venture to glance at the possible designs of the Great Ruler, and say in its secret thought, *Such was the will of Heaven!*

John, who does not relate our Lord's application of this passage of Isaiah, but applies it himself, uses much greater freedom both in quoting and in applying it. He quotes it as if the words were, "HE *hath blinded their eyes and hardened their heart;*" by which we should naturally understand the *Divine Being* to be meant; whereas, in the original words, the *Prophet* is told to do this, and the command is evidently a fine figure of speech, describing the state of things already existing in the closed eyes and ears and hardened hearts. Then John puts two passages from the old prophets together; and, not content with finding an appropriate verbal application of each to the Jewish neglect of the spiritual claims of Jesus, fancifully accounts for the one statement by the other, and materially alters the meaning of the latter in making it serve as an explanation of the former.

These very various forms and applications of this one passage from the Old Testament, as quoted four times by the writers of the New, should teach us to accept their own vague meaning when they speak of the fulfilment of Scripture, instead of attempting, from our narrower idea, to prove a fulfilment such as they never imagined.

15.

Matt. xiii. 34, 35: "All these things spake Jesus unto the multitude in parables, and without a parable spake he not unto them; *that it might be fulfilled which was spoken by the prophet,* saying, I will open my mouth in parables, I will utter things which have been kept secret from the foundation of the world."

Here Matthew finds another fulfilment of the older Scriptures, besides that which Jesus himself had suggested, in his use of the method of instruction by parables, or illustrative comparisons. The prophet here alluded to is one of the psalmists; no prophet at all in the sense of prediction, but a true Jewish prophet in the wide sense of *out-speaker* or teacher. The Psalm in question is not predictive, but historical and didactic intirely. The reference is to Psalm lxxviii. 2, which is very loosely quoted,—from memory probably, and with sufficient exactness for Matthew's idea of an illustrative quotation, which is all he means by saying, *that it might be fulfilled;* but not with that exactness, either of quotation or of application, which he surely would have studied, if he had meant what so many Christian interpreters will have him mean. The Psalm quoted says,

> "I will open my mouth in a parable;
> I will utter dark sayings of old;"

the second line corresponding in sense, but not in words, to Matthew's citation. And the term rendered *parable* in the Psalm, means many things besides such parables as our Lord's allegories. It is the title of the book of Proverbs, and means any weighty saying, or any figurative saying. (See Vol. I. p. 371.) Here, then, the *fulfilment of a prophet's words* is, the appropriate application of a psalmist's.

16.

Matt. xv. 7—9: "Ye hypocrites! *well did Esaias prophesy of you*, saying, This people draweth nigh unto me with their mouth and honoureth me with their lips, but their heart is far from me. But in vain do they worship me, teaching for doctrines the commandments of men."

Mark (vii. 6, 7) has a parallel passage.

Isaiah xxix. 13, is the passage referred to. It is descriptive of the men of the prophet's own time (the men who have eyes to see, but perceive not; and ears to hear, but understand not); it is applicable to others besides, and is applied by Jesus to the men of his day. *Well did Esaias prophesy of you*, is simply equivalent to saying, *The prophecy of Esaias well describes you.*

17.

Matt. xxi. 4, 5 (Christ's triumphal entry into Jerusalem):

"All this was done, that it might be fulfilled which was spoken by the prophet, saying, Tell ye the daughter of Sion, Behold, thy King cometh unto thee, meek and sitting upon an ass, and a colt the foal of an ass."

Mark (xi.) and Luke (xix.) narrate the incident, but without adducing the prophecy as fulfilled. John quotes the prophecy more briefly thus (xii. 14, 15):

"And Jesus, when he had found a young ass, sat thereon, as it is written, Fear not, daughter of Zion; behold, thy King cometh sitting on an ass's colt."

The passage referred to is Zechariah ix. 9:

"Rejoice greatly, O daughter of Zion;
Shout, O daughter of Jerusalem;
Behold, thy King cometh unto thee:
He is just and having salvation [bringing deliverance],
Lowly and riding upon an ass,
And upon a colt, the foal of an ass."

See Vol. I. p. 451, for the connection and original meaning of Zechariah's words. They were taken by the Jews as pointing to a coming temporal Messiah. Jesus, when he had shewn in his life and ministry the purely spiritual nature of that office, openly claimed to be the Messiah by thus enacting the scene described by the prophet. And his countrymen understood his meaning. So he *fulfilled* what was spoken by the prophet; though Zechariah may have anticipated an earlier king, whose reign would be a temporal sovereignty, peaceful and happy for Israel.

18.

Matt. xxi. 13 (also Mark xi. 17, and Luke xix. 46). On "cleansing" the temple, Jesus said: "*It is written*, My house shall be called the house of prayer; but ye have made it a den of thieves." (Compare Is. lvi. 7 and Jerem. vii. 11.)

Matt. xxi. 16. When the children cried, Hosanna to the Son of David, "Jesus saith unto them, Yea, have *ye never read*, Out of the mouth of babes and sucklings thou hast perfected praise" (compare Ps. viii. 2).

To his parable of the faithless husbandman dispossessed of the vineyard, he adds:

Matt. xxi. 42 (also Mark xii. 10, 11, and Luke xx. 17): "*Did ye never read in the Scriptures*, The stone which the builders rejected, the same is become the head of the corner; this is the Lord's doing, and it is marvellous in our eyes" (compare Ps. cxviii. 22, 23).

These, like many similar instances, are appropriate quotations, illustrative and striking, but not generally thought to be predictive of Gospel incidents, because not introduced by the assertion, *then was fulfilled.* Yet there seems no superior appropriateness or directness of applicability in some of the passages already examined where that phrase occurs. That phrase must, in short, be taken as equivalent to these: "It is written," "Did ye never read in the Scriptures;" and we shall thus find the true principle on which the Old Testament is perpetually quoted in the New.

19.

Matt. xxii. 41—45 (also Mark xii. 35—37, and Luke xx. 41—44): "While the Pharisees were gathered together, Jesus asked them, saying, What think ye of (the) Christ? whose son is he? They say unto him, The Son of David. He saith unto them, How then doth David in spirit call him Lord, saying, The Lord said unto my Lord, Sit thou on my right hand, till I make thine enemies thy footstool? If David then call him Lord, how is he his son?"

The Psalm thus quoted by our Saviour is the cx., which, if any one could read it without knowing that it was thus referred to in the New Testament, would be naturally regarded as written in celebration of a victorious Jewish king, "the rod of whose strength should be sent forth from Zion," and who should "rule in the midst of his enemies;" "at whose right hand Jehovah would strike through kings in the day of his wrath," "ruling among the heathen, and filling the places with dead bodies." All these expressions in the Psalm are plainly indicative of its original design, and little suitable indeed to a direct description of Jesus Christ. The Psalm is intitled, "a Psalm of David," which may equally mean, "a Psalm for David," or "on David;" and it may suitably be regarded as written on occasion of his victories over his enemies and his firm establishment on the throne. The Jews further regarded it as applicable to their expected Messiah, who was also, in their idea, to be a warrior prince; and perhaps even as predictive of him. Then they spoke of the Psalm as written *by* David, mentally contemplating ("in spirit") a future and greater king. And on their own principles of interpretation our Saviour here argues with them.

His argument is often thought to have been designed simply to puzzle and confound his Pharisee persecutors. I believe it was designed, indeed, to confound them, but by the very reverse process to that of puzzling them, namely, by convicting, if not convincing. No Jew could be really at a loss to say how the expected Messiah king was to be both David's Lord and David's Son. Any one of them could, *if he had chosen*, have answered: "He is to be his Son, by descent from the royal house; he is to be his Lord, by reason of the wider and more glorious empire which he will set up." "Great David's greater Son" (whether temporal or spiritual greatness were intended), expresses the whole idea. But the Pharisees did not choose to give this reply, lest it should seem applicable to the claims of Jesus himself. They *could not* answer him, because they *would not*. Their answer would have recoiled upon themselves; as just before

(Matt. xxi. 25), when Jesus asked them whether John the Baptist's mission was "from heaven or from men," and they were too politic to say either the one or the other, but replied, "We cannot tell." "Neither do I tell you," retorted Jesus, "by what authority I do these things." But the parallel which he had suggested would have made the same answer obviously applicable to the claims of John and to his own; and just so, the candid Jewish answer to this question about David's Son and David's Lord, would have too evidently included him in its terms as, possibly at least, the Christ. So they "could not tell."

20.

Matt. xxiv. 15 (also Mark xiii. 14): "When ye therefore shall see the abomination of desolation, spoken of by Daniel the prophet, stand in the holy place."

Daniel xii. 11 is here alluded to, and is as follows:

"And from the time that the daily sacrifice shall be taken away, and the abomination that maketh desolate set up, there shall be a thousand two hundred and ninety days."

The desolating abomination was a heathen army. Daniel's words had plain reference to the Syrians under Antiochus Epiphanes; our Lord's prediction speaks in the same terms of the Romans. He uses Daniel's appropriate and descriptive expression, but does not mean that his words were a prediction of the Roman conquest of Judea, *which he now himself foretels.*

21.

Matt. xxvi. 24: "The Son of Man goeth *as it is written of him:* but woe unto that man by whom the Son of Man is betrayed!"

Mark xiv. 21: "The Son of Man indeed goeth, *as it is written of him:* but woe," &c.

Luke xxii. 22: "And truly the Son of Man goeth, *as it was determined:* but woe unto that man by whom he is betrayed!"

(Mark, ix. 12, on another occasion says, Jesus told his disciples, Peter, James and John, "How *it is written* of the Son of Man, that he must suffer many things, and be set at nought.")

It is not easy to find any passage in the Old Testament which declares in plain terms that the Messiah should be put to death. Certainly the Jews had no idea of anything of the kind. Even our Lord's disciples revolted from his first suggestion of it. "Be it far from thee, Lord," said Peter impetuously; "this shall not be unto thee!" (Matt. xvi. 22).

It is observable that Luke, in recording our Lord's words as above, makes him say, not *as it is written*, but *as it was determined;* and some interpreters take the phrase *as it is written* to be simply equivalent to this. They refer us to such passages as that in Psalm cxxxix. 16: "*In thy book* all my members *were written*, when as yet there was none of them." But it may be doubted whether Matthew meant thus simply to say "as decreed by Providence," or "as written in the book of the Divine purposes." He continually refers to the incidents of Christ's life as written *in the Scriptures*, or *in the Prophets:* and he quotes the Scriptures more frequently, and perhaps more loosely, than the other evangelists. May not the phrase, as used here, bespeak merely this habit of the Jewish mind, through which the writer inadvertently assumes that a particular incident must have been foreshadowed in scriptural language, though he does not quote any such language, and we cannot even find any? Luke, at least, makes Jesus say "determined," not "written."

22.

Matt. xxvi. 31 (also Mark xiv. 27): "Then saith Jesus unto them (the disciples), All ye will be offended because of me (will fall away from me) this night: for it is written, I will smite the shepherd, and the sheep of the flock shall be scattered abroad."

It is not certain whether the quotation is to be taken as a continuation of our Lord's own words, or as the evangelists' addition in recording what Jesus had said. Probably the latter; for John, who was present, does not give the quotation (xvi. 32). The passage "is written" in Zechariah xiii. 7, 8:

"Awake, O sword, against my shepherd,
And against the man that is my fellow,
Saith the Lord of hosts.
Smite the Shepherd, and the sheep shall be scattered;
And I will turn mine hand upon the little ones.
And it shall come to pass that in all the land (saith the Lord)
Two parts therein shall be cut off and die;
But the third shall be left therein."

This is certainly a picture of warlike invasion. The connected lines, not quoted in the Gospels, shew this. Probably the passage refers to the Assyrian invasion of the kingdom of Israel, and its subversion by Shalmanezer. (See Vol. I. pp. 413 and 452.) It is only as illustrative, by the figure so aptly employed, and not as predictive of Christ's death and the temporary dispersion of his disciples, that Jesus, or his evangelist, applies it to the occasion which so naturally suggested the beautiful and tasteful image—"*It is written*, I will smite the shepherd," &c. Like many other quotations, it is not scrupulously exact. But it is exact enough for illustration, though not for prediction dogmatically declared to be fulfilled.

23.

Matt. xxvi. 53, 54: "Thinkest thou that I cannot now pray to my Father, and He shall presently give me more than twelve legions of angels? But how then shall the Scriptures be fulfilled, that thus it must be?" (See Mark xiv. 49, more vaguely.)

The remarks under No. 21 are applicable here. Matthew alone preserves these specific words of Jesus. I cannot resist the feeling that the allusion to the fulfilment of scripture is Matthew's in recording them, not Christ's in speaking them.

24.

Matt. xxvi. 56, after relating the apprehension of Jesus by the officers of the chief priests:

"But all this was done, that the Scriptures of the prophets might be fulfilled."

This allusion again is not specific; and we can only say, in general terms, that the prophecies regarded by the Jews as predictive of the Messiah, had not led them to expect a suffering and persecuted prophet like Jesus: but the apostles of Jesus, when they gained a truer idea of the Messiah from the facts of his life and death, no doubt recurred to the Old-Testament Scriptures with a truer feeling, and thenceforth rejected from their interpretation all that was inconsistent with the now realized mission, if they did not also see some *written* intimations of the Messiah's sufferings and death, where, like other Jews, they had overlooked them before. That the old Scriptures were, in the largest and truest sense, amply fulfilled, must have been the abiding thought of those who saw Judaism expiring after having given birth to Christianity. And this is a sufficient vindication of any vague and general allusions like that now before us.

25.

Matt. xxvii. 9, 10 (in the account of Judas's remorse and suicide):

"Then was fulfilled that which was spoken by Jeremy the prophet, saying, And they took the thirty pieces of silver, the price of him that was valued, whom they of the children of Israel did value, and gave them for the potter's field, as the Lord appointed me."

There is no such passage in Jeremiah; but in Zechariah (xi. 13) we find, no doubt, the place intended, under a very excusable mistake of the name. It is very loosely quoted, in point of words, as a comparison of the two will shew; while, in point of meaning, it must be plain to any unprejudiced reader, that there is the very slightest possible link of connection between them. "Thirty pieces of silver" occur in both transactions; and this, with the mention of a "potter," seems the extent of the resemblance. The passage in Zechariah (xi. 10—14) carries its own interpretation too plainly to be misunderstood. (See Vol. I. p. 451.) The prophet is directed (ver. 4) to "feed the flock of the slaughter, whose possessors slay them, and hold themselves not guilty." He takes his two crooks, *Beauty* (or *Favour)* and *Bands*, the one denoting the Divine mercy, the other the brotherly union that should prevail between the kingdoms of Judah and Israel. Presently he cuts asunder the crook *Favour*, to symbolize the breaking of the covenant between God and the people of Israel. Then he demands his wages for his services as shepherd; and being insulted by the offer of thirty pieces of silver, he "casts them to the potter in the house of the Lord," and then cuts asunder his other crook, *Bands*, to "break the brotherhood between Judah and Israel" (to signify that it was broken.).

"And I said unto them, If ye think good, give me my price; and if not, forbear. So they weighed for my price thirty pieces of silver." (This appears, from Ex. xxi. 32, to have been the legalized value of a slave; and the insult was felt by the prophet.) "And the Lord said unto me, Cast it unto the potter.

A goodly price that I was prized at of them! And I took the thirty pieces of silver, and cast them to the potter in the house of the Lord" (12, 13).

This *potter* in the house of the Lord is a great perplexity to the interpreters, and in all probability the original Hebrew was "the treasury," a word not much unlike (אוצר instead of יוצר). The Septuagint has "the furnace," *χωνευτήριον*; and Matthew has "the potter," *κεραμεὺς*, and tells us that the priests bought the *potter's field* to bury strangers in, as the fulfilment of these words. Let this quotation be tried by the rules of quotation, and it may be justified; but any one who insists upon the relation of prediction to fulfilment between the words of Zechariah and the incident in the Gospel history, and who ascribes miraculous inspiration to Matthew's very free and loose quotation of Zechariah's words as Jeremiah's, is labouring hard (whether knowingly or ignorantly) to bring contempt upon the Scriptures and upon Religion.

26.

Matt. xxvii. 35: "And they crucified him, and parted his garments, casting lots; that it might be fulfilled which was spoken by the prophet, They parted my garments among them, and upon my vesture did they cast lots."

John (xix. 23, 24) gives it more minutely:

"Then the soldiers, when they had crucified Jesus, took his garments, and made four parts, to every soldier a part; and also his coat: now the coat was without seam, woven from the top throughout. They said therefore among themselves, Let us not rend it, but cast lots for it, whose it shall be: that the scripture might be fulfilled, which saith, They parted my raiment among them, and for my vesture they did cast lots."

In Griesbach's Greek Testament, it will be seen that the passage beginning with the words, *that it might be fulfilled*, is not really a part of Matthew's Gospel. Mark and Luke, each of whom mentions the parting of the garments and casting lots, make no allusion to this passage in the Old Testament. Nor does Matthew, in his true text. John does, as above shewn. We must therefore suppose that the quotation occurred (as it very naturally might) to some reader or transcriber of Matthew, who may have marked it at first only in the margin of his manuscript, and that a later transcriber inserted it. Whence it is found in the text in some copies, but not in the most ancient. The quotation is from Psalm xxii. 18, and verbally agrees with the Septuagint. The wonder is, to find that it was not really quoted by Matthew. Whoever added it to his narrative, did so, apparently, in the very same spirit of illustrative quotation which prevails throughout the genuine portions of his Gospel. The Psalm was written, there is no reason to doubt, by David, and in reference to some period of distress and difficulty in his own life. Bishop Young says, "However some of the circumstances in this Psalm do most surprisingly indeed accord with the incidents of Christ's life and death, yet there are others which seem unequivocally to shew that they cannot be considered as prophecies of him." (*New Translation of the Psalms*, quoted by Wellbeloved *in loco.)*

27.

Matt. xxvii. 46: "And about the ninth hour Jesus cried with a loud voice, saying, Eli, Eli, lama sabachthani? that is to say, My God, my God, why hast thou forsaken me?" (Also Mark xv. 34.)

These are the opening words of the Psalm last mentioned. How naturally did they occur to the feelings of the Saviour in agony! And, though he said no more aloud than these few words, we naturally suppose him to have gone on mentally reciting other parts of that beautifully appropriate meditation. It is not a cry of anguish throughout, but expresses strong confidence in the mysterious Providence which seems, to mortal apprehension, to have forsaken the sufferer. Surely the dying Saviour dwelt with comfort upon such reflections as these, which follow in the course of the Psalm:

"He hath not despised nor abhorred
The affliction of the afflicted;
Neither hath He hid his face from him.
But when he cried unto Him, He heard.
* * * *
They shall praise the Lord that seek Him.
Your heart shall live for ever.
All the ends of the world shall remember,
And turn unto the Lord;
And all the kindred of the nations shall worship before Thee."

We have thus gone through the Old-Testament quotations in Matthew's Gospel which claim to have been *fulfilled* in the Gospel history, putting side by side with them the parallel quotations in the other Gospels, and comparing them with the original passages in the Old Testament. We have now to mention such as are found in one or more of the other Evangelists, but not in Matthew. Mark has only one such, and he has it in common with Luke.

28.

Mark xv. 28: "And the Scripture was fulfilled which saith, And he was numbered with the transgressors."

Luke xxii. 37: "For I say unto you, that this that is written must yet be accomplished in me, And he was reckoned among the transgressors; for the things concerning me have an end."

The words are in Isaiah liii. 12, occurring in that beautiful and affecting description of the "servant of God" as a "man of sorrows," from which there are other quotations in Matthew already cited. (See Nos. 9 and 12.)

The Gospel of Luke supplies a few additional quotations from the Old Testament not already adduced.

29.

Luke i. 54, 55: "He hath holpen his servant Israel, in remembrance of his mercy; as He spake to our fathers, to Abraham, and to his seed for ever."

These words, in Mary's beautiful song of gratitude, beginning, "My soul doth magnify the Lord," refer to the divine promise made to Abraham, that "in his seed all the nations of the earth should be blessed" (Gen. xviii. 18), and anticipate the approaching fulfilment of that promise. The whole song is further illustrative of our present inquiry into the spirit of scriptural quotation, as it is largely made up of expressions from many parts of the Old Testament, put together simply as appropriate in sentiment, and not as believed to be predictive of the events to which she applies them. The references in the margin of the Bible will enable any one to trace such portions of Mary's song to their original places in the Old Testament.

30.

Luke i. 67—79, is a highly illustrative passage:

"And his father Zacharias was filled with the holy spirit, and prophesied, saying,

Blessed be the Lord God of Israel;
For He hath visited and redeemed His people;
And hath raised up a horn of salvation for us
In the house of His servant David;
(As He spake by the mouth of His holy prophets,
Which have been since the world began;)
That we should be saved from our enemies,
And from the hand of all that hate us;

To perform the mercy promised to our fathers,
And to remember His holy covenant;
The oath which He sware to our father Abraham,
That He would grant unto us,
That we, being delivered out of the hand of our enemies,
Might serve Him without fear,
In holiness and righteousness before Him
All the days of our life.
And thou, child, shalt be called the Prophet of the Highest;
For thou shalt go before the face of the Lord to prepare His ways,
To give knowledge of salvation unto His people
By the remission of their sins,
Through the tender mercy of our God;
Whereby the day-spring from on high hath visited us,
To give light to them that sit in darkness and in the shadow of death,
To guide our feet into the way of peace."

There is little or nothing in the above spirited passage that can be said to be directly quoted from any of the "holy prophets" of the Old Testament, except the apostrophe to his child as "Prophet of the Highest, to go before the face of the Lord;" but it is quite in the spirit of many of them when anticipating the vaguely imagined future of the Jewish nation and their religion. Zacharias's words express the ideal Judaism of the expected Messiah's reign, as mixed up of temporal and of spiritual blessings. The "horn of salvation" bespeaks the hope of a temporal deliverance, such as is afterwards repeated in the expectation of being "saved from our enemies" and "delivered out of their hand;" while the concluding verses shew the more spiritual side of the Jewish expectation as it prevailed in the time of Jesus Christ. The prophets are appealed to rather than quoted.

Then this poetical effusion of Zacharias's, we shall do well to notice, is called *prophesying*. Yet it is not a prediction, but a declaration that things formerly predicted are now come to pass. To prophesy, was to utter fervent religious thoughts, whether didactically, or in exhortation, or in devotional acts, or in prediction. And the Holy Spirit, ascribed on such occasions to the prophet, was not understood to be always miraculous. This has been fully explained in connection with the Schools of the Prophets (Vol. I. p. 276, &c.). Zacharias, filled with holy feeling, prophetized in the language above quoted, faithfully catching and communicating the spirit of many parts of the Jewish Scriptures, while scarcely in any case pointedly quoting a single passage. And he vividly illustrates the feeling of the Jews in the time of Christ, while trying to recognize the fulfilment of their national expectation in the events transacting before their eyes.

31.

Luke iv. 16—21: Jesus "came to Nazareth * * * and went into the synagogue on the sabbath-day, and stood up for to read. And there was delivered unto him the book of the prophet Esaias; and when he had opened the book, he found the place where it was written, The Spirit of the Lord is upon me, because he hath anointed me to preach the Gospel to the poor: he hath sent me to heal the broken-hearted, to preach deliverance to the captives, and recovering of sight to the blind, to set at liberty them that are bruised, to preach the acceptable year of the Lord. And he closed the book, and he gave it again to the minister (attendant), and sat down. And the eyes of all them that were in the synagogue were fastened on him. And he began to say unto them, This day is this scripture fulfilled in your ears."

Fulfilled indeed! Yes, truly; verified beyond the truth even of the great events respecting which it was originally spoken. They are the words of the younger Isaiah (lxi. 1—3), the herald of the return from Babylon, who says of himself and in his own person, "The spirit of the Lord God is upon me * * to preach good tidings unto the meek," &c.; and who goes on to say, "They shall build the old wastes, and raise up the former desolations, and they shall repair the waste cities, the desolations of many generations." Here is a worthier fulfilment now, but not the accomplishment of a prediction. "The scripture of Isaiah was that day fulfilled" (says Dr. Sykes, in his Essay on the Truth of the Christian Religion), "no otherwise than as Jesus did preach the acceptable year of the Lord in one sense, as Isaiah had done before him in another sense. Not that our Saviour meant any double completion of prophecies; but he applied or accommodated the words of Isaiah to the present occasion; and they were equally true in both instances, in that which the prophet used them, and in that which Jesus used them; and consequently the term *fulfilled* does not signify a designed event accomplished, or that the Messiah was in the intention of Providence to preach upon these words in the synagogue at Nazareth, but only this, that the words of Isaiah are this day *verified*." (Essay, pp. 263, 265, quoted in Palfrey's Relation, &c., p. 149.)

32.

Luke xviii. 31—34: "Behold, we go up to Jerusalem, and all things that are written by the prophets concerning the Son of Man shall be accomplished (or, will be accomplished, fulfilled or completed, *in* the Son of Man). For he will be delivered unto the Gentiles, and will be mocked, and spitefully entreated, and spitted on: and they will scourge him, and put him to death; and the third day he shall rise again. And they understood none of these things; and this saying was hid from them, neither knew they the things that were spoken."

In Nos. 21 and 24, I mentioned how rare the passages are in the Old Testament which suggest, or even admit, the idea of a suffering Messiah. No such idea had possessed the Jewish mind, at any rate, in the time of Jesus. He infused it with difficulty into the minds even of his disciples, with the strong evidence of the facts of his life to aid the conviction. On the occasion now before us, "the disciples *understood none of these things.*" If they did not understand his assertion of his impending sufferings, death and resurrection, they certainly did not understand that such events were indicated in the Scriptures. Indeed, Isaiah liii. is the chief passage that seems, even in retrospect, to bear strongly upon this view of the Messiah's history. So that we must take the reference to the Old-Testament Scriptures in connection with the disclosure of the approaching sufferings of the Messiah, as importing rather that their fulfilment was shewn to be consistent with his suffering state, than that their testimony clearly proved it. Here Jesus tells his disciples, in fact, that insult, suffering and death awaited him, and that glory would follow; and thus all the great pointings of the Scriptures would be realized, though very differently from the manner in which they had been accustomed to read those Scriptures hitherto. Contrary to the general expectation, and even the obvious letter on which it is founded, the great design and real spirit of the Law and the Prophets will be realized in the Gospel of a crucified Messiah.

33.

Luke xxi. 22: "These be the days of vengeance (punishment), that all things which are written may be fulfilled."

Our Lord is here predicting the destruction of Jerusalem. His own prophecy contains the things to be fulfilled. But in what sense can they be called *the things which are written*, at the moment when he spoke them?

Either the expression was not his in speaking, but Luke's afterwards in writing them, or it is a phrase denoting the Divine purposes,—the things written in the Divine will.

34.

Luke xxiv. 25—27: "Then said he unto them (to Cleopas and the other disciple on the way to Emmaus on the resurrection-day), O fools, and slow of heart to believe (slow in believing) all that the prophets have spoken! Ought not Christ to have suffered these things, and to enter into his glory? And beginning at Moses and all the prophets, he expounded unto them in all the Scriptures the things concerning himself."

Luke xxiv. 44—47: "And he said unto them (the apostles), These are the words which I spake unto you, while I was yet with you, that all things must be fulfilled which were written in the Law of Moses, and in the Prophets, and in the Psalms, concerning me. Then opened he their understanding, that they might understand the Scriptures, and said unto them, Thus it is written, and thus it behoved Christ to suffer, and to rise from the dead the third day; and that repentance and remission of sins should be preached in his name among all nations, beginning at Jerusalem."

This very comprehensive reference, by our risen Lord himself, at the end of the third Gospel, to the testimony of Moses and the Prophets concerning himself, seems a suitable occasion for a general summary of the subject on the part of the present writer.

How deeply, yet how fruitlessly, has every studious reader regretted, that the evangelist, who tells us of these conversations of Jesus after his resurrection, has not also preserved the substance at least, if not all the details, of the exposition which he gave of Moses and the Prophets as referring to him! Vain is the regret. We can only imagine what it is probable that he may have said, by what we know him to have really said and done on other occasions throughout his mission. We cannot reproduce the lost conversation itself; but we may perhaps realize pretty justly its general purport and substance.

We cannot doubt that he had both a *negative* and a *positive* exposition to make. While he expounded what Moses and the Prophets had really said that had proper reference to him and his Gospel, he surely must have also deprecated and put his *veto* upon many ideas which they were generally supposed, by the Jews of his day, to have taught;—ideas believed by Cleopas and his companion among the rest, who "trusted that it had been he which should have redeemed Israel," and (as shewn in this very expression) trusted that he would have been a warrior prince, and would have delivered them from their subjection to the Romans, and made Israel again an independent and powerful kingdom. The very topic on which he found them talking shews how deeply they were still possessed with the idea of a temporal Messiah (derived, as they believed, from the prophets, if not from Moses), how they had watched his life and ministry with these hopes (not altogether unmingled, let us trust, with higher and purer ones), and finding these hopes extinguished by his crucifixion, were perplexed and sad when he met them. His first words to them are carefully preserved by the evangelist—"O foolish and slow of heart at believing all that the prophets have spoken!" You think you are believing the prophets, in looking for one who shall make Israel again a people of renown. You take the Messiah to be a sceptred warrior. And you will "look for another," as this who is come does not suit your idea! Foolish and slow of heart! You have not apprehended the real spirit of the Law and the Prophets, which prophesied until John and are to give place now to the more spiritual kingdom of heaven.

You must unlearn that idea of a temporal Messiah and an outward reign. If you read it in the prophets, you must regard it as their patriotic desire and hope, but not as a divine promise through them. You must read again the various intimations of the times to come, with unprepossessed and spiritual vision. You must carry forth the idea of a progressive religion, dawning in Eden and glowing amid the dwellings of the patriarchs, matured (while somewhat hardened) into system by the Lawgiver, and refined and spiritualized in the instructions of your poets, sages and prophets; you must abate something from this national and exclusive notion, and see Judaism as the germ of a world-wide faith; you must refine somewhat this outward and temporal idea, and think of a kingdom of heaven *within*, the kingdom of religion in the heart; and then say if it was not fitting that Christ should suffer these things and enter into his glory.

Our Lord's own deportment throughout his mission is a sufficient clue to what we naturally think must have been his exposition on this *negative* side of the question. He would not call himself the Messiah in public; but having lived the true Messiahship in its spiritual beauty and glory, he at last publicly avowed himself by that name, and was crucified for the avowal. Now risen from the dead, he, no doubt, expounds Moses and the Prophets as not precluding, but rather favouring, on the true and large view of their scope and purpose, this spiritual Messiahship. No doubt he deprecates the tendency of the Jewish mind to dwell upon the vulgar idea of outward royalty in connection with the reign of religion. He deprecates the Jewish thirst for war and conquest, and describes the purer royalty of one who should sway the hearts of men of all nations and kindred and tongues. He gives prominence to every more spiritual thought in their national hope; and wherever prophets announce a Prince of Peace and anticipate an age of peace, he points to these as the real attributes of the Messiah's reign, and makes peace itself a word of diviner blessing to the inward soul than even the prophets had meant it to convey.

Then, again (still judging by his conduct throughout his mission), we naturally suppose that the risen Jesus, in expounding Moses and the Prophets, may have pointedly shewn that many things generally regarded by his countrymen as spoken concerning him, had really no allusion to him at all, at least not as direct predictions of his work and office. We have seen how free and loose was the Jewish habit of scriptural quotation. When his disciples would quote Elias as an example for calling down fire from heaven, we know how he rebuked them (Luke ix. 54, &c.) for that application of Scripture. To the Sadducees, in reproval of their gross and sceptical interpretation of the Law of Moses, he said, "Ye do greatly err, not knowing the Scriptures nor the power of God" (Matt. xxii. 29, &c.). And to Pilate, when charged with treason against Cæsar by those who knew he claimed to be the Messiah, he said, "My kingdom is not of this world." All applications of scriptural language, however prevalent in Jewish use, and however exalting to the kingly power and magnificence of him to whom they were popularly applied, he must, we think, have at least passed by, if not more actively disclaimed, in expounding in all the Jewish Scriptures the things concerning himself.

But I think it probable that he would dwell more on the *general spirit* of Moses and the Prophets, than upon any particular passages and words. Certainly their general bearing upon the Gospel Age to come is much more easily traceable than their verbal references to it.

If Jesus on this occasion shewed, in broad, bold lines of light, the relation of the opening to the closing dispensation,—the fitness of the Jewish religion to prepare men's minds for still better things, and its unfitness to be regarded as itself the good that could satisfy the religious wants of the human race in all ages;—if he only repeated from his Sermon on the Mount some of his illustrations of the mode of enlarging the Jewish morality into the Christian, and, from his conversation with the woman of Samaria, his enlargement of the idea of worship from that which the Jew localized in Jerusalem and the Samaritan on the holy Mount Gerizim, into the simply grand Christian idea that "God is a Spirit, and they that worship Him must worship Him in spirit and in truth;"—if he did this and no more, the disciples on the way to Emmaus might feel that they thenceforth really understood Moses and the Prophets in their relation to the Christ now manifested, and might be satisfied that it behoved Christ even to suffer as he had done, and to enter thus upon his glorious reign! Of textual quotations, they might never see the end; but the great relation of the Law to the Gospel, of Moses and the Prophets to Christ, is not to be obscured by textual difficulties, nor does it depend for its developement upon textual niceties. The true spirit of progressive Judaism developes itself into active sympathy with the spirit of the opening Gospel.

From this broad and elevated point of view, let us now briefly glance at the contents of those Old-Testament Scriptures in which Moses and the Prophets have, virtually throughout, and verbally and expressly in some places, spoken the things concerning Christ.

He "began at Moses." The testimony of Moses to Christ and Christianity is twofold: (1) as historian of the patriarchal dispensations of religion before his own time, and (2) as himself the Lawgiver to the Jewish people. Looking back from the Christian point of view, we see in those simple records of the primitive race of men, and of the communications which they were permitted to hold (through some undescribed agency or other) with the Divine Being, a manifest intimation, from the very first, of the care of the Almighty Father for the spiritual happiness of His children. The religious ideas, that God is One, that God is good, that God loveth righteousness and hateth iniquity, were the blessed gift of His earliest revelations to those with whom He walked in Eden, to those whom He saved from the flood, and to Abraham, Isaac and Jacob, among whose tents He dwelt. This primitive religion of the ancestors of the Jewish race, contrasting, as it painfully does, with the earliest records of religion everywhere else in the world, plainly bespeaks the Divine intervention in the past, and therein tells of the Christ that was to come. Whether particular passages interspersed throughout its venerable records have a more direct verbal reference to him or not, where their language is, to say the least, strikingly applicable;—whether, in the enmity between the serpent and the seed of the woman, there be special reference to Christ, or to all that is good in all human beings, and perfectly good in Christ, their spiritual head;—whether Noah's preservation was rightly understood by the Jews to testify simply the approval of God towards the righteous in his own age, or was also designed at the time (as Christians have since commonly understood it) to point to the future salvation by Christ;—and whether Abraham took the promise, that "in his seed all the nations of the earth should be blessed," as merely giving the temporal hope which the Jews chiefly cherished in point of fact, or whether he took it in anticipation, as we may in retrospect interpret it, to portend the spiritual blessings of Christ's Gospel for all the nations of the world;—at any rate, the divine *facts* are here in the books of Moses, those facts through which Almighty God was preparing the germ of pure religion for its future developement through many stages, till it should blossom into the Christian morality and the Christian hope. "Beginning at Moses," the risen Lord doubtless expounded these great features of the patriarchal religion as "things concerning himself."

Then Moses, as Lawgiver, has his own personal testimony also to give. He carries revealed religion a great step forward. Recording the patriarchal revelations, he himself further reveals the LAW. What does it tell of Christ?

In its whole character and provisions, the Law is evidently temporal, local, and therein prospective. Local and limited it must have been always felt to be, through the very nature of its ceremonies and its single place of sacrificial worship. Their outside, carnal character must have made every spiritual-minded Jew look for an inward meaning, if not for a future fulfilment and abolition, of the ceremonies themselves. Jesus Christ, reviewing the completed ages, declares them fulfilled in his Gospel, and sees in them the preparation, and virtually the prediction, of the coming Age. These ceremonies were the "shadows of the true tabernacle." "The Law was the schoolmaster to bring men to Christ." If we did not find one word recorded, by which the Lawgiver could be proved to have looked forward to far future days, his work itself is plainly predictive. It is the prophecy, or rather the promise, of the good God, that He will still watch over the spiritual instruction and developement of the human race.

But Moses spoke, in express words and in a most emphatic way, a prediction, which, if it does not point to

Jesus solely or peculiarly, includes him and is completed in him. He solemnly said to the people of Israel:

"The LORD thy God will raise up unto thee a Prophet from the midst of thee, of thy brethren, like unto me; unto him ye shall hearken; according to all that thou desiredst of the LORD thy God in Horeb in the day of the assembly, saying, Let me not hear again the voice of the LORD my God, neither let me see this great fire any more, that I die not. And the LORD said unto me, They have well spoken that which they have spoken. I will raise them up a Prophet from among their brethren, like unto thee, and will put my words in his mouth; and he shall speak unto them all that I shall command him. And it shall come to pass, that whosoever will not hearken unto my words which he shall speak in my name, I will require it of him. But the prophet, which shall presume to speak a word in my name, which I have not commanded him to speak, or that shall speak in the name of other gods, even that prophet shall die. And if thou say in thine heart, How shall we know the word which the LORD hath not spoken? When a prophet speaketh in the name of the LORD, if the thing follow not, nor come to pass, that is the thing which the LORD hath not spoken, but the prophet hath spoken it presumptuously: thou shalt not be afraid of him" (Deut. xviii. 15—22).

The simplest and most obvious meaning to ascribe to these words is, that a succession of prophets (or teachers, in the large Jewish sense of the word) should arise—men like Moses—to mediate the Divine commands towards their fellow-men. (See Vol. I. p. 276.) Such a succession of prophets was given; and the series was crowned by Jesus and his apostles. In two of the earliest recorded apostolical discourses, one by Peter and the other by Stephen (Acts iii. 22, 23, and vii. 37), these words of Moses are most appropriately and powerfully quoted as fulfilled in Jesus Christ. There is no difficulty in expounding to the very letter, in the Scriptures of Moses, these things as "concerning Christ."

"And all the prophets," the risen Teacher also appealed to. Not minutely, textually and verbally, one would think, was it possible for him, that afternoon, to run through the multitude of books thus designated. Nor, as already hinted, should we in that manner gain the clearest, broadest and truest idea of the foreshadowing of the Gospel in the Jewish Scriptures. The plainest and strongest testimony of these prophets to the Christ as destined to come, is found in the general character of their writings;—so unsacerdotal, so anti-ceremonial, so purely moral, are the representations they constantly give of religion;—so well do they fulfil the service of purifying and refining Judaism, till it becomes in their hands almost a practical anticipation of Christianity. The Jewish prophets (as we have continually observed in analyzing their writings) always make prominent the *moral* and *devotional* side of Judaism. If there was a danger of sacrifice and ceremony being preferred to virtue and holiness of heart,—if the ceremonial priesthood were liable to degenerate into formalists and pharisees,—the succession of Jewish prophets was the healthy antidote to this tendency. They are the preachers of pure morals. They make light of the ceremonies, which were still obligatory under the Law. They turn men's minds altogether to the practice of virtue and spiritual piety. In this they are really the prophets of the Christ to come. They are preparing the way, whether consciously or unconsciously, for his Gospel.

Meanwhile, these prophets (as we have already seen) are all full of a vague idea of a bright future about to dawn. It is indeed a Jewish future, a national hope, and yet including the Gentiles also as the destined recipients of spiritual blessings from Judea. Very vague, but most genial and most true to the aspiring and trustful dictates of the religious nature, is this Jewish hope, which expresses itself in the words of many of these prophets, and which never found itself satisfied till, in the days of Jesus of Nazareth, it consented at last to part with its temporal and outside dress, and recognize in him the spiritual Saviour for whom it inly yearned. The Apostle Peter speaks of these older prophets as having "inquired and searched diligently, what, or what manner of time, the spirit of Christ which was in them did signify, when it testified beforehand the sufferings of Christ and the glory that should follow;" and adds, that it was revealed to them "that, not unto themselves, but unto us, they did minister these things,"—"things which the angels desire to look into" (1 Pet. i. 10—12). So the writer of the Epistle to the Hebrews, after enumerating the men of faith in olden times, says, "These all, having obtained a good report through faith, received not the promises, God having provided some better thing for us, that they should not, without us, be made perfect" (Heb. xi. 39, 40). In this way all the prophets, in their vaguest longings for the dimly-seen future, and under a sense of the incompleteness of the dispensation in which they stood, put upon record thoughts and aspirations which, in spirit at least, and in the great interpretation of events, were claimed by Christ as among "the things concerning himself."

And among these "prophets" are also included, according to Jewish usage, the psalmists, and generally all the devotional and moral writers of the Jewish Scriptures. The Psalms, the Proverbs, the Ecclesiastes, the book of Job, all develope (like the Prophets more strictly so called) the moral and devotional side of Judaism, and in so doing they are truly anticipators of Christianity and pioneers of its way. While the Jewish ceremonies filled the books of Moses, and occupied not only the temple services but many home incidents in the life of the pious

Jew, tempting the Pharisaic spirit to ostentation and arrogance,—these books of Jewish morals and devotion, and of earnest, reverent speculation upon God's high providence and man's faculties, duties and hopes, were the nutriment of the inner religious life to this nation who worshiped the One spiritual God. And those who had most deeply imbibed the moral and devotional spirit of these Jewish Scriptures, were the least "slow of heart" to perceive how they pointed to "something better" as in reserve, and to welcome that something better when given in Jesus Christ.

In this way at least, with however much or however little besides of mere verbal reference, the Scriptures of Moses and the Prophets point to Christ and are fulfilled (completed, verified, accomplished, made one grand whole) in him.

We have now examined all the alleged predictions from the Old Testament that are quoted in the first three Gospels. There are a few additional ones in John's Gospel still to be considered. They will require very brief comment. They are generally very free, and sometimes loose, quotations; and their application is usually such as at once declares itself simply illustrative, and not strictly predictive. These will complete this long chapter, and will fairly establish the rule of interpretation applicable to the Old-Testament quotations in the remaining books of the New.

35.

John i. 51: "Hereafter ye shall see heaven opened, and the angels of God ascending and descending upon the Son of Man,"

seems a pretty plain allusion to Jacob's vision (Gen. xxviii. 12), in which that patriarch saw the angels of God ascending and descending on the ladder, or flight of steps, from earth to heaven. Jesus Christ does not, indeed, quote this as a prophecy of his own spiritual intercourse with the Divine Being, but uses it as an illustration, appropriate and tasteful. It would have had the same force exactly if the evangelist had added, "Then shall the Scripture be fulfilled."

36.

John ii. 17 (on the cleansing of the temple): "His disciples remembered that it was written, The zeal of thine house eateth me up."

The quotation is from Ps. lxix. 9, a Psalm ascribed to David; and if written originally by David, probably adapted afterwards to the Babylonian or Syrian times of persecution:

"For the zeal of thine house hath eaten me up;
And the reproaches of them that reproached thee are fallen upon me."

The disciples remember it as a record of the past; they apply it as suitable to the present.

37.

John iii. 14, 15: "As Moses lifted up the serpent in the wilderness, even so must the Son of Man be lifted up; that whosoever believeth in him should not perish, but have eternal life."

(See Numbers xxi. 6—9.) It is a comparison, tasteful and forcible, to the Jewish mind especially;—it is an application, a fulfilment, without regarding the former event as a type or prediction of the latter. It is like "the sign of the prophet Jonah" (in No. 13); a verbal coincidence suggesting the reference.

38.

John v. 39, 40: "Search the Scriptures (Jesus said to the

Jews), for in them ye think ye have eternal life; and *they are they which testify of me.*"

This general reference opens, but without settling, the whole subject, as fully discussed in No. 34.

39.

John v. 46, 47: "Had ye believed Moses, ye would have believed me; for *he wrote of me.*"

No doubt the celebrated passage, "A prophet shall the Lord raise up, like me," &c., already considered in No. 34.

40.

John vi. 14, 15: "Then those men, when they had seen the miracle that Jesus did, said, This is of a truth that *Prophet that should come* into the world. When Jesus therefore perceived that they would come and take him by force, to *make him a king*, he departed again to a mountain himself alone."

Here is the Jewish expectation of a prophet, and of that prophet as a king.

41.

John vi. 45: "It is written in the prophets, And they shall be all taught of God. Every man, therefore, that hath heard and hath learned of the Father, cometh unto me."

The allusion is to one or both of the following passages, in which the Jewish future is earnestly anticipated as an age of purer religion:

Is. liv. 13:
"And all thy children shall be taught of Jehovah;
And great shall be the peace of thy children."

Jerem. xxxi. 33, 34:
"After those days, saith Jehovah,
I will put my law in their inward parts,
And write it in their hearts;
And I will be their God, and they shall be my people.

And they shall teach no more every man his neighbour,
And every man his brother, saying, Know Jehovah:
For they shall all know me,
From the least of them unto the greatest of them, saith Jehovah."

42.

John vii. 37—39: "Jesus stood and cried, saying, If any man thirst, let him come unto me and drink. He that believeth on me, as the Scripture hath said, out of his belly shall flow rivers of living water. (But this he spake of the Spirit, which they that believe on him should receive," &c.)

These very words are nowhere to be found in the Scripture. The passages most like are the following:

Prov. xviii. 4:
"The words of a man's mouth are as deep waters,
And the well-spring of wisdom as a flowing brook."

Is. xii. 3:
"Therefore with joy shall ye draw water out of the wells of salvation."

Is. xliv. 3:
"For I will pour water upon him that is thirsty,
And floods upon the dry ground:
I will pour my spirit upon thy seed,
And my blessing upon thine offspring."

Is. lviii. 11:
"Thou shalt be like a watered garden,
And like a spring of water whose waters fail not."

Evidently the general figure, and not the precise words, is designed to be reproduced. Probably the customary phrase, "As the Scripture hath said," is introduced by the evangelist, and does not belong to our Lord's own words.

43.

John viii. 56: "Your father Abraham rejoiced to see my day: and he saw it, and was glad."

The promise to Abraham, in Gen. xii. 3 and xxii. 18, is, that "in his seed all the nations of the earth should be blessed;"—a blessing conferred upon us through the history of the Jewish nation as the seed of Abraham, completed in Jesus Christ in "the end of the ages."

44.

John xi. 49—52, is a curious passage, where the evangelist, recording the advice of Caiaphas to put Jesus to death (because "it was expedient that one man should die for the people, and that the whole nation perish not"), says that the high-priest "*did not speak this of himself, but prophesied* that Jesus should die for that nation, and not for that nation only, but that he should gather together in one the children of God that were scattered abroad."

Certainly the language of Caiaphas himself bears no such meaning, nor can we ascribe any such thought to the mind of the high-priest. But John, in retrospect, gives his words a meaning derived from the progress of events. He says, in effect, that the words received a higher fulfilment than they had designed. They admitted a meaning which the speaker little thought of. They were a prophecy of a death fraught with more than Jewish and temporal deliverance.

I allude to this (which is no quotation from the Old Testament) as explanatory of the system of verbal illustration and parallel, so familiar to the New-Testament writers. If John finds the fulfilment of the high-priest's hostile words in a spiritual and Christian sense, it was far more obvious to appropriate the expressions of the Hebrew prophets, psalmists and sages, whenever applicable.

45.

John xii. 34: "The people answered him, We have heard

out of the Law that Christ abideth for ever: and how sayest thou, The Son of Man must be lifted up?"

The Jews had a notion that their Messiah should be immortal on earth. They said they had "heard it out of the Law." But we search Law, Prophets and Psalms, in vain for any such statement. The wish was father to the thought. Prejudice likes to quote high authority, and believes that its own opinions are in Scripture, though it cannot quote chapter and verse for them.

Such passages as the following,—Ps. lxxxix. 36, 37, cx. 4, Is. ix. 7, Ezek. xxxvii. 25, Dan. ii. 44, Micah iv. 7,—are referred to in the margin of the Bible as probably alluded to in this popular impression. They do not say that the king shall never die, but that the *kingdom shall be everlasting*. Truly, an important distinction!

46.

John xiii. 18: "I speak not of you all: I know whom I have chosen: but (that the Scripture may be fulfilled), He that eateth bread with me hath lifted up his heel against me."

The quotation is from Ps. xli. 9, written by David in sickness, when, to add to his bodily affliction, he had the desertion of one or more friends to complain of. Ahithophel is commonly understood to be pointed at in the words:

"Yea, mine own familiar friend in whom I trusted,
Which did eat of my bread, hath lifted up his heel against me."

The quotation is apt and touching, yet not perfectly appropriate. Judas was not Christ's familiar friend, nor did he eat of his bread in the sense of the original. Our Lord therefore adapts the expression by omitting the one phrase and changing the other into "eateth bread *with me*." The words, "that the Scriptures," &c., may be John's, not Christ's.

47.

John xv. 25: "This cometh to pass, that the word might be fulfilled that is written in their Law, They hated me without a cause."

The *word* was fulfilled; but it was a mere word, not a prediction. The words are not even in the Law proper, but in various Psalms. The psalmist speaks of some who hate him without cause, and fight against him without cause (Ps. xxxv. 19, lxix. 4, cix. 3). Such words were indeed verified in him who was "holy, harmless and undefiled, and separate from sinners."

48.

John xvii. 12: "Those that thou gavest me, I have kept (and none of them is lost but the son of perdition); that the Scripture might be fulfilled."

There is nothing to be found respecting the "son of perdition," nor indeed is there any prediction of Judas whatever in the Old Testament. The recurrent phrase, "That the Scripture might be fulfilled," seems to have dropped in here, as it were, mechanically from the evangelist's pen. It is wisely suggested, indeed (see Palfrey, p. 182), "that the fulfilment of Scripture here brought to view refers, not to the loss of the son of perdition, but to the *keeping* of the other disciples." This is very likely; but still the fulfilment is not verbal; for there is nothing to be found in the Old Scriptures applicable in words to those whom he had "kept." The fulfilment of Scripture is in the wide sense of the establishment of the Gospel. This was taking place through the faithfulness of those respecting whom Jesus says, "While I was in the world, I kept them in thy name, and none of them is lost (but the son of perdition); that the Scripture might be fulfilled."

It will be observed that the evangelist, presently after,

notes with equal care the fulfilment of his Master's words just now spoken. In xviii. 8, 9, when Judas and the officers come to apprehend him, he says, "If ye seek me, let these go their way;" and John immediately adds, "That the saying might be fulfilled which he spake, Of them which thou gavest me have I lost none." Not the highest and worthiest fulfilment of his Lord's words; but we see how strong is the desire of noting coincidences, parallels or other fulfilments.

49.

John xix. 28: "After this, Jesus, knowing that all things were now accomplished, that the Scripture might be fulfilled, saith, I thirst."

Theologians have spent idle time, to no purpose, in searching for any Scripture that says this. Probably the phrase about fulfilment should be taken with what goes before, not with what follows. And then we have the better and higher sense brought out: knowing that all things were accomplished in fulfilment of the Scriptures, Jesus had, at length, and not till then, a thought to spend upon his own sensations of agony, and said, I thirst. Beautiful and true this meaning! But the continually-recurrent phrase is so purely parenthetical, that it might easily be spared, or might seem to have been somewhat carelessly and mechanically thrown in, perhaps by a transcriber.

50.

John xix. 36: "These things were done, that the Scripture should be fulfilled, A bone of him shall not be broken."

The Scripture spoken of (Exod. xii. 11 and 46), describing the ceremony of the passover, directs that it be eaten in haste, with sandals on feet and staff in hand, as by men preparing for flight, and that not a bone of the paschal lamb shall be broken (which men would do when they had time leisurely to taste the marrow). The alleged *fulfilment* is, the omission of the soldiers at the cross to break the legs of Jesus, who was dead already! It seems, at first sight, one of the most far-fetched and inappropriate of applications. The intelligence of the reader revolts; his good taste is offended. Such a comparison could scarcely have occurred to the evangelist at the awful hour of the crucifixion. But he wrote his Gospel long years afterwards, when the cross of Christ was looked at with less of anguish and more of exultation, and when the comparison had grown familiar (which we see in 1 Cor. v. 7) of Jesus Christ to the Jewish passover, as the great deliverance from the bondage of the Law. So, with this expressive figure in his mind, the evangelist finds a detailed resemblance, where a better taste would still avoid the details. At all events, this *fulfilling of Scripture* shews very decisively how wide and lax the use of that phrase was.

51.

The next verse is an equally lax accommodation of ancient Scripture to passing incident:

John xix. 37: "And again, another Scripture saith, They shall look on him whom they pierced."

In Zech. xii. 10, the Almighty, representing himself (in the words of the prophet) as grieved and wounded by the ingratitude of his people, says,

"And I will pour upon the house of David,
And upon the inhabitants of Jerusalem,
The spirit of grace and of supplications;
And they shall look upon (to) me whom they have pierced,"
&c.

This is no prediction of the Gospel event, nor is the

application very suitable; but the passage associated itself in the evangelist's mind with the event he was describing.

52.

John xx. 9: "As yet they knew not the Scripture, that he must rise again from the dead."

The disciples at the sepulchre are the persons spoken of. It is impossible (as already observed) to find any Scripture of the Old Testament which clearly foretels the rising of Christ from the dead. No such expectation had been formed by the most religious Jews from their study of the Scriptures. But those Scriptures must, at least, be so interpreted as not to preclude such a consummation. They must be so read as to permit the great and true fulfilment. And this is the meaning of the verse before us. They did not so understand the Scriptures as to admit the thought of a resurrection. They soon learnt to read them as not precluding it; and God was his own interpreter for all besides, in the new religious history now opening to the world.

PART I.

THE FOUR GOSPELS;

OR, CHRISTIANITY AS TAUGHT BY JESUS CHRIST HIMSELF.

THE simplest and most obvious division of the books of the New Testament is into two parts:

I. The four Gospels, or histories of the life of Jesus Christ, presenting the earliest scriptural aspect of Christianity, as taught by the Founder himself; and

II. The Acts of the Apostles and the apostolical Letters to various churches and individuals; which present the second scriptural aspect of Christianity, in the preaching and writings of the apostles of Jesus Christ after his death, and in their controversies with Jews on the one hand and Gentiles on the other.

These two divisions embrace all the books of the New Testament, except the Apocalypse, or Revelation of St. John, which is quite of a different kind from all the rest, and must be reserved for distinct consideration.

The order in which the books of the New Testament were written, was very different from that in which they stand conveniently arranged for our Christian use. First the histories, and then the illustrative epistles, is plainly the true order for the reader; but the reverse was the order in which the books were written, namely: epistles first, in aid and illustration of the oral preaching of the Gospel, and the retrospective record of that preaching afterwards, when the eye-and-ear-witnesses of the ministry of Jesus were fast resigning their work to others' hands. Then, and not till then, were the Gospel histories written, to supply to future ages the knowledge of the things hitherto attested by word of mouth. Some of St. Paul's letters were, no doubt, the earliest written books of the New Testament. While he was addressing these to various churches and individuals, on occasions arising out of his ministry, the four Gospels were still unwritten; and if (as is very likely in itself, and seems clear from the opening verses of Luke's Gospel) there already existed some more or less full records of the life and actions, the instructions and miracles, of Jesus Christ, which had been compiled and preserved by his personal friends and disciples, these were not in general use at any rate, nor were they the means by which the Gospel was in those days chiefly promulgated. The early Christian churches learnt their Christianity by hearing, not by reading. The apostles preached the history of Christ, before any of them wrote it.

Dr. Lardner regards the Epistles to the Thessalonians as the earliest written books of the New Testament, dating them A.D. 52. The rest of St. Paul's letters he refers to the period from 52 to 62; the Hebrews he dates 63; the Epistle of James, 61 or 62; those of Peter, 64. Then he places the Gospels of Matthew, Mark and Luke, and Luke's history of the Acts of the Apostles, about 63 and 64; Jude's Epistle, 64 or 65; John's Gospel, 68; his First Epistle about 80; and his Second and Third between 80 and 90; and the Revelation, 95 or 96. (Plan prefixed to Hist. of Apostles and Evangelists, Kippis's Edit., Vol. VI.) I am not aware that more modern criticism has done anything to invalidate the general correctness of this chronological scheme. Its leading features are quite in accordance with the motives naturally ascribable to the writers of the Epistles and the Gospels respectively; and it is fully borne out by the internal marks of authorship which the books themselves present. A much later period has indeed, by some German critics, been ascribed to the four Gospels; but this has been done in defiance of the testimony alike of Christian and of Heathen* antiquity, and on the strength of conjectural arguments alone, the chief attractions of which appear to have been their ingenuity and their boldness. I shall glance at these in their place; but shall not give them a greater proportionate claim on my reader's time than I have found them to command over my own convictions.

THE FOUR GOSPELS, by Matthew, Mark, Luke and John, are four several biographical accounts of Jesus Christ,—four several memoirs, or histories of his life and teaching.

The word *Gospel* is continually applied in these books to the *substance of Christ's mission:* thus, "he preached the Gospel;" "repent and believe the Gospel." Properly denoting the substance of Christ's mission, it is also prefixed to the memoirs of that mission as their title. The original Greek word is *evangel*, literally meaning *good-tidings* (a truly descriptive name for the revelation of God in Jesus Christ); whence come our English words *evangelist* for the writer of the history, and *evangelical* for the nature of the contents. *Gospel* is an Anglo-Saxon word, with exactly the same meaning,

* Celsus, the acute and elaborate opponent of Christianity, who wrote about A.D. 176, attests the leading Christian facts by his comments on some of them and his perversions of others; and proves the existence, in his time, of many books of the New Testament, by his quotations from them. (See Lardner, Vol. VIII. p. 9, &c.)

namely, *good-spel*, or else *God's spel;* "good news," or "God's news;"—a beautiful and true description of the contents of these books. So we have here *God's tidings* according to Matthew, who has written the life of Jesus Christ; then we have the same "Gospel" according to Mark; the same again as written by Luke; and the same as written by John;—one history from four different pens.

The biographical form in which the Christian religion was given and has been preserved, is remarkable. Christianity is essentially the record of a life. The religion of Jesus is inseparable from his personal history, and from the picture which that history gives us of his character. Should any one endeavour to tabulate the doctrines of the Gospel in systematic order, or to arrange its precepts into a code of morals, apart from the living history of its great Prophet, the result would be but as the dead ashes of a plant in the chemist's crucible, from which all vitality and fragrance were evaporated. The scene, the circumstance, the occasion, at once gives to the doctrine or the precept the special form by which it may seem, at first sight, limited, and also directs us to the principle in which we may find its universality. Jesus Christ is continually, in evident unconsciousness himself, the central figure in our conception of Christian faith and duty. We cannot separate him in our thoughts from what he said and daily realized of a Heavenly Father's providence, watchful and kind, and a fatherly bosom open to prayer. We cannot separate him in our thoughts from the precepts of benevolent love and self-sacrifice which gain their true sanction in his life. We cannot detach the characteristic parable from its speaker, nor the characteristic miracle from its worker, whose soul is embodied in the word and the act. We cannot realize, in our own persons, the happiest inspiration or the most blessed solace of religion, otherwise than through tacit sympathy with his heart's anguish and his spirit's peace. Jesus Christ is himself the Gospel.

It has not been so with other religious leaders, inspired or uninspired. In no other case does the personal life and history of the founder occupy this prominence.

Judaism was what it was, as a system, apart from the personal character of its founder. His laws do not tell us what Moses himself was. They may give us a glimpse of his intellectual ability, but nothing more. They are best understood when *codified*, or arranged in a tabular view under their appropriate headings. And, so arranged, they shew an outward system well adapted for the world's special, yet temporary, needs; because what the world then needed was a system of outward laws and ordinances, not merely a moral and spiritual influence addressing the individual heart and conscience.

Mahomet, professing to receive both Judaism and Christianity, and to improve upon them both, seems not to have appreciated the progress that had taken place from the old law of "the letter," to the new "law of the spirit of life in Jesus Christ;" and his religion is contained in chapters propounding doctrines and enjoining duties as professed *oracles*, in imitation of the Law of Moses, but more absolute in their style, and declared to have been verbally dictated by Heaven. His life was chiefly an illustration of that part of the Koran which bids the true believers propagate their religion by the sword.

Socrates is, of all ancient uninspired teachers, the one whose personal individuality enters most into his teaching. He himself wrote nothing; and what is preserved of his instructions by two of his disciples is in the form of dialogue, often implying some personal traits of an illustrative kind; while the dialogue itself is always conducted in that peculiar manner of question from the teacher, tending to draw out the desired answer from the learner's own thought, which has earned the name of *Socratic*. But what we thus know of the mind of Socrates is intirely in its *intellectual* aspect. So far as he touches upon directly religious questions, it is intellectual convictions that he brings out; and in morals (his chief subject), his purpose is to elicit the *theory* of morality. Thus it is altogether as a *reasoner* that we know Socrates through his biographers. Xenophon's *Memorabilia* are the intellectual memoirs of his master; and Plato's *Dialogues* are intellectual sketches of him, whether real or imaginary. His reasonings live among the precious remains of ancient thought. But of the *man*, whose personal influence upon the intellect of his countrymen was so wide in his life-time, the world's heart and life now retain no perceivable trace.

The influence of the Christian religion, wonderful and wide-spread as it is and has been, is, in short, the influence of A LIFE;—that influence in part intellectual, producing convictions of high religious truth; but chiefly moral, devotional and practical, suggesting aspirations of faith and prompting to works of love and duty. This life is written in the books of the four evangelists, Matthew, Mark, Luke and John.

It has already been mentioned that various other narratives of the life of Jesus (in whole or in part) were in very early times current, besides these four,—a fact attested by Luke in the introduction to his Gospel. How many such there may have been, we know not; nor do we know whether any of them pretended to the character of a complete history of our Saviour's ministry. Perhaps they were chiefly fragments, such as naturally precede the production of a full memoir. Certain it is, however, that, before the end of the second century, these four were in universal use, and were the only ones in use among Christians,—a fact implying that they had already been used so long as necessarily to refer their composition back to the very times when their reputed authors lived.*

The old Fathers of the church presently found abundant reasons—ingeniously mystical—to account for this notorious fact that there were just four Gospels, and no more nor fewer;—reasons, in short, why there must be four and could not be more. Such reasonings, fanciful and absurd as they are, plainly attest the facts. Irenæus (who flourished about 178) says:

"Nor can there be more or fewer Gospels than four. For as there are four regions of the world in which we live, and four catholic spirits [cardinal winds?], and the church is spread all over the earth, and the Gospel is the pillar and foundation of the church, and the spirit of life; in like manner was it fit it should have four pillars, breathing on all sides incorruption and refreshing mankind. Whence it is manifest, that the Word, the founder of all things, who sits upon the cherubim and upholds all things, having appeared to men, has given us a Gospel of a four-fold character, but joined in one spirit.

* Professor Norton computes, from ingeniously obtained but very rational *data*, that at the end of the second century there were probably not fewer than 60,000 copies of one or other of the Gospels diffused over the world. (Genuineness of the Gospels, I. 32.) Of course I am not ignorant of the theory of certain modern German critics, which supposes the time of Irenæus (when these four histories are so distinctly spoken of as *the* histories of Jesus Christ) to have been the time at which they were *first written*, and that they at once superseded all the other histories of the Saviour by the simultaneous assent of Christians everywhere, who agreed to receive them as the works of Christ's apostles and contemporaries, though hitherto unknown, and to put intirely out of use (and out of existence too) all other well-known books of earlier date. A theory so little accordant with our conscious experience of human conduct and motive, may serve for the exercise of intellectual sword-fencing, but need not detain us in our search into the actual characteristics of the Gospel histories. English theology may have less subtlety, but it demands more solidity than these wire-drawn theories yield.

The Gospel according to John declares his primary and glorious generation from the Father: 'In the beginning was the Word.' But the Gospel according to Luke, being of a priestly character, begins with Zacharias the priest offering incense to God. Matthew relates his generation which is according to man: 'The book of the generation of Jesus Christ, the Son of David, the Son of Abraham.' Mark begins from the prophetic spirit, which came down from above to men, saying, 'The beginning of the Gospel of Jesus Christ, as it is written in Esaias the prophet.'" (See Lardner, II. 158.)

Gregory of Nazianzum (about 370) says: "Matthew wrote for the Hebrews, Mark for the Italians, Luke for the Greeks; for all that great herald John, enlightened with the heavenly mysteries." (Lardner, IV. 408.)

Presently Christian art began to memorialize the four evangelists in those fanciful emblems which ecclesiastically represent them even in our times. Matthew is painted and sculptured as a Man or a Cherub, Mark as a Lion, Luke as an Ox, and John as an Eagle. Mrs. Jameson, in her beautiful book on Sacred and Legendary Art (Vol. I. p. 98), gives this very interesting account of the growth of these emblems:

"The earliest type under which the four evangelists are figured is an emblem of the simplest kind: four scrolls placed in the four angles of a Greek cross (+), or four books (the Gospels), represented allegorically those who wrote or promulgated them. The second type chosen was more poetical,—the four rivers which had their source in Paradise. Representations of this kind, in which the Saviour, figured as a lamb holding the cross, or in his human form, with a lamb near him, stands on an eminence, from which gush four rivers or fountains, are to be met with in the catacombs, on ancient sarcophagi preserved among the Christian relics in the Vatican, and in several old churches constructed between the second and the fifth century.

"At what period the four mysterious creatures in the vision

of Ezekiel were first adopted as significant symbols of the four evangelists, does not seem clear. The Jewish doctors interpreted them as figuring the four archangels, Michael, Raphael, Gabriel, Uriel; and afterwards applied them as emblems of the four prophets, Isaiah, Jeremiah, Ezekiel, Daniel. By the early oriental Christians, who typified the whole of the Old Testament, the transfer of the emblem to the four evangelists seems obvious and easy: we find it alluded to as early as the second century. The four 'beasts' of corresponding form in the Revelation, which stood round the throne of the Lamb (iv. 7), were likewise thus interpreted. But it was not till the fifth century that we find these symbols assuming a visible form and introduced into works of art. In the seventh century, they had become almost universal as distinctive attributes."

Before examining the special character and contents of each Gospel, we must speak of the first three collectively.

Structure of the First Three Gospels.

Every attentive reader of the New Testament must have noticed that the Gospels of Matthew, Mark and Luke very closely resemble each other in many parts, and that the Gospel of John is very different in its contents from the other three. The first three have parallel passages almost throughout, while in John almost everything is additional to the contents of the others. A *Harmony* of the Gospels, where they are arranged side by side in parallel columns, shews this very plainly. The fourth column is almost uniformly empty where two of the others, or perhaps all the three, are filled; and where the fourth is filled, there is seldom anything corresponding to it in any of the other three, till we come to the concluding passages of our Saviour's history. It is clear that the first three Gospels have a certain common groundwork (whether explainable by us or not) which the fourth scarcely shares, and that the materials of John's Gospel are almost intirely additional to those of the rest. So long since as the beginning of the fourth century, the ecclesiastical historian, Eusebius, drew up what he called his Ten Canons or Tables of the Gospels, distinguishing those parts of the history of Jesus which were found in all the four Gospels, those found in three of them, those in two, and those found in only one.

It is further observable, that the correspondence among the first three evangelists often extends even to a *verbal* agreement. There are frequently many verses in succession almost word for word the same in two or three of these writers. This occurs chiefly, indeed, in reporting the words spoken by Christ, and in detailing incidents with which conversations are mixed up; but it is also the case in simple narrative, where it cannot be explained by any degree of correctness of memory on the part of independent narrators. These correspondences so curious, coupled with diversities equally striking, will be seen at a glance in the columns of any good Harmony* of

* The newest, and perhaps the best, English Harmony is that of the late Dr. Lant Carpenter (1835). The great use of a Harmony of the Gospels is, to present in one view all the various accounts of the same incident; the fuller description of which in one narrative compensates the more meagre account given of it in another; and the diversities respecting which are, to an intelligent reader, full of truth and instruction, as shewing how the same fact may appear to different witnesses from different points of view, and as giving evidence, therefore, of the essential credibility of the Gospel narratives. The less intelligent reader may be startled and shocked at these diversities, which are sometimes really irreconcilable in various minute particulars; especially if he has also imbibed the idea of a verbal inspiration as belonging to the Scriptures, which naturally seems to him to preclude the possibility of those little inconsistencies which the Harmony discloses as existing in fact. We may add, that the compilers of Harmonies (to whose laborious painstaking all thanks are due) have sometimes, in their enthusiasm for *harmonizing,* inwoven into the history a sort of double statement of certain events, where the wiser, as the more obvious, course might have been, to suppose that the occurrence is narrated by the different historians with essential truth, but circumstantial variations, irreconcilable in themselves, yet not of vital moment to reconcile.

the Gospels. They have given occasion to many curious speculations about the composition of the first three Gospels, at which we must briefly glance. But first, a few examples shall be introduced of those phenomena which ingenious critics have laboured so hard to explain. No one can compare the parallel accounts without feeling that they have some bond of connection, or are referable, to a certain extent, to a common origin. But whether that origin was documentary or oral, or both, is a question that has given rise to theories more clever perhaps than wise.

Here are the three accounts of the calling of Matthew to the apostleship, his farewell entertainment to his fellow tax-gatherers or publicans, and Christ's doctrine on fasting.

Matt. ix. 9—17:

"And as Jesus passed forth from thence, he saw a man, named Matthew, sitting at the receipt of custom: and he saith unto him, Follow me. And he arose, and followed him. And it came to pass, as Jesus sat at meat in the house, behold, many publicans and sinners came and sat down with him and his disciples. And when the Pharisees saw it, they said unto

Mark ii. 13—22:

"And he went forth again by the sea side; and all the multitude resorted unto him, and he taught them. And as he passed by, he saw Levi the son of Alpheus, sitting at the receipt of custom, and said unto him, Follow me. And he arose, and followed him. And it came to pass, that, as Jesus sat at meat in his house, many publicans and sinners sat also together with Jesus and

Luke v. 27—39:

"And after these things he went forth, and saw a publican, named Levi, sitting at the receipt of custom: and he said unto him, Follow me. And he left all, rose up, and followed him. And Levi made him a great feast in his own house: and there was a great company of publicans and of others that sat down with them. But their scribes and Pharisees mur-

(Matt.)

his disciples, Why eateth your Master with publicans and sinners? But when Jesus heard that, he said unto them, They that be whole need not a physician, but they that are sick. But go ye and learn what that meaneth, I will have mercy, and not sacrifice: for I am not come to call the righteous, but sinners to repentance.

(Mark.)

his disciples: for there were many, and they followed him. And when the scribes and Pharisees saw him eat with publicans and sinners, they said unto his disciples, How is it that he eateth and drinketh with publicans and sinners? When Jesus heard it, he saith unto them, They that are whole have no need of the physician, but they that are sick: I came not to call the righteous, but sinners to repentance.

(Luke.)

mured against his disciples, saying, Why do ye eat and drink with publicans and sinners? And Jesus answering, said unto them, They that are whole need not a physician; but they that are sick. I came not to call the righteous, but sinners to repentance.

(Matt.)

Then came to him the disciples of John, saying, Why do we and the Pharisees fast oft, but thy disciples fast not? And Jesus said unto them, Can the children of the bridechamber mourn, as long as the bridegroom is with them? but the days will come, when the bride-

(Mark.)

And the disciples of John and of the Pharisees used to fast: and they come and say unto him, Why do the disciples of John and of the Pharisees fast, but thy disciples fast not? And Jesus said unto them, Can the children of the bridechamber fast while the bridegroom is with them?

(Luke.)

And they said unto him, Why do the disciples of John fast often, and make prayers, and likewise the disciples of the Pharisees; but thine eat and drink? And he said unto them, Can ye make the children of the bridechamber fast, while the bridegroom is with them? But

(Matt.)	*(Mark.)*	*(Luke.)*
groom shall be taken from them, and then shall they fast. No man putteth a piece of new cloth unto an old garment; for that which is put in to fill it up taketh from the garment, and the rent is made worse. Neither do men put new wine into old bottles; else the bottles break, and the wine runneth out, and the bottles perish: but they put new wine into new bottles, and both are preserved."	as long as they have the bridegroom with them, they cannot fast. But the days will come when the bridegroom shall be taken away from them, and then shall they fast in those days. No man also seweth a piece of new cloth on an old garment: else the new piece that filled it up taketh away from the old, and the rent is made worse. And no man putteth new wine into old bottles: else the new wine doth burst the bottles, and the wine is spilled, and the bottles will be marred: but new wine must be put into new bottles."	the days will come, when the bridegroom shall be taken away from them, and then shall they fast in those days. And he spake also a parable unto them: No man putteth a piece of a new garment upon an old; if otherwise, then both the new maketh a rent, and the piece that was taken out of the new agreeth not with the old. And no man putteth new wine into old bottles; else the new wine will burst the bottles and be spilled, and the bottles shall perish. But new wine must be put into new bottles; and both are preserved. No man also having drunk old wine straightway desireth new: for he saith, The old is better."

And here are the three accounts of the cure of the lunatic boy;

Matt. xvii. 14—18:	Mark ix. 14—29:	Luke ix. 37—42:
"And when they were come to the multitude, there came to him a certain man, kneeling down to him, and saying, Lord, have mercy on my son: for he is lunatic, and sore vexed: for ofttimes he falleth into the fire, and oft into the water. And I brought him to thy disciples, and they could not cure him.	"And when he came to his disciples, he saw a great multitude about them, and the scribes questioning with them. And straightway all the people, when they beheld him, were greatly amazed, and running to him saluted him. And he asked the scribes, What question ye with them? And one of the multitude answered and said, Master, I have brought unto thee my son which hath a dumb spirit: and wheresoever he taketh him, he teareth him; and he foameth, and gnasheth with his teeth, and pineth away; and I spake to thy disciples that they should cast him out; and they could not.	"And it came to pass, that on the next day, when they were come down from the hill, much people met him. And behold, a man of the company cried out, saying, Master, I beseech thee, look upon my son: for he is mine only child: and, lo, a spirit taketh him, and he suddenly crieth out; and it teareth him that he foameth again; and, bruising him, hardly departeth from him. And I besought thy disciples to cast him out; and they could not.
Then Jesus answered and said, O faithless and perverse generation! how long shall I be with you? how long	He answereth him and saith, O faithless generation! how long shall I be with you? how long shall I suffer you?	And Jesus answering said, O faithless and perverse generation! how long shall I be with you, and suffer

(Matt.)

shall I suffer you? bring him hither to me. And Jesus rebuked the demon; and he departed out of him: and the child was cured from that very hour."

(Mark.)

bring him unto me. And they brought him unto him: and when he saw him, straightway the spirit tare him; and he fell on the ground, and wallowed foaming. And he asked his father, How long is it ago since this came unto him? And he said, Of a child: and ofttimes it hath cast him into the fire, and into the waters, to destroy him; but if thou canst do anything, have compassion on us, and help us. Jesus said unto him, If thou canst believe, all things are possible to him that believeth. And straightway the father of the child cried out, and said, with tears, Lord, I believe; help thou mine unbelief. When Jesus saw that the people came running together, he rebuked the foul spirit, saying unto him, Thou

(Luke.)

you? bring thy son hither. And as he was yet a-coming, the demon threw him down, and tare him. And Jesus rebuked the unclean spirit, and healed the child, and delivered him again to his father."

(*Mark.*)
dumb and deaf spirit, I charge thee, come out of him, and enter no more into him. And the spirit cried, and rent him sore, and came out of him: and he was as one dead; insomuch that many said, He is dead. But Jesus took him by the hand, and lifted him up; and he arose. And when he was come into the house, his disciples asked him privately, Why could not we cast him out? And he said unto them, This kind can come forth by nothing but by prayer and fasting."

These instances may sufficiently illustrate the kind of resemblance and diversity which prevail among the evangelists in narrating the same incidents. The closest verbal resemblances are found where the words of Christ or those with whom he converses are recorded; and it must be borne in mind that the chief part of the Gospel history is either of this *interlocutory* kind, or else contains the parables and other discourses of our Lord. The amount of mere narrative unmixed with conversation, is very small indeed; and whenever or however the first record of any of these incidents may have been put into writing, it is plain that the previous oral record must have kept its order and spirit in men's minds far more easily and more faithfully through this intermixture, than could have been the case with any mere narrative with little or no conversation alternating. Some of our Lord's conversations, and other incidents also of the Gospel history, are placed, by the different evangelists, in very various order of time; and it is evident that, in all such cases, one or other of the narrators must be mistaken as to some particulars of time or circumstance. This fact seems also to defy the idea of their having copied from each other, or from any complete narrative of earlier date than their own.

The parallel columns above shew also a very interesting characteristic of Mark's Gospel, which is of great importance in any attempted theory of the origin of the three. Mark's, though much the shortest of them all, is in many of its individual passages the longest and most full of detail, abounding in those graphic little touches of incident or circumstance which seem almost to bespeak an eye-witness. This is well shewn in the second of the above parallels; and there are other similar instances, which seem quite decisive against the idea sometimes suggested, that Mark is an epitomizer of Matthew's longer Gospel. It is not the character of an epitome or abstract to leave out large and important portions of the original and longer work (the Sermon on the Mount, for instance, is not in Mark at all), and to lengthen many of the parts preserved. Whether any satisfactory theory has yet been suggested to account for the mixed harmony and divergency of the Gospel narratives, it may be difficult to pronounce. Nor is it reasonable, indeed, to expect that we can, by the exercise of the subtlest criticism, resolve those ancient books into the elements from which their writers may have composed them eighteen centuries ago, and decide precisely which parts had been previously put into writing, and how those more ancient writings were used by our evangelists,—which parts were current in apostolical forms of oral instruction, and which were derived from the personal knowledge and memory of the individual writer, or of those to whom he had special access. We do not attempt thus to resolve other ancient histories and biographies. Xenophon wrote memoirs of his master Socrates (the *Memorabilia)*; and Plato, another disciple, wrote those immortal *Dialogues* in which he is understood to have ascribed to his master some of his own philosophical refinements, in addition to the strong wisdom of Socrates himself. But no one thinks it necessary to ask (still less, to answer or to guess) what earlier records of the instructions of Socrates may have existed before Xenophon and Plato wrote. There may possibly have been older written memoranda of that great teacher's doings and sayings, on which, as well as on the faithful stores of memory, the memoir writers of the great heathen Sage could draw. There may have been;—or, there may not have been. If there were, no doubt Xenophon at least, as more truly the biographer, used them intelligently and faithfully. If there were not, he at least diligently put into writing what was already cherished in many a faithful and loving disciple's memory as well as his own. *We* cannot, however, reach farther back than to Xenophon and Plato. They are *to us* the original biographers of Socrates. And so are the evangelists *to us* the original biographers of Jesus Christ. We can go no higher than their works. Of whatever there was previously written in their day, no doubt they made the best use that they could. But whatever that may have been, it is all long since lost. The evangelists are *to us* the original authorities. Still, if Plato had written *Memorabilia* as well as Xenophon, or (to make the case truly parallel) if two other disciples had produced memoirs of that simple kind, while Plato's Dialogues gave us (as they do) his master's philosophy as seen through the medium of his own,—scholars would, no doubt, have found it a curious and interesting task to *harmonize* the three memoir writers, and also to look at the whole life from the point of view assumed by the fourth. And if they ventured to conjecture the prior existence of some primitive memoir or memoirs, they would put forth the idea very modestly as a mere literary theory, and would not consider it any detriment to the authority of the extant memoir writers, that they probably had access to still earlier memoranda of the life of Socrates. If they found (as no doubt they would have done) great verbal agreements as well as great differences in the three *synoptical** memoirs of the Sage, they might perhaps have accepted the theory of partial records of an earlier date, to account for the correspondence; or they might perhaps have thought it a sufficient explanation, to remember how weighty his sayings often were in meaning, and how terse and striking in their style of expression, and how it was the habit of his most devoted pupils to recal them to each other's thoughts whenever they met, reciting them in affectionate emulation, and supplying each other's defects of memory, till they had almost gained, in this their oral publication, the form in which Xenophon presently afterwards perpetuated them beyond further risk of change.

Just such intelligent questionings are appropriate, and just to such an extent are theories allowable (and no farther), on the origin of the Gospel histories.

* A term applied by critics to the first three Gospels, as severally or conjointly furnishing a *synopsis*, or general view, of the life of Christ; while St. John's Gospel presents certain passages in full detail, but not a general history of the whole.

In Marsh's Michaelis * (Vol. III. Pt. ii.), there is a most learned *Dissertation on the Origin and Composition of the Three First Canonical Gospels*, in which all the leading hypotheses on the subject are enumerated and described. He first mentions those "authors who suppose that the succeeding evangelists copied from the preceding," and examines Griesbach's hypothesis in particular, who considered Mark's Gospel to have been copied from the other two. All these theories are pronounced unsatisfactory. If copying is the admitted explanation of resemblances, those diversities in the supposed copyist which seem the reverse of improvements, form difficulties more formidable to the theory, than any resemblances which it solves are arguments in its favour. "The authors who suppose that our evangelists made use of a common document or documents," are next reviewed, and Eichorn in particular; and then "the authors who have united both of the preceding suppositions." It is scarcely possible, in reading all these numerous and contradictory schemes (if we have patience indeed to read through them), to avoid being impressed with the thought, how utterly fanciful and arbitrary they all are. The learned translator of Michaelis, however, has an hypothesis of his own, which he considers quite unexceptionable and satisfactory. It is somewhat complicated and very precise. It tells us (conjecturally, but decisively) the very sources of every part of each of the first three Gospels, and explains all their agreements and all their diversities as clearly as if he had seen the evangelists at their work, with the older Greek and Hebrew Gospels before them! The following is Dr. Marsh's own description of his hypothesis, which, he says, "will solve

* Introduction to the New Testament, by John David Michaelis, late Professor of the University of Göttingen, &c.; translated and augmented with Notes, &c., by Herbert Marsh (afterwards Bishop of Peterborough).

the phenomena of every description in a very satisfactory manner, and in a manner perfectly consistent with divine inspiration:"

"St. Matthew, St. Mark and St. Luke, all three used copies of the common Hebrew document א: the materials of which St. Matthew, who wrote in Hebrew,* retained in the language in which he found them, but St. Mark and St. Luke translated them into Greek. They had no knowledge of each other's Gospels; but St. Mark and St. Luke, besides their copies of the Hebrew document א, used a Greek translation of it which had been made before any of the additions, α, β, &c., had been inserted. Lastly, as the Gospels of St. Mark and St. Luke contain Greek translations of Hebrew materials, which were incorporated into St. Matthew's Hebrew Gospel, the person who translated St. Matthew's Hebrew Gospel into Greek, frequently derived assistance from the Gospel of St. Mark, where St. Mark had matter in common with St. Matthew; and in those places, but in those places only, where St. Mark had no matter in common with St. Matthew, he had frequently recourse to St. Luke's Gospel." (Vol. III. Pt. ii. p. 361.)

To accept this hypothesis, must require a rare union of deep critical skill, vivid imaginative power and self-reliant judgment, such as I neither profess nor expect in my reader. It is a mere hypothesis for the very learned and very clever; it is no solution to the many careful and earnest students of the New Testament.

I must add, however, that the supposition of "a common document or documents" having been used by the writers of the three Gospels, is held under two very different views of the virtual authenticity of those histories. Eichorn does not regard the apostle Matthew and the apostolic men Mark and Luke, as really the republishers of those older Hebrew and Greek documents; but sup-

* St. Matthew's Gospel is known to us only in Greek, but it is an ancient and still prevalent opinion that it was originally written in Hebrew, and translated, by himself or some one else, into Greek as we have it.

poses the Gospels under their names to have been written by unknown authors near the end of the second century, and the Hebrew and Greek documents themselves to be later than the days of the apostles. Michaelis and his translator, on the other hand, believe the three Gospels to be the genuine works of Matthew, Mark and Luke, and the Hebrew and Greek documents to have been such productions as Luke alludes to in his already quoted introduction, "Forasmuch as many have taken in hand," &c. Of Eichorn's hypothesis, so utterly destructive of the genuineness of the Gospel histories, Professor Norton speaks as follows, and not without adducing ample proof of his statements respecting the four Gospels:

"The *original Gospel* is regarded by Eichorn, not only as the common source of our first three Gospels, but likewise of certain apocryphal Gospels which were in use before them. These, according to him, were the following: the Gospel of the Hebrews; the Gospel of Marcion; the Memoirs by the Apostles, used by Justin Martyr; the Gospel adopted by Cerinthus and his sect; Gospels used by Tatian in composing his Diatessaron;* and those used by the Apostolic Fathers. These Gospels, and our first three Gospels, are all supposed to have been so intimately connected as to prove their derivation from a common original; and the knowledge which we possess respecting their contents is regarded as illustrating the process of change and growth which they had all gone through. I shall, in the course of this work, remark, under the proper heads, upon the Gospels mentioned by Eichorn, and endeavour to shew that the Gospel of the Hebrews was probably, in its primitive state, the Hebrew original of St. Matthew; that the books used by Justin were our four Gospels; that there is no reason to doubt that the *four* Gospels, which, toward the end of the second century, Tatian, who had been a disciple of Justin Martyr, made the basis of his Diatessaron, were the four canonical Gospels; that Marcion had a mutilated copy of St. Luke,—a fact which, in

* Diatessaron, *four-fold narrative, or book formed out of four.*

consequence of the examinations that have taken place since Eichorn wrote, seems now to be generally undisputed; that the scanty, uncertain, contradictory information respecting Cerinthus and his sect, affords no ground for the conclusion that they used a peculiar Gospel; and that there is nothing in the writings ascribed to Apostolic Fathers which may justify the supposition that, previously to the general reception of our four Gospels, other Gospels were in circulation among Christians as authentic histories of Christ." (Norton's Genuineness of the Gospels, Vol. I. pp. 61, 62.)

The accomplished New-England divine just quoted, after carefully reviewing the theory of an *original Gospel* as put forth by Eichorn and by Michaelis, proposes the following very simple theory for explaining "the striking correspondences in matter and language which exist among the first three Gospels." He reminds us that "the discourses of the apostles and first preachers of Christianity must have consisted, in great part, of narratives of the life of Jesus;" and that "all the information which we now derive from the first three Gospels, must have been orally communicated by them over and over again." After further observations in the same strain, he says:

"We conclude, then, that portions of the history of Jesus, longer or shorter, were often related by the apostles; and it is evident, that the narrative, at each repetition by the same individual, would become more fixed in its form, so as soon to be repeated by him with the same circumstances and the same turns of expression. Especially would no one vary from himself in reporting the words of his Master.

"We have next to consider, that the apostles, generally, would adopt a uniform mode of relating the same events. The twelve apostles, who were companions of our Saviour, resided together at Jerusalem,—we know not for how long a period, certainly for several years,—acting and preaching in concert. This being the case, they would confer together continually;

they would be present at each other's discourses, in which the events of their Master's life were related; they would, in common, give instruction respecting his history and doctrine to new converts, especially to those who were to go forth as missionaries. From all these circumstances, their modes of narrating the same events would become assimilated to each other. Particularly would their language be the same, or nearly the same, in quoting and applying passages of the Old Testament as prophetical, and in reciting the words of Jesus, whose very expressions they must have been desirous of retaining. But the verbal agreement among the first three Gospels is found, as we have seen, principally where the evangelists record words spoken by Christ or by others, or allege passages from the Old Testament. Elsewhere there is often much resemblance of conception and expression, but, comparatively, much less verbal coincidence.

"Previously, then, to the composition of the first three Gospels, we may believe that the narratives which they contain had assumed, in the manner explained, a form more or less definite. Matthew, an apostle, would commit to writing those narratives which he and the other apostles had been accustomed to communicate orally. Mark and Luke, who derived their knowledge from the apostles, would record those narratives which they had heard from them. But if the accounts of the apostles had been committed to writing by ever so many different historians, still, the written agreeing with the oral accounts, and the oral accounts agreeing with each other, all those accounts must have had a striking correspondence. But, however definite might be the form which any oral narrative had assumed, still there would be variations of language, and minor circumstances would be omitted or inserted, as it was orally related by different individuals, or by the same individual at different times, or recorded by different writers. We should expect, therefore, to find, in histories in which these narratives were collected, such intermingled agreements and variations as appear in the first three Gospels. Thus, then, generally, may the resemblance between the first three Gospels be explained. In the oral narratives of the apostles, we find their common archetype, an archetype, from its very nature, partly fixed and partly fluctuating, and such, therefore, as is required to account at once for their coincidence and their diversity." (Genuineness, Vol. I. pp. 288, 289.)

Further explanations and illustrations of this very simple and natural theory follow, which I have not room to quote. That it will solve all the phenomena to the satisfaction of the minutely learned, I do not undertake to say; but it throws a broad light of sound sense upon a subject hitherto treated in too recondite and learned, and far too technical, a manner. And it may be observed, that Mr. Norton's theory, though it makes no reference to the documents alluded to by Luke, does not preclude them from some little share in the explanation of *verbal* coincidences, as there is no reason why Matthew or Mark may not have hit upon some of the very documents mentioned by Luke.

In this position, then, I am quite content to leave the various theories,—some so complex, and one at least so simple,—by which it is sought to explain how the first three Gospels were, or may have been, formed; and shall now enter upon the investigation of their respective characters and contents, as they have come down to our hands.

I propose to take them, not exactly in the order in which they usually stand; but to begin with Mark's Gospel, as being the shortest and simplest, and containing, as already mentioned, scarcely any incident or discourse that is not found in one or both of the others. That Mark's Gospel was the first written, and may even have been seen by the other evangelists, is indeed the opinion of some;* but there can be no doubt that, if our

* See on this subject a very able and luminous article in the Prospective Review, Feb. 1850, oddly misintitled, by the printer, "The Relation of the Third to the First Two Gospels." Its subject is, *The Relation of Mark's Gospel to those of Matthew and Luke.*

purpose is simply to gain a clear idea of the respective histories of Christ's life furnished by the four evangelists, Mark is the one for us to begin with. We shall find in him the simplest and briefest outline of Christ's life; yet such as he (and Peter also, if the latter sanctioned his publication) must have regarded as a sufficient account of the origin of the Gospel. If we next take up Matthew, we may gain a clear idea of the very interesting additions which he contributes to the life and ministry of our Saviour, and of the special characteristics of his Gospel. Examining Luke next, we shall find further additions of a very valuable order, and introduced in a very singular manner, which are peculiar to him alone. And John, who wrote considerably after all the others, will form a supplement to the narratives of them all, introducing chiefly fresh materials which they almost intirely omit.

To each of these histories, it is an obvious course to prefix such personal particulars as can be ascertained respecting their several writers. Not only is this necessary to give us confidence in the authenticity of the history, but it adds wonderfully to the interest we take in it, to find a life-like individuality pervading the *work of each narrator*, in addition to that which inspires the life and character of him who is the subject of all the four.

THE GOSPEL ACCORDING TO MARK.

The evangelist Mark is made known to us by several glimpses in the New-Testament Scriptures. The first mention of him is in an incidental allusion to his mother's house, as a well-known place of resort for the Christians at the time of their persecution by Herod Agrippa (A.D. 44), who, after putting to death James the brother of John, imprisoned Peter with a view to gain popularity among the Jews. Peter, when unexpectedly, and perhaps miraculously, set free, betook himself at once, while it was yet night, "to the house of Mary the mother of John, whose surname was Mark, where many were gathered together praying" (Acts xii. 12). This John, surnamed Mark, was afterwards the writer of the Gospel bearing that name. His mother's house, we here perceive, was a well-known place of Christian meeting; and she and her son, we naturally infer, were early disciples, —perhaps disciples of Jesus personally before his death.

John was his Hebrew name; Mark, or Marcus, his Roman surname,—when or why added we do not know. But, in the absence of family surnames among the Jews, personal ones were very commonly assumed, with or without special suggestive occasions,—being, in fact, almost necessary in order to distinguish one John, or Joses, or Thomas, from another. Our evangelist is generally spoken of as Mark, occasionally as John, and sometimes by both names. Some persons have very needlessly fancied there were two Marks in the New Testament, and that John Mark was a different person from Mark the evangelist. There seems no more room for this supposition than for that of another Peter besides Simon Peter.

Some of the ancient ecclesiastical writers (but not the most ancient) imagined Mark to have been one of the seventy disciples whom our Lord sent two by two before him to preach through Galilee (Luke x.); but this is mere supposition, and seems hardly consistent with the fact that he has not himself mentioned this mission of the seventy.

Some more modern critics think Mark was himself the young man whom he describes (xiv. 51, 52) as having hastily risen from his bed, and mingled, almost naked, with the crowd, when disturbed in the middle of the night by the noise attending the apprehension of Christ in the Garden of Olives. This again is mere conjecture, bespeaking the natural desire to find the future historian of these events himself present, in some of them at least, and observant of them at the time they happened. If Mark really was this young man, that might, indeed, sufficiently account for his relating an incident of so little importance to the general history, and which he alone of the four evangelists has mentioned.

In the further history of the book of Acts, we find him connected with the ministry of the apostles in the following incidents. In chap. xiii., he goes with Barnabas and Saul, as their "minister" or attendant, on their journey to Cyprus and Asia Minor; but it afterwards appears (ver. 13) that he parted from them in Pamphylia in the midst of their expedition; and the most obvious conclusion to draw from the tone of the narrative is, that he had done so through faint-heartedness. For, in ch. xv. 37—40, he is at Antioch again among the disciples; and when Paul and Barnabas propose to "go again and visit our brethren in every city where we have preached the word of the Lord, and see how they do," Barnabas would have taken John Mark with them, but Paul refused on account of his previous desertion. Their "sharp contention" on this subject resulted in Paul and Barnabas taking different routes, the former choosing Silas as his companion, and the latter taking with him Mark. Paul's stern refusal to receive Mark again, seems indicative of his own determined character and zeal; while the greater tenderness of Barnabas to the young man's first weakness, is partly explained by the fact of relationship between them, Mark being his nephew. This fact transpires in Col. iv. 10, where Paul calls him "sister's son to Barnabas."* Of the further proceedings of Barnabas, with Mark as his companion, we hear nothing more than that they went to Cyprus, Barnabas's native country; while Paul and Silas took the reverse course, through Syria and Cilicia, in revisiting the cities where Paul had before preached. The historian of the Acts follows the course of Paul from this time, and does not mention either Barnabas or Mark again.

The remaining glimpses which we catch of Mark are in the Epistles of Paul, and in one of Peter's; and these shew that he had fully reinstated himself in the approval of the unyielding apostle of the Gentiles, and was tenderly regarded by Peter.

In two letters of Paul's from Rome, we find that Mark is with him. In that to the Colossians (iv. 10), he seems to contemplate sending him to them,—into the very neighbourhood, that is, of Mark's former faint-heartedness and disgrace,—for he thus commends him contingently to their kind notice: "Aristarchus my fellow-prisoner saluteth you; and so does Marcus, sister's son to Barnabas; touching whom ye received commandment: if he come unto you, receive him." And in his letter to Philemon (24), Paul salutes his friend from Marcus, as one of his fellow-labourers. Then in the second letter to Timothy (iv. 11), which he wrote from Rome when awaiting his final trial there, he asks for Mark to come to him, in terms which shew a high appreciation of his worth and an intimate personal acquaintance: "Only Luke is with me. Take Mark and

* So Barnabas was brother to the Mary at whose house the disciples were praying when Peter reappeared from prison. But Barnabas was a Levite of Cyprus (Acts iv. 36); whence some have concluded that Mark was a Levite too; which does not absolutely follow, as we do not know to what tribe Mark's father belonged, though the presumption may be in favour of a marriage in the same tribe.

bring him with thee, for he is profitable to me for this ministry."

In this way Mark is connected with the history and ministrations of the apostle Paul. There is another passage of the New Testament which links him, briefly but very emphatically, with Peter; and the earliest ecclesiastical traditions fill up his history in connection with this latter apostle, in a manner to which it is impossible to refuse a general, and almost a minute, assent.

In Peter's First Epistle (v. 13), addressed to the scattered Christians of Asia Minor, he gives this salutation: "The church that is at Babylon, elected together with you, saluteth you; so doth Marcus my son." By *Babylon*,* he has been generally understood, from very ancient times, to have meant Rome, where both he and Paul were put to death, A.D. 65, in Nero's persecution. The testimony of the ancient church is uniform, to the effect that Peter spent some years (three or four, more likely than twenty-five) in Rome, and that Mark was his intimate companion there. Probably they had been much together in Jerusalem in previous years. From the endearing phrase which he uses, "Marcus my son," some have argued that Mark was his convert, and had been baptized by him. But this is quite a needless inference. An elderly apostle might very well speak of a younger fellow-labourer in the Gospel as his son. Nothing more natural or more affectionate. St. Peter's brief mention of him in this Epistle is an epitome of the mutual relation between the apostle and the evangelist, which the traditions of the Christian church have filled up with details seldom varying much from each other,

* An ingenious conjecture proposes *Chalybon* in Asia Minor, instead of Babylon; the figurative use of Babylon for Rome not being likely, and the real Babylon being supposed out of the question. But why not the real Babylon?

and on the whole perfectly credible. These ecclesiastical traditions are given in full by Lardner in his History of the Apostles and Evangelists (Vol. VI. pp. 82—92), and many of them in Jones's Canon of the New Testament (III. 52—72).

The ancient writers all agree in representing Mark as the companion of Peter; and several call him his *interpreter*, with reference, apparently, to the belief of his having composed this Gospel with Peter's sanction and aid. They all agree that he wrote it from the materials gained through his intercourse with that apostle,—some saying that he wrote it before Peter's death, others after, —some that he did it at the apostle's instigation and from his verbal dictation, others on his own suggestion and with less direct aid from Peter. There is a general agreement also to the effect that, after the death of Peter, Mark preached the Gospel in Egypt, where some say he wrote his history, though the general testimony makes him to have published it in Italy, if not at Rome. Nor need we dispute the current opinion that he died in Alexandria, or the neighbourhood. The Roman Catholic Church believes that his remains were afterwards brought to Venice, of which state he is the tutelar saint.

The internal characteristics of Mark's Gospel fully bear out the above idea of its origin, as written in Italy, and virtually representing the apostle Peter's view of the life of Christ.

If it was published in Rome or the neighbourhood, and designed more immediately for circulation among Gentiles and Gentile Christians, this circumstance would fully explain and justify its brevity, since this characteristic arises chiefly from the omission of things more interesting to Jewish Christians than to Gentiles. For instance, Mark says nothing about the genealogy of

Christ,*—a matter all-important to the Jew, a thing of pure indifference to the Gentile; nor about his miraculous birth,*—an idea somewhat conciliatory to the Jewish prejudices felt against his lowly parentage, but to the Roman mind too commonplace an incident to seem impressive among the multitude of its mythological demigods and heroes of preternatural descent. Mark's account of the temptation in the desert is very briefly given in a single verse. He omits all mention of the Sermon on the Mount, in a large part of which Jewish sayings are examined and christianized. He omits the Saviour's denunciations against Bethsaida, Chorazin and Capernaum, which cities are compared to Tyre and Sidon and to Sodom; also the allusion to Jonah and Nineveh, and the illustration of the increasing wickedness of "this generation" derived from the Jewish demonology;—all which allusions would certainly have been destitute of impressiveness (if not of meaning) to Roman readers. He does not relate the cure of the centurion's servant on our Lord's arrival at Capernaum, which (it is ingeniously suggested) Peter might not have witnessed if, as was very natural, he went to his own home in that city immediately on their arrival. Then it is observed that he occasionally uses the very Hebrew words spoken by Christ on certain solemn occasions, but thoughtfully supplies the interpretation. How natural that the warm-hearted Peter, in narrating the potent miracle of which he had been an eye-witness, should have preserved the very words, *Talitha cumi*, and that Mark should have explained them for Roman readers, "Damsel, arise" (Mark v. 41); and that other word on another occasion, *Ephphatha*, "be opened" (vii. 34); not to mention the

* Some consider these omissions to be a strong presumption in favour also of the earlier authorship of Mark's Gospel.

Hebrew words of Christ on the cross *(Eli, Eli, lama sabachthani)*, preserved by Matthew also!

It is further remarked (and the observation is as old as Eusebius and Chrysostom) that Peter's essential authorship of this Gospel is revealed in those passages which relate to himself personally. His impetuous and ardent character necessarily makes him the most prominent of all the apostles in every history of their Master's life. But Mark's manner of narrating the various incidents in which Peter is conspicuous, bespeaks a pen instructed, if not guided and restrained, by Peter himself; for everything creditable (as most of those incidents essentially are) to Peter is told in a quieter way than by the other evangelists, or is not told at all; whereas the sad story of his denial of Christ is given most unreservedly, while most penitentially, in Mark. Here is, in Mark's Gospel, no pronouncing Peter blessed and giving him the keys, on his confession that Jesus is the Christ (viii. 29, 30, compared with Matt. xvi. 16—); no walking on the water to meet Jesus (vi. 45—50, compared with Matt. xiv. 28, &c.); no fish with the tribute money in its mouth (Matt. xvii. 24—27); no mention of Christ's special prayer for Peter that his faith might not fail (Luke xxii. 31, 32); no casting himself into the sea to meet Christ after his resurrection; no charge from Christ to Peter to feed his sheep and his lambs; nor prediction of his martyrdom, as preserved by John, xxi. 7, 15—18, 19. Mark has omitted these and similar incidents. Such delicate yet clear and most interesting hints of indirect authorship (which are more particularly enumerated by Jones and Lardner in the places above referred to), place the evangelist Mark in close alliance with the apostle Peter as an historian of Christ.

I have already stated and shewn (pp. 251—257), when speaking collectively of the first three Gospels, that

Mark's, while much the shortest altogether, is in particular places remarkably full and minute. It has, in this respect, all the signs of being the work of an *eye-witness*. A few special instances out of many will illustrate this feature of Mark's Gospel. In the call of James and John to the apostleship (i. 20), Mark alone mentions their leaving behind them "the hired servants," as well as their father Zebedee, in the vessel. When Matthew and Luke mention the cure of Simon Peter's mother-in-law in Simon's house, Mark (i. 29, 30) calls it the house of Simon and Andrew (here is Peter's respect for his brother), and mentions James and John as being present also. In the cure of the paralytic (ii. 4), Mark describes the "uncovering the roof" (the verandah, apparently), in order to let down the sick man from above. In the voyage across the lake (iv. 36—38), the eye-witness has mentioned the unessential yet graphic particular, that "there were also with him other little ships," and has described Jesus (as doubtless he saw him) as "in the hinder part of the ship asleep on a pillow." The facts might be quite true, and sufficient for history and for faith, as Matthew and Luke give them, without these minute touches; but they are more graphic and lifelike with these additions, which make us feel that the virtual narrator (whether his own penman or not) had seen what he describes. Many more such instances might be quoted; but these are sufficient to shew the kind of internal signs which confirm the ancient tradition, in itself so probable and so interesting, that Mark has given us essentially a *Gospel according to St. Peter*, having heard its incidents recited again and again in their warm and living vigour by that noble-hearted and true though once faltering apostle, whom Christ himself surnamed (though Mark does not tell us this) the *Rock* of his church. (See Matt. xvi. 18.)

The public life of Christ, thus recorded by Mark for the instruction of Peter's disciples and hearers at Rome, embraced the following series of events and instructions, which it is useful to present in distinct abstract (with such notices of time and place as occur in it), by way of a Gospel outline, to be afterwards filled up from the other evangelists. The marks of *time or place* are distinguished by *italic type*.

ABSTRACT OF MARK'S GOSPEL.

Ch. i. John the Baptist's ministry in the *wilderness, east of the Jordan*, and the baptism of Jesus by him. 12. The temptation of Jesus. 14. Preaching of Jesus in *Galilee*, after John's imprisonment. 16. Calling of Simon and Andrew, James and John. 21. *Capernaum:* teaching with authority in the synagogue; the man with an unclean spirit cured. *House of Simon and Andrew:** cure of Simon's mother-in-law; of many sick persons. Retirement and prayer in a solitary place. 38. Tour through the *next towns*, and preaching in their synagogues. A leper cleansed.

Ch. ii. Return to *Capernaum*. Cure of the palsy. Teaching by the shore of the *Lake, or Sea, of Galilee*. 14. Call of Levi the son of Alpheus. Jesus eats in his house with publicans (Roman tribute-takers). 18. Question of fasting argued with John's disciples and the Pharisees. 23. Plucking the corn† on the sabbath, and Christ's lesson on the subserviency of the sabbath to humanity.

Ch. iii. Teaches again in the synagogue. Cure of the withered hand. 6. Pharisees confer with the Herodians.‡

* Reasonably conjectured to have been the abode of Jesus when in Capernaum and the neighbourhood.

† Allowed by the Jewish Law, and also as regards grapes in a vineyard (Deut. xxiii. 24, 25), provided no sickle was used, and nothing carried away. The Law laid no restriction as regards the sabbath. Pharisaic tradition had discovered that scruple, unknown to Moses.

‡ A name synonymous with *Romanising*; as Herod Antipas, the tetrarch of Galilee, was a mere puppet in the hands of Rome. But the name Herodian saved the patriot pride of this essentially Roman faction.

7. Jesus teaches by the *sea-side*, using a small ship to avoid the multitude, who come from Galilee, Judea and Jerusalem, Idumea, Peræa, and Tyre and Sidon. 13. Jesus goes up a mountain,* and appoints the twelve apostles. 22. Scribes come from Jerusalem to oppose him. 31. His mother and his brethren are anxious for his safety, if not doubtful of his self-possession.

Ch. iv. Jesus teaches again by the *sea-side*. Parables of the sower, &c. 35. Crosses the lake. Stills the storm.

Ch. v. In the *country of the Gadarenes*, east of the lake. Cures the maniac who lived among the tombs. "The demons enter the swine."† 21. In *Galilee* again. Raises Jairus's daughter, and cures the woman on the way.

* Probably the scene of the Sermon on the Mount, of which, however, Mark gives no record.

† This is the only *destructive* miracle performed by Jesus (for the emblematic blighting of the barren fig-tree does not deserve to be so described). In this instance of the swine, serious objections have been felt by tender religious minds. The sacrifice of property belonging to an unknown owner is vindicated by the consideration that such property was illegal and immoral. A Jew keeping swine would feel himself deservedly punished by their destruction. As for the poor swine themselves, I know not that humanity to animals would have insisted on reserving them for the butcher. But the full vindication of the scene is found, perhaps, most simply by thoroughly *realizing* it. When we read that "all the demons besought him, saying, Send us into the swine, that we may enter into them," of course we understand that the voice of the poor maniac himself spoke these strange words. He, for the moment, personated the supposed demons within him: "My name is Legion, for we are many," he said before, v. 9; and Legion was unwilling to be dispossessed of his comfortable dwelling-place in a human body, and sent back into "desert places" to seek rest and find none. This explains the reluctance of many demoniacs to be cured. Those who, in their own disordered feeling, impersonated the evil spirits, shrunk, of course, from the approach of Christ's miraculous mercy; while the few who retained their own personal consciousness, and felt themselves to be "grievously vexed with demons," hailed him as a deliverer. *Legion* reads the intent of Jesus, and desperately says, "If thou send us out, suffer us to go into the herd of swine" (Matt. viii. 31). Truly a mad request! Jesus quietly pursues his benevolent purpose, and in his usual language (as the only intelligible language) bids the demons come out;—the maniac suits the action to the word;—*Legion* goes into the swine,—that is, the maniac rushes wildly amongst them; they run before him down the steep into the lake;—*Legion* is gone; and *the man* remains, "restored to his

Ch. vi. Jesus goes to "*his own country*" (*Nazareth*), and teaches in the synagogue "without honour;" then in the villages around. 7. Sends out the twelve by two and two. 14. Herod, tetrarch of Galilee, hears of Jesus, and guiltily thinks it is John the Baptist risen from the dead. Murder of John retrospectively narrated. 30. The apostles return, and Jesus takes them by *ship to a solitary place*. Multitudes follow, and he feeds the 5000 miraculously. 46. Sends his disciples away in the ship, and joins them, walking on the water. 53. They land *in Gennesaret* (on the west side), where he performs many miraculous cures.

Ch. vii. Pharisees and scribes from Jerusalem rebuke him for neglecting the traditions of the elders, and he vindicates morality against ceremonialism. 14. Unclean meats and unclean thoughts. 24. Jesus in the neighbourhood of *Tyre and Sidon*. Cures the Syro-phœnician woman's child. 31. Thence to *Decapolis* (north-east of the sea of Galilee), where he gives speech to the deaf mute (a miracle recorded only by Mark), and (viii. 1) feeds the 4000.

Ch. viii. 10. By ship to *Dalmanutha* (supposed to be south-east of the lake), where the Pharisees ask for "a sign," and he departs "to the other side," the disciples reasoning about the "leaven of the Pharisees" on the way. 22. At *Bethsaida*, in Galilee, Christ cures a blind man (another miracle mentioned by Mark alone). 27. Is in the towns of *Cæsarea Philippi* (north of Galilee); asks his disciples, who men say he is; forbids them to call him by the title Christ; tells them he must be put to death, which Peter deprecates, and is rebuked by his Master. 34. He warns the people what self-sacrifice discipleship required.

Ch. ix. 2. The transfiguration occurs on a mountain, probably in the neighbourhood last mentioned, though generally reputed to have been Mount Tabor, in Galilee. (This was a

right mind." Truly an affecting and genuine picture is this, in however quaint a garb! and most of all in its conclusion, where the restored man desires to follow his benefactor, who most considerately forbids him: "Howbeit, Jesus suffered him not, but saith unto him, Go home to thy friends, and tell them how great things the Lord hath done for thee, and hath had compassion upon thee." (See, on demoniacal possession, Vol. I. p. 56, &c.)

vision of Moses and Elijah, the Lawgiver and the great Prophet of Judaism, speaking with Jesus about his destined death.) 14. On coming down, Jesus cures the dumb demoniac child, whom his disciples could not. 30. They pass quietly through Galilee to *Capernaum*, where the disciples dispute who should be greatest in the kingdom of heaven, and Jesus makes a little child their teacher. 38. Bids them consider as on their part those who do not actively oppose them.

Ch. x. Jesus goes "*into the coasts of Judæa by the farther side of Jordan*" (the beginning of his final journey through the Persea, to avoid passing through Samaria on his way to the last passover at Jerusalem). The Pharisees "tempt him," and he answers them. 13. He blesses children. 17. Answers the young man, what he should do to inherit eternal life. 28. Speaks of the first in privileges being last in blessing, and the last first. 32. On the way to Jerusalem, tells the astonished twelve what is to happen to him there. James and John ask to sit on his right hand and on his left in his kingdom; and he gives them all a lesson of humility. 46. They come to Jericho, where (as he departs) he gives sight to blind Bartimeus (son of Timeus).

Ch. xi. Arriving at Bethphage and Bethany on the Mount of Olives, near Jerusalem, he makes his public entry as Messiah into the fatal city. 12. The barren fig-tree is cursed, as the emblem of the barren and devoted Jewish state. 15. Jesus cleanses the temple; returns each evening to Bethany during the feast of the passover; and (27) confronts the chief priests, scribes and elders in the temple, who demand his "authority for doing these things."

Ch. xii. He teaches by parables. The vineyard let to faithless husbandmen. The stone rejected by the builders and made head of the corner. 13. The Pharisees and Herodians and (18) the Sadducees are successively foiled in their assaults; and (28) the scribe, understanding the supremacy of the two great commandments, is declared not far from the kingdom of God. 35. Jesus warns the people against the Scribes and Pharisees, and (41) blesses the widow's two mites.

Ch. xiii. In sight of the temple and its admirable structure, Jesus foretels the time when "there shall not be left one stone upon another that shall not be thrown down." 3. On the Mount of Olives, he foretels to Peter, James, John and Andrew, the destruction of Jerusalem with more minuteness.

Ch. xiv. The *passover* draws on. In *Bethany*, in the house of Simon the leper (the same, probably, as that of Martha, Mary and Lazarus*), a woman (Mary, as explained by John) anoints Jesus with precious ointment; and Judas reveals his own covetousness, and bargains to betray Christ. 12. Jesus, with the twelve, celebrates the passover in the house, apparently, of some well-known disciple, and (22) institutes the Lord's Supper. 26. They go out to the Mount of Olives, where Christ foretels his desertion by all his friends, and Peter's denial of him. 32. The prayer and sorrow in the garden. 43. The betrayal. 47. The attempted rescue by one who drew a sword (and whom we should have recognized at once as Peter, if John's Gospel did not afterwards mention his name). 53. The examination before the high-priest. 65. The insults. 66. Peter's denial.

Ch. xv. The trial before Pilate. 15. The condemnation. 16. The soldiers' insults. The crucifixion. 39. The centurion at the cross. 40. The women. 42. The burial in the tomb of Joseph of Arimathea.

Ch. xvi. The intended embalming by the women after the sabbath, and the discovered resurrection. 9. Christ appears to Mary of Magdala.† 12. To two disciples in the country

* The supposition that Martha was the widow of one Simon, who some time in his life had been leprous, and so gained this surname, would harmonize several expressions and account for certain facts in the history. In John's account of this incident (xii. 1—8), Martha "served," proving that she was in her own home; and Mary is expressly named as the woman who anointed Jesus. Bethany is "the town of Mary and her sister Martha" (John xi. 1); and Lazarus, probably a very young man, lives with his sisters, not they with him. This home is never called the house of Lazarus. In Luke x. 38, it is "Martha's house" explicitly. Simon, the leper, never makes his appearance in any of the incidents at Bethany. But on the above supposition, the house where his widow lived with her sister and brother would naturally bear his name still.

Michaelis, however, supposes the entertainment to have been given in the house of a friend, in which Martha, "who was a diligent housewife, prepared the table." (Introd., Vol. III. Pt. i. p. 20.)

† The last twelve verses of Mark's Gospel (9—20) are of somewhat

(Cleopas, according to Luke, was one of them, on the way to Emmaus). 14. Then to the eleven, whom he commissions to "preach the Gospel to every creature," and to whom he promises miraculous attestations. 19. Then he is "received up into heaven;" and they go forth everywhere preaching, "the Lord working with them, and confirming the word with signs following."

Such is a simple abstract of the history of Christ's public life and ministry, as recorded by Mark. By this account of the matter, our Lord's personal labours would seem to have been confined chiefly to Galilee, while also reaching to the other side of the Lake eastward, to Cæsarea Philippi northward, and the neighbourhood of Tyre and Sidon westward,—until his fatal journey to Jerusalem at the last passover. We shall afterwards find, however, that he was present at Jerusalem at other Jewish festivals (probably at each as it occurred during his short public ministry), returning thence to Galilee. Whatever may be the cause, Mark confines his history (as Matthew and Luke also do theirs) to the transactions in Galilee and the neighbourhood, until that last journey to Jerusalem. John's Gospel alone supplies the incidents at Jerusalem at the previous festivals.

As regards that part of our Lord's ministry which was transacted in Galilee, Matthew and Luke will be found to add many things omitted, and to enlarge upon things

doubtful authenticity, being absent from one of the four principal MSS., and marked as doubtful in many of less value. (See Griesbach's Greek Testament.) Yet one can hardly imagine that the author could consider his work as finished at verse 8. That would have been an end without a conclusion, and very inconsistent with the orderly method observed in the introduction of this Gospel, which opens with an appropriate title: "The beginning of the Gospel of Jesus Christ, the Son of God." The last twelve verses form, in fact, a most appropriate and regular ending; the little repetition (in the 9th verse) of part of what had been said in the first, being no more than is easily explained if we suppose this conclusion to have been the author's own rapid summary of the Gospel history after the resurrection of Jesus.

briefly mentioned, in Mark. Most particularly, they give a large additional store of our Lord's parables and other instructions. It cannot fail to be observed, however, that they often materially vary from the *order* in which Mark has related certain incidents common to them all. And the order again varies often between Matthew and Luke. Nor is this surprising, nor really important. Whether certain instructions were given by Christ before or after certain others,—whether a miracle upon a blind man preceded or followed, by a few weeks or months, one performed upon a paralytic,—is of no religious importance. One can imagine Peter, and the other apostles in like manner, storing up each incident and each parable, and repeating them very carefully to other disciples again and again, while comparatively negligent of their exact order of time, and presently forgetful of it. The only misfortune is, when readers demand from these writers, or ascribe to them, an infallibility of chronological memory, which they do not exhibit nor profess; and when, finding the three or four assumed infallible memories to be inconsistent with each other in point of fact, they are weakly apprehensive for the credit of Christianity, thus staked upon a fiction of their own false reverence. Any Harmony of the Gospels will shew the real state of the case, in the frequent transpositions which it has been found necessary to make of portions of each Gospel, in order to bring side by side such portions as are parallel to each other.

I shall now analyze the other Gospels in turn, to see how they severally enlarge the materials thus far presented by Mark; and shall preface each, as I have done his, by a biographical notice of the author. And, without disparaging the meritorious labours of the Harmonists, who have endeavoured, often with considerable success, to reconcile together, by various allowable suppositions, the seeming discrepancies of statement in the different writers, I may hope the plan here adopted may, in its turn, help to give a distinct view both of the harmony and the discrepancy, by presenting a clear outline of the Gospel incidents themselves, and of the varied order and different degrees of fulness with which they are narrated by the different evangelists.

THE GOSPEL ACCORDING TO MATTHEW.

It is by no means clear whether Matthew's or Luke's Gospel was the earlier written; nor, indeed, that Mark's was the earliest of the three. Considering them all to have been produced about the same time, and independently of each other, we are endeavouring merely to adopt that *order of perusal* which will leave the clearest impression of their respective contents. With this view, we have first analyzed Mark's, the shortest and simplest of the three. It is of little importance whether we take Matthew's or Luke's next. But Matthew's has a special claim to precedence, in the fact that he was an apostle of Christ, and an eye-witness, therefore, of most of the events recorded by him;—at least, of those occurring after his ninth chapter, where his own call to the apostleship is narrated; and no doubt also of many things preceding his call, and his mingling in which may have led to it and justified it. The fact of his apostleship disposes some Harmonists to prefer his order of events to that of Mark or Luke, where they differ. Yet it is thought, on the other hand, that Matthew has, in several instances, brought together into one passage discourses or events properly belonging to several occasions, through their similarity of character. These are questions of accuracy of memory on the part of the several evangelists, on which we may well despair of deciding between Matthew and Peter (as represented by Mark), or the unknown testimonies appealed to by Luke.

Matthew gives the following account of his own call to the apostleship:

"And as Jesus passed forth from thence (Capernaum?), he saw a man, named Matthew, sitting at the receipt of custom: and he saith unto him, Follow me. And he arose, and followed him. And it came to pass, as Jesus sat at meat in the house, behold, many publicans and sinners (tribute-takers and Gentiles?) came and sat down with him and his disciples. And when the Pharisees saw it, they said unto his disciples, Why eateth your Master with publicans and sinners? But when Jesus heard that, he said unto them, They that be whole need not a physician, but they that are sick. But go ye and learn what that meaneth, I will have mercy and not sacrifice: for I am not come to call the righteous, but sinners to repentance" (Matt. ix. 9—13).

In Mark (ii. 13—17) and Luke (v. 27—32), there is evidently the same history; but, instead of Matthew being its subject, we are surprised and perplexed to find that the person in question is named *Levi*. Mark calls him "Levi the son of Alpheus," and also specifies that he was receiving custom near the sea-side,—that is, the side of the Lake of Galilee. He was one of the Roman publicans, or tribute-collectors, though himself a native Jew; and it is probable that he was collecting a toll upon passengers and merchandize crossing the Lake.

But was Matthew the same person as Levi? Or were they two publicans, both called at the same time? And if two different persons, both called by Christ, did they both become apostles, or was Levi merely a disciple? And why does Matthew mention his own call merely, without alluding to Levi; while Mark and Luke mention only Levi, without a word about Matthew?

It is a curious and perplexing question of personal identities, and both sides of the question have had their advocates from the most ancient times to the present.

Perhaps the most common opinion is, that Levi was only a surname for Matthew, the apostle and evangelist. But how is it, then, that Mark and Luke, who call him Levi on this occasion, call him Matthew in their lists of the apostles? (Mark iii. 18, and Luke vi. 15; also Acts i. 13). The passages now enumerated are absolutely all in which either Matthew or Levi is mentioned, and we must be content to leave the matter in some doubt. But the patronymic given to Levi by Mark, of "son of Alpheus," seems to shew that Levi was not Matthew. For, in all the lists of the apostles, we have "James the son of Alpheus," also known as James the Less, or the younger (Mark xv. 40), to distinguish him from James the son of Zebedee; and Paul further designates this James the son of Alpheus, "James the Lord's brother" (Gal. i. 19). Then again, in the lists of the apostles, there is a Judas, the brother of this James, the "Judas not Iscariot" (John xiv. 22),—the Jude whose Epistle stands among the New-Testament Scriptures; and these two names, James and Jude, are also enumerated among the "brethren" of Jesus by Matthew (xiii. 55, 56): "Is not this the carpenter's son? Is not his mother called Mary? And his brethren, James and Joses and Simon and Judas?" (See also Mark vi. 3.) Now, if Matthew was the same as Levi the son of Alpheus, he must have been one of the Lord's "brethren" (whatever degree of relationship we understand to be implied in that term). But he is not mentioned among them, though four brothers are mentioned by name. Nor is there any hint of Matthew's sustaining such a relationship; while, in all the three lists of the apostles (which I shall now give side by side), James is expressly described as son of

Alpheus, and Judas is called his brother by Luke. With these parallel lists before us, I shall now take the opportunity, not merely of distinguishing Matthew from Levi, but also of identifying some of the less conspicuous apostles under their various surnames, and of tracing the family connection which subsisted between some of them and our Lord.

The following are the lists of the apostles as given by Matthew, Mark and Luke respectively, in the very words of each. Luke repeats the same names in the book of Acts in a slightly varied order. (See Acts i. 13.)

By Matthew (x. 2—4).	By Mark (iii. 14—19).	By Luke (vi. 13—16).
"Now the names of the twelve apostles are these:	"And he ordained twelve, that they should be with him, &c.:	"He chose twelve, whom also he named apostles:
(1) Simon, who is called Peter and	(1) And Simon he surnamed Peter;	(1) Simon (whom he also named Peter),
(2) Andrew his brother;	(3) and James the son of Zebedee,	(2) and Andrew his brother,
(3) James the son of Zebedee, and	(4) and John the brother of James (and he surnamed them Boanerges, which is, The sons of thunder);	(3) James
(4) John his brother;	(2) and Andrew,	(4) and John,
(5) Philip and	(5) and Philip,	(5) Philip
(6) Bartholomew;	(6) and Bartholomew,	(6) and Bartholomew,
(7) Thomas, and	(8) and Matthew,	(8) Matthew
(8) Matthew the publican;	(7) and Thomas,	(7) and Thomas,
(9) James the son of Alpheus, and	(9) and James the son of Alpheus,	(9) James the son of Alpheus,
(10) Lebbeus, whose surname was Thaddeus;	(10) and Thaddeus,	(11) and Simon called Zelotes,
(11) Simon the Canaanite, and	(11) and Simon the Canaanite,	(10) and Judas the brother of James,
(12) Judas Iscariot, who also betrayed him."	(12) and Judas Iscariot, which also betrayed him."	(12) and Judas Iscariot, which also was the traitor."

In the first list, Matthew's, I have numbered the names from 1 to 12; and in the other lists, I have placed opposite to each name the number to which it seems to correspond in Matthew's. With most of the names there is no difficulty or doubt. Even their general order is the same in all the three lists, with a few inversions only.

The two pairs of brothers, Simon Peter and Andrew, James and John, stand first in all, only that Andrew's name is varyingly linked with that of his brother, or postponed to those of James and John, who were frequently united with Peter in nearer attendance upon Christ.

The history and character of Peter are conspicuous in the Gospel history. James and John, the sons of Zebedee, are also well known. The name *Boanerges* was probably applied to them by our Lord on occasion of their proposing (Luke ix. 54), to "command fire from heaven" upon the Samaritan villagers. The tragical death of James in Herod's persecution (Acts xii. 2) seems to shew that he was early prominent as a preacher of the Gospel. Of John, "the disciple whom Jesus loved," we shall say more when we come to his Gospel. Andrew makes no figure in the history; but he appears (John i. 40) to have been a disciple of John the Baptist, and, as such, was "looking for the kingdom of God;" and he seems first to have pointed the attention of his more ardent brother, Simon, to the probability of Jesus proving to be the Messiah. He says a few words in the miracle of feeding the five thousand (John vi. 8).

Philip stands fifth in all the lists. He was of Bethsaida, the city of Andrew and Peter; and his first interview with Jesus, and his conversation with Nathaniel thereupon,—that "Israelite indeed without guile," yet full of prejudice (to whose confident objection—"Can there any good thing come out of Nazareth?"—he calmly replies, "Come and see"),—is a scene highly creditable to the characters of both parties (John i. 43—51). Nathaniel, according to this narrative in John's Gospel, appears to have become a disciple, and, we naturally presume, an apostle; and he is mentioned also among the apostles in John xxi. 2. But there is no Nathaniel in any of the above lists. Probably he was the same as Bartholomew, who stands next to Philip, and whose name appears nowhere else. Bartholomew is a mere patronymic, in fact, meaning the *son of Tholomew;* and the sixth apostle in Matthew's list, there can be little doubt, was Nathaniel, surnamed Bartholomew, or the son of Tholomew (or Ptolemy). *Bar* in Syriac, is equivalent to *Mac* in Scotch, *O'* in Irish, and *Ap* in Welsh.

Thomas stands next. He only comes forward individually on three occasions in the history. The first time is (John xi. 16) when Jesus, hearing of the illness of Lazarus, is dissuaded by the more timorous of his disciples from going into Judea again, lest the Jews should stone him; but Thomas bravely said, "Let us also go, that we may die with him." The second occasion shews him as a somewhat literal-minded and hard-headed reasoner (John xiv. 5), when—in reply to his Lord's words, "Whither I go ye know, and the way ye know"—he confesses, with fearless sincerity, "Lord, we know not whither thou goest," and objects, "*how can we*, then, know the way?" The third occasion is what is generally called the incredulity of the apostle Thomas (John xx. 24—29), when, if he was dogmatic in his doubts and unreasonable in his demand for proofs which might not have been granted, the satisfaction of his incredulity affords a proportionately strong evidence for us of the reality of Christ's resurrection from the dead.

Matthew is coupled with Thomas in the three lists,

which run variously, "Thomas and Matthew," or "Matthew and Thomas." It is observable that he is described as the *publican* only in his own list (where he puts himself *after* Thomas), as if Mark and Luke would omit the mention of an employment naturally in little favour among the Jews, however honourably it might be filled by the individual; while he himself, however, disdains to take advantage of so simple an omission, and boldly writes himself "Matthew the publican." This is true dignity of soul. The mind is the standard of this man.

James the son of Alpheus stands ninth in all the lists. Omitting Judas Iscariot (which designation probably means Judas of Kerioth, or Carioth, a town mentioned in Joshua xv. 25), whose abortive name is marked with disgrace in the three lists, and disappears from that in the book of Acts, there remain James's brother Judas (according to Luke's list), and Simon, variously called the Canaanite and Zelotes. But instead of the name "Judas the brother of James," we have in Matthew's list "Lebbeus, whose surname was Thaddeus," and in Mark's simply "Thaddeus." There can be no reasonable doubt that the same apostle is meant by all three; and it is easy to understand how, when the name Judas had been made infamous by Iscariot's treachery, any surname of the other Judas might come to be used by his friends, and by himself too, in preference. In the Gospel history, during the companionship of Iscariot, this Judas is spoken of (John xiv. 22) as "Judas not Iscariot," for clear distinction's sake; and afterwards he is known as Judas the brother of James, as Lebbeus, or as Thaddeus.

And now this surname, Lebbeus, so like Levi with a latinized ending, throws us back upon the inquiry, whether Levi the publican, whose call is related by Mark and Luke, is the same person, or not, with Matthew the publican who relates his own call in his own Gospel. And we are strongly tempted to identify Levi with the tenth name among the apostles. Let us recall the links of evidence: "Levi the son of Alpheus" is the person called to discipleship, if not to apostleship, in Mark; "Levi" simply in Luke; a publican according to both. In Luke's list of the apostles, there is Judas the brother of James and son of Alpheus, who in Matthew's list appears as "Lebbeus, surnamed Thaddeus," and in Mark's simply as Thaddeus. This is certainly strong evidence in favour of Levi's identity, not with Matthew, but with Jude Lebbeus, surnamed Thaddeus. Michaelis (Vol. III. Pt. i. pp. 97, 98) maintains that Matthew and Levi were two different persons, both tribute-takers, and called on the same day; though he does not identify Levi with Lebbeus, nor suppose he was an apostle at all. He thus endeavours to account for the omission of Levi's call in Matthew's Gospel, and of Matthew's in the other two:

"As it was of more importance to the readers of St. Matthew's Gospel to be informed of the call of its author to the apostleship, than of the call of Levi, especially if Levi was not called to be an apostle, it is easy to conceive the reason why St. Matthew mentioned only his own call, and was silent in respect to that of Levi. St. Mark and St. Luke, on the contrary, might without impropriety be silent in respect to St. Matthew, and mention only the call of Levi,—partly because Levi, as being the son of Alpheus, was related to Christ, and perhaps through this relationship occasioned the call likewise of St. Matthew; and partly because perhaps Levi was the principal, and St. Matthew only an inferior, person in the tribute house;—a supposition which is not improbable, as St. Mark expressly relates that the entertainment which was given to Jesus on this occasion was in the house of Levi, and St. Luke describes also Levi as the master of the feast; whereas St. Matthew, after having related his own call, does not say that the entertainment was given in *his* house, but says only, 'As Jesus sat at meat in *the* house.'"

Simon the Canaanite, in Matthew and Mark, is called Simon Zelotes (or, the Zelot) by Luke, implying that he was (or, more likely, had been) connected with that politico-religious party whom Josephus describes (War, IV. vi. 3). It is observable that there is a Simon among "the brethren of Christ" above mentioned; but the name is too common to justify the inference that Simon Zelotes was another of the family of Alpheus.

Let us now endeavour to ascertain in what sense, possibly or probably, the family of Alpheus were *brethren and sisters* of our Lord. It is generally supposed that, in Jewish phrase, cousins would be included in this designation. If brought up together on terms of constant intimacy, this is very probable; otherwise it is not so clear. The name of Alpheus's wife, we learn (from Mark xv. 40, and xvi. 1), was Mary. She is "the other Mary" in Matthew (xxviii. 1). In John (xix. 25), she appears as the second of the three Marys standing by the cross, and as sister to our Lord's mother: "Now there stood by the cross of Jesus his mother, and his mother's sister Mary the wife of Cleopas, and Mary Magdalene."* And here arise new intricacies of Scripture relationship. Our Lord's own mother was named Mary. *Her sister Mary* therefore can scarcely have been her own sister, but probably her sister-in-law; being either her brother's wife, or the sister of her husband Joseph. So Joseph's sister Mary, we conclude, was wife to Cleopas; or else Cleopas was Mary's own brother, and his wife was another Mary. Are Cleopas and Alpheus, then, the same person? Or is Cleopas (as some have suggested) the second husband of Alpheus's widow? The latter supposition is not necessary, since Alpheus and

* These are not four women, but three. "His mother's sister Mary the wife of Cleopas," must be read without a stop after *sister*. The conjunction *and* is carefully placed between the different persons.

Cleopas (or Clopas) are merely different ways of putting the same Hebrew name into a Greek form.* And now Alpheus ceases to be a mere patronymic to one or perhaps two of the apostles; for we find him, under his varied name of Cleopas, to be one of the disciples on the way to Emmaus, with whom Christ conversed after his resurrection, "expounding unto them in all the Scriptures the things concerning himself" (Luke xxiv. 18).

We have, then, this result with great clearness:

Alpheus or Cleopas was husband to "the other Mary," who is called sister to our Lord's mother, and whom we take to have been own sister of Joseph, or else Alpheus to have been own brother to our Lord's mother. Alpheus had a son James among the apostles, "the Lord's brother,"—James the younger, the writer of the Epistle; and another, "Judas not Iscariot," who is also called Lebbeus and Thaddeus, and probably was the same as "Levi the son of Alpheus," who was a publican, or Roman tribute-collector, before Christ called him. Alpheus had also two more sons, Joses and Simon, and some daughters whose names are not mentioned. And these sons and daughters are all called Christ's brothers and sisters.

If Mary, our Lord's mother, was a widow, as is universally believed, and especially if she became so when Jesus was young, and if she and her son resided thenceforth with Alpheus and his family, the cousins all growing up together from childhood as brothers and sisters, these interesting phenomena of relationship are all satisfactorily explained, and "the other Mary" is a term of

* The Hebrew is חלפי, *Ch*, *l*, *p* (or *ph*), *i*. Sounding the first letter gutturally, supplying vowels and adding a termination, we have Κλωπᾶς, or Κλεόπας. Softening the first letter, we get Ἀλφᾶιος, like Ἀγγαιος, from חגי, Haggai the prophet. See Kuinoel on John xix. 25—27, who, however, very needlessly makes Κλεόπας, in Luke xxiv. 18, a different person from Κλωπᾶς, as well as from Ἀλφᾶιος.

simple and natural endearment for a near relative, instead of seeming a vague or formal description of an indifferent person.*

From this digression (which I trust may be found useful and suggestive to the reader of the Gospel history in general), we must return to what immediately concerns St. Matthew and his Gospel in particular.

Little or nothing is known of his personal history beyond the record of his call to the apostleship. Tradition variously says, he preached in Ethiopia, Parthia and Persia. The time, place and manner of his death are quite unknown.

As to Matthew's Gospel, the ancient testimonies generally agree in representing it as having been written more directly for the use of the Jews and Jewish Christians, and (it would seem) originally in the Hebrew language. It is sufficient here to quote one or two. Irenæus, Bishop of Lyons about A.D. 178, says:

"Matthew, then among the Jews, wrote a Gospel in their own language, while Peter and Paul were preaching the Gospel at Rome and founding the church there. And after their exit (death), Mark also, the disciple and interpreter of Peter, delivered to us in writing the things that had been preached by Peter. And Luke, the companion of Paul, put down in a book the Gospel preached by him. Afterwards John, the disciple of the Lord who leaned upon his breast, likewise published a Gospel whilst he dwelt at Ephesus in Asia." (Lardner's Hist. of Apostles and Evangelists, Works, VI. 49.)

* I am not ignorant of the ecclesiastical tradition sustained by Epiphanius, to the effect that a Cleopas was the brother of Joseph of Nazareth,—consequently uncle to Jesus; nor of that cited by Theophylact, to the effect that "the other Mary" and Salome (the mother of James and John) were daughters of Joseph by the widow of his brother Cleopas,—consequently half-sisters to Jesus. (See Jones on Canon, I. 445; Lardner, V. 328.) But the former tradition gives us no help, and the latter would perplex instead of solving the scriptural facts.

Jerome, in the latter part of the fourth century, says:

"Matthew, called Levi, of a publican made an apostle, first of all wrote a Gospel in Judea in the Hebrew language, for the sake of those of the circumcision who believed. Who afterwards translated it into Greek is uncertain." (Ibid. 51.)

Ecclesiastical tradition has varied as to the time when Matthew wrote his Gospel. Some writers have said it was eight years after the ascension of Christ, and some fifteen. But the older testimony of Irenæus, which Lardner considers as decisive, would place it A.D. 63, 64 or 65.

That it was originally written in Hebrew, is doubted by many learned men, who think that the Greek, as we have it, is the original Gospel of Matthew, and that it was translated into Hebrew at an early period. There certainly was a Gospel in Hebrew, in early times, which is now lost. The Greek of Matthew's Gospel, as we have it, is the original *to us*, at any rate. It presents no clear signs of being a translation; nor is there any apparent reason why Matthew, though addressing it especially to the Hebrew Christians, should have written it in Hebrew, any more than James's Epistle "to the twelve tribes scattered abroad," or Peter's to the "scattered strangers," or the Epistle to the Hebrews itself, should have been written in Hebrew. Greek was the usual written language even of the Jews in those days.

Abstract of Matthew's Gospel.

[The passages inclosed thus in brackets have their parallels in Mark. The type without brackets denotes what is in Matthew, but not in Mark. The comparison of the contents of the two Gospels is thus rendered easy and interesting. Italics still point attention to marks of *time and place*.]

Matt. i. 1. The genealogy of Jesus Christ, or at least of Joseph, the husband of his mother, is traced up to Abraham. Fourteen names are cited from Abraham to David inclusive, fourteen from David to Josiah inclusive, and fourteen from Josiah to Joseph inclusive, as a sort of *memoria technica*, some generations being omitted. 18. The miraculous birth of Jesus Christ at *Bethlehem*.

Ch. ii. 1. The visit of the astrologers from the east, who had "seen his star" and came to do him homage. Herod's massacre of the Bethlehem children, while Joseph and Mary take refuge in *Egypt*, returning on Herod's death to *Nazareth*.*

* These first two chapters (and, in a slightly less degree, the first two of Luke's Gospel) involve us at once in great critical difficulties, to which it is foolish as well as useless to attempt to shut our eyes.

The genealogical table, if it proves (as it professes to prove) our Lord's descent from David, necessarily disproves that miraculous birth which is immediately afterwards related. For, according to the genealogy, Jesus is *the son of Joseph;* which, according to the miraculous birth, he is not. There is no allusion to Mary's pedigree either here or in Luke's genealogical list; which latter differs, indeed, irreconcilably from Matthew's, but is, like it, the professed pedigree of Joseph, not of Mary. The genealogy and the birth are thus irreconcilably at variance.

Then the stories of Herod and the Wise Men have a somewhat apocryphal air; and the flight into Egypt seems needlessly distant in the circumstances, and is connected by the historian with a very weak misapplication of one supposed scriptural prophecy—"Out of Egypt have I called my son"—and with a tasteless, if not ignorant, pun upon another quotation: "He shall be called a Nazarene." (See before, p. 188, No. 3, and p. 190, No. 5.)

These considerations have led some critics to reject the first and second chapters as not really written by Matthew, and to consider his work as properly opening at iii. 1, with the ministry of John the Baptist, as Mark's does. But such conjectural criticism cannot be allowed to alter the text of Scripture. These chapters stand at the beginning of all existing manuscripts of Matthew's Gospel; and there, in the light of honest criticism, they must stand, part and parcel of the work.

But it does not follow that all parts of one book are equally credible. What Matthew wrote may and must have been derived from different sources, and its different parts may have possessed various degrees of certainty in his own mind. Of many things in his Gospel (and those, no doubt, the leading events) he was an eye-witness, and therefore is the best possible evidence. But some things, even after his call, and many before it, which he has related in his Gospel, had not been witnessed by himself

[Ch. iii. 1. Preaching of John the Baptist (more fully described here by Matthew), and the baptism of Jesus in the *Jordan.*]

personally, and must therefore have been derived from the testimony of others. This is the case with all historians. We cannot all see everything with our own eyes.

Now the subject-matter of these first two chapters goes back to a period *thirty years previous* to all the rest of the narrative. When Jesus was about thirty years old, Matthew first associated himself with him as a disciple. We have no reason to believe that, until his baptism by John, our Lord had sought or attracted any public notice whatever, or that his infancy was reputed to have been marked by miracle. About A.D. 30, Matthew becomes a disciple of Christ. He mixes with the disciples thenceforth, learns all the sayings and doings of Jesus up to that time, and observes them from that time forward; follows him till his death, and testifies, with the rest, after his resurrection, to his completed Messiahship. Then, after about thirty years more, when time is thinning the ranks of the personal companions of Jesus, Matthew is impelled, like some others, to record in writing the history of his Master's deeds and words. Is he fifty, or is he sixty, years of age himself? He records the transactions of his own ripe manhood during the year or two when he had been an attendant upon Jesus, hearing all that he said and watching all that he did in public, and often hearing explanations in private of his mysterious course of action. The public ministry of Christ, Matthew had witnessed when a young or middle-aged man, and he wrote an account of it in his mature life, having heard and repeated the various details continually from the one time to the other. But to these transactions of Christ's manhood and his own, he prefixes an account of certain things said to have happened thirty years earlier still,—things connected with the birth and infancy of him whom he first knew at thirty years of age. Is it not evident at once, on this mere statement of the case, that the testimony of Matthew to the events of Christ's public ministry stands upon a very different footing from his record of Christ's birth? The one is his own account of things which he personally knew and remembered; the other is an account of things told him at second-hand, as having occurred much earlier, and possessing little notoriety at the time of the main history; and which, of course, he only gives us as at second-hand, and we ought to receive accordingly. When Matthew wrote, the public events of thirty to thirty-three years before were quite notorious and well ascertained; but the private occurrences of sixty-three years before were not so well ascertained, nor so clear of fable and exaggeration. That the birth of Jesus had excited no special interest during his public life and ministry, seems plain from the absence of all allusions to its miraculous character in the records of his ministry. He is spoken of as "the son of Joseph," without a hint on the part of the evangelists that the fact was otherwise. (Luke iv. 22; John i. 45, vi. 42.) But we know very well

[Ch. iv. 1. Temptation of Jesus (more fully here by Matthew). 12. Jesus in *Galilee*, after hearing of John's imprisonment. 18. Calling of Simon and Andrew, James and John.]

that, before thirty years had passed over his death, the lowliness of his birth and condition and the scandal of his cross became the occasion of false shame to many of the half-persuaded among both Jews and Gentiles; and when mystical ideas began to veil the reality of the crucifixion, there was room for the growth of others tending to glorify the birth. This being the case, what was the duty of the faithful biographer, who knew, of his own personal knowledge, the events of Christ's ministry, and had heard from others the story of his birth? Shall he omit the hearsay evidence, and proceed at once to the known facts? Or may he prefix the current traditions of the birth to his memoirs of the middle life, and trust to the discrimination of his readers to understand that the interval of thirty years necessarily puts the two parts of his narrative on very different footings of evidence?

Matthew has done the latter; and we do him great injustice if we receive as of equal credibility things resting on such palpably different kinds of evidence. Surely he must himself have been conscious of the incompatibility of the miraculous birth with the genealogical derivation of the Christ from David through Joseph of Nazareth. But he had found (we know not where) this genealogy, and he had received (we know not whence) the narrative of the miraculous birth; and he has given them both as he received them, leaving us to judge of them as we best can, and not expecting us to suppose he *could* personally accept them both, nor thinking that we should ever imagine ourselves bound to do anything so inconsistent.

In this reasonable and natural way, I suppose, we must deal with the difficulty before us. We cannot reject from the document, as spurious, either of these irreconcilable statements; but we can easily distinguish between the unknown testimony (perhaps mere popular rumour) on which Matthew has introduced the very questionable story of the miraculous birth, together with the testimony (also unknown, but no doubt documentary) which has traced the pedigree of Jesus through Joseph as his father;—between these and the direct personal evidence with which he narrates the public ministry of Jesus, to which he himself, in the full vigour of his manhood, was an eye-witness, and in which he himself took part. In any biography, except a scriptural one, such a distinction would be at once taken as a matter of course. Why the Scriptures alone should be refused the commonest literary and critical justice by their admiring friends, I know not; nor why, in religious matters alone, it should be expected that we can admit contradictory statements, without feeling that one of them must be, in some way or other, a mistake. I cannot possibly believe both that the pedigree of Jesus was as here stated, and that he had (as also here stated) no paternal pedigree at all! Matthew may have done his duty in submitting these contradictory materials to his readers' decision. Let us

Ch. v. 1. The Sermon on the Mount (a hill near *Capernaum*), containing:—2. The Beatitudes, or blessings of Christian discipleship; 17. A running commentary on the Law and the Prophets, as about to be completed in Christ, and a review of various perverted scriptural maxims, and other maxims of popular morality, in the light of Christian truth, purity and benevolence; Ch. vi. 1. Precepts on alms, fasting and prayer; 9. The Lord's Prayer; 19. Precepts of religious-mindedness; Ch. vii. 1. Of tenderness in condemning others; 6. Of Christian caution and prudence; 7. Of confidence in prayer; 12. The golden rule completing the Law and the Prophets; 13. The broad way and the narrow one; 15. Cautions against false teachers; the test of conduct; 24. The house upon a rock and the house on the sand; 28. The perceived contrast between Christ's mode of teaching "with authority," and that of the scribes as expounders merely.

[Ch. viii. 2. The leper cleansed.] 5. The centurion's servant cured of palsy at *Capernaum*, and Christ's blessing on this Gentile's faith.* [18. Jesus crosses the lake to *Gadara*; stills the storm; cures the two maniacs (Mark mentioned only one) among the tombs.]

[Ch. ix. 1. Comes to "his own city" (perhaps *Capernaum* is here meant), where he cures the palsied man (as narrated *earlier* by Mark). 9. Call of Matthew, while sitting at the receipt of tribute. Jesus eats with the "publicans." 14. Question of fasting argued with John's disciples. 18. Jairus's daughter

do our duty; and let us do him the justice of supposing he expected us to discriminate.

* Faith, that is religious susceptibility and trust, seems to have been demanded usually, perhaps always, as a moral prerequisite for receiving Christ's miraculous benefits. It might be manifested by the person more immediately, or by others more remotely, concerned; but it is generally shewn, if not expressed in words, by some one or other. This is a beautiful fact, which has been strangely perverted into a sceptical argument against the reality of Christ's miracles, as depending (it is alleged) on the faith of the parties cured. They did *not* so depend. The party cured was, in the present case, a servant, and the person expressing the faith was his master. The faith of either might have been a *moral* reason for the miracle being done; but in no sense could any faith on the centurion's part have acted restoratively upon his palsied servant.

raised (Matthew does not mention the father's name). The woman on the way cured.] 27. Two blind men restored to sight. 32. A dumb demoniac cured.

[Ch. x. 1. The twelve apostles commissioned and sent forth to proclaim that "the kingdom of heaven is at hand." (Christ's instructions to them are here given much more fully than by Mark.)]

Ch. xi. 1. John the Baptist, having heard in prison of Christ's miracles, sends two of his disciples to ask whether he is the expected Messiah or not,—seemingly implying, on his own part, a difficulty in reconciling the Jewish hope with the actual ministry of Jesus, and perhaps also gently hinting his own wondering sense of personal neglect, as the forerunner of the Prince Messiah. Jesus desires them to report to their Master what they have seen and heard; and then, turning to the multitude, he speaks of John as a true prophet indeed, and "the Elias who was to come." He reproves the waywardness of the people, laments for the cities that had heard his mission with indifference, and invites those that labour and are heavy-laden to find rest in him.

[Ch. xii. 1. The disciples pluck corn on the sabbath, and Jesus rebukes the sabbatarianism of the Pharisees. 9. Cure of the withered hand in the synagogue. 14. The Pharisees plot and Jesus retires. 22. Cures a blind and dumb demoniac, and encounters the Pharisees in argument when they ascribe his miracles to Beelzebub. 46. "His mother and his brethren" come in search of him. (These incidents are placed earlier by Mark. Matthew gives the encounter with the Pharisees much more fully, after mentioning the cure of the demoniac, which is not mentioned by Mark, as the immediate occasion of the discussion.)]

[Ch. xiii. 1. Jesus teaches by the *sea-side*. Parables of the sower, &c. (That of the tares and the wheat is preserved by Matthew alone.) 53. Jesus goes into his own country (*Nazareth*, plainly); but does not many mighty works there, because of their unbelief.]

[Ch. xiv. 1. Herod hears of Jesus, and thinks it is John the Baptist risen from the dead. The murder of John narrated. Jesus and his disciples depart *by ship to a desert place*. The five thousand are fed *beyond the Lake.* Jesus sends his disciples on board, dismisses the multitude, and retires up a mountain to pray. Walks on the water to them, and lands on the west side. (Matthew adds the characteristic incident of Peter walking on the water and then doubting and beginning to sink.)]

[Ch. xv. 1. Scribes and Pharisees from Jerusalem arraign him at the bar of tradition, and are convicted by him in the court of morals. 21. The cure of the *Canaanite* woman's demoniac child near *Sidon.* 29. Jesus returns to the *Sea of Galilee,* cures many (Mark has specified the deaf mute), feeds the 4000, and takes ship to the neighbourhood of *Magdala* (Mark says *Dalmanutha:* he may have visited both.)]

[Ch. xvi. 1. Pharisees and Sadducees demand a sign in the sky, and he crosses to "the *other side.*" The leaven of the Pharisees. In *Cæsarea Philippi,* Jesus asks his disciples, Who men say he is; promises Peter the keys of the kingdom of heaven (not mentioned by Mark), on his confession of him as the Christ; foretels his death; which Peter deprecates, and is then rebuked as a Satan and a stumbling-block.]

[Ch. xvii. 1. The transfiguration. 14. Cure of the lunatic child.] 24. Jesus *at Capernaum,* pays tribute-money for himself and Peter (probably the customary contribution to the temple).

[Ch. xviii. The disciples dispute who should be greatest, and are answered from the little child. (Matthew here gives much more fully Christ's discourse on divine and human forgiveness, including his parables of the lost sheep and the unforgiving creditor.)]

[Ch. xix. Jesus goes to the *other side of Jordan,* through the *Peræa.* The Pharisees "tempt him," and he replies. He blesses children; answers the young man how he may inherit everlasting life. The "first that shall be last, and the last that shall be first."]

Ch. xx. 1. Parable of the labourers in the vineyard, foreshadowing the welcome of the Gentiles into the Gospel dispensation. [17. *Going up to Jerusalem,* Jesus tells the twelve of his approaching death. James and John (their mother accompanying them) ask to sit on his right and left, when he shall assert his kingly state. He bids those who would be great in his kingdom, be chief in service. 29. Two blind men restored to sight as he leaves *Jericho*. (Mark mentions only one, but him by name, the son of Timeus.)]

[Ch. xxi. 1. Jesus makes his public entry into *Jerusalem* as Messiah. 12. Cleanses the temple. 17. Goes to *Bethany* to lodge. 18. Devotes the barren fig-tree. 23. Teaches in the temple, and answers the priests and elders who demand his authority.] 28. Parable of the two sons (imaging the Jews and the Gentiles; the one assenting, but disobeying; the other refusing, but afterwards repenting and obeying. [33. The vineyard let out to husbandmen. 42. The stone rejected by the builders.]

Ch. xxii. 1. The parable of the marriage feast and the man who had refused to accept a marriage garment. [15. The Pharisees and Herodians seek to ensnare Jesus about tribute-money. 23. The Sadducees also respecting the resurrection. 34. The scribe is taught the two great commandments. 42. Christ the son and lord of David.]

Ch. xxiii. 1. Fearful woes against the Scribes and Pharisees, "the hypocrites" (reported in full by Matthew, only glanced at by Mark).

[Ch. xxiv. Destruction of the temple and city foretold, in the coming of the Son of Man and the completion of the age.*]

Ch. xxv. 1. Parable of the ten virgins. 14. The talents. 31. The sheep and the goats.

[Ch. xxvi. 1. The passover at hand. 6. Jesus in the house of Simon the leper, at Bethany. 14. Judas bargains with the priests. 17. Celebration of the passover and institution of the Lord's Supper. 30. Mount of Olives. 47. Betrayal. 57. Examination before Caiaphas. 69. Peter's denial.]

[Ch. xxvii. 1. The trial before Pilate.] 3. The remorse and suicide of Judas. [11. The trial continued. The condemnation. The soldiers' insults. The crucifixion.† The

* *ἡ συντέλεια τοῦ αἰῶνος*, in *Common Version*, "the end of the world." Compare Matt. xiii. 39: "The harvest is the end of the world." Compare also Heb. ix. 26: *ἐπὶ συντελείᾳ, τῶν αἰώνων*; *Common Version*, "Now once *in the end of the world* he (Jesus) hath appeared;" surely, rather, "*the end* or completion *of the ages*." (See note, p. 301.)

† In Matthew (xxvii. 52, 53), there is a very curious and perplexing

centurion's confession. The women. 57. The burial.] 62. Pilate grants a guard for the sepulchre.

[Ch. xxviii. 1. The resurrection.] 11. The guards tampered with, and promised impunity by the priests. [16. Christ meets the eleven disciples in Galilee, and gives them his parting commission to preach the Gospel.]

Note referred to p. 300.

A large and solemn inquiry opens here, and one beset with critical difficulties. Our Lord's predictions in Matt. xxiv. and xxv. are generally considered to have reference to two distinct subjects: first, to the destruction of Jerusalem by the Romans "before this generation shall pass;" and, secondly, to the last judgment,—that is, to the retribution of the future life, whether conceived of as awaiting each person on his death, or to be pronounced collectively (dogma beyond imagination!) upon all races and generations of men at some future period described as "the end of the world." Now the most careful and earnest readers find it impossible to decide exactly how much of this prophecy relates to the one subject, and how much to the other, and where and how the transition is made from the one to the other.

Comparing these two chapters of Matthew with the corresponding parts of Mark (ch. xiii.) and of Luke (ch. xxi.), we find the topics of Matthew's former chapter (xxiv.) repeated by Mark and Luke, while those of his latter chapter (xxv.) are peculiar to Matthew, namely, the parables of the ten virgins, the talents, and the sheep

statement inserted here, which no other Gospel contains, namely, that "many bodies of saints who had fallen asleep were raised; and they came forth out of the tombs after his resurrection, and entered into the holy city, and appeared unto many." The passage has a very legendary look; and some critics conjecture that it was not written by Matthew. But all the MSS. have it. It at once brings to mind Dan. xii. 1, 2, where it is said that "Michael, the great prince, on behalf of the children of Israel shall stand up, * * and the people shall be delivered, every one that shall be found written in the book. And *many of them that sleep in the dust of the earth shall awake, some to everlasting life, and some to shame and everlasting contempt.*" The Jews, no doubt, expected this kind of resurrection to accompany their Messiah's reign; and we are strongly tempted to conjecture that a legend to this effect has crept into Matthew's Gospel with no sufficient authority. The second book of Esdras, and some other parts of the Apocrypha, attest the expectation. It can hardly be an essential of Christian belief, to maintain that it was fulfilled.

and goats (the talents being, however, in a somewhat varied form, described by Luke (xix. 12, &c.) as spoken by our Lord on the way up to Jerusalem, with a view to repress the expectation that the kingdom of God would immediately appear). The common interpretation seems to consider the twenty-fourth chapter of Matthew, and the whole parallel record in Mark and Luke, as a prophecy of the destruction of Jerusalem and its attendant circumstances, and the additions in Matthew's twenty-fifth chapter as referring to the great future judgment. Yet there are expressions both in Mark and Luke, as well as in the earlier part of Matthew's record, which it seems difficult to explain and justify as referring simply to the coming of the Son of Man in the destruction of Jerusalem. Nor must we forget that Luke has placed the parable of the talents almost immediately before, and that Mark has a few words apparently suggested by it (xiii. 34). And if our Lord really made the supposed transition from the one topic to the other, it is strange indeed that the greater topic should scarcely make its appearance at all in the reports of Mark and Luke, while the minor one (not small in itself, but only by comparison) is as fully recorded by them as by Matthew.

There is another view of the matter, far more simple and obvious, more agreeable surely to the nature of the case, and at the same time confirmatory, in a remarkable degree and a most interesting manner, of the antiquity and genuineness of these three Gospels. In some of St. Paul's Epistles, there are plain traces (which will be pointed out when we come to them) of a notion which is well known to have prevailed in the early Christian church, to the effect that the *end of the world* was at hand; that phrase being understood to imply some intire change from the conditions of our present physical existence, and the beginning of a different order of human life, perhaps not upon this planet Earth. And this kind of expectation continued to be held, strongly though vaguely, by many Christians for a long time, only giving way to the millenarian idea as its successor. The prophecy of Jesus before us, and the parts of Paul's Epistles above referred to, were regarded as sanctioning it.

But what if this idea, of an approaching termination of the present mortal state of man and the opening of an immortal one as the new Messianic kingdom, prepossessed the minds of our Lord's Jewish disciples both while they heard, and also when they wrote down, his prophecy of the end of the Jewish age and the coming of the Son of Man in the establishment of the Christian age? The destruction of Jerusalem was, in point of historical fact, the definite period of time at which we must fix the absolute end of the Jewish dispensation as having occurred. Till then, the Law was. Since then, the

Law has been impracticable. Hence the propriety and force of the prophetic description given of that time as the "end of the age" (not of the world), and as "the coming of the Son of Man." Judaism had then fulfilled its course. The Son of Man was thenceforth the spiritual head of mankind. And now "the Son of Man having thus come in his glory," Judaism having given place to Christianity, and the moral and religious principles of the latter being propounded as the everlasting principles of the Divine government over mankind, we can see how the parable of the Sheep and the Goats is truly descriptive of the Divine judgment over human actions both here and hereafter, whether we further interpret the parables of the Virgins and of the Talents from the same point of view, or regard them as more particularly designed to inculcate watchfulness in looking for the secular signs of the coming end of the Jewish age. We have only to realize the fact of our Lord's Jewish disciples being thus prepossessed with the idea that the end of the Jewish age would be the end also of this mortal state, and we account for a certain involuntary colouring of the prophecy, where its imagery, as we have it, seems to us scarcely appropriate to the occasion as tested by the historical fulfilment; while, however, that fulfilment is most wonderfully exact in many minute descriptions of things connected with the siege of Jerusalem.

Now this mixture of an idea which was not in fact fulfilled, with the record of a prophecy so remarkably fulfilled in its palpable points, is one of the strongest imaginable proofs of the antiquity and genuineness of the books in which the record is preserved. Had the evangelists written *after* the destruction of Jerusalem, they could not surely have made such a mistake. Fact would then have interpreted their Master's prophecy, and recalled its very words to them, preventing any such confusion of mind in those who were recording it to the best of their memory. The books which record Christ's prophecy (obscured as the record is with phrases naturally suggesting something more than really happened) *must* have been written *before the year A.D.* 70, when Titus destroyed Jerusalem. Literary evidence could not be stronger. No one forging Gospels in the second century, for the supposed credit of Christianity, would have ascribed to Jesus a prophecy of doubtful fulfilment. When Jerusalem was actually destroyed, it would have been easy to write a more clear *retro-prediction*. The most pointed parts respecting Jerusalem could not, indeed, have been made more clearly appropriate; but those other parts would surely have been omitted or modified, which seem more suitable to the end of the natural world than to that of the Jewish age merely. For these parts necessarily impugn either the truth of the prophecy or the exactness of the record; and the latter may innocently fail in the points alluded to, while its veracity is unimpeachable.

I have not seen this argument anywhere stated; but I feel confident of its soundness. The fear of free scriptural criticism has kept it too long unstated; but it is a very pearl of moral evidence amid textual doubts and difficulties. It proves that the first three Gospels must be more ancient than the year 70, when Titus destroyed Jerusalem and the Jewish age ended. Christ's prophecy would have been differently written, if it had not been written till after that event.

Allowing thus for the accidental, yet natural, admixture by the evangelists, of the prevailing idea respecting the coming end of the present order of sublunary things, in their record of Christ's prophecy of the destruction of Jerusalem, we shall still have to decide whether any parts of his discourse have reference or not to what is called the Last Judgment, or the allotments of happiness and misery in a future state. And it will seem more in accordance, surely, with the natural order of his subject, to consider him as describing the *Gospel age on earth* (reaching, with its spiritual hopes and aims, from earth to heaven) *as about to ensue on the ending of the Jewish age*, than to imagine that he passes on at once from the destruction of Jerusalem to the judgment scene of another life. Having foretold the completion of the Jewish age and the cessation of the authority of the Jewish Law, he goes on (according to this view of the matter) to sketch some of the moral and religious principles of the Christian age that shall succeed. The new dispensation is to be based on the universality of God's providence,—open to every creature of God, knowing no distinction of nation, or kindred, or tongue, or people. It is a republication of the everlasting truths of natural religion, drawn forth from behind the veil of nature's doubts, and sanctioned and endeared by revealed authority and revealed love. It makes Jew and Gentile all one before the Heavenly Father of all. The Jews whom the tutelage of the Law has brought to Christ, it releases from the bondage of their many ceremonies, and accepts into the service of a spiritual faith and the good works of righteousness. Those Gentiles who do by nature many of the things contained in the Law, it recalls at once from their idolatry and their ceremonialism, into the equal service of the same spiritual belief, and the same pure and high-toned morality. This is the reign of Christ on earth. Of these great religious principles, he is personally the emblem and representative. And the prevalence of these great principles is the true characteristic of Christendom, as the kingdom of Christ, the kingdom of God, the kingdom of heaven on earth.

Now these, the admitted characteristics of Christian faith and morality, are described as in operation in these admirable parables of our Lord,—the ten virgins, the talents, the sheep and goats. They form so many manifestoes of the moral laws of Christ's kingdom.

This new kingdom is compared in its rise to the expected, yet uncertain, approach of the bridegroom to a wedding-feast; for which these *Ten Virgins* are waiting, lamps in hand, some wisely prepared, but others betraying the most foolish want of forethought. How aptly and forcibly are the characteristics of the Gospel dispensation represented in this parable, by the happy and rejoicing image of a wedding-feast! Our Saviour delights in the reproduction of this image, in which he is himself the bridegroom. Loving, hopeful, trusting and rejoicing, is the Christian's faith. And most truly do these virgins represent the wisdom with which the heavenly King is prepared for and welcomed in some hearts, and the foolish, reckless unpreparedness with which others neglect the necessary means of sharing the blessedness he offers!

The Talents is a picture of human life in its most deeply religious and moral aspect, as seen from Christ's own point of view, as the gift of Almighty God, and especially as designed to be perpetuated beyond the present state. The Gospel which throws this religious light around our condition, speaks of all our faculties, possessions and opportunities, as trusts committed to our fidelity, and for our use or neglect of which, whether few or many, we shall be held accountable. A doctrine to which conscience assents, wherever it has light enough to apprehend the doctrine itself. A doctrine to the truth of which our present life continually bears witness in its spiritual retributions of good and evil, making the spiritual future of another life the firm resting-place of conscience as well as of affection.

And on this same view of these grand parables, as illustrating the sway of the new kingdom of Christ now proclaimed on earth and reaching to the life to come, the concluding one of the *Sheep and Goats* declares, in terms most unequivocal, that the eternal principles of the Divine administration approve and reward the virtues of man to man, and discountenance and punish all neglect of mutual duty. "When the Son of Man shall come in his glory," does not, according to this view, point to some still future appearing, but to the now existing order of his heavenly kingdom upon this earth. He is even now upon the throne of his glory, with the holy angels of Truth, Virtue, Justice, Peace, Mercy, around him. Before him *are* gathered all nations, recognizing him of Nazareth as their common Lord and Teacher, Guide and Judge. "His law is gone forth from Zion, and the word of the LORD from Jerusalem." To their own consciences, if not to each other's perception, he divides the sheep from the goats by moral tests, the tests of conduct. And the King is continually saying to the righteous, in the recorded promises of his Gospel, softly echoed by their own consciences, that they are the blessed of their Father, and already inheriting his kingdom. And when they do good to their fellow-men for Christ's sake, as well as at the bidding of their common humanity, they thankfully know and meekly feel what he so graciously says of its being *done unto him*. And if they on the left hand pretend not to know how any duty they can do can reach the Prince of this heavenly kingdom, their consciences can no longer sophisticate with him when he explains—"Inasmuch as ye did it not to one of the least of *these my brethren*, ye did it not to me." So these must go away from his sentence, as often as he thus pronounces it, into the punishments of this age of clearly announced spiritual retribution, and the righteous into its blessed life continually more and more abundantly.

These are, beyond question, the great principles of the Divine Government itself;—the principles upon which it has, doubtless, ever been conducted, however little or however fully known to mankind;—principles clearly proclaimed and published by the Gospel, and understood by men's reason and accepted by their consciences, as eternally right and just and kind. The kingdom of heaven on earth, in which Christ is supreme, is thus the reign of pure morals and vital piety and heavenly faith. Would that all Christians knew it as such, and such only!

THE GOSPEL ACCORDING TO LUKE.

THE third Gospel in our canon, and the book of the Acts of the Apostles, were written by the same pen. This appears from the opening of each, where they are severally dedicated to a person named Theophilus, while the opening of the Acts also refers to the "former treatise," and carries the history forward from the point at which it was left in the Gospel.

Universal Christian antiquity ascribes these two books to Luke, the companion of the apostle Paul in many of his travels. We therefore consult the history and letters of St. Paul, to see what light they can throw upon the personality of Luke.

Writing to the Colossians from Rome during his detention there before his trial, Paul sends greetings from Luke among others: "Luke, the beloved physician, and Demas, greet you" (Col. iv. 14). This passage, incidentally informing us of his calling in life, seems to vouch for fair education and ability on the part of Luke, though we must be well aware that the profession of physician did not, in those days, bear rank proportionately to its position among us. The literary qualities of the writings of Luke fully bear out this account of him. His style is above the average of Hebrew Greek writers, approaching nearer to the flowing ease of classical Greek, while yet full of Hebraisms of thought and phrase.

In the letter to Philemon, who lived at Colosse (as inferred from Col. iv. 9),—a letter written also at Rome at the same time as that to the church of the Colossians,—Paul again mentions Luke as among his fellow-labourers: "There salute thee Epaphras, my fellow-prisoner in Christ Jesus, Marcus, Aristarchus, Demas, Lucas, my fellow-labourers" (Philem. 23, 24).

Then, in his second letter to Timothy, written also from Rome, but at a later period of his detention there, Paul says (2 Tim. iv. 11), "Only Luke is with me," and bids Timothy bring Mark with him when he comes, Demas having forsaken him through "love of the present world," and his other companions having been sent by him into various quarters.

Turning now to the history of St. Paul as given in the book of Acts, we find that the writer is evidently present during the transactions of a large part of the history, as he uses the form *we* in his narrative. This expression first occurs in xvi. 10, 11, where Paul is in Troas (near the site of old Troy, at the N.W. corner of Asia Minor), and a vision appears to him entreating him to go over into Macedonia. Then the historian proceeds: "After he had seen the vision, immediately *we* endeavoured to go into Macedonia, assuredly gathering that the Lord had called us for to preach the Gospel unto them." It is generally supposed from this, that Luke first joined Paul and Silas at or near Troas, on this journey. The same form of expression, *we*, is continued till the 17th verse, when it vanishes for a while, to reappear in chap. xx. at the 5th verse, where it is said, "These, going before, tarried for *us* at Troas." It were a needless scruple, however, to doubt that Luke was with Paul and Silas, more or less, during their intervening journeys through Amphipolis, Apollonia, Thessalonica, Berea, Athens, Corinth and Cenchrea, the voyage thence to Ephesus and back again into Macedonia, till the embarkation from Philippi for Troas on the way to Jerusalem. Paul and Silas being the prominent actors in all these scenes, the narrator's word is usually *he* or *they*, except when he describes the journeying and voyaging from place to place, when he generally includes himself in the collective form *we*, but still without mentioning his own name. This form occurs sufficiently often throughout the rest of the book, to shew that the writer accompanied the apostle Paul to Jerusalem, and, never losing sight of him (so to speak) while he was imprisoned at Cæsarea, sailed with him in the same ship to Rome, where he appears to have stayed with him, as already attested by Paul's letters themselves, during the two years' imprisonment, with which event the book of Acts closes.

It has been made a question whether Luke was a native Jew, or a Jewish proselyte, or a Gentile, before his conversion to Christianity. Each of these views has been held. But he could hardly have been a mere Gentile convert, to have accompanied Paul to Jerusalem without scandal, when the fact of the apostle's having been seen with Trophimus, an Ephesian, in the city, raised a rumour against him of his having brought Greeks into the temple and polluted it (Acts xxi. 28, 29). And, on the other hand, Paul's mode of mentioning him to the Colossians, above quoted, seems to shew that he was not a native Jew at any rate; for it is after enumerating Aristarchus, Mark, and Jesus called Justus, as his only fellow-workers "of the circumcision" who have been a comfort to him in his bonds, that he adds the salutations of Luke and Demas. Taking the enumeration as rigidly as possible, and allowing nothing for an after-thought (which is, however, conceivable), this mention of Luke, separately from the Jewish fellow-workers, would be sufficiently explained by supposing him to have been a Gentile by birth, but a Jewish proselyte before his conversion to Christianity. We cannot, of course, tell when his conversion to Christianity took place; but had it been effected by Paul's preaching (as some have supposed), we should probably have had some allusion to it in the writings of the one or the other. Probably he was of much longer standing in the Christian church. His companionship with the great apostle of the Gentiles is, perhaps, enough to account for a certain manner observable in his Gospel,—from which some have argued that he was a Gentile till he became a Christian,—where he speaks of the Jews and their institutions as if not including him personally. Thus (Acts i. 19) he speaks of the field to bury strangers in, bought with Judas's desecrated money, as "called in *their* proper tongue Aceldama, or the field of blood," as if it was not his own native tongue too. But this kind of phrase is common to the other evangelists also, who all evidently look at the Gospel in its relation to the wide world of nations and kindreds and tongues and peoples, and often explain little Jewish specialties as if conscious that they were writing for a wider sphere of readers. (See Matt. xxviii. 15; Mark vii. 3; John v. 1.)

The name of *Lucius* (differing in the original from Luke or Lucas, just as much as the latter does from Lucius in English letters) occurs twice in the apostolical memoirs and letters, and is thought by some to belong, in one instance or in both, to our evangelist. But this is very doubtful; and so are some other opinions respecting St. Luke, which I shall mention as mere conjectures.

In Acts xiii. 1, Lucius of Cyrene is mentioned with Barnabas and other "prophets and teachers," at Antioch, in Syria, by whom Barnabas and Saul were designated, by fasting, prayer and laying-on of hands, to their first mission to the Gentiles. This seems to be the origin, so far as it is traceable in Scripture, of the common opinion that Luke was a native of Antioch, though it would strictly prove him merely a resident there, but native of Cyrene, in the north of Africa.

In Paul's letter to the Romans (xvi. 21), a Lucius sends his greetings, together with those of Jason and Sosipater; and the apostle calls all the three his "kinsmen." To the assumption that this Lucius is our evangelist, it is objected, that if Luke the historian had been thus akin to Paul, the fact would have been likely to transpire in his own history in the Acts. But his modest reserve respecting himself in that history, even when including himself with the principal actors as their fellow-traveller, in the terms *we* and *us*, might sufficiently explain his omission, whether to speak of his relationship to the apostle, or to identify himself with the Lucius of Cyrene, whom he names in the third person only. But these are mere possibilities and conjectures.

It has been a favourite idea with both ancient and modern commentators, that Luke is the person referred to by St. Paul in his second letter to the Corinthians

(viii. 18), when he says, "We have sent with him (with Titus) the brother *whose praise is in the Gospel* throughout all churches; and not that only, but who was also chosen of the churches to travel with us with this grace" (this gift to the church at Jerusalem). The apostle may allude to Luke, but we cannot be sure that he does. Some have supposed him to mean Barnabas, and some Mark; so intirely conjectural is the opinion. The idea of proving that Luke or Mark had already written his "Gospel," from the expression that his praise is *in the Gospel*, is very far-fetched, as the phrase is equally applicable to a spoken as to a written Gospel.

It has been imagined, again, that Luke was one of the Seventy disciples, whose mission, it is curious to observe, he alone of the four evangelists mentions. This, again, is mere conjecture (as it is in respect to St. Mark); and it is an improbable conjecture if we take Luke to be Lucius of Cyrene, resident at Antioch when first we hear of him, both places being remote from Galilee, where undoubtedly the Seventy dwelt.

It is also a tradition that Luke was one of the two disciples who met Jesus after his resurrection on the way to Emmaus,—an occurrence barely mentioned by Mark, and more particularly by Luke (xxiv. 13—), with many very interesting details of the interview. Luke tells us that the name of one of these disciples was Cleopas, but does not hint who the other was. If it was himself, his modest withdrawal of himself from notice in the Acts makes it likely that he should have omitted to obtrude his own name here. But this, again, is a mere conjecture.

We have found scriptural evidence of his being a physician. In the middle ages a tradition became prevalent to the effect that he was a painter; and portraits then existing of the Virgin were ascribed, in undoubting faith, to his pencil. But we must still distinguish between the few facts known respecting him, and the many fancies, conjectures and possibilities.

As to the time when Luke wrote his Gospel, opinions vary. Some make it earlier than Matthew's. Some make it the third in the order of composition, as of place in the canon. It is plausibly conjectured that he may have found leisure, as well as suggestion, to write it while Paul was a prisoner at Cæsarea before being sent to Rome; or that, during the two years of his residence at Rome with Paul, he may have written both it and the book of Acts. The former date would be A.D. 58—60; the latter, 61—63. There have been many traditions on this subject. A prevailing opinion (in which Lardner acquiesces) is that he wrote, or at least published, his Gospel and the Acts in Greece, where tradition says that he resided, after the expiration of Paul's first captivity at Rome, till his own death.

As to the qualifications possessed by Luke for writing a history of the ministry of Jesus Christ, it has been customary to dwell (not very appropriately or wisely) upon the fact of his being the companion of Paul. But Paul was not one of the original witnesses of the Gospel facts, except from a distance and as an uncompromising opponent; and whatever we may think of the nature of his supernatural communications with the risen Saviour, we shall not increase the credibility of Luke's Gospel by regarding his testimony to the facts of Christ's life as derived from Paul. As we have seen, Luke's own personal concern in those events as one of the Seventy, or as the companion of Cleopas, is a mere matter of presumption. But he plainly tells us himself, in the preface to his Gospel, the grounds on which he claims attention and credit to his statements; and these grounds are the reports of "eye-witnesses and ministers of the word."

"Forasmuch as many have taken in hand to set forth in order a declaration of those things which are most surely believed among us, even as they delivered them unto us, which from the beginning were eye-witnesses and ministers of the word; it seemed good to me also, having had perfect understanding of all things from the very first, to write unto thee in order, most excellent Theophilus, that thou mightest know the certainty of those things wherein thou hast been instructed" (Luke i. 1—4).

The allusion to the "many others" who have undertaken the same theme, has caused much fruitless discussion. Does Luke write his Gospel in order to discredit those writers and to correct their mistakes? Such appears to be the general impression among theologians, who agree that he cannot allude to any of the four Gospels, and seem disposed to infer that he must therefore allude to some absurd "apocryphal" productions or other, which he designs to discredit and supersede. Yet his tone is not that of disapproval when he says, "It seemed good to me also." He puts himself pretty much upon a level with those whom he speaks of, but seems to profess to do more systematically and completely (having had perfect understanding of all things from the very first) what they may have done in fragments. I have already implied this view of his meaning, as the most obvious at once and the most satisfactory. Luke's own acquaintance with the eye-witnesses of the Word was, no doubt, ample. Whether personally attendant upon any part of Christ's ministry or not, he was in Jerusalem with Paul when many of the apostles were there, and multitudes of other living witnesses were to be found in Galilee and other parts of Palestine.

We are naturally curious to know who this Theophilus was, who is distinguished by having one of the four Gospels and the book of Acts inscribed to him. The title "most excellent" (κράτιστε), though given to rulers, as by the hireling orator Tertullus to Felix ("most noble Felix," Acts xxiv. 3), was not a courtesy exclusively paid to them. Theophilus was, no doubt, a leading Christian in whatever neighbourhood Luke first published his Gospel; but we know nothing whatever of him personally. It is, however, a curious fact, which we have on the authority of Josephus, that a Jew of this name had been made high-priest by Vitellius, the Roman governor of Syria, about the time of the death of Tiberius (A.D. 37), and was deposed by Agrippa (the "king Agrippa" of Acts xxv.), whom Claudius reinstated in the dignity of king, and who gave the priesthood to a brother of his own wife. Some have imagined that this Theophilus may have become a Christian, and been the person to whom Luke dedicated his histories. But such conjectures are an amusement rather for curious thought, than materials of religious knowledge.

Let us now proceed to an analysis of Luke's Gospel. It contains some highly valuable additions to the contents of the others, principally from the tenth to the eighteenth chapters, or thereabouts, which are introduced in a very curious manner. These additions consist, first, of the mission of the Seventy, and then of a multitude of parables and discourses of Christ (few of which are in the other Gospels), given by Luke without any distinct marks of time or place, and with very few incidents interspersed. Among the parables and discourses thus specially preserved by Luke, are those of the Rich Man enlarging his barns and laying up goods for many years; the Barren Fig-tree allowed to stand another year; the Neglected Invitation; the Returning Prodigal; the Unjust Steward; the Rich Man and Lazarus; the Unjust Judge; and the Pharisee and Publican. This enumeration is sufficient to intitle Luke to the gratitude of Christendom. The manner in which these additions are introduced is remarkable, and is very puzzling to such critics as insist upon the exact *when* and *where* and *how* of everything recorded. They occur after the announcement (ix. 51) that Jesus, "the time having come for his being received up, steadfastly set his face to go up to Jerusalem." This was his last journey thither, and lay through the Perea, as narrated by the other evangelists, the Samaritans not allowing him to pass through their land (ix. 53). Then, in xvii. 11, he appears to be still only setting off "through the midst (that is, along the common borders) of Samaria and Galilee;" and, in ch. xviii., he passes through Jericho, as in the other Gospels. Critics have endeavoured to find a reason for this arrangement—presuming it to be a deliberate arrangement, though plainly not a chronological one—by supposing that the mission of the Seventy was to the Perea, and that Luke afterwards collected in that neighbourhood, from various survivors of these Seventy, the materials here introduced into his Gospel, some of them being indeed common to the other Gospels, but most of them peculiar to his; and that he introduced them in the mass, as he had gathered them, without attempting the hopeless task of assigning them to their respective times and places. Whether such a critical theory be deemed satisfactory or not, the chapters in question (known to critics as Luke's *Gnomology)* must be regarded as partaking the character of anecdote rather than of connected history. They are invaluable in their contents; and, as regards some of them especially, our great surprise is to find that they are preserved in only one of the evangelists. Perhaps the truest reflection would be to the effect, that in all probability a great multitude of equally striking sayings and doings of Christ are lost to history, after all that the four evangelists have jointly and severally preserved; so as to justify, to oriental taste at least, the bold hyperbole with which John's Gospel ends: "And there are also many other things which Jesus did; the which, if they should be written every one, I suppose that even the world itself could not contain the books that should be written."

Abstract of Luke's Gospel.

[The passages inclosed thus, in *square* brackets, have their parallel passages in Mark.]

(Those inclosed thus, in *round* brackets, have parallels in Matthew.)

[(Those inclosed thus, in *both brackets*, have parallels in both Mark and Matthew.)]

Those peculiar to Luke are without brackets. Italics, as before, draw attention to intimations of *time* and *place*. The order of events in Luke's Gospel differs very much from both the others.

Ch. i. 1. Introduction, and dedication to Theophilus. 5. Angelic announcement of the coming birth of John the Baptist, to his father Zacharias officiating at *Jerusalem*. 26. Similar announcement of the coming birth of Jesus, to his mother Mary, in *Nazareth*. 39. Mary visits Elizabeth in the hill-country of *Judah*. Poetical salutation by Elizabeth. 46. Mary's song, finely expressive of the Jewish idea of a temporal deliverer. 57. Birth and naming of John. Zacharias "prophesies" the current Hebrew hope.

Ch. ii. 1. Census ordered by the emperor Augustus.* (Joseph goes to *Bethlehem* to be registered, being of the lineage of David, taking Mary with him, and the child is born there). Announcement to the shepherds, and their visit to *Bethlehem*. 21. The child is named Jesus. 22. The mother's

* This census or registration seems to have been ordered by Augustus on occasion of Herod's death, while he was undecided how to dispose of Judea. It was suspended, apparently, when he determined to make Archelaus tetrarch, and resumed on the deposition of the latter ten years afterwards, Cyrenius being then prefect of Syria.

purification according to the Law. 25. Simeon's song of thanksgiving, and Anna's prophesying to those who "looked for redemption in Jerusalem." 41. The *passover*, when Jesus was *twelve* years old, the time at which boys might first partake.

[(Ch. iii. 1. Ministry of John the Baptist, very carefully dated by Luke in the *15th year of the Emperor Tiberius.** 21. Baptism of Jesus.)] (23. Genealogy of Joseph, irreconcilably varying from that given by Matthew.†)

* A.D. 29, according to the common chronology; but it is generally understood that the birth of Jesus was one, two, or perhaps three years earlier than the received era.

† The same kind of difficulties, if not absolutely in the same degree, beset the introductory chapters of Luke's Gospel, as the corresponding parts of Matthew's; and they must be honestly acknowledged here, as in the other instance, and the same general principles of explanation must be applied.

It has indeed been thought that Luke's account of the birth of Christ does not necessarily imply that it was miraculous in a sense inconsistent with his genealogical descent as traced through Joseph from David; and we are reminded that the birth of John the Baptist is here described as, in another sense, miraculous also. But, while the phraseology of Matthew is certainly more explicit on this point, that of Luke can hardly be said to imply less. Referring to what I have before said on Matthew's history of the birth of Jesus, for the true estimate of the lower degree of credibility necessarily attaching to these parts of a biography, the real interest of which began to be felt thirty years later, I would now observe that the introduction here supplied by Luke is, under that modified view of its credibility, highly interesting and beautifully poetical. The intercourse of the cousins, the destined mothers of the Messiah's forerunner and of the Messiah himself, is finely imagined; and the angelic announcements to them, as also the "prophesyings" of Zacharias, Simeon and Anna, precisely represent, and in vivid colours too, the temporal hope of the Jewish nation in reference to their expected Prince. Read as illustrations of this attitude of the Jewish mind—which was its attitude of expectant desire for centuries—they are intensely interesting and beautiful. Nor is it difficult to conceive the process through which these traditions might grow in minds half believing that Jesus was the Christ, but not relinquishing their hope of a temporal Messiah, and trusting, even after his death, that he would come again and fulfil their idea. So long as the temple stood, Judaism was unrepealed, and its abolition was a thought incredible to the mind of many a Jewish Christian. The birth and infancy of the Baptist and the Christ were retrospectively imagined from this point of view; while the facts of their mature manhood, in their respective public ministries, were too unyieldingly impressed upon the memories of living men, and written even upon the world's great events,

[(Ch. iv. 1. Temptation of Jesus, as fully as in Matthew. 14. He teaches in the synagogues of *Galilee*. 16. Is rejected at *Nazareth*, Luke's account of the scene in the synagogue of Nazareth being the fullest, and placed *earlier* than by the others.)] [30. At *Capernaum* his word was with power. Man in the synagogue with unclean spirit cured.] [(38. Cure of Simon's mother-in-law and many more.)] [42. Retirement to a desert place.]

Ch. v. 1. Miraculous draught of fishes in Simon's boat on the *Lake of Galilee*. [(10. Call of Simon and Andrew, James and John. 12. Cure of the leper. 17. Cure of the palsy. 27. Call of Levi. 29. Feast in Levi's house. 30. Murmuring of the Pharisees about "publicans and sinners." 33. Question of fasting.)]

[(Ch. vi. 1. Plucking the corn on the sabbath. 6. Withered hand healed in the synagogue. 12. The twelve apostles chosen on a hill.)] (17. The "Sermon on the Mount," much abbreviated, as compared with Matthew's account, and stated by Luke to have been spoken by Jesus on his coming down from the mountain and standing on the plain. Luke has preserved various other scattered portions of this discourse in his "Gnomology.")

(Ch. vii. 1. Centurion's servant cured at *Capernaum*.) 11. Raising of the widow's son at *Nain*. (18. John the Baptist's message. Christ's reply and his testimony to John.) 36. The woman that had been a sinner* anoints the feet of Jesus as he reclines at meat in the house of Simon the Pharisee.

[(Ch. viii. 4. Parable of the Sower. 16. Of the Lamp set on a stand. 19. His mother and brethren are anxious about

to allow of their being similarly represented. Hence we have, in Luke's Gospel, a Jewish Messiah's imaginary infancy prefixed to the authentic memoirs of the World's Christ in his manhood and public ministry.

* By one of those popular fallacies which seemingly, through having no foundation in fact, are the more adhesive in the idea, this woman is generally confounded with Mary of Magdala, who was no sinner, but a great sufferer, "out of whom had gone seven demons." (See Luke viii. 2.) Christ had cured her of a disordered mind. This other woman, apparently, he had won back from sin, and she here shews her gratitude. The popular meaning of *Magdalen* is a foul libel upon the scriptural person so named.

Jesus. 22. Crossing the lake, he stills the storm. 26. Cures the fierce demoniac in *Gadara*, and returns to the Galilean side. 41. Jairus's daughter. 43. The woman cured on the way.)]

[(Ch. ix. 1. Jesus sends out the twelve apostles. Luke's account is very brief, and he has in his Gnomology, ch. xii. 2—12, many sayings that are given by Matthew in the charge to the apostles. 7. Herod's alarm at Christ's miracles, thinking that John the Baptist was risen. 10. The return of the Twelve, and miracle of the Five thousand near *Bethsaida*. 18. What men were saying about Jesus. He announces his destined death, and bids his followers expect persecution. 28. The transfiguration *eight days after*. 37. The *next day*, cure of the dumb demoniac. 46. Debate who should be greatest in the Messiah's kingdom.)]

Ch. ix. 51. The "Gnomology" begins :*

Jesus, "steadfastly setting his face *to go up to Jerusalem*," sends messengers before him, who are repulsed in a *Samaritan* village. James and John—called Boanerges by their gentle Lord, probably, on this occasion—would have called down fire from heaven. (57. Jesus discourages lukewarm followers.)

Ch. x. The Seventy disciples are sent forth "two and two before his face into every city and place whither he himself would come." (His instructions to them are in part reported by Matthew, in chapters x. and xi., as spoken on quite a different occasion.) 17. The Seventy return to him. 25. The parable of the Good Samaritan, in reply to the lawyer's question. 38. Christ at *Bethany* in Martha's house,—perhaps when attending the feast of the dedication of the temple in November or December, if order is at all preserved in this Gnomology.

Ch. xi. 1. The Lord's Prayer dictated on the request of one

* I know not who first gave this name to these chapters of Luke's Gospel, a name literally meaning *sententious instruction*, and not more specially applicable to this part than to many others of the Gospel history. It might be more correctly described as *Anecdotes*, or *Memorabilia* in the Xenophontean sense, being somewhat miscellaneous and regardless of chronological sequence, while certainly containing many of the most weighty and sententious of our Lord's instructions.

of the disciples, and precepts how to pray added. (Matthew gives it in the Sermon on the Mount, somewhat varied in words, and the accompanying instructions with similar variations.) [(14. Cure of a dumb demoniac. Christ confutes those who say he casts out demons by Beelzebub.)] (29. The evil generation rebuked for seeking a sign. Son of Man to be a sign like Jonah. 33. Light and darkness,—passages from Sermon on the Mount.) 37. Jesus dines with a Pharisee, and discourses of inward and outward cleanliness. [(42. Some passages are similar to the "woes" to the Pharisees in Matthew xxiii. and Mark xii., as spoken at Jerusalem.)]

Ch. xii. 1. Cautions against hypocrisy (some verses like parts of Christ's counsels to the Twelve in Matt. x.). 13. Against covetousness: parable of the Rich man laying up "much goods for many years." (22. Precepts against anxiety, like Sermon on the Mount, Matt. vi. 25—34. 35. To be ready for the Lord's coming; some verses like Matt. xxiv. 43, 44, and 45—51.) 49. Jesus foretels divisions respecting himself. Ch. xiii. 1. That calamities are not necessarily judgments, as in the case of Pilate's cruelty and the falling of the tower of Siloam. 6. Parable of the Barren fig-tree spared another year. 10. The infirm woman in the synagogue healed on the sabbath. (18. Parables of the Mustard-seed and the Leaven, as in Matt. xiii.) 22. Christ is "*journeying toward Jerusalem.*" 23. Answers the inquiry, Are there few that be saved? chiefly in phrases occurring also in the Sermon on the Mount. 31. Christ is told of Herod's designs against him. 34. Laments for Jerusalem (as on the spot in Matthew xxiii.).

Ch. xiv. 1. Eats bread with a chief Pharisee on the sabbath, and heals the dropsical man. 7. Comments on the struggle for chief places at table. 12. Suggests to his host to entertain those who cannot recompense him. 15. Parable of the slighted Invitation, and its extension to wayfarers and the poor. 25. Great multitudes following, Christ bids them count the cost.

Ch. xv. 1. Parable of the Lost sheep (the germ of which is in Matt. xviii. 12); 8. The Lost money; 11. The Prodigal son.

Ch. xvi. 1. Parable, to his disciples, of the Unjust steward. 14. The Pharisees interpose. 19. Parable of the Rich man and Lazarus.

[(Ch. xvii. 1. Causes of offence must be. 3. Precept of mutual forgiveness.)] 5. The best servants of God can do no more than their duty. GNOMOLOGY PERHAPS ENDS HERE. 11. As he went to Jerusalem, he passed *between Samaria and Galilee.* Cure of the ten lepers. 20. Pharisees ask when the kingdom of God will come. Christ's reply is in part similar to his prediction of the destruction of Jerusalem nearer the end of the Gospels.

Ch. xviii. Parable of the Unjust judge, to the end that men ought to pray continually; 9. Of the Pharisee and Publican, spoken to "certain who trusted in themselves that they were righteous and despised others." SOME MAKE GNOMOLOGY END HERE. [(15. Christ blesses infants. 18. Tells the young ruler how he may inherit eternal life. 31. Speaks to the Twelve, *while going up to Jerusalem*, of his approaching death, and "they understood none of these things." 35. Approaching Jericho, he gives sight to a blind man.*)]

Ch. xix. 1. *At Jericho*, in the house of Zaccheus. 11. Parable of the Ten pounds, to correct the idea "that the kingdom of God would immediately appear." (Compare the parable of the Talents in Matt. xxv.) [(28. At *Bethany* and *Bethphage.* Public entry into *Jerusalem.* Cleansing of the temple.)]

[(Ch. xx. 1. Priests and scribes demand his authority. 9. Parable of the Vineyard and the unfaithful husbandmen. 19. The priests and scribes plot against him. 22. Question of paying tribute to Cæsar. 27. The Sadducees' question of the resurrection, &c. 45. Jesus warns the people against the scribes, less fully than in Matthew.)]

[Ch. xxi. 1. The widow's mites.] [(5. Prophecy of the destruction of Jerusalem and the temple, to take place before "this generation" shall pass away.)]

[(Ch. xxii. 1. The passover. Judas bargains with the priests. Institution of the Lord's Supper.)] 24. Strife among the apostles, which should be greatest. 31. Warning to Peter. [(39. Jesus goes to the Mount of Olives. 47. The betrayal and

* Matthew and Mark say it was in *leaving* Jericho; and Matthew says there were two blind men. Mark says one, and gives the name, Bartimæus. Such circumstantial differences attend essential historical truth; but they defy the theory of writing by Divine inspiration.

attempted rescue. 54. Peter's denial. 66. Examination before the Sanhedrim, very briefly given by Luke.)]

[(Ch. xxiii. 1. Trial before Pilate.)] 7. Pilate sends Jesus to Herod, and the two rulers "are made friends." [(13. The trial resumed. 24. The condemnation.)] 27. Christ bids the women who follow him weep not for him, but for themselves and their children. [(33. The crucifixion.)] 39. The penitent thief on the cross. [(50. The burial.)]

[(Ch. xxiv. 1. The resurrection.)] [13. Jesus appears to Cleopas and another on the way to Emmaus, and "expounds to them in all the Scriptures the things concerning himself,"—very briefly mentioned by Mark. 36. He appears to the eleven at Jerusalem, and eats with them.] 44. "He opens their understanding, that they might understand the Scriptures,"—leads them out to Bethany, and there, while blessing them, ["was parted from them and carried up into heaven."]

THE GOSPEL ACCORDING TO JOHN.

THE fourth Gospel is peculiarly interesting and valuable, whether we consider its contents or its author. It is not a repetition of the other Gospels, but consists almost intirely of additional materials, which have been preserved by the favourite apostle and intimate friend of Christ, "the disciple whom he loved."

John was the younger brother of James. Their father Zebedee was a fisherman on the Lake of Galilee,—of comfortable condition, apparently, in his way of life, employing hired servants (Mark i. 20) to help him and his sons. Occasionally, if not constantly, they fished in partnership with Simon and Andrew (Luke v. 7 and 10). The mother's name was Salome; and she is mentioned among the Galilean women who "ministered to Jesus" of their substance, and also as coming to his tomb to anoint his corpse (Matt. xxvii. 56; Luke viii. 3; Mark

xv. 40, xvi. 1). Some ecclesiastical traditions make her to have been the daughter of Joseph of Nazareth by his first marriage, and thus half-sister to Jesus ; but there is not a trace of any such relationship in the Scriptures.

John is believed to have been a disciple of John the Baptist before he was called to the apostleship. This is a natural inference from his own narrative (i. 35—40), where Andrew is named as one of two disciples of the Baptist, and the writer is supposed to be the other. Not unlikely the two pairs of brothers, Andrew and Simon, James and John, were all disciples of the Baptist and expectants of the kingdom of heaven. It is remarked that our evangelist always names him simply as *John*, without adding the designation *Baptist;* which the other evangelists usually add, by way of distinguishing him from this apostle, while the apostle never thinks of being confounded with so celebrated a man as his former master. A delicate but reliable hint of such having been their relationship!

The brothers, James and John, and the other two, Peter and Andrew (though Andrew is not so uniformly mentioned as Peter), were evidently admitted to a more intimate and confidential intercourse with our Saviour than the rest of his disciples. The three alone were with him at that early miracle of the raising of Jairus's daughter; they alone were with him on the Mount of transfiguration, and in the Garden of his agony. Of each pair of brothers, one is more prominent than the other. Peter's energy quite throws Andrew into the shade, and John's affection is more attractive even than James's heroic martyrdom.

The request of James and John, seconded by their mother, that they might sit one on the right and the other on the left hand of Jesus in his kingdom (Matt. xx. 20—), seems to shew them somewhat presuming upon this intimacy, while deeply imbued with the Jewish notion of a temporal Christ. And their suggestion, on another occasion, to call down fire from heaven upon the Samaritans (Luke ix. 54), betrays a hasty zeal little in accordance with the mature character of John as estimated from his writings. Probably it was on this latter occasion, or in reference to it (as already observed), that our Lord reprovingly designated these two brothers *Boanerges* (sons of thunder), though theologians are not wanting who make it a term of praise applicable to their distinguished eloquence, reminding us how it was said of Pericles that "he thundered, lightened, and threw all Greece into confusion."* This designation is only mentioned once, namely, in Mark's list of the apostles (iii. 17), and does not seem to have been cherished by themselves or others, as a surname of pleasant association might have been.

John is personally known to us through his writings, rather than through numerous biographical incidents and actions. These latter are not abundant, either within or beyond the scriptural period.

It is allowed on all hands that he was young when attendant upon Jesus; that he was the youngest of all the apostles, and possibly the only one younger than our Lord himself. In West's immortal picture of "Christ Rejected," John is presented to the sight, as he most naturally occurs to the thought, with a countenance of almost feminine sweetness and tenderness, the eye beaming with intelligence, yet melting with affection. His personal qualities, joined with his youth and devotedness, must have earned for him the pre-eminent place in his Master's regard which he plainly held. His simple-hearted use of the phrase, "disciple whom Jesus loved," as a modest synonym for his own name, shews how fully

* Aristoph. Achar. 531.

and unenvyingly it must have been yielded to him. The facts which prove him to have held this high place in his Lord's regard, are, first, his reclining at the paschal table in the place of honour, next to the Master of the feast ("lying on his bosom" denotes precisely this, the head of each person being near the breast of the one next above him); and, secondly and most decisively, his receiving as his Master's dying bequest the care of his widowed mother. "Behold thy son," "Behold thy mother," was all that needed to be said; "and from that hour that disciple took her to his own home." Probably John was the "other disciple"* whose name he does not mention (xviii. 15), who accompanied Peter into the high-priest's palace to watch the proceedings, when their Master was apprehended. He alone, of all the twelve, had fortitude to follow him thence to the crucifixion.

After the death and resurrection of his Master, John is prominent in exertion and danger as the companion of Peter (Acts iii. iv. v.); and, after the martyrdom of Stephen, he is sent with Peter, on behalf of the apostles, to Samaria (viii. 14), to confirm the work which had been begun by the deacon Philip in that city. It is generally believed that John, on his return thence, stayed in Jerusalem or the neighbourhood as long as the mother of Jesus lived, which, according to Eusebius, was till about A.D. 48, or eighteen years after the crucifixion. He was still at Jerusalem fourteen years after Paul's conversion, that is A.D. 50, as appears from Gal. ii. 1—9; but all trace of his being there after that time vanishes. Ephesus is his next ascertained abode; but he does not seem to have been there during the period to which the

* How that other disciple "was known unto the high-priest," it is quite useless to conjecture. Some think it may not have been John, but Judas, who was indeed too well known, at least to the high-priest's attendants; but it is not likely that Peter would have availed himself of *his* introduction, nor that Judas would have had the hardihood to be there himself.

book of Acts and Paul's Epistles belong, as he is never mentioned, though Ephesus is often the scene referred to, both in the history and by letter. He may have been in other parts of Asia Minor, perhaps founding some of the seven churches referred to in the *Revelation;* but he can hardly have fixed his residence at Ephesus till after the deaths of Paul and Peter, A.D. 65. It is the uniform tradition of antiquity, that he spent many years, in the latter part of his life, in that city; that he was banished to Patmos, a small island in the Ægean, by the emperor Domitian (one writer, indeed, says by Claudius,* but this seems quite a mistake); and that, on the tyrant's death, he returned to Ephesus, and died there at a very advanced age. Domitian died A.D. 96; and the date of John's death is believed to be 100 or 101. Eusebius puts it in the reign of Trajan, which began A.D. 98. His probable age at the time of his death depends upon our impression of his age when he first attended our Lord. If he was ten or twelve years younger than Jesus, attaching himself to his Master at seventeen or eighteen years of age, this would make him close upon ninety when he died. He is generally supposed, however, to have been twenty-four or twenty-five when he was called by Jesus, and to have lived to ninety-five or ninety-six; while some will have him to have been about the same age as Jesus, and to have lived to be upwards of a hundred years old. He seems to have been the only one of our Lord's apostles who survived the destruction of Jerusalem by Titus, A.D. 70; and he has preserved the remarkable prediction of Jesus to the effect that he should survive till that "coming" of his Lord. (See John xxi. 20—24.)

* Claudius made a decree banishing the Jews from Rome, A.D. 51 (Acts xviii. 2); but this would not have induced a Christian apostle, if residing at Ephesus, to exile himself to Patmos.

The questions when and where John wrote his Gospel, can only be answered proximately. Opinions vary as to whether he wrote it before, or after, the destruction of Jerusalem. It is observable that he has not recorded our Lord's prophecy of that event; so that the argument by which we infer the other Gospels to have been previously written (from a certain confusedness in their records of that prophecy), has no place as regards John's Gospel. Yet, if he was acquainted with the other Gospels (as is generally supposed), and wrote after the destruction of Jerusalem, we might perhaps wonder at his not noticing the prophecy for the sake of pointing to its fulfilment. And it is further observed that he speaks of Jerusalem as still apparently unchanged: "There *is* at Jerusalem, by the sheep-market, a pool," &c. (v. 2). It has been thought that the manner in which John has recorded Christ's prophecy of Peter's death (xxi. 18, 19), without stating that his death had occurred, must date the composition before that event, namely, before A.D. 67; but this is a doubtful argument, for the 19th verse would have been highly appropriate if Peter's death was notorious when John wrote: "This spake he, signifying by what death he should glorify God." Lardner thinks John may have written his Gospel about A.D. 68. It is generally admitted that John had seen the other Gospels, or one at least of them. The remarkable diversity between his Gospel and all the rest, his omission of almost all that they have recorded, and his recording almost exclusively things which they have omitted, seems to prove design on his part with reference to what they had already done.

This difference between the contents of John's Gospel and all the rest did not escape the notice of the ancients, though they have not described it with perfect exactness. Eusebius writes thus: "The three first written Gospels being now delivered to all men, and to John himself, it is said that he approved them and confirmed the truth of their narration by his own testimony, saying that there was only wanting a written account of the things done by Christ in the former part and the beginning of his preaching. And certainly that observation is very true. For it is easy to perceive that the other three evangelists have recorded only the actions of our Saviour for one year after the imprisonment of John," &c. (See Lardner, IV. 225.) Now this is a very imperfect account of the object of John's Gospel, as judged by the execution. It is true that he has supplied some incidents prior to John the Baptist's imprisonment. But it is not true (as implied) that the other Gospels begin from that period, nor that his ceases with it. As far as ch. x. 21 of John's Gospel seems to belong to this earlier period; and all the rest belongs to the last four or five months of our Lord's life, namely, from the feast of Dedication in the end of November or December, to the Passover at the Easter following.

If we were to describe the most palpable difference between the contents of John's Gospel and those of the other three, it would be by saying, that they record chiefly our Lord's doings in Galilee and the neighbourhood, and he chiefly those which occurred at Jerusalem at the annual feasts. From the first three evangelists we should not know that our Lord had taught in Jerusalem at all, except at the passover at which he was crucified. From John, on the other hand, we might suppose him generally there, except at "the beginning of his miracles in Cana of Galilee" (ii. 1—11), and on a second visit when he passed through Samaria, and healed the nobleman's son at Capernaum (ch. iv.), and when (perhaps the same period) he fed the 5000 in the wilderness beyond the Lake of Galilee, as recorded by John in his sixth chapter to have occurred when Jesus "would not walk in Jewry because the Jews sought to kill him." This difference of materials is perfectly intelligible if we suppose that, until the last passover, our Lord was not accompanied by more than a few of his apostles in his journeys to Jerusalem, and that Matthew was not of the number, but that John always was. Nothing more natural and simple. In the accounts of his earlier visits to Jerusalem, disciples are seldom named as accompanying Jesus, and then not in a way to mark them as apostles. And there are repeated indications of a studied quietness and unostentatiousness of demeanour on the part of our Lord on these occasions; as also of the need of such caution, to avoid exciting an enthusiasm which his spiritual Messiahship could not satisfy. To the feast of Tabernacles, we read that he "went up not openly, but as it were in secret" (vii. 10; see also xi. 54, 56). Assuming that John was his companion on all these occasions, and no other apostle uniformly nor often, we see at once how the occurrences at Jerusalem would be the principal addition he had it in his power to make, and the most important possible addition to his Master's memoirs as hitherto written. The festivals which St. John thus records are, in the words of Dr. Carpenter, "a previous Passover, a festival which we have reason to regard as the Pentecost, a feast of Tabernacles and a feast of Dedication. If the ministry of Christ included only two passovers, then he has recorded transactions at every festival." (Harmony, Introd. p. xxxii.)

In recording these transactions, John is particularly careful to note every demonstration made by our Lord of his claims to the character of the Messiah, and every encounter in which he engaged with the Jewish priests and rulers on the subject of his claims. And in these and all other incidents, he gives at full length and with all the verbal exactness that a young and affectionate memory could ensure, the various discourses of his Master and his conversations with his insidious foes. These conversations and discourses cannot, of course, be taken to be *verbatim* and *literatim* as our Lord spoke them. They are too long for the exactest memory to have retained from once hearing; but their substance was in each case so marked, and their course of thought or argument so clear and consecutive, that we need not hesitate to feel ourselves *practically* possessed of the words of Jesus, especially as John has retained the first personal form in reporting them.

John's own avowal of his purpose in writing his Gospel quite agrees with these its observable characteristics. "These are written," he says near the end (xx. 31), "that ye might believe that Jesus is the Christ, the Son of God; and that believing, ye might have life through his name." To prove that Jesus is "the Christ, the Son of God," was the purpose, doubtless, of each of his biographers. The first three had traced his heaven-guided course, as he taught and wrought miracles in Galilee, Phœnicia, the Decapolis and Peræa, and in his last and fatal visit to Jerusalem; John was able to narrate his former visits also, which had taken place more privately, yet always conspicuously enough for a strong interest to centre upon him and strong enmity to threaten him. While the others had narrated his encounters with Priests and Pharisees who came from Jerusalem into the provinces, John could disclose the progress of events and reasonings in the capital itself, from which those artful deputations successively emanated, and could thus complete the detail of wonderful works and words which declared his beloved Master to be the Christ of the world.

John gives especial prominence to every declaration

of Jesus in which he avows his divine authority and, whether more or less plainly, his character of Messiah. Our Lord's reserve as to the verbal use of this title is indeed marked enough even in what this Gospel records; but John seems carefully to preserve every expression in which Jesus sets forth his divine commission, and never loses sight of his own declared theme, that Jesus is "the Christ, the Son of God," through whose name the believer "might have life."

The same clear and emphatic purpose is evident in the opening of John's Gospel; than which nothing can be more appropriate or forcible, if considered as bearing upon the apostle's expressed design. That celebrated and much controverted Proem begins with tracing the commission and the powers of Jesus to their divine source. While two of the other evangelists have preserved certain dubious, difficult and self-contradictory traditions of a miraculous bodily birth, John has simply and most emphatically declared the divinity of those *spiritual gifts* which constituted Jesus *the Christ*. We have already noticed (Vol. I. p. 373) the fine personifications of the divine *Wisdom* in the book of Proverbs, and (II. 24—27) the yet more remarkable representation common among the Jews shortly before the Christian era, both of the divine *Wisdom* and of the divine *Word*. It is further to be observed, in illustration of the meaning of this latter phrase, that the Jewish Targums, or Paraphrases on the Jewish Scriptures (the oldest of which seem to have been written not long before or not long after the time of Christ), continually use the expression *the Word of God*, where the original has the Sacred Name simply. Thus in paraphrasing the verse, "Moses brought forth the people out of the camp to meet with God" (Ex. xix. 17), the Targum expresses it, "Moses brought forth the people to meet with the

Word of God." And (Job xlii. 9), "Jehovah accepted Job," is expressed in the Targum, "The *Word of Jehovah* accepted Job." This phrase is continually used in this manner by these writers, instead of the simple name, God or Jehovah, where it is impossible to see any reason or propriety in the usage, except that it had become the habitual Jewish phrase to denote the acts and manifestations of the Supreme Being. Perhaps it bespoke a feeling of reverence for the Sacred Name, like that which induces the Jews to this day, when they read their Scriptures aloud, to substitute *Lord* for *Jehovah.* A scruple imitated, by the by, in our Common Version, beyond the Jewish superstition (if such we call it), where LORD is printed instead of Jehovah, and not merely substituted in reading. (See Lardner's Works, VI. 215—217.)

By the *Word*, then, or the *Word of God*, or the *Word of Jehovah*, the Jews of the times of the Apocrypha and of the time of Christ, sufficiently understood to be meant the Divine attributes, or will, or agency; and by tracing up the mission of Jesus to the Word of God as its source, St. John, in effect, declares at the very outset the same theme which he tells us at the close he has endeavoured to illustrate, namely, "that Jesus is the Christ, the Son of God." Any subtle metaphysical refining upon the nature of the Logos, or Word, seems out of place, when we remember that those to whom our Lord spoke of himself, and to whom John wrote of him, under this title, had a fixed meaning already attached to it. Our evangelist uses language so similar at the beginning of his first Epistle, that it is inevitable to bring the two passages side by side, for comparison and mutual explanation. They run thus:

Proem to the Gospel of John: "In the beginning was the Word; and the Word was with God, and the Word was God. The same was in the beginning with God. All things were made (or done) by him (or it), and without him (or it) was not anything made that was made. In him (it) was life, and the life was the light of men. * * * And the Word was made flesh."

Proem to the first Epistle of John: "That which was from the beginning, which we have heard, which we have seen with our eyes, which we have looked upon, and our hands have handled, of the Word of Life (for the Life was manifested, and we have seen it, and bear witness, and shew unto you that eternal Life which was with the Father, and was manifested unto us); that which we have seen and heard declare we unto you."

We cannot but notice the parallel and often identical phrases in these two introductions:

In the Gospel there are these:	*In the Epistle* these:
In the beginning.	From the beginning.
The Word.	The Word of Life.
The Word was with God.	The Life was with the Father.
The Word was made flesh.	The Life was manifested.
The Life was the light of men.	We have seen it (the Life).

And it is particularly observable that having, in the Epistle, called the divine Word the *Word of Life*, the apostle thenceforth speaks of *the Life* just as he does of *the Word* in the proem to the Gospel. In each case he evidently speaks of *all that was supernatural* in the personal endowments of Jesus, *all that constituted him the Christ* or Messiah, the beloved Son of God. Dr. Lardner writes as follows:

"What St. John says in the introduction, appears to me agreeable to the main design of his Gospel. He therein shews, that Jesus came and acted by the authority of God, the Creator of the world, the God and Supreme Lawgiver of the Jewish people. The eternal word, reason, wisdom, power of God, which is God himself, by which the world had been made, by which he dwelled among the Jews in the tabernacle and the temple, dwelled and resided in Jesus in the fullest manner; so that we, his disciples, and others who believed in him, saw and clearly discerned him to be the promised Messiah, the great prophet that should come into the world." (Hist. Ap. and Evang., Works, Vol. VI. p. 213.)

It seems quite needless to seek explanation of the special aim of John's Gospel (where many learned men have sought it) in the supposed prevalence of various heresies in the apostolical church, and John's supposed desire to discountenance them. A very undignified view of the evangelist's office would this be. He vindicates for himself a far higher aim in his own statement of his object, as being to prove "that Jesus is the Christ, the Son of God." He has stated his Master's claims; by which the doctrines of orthodox and heterodox alike must be tried.

There is a peculiarity in the style of John's Gospel which can hardly fail of striking an intelligent reader; namely, his frequent use of *explanatory parentheses.* They seem usually to arise out of his desire to give precise and full information, and to preclude misapprehension. When they occur in narrative, they can have only this effect; but when they occur in the midst of a discourse of the Saviour's, it is sometimes difficult to separate the words of Jesus from the comment of the evangelist. Thus, in the conversation with Nicodemus (ch. iii.), there are several evident parentheses inserted by the evangelist; and there are also other passages respecting which it is difficult to decide whether they are the words of Jesus speaking, or of John recording and explaining. I mark the former thus, (   ); the latter thus, [   ]:

"Jesus answered and said unto him, Art thou a master of Israel, and knowest not these things? Verily, verily, I say unto thee, [We speak that we do know, and testify that we have seen; and ye receive not our witness.] If I have told you earthly things, and ye believe not, how shall ye believe, if I tell you of heavenly things? And no man hath ascended up to heaven, but he that came down from heaven, (even the Son of Man which is in heaven.) And as Moses lifted up the serpent in the wilderness, even so must the Son of Man be lifted up: that whosoever believeth in him should not perish, but have eternal life. For God so loved the world, that he gave his only begotten Son, that whosoever believeth in him should not perish, but have everlasting life. For God sent not his Son into the world to condemn the world; but that the world through him might be saved. [He that believeth on him is not condemned: but he that believeth not is condemned already, because he hath not believed in the name of the only begotten Son of God.] And this is the condemnation, that light is come into the world, and men loved darkness rather than light, because their deeds were evil. [For every one that doeth evil hateth the light, neither cometh to the light, lest his deeds should be reproved. But he that doeth truth cometh to the light, that his deeds may be made manifest, that they are wrought in God"] (iii. 10—21).

Again, in the latter part of this chapter, the words of John the Baptist probably end at ver. 30, "He must increase, but I must decrease;" and the rest are probably the words of the evangelist. Yet some part at least might be included in the testimony of John the Baptist; and different readers will perhaps divide the passage differently between the Baptist and the historian.

In the first nine verses of the next chapter there are three passages marked as parentheses in the Common Version, the last of which may possibly be taken by some to be a parenthetical remark of Christ's, but is much better understood as the explanatory remark of John, and is an instance of the kind of ambiguity elsewhere found in the discourses of Jesus as recorded by

John. The three passages now alluded to are marked below in round brackets ( ) as in the Common Version; and there are other sentences also illustrative of the careful and circumstantial character of John's narrative which I distinguish by the square brackets [ ].

"When therefore the Lord knew how the Pharisees had heard that Jesus made and baptized more disciples than John (though Jesus himself baptized not, but his disciples), he left Judea, and departed again into Galilee. [And he must needs go through Samaria.] Then cometh he to a city of Samaria, which is called Sychar, [near to the parcel of ground that Jacob gave to his son Joseph.] Now Jacob's well was there. Jesus therefore, being wearied with his journey, sat thus on the well: [and it was about the sixth hour.] There cometh a woman of Samaria to draw water: Jesus saith unto her, Give me to drink. (For his disciples were gone away unto the city to buy meat.) Then saith the woman of Samaria unto him, How is it that thou, being a Jew, askest drink of me, which am a woman of Samaria? (for the Jews have no dealings with the Samaritans") (iv. 1—9).

This subject is well and fully elucidated in the *Christian Reformer* for August, 1835. But the careful reader of St. John's Gospel will not fail to observe continual illustrations for himself, analogous to the foregoing.

Abstract of John's Gospel.

[The passages printed in square brackets are those which have already occurred in one or more of the first three Gospels; the letters M. MK. L. distinguishing which of the three. Those not in brackets are peculiar to John's. The proportion of the latter is very great indeed, as will be seen at a glance. The order in which John records events gives no trouble to the Harmonists, with the exception of his sixth chapter.]

Ch. i. 1. Proem: The divine Word the source of life and light in the spiritual new creation. John the Baptist "sent from God." The Word the true light. The Word made flesh.

John's testimony. Moses fulfilled in Christ. 35. The calling of Andrew and (apparently) John; of Simon, Philip and Nathanael.

Ch. ii. 1. Marriage-feast at *Cana* of *Galilee*, and Christ's first miracle there.* 13. The *Passover (our Easter)*. Jesus at *Jerusalem;* drives the traders out of the temple;† predicts his own death. Many believe when they see his miracles, but he does "not commit himself unto them."

Ch. iii. 1. Christ's conversation with Nicodemus, that disciple secretly, who came by night for fear of the Jews, and is told he must be baptized and confess Christ in open daylight, if he would enter the kingdom of God. 22. Jesus, in *Judea*, receives disciples by baptism. Magnanimity of John the Baptist on being informed of it.

Ch. iv. 1. Conversation between Jesus and the woman of *Samaria*. Spiritual worship acceptable to the Father, and all places holy for its offering. Jesus declares himself the Christ. Many Samaritans believe on him. 43. In *Galilee* at *Cana*, Jesus cures the nobleman's son, ill at Capernaum.

Ch. v. "A feast of the Jews" (seemingly *Pentecost*, or the feast of Weeks, held seven weeks after the Passover, whence our *Whitsuntide*. Some think it to have been the feast of *Purim* (see Esther ix. 19) a month before the Passover, and suppose eleven months to have passed since ch. ii. 13). Jesus, at *Jerusalem*, cures the infirm man at the pool of Bethesda‡ on

* A simple, beautiful and gracious act, comparatively private, and performed probably when only a few of the apostles had been called, but at which John no doubt was one of the "disciples" present, has been left to his affectionate pen to preserve from falling into oblivion.

† This is narrated by all the other three, as having been done at the *last* passover of our Lord's ministry. John, who puts it at the first passover, says nothing about it in connection with the last. This is very curious. There is no reason, however, why it cannot have been done twice, and John supplies the omitted instance without repeating the one already recorded by others.

‡ Part of verses 3 and 4 (about the moving of the water when an angel came down and troubled it and gave it the healing virtue) are of doubtful authenticity, as marked by Griesbach in his critical edition. Such was, no doubt, the popular Jewish tradition; but the doubt is, whether John vouches for it. According to some of the best MSS., he does not. This is

the sabbath. 17. He vindicates himself against the sabbatarian scruple, and avows his divine commission as Son of Man and Son of God, as predicted by Moses and fulfilling the Scriptures.

[Ch. vi. 1. Jesus went *over the Sea of Galilee*. The *Passover* near.* The feeding of the five thousand in the wilderness,

just the kind of instance in which the questionable verses might have been written as a marginal note by some one who believed the tradition, and copied into the text by a subsequent transcriber.

* This passover is the perplexity of the New Testament chronologists. Without it, the series of Jewish feasts would be recorded in John's Gospel in their regular order; for a Passover has already been recorded in ch. ii., and (seemingly) a Pentecost in ch. v.; then, in ch. vii., we have the feast of Tabernacles (in autumn); at x. 22, the feast of the Dedication of the Temple (November or December); and at xi. 55, the fatal Passover approaches, which fills the remainder of the history. These would form a regular series from passover to passover again, every one of them finding Jesus duly at Jerusalem. But if this passover, parenthetically named in ch. vi. as *at hand*, is to be taken as a different one from both the others, and as alluded to here in its proper place, we must then suppose that a whole year is left intirely blank by John in his history of our Lord's ministry. Were it not for this allusion (for it is only an allusion, in parenthesis—"And the passover, a feast of the Jews, was nigh"), no one would deliberately maintain our Lord's public ministry to have extended over a longer period than that included between two passovers, with a short time preceding the first. It has been conjectured that the word *passover* should be omitted from the text, which would then run, "Now a feast of the Jews was nigh," and that feast would be the *Tabernacles*, which is described in ch. vii. For this conjecture there is no MS. authority whatever. Nor does it seem likely that John, who usually dates so carefully, should have dated anything so vaguely as by saying "*a* feast of the Jews was nigh." Better omit the whole verse conjecturally, and we then should find no difficulty in placing this visit to the east of the Sea of Galilee between the Pentecost and the Tabernacles. But, if we do not venture thus to omit the verse from our "note of time," and yet do not think it necessary to intercalate a year in our Lord's history which is left blank by his historians, the alternative is (that adopted by Dr. Carpenter in his Harmony), to suppose that the passover here mentioned as nigh at hand is the *final* passover, and that the events related in this ch. vi. really belong to a later period, namely, to xi. 55, where it is again said "the Jews' passover was nigh at hand." But this supposition, be it observed, does not mean that the several portions of John's Gospel have been displaced; it implies displacement by the evangelist himself. He could not have recorded this visit to the eastern shore of the Sea of Galilee, between his account of the feasts of Pentecost and Tabernacles, if he had remembered that it happened between the Dedi-

M. MK. L.] 14. Jesus fears they will seek to make him a king by force. [16. He walks on the water. They come to Capernaum, M. MK.] 22. His discourse in the synagogue at Capernaum on "the true bread from heaven." The gross misconstruction of his words by the Jews, whom, unable to enlighten, he purposely revolts by saying they must eat his flesh and drink his blood. 60. Many disciples fall away. Peter confesses him to be "the Christ, the Son of the living God."

Ch. vii. 1. Jesus in *Galilee*, because the Jews in Judea sought his life. 2. *Feast of Tabernacles (autumn)* at hand. 10. Jesus *goes up to the feast* privately. 11. Much discussion at Jerusalem respecting him and his claims. 37. He teaches in the temple. 45. Officers sent to apprehend him return awed and confounded, declaring that "Never man spake like this man." Nicodemus puts in a word on his behalf—"Doth our law judge any man before it hear him?" &c.—and is taunted for it: "Art thou also from Galilee?" 53—viii. 11. The adulteress brought before Jesus as he taught *in the temple* the next day, and his judgment upon her and her accusers.* 12. His discussion with Pharisees and other Jews respecting his claims upon them as children of Abraham.

cation and the next Passover. The knot is cut most effectually by deciding that the parenthetical verse (vi. 4, "And the passover, a feast of the Jews, was nigh") confuses the chronology, and ought to be disregarded as a mistake one way or other, though we cannot tell how. If the feast in ch. v. was the feast of *Purim*, of course the Passover is here in true order. The difficulty then is to suppose that the events from ch. ii. 13 to v. 1 occupied eleven months. The unoccupied time still oppresses us. The incident recorded in this ch. vi., the feeding of the 5000, is narrated by all the other three evangelists; but our Lord's discourse the day after in the synagogue of Capernaum, arising out of his miracle in the wilderness, is preserved by John alone, and this may perhaps be his reason for retracing in this instance the ground already traversed by them. John is also the only one who mentions (vi. 14, 15) that the enthusiasm of the people, on occasion of the miracle, made Jesus fear that they would "take him by force to make him a king,"—one of the symptoms which this evangelist is always on the watch to note, of our Lord's claims, and their admission, rejection or misapprehension.

* This passage is of doubtful authenticity, though perfectly credible. It is wanting in the very best MSS., and presents an uncommon variety of readings in those which have it. Griesbach marks it accordingly as probably to be omitted. Scholz thinks it genuine.

Ch. ix. 1. Christ's cure of the man blind from birth, and his repudiation of the prevailing doctrine that sin is the cause of all human sufferings.

Ch. x. 1. His discourse about the Good Shepherd and the Door of the Sheep-fold. 22. The *feast of the Dedication (November or December).* Jesus at *Jerusalem*, walking in Solomon's portico, is asked to say plainly whether he is the Christ. Avoids the *name*, but appeals to his works "done in his Father's name," calls himself "the Son of God," and declares himself "one with the Father:" "The Father is in me, and I in him." 39. He eludes the attempt to take him, by going to the *east of the Jordan*,* where John had baptized.

Ch. xi. 1. While there, he hears of the illness of Lazarus, of *Bethany*, and, after two days' delay, returns into *Judea*, and raises Lazarus from the dead. 47. The fame of this miracle spreads, and the Pharisees in the Council decide from that time to put Jesus to death. 54. He "therefore walks no more openly among the Jews," but goes to a city called Ephraim, near the wilderness.† 55. *The final Passover (our Easter)* at hand. Much speculation as to his coming or not to the feast.

[Ch. xii. 1. Six days before the passover, he comes to *Bethany*, to the house of Lazarus and his sisters, where Mary anoints his feet; and Judas, pretending care for the poor, reveals his own covetousness, M. MK. 12. Jesus makes his triumphal entry into Jerusalem, M. MK. L.] 20. The Greek Jews (Gentile proselytes?) desire to see Jesus. A voice in the temple attests him. 32. He predicts his own death. 44. Solemnly declares himself sent and instructed by the Father.

Ch. xiii. 1. Additional incidents at the Last Supper. Jesus washes the disciples' feet. [21. Declares that one of the

* To this period careful Harmonists refer the incidents and discourses recorded in Luke's Gospel, xiv. xv. xvi., which seem to have taken place in the Peræa, and form, perhaps, the most interesting part of Luke's *Gnomology*.

† To harmonize John's Gospel with the others, we must suppose our Lord to have gone thence into Galilee, Decapolis, and further northwards to Cæsarea Philippi, teaching and working miracles, before setting out on his final journey from Galilee through the Peræa to Jerusalem. John omits all this.

Twelve is about to betray him, M. MK. L. 24. Points out Judas as the traitor, M.] 31. His pious reflections when Judas is gone out.

Ch. xiv.—xvi. His discourse during and after the passover, consoling his disciples and instructing them for their approaching duties. They do not, even yet, thoroughly admit the idea that he is about to die. (I attempt no abstract of this discourse, nor of the next chapter.)

Ch. xvii. His prayer for them and for their disciples.

[Ch. xviii. 1. Gethsemane. 3. The betrayal. 13. The examination in the high-priest's house, M. MK. L.] 19. Jesus refuses to declare his pretensions, alleging the openness with which he had taught; 22. Is struck by an officer. [Peter's denial of Christ, M. MK. L. 28—xix. 24. Jesus is brought before Pilate, condemned and given up for crucifixion, M. MK. L.; but John has many new particulars.]

Ch. xix. 25—27. Jesus, on the cross, commits his mother to the care and protection of "the disciple whom he loved." 31—37. The soldier pierces the side of Jesus with his spear. [38. The burial, M. MK. L.]

[Ch. xx. The resurrection discovered, M. MK. L.] John has additional particulars in verses 4—17, describing how he and Peter found the grave clothes in the sepulchre, and Mary of Magdala's conversation with Jesus, "supposing him the gardener." [19—23. Jesus appears to the apostles, MK. L.] 24—29. Appears again and convinces Thomas, who was absent the time before. 30. The evangelist declares his purpose in writing the Gospel, "that ye might believe that Jesus is the Christ, the Son of God; and that believing ye might have life through his name."*

Ch. xxi. 1. Jesus appears to Peter, Thomas, Nathanael, John

* Some think the Gospel properly ends here, and that the following chapter is not genuine. But so needless, while so large, a conjecture is not to be admitted against the evidence of manuscripts. There is no critical ground for doubting that John wrote ch. xxi. as well as the rest. It is possible, indeed, that he may have originally finished with ch. xx., the last verse of which, just quoted, is very like a conclusion; and he may have added another chapter afterwards. We must take it, at least, as we find it. The last chapter looks like a supplement, and we may be thankful that he has added it.

and another, at the *Sea of Galilee*, when they are fishing. 7. Is disclosed by the great draught of fishes. 15. Charges Peter thrice to feed his flock, and foretels that apostle's death by martyrdom. 20. Foretels that John "shall tarry till he comes." 23. The thoroughly oriental, if we do not call it a somewhat hyperbolical, conclusion, that if all the things which Jesus did were written, "even the world itself could not contain the books that should be written," is highly appropriate to St. John's Gospel, which (as is manifest in the foregoing outline) consists almost intirely of additional materials, to those which had previously been given forth as a sufficient exhibition of the doctrines and claims of Christianity.

UNIVERSALLY-ADMITTED CHRISTIAN PRINCIPLES, AS DEDUCED FROM THE FOUR GOSPELS.

THE conclusion of the four Gospels, which describe Christianity as it was set forth by its Founder, may seem an appropriate place for attempting something like an abstract or summary of the principles which, according to those books, constitute the religion of Jesus Christ.

What we learn from the four Gospels may be truly and properly called *evangelical* Christianity. For who shall teach it in greater purity than it was taught by its Founder? The Acts and Epistles will shew us how the apostles of Christ preached this Gospel after his death, how they reviewed his completed work, and how they reasoned respecting it with Jews and with Gentiles; but in the books already analyzed we have the sacred record of the Gospel in his own life and person; above which we cannot ascend, and in accordance with which, assuredly, the apostles preached and wrote afterwards in his name.

Paying no regard, therefore, to human systems of faith, we may, without much difficulty, enumerate certain great religious principles, whether in the way of belief, duty or influence, which are admitted, by the most thoughtful and practical Christians of every sect and name, to be characteristic of Christianity,—whatever other ideas, of more disputable order, may be also thought essential to it, or non-essential, by different classes of Christians. I wish, if possible, to keep free from merely doctrinal debate in this enumeration. And it is clear to most Christians who have risen above a merely literal and wordy idea of religion, that Christianity is not to be described adequately by any mere doctrinal articles or creeds whatever.

Christianity is a Spirit and a Life; not a ceremonial, nor a system, nor a creed. It is to be described rather than defined. We are not to tabulate its doctrines, precepts and promises merely; but rather to confer with the Teacher himself in his recorded life and example. The perusal of the four Gospels is calculated to impress any unprejudiced reader, of a practical and devotional turn of mind, with the truth of this statement. Jesus Christ's Life and Example constitute the Gospel. What he said is inseparable from what he did and was. The peculiar religious power of the Gospel has been already described as traceable to this, its *biographical* character (p. 244, &c.).

But while regarding this living spiritual influence as the chief characteristic of Christianity, as read in the four Gospels, we also find certain grand beliefs, duties and hopes attested by it, which admit of articulate voice and description. Thus:

(1.) The conviction, "that Jesus is the Christ, the Son of God," is, according to the apostle John, the foundation belief of Christianity; as in the common sense of language it must be. He tells us he wrote his Gospel to prove this; and the same is evidently the purpose of the other evangelists also throughout theirs.

(2.) This belief is implied in our reception of the Life of Jesus as genuine and exemplary; for he expressly claimed, by act and word, to be received as the Christ. And this belief implies the acknowledgment of his power and authority to teach in the name of the Almighty.

(3.) As the Christ, Jesus is connected with the Jewish dispensation, while rising above it and superseding it. He fulfils it, and so ends it.

(4.) He sets forth the One God, Jehovah, not as the God of the Jews only, but of Samaritans and Gentiles too.

(5.) He makes Him known under the hitherto unknown attributes of the "Heavenly Father," and gives enlarged and endearing views of Divine Providence as exercised by such a Being.

(6.) He fulfils the ceremonial Law, and brings it to an end, declaring Virtue sufficient every where, without sacrificial offering; and Repentance and Amendment every where the true and sufficient atonement for sin.

(7.) Making the worship of God strictly spiritual, he declares that the Divine Mercy-seat is always accessible to human prayer, and the Holy Spirit of God ready to meet the spirit of man, whether imploring help in trouble, or help against temptation, or rising in grateful praise, or in virtuous and pure aspiration.

(8.) The Moral Precepts of Jesus, not systematically given, nor capable of being formed into a system, teach us that good and evil are in the heart and motive, and that our actions should be done with constant reference to the will of Him who seeth in secret and will reward openly.

(9.) All his morality is such as seems to regard man as a spiritual and immortal being. His unhesitating doctrine of Immortality quickens the spiritual nature within us; and the quickened spiritual nature feels in itself the suggestion, and welcomes the assurance, of immortality. This influence is reciprocal.

(10.) All these great religious principles are illustrated and enforced in the person and example of Jesus Christ himself;—ever looking up to God with intire faith, serving man with lowly kindness, and blending the interests of time with those of eternity.

(11.) Jesus Christ foretels his own death and resurrection from the dead. And this one fact in his Messiahship, prospective only during his life, is made more prominent in the preaching and writings of his apostles when realized after his death, than it had been in his own preaching, though often predicted by him. They preach "Jesus and the Resurrection;"

not simply his living history, but its completion in his death and resurrection from the dead. This is the great modification which the preaching of the Gospel has to undergo in its second scriptural period.

The great principles now enumerated make their appearance very inadequately (it must be confessed) in the Abstracts above given of the contents of the four Gospels. They are fully manifest only to the reader of the Gospels themselves; and not to every reader, nor on every reading. It is the intelligent, at once, and earnest, practical and devotional reader, reading frequently, who fully learns, even from the Gospels themselves, what Christianity is. Experimental Christianity is the real evangelical faith. Its elements are soon learnt. It requires the life to practise them.

PART II.

THE ACTS AND LETTERS OF APOSTLES;

OR, CHRISTIANITY AS PREACHED AND DEVELOPED AFTER THE DEATH OF ITS FOUNDER.

A NEW developement was given to Christianity soon after the death and resurrection of its Founder. His personal ministry had not extended beyond the borders of Palestine; nor had his apostles gained the idea that the Gospel was designed for any but Jews, though in his recorded words and actions we find plain proofs that Jesus himself had contemplated mankind at large as the subjects of his kingdom. Shortly after his resurrection, however, his apostles are found rising to a wider view of their mission; and having now before their eyes his completed work and ministry, as the sum and substance of their appointed message to the world, they carry it beyond the limits of Palestine, and offer it henceforth without distinction to Gentiles and to Jews. How this enlargement of view took place in the minds of our Lord's Jewish apostles, is explained in the book of the Acts; in which book a new and most active and successful agent in the work presents himself in the person of Paul, pre-eminently the "Apostle of the Gentiles." Controversies ensue, as was naturally to be expected, on the part of the Christian apostles with Jews on the one hand

and Gentiles on the other; and a record of the most important and interesting of these is preserved to us in the Acts and the Epistles. This second stage of Christianity now opens before us in the remaining New Testament Scriptures.

The spread of the Greek language and civilization over the South of Europe, the West of Asia and the North of Africa, has been noticed as one of the great providential preparations for the diffusion of the Gospel. The agglomeration of all these countries as provinces of the vast Roman empire, throughout all parts of which a more constant intercourse was sustained, for purposes alike of government and of trade, than had ever before prevailed among such remote parts of the world, was another great preparation for the same end. As the Greek language was the *intellectual* instrument of communication, the Roman administration supplied the *material* means. The ships that bore government officials and commercial freights to and fro, across the Levant and Archipelago, often carried with them apostles and evangelists as missionaries, and sometimes as prisoners for Christ's Gospel.

Another leading circumstance which greatly aided, on the whole, while partially obstructing, the progress of the Gospel, was the previous settlement of Jews in every principal city and place throughout the empire. These "Jews of the dispersion" found in the widely-extended Roman rule, the greatest facilities for locomotion and traffic; and though despised for their "superstition," and sometimes cruelly persecuted, they were generally tolerated as convenient in secular life. Wherever the apostles of Christ went, they found a society, and generally a synagogue, of Jews; and to them first they proclaimed the glad-tidings of Jesus Christ; to the Gentile population afterwards. Their success was various.

In some places the Jewish population welcomed their mission; in others, they were its chief opponents. The Roman officials generally regarded, or at least represented, the Christians as a mere sect of Jews, in consequence of these visible marks of connection. But in many places the proportion of Gentile converts was so great as to defy such a representation from the very first.

Thus the Greek, the Latin and the Hebrew cultures were united in the earliest progress of Christianity, as their languages had been in the inscription over the Cross!

We must not expect to find in the New Testament Scriptures (nor indeed any where else) a complete and systematic account of the preaching of Christianity by the apostles; or, if we do, we shall be wofully disappointed. The book of Acts does not pretend to be a history of *all* the acts of *all* the apostles. It contains, indeed, only part of the actions of a very few of them. The acts of many of them are quite unknown, except in the vaguest and most uncertain traditions. Then the Epistles (a large proportion of them being the work of one writer, Paul), having been occasioned, like all genuine letters, by special circumstances naturally calling them forth, do not form anything that can be called a *cycle* of Christian doctrine and instruction, though their contents are very various and are inestimable to the earnest student of Christian truth, who is satisfied to use them for what they really are. Let us take these books, then, as we find them, and endeavour to ascertain their real character and worth.

THE ACTS OF THE APOSTLES.

In speaking of the Gospel of Luke, we have already stated all that is known of the author of the book of Acts, which is attested by all Christian antiquity to be the work of the same pen. We now enter at once, therefore, upon the character and contents of the book itself.

By the title, *Acts of the Apostles*, some would have us understand the history of Peter and Paul to be meant, as their actions are chiefly recorded in this book, and the title in its largest sense is thought to be hardly warranted by the contents. But the narrative is certainly not restricted to the acts of Peter and Paul; for we have John united with Peter in the early part of the book,—and it records the death of his brother James, and afterwards introduces the other James as presiding over the council of the apostles at Jerusalem, who are mentioned collectively, though no further individually. Whether the title, Acts of the Apostles, was given by Luke himself to the book, may be doubtful; but it cannot reasonably be taken in any less obvious sense than that of the history of the apostles generally, so far as came within the scope of the writer to narrate, or perhaps so far as was credibly known to him.

Learned men have perplexed themselves to find out the precise *purpose and scope* which Luke proposed to himself in writing the Acts. They think he cannot have designed a complete history of the Christian Church from the death of its Founder downwards; for it is not a complete one. So, some say, he wrote to shew that Christianity was designed for both Jews and Gentiles; some, that he meant to give a history of Peter's and

Paul's labours; and some would find his special purpose in the personal wants (altogether conjectural) of his unknown patron Theophilus, to whom both the Gospel and the Acts are dedicated. But what if Luke's design was simply *to tell all he knew* about the diffusion of Christianity since Christ's death; as, in his Gospel, he had told all he could learn of its preaching by Jesus Christ himself! This is perhaps too simple a theory to satisfy learned and ingenious critics; but it may be the likeliest account to give of the origin of a book so unpretending in its character. In the incidents of the chief part of the book, from ch. xvi. to the end, the narrator was the companion of Paul, and it was natural and right that he should give the details of that apostle's acts with the greatest fulness. If we ask what were probably his materials for the earlier part of the history, in which there is no proof of his having been present at Jerusalem, where the scene chiefly lies,—the most natural and satisfactory answer is that which we derive from his own avowal in the opening of his Gospel, namely: that he informed himself diligently by conferring with those "who from the beginning were eye-witnesses and ministers of the word." Perhaps, when he wrote the Acts, there were already some written documents existing, which recorded the early proceedings of the apostles at Jerusalem; as there were certainly others relating to the actions and discourses of the Saviour. By means of these, or of personal intercourse with the apostles, he considered that he "had perfect understanding of all these things from the very first;" and so thought it good "to write them in order."

I proceed to the analysis of the book of Acts.

Abstract of the Book of Acts.

[The first eight chapters relate the general history of the infant church of Christ in Jerusalem down to the martyrdom of Stephen, and the planting of Christianity throughout Judea and Samaria by the apostles and their first converts when scattered abroad in the more general persecution of the church which ensued.*]

Ch. i. 1. The opening of the book refers to Luke's Gospel as "the former treatise," and recapitulates, with a little added detail, the parting promise of Jesus to his apostles that he would send the Holy Spirit, and his injunction to them to remain in Jerusalem till they should receive it. It also repeats the account of the *Ascension* of Jesus Christ, which is briefly and vaguely given in the Gospels of Mark and Luke, and is here more particularly stated to have taken place *forty days* after the Resurrection; the fact itself being intirely omitted by Matthew and by John.† 15. The eleven apostles choose, by ballot appa-

* Once for all, I must here make the largest acknowledgment of my obligations to the splendid work of Messrs. Conybeare and Howson, recently published, on the Life and Epistles of Paul, which brings together all that is known, and suggests perhaps all that can be imagined, in illustration of the subject. The work is only faulty (if fault may be found with it) through excess:—too sumptuous in style and costly in price for wide circulation; too full for any but professional or semi-professional readers; and perhaps too minute, both in its remotely connected details and in the conjectural reproduction of parts left blank by the narrator, for any but very patient and very imaginative readers. It has put into a living form, however, all the learning of Lardner and the older theologians, and all the pictorial knowledge of later travellers and artists. Kuinoel's Commentary is invaluable in the Acts, as in the Gospels. Nor must I omit to name an English Commentary on the Acts, just published (1854), by W. G. Humphry, B.D., examining chaplain to the Bishop of London.

† Mark's account of the Ascension is in these words (xvi. 19):
"So then, after the Lord had spoken unto them, he was received up into heaven, and sat on the right hand of God."
Luke's, in his Gospel, is as follows (xxiv. 50, 51):
"And he led them out as far as to Bethany; and he lifted up his hands

rently,* after solemnly invoking the direction and blessing of God upon their choice, Matthias, in the room of Judas Iscariot,†

and blessed them. And it came to pass, while he blessed them, he was parted from them and carried up into heaven."

His account at the beginning of the Acts is as follows (i. 1—3 and 9—11):

"The former treatise have I made, O Theophilus, of all that Jesus began both to do and teach, until the day in which he was taken up, after that he through the Holy Spirit had given commandments unto the apostles whom he had chosen: to whom also he shewed himself alive after his passion by many infallible proofs, being seen of them forty days, and speaking of the things pertaining to the kingdom of God. * * * And when he had spoken these things, while they beheld, he was taken up; and a cloud received him out of their sight. And while they looked steadfastly toward heaven, as he went up, behold, two men stood by them in white apparel; which also said, Ye men of Galilee, why stand ye gazing up into heaven? This same Jesus, which is taken up from you into heaven, shall so come in like manner as ye have seen him go into heaven."

The omission of all record of this event by Matthew and John (the two apostle-evangelists, the eye-witnesses) is quite inexplicable. It seems as if they had regarded the resurrection of Jesus as the concluding scene of his Messianic history. At any rate, they trace it no further. But from that well-attested event, the thoughtful mind necessarily goes on to infer something that may be properly called an ascension; that is, the transference of the risen Jesus from this state of mortal existence to his immortal state. Yet all speculation as to the manner in which it may have taken place seems perfectly vain, unless we could first know the nature and locality of his present state of existence. Then we might perhaps reverently dare to ask, what became of the bodily form in which he died, and in which identically he rose and shewed himself to his disciples. The known philosophy of the solar system now, of course, puts out of question that ancient venerable faith which placed heaven locally above the clouds; so that, if we accept as literally as possible the account of St. Luke, that he was "taken up, and a cloud received him out of their sight," we can only regard the outward miracle thus described, as having been designed to

* This is the natural inference from the description. They proposed two, *ἴστησαν δύο*, and gave in their lots, *ἔδωκαν κλήρους αὐτῶν*; and the lot fell upon Matthias.

† The account of Judas Iscariot's death here given in Peter's address, can scarcely be reconciled with the history in Matthew (xxvii. 3—10). But what is the harm of the discrepancy? The only harm is in trying to prove them consistent and both infallibly correct. The credit of the historians does not require this, and the diversity forbids it.

to be "a witness with them of the resurrection of Jesus," that is, as a twelfth apostle.

Ch. ii. 1. On the day of Pentecost (our Whitsuntide) next after the death of Jesus, the apostles receive the gift of the Holy Spirit; the immediate and conspicuous result of which is, to enable them to speak the various languages native to the Jews then assembled at Jerusalem from the various countries of Eastern Europe, Western and Middle Asia, and North Africa.* 14. Peter (the *Rock* of the church's foundation) stands forth and declares this to be the fulfilment of Jewish prophecy, quoting appropriate words from Joel; and then proclaims the divine mission of Jesus as "a man proved to be from God by miracles, wonders and signs which God did by him;" adduces two of the Psalms of David as applicable to his resurrection and his Messianic authority; and concludes with attesting to "all the house of Israel," "that God hath made that same Jesus whom ye crucified, both Lord and Christ." 37. Those who are convinced are baptized, and three thousand souls are added to the church that day. 44. In a

symbolize to the outward eyes of the disciples the fact of his transference to that spiritual state of being, the nature and locality of which are still wholly unrevealed. The words of what is called the *Apostles' Creed*, that "He ascended into heaven and sitteth on the right hand of God the Father," may have been meant literally when they were penned, but can have only a figurative or suggestive meaning now, in the minds of those who use them thoughtfully.

The Ascension of Jesus, in point of fact, is seldom referred to in the Acts and Epistles as a specific matter of Christian belief or interest. But the case is quite different as regards his Resurrection, which is the perpetual theme of express attestation and of full-hearted allusion. Christ living on earth, teaching, healing, doing good,—Christ dying,—Christ risen,—Christ exalted to the right hand of Divine power,—are the favourite topics. But Christ in the act of ascending, is not a point which the understanding grasps or on which the affections dwell. It is but the transition period, inferred rather than appreciated by distinct thought.

* The scene here described seems to present the apostles to our view as severally surrounded by a group of persons from one particular country, and addressing each group in their native language. It seems a very forced interpretation to think (as has been maintained) that the miracle was upon the *hearers*, making them hear their own different languages from one speaker.

certain sense, the apostles and their converts have "all things common;" but not in the modern sense of a community of goods. At their own option, but without any constraint or compulsion, many of them sell their lands and goods, and bring the proceeds, which are "parted to all as every man has need." But it was not only "their own, to do as they pleased while it remained" in their own hands, but even "after it was sold, it was still in their own power," as declared shortly afterwards by Peter to Ananias and Sapphira.

Ch. iii. 1. Peter and John, going up to the temple at the usual hour of prayer, bid the cripple at the temple gate, "In the name of Jesus Christ of Nazareth, rise up and walk." 12. This miracle having excited great interest, Peter sets forth to the assembled multitudes the claims of the gospel of Christ, declaring that the miracle now done is a proof that the God of Abraham, Isaac, Jacob and the Patriarchs has glorified his Son Jesus, whom they had denied and crucified (thereby fulfilling the prophetic counsel of God). He exhorts them to repent, and seems to anticipate (ver. 20) that Jesus Christ shall be sent again from heaven in "the times of restitution of all things;"* quoting Moses as having promised "a prophet like himself," and adducing the earlier promise to Abraham, that "in his seed all the kindreds of the earth should be blessed," as now fulfilled in Jesus Christ, whom God has sent "to bless you, in turning away every one of you from his iniquities."

Ch. iv. 1. The captain of the temple (the head of the band of Levites on guard), under orders from the priests, of the Sadducean† party principally (who are alarmed at the growth

* The remains, surely, of the Jewish Messianic thought; in which thought was the origin of the early Christian expectation of the end of the world being at hand.

† The Pharisees, whose hypocrisy and parade our Lord had rebuked, had been his most active persecutors. But the Sadducees seem to have been now roused to hostility against the apostles, by the prominence given in their preaching to the announcement of Christ's resurrection; "for the Sadducees say that there is no resurrection, neither angel, nor spirit" (Acts xxiii. 8). But the Pharisees, with Saul among them, were presently afterwards eager for Stephen's death, regarding the apostles, like their Master, as subverters of the Law of Moses.

of the new sect, now numbering about 5000), apprehends Peter and John, and brings them the next morning before the Sanhedrim, who demand, "By what power, or by what name, ye have done this?" Peter, still the spokesman for both, declares that it is "by the name of Jesus of Nazareth, whom they had crucified, whom God had raised from the dead;" and that his is the "only name under heaven given unto men whereby we must be saved."* 13. The Sanhedrim forbid them to speak or teach any more in the name of Jesus; but they refuse to pledge themselves to obey human rulers rather than God, and are let go. 23. The beautiful thanksgiving prayer of the collective apostles on their return to them, is a model, *mutatis mutandis*, for social Christian worship. 31. A new effusion of the Holy Spirit enables them to "speak the word of God with boldness." 33. The success of the apostolic preaching is described by saying, "With great power gave the apostles witness of the *resurrection* of the Lord Jesus;" which crowning fact of their Master's history is the leading topic of their preaching everywhere. 36. Barnabas (afterwards the companion of Paul in one of his journeys) sells his land and "lays the price of it at the apostles' feet."

Ch. v. 1. Ananias and Sapphira, having sold some property, bring only part of its price, as if the whole; and being severally convicted of dishonesty and falsehood by Peter, severally fall down dead.† 17. After continued miraculous cures of sick people, the high-priest and Sadducean party imprison "the apostles" (that is, Peter certainly, for he is named; John, no

* σωθῆναι. The Greek word covers a larger extent of meaning than any English word that can be adopted. It includes both the bodily healing and the spiritual. So, in Peter's use of it, the meaning rises from the less to the greater; from the cure of the cripple to the gift of everlasting life.

† Some think they had committed this fraud with a view to test the supernatural knowledge of the apostles; others think they wished secretly to hold something in reserve, in case the Christian community should be soon broken up. Whether there was anything miraculous in their sudden deaths is doubted, and is not asserted in the narrative. Peter does not even predict that of Ananias. Conscience, convicted and alarmed by an unimagined detection and public exposure, may be thought sufficient in his case; and the added horror of her husband's death, possibly in that of Sapphira.

doubt, who has been thus far always prominent with him; and some other or others not named). They are miraculously rescued from prison, and found teaching in the temple the next day; are brought unresistingly before the Sanhedrim; and, to the complaint that they have disobeyed the previous prohibition by continuing to preach, they nobly reply, "We ought to obey God rather than men." Peter, again the spokesman, repeats that the crucified Jesus has been exalted by God to be a Prince and a Saviour, and that the spiritual gifts of his apostles, as well as their oral testimony, prove his claims. 33. The irritation of the Sanhedrim is kept in check by the prudence of Gamaliel, a learned Pharisee (the Jewish teacher of the future apostle Paul), who advises them to let the men alone, and trust that, "if their work be of men, it will come to nought; whereas, if it be of God, they cannot overthrow it, and might be found fighting against God." He reminds them of the fate of two recent pretenders to divine authority, Theudas, and Judas of Galilee, as illustrations of the wisdom of his doctrine of forbearance.* So the apostles were beaten and again forbidden to preach their Master's gospel; and, being dismissed, "rejoiced that they were counted worthy to suffer shame for his name; and daily in the temple and from house to house ceased not to teach and preach the glad-tidings that Jesus is the Christ."

Ch. vi. 1. The church at Jerusalem having grown numerous, and some complaints and jealousies arising on the part of the Grecians (the foreign Jews) against the Hebrews (the Palestinian Jews) about the distribution of alms to the needy, seven deacons are appointed to manage the secular affairs of the church. The apostles pray and put their hands on them, thus

* Nothing is known, beyond what Luke has here hinted, of the particular pretensions and proceedings of this Theudas. A later Theudas, about A.D. 45, is mentioned by Josephus (Ant. xx. 5); and Whiston supposes the Theudas named by Gamaliel may have been one of the impostors before mentioned in Josephus, in Ant. xvii. 10. The fanatical revolt of Judas, named by Gamaliel, is fully detailed by Josephus (Ant. xviii. 1). Such false Christs were numerous,—the product of the Jewish national expectation then prevalent.

designating and blessing them.* 8. Stephen, one of these deacons, "full of faith and power, did great wonders and miracles among the people;" and coming into discussion with Jews of various synagogues,† was accused by them before the Sanhedrim, of having spoken "blasphemous words against Moses and against God," to the effect that Jesus of Nazareth would destroy the holy place and change the customs which Moses had delivered;—a very intelligible perversion, on their part, of the Christian doctrine, according to which the Law is fulfilled and superseded.

Ch. vii. 1. Stephen defends himself before the high-priest in a rapid summary of the Jewish history from Abraham downwards, at each step dwelling upon its spiritual and comprehensive import, and pointing out the prospective and progressive character of Divine Revelation. He has arrived (ver. 48) at the building of Solomon's temple, and in that connection says, most appropriately to the immediate accusation against him, "Though indeed the Most High dwelleth not in temples made with hands, as saith the prophet, Heaven is my throne, and earth is my footstool; what house will ye build me? saith the Lord; or what is the place of mine abode? Hath not mine hand made all these things?" And here (ver. 50) it is evident that his address was interrupted by the clamour and violence of those who felt the appropriateness of the defence; and in the remaining three verses, the doomed martyr can only remind

* Hence, by false imitation, the modern "imposition of hands." In apostolic days it meant simply the *designation* of the person on whom the blessing, whether natural or supernatural, was implored. Laying on hands did not give the power of the Holy Spirit. In the instance before us no such power is stated to have been then given.

† Synagogues were very numerous in Jerusalem, and each set of foreign Jews seems to have had its own. The synagogue of the Libertines (Libertini, or Roman freedmen properly) has perplexed interpreters; but Tacitus (Ann. ii. 85) says there were 4000 of them in Rome, and that Tiberius banished some to Sardinia, and ordered the rest to quit Rome. It is conjectured that they were chiefly the descendants of Pompey's prisoners of war. These Libertini, and the Jews of North Africa (who seem to have formed one synagogue), and those also of Cilicia and Asia Minor, were Stephen's persecutors. Saul, doubtless, was prominent as a member of the Cilician synagogue.

them that they are treating him as their fathers had done the prophets, and as they themselves had treated the "Just One." 54. His sublime martyrdom follows. He sees a vision of his glorified Saviour, and exclaims, "Lord Jesus, receive my spirit;" "Lord, lay not this sin to their charge." So he fell asleep! Saul, the future apostle Paul, stood by, taking charge of the mantles of those who stoned him, "consenting unto his death," yet doubtless receiving impressions of a very different ultimate tendency.

Ch. viii. 1. The persecution of the Christians* at Jerusalem proceeds, Saul being a prominent actor in it. Driven from Jerusalem (where, however, the apostles remained), the Christian disciples preach elsewhere throughout Judea and Samaria. 5. Philip the deacon preaches in a city of Samaria; and Peter and John presently go down and pray for the new disciples, that they may receive the Holy Spirit. Simon the magician, or sorcerer, pretending conversion and having been baptized, offers to purchase the power of communicating spiritual gifts, and is indignantly denounced by Peter as "still in the gall of bitterness and the bond of iniquity." 26. Philip, having returned to Jerusalem, goes southward towards Gaza, and being overtaken by the chamberlain of the Queen of Ethiopia, or

* This persecution, instigated by the Sanhedrim, seems to have been unheeded and unchecked by the Roman governor. The illegal and tumultuous execution of Stephen was not called in question. It is not quite certain, for want of exact dates, who was the Roman procurator of Judea at this time. Pilate was recalled A.D. 37, just reaching Rome to find Tiberius dead. Marcellus was then appointed temporarily by the governor of Syria, and superseded presently by Marullus, whom the new emperor Caligula appointed. The Sanhedrim, during this period, would be under no immediate fear of their Roman masters. Caligula, on his accession, made Herod Agrippa (grandson of Herod the Great) king of Trachonitis, &c.; and in A.D. 41, Claudius made him nominal king of Judea and Samaria also, as we find him soon afterwards in the book of Acts, when instigating a savage persecution against the Christians. On his death, A.D. 44 (Acts xii. 23), Claudius thought his son Agrippa too young to succeed him, and Judea became again a Roman province under Fadus. But the young Agrippa succeeded his great-uncle Philip in the tetrarchy of Ituræa, &c., and was called king by courtesy. He was the "king Agrippa" who went to Cæsarea to salute Festus on his coming to his province, and before whom Paul gave an account of his life and conversion (Acts xxv. xxvi.).

Upper Egypt, who was a Jew returning from one of the national feasts at Jerusalem, preaches Jesus to him and baptizes him.

Life of Paul.

The ninth chapter relates the conversion of Paul, the persecutor of Stephen, and his call to the apostleship of the Gentiles. His history fills the rest of the book of Acts, except the three chapters next ensuing (x.—xii.), which tell us how Peter was taught to regard the Gentiles as admissible to the kingdom of Christ, and narrate the persecution of the church by Herod Agrippa and his miserable death. And as Paul's history is thus prominent through the rest of the book of Acts, so his writings occupy the larger part of the remaining pages of the New Testament.

The relation of Paul to the Gospel history is therefore of the highest interest and importance; and it is desirable to set his life and character in the clearest possible point of view. He is introduced to us in the book of Acts without explanation or description, further than as a young man at whose feet the witnesses against Stephen deposited their clothes while stoning him,—as consenting to Stephen's death, making havoc of the church, and committing men and women to prison,—and now as going to Damascus with letters from the high-priest* to the synagogues there, authorizing him, if he found any "of this way" in that city, to bring them bound to Jerusalem.† But his earlier history is not altogether unknown. In his self-vindications on two occasions in the book of Acts, and in his various letters, we find many interesting particulars preserved relative to his origin and early history. After consulting these (and vainly wishing they were more full), we may take the book of Acts as his biography from the death of Stephen, inserting, in foot notes, the few additional particulars derivable

* It seems a natural inference from Paul's expression afterwards (Acts xxvi. 10), that he was himself a member of the Sanhedrim, as he says he gave his *vote* against those who were put to death; *κατήνεγκα ψῆφον*.

† The Romans recognized and supported the religious authority of the Sanhedrim at Jerusalem over the Jews in all parts of the empire.

from his own letters, marking carefully the occasions on which those letters seem to have been respectively written, and adding the little that is known or inferred of the apostle's history after the somewhat abrupt and disappointing termination of the book. This will be the best possible preparation for the perusal of Paul's Epistles, which will come next in order.

Saul—for such was his original name—was a native of Tarsus, the chief city of Cilicia, of which province it had been made the capital by Pompey. Saul was of pure Jewish pedigree, "a Hebrew of the Hebrews," "of the tribe of Benjamin;" which last fact may sufficiently account for his having been called after the name of the first Jewish king, who had been of that tribe and whose name might naturally become frequent in his tribe ever after,—as a name less fabulous than Arthur, if less loved than Alfred, among English families.

Tarsus was "no mean city." Its antiquity was higher than clear history reaches. Its geographical position,—near the north-eastern corner of the Levant, and on the highway from Greece to Persia, or from Rome into Syria,—had made it well known in the histories of all those countries. It ranked high in letters and philosophy, so as to be compared by Strabo to Athens and Alexandria. It had taken the part of Julius Cæsar in the civil war, had been made a free city by Antony, and been lately exempted by Augustus from taxes. Jews were numerous in Tarsus.

Saul was born here, probably a few years after the birth of Christ. So, at least, we judge from his being called a young man at the death of Stephen, A.D. 37,* and playfully calling himself "Paul the aged" in his letter to Philemon (ver. 9), written about A.D. 62. If born A.D. 7 (of the common era), he might be 30 years old on the former occasion, and 55 on the latter. Some make him younger than this by eight or nine years. Some will have him older.

Of his parentage we know nothing, but that his father was a Pharisee (Acts xxiii. 6). He had a sister, whose son gave timely information of his intended assassination by some Jewish zealots (Acts xxiii. 16); and he enumerates various "kinsmen" by name (perhaps mere *tribesmen*, Benjamites) in his letter to the

* Kuinoel's Prolegomena, p. xix.

Romans (xvi. 7 and 11), as residing in the great city. His father was a Roman citizen, and Paul was "free-born." How this franchise had been gained, is matter of mere conjecture; but there were a great number of Jewish *Libertini*, or freedmen, who had received their freedom for faithful service in the Roman armies; and this may perhaps have been the case with the father of Saul of Tarsus. The youth was brought up to the trade of a tent-maker (Acts xviii. 3), for which Tarsus was locally somewhat celebrated,—a cloth called *Cilicium* being woven of goats' hair, the produce of the neighbouring mountains, and much used in tent-making. We cannot assign the exact worldly condition of the family from this fact, as it was the laudable custom of religious Jews to give their sons a trade as a resource, even if themselves wealthy. Tent-making was a very extensive business in those days of distant travelling between Rome and her provinces.

A first-rate education, according to the standard of his day, was unquestionably given to young Saul; and his natural abilities are shewn by his life and writings to have been of a very high order. He was acquainted with Greek classical literature and philosophy; for he quotes some of its poets and copes with some of its philosophers. But his education was strictly such as a Jew, zealous for the Law, might give his son. Like other *Hellenist* Jews (those living among Greek populations), he used the Greek language, probably as freely as the Hebrew. He quotes, in his Epistles, from the Greek of the Septuagint; and addresses the chief captain in Greek, at Jerusalem (Acts xxi. 37), before speaking to the multitude in their native Hebrew or Syriac. His education was completed at Jerusalem under Gamaliel, that "Pharisee and teacher of the Law, had in reputation among all the people," whose prudence and forbearance, mentioned a few chapters before (v. 34), strongly contrast with the headstrong and cruel zeal of his pupil Saul as persecutor of the church; in which attitude he presents himself in this ninth chapter. He seems to have been resident in Jerusalem during this interval (Acts xxvi. 4); and had probably noticed with contempt the interest excited by the recent career of Jesus of Nazareth. He now volunteers to be the emissary of the Sanhedrim to Damascus, and obtains letters from the high-priest to the synagogues there, ordering the surrender of all Christian believers among the Jews in that city.

Damascus is perhaps the oldest existing city in the world, dating back to the time of Abraham (Gen. xv. 2, if indeed it was a *city* in his time), and still calling forth the admiration of travellers by its peculiarly beautiful situation. It was about 40 miles N. E. of Cæsarea Philippi, and 130 or 140 from Jerusalem. It had been the head of the Syrian kingdom in the times of the Jewish monarchies, and had fallen with Israel under the Assyrian power, and then successively under the Babylonian, Persian, Græco-Syrian and Roman rule. The Jews were very numerous in it. If we may believe Josephus (Wars, ii. 20, § 2), 10,000 of this people were slain there in the reign of Nero. It is difficult to ascertain its precise political relations at the time of Paul's conversion. But it appears, from an allusion in one of his letters (2 Cor. xi. 32), to have been at that time under the sway of Aretas, the king of Arabia. This prince was at variance with Herod Antipas, tetrarch of Galilee, his son-in-law, whose faithlessness to the daughter of Aretas, and whose shameful connection with Herodias, his brother Philip's wife, were reproved by John the Baptist at the sacrifice of his own life. It is conjectured that Caligula, who on his accession to the empire, A.D. 37, banished Antipas, may have conferred the government of Damascus upon Aretas. All we know is, that the latter was in possession at this time.—We resume the abstract of the book of Acts.

Conversion of Saul, A.D. 36 (?).*—Ch. ix. Travelling to Damascus with the intent to root out the Nazarene heresy,† when near his journey's end, a sudden miraculous light shone round him, and a voice called to him, in the Hebrew language,‡

* The dates are taken henceforth from Conybeare and Howson. Kuinoel puts the conversion of Saul A.D. 40.

† It seems implied that Saul had good reason to know that there were Christians already at Damascus, whether fugitives from Judea or converted Damascene Jews.

‡ See Acts xxvi. 14. Paul twice gives an account of his own conversion; first in his speech to the Jews when apprehended by them in Jerusalem

"Saul, Saul, why persecutest thou me?" To his astonished and trembling inquiry, "Who art thou, Lord?" the voice replies, "I am Jesus whom thou persecutest. [It is hard for thee to kick against the goads.*]" The voice then bids him go to Damascus and wait till "it shall be told him what to do." Blind with the effects of the vision, he is led into the city by his companions (the servants and officers of the Sanhedrim, it is presumed), and remains dark and fasting for three days at the house of one Judas, in the Straight Street.† Meanwhile, a Christian disciple in Damascus, by name Ananias, has seen a vision directing him to visit Saul,—of whom he has before heard as the zealous persecutor of the Christian church,—and to put his hand on him for the restoration of his sight. Ananias does so; Saul recovers his sight at the touch, is filled with the Holy Spirit, is baptized (by Ananias, we naturally conclude), and after remaining some days with the disciples at Damascus, enters the synagogues and preaches that Jesus is the very Christ. "After many days were fulfilled" (ver. 23), the Jews of Damascus laid a plot against his life, and he escaped from the city by night, being let down from the city wall (from some house, probably, adjoining the wall) in a basket.‡

and rescued by the Roman captain (ch. xxii.), and again before Festus and Agrippa at Cæsarea (xxvi.). Between these accounts and the narrative in ch. ix., there are circumstantial variations, of no real moment except to the asserter of their plenary inspiration, and to the unbeliever who takes up the argument thus prepared for him.

* Griesbach omits this clause. It seems to have crept in from ch. xxvi. 14, through the association of thought in some copyist's mind. A good illustration of textual variations.

† Such involuntary indications of authenticity as these minute particulars furnish, should be noticed by the careful reader.

‡ An important passage in Paul's history is here omitted by St. Luke, which is supplied by himself in his Epistle to the Galatians,—namely, his spending the principal part of three years in Arabia and in a second visit to Damascus. Paul's own words are as follows (Gal. i. 15—21):

"When it pleased God, who separated me from my mother's womb, and called me by his grace, to reveal his Son in me, that I might preach him among the heathen; immediately I conferred not with flesh and blood: neither went I up to Jerusalem to them which were apostles before me; but I went into Arabia and returned again unto Damascus. Then, after three

When he came to Jerusalem again, and tried to join the Christians there, they, very naturally, "were all afraid of him, and believed not that he was a disciple," till Barnabas attested the reality of his conversion, and described his bold avowal of the name of Jesus at Damascus. It is conjectured that Barnabas, himself a native of Cyprus, may have been acquainted with Paul in early life; and if so, what more likely than that, on the news of Paul's defection from Judaism being brought back to Jerusalem by the officers of the Sanhedrim who had accompanied him, Barnabas should have hastened to Damascus to welcome his accession to the blessed faith which he himself had earlier found? Paul was then received among the Christians, and for about fifteen days "spake boldly in the name of the Lord Jesus, and disputed against the Grecians" (the Hellenistic Jews); till their violence against him suggested his retirement,* and he went to Cæsarea, and thence (by ship, no doubt) to Tarsus, his native place. There is no record pre-

years, I went up to Jerusalem to see Peter, and abode with him fifteen days. But other of the apostles saw I none, save James, the Lord's brother. Afterwards I came into the regions of Syria and Cilicia."

Arabia is a word of very vague meaning, being used to denote not only the country south of Judea (of which Petra was the capital), but also to include the desert country east of Judea. And during the dispute between Aretas and Herod already alluded to, and the possession of Damascus itself by Aretas, there is no knowing how near or how far off Paul may have made his Arabian sojourn during this period. We can hardly be wrong in supposing his object to have been to gain time for thought and reflection, amid the revolution which was taking place in all his religious ideas and feelings. This three years' interval between Damascus and Jerusalem is the best possible answer to the suggestion, that the Christian preaching of Saul was dictated by a hot enthusiasm which mistook its own strong emotions for a supernatural call to the apostleship. Whether this persecution at Damascus cut short his first or his second visit there, we cannot tell; but after the second, he came to Jerusalem, where it appears the only apostles whom he saw were Peter and James. "Afterwards (says he to the Galatians) I came into the regions of Syria and Cilicia;" and his departure from Jerusalem to Tarsus, here in the Acts, is plainly the parallel period.

* In Acts xxii. 17—21, the apostle says he was also warned, by a vision of the Saviour appearing to him when praying in the temple, to get quickly out of Jerusalem; and was informed, when reluctant to leave the post of exertion and danger, that his specific destination henceforth should be to preach to the Gentiles.

served of his intercourse with Peter and James at Jerusalem during the period above named; but we cannot doubt that it must have brought the new convert into intimate acquaintance with the history of the earthly life and ministry of the now glorified Saviour, who had miraculously appeared to him to claim his services as an apostle.

The conversion of Saul is a point of great interest in the external evidence of Christianity, on which argument has been elaborately spent.* The subject will not be *argued* in these pages; but the scriptural statements may be presented, it is hoped, in a clear and succinct manner as they occur, and those intellectual and moral qualities of the Apostle of the Gentiles may be thus developed, instead of argued, on the perception of which the decision of his claims to a supernatural call is virtually made in each thoughtful mind.

A period of rest from persecution now ensued (ix. 31):

"Then had the churches rest throughout all Judea and Galilee and Samaria, and were edified; and walking in the fear of the Lord, and in the comfort of the Holy Spirit, were multiplied."

The persecution which had arisen in reference to Stephen had died down; many of its subjects had doubtless fled from Jerusalem into Galilee and Samaria, and the leading persecutor had become an apostle. It is conjectured by some, that the insane folly of Caligula, who about this time (A.D. 39) ordered his statue to be erected in Jerusalem, and thus goaded the Jews to the point of rebellion, may have been another cause of the cessation of all active measures on the part of the Jews against the Christians, when the highest sanctity of their own religion was in danger. (See Jos. Ant. xviii. 8.) Whether ascribable to this cause in part or not, "the churches had rest." It is here observable that they were *churches*, and not one collective church.

Peter, passing through "all quarters," visits Lydda, Saron

* It may be sufficient to allude to Lord Lyttleton's "Observations on the Conversion and Apostleship of St. Paul;" and, on the other hand, to mention Gamaliel Smith's (Jeremy Bentham's) "Not Paul, but Jesus," as a specimen of microscopic objections founded on the consciously false assumption of a verbal inspiration being claimed by the Scriptures.

and Joppa; and, while in the last-mentioned place, he is divinely instructed to regard Gentiles as eligible, equally with Jews, to the privileges and hopes of the Gospel.

Ch. x. 1. Cornelius, a Roman centurion stationed at Cæsarea as captain of the Italian band (which name seems to denote that it was composed of native Italians, if not Romans, and in no degree of *provincial* recruits, while its commander, bearing a distinguished Roman name, was nevertheless a popular man among the Jews), has seen a vision, directing him to send to Joppa for Peter; while the latter, shortly before the arrival of the messengers, sees that emblematic vision which forbids him any longer to look upon the Gentiles as unclean.

Here, then, is another important stage of developement realized by the catholic spirit of the Gospel. It has already welcomed Hellenist Jews and Samaritans; it now opens the hearts and minds of its apostles to the Gentiles also; while beyond the limits of Judea, the newly-converted Saul is already sounding the same note of religious equality among the mixed Jewish and Greek population of Tarsus and Cilicia. Peter, thus at length freed from the lingering prejudice which had made him and his fellow-apostles regard Christianity as a blessing for the covenanted people alone, goes cheerfully to Cæsarea, and avows before Cornelius and his assembled friends the newly-apprehended truth (34, 35), "that God is no respecter of persons, but that in every nation he that feareth Him and worketh righteousness, is accepted of Him." He tells the wondrous story of Christ's life; and while he speaks, the Holy Spirit falls on all his hearers, enabling them to speak other languages than their own. The Jewish Christians who had accompanied Peter were astonished; but the inference was irresistible, that those on whom the Spirit had fallen might be baptized and received into the church. Peter, on the urgent request of his new converts, stays there "certain days."

In the next chapter (xi.), Peter has to vindicate his new catholicity of view to his fellow-apostles and brethren in Judea, some of whom were greatly scandalized by his "eating with uncircumcised men." He simply recites the history of the last few days, and "when they heard these things, they held their peace and glorified God, saying, Then hath God also to the Gentiles granted repentance unto life."

19. Meanwhile, some of those who had been scattered abroad in "the persecution that arose about Stephen," had been preaching the Gospel in Phenice, the island Cyprus, and the important city of Antioch, but to Jews only; except that some from Cyprus and Cyrene (who perhaps had previously heard of the conversion of Cornelius) seem to have ventured to preach to Gentile Greeks* at Antioch. The historian devoutly says, "The hand of the Lord was with them; and a great number believed and turned unto the Lord." The church at Jerusalem, hearing these things, send Barnabas to Antioch, with whose aid "much people was added unto the Lord." He presently goes to Tarsus to seek Saul. What the latter had been doing in the interval, ever since his retiring to Tarsus, we cannot positively know; but it is probable that he had founded some of those churches in Cilicia of which we read in xv. 41. Saul returns with Barnabas to Antioch, where they both remain a whole year, teaching and worshiping with the church. During this period, a prophet from Jerusalem, named Agabus, predicted a great dearth as impending, "which came to pass in the days of Claudius Cæsar," and in relief of which the disciples at Antioch sent alms to Jerusalem by the hands of Barnabas and Saul.† The name of CHRISTIAN was now first used to describe the disciples of Jesus. 26. "The disciples were called Christians first in Antioch." This name was probably given to them by the Roman population, as it is of Roman form, like *Pompeian*, *Marian*, &c.; and was most likely meant to be simply descriptive of their discipleship to one whom they continually spoke of as Christ. The word *Christian* is only used twice more in the New Testament. One instance is where Agrippa said to Paul, after the eloquent pleading of the apostle before him and Festus, "Almost thou persuadest me to be a Christian" (Acts xxvi. 28). The other instance is in the First Epistle of Peter,

* *Greeks*, ἕλληνας; not *Grecians*, ἑλληνιςὰς; seems admitted to be the true reading.

† There is nothing more said about this visit of Barnabas and Saul to Jerusalem. They seem to have returned to Antioch immediately on completing their charitable errand.

who says to the dispersed and persecuted (iv. 16), "Let none of you suffer as an evil-doer; but if any man suffer as a Christian, let him not be ashamed, but let him glorify God on this behalf." Both these instances are later than the period when the name is mentioned as originating at Antioch. The followers of Jesus are called *disciples* in the four Gospels; and in the Acts and Epistles they are also spoken of as the *brethren*, *believers*, *saints* or holy people, and collectively as the *Church of Christ* or the *Church of God.* Their Jewish opponents called them Nazarenes and Galileans. When the Romans at Antioch spoke of them as Christians, they accepted the name at once, as not merely descriptive but honourable.

ANTIOCH becomes, from this time, the centre of action for the Christian mission to the Gentiles; and what may be called the second part of the book of Acts begins here, its interest centering upon the missionary labours of Saul. As far as concerned the progress of the Gospel among the Gentiles, there can be no doubt that this withdrawal from Jerusalem was very desirable. Christianity no longer seemed, in the eyes of the world, to be a matter of mere Jewish interest; nor could the Christians any longer be fairly regarded as a sect of Jews. The Gospel now took its place visibly among the great interests of human life. And it is a remarkable and important fact that its success was at once so decided in the important city of Antioch.

As the Roman capital of the province of Syria (to which Judea was a sub-province), Antioch was the most central and conspicuous place in the eastern part of the Roman empire; the place of all others to give notoriety to any new movement of Eastern thought.

It was situated about twenty miles up the river Orontes, which empties itself into the N.E. corner of the Levant, just south of the bay of Issus, and opposite to the N.E. corner of the island of Cyprus. It was built by Seleucus Nicator about 300 years B.C., and was made the capital of the Greek kingdom of Syria. It grew and flourished, and was famous for its commerce, being on the direct road from Europe into the heart of Asia. Seleucia, on the sea-coast near the mouth of the

Orontes, was the growth of the same period. Antioch became one of the three principal Christian Sees, or Patriarchates, of the second century, the others being Rome and Alexandria; to which were added Constantinople in the fourth century, and Jerusalem in the fifth.

The narrative of St. Luke returns now to the church at Jerusalem:

Ch. xii. 1. Herod* Agrippa, in whose person the Jewish monarchy was nominally restored, seems to have sought popularity among the Jews by persecuting the infant church of Christ. He put James the son of Zebedee to death; and, "because he saw that it pleased the Jews, he proceeded further to take Peter also." Peter is delivered from prison by an angel, and after rejoining the disciples at the house of Mary the mother of John Mark (the evangelist Mark), he departs "to another place" not mentioned,—for safety, doubtless. 20. The death of Herod takes place in the theatre of Cæsarea, amid gorgeous pageantry and loathsome flatteries.† 24. Barnabas and Saul, having fulfilled their charge at Jerusalem, return to Antioch, taking with them John Mark (who was nephew to Barnabas).

Paul's first journey, with Barnabas and Mark, starting from Antioch, A.D. 48.—Ch. xiii. The prophets and teachers at Antioch, on the suggestion of the Holy Spirit,‡ designate Barnabas and Saul by fasting, prayer and laying on of hands, for a mission to places apparently not fully defined at first. 4. They go down to Seleucia, and sail thence to Cyprus, the native country of Barnabas, taking with them John as their "minister" or assistant; land at Salamis at the east end of the island, and preach in the Jewish synagogues. 6. Thence they traverse the island to Paphos at its western extremity; where the "deputy of the country," Sergius Paulus, resided,

* Herod was made nominal king of Judea by Claudius on his accession, A.D. 41, and died A.D. 44. As, up to this time, the chronology of the book of Acts is somewhat unsettled, a fixed date here is very valuable.

† Josephus, Ant. xix. 8, gives a similar account.

‡ It is vain to conjecture how this was conveyed; whether outwardly signified, or merely inferred from the unanimity with which, while ministering to the Lord, they determined upon the mission and the men.

and a Jewish sorcerer, Barjesus (called also Elymas, or *magician)* seems to have been under his patronage;—no uncommon illustration of the mixture of credulity and scepticism in respectable Romans in the Imperial times. The deputy, or proconsul,* sends for Barnabas and Saul, desiring to hear the word of God. Elymas endeavours to counteract their influence, and is reproved by Saul and afflicted with blindness "for a season." The proconsul becomes a believer.

From this moment the apostle is uniformly called PAUL, as up to this time he has been uniformly *Saul*, the transition being marked by the historian, at ver. 9, by using both names: "Saul, who is also Paul." It is a matter of curious conjecture to decide why this change was made, and why just at this time. Some think he bore both names from childhood. The one being Hebrew, and the other Roman, with only the difference of the first letter, it is very credible that the Romans among whom he mixed might, even involuntarily, give him the name they were most used to pronounce. It is not improbable that he might, if already called by the one name by his old Jewish friends, and the other more commonly by his new Gentile associates, deliberately prefer the latter when he is now setting forth as Apostle of the Gentiles; and it is also possible that a delicate compliment may have been designed

* The Roman provinces were at this time of two orders, Imperial and Consular. To the former class, the emperor sent a Prætor as military governor, to remain during his pleasure; to the latter, the senate nominated a Proconsul as civic governor for the year. Augustus had taken into his own hands for military government the most disturbed provinces, and given the quieter ones to the senate. Many re-adjustments were afterwards made. The older commentators (Grotius among them), believing Cyprus to have been an imperial province, supposed that Luke had made a mistake, though a pardonable one, in calling Sergius Paulus ἀνθύπατος, or proconsul. But a Greek coin has been found, of the reign of Claudius, bearing the inscription κυπρίων (of the Cyprians), and ἀνθύπατος as the title of the governor Proclus, who succeeded Sergius Paulus (see Marsh's Lectures on the Authenticity, &c., xxvi.). And all the time it was clear, on a careful reading of Dio Cassius, that Augustus, who in the first instance retained Cyprus as an imperial province, had afterwards given it and Galatia to the senate in exchange for Dalmatia. Luke's designation, "proconsul," is therefore quite right; and this minute exactness sustains the claim of the writer of the book of Acts to have been contemporary with the events.

by him towards the proconsul of Cyprus, in using the name of his distinguished convert as his own. At all events, he is Paul the Apostle uniformly from this time in the book of Acts, and in all his own Epistles, which were all written subsequently to this journey through Cyprus.

13. From Paphos in Cyprus, Paul and his friends sail across to Pamphylia (on the S. coast of what we now call Asia Minor), the province adjoining Cilicia to the W. At Perga, a town in this province, John Mark faint-heartedly leaves them and returns to Jerusalem. 14. Paul and Barnabas travel inland to Antioch in Pisidia,* where Paul (being invited to do so) speaks in the Jewish synagogue. His address, reported in this chapter, is quite in the style of those of Peter and Stephen in the earlier chapters, expounding Christianity as the destined fulfilment of Judaism. The service being over, they were urgently requested to preach the same words again the next sabbath (or rather between that and the next sabbath†). They conversed, accordingly, with native Jews and proselytes; and "the next sabbath-day came almost the whole city together to hear the word of God." Whether Gentiles were among the audience, or whether the apostle's doctrine of equal religious privileges for Jew and Gentile was the sole cause of offence, the more exclusive Jews now oppose Paul; and he and his companion thereupon take their ground independently of the synagogue:—46, 47: "Then Paul and Barnabas waxed bold, and said, It was necessary that the word of God should first have been spoken to you: but seeing ye put it from you, and judge yourselves unworthy of everlasting life, lo, we turn to the Gentiles. For so hath the Lord commanded us, saying, I have set thee to be a light of the Gentiles, that thou shouldest

* The Antiochs were very numerous. This "Antioch in Pisidia" must not be confounded with the Antioch in Syria, from which Paul and Barnabas set out. The Syrian capital is always simply ANTIOCH when spoken of in the New Testament. Pisidian Antioch was a Roman colony.

† "Betwixt and the next sabbath," is a familar English phrase nearly equivalent. The Received Text makes the *Gentiles* request this; but Griesbach's has nothing about Gentiles. There were "religious proselytes" there (ver. 43); that is, Gentile converts or Hellenist Jews; and, on the following sabbath, even Gentiles seem to have also obtruded into the synagogue, to the great horror of zealous Jews.

be for salvation unto the ends of the earth." The Gentiles receive this decision with enthusiasm, and the word is published "throughout all the region." The Jews prevail, however, in driving the apostles out of the city; who, emblematically of their independent and high purpose, "shake off the dust of their feet against them," and proceed to Iconium. This and the next two towns were in Lycaonia, the central province of Asia Minor, north of Cilicia, and separated from it by Mount Taurus. Ch. xiv. 1. At Iconium, they went first into the Jewish synagogue; many, both Jews and Greeks, believed, and "they abode there long;" but the unbelieving Jews stirred up the Gentiles, and the apostle and his companion quietly retreated to Lystra and Derbe. There is no mention of a synagogue in either of these towns, and their audience seems to have been chiefly composed of Gentiles.* A cripple among the audience is healed by Paul; whereupon these heathens cry out, "The gods are come down to us in the likeness of men." They call Barnabas Jupiter (no doubt the larger and handsomer man of the two), and Paul Mercury, as being "the chief speaker;" and the priest of Jupiter comes out with oxen and garlands to offer sacrifice to them. That most eloquent, unpremeditated address was then hurriedly spoken to them by Paul, yet scarcely availed to restrain the idolatrous demonstration: "Sirs, why do ye these things? We also are men of like passions with you, and preach unto you that ye should turn from these vanities unto the living God, which made heaven, and earth, and the sea, and all things that are therein: who in times past suffered all nations to walk in their own ways; nevertheless, he left not himself without witness, in that he did good, and gave us rain from heaven, and fruitful seasons, filling our hearts with food and gladness." 19. But the persecutors from Antioch and Iconium still follow the steps of our apostle; and he is severely stoned

* But doubtless there were some Jews in these places, and it is probable that Timothy was among Paul's hearers; for, on Paul's second journey thither (Acts xvi. 1), he took Timothy away with him thence,—"the son of a certain woman which was a Jewess and believed, but his father was a Greek; who was well reported of by the brethren that were at Lystra and Iconium."

at Lystra by the same ignorant multitude who just before would have worshiped him. He goes on, however, to Derbe, Barnabas still accompanying; and having preached the Gospel there and made many disciples, they return the way they had come, and appoint elders to preside over the church in each place, Lystra, Iconium, Antioch, Perga; thence they go to Attalia, on the coast, and sail to the Syrian Antioch, "from whence they had been commended to the grace of God for the work which they had now fulfilled." They report to the assembled church "how God had opened the door of faith unto the Gentiles. And there they abode long time with the disciples." This ends the first missionary journey of St. Paul.

The "Council of Jerusalem," A.D. 50 or 51.—The question of the continued obligation of the Jewish Law upon Christians, and of the necessity of Gentile converts submitting to it, was not finally settled by Peter's vision. Long-established ideas are not so easily parted with. Many Jewish Christians continued to believe the Law obligatory, not only upon themselves, but upon the Gentile believers too. And while Antioch was the centre of Paul's mission to the Gentiles, many of the brethren at Jerusalem looked with dissatisfaction upon their free admission into the Christian church. So, on the return of Paul and Barnabas to Antioch, they found a formidable controversy awaiting them, which Paul had ever afterwards to wage, by letter as well as in person, throughout his ministry. It is the key to his letters to the Galatians and Romans especially.

Ch. xv. 1. "Certain men who had come down from Jerusalem were teaching the brethren and saying, Except ye be circumcised after the manner of Moses, ye cannot be saved."

After "no little dissension and disputation" at Antioch, it was agreed to send Paul and Barnabas and others* "to Jerusalem to the apostles and elders about this question." On their way through Phenice and Samaria, they caused great joy by declaring the conversion of the Gentiles; and on arriving at Jerusalem, they gave an account, before the apostles, the

* Titus, a Gentile convert, was one of these others (Gal. ii. 1).

elders and the church, of their late successful mission among the Gentiles. It was, as we might expect, the converted Pharisees (ver. 5) who insisted upon the necessity of imposing the Law upon the Gentile believers. The apostles and elders being assembled, Peter told over again how God had bidden him preach to the Gentiles, and deprecated the idea of putting "a yoke upon the neck of the disciples, which (he said) neither our fathers nor we were able to bear." Then Paul and Barnabas having given their narrative amid marked silence and attention, James,* in a very conciliatory manner, fortifies Peter's argument by quoting various prophetic allusions to the Gentiles, and suggests to the meeting, "not to trouble" those Gentiles who are turned to God, but merely to urge them to "abstain from pollutions of idols, and from fornication, and from things strangled, and from blood,"—those heathen practices which were most offensive at once to Jewish feelings and to the purity of both Jewish and Christian worship.† This suggestion was adopted and embodied in a very kindly letter

* This is James the Less, or Younger, "the Lord's brother" (cousin ?), "the son of Alpheus," as he is variously called in Scripture; "James the Just," in ecclesiastical history. He seems to have been the president of the apostles.

† That a sin against morality is here classed with offences against the ritual law of Moses, is a sad record of the fact that it was almost uniformly connected with the ritual of idolatrous ceremonies in heathen temples! Here is one of those points of contrast which proclaim the Jewish ceremonialism to have been divine in its origin and elevating in its influence.

St. Paul alludes to this deliberation in Gal. ii. 1—10, where he speaks with great warmth in defence of the freedom of the Gentiles, and with strong indignation towards "false brethren." James, Cephas and John, he says, agreed thenceforth to preach to the Jews, while he and Barnabas should to the Gentiles, the latter promising to remember the poor Christians in Judea. In the following verses he mentions an incident not named in the Acts, and not very creditable to Peter's consistency:

"But when Peter was come to Antioch, I withstood him to the face, because he was to be blamed. For before that certain came from James, he did eat with the Gentiles; but when they were come, he withdrew and separated himself, fearing them which were of the circumcision. And the other Jews dissembled likewise with him; insomuch that Barnabas also was carried away with their dissimulation. But when I saw that they walked not uprightly according to the truth of the Gospel, I said unto Peter before them all, If thou, being a Jew, livest after the manner of Gentiles, and not to the Gentile brethren in Antioch, Syria and Cilicia; while Judas, surnamed Barsabas, and Silas, "chief men among the brethren," were commissioned to accompany Paul and Barnabas to Antioch, and explain the matter further by word of mouth. "Being prophets also themselves, they exhort the brethren and confirm them." Silas remains at Antioch (34) when the rest of the deputation returns home.

Second journey of St. Paul from Antioch (with Silas and Timothy), A.D. 51.—Ch. xv. 36. "After some days," Paul proposes to Barnabas to re-visit their newly-formed churches in Asia Minor. But, on Barnabas proposing to take Mark with them (who seems to have come from Jerusalem with this purpose), Paul would not consent, on account of his recent desertion; so they separate,* and Barnabas sets off with Mark for Cyprus, while Paul, with Silas for his companion, takes the reverse direction through Syria and Cilicia, among his earliest churches (to which the Jerusalem letter is addressed), and so to Derbe and Lystra, of his later planting. Here (xvi. 1) he finds his young convert† Timothy, whom, as the son of a mixed Jewish and Greek marriage, he now circumcises, with a view to conciliate the Jews in those parts. Having travelled through Phrygia and Galatia, and being forbidden by the Holy Spirit to preach in the province of Asia, and also

as do the Jews, why compellest thou the Gentiles to live as do the Jews!" (Gal. ii. 11—14).

How soon after the meeting at Jerusalem this visit of Peter's to Antioch occurred, is doubtful. Perhaps before Paul's second journey. That no permanent ill-will resulted between these two distinguished men is plain, however, from Peter's mention of Paul (2 Pet. iii. 15) as "our beloved brother," and is characteristic of the candour with which he could confess himself to have been in the wrong.

* If the dispute at Antioch between Peter and Paul had only just occurred, in which "Barnabas also was carried away with the dissimulation," this would further explain the occasion of his separation from Paul. We have no record of Barnabas from this time, but a kindly allusion to him on Paul's part five or six years after (1 Cor. ix. 6).

† "My own son in the faith" (1 Tim. i. 2); "My dearly beloved son" (2 Tim. i. 2). He had probably been converted on Paul's previous visit to Lystra.

in Bithynia, they pass by Mysia to Troas.* Here Paul has a vision directing him to cross over to Macedonia, and the Christian mission is planted accordingly, for the first time, in Europe. Luke apparently joins them at Troas, as the narrative here assumes the first personal form (ver. 10): "*We* endeavoured to go into Macedonia," &c. A fair wind carries them "with a straight course" in two days past Samothrace to Neapolis, whence they have a few miles only to travel to Philippi, "the chief† city of that part of Macedonia, and a Roman colony." The Jews in Philippi are few; they have no synagogue, but a "place of prayer," outside the city, by a river-side, where Paul and his companions meet a company of Jewish women on the sabbath. Among them was one named Lydia, from Thyatira‡ in Asia, a seller of the celebrated purple dye, who "was baptized and her household," and who hospitably constrained the apostle and his companions to stay at her house. An unfortunate insane girl (apparently a slave), whom the Jews would have called a demoniac, but who in this Græco-Roman city is described as "possessed with a spirit of Python" (or Apollo), and whose strange, but often shrewd, utterances were received for oracles (as has often been

* All these names denote parts of what we now call *Asia Minor*. *Phrygia* was a vague term for the central part, and included *Galatia*, so called from its population being chiefly Gauls. *Asia* means the Roman province so called, comprising the whole west or Ægean coast, and reaching inland till it meets *Bithynia* lying on the Propontis and Euxine, the vague borders of *Phrygia* in the centre, *Pisidia* next southward, and *Pamphylia* on the Levant coast. *Mysia* was the old name of the north part of this province of Asia, which included also the old *Lydia* and *Caria*. *Troas* (which also denoted the north-west corner around old Troy, "the Troad") is here the sea-port town, Alexandria Troas more properly, somewhat south of old Troy.

† *πρώτη τῆς μερίδος τῆς μακεδονίας πόλις*, literally, the *first* city. Amphipolis was the capital of that part of Macedonia; so some take it to mean *the first city Paul came to*; but that, again, was Neapolis. A very tempting conjectural reading is, *πρώτης μερίδος*, "a city of the first part of Macedonia," for this part was called *Macedonia prima*. Or (if we keep the common reading) we must translate it "*a* chief city." Luke's exactness need not be questioned, at any rate.

‡ Was her conversion the first seed for the growth of the Gospel in her own city, when she returned home? Thyatira was one of the seven churches of *Asia*, in Rev. i. 11, of which the New Testament tells us nothing more.

the case with such persons among the illiterate in many countries), to the no small gain of her owners,—follows the apostles' company day after day, crying out, "These men are the servants of the Most High God, which shew unto us the way of salvation." Paul cures her disordered mind by commanding the spirit, in the name of Jesus, to come out of her. "Her masters," enraged at the loss of their wicked gains, drag Paul and Silas* before the propraetors, and charge them with introducing unlawful Jewish customs. They are summarily scourged and imprisoned; but while, at midnight, they sing praises to God, the prison doors are miraculously opened and all its inmates set free. The jailor (who was responsible with his life for their safe custody) attempts suicide (like a real Roman in such a case); but Paul restrains him by that commanding moral power which he often shewed, and tells him they are not going to escape. The jailor is converted, with all his household. In the morning, the propraetors, on being informed by the jailor of what had happened, sent the lictors to set the prisoners free. But Paul, now hinting his Roman citizenship, to the great alarm of the magistrates, refuses to be thus "thrust out privily;" and the propraetors come apologetically in person and beg them to leave the city.† They do so at their early leisure,‡ after again visiting the brethren at the house of Lydia.

Ch. xvii. 1. Passing through Amphipolis and Apollonia,

* Luke and Timothy were probably less conspicuous, or perhaps not with them at the very time of the miracle.

† If it is asked, why Paul did not assert his citizenship to prevent the illegal scourging (as on a later occasion at Jerusalem he did), the obvious answer is, that Silas was not a Roman citizen, and Paul was too generous to desert his friend. He might speak roundly of Roman citizens (in the plural) having been beaten illegally, but could not have said, *We are* Roman citizens, to prevent the infliction.

‡ Paul, Silas and Timothy, that is. Luke, apparently, stays behind, the narrative dropping again into the third person, and becoming less minute and vivid than in the visit to Philippi. He seems to have joined Paul again at Philippi on his third journey (xx. 5), where the narrative says *we* and *us* again. Did he consolidate the church at Philippi meanwhile? or return to Troas? or travel in his own professional career? or as missionary of the Gospel? (See Conybeare and Howson, I. 334.)

they come to Thessalonica, "where was a synagogue of the Jews," implying that there was not in the other two places. Jews were very numerous in Thessalonica. It was the capital of Macedonia Secunda, and the most populous and commercial place in the whole province.* Here Paul and Silas addressed the Jews first, for three successive sabbaths, especially explaining the death and resurrection of the Messiah. Some Jews believed; "devout Greeks"† more numerously; and of "the chief women not a few;"—Jewish wives, possibly, of some of the leading men in the city. There is nothing more said about Gentile converts here; but, from 1 Thess. i. 9, we learn that the Thessalonian church was principally composed of Gentiles, and the reception of these Gentiles may probably explain what now happened. For the unbelieving Jews raised a riot and attacked the house of Jason,‡ where they expected to find Paul and Silas; they bring Jason to bail before the rulers;§ and the brethren prevail upon the apostles to go forward to Berea.

11. The Berean Jews are applauded for their diligent searching of the Scriptures and investigation into the claims of the alleged Christ. Many of them consequently believed; and not a few Greek women of high rank, and men also. But the Thessalonian Jews follow the apostle's steps and excite the mob; so that the brethren thought it prudent to send Paul away. He embarked, probably, from some neighbouring sea-port for Athens (14); or he may have taken the direction of the sea coast by land. Silas and Timothy are to join him at Athens; but, while he is waiting for their arrival, his ardent zeal cannot restrain itself in the view of the countless forms

* The modern Greece and South Turkey (from Mount Hæmus southward) was divided into three Roman provinces, namely, Macedonia in the north-east, Illyricum north-west, and Achaia in the south, the last being nearly identical with the present kingdom of Greece. Macedonia was divided into *prima*, *secunda*, *tertia* and *quarta*.

† It is a question whether these were proselytes to Judaism, or simply non-idolatrous Gentiles, like Cornelius the centurion.

‡ Possibly a kinsman, or tribesman, of Paul. See Rom. xvi. 21.

§ *πολιτάρχαι*. The politarchs. Thessalonica was a free city, and its magistrates were neither proconsuls nor propraetors.

of idolatry raised on all hands to gods known (as supposed) and unknown. The Athenians had the reputation, among Greek writers, and also with Josephus, of being the most religious of the Greeks (εὐσεβεστάτοι); and Paul tells them (when, after many private discussions with Jews, devout persons, and any that met him in the Agora, he was brought before the Areopagitic Council) that he observes their "carefulness in religion" * (δεισιδαιμονεστέροι). His noble and well-known speech in the presence of Stoics and Epicureans, Judges of the Areopagus, Greeks of all classes, and Jews, seems to have been cut short by the impatience of some who scoffed when he talked of "the resurrection of the dead." One of the Areopagite judges, Dionysius, however, became a Christian, and a woman named Damaris and others; but we hear nothing more in the New Testament about the church at Athens; and the Gospel seems, as a general rule, to have taken deeper root in the more active mercantile populations, than in this city of philosophy and art. Its next scene is a commercial place.

Ch. xviii. 1. Paul goes from Athens to Corinth, then the capital of the province of Achaia, and a Roman colony,—a place of great trade, having been rapidly rebuilt since its destruction by Mummius, and peopled by a mixed population of Greeks, Jews and Romans. Here he meets Aquila, a Jew of Pontus (south-east coast of the Euxine Sea), and Priscilla his wife, who have been driven from Rome by the decree of Claudius against the Jews.† They are tent-makers by trade, like Paul, and he resides and works with them, attending the synagogue every sabbath, and persuading both Jews and Greeks. Aquila and Priscilla become, apparently, his converts at this time. Silas and Timothy rejoin him here. The Jews violently opposing, he "goes to the Gentiles." A proselyte named Justus (the name arguing him a Roman) opened his house, which "joined hard to the synagogue," for the

* Conybeare and Howson, I. 389. Perhaps "tendency to superstition" was gently, though not offensively, hinted in the phrase used by Paul. (See *Christian Reformer*, Nov. 1847.)

† A.D. 52 probably. They are at Rome again when Paul writes to the church there (xvi. 3), A.D. 58.

apostle's preaching. Crispus, the head of the synagogue, is converted, with his family. The Lord, in a vision, assures Paul that he has much people in Corinth; and the apostle stays there a year and a half, teaching the word of God among them.* We cannot doubt that his labours and those of his companions extended to many other towns of Achaia, from its metropolis. Gallio, brother of the philosopher Seneca, was proconsul at that time (ver. 12), a man of singular virtue, just and humane, while easy-tempered. The Jews brought Paul before him on the charge of "persuading men to worship God contrary to the Mosaic Law." Gallio at once refuses to interfere in a matter of "words and names and the Jewish Law," and rightly and clearly defines his own office to be the redress of wrong and wickedness. The discomfiture of these Jewish plaintiffs was matter of amusement to the Greek spectators, who took Sosthenes,† the chief of the synagogue, and beat him before the very judgment-seat, Gallio not interfering. From Corinth (that is, from its port Cenchrea), the apostle sails, with Aquila and Priscilla, for Ephesus, the capital of the province of Asia, Paul himself meaning to attend an approaching festival at Jerusalem. At Cenchrea, either he, or Aquila more likely (for the construction is ambiguous), ends a voluntary vow, something like that of the Nazirite, by cutting his hair, which during the vow had been allowed to grow long. Here we lose sight of Silas; whether left behind at Corinth, or whether (as some think) he accompanied Paul to Jerusalem and stayed there, the narrative does not say.‡ Tradition idly makes him to have been the first bishop of

* Here the two letters to the Thessalonians were written; and in the greetings of both of them, the names of Silas and Timothy are united with that of Paul. From 1 Thess. iii. 1—6, it appears that while Paul was alone at Athens, he had commissioned Timothy to go back to Thessalonica "to establish and comfort them in the faith." On Timothy's return to him at Corinth, the first letter to the Thessalonians is written, and the second a few months later.

† It is possible, but by no means certain, that this is the Sosthenes named as a Christian brother afterwards (in 1 Cor. i. 1), as being with Paul at Ephesus.

‡ Silas (Silvanus is the same name) is afterwards the bearer of Peter's First Epistle to the Christians in Asia Minor (1 Pet. v. 12).

Corinth. Timothy is at Ephesus in ch. xix. 22; whence it is fair to conclude that he sailed with the party from Cenchrea. Arrived at Ephesus, Paul visits the synagogue and reasons with the Jews; he is pressed to stay, and promises to return after the approaching festival. He re-embarks (perhaps in the same vessel) for Cæsarea; and we are then merely informed that, "when he had landed in Cæsarea and gone up and saluted the church, he went to Antioch" (ver. 22). It may be doubted whether he even reached Jerusalem at all; and some suppose that, on landing at Cæsarea, he found himself too late for the feast, and so went straight to Antioch. "*Gone up*," may be translated, "*gone ashore*;" and the church which he saluted would then be that of Cæsarea. Any how, we have no account of his going to Jerusalem; and the end of his second missionary journey has now brought him back to Antioch, in Syria, whence he had set out.

Paul's third journey from Antioch, A.D. 54.—Ch. xviii. 23. After he has "spent some time" there, he goes over all the country of Galatia and Phrygia in order, strengthening the disciples, and so to Ephesus, as promised. Here, meanwhile (ver. 24), a representative of the state of religion in a distant but most important part of the world, makes his appearance,—Apollos, an Alexandrian Jew, eloquent and mighty in the Scriptures, who has been instructed in the way of the Lord, but knows "only John's baptism." From this expression, we need not suppose that he knew nothing of what had happened in Palestine since the preaching of John the Baptist; but that, having been baptized as a disciple of John, he had not been subsequently baptized as a Christian. He knew no baptism but John's. Nor did he know the full history of Christ's life, death and resurrection. Aquila and Priscilla inform him more thoroughly, and his zeal becomes the more lively. He goes to Corinth, with letters of attestation from the brethren at Ephesus, to "water what Paul had planted," and mightily convinces the Jews that Jesus is the Christ.

Ch. xix. 1. Apollos has just left Ephesus, when Paul arrives and finds about twelve disciples (perhaps also from Alexandria) in much the same state of knowledge as Apollos lately was, having been baptized into John's baptism, and not having heard "whether there be any Holy Spirit."* They are more fully informed, are baptized into the name of the Lord Jesus, and receive the Holy Spirit. 8. For three months Paul preaches at Ephesus in the synagogue of the Jews; and then, meeting with opposition, turns to the Gentiles, who frequent his instructions in the school of one Tyrannus. This he does for two years,† extending his instructions, personally or through his companions, throughout the province of *Asia*. 11. "Special miracles" having been wrought through the agency of Paul (the cure of sick persons by handkerchiefs brought from him is particularized‡), it occurred to some itinerant Jewish exorcists to try the power of the name of Jesus in casting out demons. The madman whom they so adjured shrewdly replied, "Jesus I know, and Paul I know; but who are ye?" and turned furiously upon them, to the irretrievable discredit of their art. Many magicians publicly burned their books and confessed the cross. 21. Paul now purposes to go through Macedonia and Achaia, and thence to Jerusalem, and expresses an intention, or else a presentiment, that he must, after that, see Rome. Timothy and Erastus go before him into Macedonia; and while Paul still stays for a season, a great tumult occurs in Ephesus, excited by Demetrius the silversmith, "who made silver shrines for Diana." The temple

* Or, "whether the Holy Spirit has been given," *εἰ πνεῦμα ἅγιον ἐστιν*. So, in John vii. 39, *οὔπω γὰρ ἦν πνεῦμα ἅγιον*, is rightly translated, "for the Holy Spirit was not yet given."

† It is conjectured that, during these two years, he made a visit of a few days to Corinth, to which he may seem to allude (2 Cor. xii. 14). Ships were constantly sailing to and fro. His First Epistle to the Corinthians was written from Ephesus. It has also been supposed that during these two years he went with Titus to Crete, leaving Timothy in charge at Ephesus; and that the first letter to Timothy was written from Crete, and that to Titus on his return to Ephesus. (See Belsham's Epistles of Paul.) But Conybeare and Howson, with recent critics in general, assign a later date to both these letters.

‡ It is ingeniously conjectured that the *specialty* of these was designed to shame the addictedness of the Ephesians to the arts of magic and sorcery. But it is not clear that these are meant as the special miracles; they may be mentioned as illustrations rather of the overflowing divine energy manifested.

of Diana of Ephesus was very magnificent, the statue of the goddess very ancient, and the reputation of both very widespread. The votaries from all parts, no doubt, bought Demetrius's little silver shrines as memorials. He sees danger to his craft in the doctrine "that they be no gods which are made with hands." A tumultuous meeting takes place in the theatre. Two of Paul's companions are laid hands upon; and he himself is only restrained from following (which must have been to his almost certain destruction) by the interference of some of the Asiarchs* who were well-disposed towards him. In the theatre, Alexander, a Jew (possibly the same Alexander, the coppersmith, mentioned in 2 Tim. iv. 14), tries to "make his defence," no doubt wishing to clear himself and his countrymen of all responsibility for Paul's doings; but he is cried down. At last, the "town-clerk,"† or chancellor, or recorder, with great address, appeases the meeting, tells Demetrius it is sessions'-time, and the proconsuls are in the city, ready to settle any offences against the law, and dismisses the assembly.

Ch. xx. 1. In four verses we are briefly told that Paul left Ephesus for Macedonia,—went over those parts,—gave much exhortation,—came into Greece (Achaia),—stayed there (we presume at Corinth chiefly) three months,—and was about to sail for Syria (to visit Jerusalem, as before proposed), when a plot against him by the Jews determined him to return through Macedonia‡ instead. 5. Companions both from

* τινὲς τῶν ἀσιαρχῶν, the deputies from the towns of Asia to regulate the games and shows at Ephesus, now going on.

† γραμματεὺς. Ephesus, like most of the Greek cities, was allowed by the Romans to maintain its own internal government.

‡ Many things not mentioned by Luke in the history are assigned to this period by decisive passages in Paul's Epistles. From Ephesus, on the way to Macedonia, he went by Troas; and, preaching with success, would have stayed there longer, but was anxious to meet Titus, who was bringing him news of the Corinthian church, and who met him, in fact, when he had reached Philippi, in Macedonia. (See 2 Cor. ii. 12, 13, and vii. 6.) From Philippi he writes his second letter to the Corinthian church, and sends it by Titus (and Luke?), promising shortly to come himself. While going over the parts about Macedonia, Paul elsewhere says (Rom. xv. 19) that he had been as far as Illyricum (the conterminous province). At Corinth ("Achaia

Greece and Asia assemble at Philippi, and sail in two different vessels to Troas. The time of the year was that of the Passover, and the feast which he meant to keep at Jerusalem was therefore Pentecost. He is carrying alms from Macedonia and Achaia for the poor saints at Jerusalem. (Here, if not before, Luke is again of the party, as the forms *we* and *us* reappear.) At Troas they spend seven days, and the restoring miracle upon the young man Eutychus is performed. Paul rejoins the ship at Assos (walking across the promontory while the ship rounds it, and so, probably, gaining that last night's meeting with the church at Troas), and they sail on to Miletus. Unable, for want of time, to go to Ephesus, Paul had sent for the elders of that thriving and interesting church to meet him at Miletus, to whom he gives a most affectionate charge to pasture the Lord's* church, expressing his clear foreboding of bonds and imprisonment, and his certainty that they would see his face no more. With most affectionate and pious farewells they accompany him to the ship, which lands them at *Patara* (near the south of *Asia)*, where they fortunately meet with another ship just sailing for Tyre. Ch. xxi. 4. They stay seven days with the disciples whom they find at Tyre, and who in vain implore Paul to desist from his purpose of going to Jerusalem. They sail again from Tyre to Cæsarea, touching at Ptolemais (Acre), and saluting the brethren there. 8. At Cæsarea they are received by Philip the evangelist (or deacon, see ch. vi. 5), whose four daughters "prophesy." They tarry many days (the prosperous voyage having left them time to spare); and here Agabus (who

for three months"), it is pretty well agreed that he wrote the Epistle to the Galatians, and that to the Romans. He stays seven days at Troas on his return from Macedonia, to take advantage of the "door opened" to his preaching in that place.

* Here occurs one of the very few various readings that have any doctrinal importance. "The Church *of God* which he hath purchased with his own blood," is corrected by Griesbach, and all critical editors since his time, into "the Church *of the Lord*," in accordance with all the best MSS. It is mentioned here for the sake of stating how very few those various readings of the New Testament are which affect, or are thought to affect, any matter of distinct Christian belief. There are not more than half-a-dozen such, at the very most.

had signified the dearth in ch. xi. 28) emblematically hints Paul's imprisonment by the Jews of Jerusalem. But Paul goes bravely forward.

Paul arrested at Jerusalem and sent to Rome.—Ch. xxi. 15. At Jerusalem, Paul and his friends are gladly received by James and the elders, and narrate their manifold success among the Gentiles. He is reminded of the strong prejudices prevailing among the Jewish Christians against him, and consents, as recommended, to shew his own personal observance of the Law by defraying the purification charges of some poor brethren who have the Nazirite vow upon them. 27. Jews from Asia, knowing that he was in the temple, and having seen Trophimus, an Ephesian, with him in the city, raised a cry that he had brought Greeks into the temple and polluted it. They violently drag him forth, and are only prevented from murdering him by the timely intervention of the Roman captain with his soldiers, who apprehends him and chains him, thinking he is an Egyptian* who had lately caused an insurrection, and is astonished when he hears him speak Greek. Paul briefly tells who he is, and requests permission to speak to the crowd before being carried into the castle. From the steps of the fortress he addresses them in Hebrew, giving an account of his own early life and conversion. Ch. xxii. 1—21. They hear him attentively till he declares his mission to the Gentiles; but, at that word, their fury is renewed. The chief captain (to whose Roman ears this was all probably unintelligible) orders his prisoner into the castle, and gives him in charge to a centurion to "examine by scourging;" but Paul asserts his Roman citizenship, and is thenceforth treated accordingly. 30. The chief captain, perplexed to know what to do with his prisoner, sends him to the Sanhedrim. Ch. xxiii. 1. Grossly insulted by the high-priest (who orders him to be smitten on the face for declaring he had always lived conscientiously), Paul remonstrates indignantly and somewhat intemperately, but immediately apologizes to the sacred office, which the man had dishonoured. Then, seeing that calm

* Josephus, Ant. xx. 8, 6; Wars, ii. 13, 5.

investigation was not the purpose of the Sanhedrim, and noticing the mixture of Pharisees and Sadducees among his judges, he announced himself (with truth equal to the prudence of the avowal) to be a Pharisee and the son of a Pharisee, and added that the resurrection of the dead was a leading principle of the religious doctrines which he was called in question for teaching. The Sanhedrim being thus divided, the chief captain again claims his prisoner and secures him in the castle. 11. In the night, a vision of Jesus cheers him, and tells him he is to bear witness at Rome also. 12. A plot by some desperate Jews against his life being fortunately detected by Paul's sister's son, the chief captain sends his prisoner to Cæsarea by night under strong military escort, with an explanatory letter to Felix, the Roman Procurator. Ch. xxiv. 1. The high-priest and elders follow in a few days, with their hired advocate Tertullus. They charge Paul with being seditious and a ringleader of the Nazarene sect, and with profaning the temple. Paul (10—21) rebuts the charges of sedition and profanation by the mere statement of facts, and confesses and vindicates what they call his "heresy." Felix puts off deciding the case; sends for Paul another day to declare the faith in Christ before his Jewish wife Drusilla (and is made to tremble for a moment before the prisoner's reasoning on righteousness, temperance and judgment to come); temporizes, in the hope of being bribed to set the apostle free, sending for him often; and leaves him in bonds at last when removed from his government, "to shew the Jews a pleasure," while they were following him to Rome with complaints against his oppressive government.

Ch. xxv. 1. Festus having succeeded, the high-priest and leading Jews press for a trial at Jerusalem; but the new governor bids them come to Cæsarea, where, accordingly, they renew their various accusations, but without proof. 8. Festus, probably on perceiving that these were questions of the Jews' religion, asked Paul if he would consent to be tried before him at Jerusalem; but the latter, still using his birthright as a Roman citizen, wisely appeals to the supreme tribunal of the empire, in these manly terms: "I stand at Cæsar's judgment-seat, where I ought to be judged: to the Jews have I done no wrong, as thou very well knowest. For if I be an offender, or have committed anything worthy of death, I refuse not to die: but if it be nothing whereof these accuse me, no man may deliver me unto them. I appeal unto Cæsar." 13. Agrippa* and his sister Bernice coming to Cæsarea to salute the new governor, the latter takes occasion to mention the case of Paul; and Agrippa being curious to hear him, Paul makes before them all (xxvi.) his last-recorded public statement of his life, conversion and Christian belief.

Ch. xxvii. and part of ch. xxviii. give a minute and truly graphic account of Paul's voyage to Italy,—the tempest,—the shipwreck on the island of Malta, and the saving of the passengers and crew.†

Ch. xxvii. 1. Paul, with other prisoners, is put under the charge of Julius, a centurion of the Augustan or Imperial band, Luke being his companion, and also Aristarchus of Thessalonica (mentioned, in xix. 29 and xx. 4, as being with Paul at Jerusalem and at Philippi; and, in Col. iv. 10, as his "fellow-prisoner" at Rome). They sail in a ship bound for Adramyttium, on the coast of Mysia, touch at Sidon, and, with wind against them, coast along to Myra in Lycia. Here they go on board an Alexandrian ship sailing for Italy; and when on the coast of Crete, with wind against them and the season growing late, Paul recommends wintering there; but the centurion, guided by the opinion of the master and the pilot, determines to proceed. Storm ensues (14); and, with ship dismantled and driving before the wind, they are wrecked on the island of Malta; but, through Paul's commanding presence of mind, all lives are saved. Ch. xxviii. 7. Publius, the governor of the island, lodges them three days courteously. His father, ill of dysentery, is healed at Paul's prayer, and

* Agrippa II., the son of Herod Agrippa of Acts xii. (See note on p. 358.)

† The narrative of this voyage is quite a study in ancient seamanship. It has been most thoroughly elucidated by James Smith, Esq., of Jordan Hill (in an 8vo volume, 1848), whose conclusions are, in almost every instance, accepted by Messrs. Conybeare and Howson in their splendid work. I must be content here merely to allude to these most curious and satisfactory sources of information.

other miraculous cures are performed. They wait three months for a ship to carry them forward; when the *Castor and Pollux*, from Alexandria, takes them, by Syracuse and Rhegium, to Puteoli. "Brethren" are found resident there, and other brethren from Rome come to meet them on the road.

Ch. xxviii. 16. At Rome, the apostle, while awaiting his trial, is kept in *military custody* (that is, guarded by a soldier whose left hand is chained to the prisoner's right), but is allowed to go, thus attended, wherever he pleases, and to dwell in "his own hired house." Soon after his arrival, he calls the chief of the Jews together, to explain to them the necessity he had been under of claiming the protection of Roman law against his own countrymen in Jerusalem; and he is relieved to find that there has been no one as yet from Judea speaking harm of him in Rome. On an appointed day, he expounds the kingdom of God more fully to them; whereupon, as usual, some believed and some believed not. To the latter he then declares that "the salvation of God is sent to the Gentiles, who will listen to it;" and the historian adds, that he "dwelt two whole years in his own hired house, and received all that came in unto him; preaching the kingdom of God, and teaching those things which concern the Lord Jesus Christ, with all confidence, no man forbidding him."

With these words the book of Acts abruptly ends, not even informing us what happened to the apostle at the end of the two years' detention, but certainly suggesting the inference that after two years he regained his liberty. The few remaining facts of his history that are ascertained, or credibly believed, from other sources, shall now be briefly stated.

The two years' delay before his trial may be understood as having been in part necessary, in accordance with Roman justice, to give his accusers time (if they chose to persist) to collect their witnesses, not only from Palestine, but from Achaia, Macedonia, Asia and Syria. Probably, however, there was little disposition on the part of the Jewish Sanhedrim to prosecute the trial thus removed to Rome; nor on the part of the Roman government to undertake an inquiry so perplexing, and indeed unintelligible, to them.

While awaiting his trial, Paul wrote his letters to Philemon and to the Colossians, the (so-called) letter to the Ephesians, and that to the Philippians; from which letters we gather many facts respecting the progress of Christianity in Rome under the ministrations of the "prisoner for Christ." These will be particularized under the various Epistles where they occur. At this time, there was certainly no active public feeling in Rome against the Christians. But during Paul's residence there, and by means of it, they became conspicuous enough to suggest to Nero the idea of throwing upon them the odium of the great fire which, a few years afterwards, he was suspected of having caused.

Paul's arrival at Rome was in the spring of A.D. 61. In the spring of 63, he is presumed to have been either acquitted on trial or released without trial. As in his letters, written during his detention, to the Philippians and to Philemon of Colosse (and to the Hebrews, if that letter be his), he had expressed the hope of being set free and soon visiting them, we naturally conclude that, when set free, he did visit the churches of Asia Minor, Macedonia, Achaia and other parts; and his remaining letters imply various visits to have taken place. From his having expressed, in his letter to the Romans some years before, an intention of going to Spain, it is inferred by some (and early tradition accords, though without going into particulars) that he actually fulfilled a journey into Spain.

In the year 64, the fire at Rome took place; and in the latter part of that year, the persecution of the Christians began, in the course of which it is agreed that both Paul and Peter suffered martyrdom at Rome. Lardner (who gives little credit to the alleged journey to Spain) places their deaths in the year 65, or possibly at the end of 64. Conybeare and Howson (who stand up for the journey into Spain, and allow two years for it) place the execution of Paul in the summer of 68, only a few days or weeks before Nero's death. Some suppose Paul to have come of his own accord to Rome during the persecution; others, that he was apprehended while travelling elsewhere, perhaps at Nicopolis, in Illyricum (where he bids Titus join him for the winter, Tit. iii. 12).

If the Epistle to the *Hebrews* is Paul's, it may be supposed (as it dates itself from Italy, xiii. 24) to have been written either during or shortly after his first imprisonment. The first letter to Timothy and that to Titus were probably written during his last Asian and Macedonian tour,—the former from Macedonia, the latter from Ephesus; and the second to Timothy was written evidently during his second imprisonment at Rome, when he has been examined once before Nero, and is "ready to be offered," feeling that the time of his departure is at hand.

The events of Paul's life may be usefully presented in a tabular view, including the respective dates of his Epistles at the places where they were written, and intermingling also the most important world-dates of the same period. I take these, somewhat abridged, from Conybeare and Howson (Vol. II. p. 560). The dates connected with the supposed Spanish journey are marked as doubtful (?) in their own table, and the few that follow must, of course, be supposed earlier by three or four years, if we adopt Lardner's conclusions. The earlier dates also (prior to the year 44) are confessedly doubtful, and the events from 39 to 43 are only conjecturally ascribed to that time.

Chronology of Paul's Apostleship.

A.D.

36? St. Paul's conversion.

37? At Damascus. (Accession of Caligula, March 16.)

37, 38? Arabia, and return to Damascus.

38? Flight from Damascus to Jerusalem, thence to Tarsus.

39—43? Preaches in Syria and Cilicia, making Tarsus head-quarters, and probably undergoes most of the sufferings mentioned 2 Cor. xi. 24—26. (Accession of Claudius, Jan. 25, A.D. 41.)

44 Brought by Barnabas to Antioch, and stays a year before the famine. (Death of Herod Agrippa. Cuspius Fadus, procurator of Judea.)

45 Visits Jerusalem with Barnabas to relieve the famine.

46, 47 At Antioch. (Tiberius Alexander, procurator.)

48, 49 First missionary journey from Antioch to Cyprus, Antioch in Pisidia, Iconium, Lystra, Derbe, and back

A.D.

through the same to Antioch. (Agrippa II. made king of Chalcidice.)

50 "Council of Jerusalem." (Cumanus, procurator.)

51 SECOND MISSIONARY JOURNEY from Antioch to Cilicia, Lycaonia, Galatia,

52 Troas, Philippi, Thessalonica, Berea, Athens, Corinth; *writes* 1 *Thessalonians.* (Claudius expels the Jews from Rome.)

53 At Corinth; *writes* 2 *Thessalonians.* (Agrippa II. made tetrarch of Trachonitis, and Felix procurator of Judea.)

54 (Spring) He leaves Corinth, reaches Jerusalem at Pentecost, thence to Antioch. (Accession of Nero, Oct. 13.)
THIRD MISSIONARY JOURNEY (autumn) from Antioch (through Galatia and Phrygia) to Ephesus.

55, 56 At Ephesus.

57 (Spring) *Writes* 1 *Corinthians;* (summer) leaves Ephesus for Macedonia, where (autumn) *he writes* 2 *Corinthians;* thence (winter) to Corinth, where *he writes Galatians.*

58 (Spring) *Writes Romans;* leaves Corinth, by Philippi and Miletus, to Jerusalem (Pentecost), where he is arrested and sent to Cæsarea.

59 At Cæsarea.

60 (About August) Sent to Rome by Festus. (Felix recalled and succeeded by Festus.)
(Winter) Shipwrecked at Malta.

61 (Spring) Arrives at Rome.

62 At Rome; *writes Philemon, Colossians, Ephesians, Philippians.*

63 (Spring) Is acquitted, and goes to Macedonia and Asia Minor (Phil. ii. 24 and Philem. 22).

64 ? Goes to Spain. (Great fire at Rome, July 19, and persecution of Christians.)

65 ? In Spain. (Gessius Florus, procurator of Judea.)

66 ? From Spain ? to Asia Minor (1 Tim. i. 3). (Jewish war begins.)

67 ? (Summer) *Writes* 1 *Timothy* from Macedonia.
(Autumn) *Writes Titus* from Ephesus.
(Winter) At Nicopolis, in Illyricum.

A. D.
68? (Spring) In prison at Rome; *writes 2 Timothy.*
(Summer) Executed, May or June. (Death of Nero, middle of June.)
[65 Executed, according to Pagi and Basnage; whom Lardner follows, suggesting the end of 64 as possible.]

THE EPISTLES OF PAUL.

I SHALL next take up the Epistles of Paul in their most probable chronological order;* and, having first mentioned any new contribution which the particular Epistle in hand may offer to the facts of Paul's life, shall endeavour to give a faithful outline of its contents. In these abstracts, I shall not hesitate to modernize the customary phraseology, where by so doing I think I can better represent the ancient thought to a modern reader's appreciation. In an abstract this may be done, to a degree that is hardly allowable in a translation. But I would suggest to the thoughtful reader the great advantage that he will find from reading the Epistles of Paul in some other translation than the authorized English version. Perhaps no parts of the New Testament so much need re-translation as the Epistles, for the purpose of bringing out the correct meaning; and there is a freshness, clearness and force in many of our revised versions (added to their freedom from the unnatural divisions of chapters and verses), which makes us conscious at once that we have never before understood the

* The order in which St. Paul's Epistles stand in the common Bible, is that of the supposed importance of the churches to which they were addressed,—a very unsatisfactory plan for their intelligent perusal. I shall follow Conybeare and Howson's order, noting any important difference of arrangement by other chronologists.

apostle's meaning in the venerable columns of King James's translation.

The earliest and ablest English expositor of Paul's Epistles was the truly great John Locke. His *Paraphrase and Notes on the Epistles of St. Paul to the Galatians, Corinthians, Romans and Ephesians,* with an Essay prefixed "for the understanding of St. Paul's Epistles by consulting St. Paul himself," is an invaluable volume.

The *Essay* is distinguished by sound scriptural knowledge and good sense. After remarking on the nature of epistolary writings, and the peculiar style of thought and expression belonging to St. Paul, he rightly ascribes a great part of the difficulty of understanding his letters to their being so unnaturally cut up into chapters and verses. "If Tully's Epistles were so printed and so used, I ask whether they would not be much harder to be understood, less easy and less pleasant to be read by much than now they are?" He then gives, as the true rules for understanding St. Paul, the following: To read the whole letter through at once; and to do this several times, till we see the general subject and discover the drift and aim;—then to trace out his reasonings, expecting to find in them the same force, order and perspicuity as in his speeches;—and having followed the thread of his reasoning in any one Epistle, to compare what he says on the same subject in any other; thus making St. Paul the interpreter of his own writings.

The *Paraphrase and Notes* apply this method in detail; and so much was his method approved as to be imitated by other expositors, Mr. Peirce and Dr. Benson especially, in Paraphrases and Notes on all the Epistles which Locke had on his death left untouched.

Of new versions of Paul's Epistles I may here specify a few:

Archbishop Newcome's Attempt towards Revising the English Version of the New Testament (perhaps not free enough for the purpose now suggested).

Wakefield's (Gilbert) Translation of the New Testament (perhaps too bold for good taste, while always vigorous and fresh in style).

Conybeare and Howson's Life and Epistles of St. Paul. (A new translation of all St. Paul's Epistles is given, so explanatory as to approach often to a paraphrase.)

The New Testament (from Griesbach's Text). By a Layman. 12mo. Pickering. 1840.

The New Testament, translated from Griesbach's Text. By Samuel Sharpe. 12mo. Moxon. 1844.

To these translations and expositions must be added a recommendation of Paley's instructive *Horæ Paulinæ*. The intelligent reader of Paul's Epistles should read in connection with each letter the corresponding pages of that admirable book. For learned exposition, old *Grotius* is throughout the N. T. a host in himself. More modern expositors have added little to his *Annotationes in N. T.*

EPISTLES TO THE THESSALONIANS.

(A.D. 52, 53.)

THESE two letters are admitted to be, not only the earliest of St. Paul's writings, but the earliest written books of the New Testament.

St. Paul's second missionary journey brought him (as detailed in the Acts, xvii. xviii.) to Thessalonica, and, soon afterwards, to Corinth. The intelligent reader will here carefully re-peruse the history. (See also pp. 377—380.) These letters were written from Corinth during Paul's residence there of a year and half (A.D. 52, 53). That the church at Thessalonica consisted, chiefly if not intirely, of converted Gentiles, is plain from two passages in the First Epistle, where Paul speaks of their having "turned from idols to the service of the living and true God" (i. 9); and, again, says that they have suffered persecution from their own countrymen, as the churches in Judea had from the Jews (ii. 14). The apostle expresses the strongest affection for the Thessalonians. It appears, from the First Epistle, that while Paul was alone at Athens waiting for Timothy and Silas, whom he had left at Berea, Timothy had gone back, by his direction, to Thessalonica, to inquire after their welfare and well-doing; and it was on Timothy's rejoining the apostle at Corinth, that the first letter to the Thessalonians was written.* His strong language, in alluding to the malevolence of the Jews (ii. 15, 16), is quite appropriate to his experience at Corinth as detailed in Acts xviii. 6. The contents of the letter are in brief as follows:

Abstract of 1 Thessalonians.

Ch. i. 1. The apostle (joining the names of Silas and Timothy with his own in the salutation) thanks God for the conversion of the Thessalonians from idolatry, and their worthy conduct as Christians.

Ch. ii. 1. He refers to his own ministrations and example among them, and encourages them under the sufferings which they are beginning to experience from their heathen fellow-countrymen, just as the Jewish Christians had done at the hands of the unconverted Jews. 17. He tells them how he longed to see them again, and had intended it more than once, "but Satan had hindered;"† so he had been content to be

* The received text, in a P.S. to each of these Epistles, makes them to have been written from Athens; but those P.SS. are comparatively modern and of no authority against internal evidence. In this case the evidence seems plain enough for Corinth, as Timothy has just rejoined Paul (1 Thess. iii. 6), and this happened, not at Athens, but at Corinth, as stated in Acts xviii. 5.

† Grotius conjectures that the necessity of frequent disputations with the Epicureans and Stoics was the hindrance alluded to.

alone at Athens, while Timothy went back to them to establish and encourage them under the tribulations which he had warned them to expect. Now (iii. 6) Timothy has just rejoined him with good tidings of their faith and charity and affectionate regard for their apostle, and his heart overflows to them in this letter, and he repeats the hope that God will direct his way to them.

Ch. iv. 1. Furthermore, the apostle beseeches and exhorts the Thessalonians to maintain a scrupulous purity of conduct in respect to that sensual and degrading vice which was thought so lightly of by Greeks and Romans, and which (as we have seen) had been already reprobated in the Jerusalem letter to the Gentiles. They must not be "as the Gentiles who know not God." "He hath not called us unto uncleanness, but unto holiness."* 6. He deprecates fraud and overreaching in business, thus applying Christian morals to the active secular life of their commercial city. 9. He urges brotherly love as a duty divinely taught by Nature itself; commends them for its practice, and beseeches them to increase in it more and more; but he evidently hints (11) that some are neglecting the proper work of their secular callings (perhaps under a mistaken religious enthusiasm too easily reconciling itself to practical indolence).† 13. Probably in allusion to the tidings of some death or deaths among the church at Thessalonica, which may have been reported by Timothy to the apostle, he bids them "not sorrow even as others who have no hope." The passage is so full of critical difficulties, while so interesting to the faith of the heart, that it must be presented intire, with such elucidations as I can suggest.‡

* The frequency and earnestness of these allusions, in Paul's Epistles to his Gentile converts, ought deeply to impress the Christian reader, and especially every young man. No false delicacy shall lead me to veil such passages in these abstracts, nor prevent a more pointed reference to this urgent topic of morality, in connection with the most forcible of St. Paul's pure-minded appeals.

† Paul seems to intend a reproof for this abuse of the Christian profession, in his allusions to his own practice among them, of working diligently for his own maintenance (ii. 5 and 9).

‡ "But I would not have you to be ignorant, brethren, concerning them

Ch. v. 1. To these mysterious hints the apostle adds (in language similar to that of our Lord's prediction of his own coming) the plain avowal that the day of the Lord will come suddenly and unexpectedly, and that the Christian must therefore be always ready.

12. The Epistle concludes with affectionate exhortations to

which are asleep, that ye may not sorrow like others who have no hope. For as we believe that Jesus died and rose again, even so them also which sleep will God, through Jesus, bring with him. For this we say unto you by the word of the Lord, that we which are alive and remain unto the coming of the Lord shall not go before them which are asleep. For the Lord himself shall descend from heaven with a shout, with the voice of the archangel, and with the trump of God: and the dead in Christ shall rise first: then we which are alive and remain shall be caught up together with them in the clouds, to meet the Lord in the air: and so shall we ever be with the Lord. Wherefore comfort one another with these words" (iv. 13—18).

The obscurity of certain expressions in our Lord's prediction of the coming of his kingdom, as recorded by his evangelists, has already been freely acknowledged and remarked upon. (See *note*, p. 301.) This passage in St. Paul's earliest Epistle seems (on the broadest and most *natural* view we can take of it) to betray that confused expectation of a coming change from mortal life on earth to immortal life elsewhere, which continued, long after the apostle's days and in spite of the realized destruction of Jerusalem, to connect itself in many minds with the Saviour's prediction. We may be unwilling to think that St. Paul had so mistaken the meaning of the "word of the Lord" (through whatever channels he had heard it reported); but how else can the words before us be reasonably explained, except as expressing the conviction that he himself and some of those to whom he writes will still be alive at the coming end of this mortal state? It is "*we* that are alive and remain" (or *those of us* that are). And the mistake was not as regards the *time*, for Jesus had expressly said, "before this generation pass away." The mistake was as regards the character of the expected event. The end of the age would destroy Jerusalem and end the Law;—the new age of the Gospel, the reign of the Son of Man, would thereupon begin. Is it surprising that, while the predicted event was yet undeveloped, even apostles (if not miraculously guarded from mistake) should have erred in their expectations?

This subject recurs in the Second Epistle to the same church, amid yet more curious and difficult details, which we shall presently notice. Meanwhile, let it be observed, that the idea never re-appears with all these details in any other Epistle of Paul's; and that the only other place in which it is very distinctly implied is in the next letter he wrote, namely, the First to the Corinthians. Does not this seem as if he himself soon outgrew his own mistake?

respect the appointed elders of the church, and with other suggestions designed, as some think, for the elders, all bearing upon practical holiness. He sends the customary greeting* to the brethren, desires that his letter may be read publicly to them all, and adds (in his own hand-writing probably) his benediction.

The SECOND letter to the Thessalonian church is almost intirely devoted to one subject, which had made its appearance in the first letter, namely, the second coming of Jesus Christ. It seems to have come to the apostle's hearing, that some of the Thessalonians believed, or professed to believe, as on the authority of his teaching, or else of his letter (ii. 1, 2),† that the day of Christ was then *close at hand;* and some made this a reason, or an excuse, for neglecting the secular work of life and "walking disorderly." To remove this misapprehension of what he had said, and to rectify the disorderly living, is the object of the Second Epistle.

ABSTRACT OF 2 THESSALONIANS.

Ch. i. 1. Paul still holds out the expectation of Christ's second coming, as a source of comfort and encouragement to them under persecution, and plainly anticipates a display of retributory vengeance against the opponents of the Gospel, such

* "Greet all the brethren with a holy kiss." A custom referred to in some other Epistles. "The men and women were placed in separate parts of the building where they met for worship; and then, before receiving the Holy Communion, the men kissed the men, and the women the women. Before the ceremony, a proclamation was made by the principal deacon: 'Let none bear malice against any; let none do it in hypocrisy.'" (Conybeare and Howson, I. 427, *note.*)

† Some consider this passage to imply that a letter had been forged in the apostle's name. At the end of this Second Epistle, he lays stress upon his having written *the salutation* with his own hand, his "token in every Epistle" (his letters being usually penned by an amanuensis, except the salutation at the conclusion).

as might perhaps (though not very easily) be interpreted as a vague description of the coming end of the Jewish state; while, however, such an interpretation would be deficient, inasmuch as the persecutors of the Thessalonian Christians were not Jews, but "their own countrymen."

Ch. ii. 1. But while still anticipating the day of Christ, Paul bids them not be deceived into the idea of its *immediate* approach; for (as he had told them in person*) there will be a great falling away first; and wickedness, now working secretly, will shew itself plainly; the man of sin will stand disclosed; influences now hindering will have ceased to obstruct the developement of the evil; a strong delusion will be upon the wicked power thus spoken of; till "the Lord will consume him with the breath of his mouth, and destroy him with the brightness of his coming." The words of this remarkable passage are placed below.† 15. The apostle exhorts

* Hence half the obscurity of what the apostle has written. If we knew just what he had before *said* to them, we should better understand what he now writes.

† "Let no man deceive you by any means: for that day shall not come, except there have come the falling away first, and the man of sin be revealed, the son of perdition; who opposeth and exalteth himself above all that is called God, or that is worshiped; so that he sitteth in the temple of God, shewing himself that he is God. Remember ye not that, when I was yet with you, I told you these things? And ye know what hindereth now; so that he may be revealed in his own time. For the mystery of wickedness doth already work: only he who now hindereth will hinder, until he be taken out of the way. And then shall that wicked one be revealed, whom the Lord shall consume with the breath of his mouth, and shall destroy with the brightness of his coming: even him, whose coming is after the working of Satan, with all the power and signs and wonders of falsehood; and with all the deception of unrighteousness in them that perish; because they received not the love of the truth, that they might be saved. And for this cause God shall send them strong delusion, that they should believe the lie: that they all may be condemned who believed not the truth, but had pleasure in unrighteousness" (ii. 3—12).

This difficult passage has, of course, found many absurd interpretations. The Man of Sin has been variously taken to be the Roman power, the Pope, Napoleon, &c. The Roman Catholics are disposed to regard Mahomet, or Luther, or both, as so designated. It has been forgotten that Paul is speaking of what he expects to witness *while he and his correspondents live*, though it is not close at hand. Nearer interpretations have been, how-to steadfastness; ch. iii. 1. desires their prayers on his behalf; 6. bids them withdraw from every one whose conduct is dis-

ever, attempted. The *Man of Sin* has been taken for Caligula, who ordered his statue to be set up in the temple of Jerusalem. But that was already a past incident, when Paul wrote this letter (in the reign of Claudius) anticipating a Man of Sin.

If, however, as already hinted by me, and as acknowledged even by orthodox divines, St. Paul shared in the mistaken but general expectation that Jesus Christ was to come again in that very generation (see Conybeare and Howson, I. 431), it seems an absurd attempt to find a distinct and true fulfilment of his words in subsequent events; and their true spirit surely is to be found rather by entering into the anticipations which were natural to a religious and observant man in his circumstances, possessed with the erroneous idea of Christ's personal return to judgment as about to happen within the period of the then existing generation.

Part of the phraseology of this passage reminds us of Christ's own prediction as recorded by Matthew (xxiv. 4, 11, 24): "Take heed that no man deceive you; for many will come in my name, saying, I am Christ, and will deceive many." "Many false prophets will arise, and will deceive many." "There will arise false Christs and false prophets, and will shew great signs and wonders; insomuch that, if it were possible, they will deceive the very elect." Then the *man of sin exalting himself* in the temple of God, is not unlike the words in which the book of Daniel describes the presumptuous irreverence of Antiochus Epiphanes and the destruction of his power (Dan. vii. 25—27); and also recalls to mind another passage in Daniel (ix. 27), and our Lord's allusion to it (Matt. xxiv. 15), where the *abomination of desolation* is spoken of as standing in the holy place. We need not doubt that these passages of Jewish Scripture and of currently remembered Christian prophecy, were present often to our apostle's mind, when he thought and wrote of the expected coming of the Lord.

If we further realise the social and political circumstances amidst which he moved, and of which he was not an inattentive observer, we may perhaps be able to do some sort of justice to his expectation and advice as expressed to the Thessalonian church. We shall find these, in short, to be manly and wise under the circumstances. The leader of the Christian mission among the Gentiles, Paul finds his churches everywhere exposed to Gentile as well as Jewish persecution. The Christians are not of the world, but their Master has chosen them out of the world, and the world hates them. The surrounding heathenism is not merely a false speculation, belief or worship, but is essentially promotive of false morals and depraved practice. The whole world lieth in wickedness. The Christian church has to sustain for a while a hard but glorious conflict against all the powers of evil, till the Son of Man shall come, when (as Paul and many others trust) the mortal state will pass away, and the heavenly kingdom of the Messiah orderly, appealing to his own example of industrious self-support when among them. 17. The salutation is, he says, in his own hand: "*Thus I write: The grace of our Lord Jesus Christ be with you all. Amen.*"

be visibly substituted. Christ himself has limited the time: "This generation shall not pass till all be fulfilled." And they quite truly understand the limits of the time; only they misunderstand the *nature of his promised coming*. And when his spiritual coming shall have been realised as he designed it to be understood (in the destruction of Jerusalem some years after St. Paul's death), those who do not appreciate that fulfilment will thenceforth misinterpret the *predicted time*, and still expect his coming, generation after generation.

Paul looks around him for such signs of the times as may be already discernible. It still wants (as we know by the event) about eighteen years to the final fulfilment of Christ's prophecy in the destruction of Jerusalem and the abolition of the ceremonial worship. But, while the apostle repudiates the idea that the day of the Lord is close at hand, he thinks he sees causes in action which will, before very long, mature the predicted state of things in which it will assuredly come. The furious and malignant enmity of the Jews, and the wickedness of the Gentile world, seem to point to the crisis as not far distant. The wickedness is already at work, though in a comparatively secret manner. Some twelve or thirteen years ago, when Caligula's mad impiety almost excited Judea to open rebellion, the political crisis was with difficulty averted by the wise procrastination of the procurator, till the emperor's death removed the alarm. A more conciliating, if not a wiser, will has since wielded the sovereign power of the Roman empire (Claudius succeeded A.D. 41), and at present hinders the conflicting elements of Jewish enthusiasm or superstition and Roman worldliness from bursting into deadly fight. And "he will hinder till he be taken out of the way." But Claudius is no longer young. At 62 years of age, and never of robust health, his prospect of life is somewhat uncertain. And his adopted successor is—Nero, a very young man, but of no virtuous promise. Or more likely the succession may be disputed, and lax government ensue.

If this had been the tone of the apostle's conversation when he was with the Thessalonians (to which he alludes, ii. 5), we should say such conversation was very natural, and that his mode of alluding to "that which hindereth," in his letter to them, would be intelligible to his friends, while properly discreet on his part. Expecting, as he evidently did at this period of his ministry, that the *end of the world* would come at the end of the Jewish age then drawing to its close, was it unnatural, or otherwise than sagacious, to expect, that the repressed elements of lawlessness would break out on the next change of imperial hands, and that the troubled times ensuing would be closed by the coming of the Lord from heaven?

Claudius died and Nero succeeded within a year from this time, A.D. 54.

EPISTLES TO THE CORINTHIANS.

(A.D. 57.)

THE church at Corinth was founded by St. Paul, A.D. 52, 53, on his second missionary tour, as recorded in Acts xviii. 1—18. (See pp. 379, 380.) The apostle's converts were chiefly Gentiles. But many Jews were soon after added to the church through the ministry of Apollos (Acts xviii. 27, 28), through whom, as an Alexandrian Jew, it is just possible that some elements of mystical speculation may have been unwittingly grafted upon the simplicity of the Gospel; while, however, he is spoken of by Paul, in this First Epistle, without the slightest intimation of disapproval, and indeed with most generous appreciation as a fellow-labourer.

The first letter to the Corinthians was written from Ephesus (on the apostle's third journey), A.D. 57, as appears from ch. xvi. 8, where he says, "I will tarry at Ephesus till Pentecost;" and from ver. 19, where he

Nero's reign began well, under the influence of Seneca and Burrus; and the causes of the Jewish war did not become visibly active for some years yet. And it is well worth the notice of theologians (though I know none who have published the remark), that this mistaken expectation of St. Paul's, though he repeats it in a gentler form in his next written letter (1 Cor.) in the third year of Nero, altogether disappears from his correspondence thenceforth. It does not revive even in the letters written under the Neronian persecution, when our apostle himself was in prison for the Gospel's sake, and anticipating martyrdom. He still looks for the "appearing of the Lord," but no longer describes it as he once ventured to do. Paul's mind, no doubt, outgrew its own mistake under the teaching of events, which, however, taught many other minds in vain. It is not correct, then, to represent this expectation of the coming end of the world as the settled and uniform belief of the apostles and their times. Only in a partial sense is it a scriptural doctrine, and in no proper sense a revealed doctrine. It is a mistaken but pardonable inference from Christ's prophecy, while that prophecy was still unfulfilled; and, in Paul's mind at least, it was revoked before the real fulfilment came,—for Paul did not live to see the end of the Jewish age.

gives salutations from the churches of Asia. (For this residence in Ephesus, see Acts xix. and pp. 381, 382.) The letter was probably sent by the hands of Titus. The common *Postscript* stating it to have been written from Philippi is clearly erroneous.

In the interval between Paul's residence at Corinth and the date of this letter, while it is evident that the church had grown and in many respects prospered, other symptoms the reverse of satisfactory had manifested themselves. Party divisions had grown up, and some gross heathen immoralities had been brought in, which should have been altogether left behind by those who joined the people of Christ. The name of Apollos had been taken as a party badge by some, that of Paul by others, that of Cephas or Peter by a third party.* This last-mentioned fact seems to intimate that a Palestinian or strict Jewish party, calling themselves by the name of Peter, had grown up under the influence of those who maintained that the Law of Moses was incumbent even upon Gentile Christians. And it is equally plain that heathen philosophy, as well as heathen immorality, had infected a part of the Corinthian church with its bold denial of a future life. The apostle (iv. 15) painfully alludes to their "ten thousand guides," while he affectionately claims to be their "only father in the Gospel."

It is supposed by some,† that during the two years (Acts xix. 10) of Paul's residence in Ephesus and the neighbourhood, he may have made a short visit to Corinth. This supposition arises from his speaking, in his second

* Ch. i. 12. "And I of Christ" surely cannot be held to prove that there was a *party* so calling themselves. Is it not rather the apostle's gently ironical hint that this name, least thought of, should have been the only name for them all?

† Conybeare and Howson, II. 18.

letter, of being ready a *third* time to come to them (2 Cor. xii. 14, xiii. 1). But he does not say he *had been there twice* before. He is "*ready* a third time;" for he has confessedly changed his plan once, and instead of passing from Ephesus through Corinth into Macedonia, and then back by Corinth, as he once thought of doing, he goes first through Macedonia into Corinth, and then back through Macedonia, thus making one visit at Corinth instead of two (2 Cor. i. 16). And this change of purpose having been objected against him as a sign of weakness, he declares that he had deferred his earlier intended visit, *to spare them* (ver. 23). There is no need, then, of supposing a second visit before the date of the first letter.

Some suppose that Paul wrote an earlier letter than that which we know as 1 *Cor.* This supposition is founded upon what he says (v. 9): "I wrote you in the epistle, not to | company with fornicators" (*ἔγραψα ὑμῖν ἐν τῇ ἐπιστολῇ*). But this may refer to what he has just written* in this very letter, in verses 2 and 7 of the same chapter, and which he goes on to explain, limit and enforce.

It is quite certain, however, that the church at Corinth, or a part of them, had written a letter to the apostle, asking his opinion on various points; for he, in this letter, again and again refers to their inquiries, quoting even the words of their letter, and giving full and explicit answers. Probably this letter from Corinth had been brought to Ephesus by Stephanus, Fortunatus and Achaicus (xvi. 17); and they, or some of them, may have been the same persons as those of the household of Chloe

* *γέγραφα* would, of course, have been more strictly classical than *ἔγραψα*; but the New Testament Greek is not strictly classical; and Paul uses the very same expression, *ἔγραψα*, to the Galatians (vi. 11): "Ye see in what large letters *I have written* to you, with mine own hand."

(i. 11), from whom the apostle had learned in conversation (what their letter had not mentioned) that there were "contentions" among them.

Before writing this letter, Paul has sent Timothy and Erastus into Macedonia (Acts xix. 22); and from this letter it appears (iv. 17 and xvi. 10) that the mission of the former is to include a visit to Corinth. But of Timothy's visit we have no record, nor any allusion to it as actually accomplished. Paul himself means to come soon, "if the Lord will" (iv. 19, xi. 34), after passing through Macedonia, and probably to winter with them (xvi. 5). The fulfilment of this visit is implied in the very brief account of his subsequent visit to Macedonia and Greece (Achaia), in Acts xx. 1—4. (See p. 383.) But he wrote his Second Epistle also before going to Corinth, namely, from Philippi on his way into Achaia about a year after the date of the First Epistle.

Abstract of 1 Corinthians.

Ch. i. 1. Salutation, jointly with Sosthenes, addressed, not only to the church at Corinth, but also to all that in every place call upon the name of the Lord Jesus Christ. 4. Paul thanks God for their conversion and Christian gifts and privileges, and, in the name of these things, rebukes their party-spirit. For his own part, he is glad to remember that he had baptized scarcely any one at Corinth; so that there is no colourable pretence for a *Paul* faction, and should be for no other. He had preached the simple and pure Gospel of Christ crucified,—to Jews a stumbling-block, and to the subtle, wisdom-seeking Greeks, folly; but a divine power and wisdom to those who accept it.

Ch. ii. 1. He refers to his own manner of preaching the Gospel among them, as accordant with the simplicity and power of this divine wisdom, and not affecting the subtlety of thought or the rhetorical style of the Greek philosophies. He had come among them in weakness and fear and great trembling,* but had been sustained by the powerful manifestation of the Holy Spirit; and their faith had been based, not upon human wisdom, but upon the power of God. 7. But this Gospel is wisdom indeed to all spiritually-minded persons; and gross-minded (carnal) persons and merely intellectual (natural) persons call it folly, because they cannot appreciate it.

Ch. iii. 1. Paul has not hitherto been able to regard them as full-grown spiritual men, but as babes in Christ, animal-minded. And their present dissensions prove that they are not yet spiritual. Paul and Apollos are only ministers of God; the church is the work on which they are engaged; its members are the spiritual temple of God, to be kept holy and undefiled. 18. The world's wise man has yet to learn from on high, how all things subserve the disciples of the heavenly wisdom. All things are theirs; Paul, Apollos, Cephas, the world itself, life, death, things present and to come; all are theirs; and they are Christ's; and Christ is God's. Let the apostles be looked upon as servants of Christ and stewards of the secrets of divine revelation.

Ch. iv. 6. What he has written about Apollos and himself, he bids them take home to themselves, and cease to vaunt their own knowledge and attainments. 8. The teachers could be satisfied to be of no account, if the taught were really full and rich and royal. Paul's sharp yet genial satire here shews itself. But (14) he adds, that he does not write this to shame them, but to warn them as his beloved sons. 17. He has sent Timothy to them to bring them into remembrance of his way of Christian teaching; and he will follow soon and "discover not the words of the boasters, but their power." Shall he come (he asks them) with a rod? or in love?

Ch. v. 1. With deepest sorrow and shame on their behalf, the apostle has heard of a sin of lust existing among them, such as is scarcely known even among heathens,—"that a man should have his father's wife." And they are puffed up! "instead of mourning as they rather ought to do." 4. He

* Ill-health, say some; perhaps rather the natural anxiety which his first encounter with Greek thought at Athens had produced in his mind.

distinctly and unhesitatingly bids them dismiss the offender from the church till he repents and reforms his life. 9. He explains that in bidding them not keep company with fornicators (as also with other offenders), he does not speak of heathens outside their communion, but of brethren within. To avoid every such person, one had need "go out of the world;" but they must "put away from among themselves that wicked person."

Ch. vi. 1. The apostle reprobates the practice of appearing before the heathen tribunals to settle small disputes, instead of finding arbitrators among themselves. If the "holy people of Christ are to judge the world,"* cannot they settle little matters among themselves? But there must be something wrong when Christian brethren go to law with each other at all. They ought rather to bear wrong than to do it. Christian wrong-doing should be an impossibility. No wrong-doer can inherit the kingdom of God. Those who were such before their conversion are now washed, sanctified and justified, in the name of Jesus Christ and by the Spirit of God. 12. Does some one plead: "All things are lawful to me"?† Paul replies: Not all things are expedient. And of all things that are lawful, it is well not to be brought under the power of any. Is it said: "Food is made for the appetite, and the appetite demands food"? Yet both are temporary and mortal. And the body is not for fornication, but for the Lord, and the Lord for the body; and He who raised up the Lord will raise us up also. Christians are members of Christ; and shall the members of Christ become the members of a harlot? The apostle is most earnest upon this often-recurring aspect of heathen immorality. Flee fornication, he repeats. While other sins that men commit may seem without bodily results, this is a sin against a man's own body; and that body ought

* Traces of the outward Messianic idea are evident in such allusions as this. The "day of Christ" is anticipated throughout this Epistle, but in a far less defined form than in the Thessalonian letters. In the fifteenth chapter the most remarkable allusion occurs.

† The words apparently of their letter, quoted again by the apostle in the connection in which they were written (x. 23).

to be a temple of the Holy Spirit, who should be served by the body as well as the soul.

Ch. vii. 1. Paul next answers the questions put to him in the Corinthian letter:

First, as to the desirableness of marriage under the impending troubles. 2. Plainly it is the true preventive of sin. 7. But to the widowers and widows he says, it is good for them to remain as they are, like himself,* if they can bear it; if not, let them marry. This he says permissively; but to those who are married (10) authoritatively, in the name of the Lord, he repudiates the idea that marriage is dissolved by the impending troubles or the coming kingdom of Christ. The Christian husband or wife of an unbelieving partner is not to shake off, but to sanctify, the relationship. Only, if the unbelieving husband or wife is determined to separate, let the other consent for peace' sake. 17. In the same spirit, let every Christian continue in the condition in which he was when called: if circumcised, let him think no more of it; if not, let him by no means submit to the rite;—is he a slave, let him not care (though, if he may be made free, let him use the opportunity). If he be a servant (slave), he is Christ's freedman; if free, he is Christ's servant. 25. Then, as to giving their young women in marriage,—"considering the impending trouble," Paul thinks it best for a man to remain as he is. "If married, seek not to be loosed; if free, seek not a wife." Yet there is nothing wrong in marrying; only mortal sorrows may be the heavier to both parties. "The time is short, and the fashion of this world is passing away." The married will be more anxious about worldly matters; the unmarried more singly devoted to the things of the Lord. They must decide for themselves after all; but such is Paul's judgment, and he "thinks he too has something of the spirit of God."

Ch. viii. 1. The next subject of inquiry in the letter of the Corinthian elders was, whether a Christian might eat of meat

* This seems to shew that Paul was a widower (the ancient tradition of the church); unless by *τοῖς ἀγάμοις κἀι τᾶις χήραις* (literally, unmarried men and widowed women), we are to understand both the unmarried and the bereft of both sexes.

which had been offered to an idol.* Some scrupled to do it; but those who wrote, or some whose words were reported, talked in this style: "We know (for we all have knowledge†) that an idol is nothing at all, and that there is none other God but one. For though there be that are called gods, whether in heaven or in earth (as there are gods many and lords many), yet to us there is but one God, the Father, of whom are all things, and we unto Him; and one Lord Jesus Christ, through whom are all things, and we through him." Your fancied knowledge, says Paul, puffs you up; while a loving regard to others would at once teach you what to do. And some are not so "knowing" as you, but think they are holding communion with the idol by eating; and so their weak conscience is defiled. "But meat (you say) commendeth us not to God." No; but take care that your freedom be not a stumbling-block to weaker brethren. Better never eat flesh meat at all, than lead weak consciences into sin.

Ch. ix. 1. The apostle turns abruptly to another subject, not perhaps in their epistle, but which he knew to be in the mouths of many at Corinth who disparaged his apostolical authority. Perhaps they cavilled at his not having been one of the twelve personal attendants of Christ. Apparently they perverted against him the fine independence of spirit with which he had maintained himself by tent-making, rather than throw himself upon the limited resources of certain churches, or the tardy generosity of others. "Am I not an apostle? &c. You are the seal of my apostleship; and this is my answer to those who question my authority." 4. He asserts his apostolic right, equally with Cephas and the Lord's brothers, to be maintained by his converts, and to take a wife if he chose. They that wait at the altar are partakers with the altar; and just so, "the Lord hath ordained that those who preach his

* Just as with the Jewish sacrifices, only portions of which were actually offered, the rest of the flesh was either taken home by the offerer, or, becoming the perquisite of the priest, would naturally find its way to the shambles.

† γνῶσιν, lofty discernment, superior intelligence. It is rather a proud word (as used, at least, by some); it is the root of *Gnosticism*, both etymologically and historically.

Gospel should live by the Gospel." 15. But he has not used these rights. He is impelled to preach the Gospel, and cannot be silent; and, while independent of all men, he is ready to serve all, conciliating the Jews, as a Jew himself, so far as he can, and to the Gentiles vindicating their freedom from the Law, while "not without a law to God, but under Christ's law."

Ch. x. 1. He further warns the Corinthians against immorality and idolatry (the two constantly connected) by the history of the Jewish people. 15. He appeals to their own intelligence to acknowledge that, as in the Lord's Supper they hold communion with Christ, and the ceremonial Israelites by eating of the sacrifice are identified with the Jewish worship, so, though the idol is nothing at all, yet partaking of its sacrifice is partaking of demon worship. Does any one repeat, "All things are lawful for me"? Yes; but not all things are expedient. All things may be strictly lawful, but not all things tend to mutual improvement. Let every man be guided by his neighbour's good, rather than his own pleasure. 25. So they may eat what they buy in the shambles, without asking any question about it. And they may eat at a heathen's table, without curiously questioning the history of every dish. But, if a weak brother (who surely should not have gone to a Gentile's house at all) directs attention to the fact that something has been offered in sacrifice, "eat not (says Paul) for the sake of his conscience who shewed it." Let them follow their apostle in these things, as he follows Christ.

Ch. xi. 2. Paul censures the practice of women appearing as teachers in the church (prophesying) without a veil upon the head, which he deems a becoming sign of subjection (ver. 10) to man. 17. He severely censures the gross and almost incredible abuses which had, at Corinth, crept into the celebration of the Lord's Supper, the institution of which he recapitulates almost in the very words of St. Luke's Gospel. Luke was already well known to him, and their mutual acquaintance explains the closer verbal correspondence. This rite was, in different times and places, very variously observed. In Corinth, it seems to have been celebrated at a public meal, to which (according to an old custom among the Greeks) each person sent his own provisions. And this explains the possibility of such excesses, mixed with such neglect, as St. Paul describes, when every one begins his own supper without helping any one else, and one man is hungry and another drunken. They make no difference between this and a common meal, not realizing in any way the Lord's body as emblemed to their thoughts. Such unworthy eating and drinking brings its own judgment (ver. 29, where *damnation* is a very false rendering) in the many weak and sickly, and some dying and dead! "What!" (says the indignant apostle) "have ye not houses to eat and drink in? Tarry then for each other; and when you are hungry, eat at home. The rest I will set in order when I come."

Ch. xii. 1. The next subject is spiritual gifts (or, as some translate, spiritual *persons*); on which, if we attempt accurately to define the nature and limits of each gift, and to decide which were natural and which supernatural, the task is hopeless.* But higher lessons survive, which the apostle taught in connection with his remarks on these now obsolete gifts. 3. The very confession of Jesus as Lord argues a participation

* They are enumerated as follows (ver. 8—10):

1 Word of wisdom	λόγος σοφίας
2 Word of knowledge	λόγος γνώσεως
3 Faith	πίστις
4 Gifts of healing	χαρίσματα ἰαμάτων
5 Working of miracles	ἐνεργήματα δυνάμεων
6 Prophecy	προφητεία
7 Discerning of spirits	διακρίσεις πνευμάτων
8 Kinds of tongues	γένη γλωσσῶν
9 Interpretation of tongues	ἑρμηνεία γλωσσῶν.

And again as follows (ver. 28):

Apostles	ἀποστόλους
6 Prophets	προφήτας
Teachers	διδασκάλους
5 Miracles	δυνάμεις
4 Gifts of healing	χαρίσματα ἰαμάτων
Helps	ἀντιλήψεις
Governments	κυβερνήσεις
8 Diversities of tongues	γένη γλωσσῶν.

The four numbered in the second list are all that correspond with any in the first list.

in the Holy Spirit, which is given to the several disciples in various manifestations for the benefit of all. 12. Jews and Gentiles, bond and free, are all one body in Christ by the baptism of one spirit of holiness. The beautiful illustration of the mutual use and dependence of the members of a Christian church, from the mutual service of the parts of the human body, follows. 31. Yet let them desire and prize the best gifts, and their apostle will tell them of something far better still:—Charity, Christian love, will outlast them all. Prophesying will be done away, tongues be silent, and inspired knowledge come to an end in the church on earth, while Faith, Hope and Charity, these three abide; and the greatest of the three is Charity. "Follow after Charity."

Ch. xiv. 1. Returning to the comparative value of spiritual gifts, the apostle commends that of prophesying as the most useful to the church, and most likely to convince the unlearned and the unbelieving, though not the most showy or most coveted. 26. He gives directions for the exercise of their gifts in the church, and forbids women to speak on such occasions (though, in xi. 5, they are contemplated as praying or prophesying, in more private assemblies perhaps). All things must be done decently and in order.

Ch. xv. 1. The apostle recapitulates the proofs of Christ's resurrection as a fundamental fact in his preaching and in the Christian belief of his converts; and then addresses himself to "some among them who say there is no resurrection of the dead." These were no doubt Epicureans, in the church, or just outside of it among the relatives and friends of its members. The chapter (used in the Church-of-England burial service) is well known; but perhaps the real drift of its argument is not always seen, nor the soundness of its logic properly estimated. Paul is arguing with those who deny the possibility of a future life; the same sort of people who at Athens had mocked when he spoke of the resurrection of the dead. His argument here is in two parts: first (ver. 12), he addresses himself to those who say a future life is impossible,—that there is no such thing as a resurrection of the dead. To them he replies, that the thing has been proved possible by being shewn in fact: "If no dead rise, then Christ cannot have been raised. But Christ is risen, therefore the dead *can* rise." This is the logical argument, detached from that rich vein of feeling and poetry which the very thought of annihilation calls forth from his mind in the course of the reasoning. Paul does not pretend to prove from Christ's resurrection that all men *must* rise; that would be a *non-sequitur*. He disproves the alleged impossibility of a resurrection, by shewing that it has taken place. Then the second part of his argument (beginning at ver. 35) is addressed to the further difficulty of conceiving "*how* the dead are raised up, and *with what body* they come." Paul does not answer this question positively, but deprives it of its negative power. Foolish questioner! he says: first tell me *how* a seed grows, before you ask defiantly how the dead are raised up. Say, the seed *cannot* grow and *does not* grow, because you do not know *how*; or cease to say the dead cannot be raised, because you know not how. With what body do they come? With what body does the seed come? Not with the body that you sowed. God giveth a body as pleaseth Him. And no end of bodily forms are in His power. For every seed has its own body. Beasts, birds, fishes, men, all have their own. Bodies celestial and bodies terrestrial there are. Sun, moon, stars of differing glory. Who then shall sceptically ask, With what body the dead may come? What is sown in corruption shall be raised in incorruption. As there is an *animal body*, so there is a *spiritual body*. Say, foolish questioner, if you will, that a "spiritual body" is a contradiction in terms. Paul has used it on purpose. But there is no solecism in his argument. The Christian apostle, trusting the power of God and believing His promise, simply means to say: You need not demand *how*, but be sure it will be as promised, whether in a body, properly so called, or not. If your spirit accepts the Christian hope of immortality, the bodily question will bear postponement. No labour in the work of the Lord will be in vain.*

Ch. xvi. 1. The apostle concludes his epistle with urging a weekly collection for the poor Christians in Jerusalem, as

* The verses 23—28 and 51, 52, betray the expectation of a visible Messianic kingdom; but in a much less full and distinct form than was presented in the letters to the Thessalonians four years before.

already instituted among the Galatian churches where he has lately been. He mentions his plans for coming to them; commends Timothy to their kind reception; says he had wished Apollos to go with the bearers of this letter; gives many kind greetings; and writes the salutation with his own hand: "If any man love not the Lord Jesus Christ, let him be separated *(Anathema)*. The Lord cometh" *(Maranatha)*.

The SECOND Epistle to the Corinthians was written probably about half a year after the first (that is, A.D. 57), at Philippi most likely, certainly in Macedonia, as its own expressions imply. This year of the apostle's labours is passed over (as already remarked) in the most hasty manner in the book of Acts (xx. 1—4). But we learn the history of his mind, and in part also that of his labours, from this second letter to the Corinthians. Leaving Ephesus, after the riot of Demetrius and the silversmiths, he went to Troas, where he expected to meet Titus returning from his mission to Corinth as bearer of his first letter. Not meeting him there, and being restlessly anxious to know the state of things at Corinth, and the effect which his first letter had produced, he crossed the sea into Macedonia, where he met Titus, and was gladdened by tidings from Corinth, on the whole very satisfactory. The great immorality denounced in his first letter had been repented of and forsaken; and he feels that his friends are still worthy of his confidence and love. But the doctrinal mischief-makers are not yet silenced, and are labouring hard to destroy his reputation and influence as an apostle. Paul determines to write again before going in person to Corinth, and sends this second letter by Titus and two others (viii. 18 and 23), one of whom is generally supposed to have been Luke, as asserted in the postscript.

This letter contains no new topics, but resumes those of the first, as modified by the report of Titus. The tone of the letter is peculiarly plaintive, while warmly affectionate. The apostle seems to be labouring under an oppression of feeling which he cannot throw off. He speaks (i. 8) of the trouble he had had in Asia, when he was pressed exceedingly, above his strength, so as even to despair of life. Whether, in these words, he alludes to the alarming tumult which had driven him from Ephesus, or to other difficulties which he met with from his Jewish opponents there (and to which he refers afterwards in Acts xx. 19), or whether ill-health was in part also the obstacle to his work and the source of this oppressive feeling of his mind, is one of the many questions open to critical conjecture, on which perhaps confessed ignorance is truest wisdom. The letter is, in brief, as follows:

Abstract of 2 Corinthians.

Ch. i. 1. Salutation, jointly with Timothy, to the Christians in Corinth and in Achaia generally. 3. Paul thanks God that recent sore affliction fits him all the better to comfort others; and, as he has himself found religious comfort, he trusts they will also, and that he and they will have occasion of mutual rejoicing in the day of the Lord Jesus. 15. He had meant to come to them sooner, on his way to Macedonia, and had not been fickle in his change of plan; for he had postponed his visit simply out of tenderness to them, as he did not wish to come to them again "in heaviness."

Ch. ii. 3. He refers to his first letter, "written with many tears," not for the purpose of grieving them, but to prove his love to them. 5. The punishment which they have collectively inflicted on a certain offender against Christian morals, he rejoices to hear has been effectual; and he now bids them forgive and comfort him. 12. He tells them how at Troas, though a door of success was open to his mission, he had no rest in his spirit, because Titus did not arrive from Corinth;

so he had come forward into Macedonia, and there found the comfort he longed for. 16. "Who is sufficient for these things?" says the apostle. There is no room for self-commendation; but God has thought him worthy to be a minister of the New Covenant, the spirit of which (iii. 6) he contrasts with the literal outwardness of the Law of Moses.

Ch. iv. 1. He describes the spirit of his ministry, and (ver. 7) contrasts with its dignity and value the feebleness of the "earthen vessels" to which it is committed, and the sufferings of an apostle's life. 15. All is for the sake of others; and while the outward man perishes, the inward is renewed continually,—temporary trials leading to eternal blessedness.

Ch. v. 1. For when the earthly tent shall be taken down, there will be a mansion of God's own building prepared in the heavens; and he feels that, while he is at home in the body, he is absent from the Lord, and labours, therefore, whether present or absent, to be accepted of him.* 11. This sense of responsibility gives earnestness to his efforts; and though some call him mad, others will understand the deep sobriety of his conduct, as inspired by duty to God for the sake of his fellow-men. The love of Christ constrains him to judge, that if one died for all, his death was their death,† and the living were to live henceforth no more to themselves, but to Christ. 16. Therefore he knows no carnal distinctions between Jew and Gentile; for Christ, whom he once viewed through such a medium, is no longer seen by him as Saviour of the Jews alone: Christians are a *new creation;* God is reconciling the whole world to himself, not imputing their trespasses unto them; and this message of reconciliation is committed to Paul's hands among others. Hence his affectionate urgency (vi. 2): "Now is the accepted time, now is the day of salvation."

Ch. vi. 3. He alludes again to his own trials and sufferings (11), opening his mouth and heart to them, and inviting their

* If I mistake not, the lately definite expectation of the apostle, that the day of Christ would be visible and external, and that he should live to see it, is fast giving place in his mind, when he writes this passage, to the simpler expectation of a spiritual life immortal.

† Conybeare and Howson, II. 104.

confidence in return; and then (14) renews the injunctions of his former letter, to keep free from all participation in heathen vices.

Ch. vii. 2. He recurs to the state of anxious feeling respecting them in which he had come to Macedonia, and the comfort and joy which he had derived from the report of Titus. 8. Still, he does not regret having written that painful letter to them. It has led them to repentance; and he can now altogether confide in them.

Chs. viii. and ix. are devoted to the subject of the collection for the poor Christians in Judea. He mentions what is doing in Macedonia among brethren comparatively poor themselves, and begs the Corinthians to complete what they had begun a year ago, as alluded to in his previous letter. 6. Titus will revisit them to superintend the completion, as he had done the beginning, of this good work, and two well-approved brethren will accompany him.* An earnest and affectionate exhortation to liberality follows; the blessings of cheerful giving are upon both giver and receiver; and are not temporal only, but spiritual, drawing forth gratitude to God and love to man.

Ch. x. 1. The tone of the epistle changes at this point from gentleness and kindness to a sternness bordering upon severity and mixed with threatening, which requires us to regard it as no longer referring to the members of the Corinthian church in general, but to those Jewish disturbers of its harmony, whose machinations, though defeated, were not relinquished, and might yet become troublesome. We find, from this part of the letter, that St. Paul's detractors had descended so low as to disparage his personal appearance. He begins the subject by intreating them not to make it necessary for him to shew his bold reliance upon his own authority, against some who would measure him by a carnal standard. When the obedience of the church in general is complete, he will still be ready to punish any who are disobedient. 7. If any one thinks he is Christ's, Paul has a better right to boast of being so; and, in a delicate hypothetical way (with frequent apology and depre-

* The brother in viii. 18 is generally believed to be Luke; and the other in ver. 22 is variously supposed to be Gaius, Tychicus or Trophimus, mentioned in Acts xx. 4.

cation of any really boastful thought), he glances at his own apostolic endowments and claims. Ch. xi. 21. Hebrew birth and privileges were his as much as any one's. In the service of Christ, he was more abundant in toil and danger* than any of his detractors. Ch. xii. 1. Then, coming to visions and revelations of the Lord, he says he *knows a man in Christ* who sixteen years ago (whether in the body or out of the body, he cannot tell) had been caught up into Paradise, and heard things beyond his power to declare. He adds, resuming the first person: "And lest I should be exalted above measure through the abundance of the revelations, there was given to me a thorn in the flesh,† a messenger of Satan, to buffet me." 11. They have compelled this glorying, which seems to himself foolish. He appeals with stern seriousness to his past

* He enumerates several things unrecorded in the history:—five scourgings by the Jews, three Roman beatings (of which we read one in Acts xvi. 22), and three shipwrecks, none of which are noted in the history, for that at Malta was yet to come.

† The bodily infirmity thus confessed by Paul, and meanly thrown against him by the taunts of others, is not sufficiently defined on either hand to enable us to know what it really was. He himself merely calls it a "thorn in his flesh." But he also says (1 Cor. ii. 3) that, when he first preached at Corinth, he was with them "in weakness, and in fear, and in much trembling." And to the Galatians (iv. 13, 14), he speaks of having preached to them amid "infirmity of the flesh," by which some sort of bodily infirmity must certainly have been meant. His opponents and detractors seem to have said of him, that he was "in personal presence lowly among them, but when absent bold towards them" (2 Cor. x. 1); and, more pointedly, that "his letters are weighty and powerful, but his bodily presence is weak and his speech contemptible" (x. 10). Some of the old fathers thought the thorn in his flesh was headache, or some complaint of the head and eyes. Some tell us that he was a man of low stature, with mean aspect of body, a bald head, and an impediment in his speech. Some kind of paralytic affection has been imagined by others, which made writing difficult to him, and would account for his employing a scribe. Extreme shortsightedness is another conjecture. Mere conjectures all of them! Yet the want of a commanding presence, and the accompaniment of any kind of impediment or defective articulation, would account for all that his opponents said of him; while nothing of this kind can be supposed to have existed beyond a slight degree, if the records of his public speeches and their effect upon the audiences are borne in mind. Perhaps we should not be wrong in supposing special ill-health during the time included in the Corinthian and Galatian visits.

course among them, when he had shewn all the signs of an apostle, but abstained from burdening their generosity for his personal support. "Forgive me this wrong!" he says with gentle irony. 19. Again he earnestly urges that any who have not already repented of their heathenish sins, should do so before he comes; for he will be grieved indeed to have to shew his authority and power in punishment. He would be glad to be weak in this respect, through their being strong in virtue; "and this also we wish, even your perfection." Ch. xiii. 11. Salutations and benediction conclude the letter.

EPISTLE TO THE GALATIANS.

(A.D. 57?)

THE apostle Paul visited Galatia both on his second and third journeys (pp. 375 and 381, and Acts xvi. 6, xviii. 23); but of his labours in that province, the historian of the Acts has preserved no details whatever. The chief towns of Galatia were Ancyra, Tavium and Pessinus. It is not quite certain when and where the Epistle to the Galatians was written; but the most probable opinion makes its date to have been Corinth, A.D. 57, to which place Paul was on his way (in his third missionary journey) when he wrote the letter (2 Cor.) last analyzed. Dr. Lardner, indeed, places the Galatian letter much earlier, and supposes it to have been written from Ephesus or Corinth, A.D. 52 or 53, on Paul's second journey, and very shortly after his first visit to Galatia; while the common postscript quite erroneously makes it to have been written from Rome some years later.

Taking it as written from Corinth, A.D. 57, we suppose the apostle to have heard, on his arrival there, the unsatisfactory tidings that the Galatian churches had fallen under the influence of Judaizing teachers, who insisted upon the necessity of circumcision, and, like similar teachers at Corinth, disparaged the authority of St. Paul. These tidings might meet him at Corinth direct from Ephesus, between which places the mercantile communication was constant. The letter to the Galatians is instantly written by him and despatched. It bears all the marks of earnest urgency. Paul seems to have written it *with his own hand* throughout (contrary to his usual practice), for he points their attention to this fact as shewn in the large writing (vi. 11).* This was either a sign of haste that could not wait for an amanuensis, or of affectionate earnestness which would write personally at whatever effort.

The letter is intirely devoted to the great question of the obligation of the Mosaic law upon Gentiles,—a doctrine which Paul indignantly repudiates and disproves by the clearest arguments. He had already repudiated the idea in his letters to the Corinthians; but here he *argues* the question thoroughly,—as thoroughly, perhaps, though not so much at length, as afterwards in the epistle to the Romans, of which, indeed, this letter to the Galatians may be considered the germ.

In attempting an abstract of this most lively epistle, I shall generally keep its personal forms of address, as the only way of retaining any of its fire and force.

Abstract of the Epistle to the Galatians.

Ch. i. 1. The salutation includes "all the brethren who are with me" (probably some of those who are mentioned by name in Acts xx. 4, as returning with Paul from Achaia into Asia after this visit to Corinth). The apostle asserts, at the

* *πηλίκοις γράμμασιν*: not "how large a letter" (it is rather a short one, in fact), but *in what large letters.*

outset, his divine call to the ministry of Christ: "Paul, an apostle,—not sent from men, neither by man, but by Jesus Christ, and God the Father who raised him from the dead." 6. He plunges at once into the subject of his letter:—I wonder at your changeableness,—to leave Christ so soon for a different Gospel (which is, indeed, nothing but this,—that some troublesome people wish to subvert the Gospel of Christ). Let any one who preaches a different Gospel be rejected *(Anathema)*. Do you think I seek the favour of men? or of God? If the former, I should never have taken up the ministry of Christ at all. 11. He appeals to the notorious facts of his own life, and particularizes others less known:—his Jewish education and persecuting zeal against the Christian church; his conversion, neither caused nor followed by personal conference with the other apostles, but produced by divine communication, and matured also by retirement in Arabia and Damascus. Not till three years after his conversion had he seen Peter and James at Jerusalem; and fourteen years after it, he had gone with Barnabas and Titus to the "Council of Jerusalem," on this very question of imposing the Jewish Law upon Gentiles, and had vindicated the freedom of the latter from the attempts of false brethren. Ch. ii. 6. But on this occasion he had gained no new instructions even from the chief apostles of Christ, James, Peter and John, who had agreed to preach to the Jews, while Paul and Barnabas should go to the Gentiles,—the latter promising to remember the poor brethren in Judea (Paul's constant care). 11. Afterwards, at Antioch, he had withstood Peter to the face for his weak dissimulation on this very subject. "If a Jew has overcome in his own person the Jewish exclusive scruples, should he wish to subject the Gentiles to them? We, though born Jews, and not unholy Gentiles, know that a man is not justified by the works of the Law, but by the faith of Jesus Christ." Here, at verses 15, 16, is the *thesis* announced, which is maintained throughout this Epistle, against the false brethren who insisted upon the Gentile Christians being circumcised:

"A man is not justified by the works of the Law, but by the faith of Jesus Christ."

If Paul's own statement of his thesis had been borne in mind, we should never have heard of a controversy among Christians as to the comparative saving power of faith and of good works. The question is not between faith and good works, but between the ritual works of the Jewish Law and the spiritual influences of Christianity. And when Paul maintains that a man is *justified* by the latter without the former, we must not ascribe to his words the stiff modern theological idea of *final* or *complete justification*, but understand him to say, in language more native to the heart, that the Divine blessing is won by the spiritual service of Christianity, without the ritual works of the Jewish Law. With these obvious, but neglected, meanings restored to his principal terms,—*Faith*, *Works* and *Justification*,—there is no difficulty in understanding, nor possibility of dissenting from, his noble vindication of Christian liberty and enforcement of Christian virtue. So the letter proceeds:

Ch. ii. 17. But if, while seeking Christian justification, we make ourselves obnoxious to Legal uncleanness, is Christ the minister of sin? God forbid! For if I build up again the ritual institutions which I have done with, I, by my own act, make myself a transgressor. Having been at first under the Law, I died to the Law that I might live to God. In Christ's crucifixion I died thus to the Law; but the Christian life survives in me. I do not reject, but accept, this grace of God; for if justification were to be sought by the Law only, Christ must have died in vain.

Ch. iii. 1. O, foolish Galatians! who has bewitched you? Answer but one question: Did you receive the Spirit by the works of the Law, or by hearing the faith of Christ? Are you so foolish, when you began spiritually, as to think you can become complete with fleshly observances? Did I work miracles and communicate the Spirit to you by the Law, or by the Gospel? 6. And what was Abraham's righteousness? A living faith. Abraham's children are all those who have a

like faith, that is trust, in God, including Gentiles as well as Jews. 10. The Law leaves a curse upon the non-fulfilment of any part of its own requirements, and even its prophets declare that "the righteous live by faith." 13. Christ has redeemed us from the curse of the Law, that the blessing of Abraham may come upon the Gentiles through Jesus Christ. 15. To compare human transactions with divine: A covenant (always held sacred among men) was made with Abraham and his seed. The Law, instituted 430 years afterwards, did not annul that covenant of free divine promise, but was provisionally given until the promised seed, Christ, should come; being ordained by angels, by the hands of Moses as mediator,—God being one of the contracting parties, His people the other (but His children of the human race not being represented on that occasion).* 21. The Law, thus provisionally instituted, is not inconsistent with the Divine promises. Its use was as conductor to the school of Christ, where we are no longer under the conductor's charge, but are children of God by faith in Jesus Christ. All distinctions vanish before the great spiritual influence of the Gospel. Jew and Greek, bond and free, male and female, are all one in Christ; they are Abraham's seed and heirs, as promised.

Ch. iv. 1. The heir, while a child, is under tutelage. So was the world till the fulness of time arrived, when God sent forth His Son to redeem those who were under the Law, and give the adoption of sons to them and all others. 8. You Galatians, heathens previously, have been lately taught to know God: will you turn back to weak and beggarly elements of outward observance? 11. "I am afraid of you (says the apostle), lest I have bestowed upon you labour in vain." "Be as I am" (satisfied without the Law), "for I am as ye are" (having given up its exclusive hopes). He refers affectionately to their former reception of him, and desires to be with them again and "change his voice," that is, change *to* his voice, take his voice in exchange, converse instead of writing. 21. But you, who wish to be under the Law, why not really listen to what the Law says? Abraham had two sons; one by

* See Locke on Gal. iii. 20 (note).

Hagar the bond-woman, the other by Sarah the free-woman. These sons may be compared to the two covenants,—the one that of Sinai, answering to the existing Jerusalem,—the other to the heavenly Jerusalem. We, like Isaac, are the children of the promise, the children of the free mother.

Ch. v. 1. Stand fast, then, in the freedom given by Christ. 2. If you adopt circumcision, I tell you plainly, Christianity is of no use to you. Whoever does this, binds himself to do the whole Law of Moses. You have no more concern with Christ. You have fallen from the free gift of God's grace. In Jesus Christ, the being circumcised or not signifies nothing; but faith, which worketh by love, is everything. 7. You did run well; be worthy of your former selves. He that troubles you shall bear the punishment. 12. It would be well if the *circum*cisers would *ex*cise themselves (separate from your community). 13. But let this Christian freedom be used virtuously and benevolently. The Law itself is really fulfilled in this one precept: "Thou shalt love thy neighbour as thyself." 16. Let spiritual Christians walk spiritually, and not fulfil the lust of the flesh. The opposite works of the flesh and of the spirit are described. But those who are Christ's, have crucified the flesh with its passions and lusts.

Ch. vi. 1. The apostle suggests how to treat offenders; 6. exhorts to liberality in maintaining their church teachers; 11. points their attention to his own hand-writing; 12. charges selfishness and ostentation upon the circumcising zealots; 15. repeats that Christianity knows no difference on this score between Jew and Gentile, but requires "a new creation" everywhere. He then concludes with affectionate benedictions.

EPISTLE TO THE ROMANS.

(A.D. 58.)

THERE is no doubt whatever as to the date and other leading circumstances connected with the production of this letter, in some respects the most remarkable and valuable of Paul's writings. It dates itself and explains itself as written from Achaia (Corinth doubtless, whence the last-mentioned letter probably was sent), when the apostle is about to go to Jerusalem with the contributions of the Macedonian and Achaian churches for the poor Jewish Christians (xv. 22—26). The postscript is, in this instance, quite borne out by internal evidence, when it says that the letter was written from Corinth and sent under the care of Phebe, a deaconess of the church at Cenchrea. She is commended by the apostle, in his letter, to their good offices (xvi. 1, 2); and he particularly bespeaks their help, if opportunity should offer, in some *business* which she has in hand at Rome. Some have conjectured that it was a lawsuit. It seems reasonable to infer that she was a widow, from her independent mode of action; and she was evidently a person of consideration at Cenchrea. Paul speaks of her frequent kind offices to himself and others.

The intended journey of this lady to Rome decided Paul to avail himself of the opportunity of writing to the Christian church in the great city. He had never yet been there; and it is to this day uncertain when and by whom Christianity had been first preached in Rome. But the continual intercourse between Rome and Judea, and the residence of so many Jews in Rome, makes it pretty certain that Christianity was early known there, and that the Christian church in that city must at first have been composed of Jewish converts; while, however, it is clear from St. Paul's letter that, when he wrote, it was a mixed church of Jews and Gentiles, with the latter element apparently in the ascendant. The very numerous salutations towards the end of the Epistle include some well-known names. St. Paul expresses, near the beginning, his desire and intention soon to visit them; and towards the conclusion (xv. 18—32), he more fully explains himself to the effect, that he has hitherto avoided preaching where others had already been before him, but that, having now been as far as Illyricum, and having "no more room in those parts," he contemplates (after completing his present mission to Jerusalem) undertaking a more distant journey into Spain, and means to visit the brethren at Rome on his way. He is evidently impressed with the dangers which threaten him meanwhile at the hands of the unconverted Jews of Judea, and asks the prayers of his friends at Rome for his safety. How his worst fears were fulfilled at Jerusalem, and how differently from his intention he appeared in Rome "a prisoner for Christ," the history has already told us.

The contents of the Epistle to the Romans are of a more general and comprehensive kind than has been the case with any of those hitherto examined. It has no reference to any special circumstances or transactions of the Roman church, to most of the members of which, indeed, the apostle is personally unknown when he writes. But he has heard of their growth and general welfare. He knows the dangers and difficulties which beset them like other churches. And he handles, but in a more general way, and in a manner applicable to all Christian churches, as being without any special allusions whatever, the same topics which had borne a more pointed temporary and personal reference in other letters. There were, doubtless, in Rome the elements of the same struggle with the zealots for circumcision which had lately broken out in the Galatian churches; and Paul treats this question fully, but from a more comprehensive and (as it were) impersonal point of view. The question of clean and unclean meats, too, was sure to arise, if it had not done already, in Rome just as in Corinth; and the apostle touches this topic in more general, but clear, comprehensive and decisive terms, which remind us of the advice he had written a year ago to the Corinthians, about "things offered to idols."

The principal part of this noble Epistle is devoted to the subject of *Justification by the Christian Faith.* And here, as in the Epistle to the Galatians, it is very necessary (in order to understand St. Paul's meaning) that we endeavour to lay aside all merely modern, technical and dogmatical ideas respecting the principal terms used in the argument, namely, *Law, Works, Faith, Justification.*

The question opened in this letter is larger, and is more freely handled, than that already treated in the letter to the Galatians; while the central topic is the same in both, and many expressions are so similar as to confirm the opinion of its being written about the same time. To the Galatians the apostle vindicated the sufficiency of Christian faith for justification in the sight of God, against those carnal-minded zealots who insisted upon circumcision. The "works of the Law" had there the narrowest possible meaning, namely, the outward and bodily ceremonies of Judaism. But to the Romans the apostle now presents the same essential doctrine of the sufficiency of a spiritual Christianity from a wider point of view, not merely as in opposition to the dead works of ceremonial Judaism, but also to every other law or mode of action by which it could be pretended that men might put themselves into a state equivalent to that of Christian justification before their Maker.

Law thus stands for any definite, absolute, outside rule of conduct. And in opposition to Law, here stands *Faith,* denoting spiritual religion as the inward spring of action and emotion, whether influencing Abraham before the Law, or good men under the Law, or especially as inspiring the disciples of Christ.

Works now stand for every low and false attempt to *earn* heaven as wages for service done; and with these is contrasted the *Grace*, or free kindness, of God, as shewn in the Gospel.

And *Justification* or *Righteousness* (the former being the more suitable translation of the Greek word, and least liable to mistake) denotes the state of blessing and privilege into which Christians are called by God's mercy, but not that state of spiritual safety, assurance and presumption which it has often been taken to mean.

These terms were virtually explained long since by John Locke, in his Paraphrases of Paul's Epistles; and more laboriously by Dr. John Taylor, in his Key to the Apostolic Writings and Paraphrase of the Epistle to the Romans; from the latter of which I extract the following:

"We cannot, so far as I can see, have clear conceptions of the argumentative or controversial part of the Epistle, unless we are clear in this point: That the justification the apostle argues for is the right which we, believing Gentiles, have, through the favour and gift of God, to the blessings, honours and privileges of *his kingdom in this world;* not so as thereby to have the possession of the heavenly and eternal kingdom absolutely secured to us, but so as to be favoured with the assurance of pardon, the promises and hope of the eternal kingdom, and all proper light and means to prepare us for it, if we do not wickedly despise and abuse them. It is this notion of justification alone which corresponds to the design and end of the Epistle, to the foresaid general, collective notion of *Jews* and *Gentiles*, and makes everything lie easy and straight in the apostle's discourse and arguments." (Taylor's Preface to Romans, § 45.)

Abstract of the Epistle to the Romans.

Ch. i. 1. The salutation from Paul "to all that be in Rome, beloved of God, called to be saints," sets forth, in a long and somewhat involved parenthetical sentence, his own apostleship, the completion of the purposes of Judaism in the mission of Jesus Christ, and the equal reception of the Gentiles into the new dispensation. 8. The apostle thanks God for what he has heard of the faith of the Roman church, and expresses the desire which he has long had, and still cherishes, of visiting them. 16. He is "not ashamed of the Gospel; for it is the saving power of God to every one who has faith in it; to the Jew first, and also to the Gentile. For in it God's method of justification from faith to faith (springing from faith and received by faith) is revealed."* And from this statement of his theme, the apostle at once proceeds to its illustration and enforcement. That theme essentially is, that the Gospel is for Jew and Gentile alike; that both need it, and both are blessed with the highest spiritual good by its means. 18. Without pointedly addressing the Gentile part of the church, Paul first appeals to the native reason and conscience of man, as able to see God in His works, and discern between right and wrong in human conduct; and on the groundwork of natural religion, he declares the idolatry and wickedness of the heathen world to be "without excuse." A dreadful picture indeed he draws of the disgusting profligacy of the age,—a picture, alas! not overcharged by any means, for it is but the abstract of the varied testimonies of contemporary Latin historians and satirists. It was now the fourth year of the reign of Nero,—the age of most filthy and unblushing vice in the capital city of the world. To the Christian church at Rome especially, the apostle points to these things with the finger of earnest deprecation.

Ch. ii. 1. Without naming the Jew, St. Paul virtually addresses him next, and places him also "without excuse," if, while condemning the Gentile, he does the same things himself. 6. God will render to every man according to his deeds, to Jew and to Gentile, without respect of persons. 12. Those who have sinned, not being under a Law, will perish also

* "God's method of justification." This is Archbishop Newcome's translation, who adds in a note: "The original word is often used by St. Paul for God's treating men as just or righteous, whether by admitting them into the outward privileges of the Christian church here, or into his heavenly kingdom hereafter." It is of the former only, as the Archbishop leaves us to infer, that the apostle speaks throughout this Epistle.

without reference to Law; and those who have sinned under a Law, will be judged by that Law. What can be more equitable? 14. When the Gentiles, who have no Law, do by nature the requirements of the Law, they, though they have no Law, are a Law to themselves, since they shew that the deeds of the Law are written in their hearts, their conscience also bearing witness, and their own thoughts condemning or excusing them. 17. He now appeals to the Jew by name, as resting in the Law and making his boast of knowing God and being better instructed than the Gentile. Disobedience on his part causes the name of God to be blasphemed, and makes him virtually a heathen in the sight of heaven. So must the obedience of the Gentile make him as a child of Abraham before God. "For he is not a Jew who is one outwardly; neither is that circumcision which is outward in the flesh. But he is a Jew who is one inwardly; and circumcision is that of the heart, in the spirit and not in the letter, whose praise is not from men, but from God."

Ch. iii. 1. Is it asked then, What advantage the Jew has from the Law? "Much, every way," the apostle replies; "chiefly because to them were committed the oracles of God." Though some of them were faithless to the trust, this does not annul the faithfulness of God towards them and towards all men. 9. "Have we Jews then precedence to the Gentiles?" No; for both Jews and Gentiles have been already proved to be in a sinful state. The Jewish Scriptures themselves speak, indeed, of those under the Law as being "none of them righteous, no not one;" as having "all gone out of the way;" and use yet stronger expressions than these. 20. Therefore justification is not found through the works of the Law, but the acknowledgment of sin rather is made under it. 21. But now, *quite apart from Law*, God's method of justification has been brought to light, as attested by the Law and the Prophets. This justifying process is carried on through *faith in Jesus Christ*, for all and upon all who have that faith; for no difference is made between Jew and Gentile. All have sinned; and all are placed on a new footing of justification, freely by his grace (freely and graciously placed in the Christian state of religious blessings, motives and hopes). They have been ransomed* as from slavery by Jesus Christ. His death sets him forth also like a propitiatory offering,* to shew God's method of justifying mankind by passing over their former sins, and to shew His present method of justification, as Himself just and justifying him that has faith. 27. There is no room for boasting then. Justification must come by faith, apart from the works of the Law. God is the God of Jews and Gentiles alike. And this is the true vindication of the Law of Moses itself.

Ch. iv. 1. Look at the case of Abraham, the lineal head of the Jewish nation. His justification was on account of his faith. It was not earned by service and claimed as a debt! 9. This is clear; for Abraham was justified and blessed by God while he was still "in uncircumcision," and he received that ordinance as a seal of the justification which arose from his faith while still uncircumcised. 16. Abraham's faith is described: it was *trust* in the Divine promise. This is what was "reckoned to him for justification." 23. And similar faith "on Him that raised up Jesus our Lord from the dead," will be reckoned to us also as a justifying faith.

Ch. v. 1. "Thus justified by faith, Christians have peace with God through their Lord Jesus Christ." And they can even rejoice to suffer for his sake who died for them; assured that, having been brought from a state of enmity by Christ's death, much more, after this reconciliation, they will find salvation by participating his life. 12. *Life by Christ*, is the converse of the *mortality*† *derived from Adam* to the human race as his descendants. 15. But very different from the offence is the free gift! 18. "As the fruit of one offence reached to all men, and brought upon them condemnation, so likewise the fruit of one acquittal shall reach to all, and shall

* Illustrative figures, each appropriate, but quite distinct. The latter, which is here only glanced at, is very beautifully developed in the Epistle to the Hebrews, in which (in order to conciliate the Hebrew feeling) the writer runs an ingenious parallel between the temple service of the old dispensation and the spiritual things of the new.

† Paul's doctrine, like the doctrine of Genesis, is, that the human race became *mortal* by Adam's transgression: "By one man sin entered into the world, and death by sin."

bring justification, the source of life."* 20. The introduction of the Law made the offence more evidently abound, till the grace of God in the Gospel abounded more.

Ch. vi. 1. Can this last thought be perverted into a plea for "continuing in sin, that grace may abound"? How is that possible, when the whole life of the Christian implies that *he has already died to sin?* Baptized into Christ's death, the disciple dies to all evil and rises to newness of life. "The old man," "the sinful body," is crucified with Christ. 12. Sin must no more reign in him; for this very reason, that he is not under the Law, but under Grace. 16. To whosesoever service a man gives himself up, that is his real master. The Gentile Christian once was the bond-servant of Sin; but now he is rescued from that service, and bound to the service of Righteousness. 23. The wages of the former service is death; but the free gift of God, in the other, is eternal life.

Ch. vii. 1. As the low and sinful tendencies of human nature have been declared to be dead in the Christian disciple, Paul illustrates his freedom from the obligations of the Mosaic Law by somewhat fancifully pursuing this figure.† The Law can only bind its subjects during their life. So a woman is bound to her husband while he lives; but if he die, she may innocently marry again. And "ye also are become dead to the Law by the body of Christ," so as to be married to him who was raised from the dead. You are (or ought to be) dead to the flesh and its sinful passions, and ready to bring forth good fruit to God, "in the new spirit, not according to the old letter." 7. The apostle replies to an objection ready to arise in the mind

* Conybeare and Howson's translation.

† The comparison does not (as the critic would say) "run on all fours:" As a woman, *when her husband is dead*, may marry another, so ye, *being dead* to the Law in Christ's body, are married again to the risen Christ. But the dead do not marry again. One would have expected rather to find the comparison carried out thus: So ye, *as the Law is dead*, are married to Christ. And this seems the real thought, though confused in the logical expression. Might not *εθανατώθητε τῷ νόμῳ* be sufficiently translated, "Ye have been separated from the Law by death,"—not your own death, but that of the Law? The common reading of ver. 6 favours this idea: "*That being dead wherein we were held.*"

of a zealous Jew: "Is the Law then sin, or the cause of sin?" God forbid! Nay; I* should not have known what sin was, except by the Law. One would not have known the sin of coveting, unless the Law had said, Covet not. But sin, having taken occasion by the commandment, wrought in me all manner of coveting; † for, apart from Law, sin is dormant and, as it were, dead; and I was alive once apart from Law; but when the commandment came, sin gained new life, and I died. The Law itself is holy and just and true. Did this good thing then become death to me? O no; it was sin that became so,—that it might be shewn to be sin, as producing death by means of what was good. The law itself is spiritual. It is I, the man, that am carnal. I do not acknowledge my own actions; for "what I wish, that I do not; but what I hate, that I do." So, in doing what is contrary to my best will, I acknowledge at least that the Law is good. And it is not my own true self, not my best self, that does it, but sin dwelling in me. In my fleshly self, good abides not; "for to will is present with me; but how to perform that which is good, I find not. For the good that I would, I do not; but the evil which I would not, that I do. Now, if I do that which I would not, it is no more I that do it, but sin that dwelleth in me." The state of things, in short, is this: When I wish to do right, evil is at hand. The inward man of conscience and will delights in the law of God; but there is another law in my members warring against the law of my mind. Wretched man! What deliverance is there from this deadly body, these fleshly temptations, these carnal desires? Thank God, the deliverance is offered in Jesus Christ!

Ch. viii. 1. "There is, therefore, now no condemnation to

* It argues great simplicity in any reader to suppose that the apostle means himself personally by *I* and *me* in this curious passage. He describes the mental struggles of many Jews besides himself; the quickening of natural conscience by the Law, and its perplexity when so quickened, till a more spiritual faith was found in the Gospel. A very full abstract of this important passage is given above.

† How true is this, that the negative precept itself may suggest the evil deed, unless it suggest also the restraining motives and the opposite love of good! The thought may be excited by hearing the prohibition!

them that are in Christ Jesus; for the Law of the spirit of life in Jesus Christ hath made me free from the Law of sin and death." What was impossible to the Jewish Law with its fleshly ordinances, has been done in Christ, whom God sent in the likeness of sinful flesh to condemn sin in the flesh; so that the justification of the Law henceforth to be fulfilled shall be by our walking, not after the flesh, but after the spirit. 6. The fleshly, or carnal, mind and the spiritual mind are contrasted. If Christ be really in us, "though the body be dead because of sin, yet the spirit is alive because of righteousness." 13. To live after the flesh is death; but to mortify the deeds of the body is real life. 14. Christians are sons of God, crying Abba, our Father, in the spirit of adoption. 18. Present suffering is not to be compared to their expected blessedness. 19. The whole creation is yearning for the developement of a higher state. 23. Christians especially have realized a livelier hope, and look for their full adoption and "redemption from the body."* And while resting in hope of their salvation, they find spiritual help in their hearts before God. 28. All things, even the most afflictive, must work together for good, to those whom God hath thus foreknown and foreappointed, called and justified and made partakers of His glorious kingdom. An exulting passage concludes this chapter, with this part of the letter.

Ch. ix. 1. Paul expresses his earnest and sorrowful concern on behalf of the Jewish nation in general, who have rejected the Gospel, after so long possessing the covenanted favours of God. 3. For their sake he could wish himself rejected from Christ, if that would bring them in. 6. Not that the promise of God has failed; "for not all are Israel that are of Israel." The promise was made to Isaac, but not to Ishmael; and to Jacob again, but not to Esau. 15. And the will of God is supreme, both in the dispensation of His mercy and in the rejection of those whom He has long forborne to punish. 24. The calling of the Gentiles was anti-

* Wakefield's translation; *τὴν ἀπολύτρωσιν τοῦ σώματος ἡμῶν*; the plain meaning, in my opinion, and the only one consistent with the continual contrast between the body and the spirit.

cipated by the Jewish prophets themselves. 30. And now the Gentiles, though not seeking justification, have found it in the spiritual faith of the Gospel; while the Jews, seeking it by their Law, have not found it, because "they did not seek it by faith, but by the works of the Law."

Ch. x. 1. The apostle's desire and prayer to God for Israel is, that they may yet accept the Gospel salvation. 4. "For Christ is the end of Law for justification to every one that has faith;" 12. without distinction between Jew and Gentile. 14. The benevolent suggestion to preach the Gospel derived hence, though some will not hearken to the tidings.

Ch. xi. 1. Yet God has not cast off his ancient people. 5. There is still a faithful remnant, as in the days of Elijah,— "according to the election of grace" (chosen by Divine favour). 7. What Israel is seeking by the works of the Law, Israel collectively fails to find; but the chosen among them have found it. 11. Nor is the re-admission of the rest of the Jewish people into the Divine covenant hopeless. 12. If their fall enriches the world, how much more would their fulness! 14. Paul would provoke his kindred to emulation by the sight of the believing Gentiles received into Christian adoption. 17. He makes a beautiful appeal to the latter, as branches of a wild olive-tree grafted upon a fruitful stock, not to boast over any of the natural branches that have been broken off. 25. He declares to them "the mystery"* of the calling of the Gentiles; that blindness has fallen upon a part of Israel till the full body of the Gentiles shall have come in; and then all Israel also will accept the Christian salvation. "For (29) the gifts and calling of God are not revoked by any after-thought of His." "To Him be glory for ever. Amen."

The great argument of the Epistle here concludes, and the rest is devoted to practical advice.

* Mystery properly means *a secret*. In the Scriptures of Revelation, it frequently, if not generally, means a "*revealed mystery*,"—secret hitherto, now disclosed. The leading mystery of the kingdom of heaven was the *calling of the Gentiles*. It is often so designated by Paul (Eph. i. 9, 10; iii. 4—9)

Ch. xii. 1. The apostle exhorts earnestly to a holy and obedient life, as the believer's reasonable service; to the harmonious and unenvying use of their various spiritual gifts, and the practice of all kind and sympathizing affections.

Ch. xiii. 1. He enjoins obedience to the civil government as a religious duty.* 8. All social duties are comprised in the Christian Law of Love. 11. A vague allusion to the day of salvation being near, contrasts with some stronger ones that have been noticed in Paul's earlier letters.

Ch. xiv. 1—xv. 13. In this well-known passage (beginning, "Him that is weak in faith receive ye," &c.), St. Paul gives most admirable precepts of mutual forbearance, for the guidance of the Gentile Christians in their intercourse with those who retain the Jewish scruples about meats and days and other external observances. It is quite in the spirit of the advice to the Corinthians (1 Cor. viii.—x.), but is expressed in more general terms, not having been drawn forth by special facts, but designed to warn them against abiding dangers. 14. He courteously apologizes for speaking thus plainly to them, and is persuaded that they can remind each other of what is right. 17. He details his plans for his next ensuing labours, including (on the completion of his charitable errand to Jerusalem) an early visit to Rome on his purposed voyage to Spain.

Ch. xvi. 1. Phebe, the bearer of the letter, is commended to their good offices, and numerous salutations are addressed to Christians at Rome. 17. The apostle warns them against self-interested mischief-makers. 21. He gives the salutations of Timothy and others with him at Corinth; and Tertius, the scribe who writes for the apostle, gives his own salutation. 25. A fine doxology concludes the Epistle.

* It has been well observed that "this was written before the Imperial government had begun to persecute Christianity. It is a testimony in favour of the general administration of the Roman criminal law." (Conybeare and Howson, II. 191.)

EPISTLE TO THE COLOSSIANS.

(A.D. 62.)

THE foregoing Epistle (to the Romans) was written from Corinth on the apostle's third missionary journey. He went thence (as we read in Acts xx. 3—xxi. 17) through Macedonia, by Troas, Miletus, Tyre and Cæsarea, to Jerusalem, carrying the contributions of the Macedonian and Achaian churches for the poor Christians of Judea, as purposed by him when he wrote the letter to the Romans (xv. 25—28). At Jerusalem he was arrested and sent to Cæsarea; whence, after two years' delay, he was sent to Rome by Festus, on his own appeal from the provincial tribunal to that of the emperor. His next four letters (to the Colossians, Philemon, the Ephesians and the Philippians) were written during his detention at Rome while awaiting his trial. The nature of that custody is described at the end of the book of Acts. It allowed him, not only to "dwell in his own hired house and receive all that came in unto him," but also to write freely to distant churches and friends. Is it not probable that, in the obscurity of the Jewish accusations against him, both his conversations and his letters, thus freely permitted, may have been looked to as possible sources of illustrative evidence on the pending trial? Of that trial we have no record; but, either after trial or without trial, the apostle was certainly set at liberty.

Colosse was an ancient, but somewhat decayed, city of Phrygia, the neighbouring cities of Laodicea and Hierapolis having risen while it declined. The chief or only interest attaching to it is as the seat of an early Christian church, to which an apostle wrote a still existing letter.

It does not appear that Paul had ever been at Colosse, though some think he may have been there when he travelled, as he is twice recorded to have done (Acts xvi. 6 and xviii. 23), through Phrygia and Galatia. But, on the other hand, Paul in this letter speaks of "having heard of their faith" (just as he does to the Roman church), and not of being "thankful on each *remembrance* of them," as he does to churches planted or already visited by him. Indeed, the 7th verse of this Epistle speaks of Epaphras in terms that naturally lead us to consider him as having been the founder of the church at Colosse. They had "learned the grace of God from Epaphras;" and he (now at Rome*) had informed the apostle of their "love for him in the spirit" (i. 7, 8; iv. 12). From ch. ii. 1, also, it is natural to conclude that neither the Colossians nor the Laodiceans had seen Paul's "face in the flesh." One Archippus was at this time presbyter, or bishop, of the church at Colosse (iv. 17). Probably Epaphras, Archippus and Philemon (the last of whom will be more particularly mentioned soon, and in whose house the church at Colosse held their meetings), were among the earliest heralds of the Gospel at Colosse, having heard Paul's announcement of it at Ephesus during his long residence there (Acts xix. 9, 10). The Epistle dates itself as written during the apostle's captivity: "Remember my bonds." And the P.S. is correct in repeating, from the letter itself, that it was sent by Tychicus and Onesimus as bearers. The former, an Asiatic, probably of Ephesus, had accompanied Paul on his last journey to Jerusalem, and is named by him

* Epaphras is, in the Epistle to Philemon, of the same date exactly (ver. 23), called by St. Paul his "fellow-prisoner in Christ Jesus;" and by the same term he, in this Epistle to the Colossians (iv. 10), describes Aristarchus, a Thessalonian who had been his fellow-voyager to Rome. By "fellow-prisoners" is probably only meant that they shared his lodging, which was *his* prison, whether theirs literally or not.

afterwards in his letters to Titus and Timothy as an active emissary on similar occasions to this which now takes him to Colosse. Of Onesimus we shall learn more particulars in connection with the letter to Philemon, which was sent to Colosse by the same bearers.

The Epistle to the Colossians presents no pressing difficulties of interpretation. It has a breadth and comprehensiveness of topics which fit it for general Christian use. It implies the same view of the equality of Gentile and Jew in the kingdom of Christian faith, which was set forth with laboured argument and illustration in the letter to the Romans; but it does not *argue* the matter again. It is eminently a *practical* Epistle. And the apostle designed it to be read beyond Colosse, as he bids his friends (iv. 16), after reading it among themselves, "cause it to be read also in the church of the Laodiceans; and that ye likewise read the epistle which you will receive from Laodicea." From this last injunction we necessarily conclude that the apostle wrote at the same time, and sent by the same messengers, a letter to Laodicea. There is no such letter of Paul's, indeed, now extant by *name*;* but (as will be shewn in its proper place) the letter known as that to the *Ephesians* is, in all probability, the one here alluded to.

Abstract of the Epistle to the Colossians.

Ch. i. 1. Timothy is united with the apostle in the salutation. 3. Paul thanks God for what he hears of their Christian faith and heavenly hope, and prays for their worthy conduct as those who have been "delivered from the power of darkness,

* A short *Latin* letter under this title, made up of nineteen verses from the Epistles to the Galatians and Philippians, is evidently a more recent attempt to supply the missing letter to the Laodiceans.

and translated into the kingdom of God's beloved Son;" in whom they are ransomed, or redeemed, and their former sins are forgiven. 15. Christ is the representative of the Almighty, the first-born of the new spiritual creation, in whom all things in heaven and earth* have been created (anew).† 19. For it pleased God that "all fulness" should dwell in him, and that things on earth and things in heaven* should be reconciled together by his cross. 21. Thus the Colossians, formerly alienated in heathenism, have been reconciled; let them only be firm and true to their Christian faith. 24. As for Paul himself, he rejoices to suffer for Christ's church, while declaring the revealed mystery of Divine love to the Gentiles, and striving to present every disciple as a full-grown man in Christ.

Ch. ii. 1. The apostle expresses his anxiety for the Colossians and Laodiceans, and all churches not personally known to him, that they may be firm in Christian truth, and not lay down their Christian comforts and hopes for the adoption of any more specious doctrines. 3. The Gospel is the truest wisdom, whatever "enticing words" there may be by which any man may seek to allure them from it. 9. In Christ is the fulness of Divine inspiration; and *their* fulness is in him as the Head of the new dispensation. 11. In him they are spiritually made the people of God, burying their former sins (as it were) with Christ in baptism, and rising again thence to new life with him; while the written ordinances of the fleshly Judaism are blotted out and nailed to his cross. 16. Let them resist, therefore, the imposition of Jewish traditions respecting clean and unclean meats and holy days, and affected self-humi-

* Surely *Jews and Gentiles* must be the things in "heaven and earth" (vers. 16 and 20). See Locke's Paraphrase on Eph. i. 10, where the same language occurs (being written at the same time). The Jews were the ancient kingdom of heaven. "The whole family in heaven and earth" (Eph. iii. 15) form the Gospel kingdom.

† The full phrase is, created *anew*, *new* creation, *new* creature (2 Cor. v. 17; Gal. vi. 15). So the *new man* (Eph. ii. 15, iv. 24; Col. iii. 10). When *new* is not expressed, it is to be understood, therefore, in the apostle's descriptions of the *creation in*, *by*, or *for Christ* (ἐν αὐτῷ, δι' αὐτοῦ, εἰς αὐτὸν).

liation and angel-worship, and hold to Christ as the Head of the great body to which they belong.

Ch. iii. 1. Those who are risen with Christ from the life of the flesh, should set their affections on things above, and let their members truly die to earthly and shameful lusts, such as they once walked in while they were heathens. 8. They must put off all unsocial and unkind feelings as their "old man," having put on "the new man, who grows continually in the knowledge and likeness of Him that created him." 12. The apostle exhorts them tenderly to mutual charity and peace, and to social worship. 18. He gives special precepts to husbands and wives, children and parents, slaves and masters.

Ch. iv. 2. He asks for an interest in their prayers, that, though in bonds, he may still find an opening for his apostolic labours. 5. Cautions them how to behave towards unbelievers. 7. Refers them to the bearers of the letter for information respecting himself. 10. Greets them from Aristarchus, Mark (who, he hints, may possibly come to Colosse); from Jesus called Justus, Epaphras their fellow-countryman (whose zeal he greatly commends); also from Luke and Demas. 15. Sends salutations to Laodicea, and bids them exchange letters with that church. 17. Message to Archippus the presbyter. 18. Salutation and benediction.

EPISTLE TO PHILEMON.

(A.D. 62.)

This is a private letter to a private Christian at Colosse, on a personal matter, which the apostle wrote at the same time as the above letter to the church at that place, and sent by the same messengers, Tychicus and Onesimus. The latter was the occasion and subject of the letter to Philemon.

Onesimus was Philemon's slave. He had deserted his master, and found his way to Rome. There he came under Paul's notice and influence, and earned the apostle's strong interest and affection. Paul would have been glad to retain him in the service of the Gospel, which had set his soul free; but would not do so without Philemon's assent. But the Epistle is its own best explanation. Though private in character, it is full of Christian interest.

ABSTRACT OF THE EPISTLE TO PHILEMON.

Ver. 1. The greeting is from Paul and Timothy to Philemon and Appia (his wife, doubtless), to Archippus, "our fellow-soldier," and to the church assembling in Philemon's house. 4. Paul is thankful for what he has heard of Philemon's faith, and of his kindness and generosity towards the disciples of Christ. 8. He intercedes for the favourable reception of Onesimus,—which he might, indeed, in his apostolic character enjoin upon his friend, but he rather beseeches. 10. He calls Onesimus "his own son whom he had begotten in his bonds;"—he would have retained him with him as Philemon's representative, but will not without the master's consent. 15. "Perhaps" (Paul suggests, with admirable tact and delicacy, thus most effectually interceding for the slave's liberation)—"Perhaps for this very end he departed for a season, that thou mightest receive him back for ever; not now as a bondsman, but above a bondsman, a brother beloved; very much so by me, how much more dear to thee, being thine both in the flesh and in the Lord! If, then, thou count me as a friend, receive him as myself." 19. Paul will be accountable, if desired, for anything due from Onesimus;* but he beautifully hints Philemon's spiritual obligations to himself as his convert. He has full confidence that his friend will do more than he asks. 22. He confidently anticipates his own speedy liberation, on which he will visit Colosse; and he even desires Philemon to prepare him a lodging. The salutations are from the same persons as in the letter to the Colossians, except Jesus called Justus, who was probably unknown to Philemon (as he is to church history).

* For loss of service, perhaps. It does not imply, as some take it to do, that Onesimus had robbed his master.

EPISTLE TO THE EPHESIANS [?].

(A.D. 62.)

THAT this letter was written about the same time as that to the Colossians, is patent on the face of the two compositions. Their contents are so similar, not only in general thought and feeling, but even in verbal expression, that one can have no hesitation in ascribing them to the same time,—almost to the same day. This seems like an expansion of that to the Colossians, or the Colossians like an abstract of this. Tychicus is mentioned (vi. 21, 22) as the bearer of this also; and the P.S. states, accordingly, that it was "written from Rome, and sent by Tychicus." But that it was addressed to the *Ephesians*, as stated in the salutation and P.S., is generally admitted to be a mistake in the received copies. In many ancient copies (as asserted by Basil), the name of the church to which it was addressed was left out altogether in the salutation; and in one still existing, *Ephesus* is only put in the margin. In some ancient manuscripts, and by some ancient writers, it was called the Epistle to the *Laodiceans*.

That it cannot have been addressed to the Ephesians, is plain from its very general and indefinite mode of address, and the intire absence of all personal greetings and messages, such as must have been written to a church where the apostle had resided so long as he had done in Ephesus: and also from his speaking (i. 15) of the church to which this letter is addressed, as one whose faith and love had been *reported* to him, and who *might perhaps have heard* (iii. 2) of his doings in the dispensation of grace. These cannot have been his friends at Ephesus.

Perhaps this is the letter which he mentioned to the Colossians as having been sent to the Laodiceans. Perhaps, as some think, it was a sort of circular letter to the various churches of Phrygia (in the same way as that to the several churches of Galatia); and the *place* to which it was addressed may have been left blank in the different copies carried out by Tychicus, to be supplied according to circumstances. This would account for the old variations in the inscription. And we may perhaps account for its having been inscribed at last to the Ephesians, by copyists more zealous than discriminating, through a natural feeling of the probability that Paul *must* have written some letter or letters to a church so interesting to him as that at Ephesus. If he did, his letter to them is certainly not now in our canon; and how many more of his writings may have been lost, it is impossible to say.

ABSTRACT OF THE EPISTLE TO THE EPHESIANS (SO CALLED); PERHAPS, RATHER, TO THE LAODICEANS.

Ch. i. 1. Salutation. 3. Paul thanks God for the Gospel of Jesus Christ, in whom "He hath blessed us with all spiritual blessings in heavenly things,"* as He had designed long ages before; "gathering together (ver. 10) under one head all things in Christ, both things in heaven and things on earth." 15. He thanks God for the conversion of those to whom he is writing, and prays that they may understand and value their spiritual inheritance. 20. Christ, raised from the dead and placed on the right hand of God in the heavenly dispensation, has received full power in everything relative to "the church, which is his body, filled by Him who filleth all things."

* ἐν τοῖς ἐπουρανίοις. This phrase occurs five times in this Epistle, and nowhere else in the New Testament. Wakefield translates, *in the heavenly dispensation*, which seems the obvious sense. The Common Version says, *heavenly places*, four times (namely, i. 3, 20; ii. 6; iii. 10), and *high places* the fifth time (vi. 12), giving to it an intirely different meaning in this last instance. Neither *places* nor *things* being expressed, the latter is usually understood in such phrases.

Ch. ii. 1. Those who were lately heathens, have been made alive and brought into a state of salvation by the Divine grace, and placed with Christ in the heavenly dispensation, through no seeking of their own, but by the free gift of God. 10. They are God's workmanship, created anew in Christ for good works, and sharing with Israel the equal blessing of God,—the wall of partition between Jew and Gentile being broken down, the Law of ordinances being abolished by Christ's death, and both Jew and Gentile having access henceforth by the same spirit to the Father of all.

Ch. iii. 1. "For this cause (the apostle pursues), I, Paul, the prisoner of Jesus Christ for you Gentiles;"——"beseech you to walk worthy of the vocation wherewith ye are called," is the completion of his sentence, in the next chapter. What intervenes is a fine parenthesis, very characteristic of the fervour of the apostle's mind; in which (ver. 3) he resumes what he has just before said of the mystery of the call of the Gentiles, and then (7) exults in his own part in this ministration of Divine favour; (13) glances at his own tribulations; (14) implores the fulness of Divine love upon his friends; and (20) ascribes praise to God in a fine doxology.

Ch. iv. 1. He does not forget, however, what he was going to say, but takes up his previous words, and "beseeches them to walk worthy of their Christian calling;" especially exhorting them to unity and mutual kindness, as members of one body in Christ, having each their various gifts for the growth and health of the whole. 17. The immoralities of their Gentile state must be quite left behind; the "old man" must be put off, and the "new man" put on. 25. More particular precepts follow, enjoining truthfulness, restraint of anger, honesty, purity of conversation, kindness and forgivingness. As God in Christ hath forgiven them, let them be followers of God as dear children, and walk in love as Christ did. Ch. v. 3. The unclean vices of heathenism are most especially to be shunned. Such things should never be even named among the holy people of God. 8. Once they were in darkness, but now they are light in the Lord. 22. The relative duties of wives and husbands, (vi. 1) children and parents, (5) slaves and masters, are enforced. 10. They are exhorted to array themselves with the whole armour of God, as their defence against evil, in the heavenly dispensation; and to assail it with the word of God as their spiritual sword (a military metaphor often suggested to the eyes of the prisoner for Christ at Rome). 19. He desires their prayers; refers them to Tychicus for news of all that concerns him; and concludes with a benediction.

EPISTLE TO THE PHILIPPIANS.

(A.D. 62, probably Autumn.)

THIS Epistle bears its own date distinctly, in its subject matter and allusions. It was written from Rome, but somewhat later than those already analyzed. This is clear from several intimations of time. The apostle's imprisonment (he tells the Philippians) is now become notorious "in the whole Prætorium* and to all others;" and the Christians are waxing confident, and speaking the word fearlessly (i. 13, 14). Some of Cæsar's household (bondsmen, probably) are among his converts, who salute their fellow-believers at Philippi (iv. 22). But the lapse of time is marked in another way also. Epaphroditus was sent by the Philippians to Rome (as this letter informs us) on their hearing of Paul's imprisonment, to carry their sympathy and their pecuniary help. He has been seriously ill at Rome; his friends at Philippi have heard of his illness, and expressed their anxiety respecting him; and, on hearing of their anxiety, Epaphroditus now wishes to return to Philippi, and Paul

* *Palace*, in the Common Version. The word is used to denote Pilate's official residence, in John xviii. 28, 33, &c.; and Herod's, in Acts xxiii. 35; and may perhaps mean the Imperial Palace here, though *Palatium* was the word used by the Romans themselves. More probably *Prætorium* here means the whole establishment of Prætorian guards, to the custody of whose prefect Paul had been consigned by the centurion Julius (Acts xxviii. 16).

makes him the bearer of this letter (ii. 25—28). All this implies the lapse of a good many months.

It is also observable that, though the apostle "trusts to come himself shortly" to Philippi, yet he seems to be struggling against a prevailing feeling to the contrary. The tone of this letter is indeed less confident, on the whole, as to the probable issue of his imprisonment, than that which prevails in the letter to Philemon. If the letter now before us was written shortly after the death of Burrus, the prefect of the Prætorian guards, that event would sufficiently explain the new grounds for vague apprehension which the apostle would naturally feel. Burrus, an enlightened and virtuous man, had been, with the philosopher Seneca, guardian to Nero, and had maintained some degree of salutary restraint upon his fast maturing vices and tyranny. The circumstances of Burrus's death were not free from the suspicion of poison having been administered by Nero's orders. The influence of Seneca was from that time at an end; and the philosopher saw through the thin veil of feigned respect with which he was treated till, after two years more, the tyrant had him put to death. Burrus was succeeded in the prefecture of the Prætorian guards, by Fenius Rufus and Sofonius Tigellinus; the former, according to Tacitus, a harmless and indolent man; the latter, the active and shameless pander to Nero's vices. (See Tacitus, Ann. xiv. 51—57.) To this critical period the letter to the Philippians is assigned by Conybeare and Howson.

It is the most intirely cordial, and the most free from hints of disapprobation and censure, of all Paul's letters to the churches. This church had been founded by him on his second missionary journey (Acts xvi. 12—40); and revisited, no doubt twice, on his third journey, in going to and returning from Achaia (xx. 1—6). The Philippians had, from their first conversion, sent him occasional supplies, which he would not accept from the Corinthians (see 2 Cor. xi. 8, 9); and they had also, like the other Macedonian and Achaian churches, contributed handsomely to that collection for the relief of the "poor saints in Judea," which the apostle, on his third journey, carried to Jerusalem. In this letter he praises their faith, constancy, personal attachment and liberality. The only words of reproof occurring in it, are mildly directed to the reconciliation of two female converts, named Euodia and Syntyche. The allusions which he makes to the Judaizing party are as cautions against impending danger, not (as in his letters to some other churches) remonstrances against perversions from the faith of Christ, actually prevailing among those whom he addresses. He writes under a solemn sense of the near approach of "the day of the Lord;" but without repeating any such distinct, yet erroneous, idea of the mode of its manifestation as found utterance in his letters to the Thessalonians ten years before. At that time he wrote: "We that remain alive shall be caught up in the clouds, to meet the Lord in the air." Now, he knows not whether he shall live or die, but "to live is Christ, and to die is gain;" and, whatever be his personal fate, he believes the limit of the Saviour's prophecy respecting the end of the age must be approaching, and devoutly says: "The Lord is at hand."

Abstract of the Epistle to the Philippians.

Ch. i. 1. The salutation is jointly from Paul and Timothy, the latter having been united with the apostle in his first preaching at Philippi. 3. Paul thanks God for their Christian faith and virtue, and prays for its completion. 12. He tells them how his own imprisonment is tending to the furtherance of the Gospel; 19. speaks doubtfully of the probable issue, but trusts that Christ may be magnified whether by his life or by his death; 22. knows not what to wish for himself, but for their sakes trusts he shall still live for the furtherance of their faith. 27. He exhorts them to continued unity, to the brave endurance of persecution, and (ii. 3) to lowly-minded mutual service, after the example of Jesus Christ, who, though invested with divine powers, did not put them forth with ostentation and arrogance, but took upon him the form of a servant, and submitted to the death of the cross; in requital of which, (9) God hath highly exalted him and given him a name above every name, that Christ should be acknowledged as Lord, to the glory of God the Father. 17. Paul again reverts to his own state and doubtful prospects; declaring that, though he should be "offered upon the sacrifice and service of their faith,"* he would rejoice both in himself and with them. 19. He will send Timothy to Philippi as soon as he sees what the issue is to be as regards himself, and trusts in the Lord to come himself also shortly. 25. He now sends back Epaphroditus, their messenger, who had ministered to his wants, who has been ill at Rome, nigh unto death, for the work of Christ, hazarding even his life in his zeal to supply what they had left to him to do in ministering to the apostle.

Ch. iii. 1. He warns them against the Judaizing party, as he has before done personally, if not also by a letter now lost. That party he calls "the dogs," or unclean people (who neglect spiritual justification while vainly attempting an unattainable ceremonial holiness); he calls them evil workmen† (constructing, as they did, a false Gospel); he calls them the *con*cision, because the true *circum*cision are those who serve God spiritually, and whose only boast is in Jesus Christ, trusting no more to fleshly observances. 4. Yet he says that he himself, if any man, might have had confidence in the flesh, by reason of his pure Hebrew descent and zealous devotedness to the Law. 7. But he had given all up for the excellent knowledge of Christ; had ceased to seek his own justification by the

* Let the careful reader notice how the apostle uses the same sacrificial metaphor in reference to his own possible martyrdom, which he applies more frequently to the actual death of Christ. See also 2 Tim. iv. 6.

† *κακοὺς ἐργάτας*; so, in 2 Cor. xi. 13, they are called *ἐργάται δόλιοι*, *deceitful workers*, and false apostles.

Mosaic Law, and had gratefully accepted that of Christian faith; and now he strives only to win Christ and attain unto the resurrection of the dead. 12. Thus animated, he presses forward, and invites his friends to do so too, in the glorious emulation of the Christian race, to the mark yet distant and high above them, as citizens of heaven.

Ch. iv. 2. Personal messages ensue, intreating Euodia and Syntyche to be reconciled in the name of their common Christianity, and begging some one whom the apostle calls his "true yoke-fellow," to promote their reconciliation, as women who had before laboured earnestly with him in the Gospel. Clement, afterwards Bishop of Rome, is also mentioned by name as now labouring at Philippi. 4. Exhortations to cheerful faith and virtuous earnestness follow. 10. Paul thanks them very delicately for their gift, received through Epaphroditus, as one added to many instances of their generosity; and (22) sending special salutations from the Christians of Cæsar's household, ends this most cordial epistle with his benediction.

THE PASTORAL EPISTLES.

(A.D. 64, 65?)

THE only remaining Epistles that are Paul's by the universal consent of antiquity, are those addressed to Timothy and Titus, and known as the *Pastoral* Epistles; their purpose being to instruct these two "evangelists" in their duties, and, still more perhaps, to arm them with authority as the apostle's deputies in the organization and superintendence of certain churches. Titus's sphere of action was the island of Crete; Timothy's, apparently, Ephesus, or more probably the churches of the province of Asia generally, and perhaps those of Phrygia also.

A very curious literary question arises as to the period of St. Paul's life to which these Epistles should be referred. Some ascribe the first letter to Timothy and that to Titus to the time of the apostle's third journey, when (Acts xx.) he went from Ephesus into Macedonia and Achaia; others place them after his first imprisonment at Rome. The second to Timothy is, in either case, referred to the time of Paul's second imprisonment. The principal data are as follows:

The first Epistle to Timothy and that to Titus are, unmistakably, of nearly the same period, the thought and verbal expressions of the two being in many places almost identical, while the topics are considerably varied in other parts. Now the Epistle to Titus speaks of having left that evangelist "in Crete, to set in order the things that are wanting, and appoint elders in every city." The first to Timothy says: "I besought thee to abide still at Ephesus, when I went into Macedonia, that thou mightest charge some not to teach other doctrines;" and Paul, when writing, "trusts to come to him shortly." He also tells Titus that he means to winter in Nicopolis (presumed to be the Nicopolis in Illyricum, built by Augustus in commemoration of the battle of Actium). In the second letter to Timothy, he says, "Erastus stayed at Corinth, and I left Trophimus at Miletus sick;" which seems to imply that, when again prisoner in Rome, he had recently travelled through Miletus and Corinth.

Now if we attempt to find a place in the apostle's third missionary journey for these implied movements (of course reserving for a later time those alluded to in the second letter to Timothy), we might very easily suppose that Paul had been to Crete during the two years and more that he resided chiefly at Ephesus, that he left Titus there, and wrote to him soon afterwards. But the recorded facts of that journey are quite irreconcilable with those implied in both epistles. Instead of Timothy staying at Ephesus when Paul went into Macedonia, we find he was sent before him with Erastus (Acts xix. 22); he is with the apostle at Macedonia, and is joined with him in the salutation of the second letter to the Corinthians; and as for Titus, by whom that letter is sent to Corinth, as the first had probably been from Ephesus, and who rejoined Paul in Macedonia (2 Cor. vii. 5—7), he, it is evident, cannot have been in Crete while thus busy in Achaia and Macedonia.

The alternative view assigns these two letters to a later period of Paul's life, namely, that which ensued on his liberation from his first imprisonment.

We have found, from his letters written during that imprisonment, that he proposed visiting Colosse (see Philem. 22) and Philippi (Phil. i. 26, ii. 24) as soon as he should be set free; and we naturally take for granted, in the absence of all actual information respecting this part of his life, that, on his liberation, he carried those lately expressed resolutions into effect. Dr. Paley, who follows Bishop Pearson in assigning the Pastoral letters to this later period, expounds the two views and their respective arguments with his accustomed clearness, and thus sums up his result,—a result now generally accepted by theologians:

"Upon the whole, if we may be allowed to suppose that St. Paul, after his liberation at Rome, sailed into Asia, taking Crete in his way; that from Asia and from Ephesus, the capital of that country [province], he proceeded into Macedonia, and crossing the peninsula in his progress, came into the neighbourhood of Nicopolis; we have a route which falls in with everything. It executes the intention expressed by the apostle of visiting Colosse and Philippi as soon as he should be set at liberty at Rome. It allows him to leave 'Titus in Crete,' and 'Timothy at Ephesus as he went into Macedonia;' and to write to both not long after from the peninsula of Greece and probably the neighbourhood of Nicopolis; thus bringing together the dates of these two letters, and thereby accounting for that affinity between them both in subject and language, which our remarks have pointed out. I confess that the journey which we have thus traced out for St. Paul, is, in a great measure, hypothetic: but it should be observed, that it is a species of consistency, which seldom belongs to falsehood, to admit of an hypothesis, which includes a great number of independent circumstances without contradiction." (Horæ Paulinæ: Titus; end.)

In this "hypothesis," Paley does not leave room for the journey into Spain, which is indeed the most purely imaginary of all the incidents ascribed to Paul's life, not being required in order to account for any known facts or epistolary allusions. Those who insist upon it, suppose the apostle to have visited Asia Minor and Macedonia, according to promise, on his release in the spring of 63; then (A.D. 64—66) to have visited Spain; and on his return thence, to have again visited Asia Minor and Macedonia (the two hypotheses henceforth essentially coinciding); to have gone to Crete with Titus; to have written 1 *Timothy* and *Titus;* to have wintered perhaps at Nicopolis; and, either being apprehended there or going thence to Rome of his own accord, to have been again imprisoned; to have written 2 *Timothy* at Rome in the near prospect of death; and to have been beheaded there shortly afterwards. This insertion of the Spanish journey postpones the time of his death to the middle of 68, within a few days of the end of Nero's reign. Those who reject this journey date the catastrophe three or four years earlier, and suppose the apostle to have suffered death in the persecution of the Christians which Nero excited after the fire at Rome. That fire took place in July, 64.

Critical students fancy they trace some little change of style in these Epistles, marking their later date; and that the topics treated betoken a more advanced state of church organization (and of outward heresies also) than is seen in Paul's other letters. But it should be remembered that there are no earlier *Pastoral* Epistles with which to compare them. The heresies to be rebuked seem identical with those rebuked by Paul in other letters. They are still Jewish graftings upon the simplicity of Christian faith. Comparing the letters to Timothy with that to Titus, the careful reader finds a difference of tone appropriate to the fact, more than once alluded to, that Timothy was a *young* man, considering the solemn duties assigned to him, while we infer that Titus was older. To Timothy the apostle writes much more fully than to Titus. Of the latter we know nothing except from Paul's letters. He was one of the deputation from the church of Antioch (see Gal. ii. 1) to the "Council of Jerusalem," on the question of the obligation of the Mosaic Law upon Gentile Christians, and was Paul's companion and messenger on many subsequent occasions. He was a Gentile convert, Paul's "own son after the common faith" (i. 4). Of Timothy we learn more from the book of Acts, ch. xvi.

The contents of the three Pastoral Epistles are as follows:

Abstract of the Epistle to Titus.

Ch. i. 1. Salutation. 5. Paul had left Titus in Crete for the express purpose of setting right what still remained to be done, and appointing presbyters* (elders) or bishops* (overseers) in every city. 6. The moral and religious qualifications of an elder are described. 10. False and selfish teachers, especially the Judaizers, must be opposed. 12. Paul quotes the low character given of the Cretans by one of their own poets (or prophets). They must be duly reproved, and no heed be given to Jewish fables and human precepts.

Ch. ii. 1. The things that comport with wholesome doctrine,

* *Elders*, πρεσβυτέροι in ver. 5, are synonymous with ἐπίσκοποι, translated *bishops* in ver. 7.

are pure morals in each relation of life. The duties of aged men, of aged women, of young women, of young men, of bondsmen. 12. Zeal for good works is the true characteristic of the peculiar people of Christ.

Ch. iii. 1. Good Christians will be good citizens; having been saved from their heathen state by the love of God, washed in the laver of regeneration, renewed by His Holy Spirit, justified by His grace, and made heirs of eternal life. 8. It is a reliable saying, that those who believe in God should carefully practise good works. 9. Foolish questions and genealogies and contentions and strivings about the Jewish Law are unprofitable and vain. 10. Men who make divisions should be rejected. 12. Paul will send Artemas or Tychicus to him; and then let Titus come to Nicopolis to join him for the winter. Zenas the lawyer (of whom we know nothing) and Apollos (well known) are commended to Titus on their journey through Crete. Doubtless they bear this letter.

Abstract of the First Epistle to Timothy.

Ch. i. 1. In the salutation, St. Paul affectionately calls Timothy his "own son in the faith." 3. He reminds him of the purpose for which he had wished him to remain in Ephesus, "to charge *certain persons* not to teach differently" from what the apostle had done. 5. "The end of the commandment is love, out of a pure heart and a good conscience and faith unfeigned." 6. Ignorant sticklers for the Jewish Law do not know its true use and meaning, nor the superiority of "the glorious Gospel of the blessed God." 12. He thanks Christ for his call to the apostleship, from having been a persecutor. 18. Charges Timothy to fulfil the hopes* entertained of him by those who had designated him to the service of the Gospel (not like Hymenæus and Alexander, whom Paul had expelled from the church).

Ch. ii. 1. The apostle gives directions respecting public worship:—that prayer be made for all men, as there is one

* "Prophecies." See also iv. 14, which explains the allusion.

God over all, and one Mediator between God and men; (8) that men, and not women, should offer the public prayers. The virtues and duties which are appropriate to the latter shall be enough for their salvation.

Ch. iii. 1. The qualifications necessary for a bishop or presbyter, and (8) for a deacon, are described. 14. Paul hopes to come soon; but, in his absence, Timothy will know how to act in the church, which is "the house of God." "The pillar and ground of the truth, and confessedly a great mystery, is that of godliness (religion). He who* was manifested in the flesh, was justified in the spirit, seen by angels, preached among the Gentiles, believed on in the world, received up into glory."

Ch. iv. 1. False teachers† are making their appearance, as has been foretold; but their foolish fables must be rejected. 11. Thus let Timothy teach, and set a good example, and use his gifts diligently; and none can despise his youth.‡

Ch. v. 1. How to administer rebuke. 3. Directions for the support of destitute elderly widows. 17. How to treat the presbyters; how to decide complaints, &c.

Ch. vi. 1. Duties of bondsmen. 3. The worldliness of the false teachers. 11. Exhortations to Timothy to keep his trust faithfully, (17) to incite the rich to generosity, and (20) to avoid the profane babblings and antitheses which some people falsely called *knowledge*.

* Another of the few passages in the New Testament in which different readings affect, or are thought to affect, any of the great truths of the Gospel. With that view, I quote the passage in full. The above is Griesbach's reading, and also his punctuation, connecting part of verse 15 with 16.

† Doctrines about demons, prohibition of marriage, and abstinence from certain meats, are here particularised as the old-wives' fables to be shunned: fables and endless genealogies are repudiated in i. 4. All these speculations were Jewish, except the ascetic element in reference to marriage, which seems more like the produce of Alexandrian Platonism. The "genealogies" were probably those of the supposed angels and celestial host.

‡ *Youth* is a comparative term, in reference to one's office and duties. If Timothy was eighteen or twenty when we first meet with him in Acts xvi. (A.D. 52), he was now probably thirty or thirty-two (dating this Epistle A.D. 64).

Abstract of the Second Epistle to Timothy.

Ch. i. 1. The salutation is addressed "To Timothy my dearly beloved son." 3. Paul reminds him of his pious ancestry on his mother's side, and exhorts him to stir up the gift of God which was in him through the laying on of the apostle's hands, and to be ready to share affliction in the Christian hope of immortality. 15. The apostle has been deserted by all his Asiatic companions; among them, Phygellus and Hermogenes (persons quite unknown). But Onesiphorus, when he was in Rome, sought him out diligently, and was not ashamed of his chain.

Ch. ii. 1. Timothy must commit his instructions to other faithful men able to teach others again, and (3) be ready to take his share in suffering as a good soldier of Jesus Christ, preaching the resurrection of Jesus as the crowning fact of the Gospel. 14. He must deprecate and avoid the absurd wordy contentions of the Judaizers. 18. Hymenæus and Philetus are specified as teaching that the resurrection is already past.* 21. Let Timothy carefully preserve his own purity and gentleness.

Ch. iii. 1. The dangers of the "last days." 10. Persecution must be expected; but let him be faithful to his early religious education and his mature Christian convictions.

Ch. iv. 1. The apostle's solemn charge to the young evangelist, in certain prospect of his own death. He is "ready to be offered," and there is "laid up for him a crown of righteousness." 9. He begs Timothy to come to him speedily, as he is almost alone; for Demas has forsaken him for love of the world (after being mentioned as with him in his letters to Philemon and the Colossians). Crescens is gone to Galatia,

* Probably they held some mystical doctrine or other to the effect that the soul had risen from its previous death. Was this a wilful, or an innocent, hardening of Paul's own beautiful figurative language respecting the disciple's death to sin and resurrection to the life of righteousness? Or were these mystics weary of looking for an outward end of the world, and unable to imagine any other transition to the life immortal? This Hymenæus had been expelled from the church at Ephesus (1 Tim. i. 20).

and Titus to Dalmatia (perhaps by the apostle's desire). Had Titus wintered with him in Nicopolis, as once intended? We know not. Only Luke now remained with the captive apostle. He bids Timothy bring Mark with him. "Tychicus I send to Ephesus" (the bearer probably of this letter). 13. The commission to bring the cloak (or perhaps *case)* and books and parchments,—how genuine a touch of nature, marking the epistle as genuine! 14. Alexander the coppersmith (possibly the Jew Alexander of Ephesus) has done him much evil (or perhaps, brought many evil charges against him at his trial). 16. On the first hearing of his cause no one stood by him, but his heavenly Master alone, who gave him confidence to proclaim the Gospel in the hearing of all kinds of Gentiles. He was delivered from "the lion's mouth;" and the Lord will still deliver him from every evil, and preserve him unto his heavenly kingdom. 19. Salutations to Prisca and Aquila and the household of Onesiphorus (himself not yet perhaps returned home, though he has left Rome; or dead, as some argue). Erastus remained at Corinth (he was chamberlain or steward there, as stated in Rom. xvi. 23), and Trophimus was left sick at Miletus;—two memoranda which seem to imply that Paul had been in both those places recently, as he had also at Troas. 21. Again he urges Timothy to come before winter; and with salutations (including that of Linus, reputed the first bishop of Rome) concludes his last extant, if not his last written, epistle thus: "The Lord Jesus Christ be with thy spirit. Grace be with you all. Amen."

EPISTLE TO THE HEBREWS.

(A.D. 62 or 63?)

In speaking of the *Canon* of the New Testament, I have mentioned the different opinions prevalent in ancient times as to the authorship of the Epistle to the Hebrews. (See pp. 144—151.) Of those who did not consider it to be Paul's, in the strictest sense, some ascribed it to Luke and some to Clement of Rome, accounting for its similarity of thought to the acknowledged writings of Paul, by the close companionship of the supposed writer. Others, in ancient times, ascribed it to Barnabas; who, being himself a Levite, it has been thought, would be very likely to address himself to the argumentative removal of the Hebrew difficulties in the way of the reception of Christianity. Luther, more recently, ventured to ascribe this Epistle to Apollos the Alexandrian. It is placed, in the Common Bible, after St. Paul's undoubted Epistles, as a tacit intimation of the doubt attaching to its authorship.

We cannot wisely presume to add any more distinct opinion to that state of doubt in which the ancient testimonies have left the matter. So far, however, as the contents of the Epistle itself are concerned, it appears to be perfectly consistent with all that St. Paul had written in other directions. To mixed churches of Jews and Gentiles, and to those which consisted chiefly, if not exclusively, of the latter, he has, as we have seen, presented in various points of view the relation of the Law to the Gospel, and bravely vindicated the freedom of the Gentile Christian from all obligation to submit to the ceremonial of the Law. The argument of the Epistle to the Hebrews seems to present the same great question in its alternative point of view, namely, as affecting Jewish Christians. The writer represents Christianity as the consummation of the Divine purposes which had been gradually unfolded through all past ages. He looks upon the Jewish ceremonial worship (still going on) as about to cease at a near approaching day; and labours to reconcile the Jewish mind to the loss of all those venerated rites, by representing them as mere shadows and symbols of the more spiritual dispensation which has now arisen. Whether regarded as designed merely to satisfy the remaining scruples of the Jewish Christians, or also to influence the unbelieving Jews, nothing can be more appropriate, nor more essentially true, than the parallel thus drawn between the outward priesthood and ritual of the Law of Moses and (so to speak) the spiritual priesthood and service of the Gospel. This reconciling parallel was as true to the perception of the Hebrew Christian, as the blessed contrast between the two dispensations was to that of the Gentile.

The quotations from the Old Testament occurring in this Epistle, are made in so very free, and indeed so loose a manner, that some persons have been reluctant to ascribe them to Paul. Yet there are very similar, though not so numerous, instances of the same kind in his acknowledged Epistles; and indeed, after what we have said (pp. 178—240) on the quotations occurring even in the Gospels, there ought to be no surprise felt in finding the extreme of freedom exercised in epistolary quotation, especially to *Hebrews*.

Critics have endeavoured to conjecture what particular church of Hebrew Christians it was to whom the Epistle was immediately sent. For, though it has not the customary address of ancient letters prefixed, it plainly *is* a letter to a particular society or neighbourhood, and not a mere circular or general address to Hebrews or Hebrew Christians at large. This is plain from such personal allusions as occur in ch. vi. 10, where the writer speaks of their "work and labour of love in ministering to the saints;" and in xiii. 19, where he hopes "to be soon restored to them." In attempting to define the original and immediate purpose of the Epistle, some assume that it was addressed to the Jewish Christians at Jerusalem, as the chief of the Jewish churches; while others (especially those who ascribe the authorship to Apollos) suppose it to have been addressed to the Alexandrian church.

The chief argument for the latter idea is, that the recognition of their liberality to the saints is thought more appropriate to the Alexandrian Christians, who (like the other Jews there) were rich, than to the Jerusalem Christians, who were poor. But what if this "ministration to the saints" was, in part, the distribution of the collections from Macedonia, Achaia and elsewhere, dispensed by the Jerusalem church to the poor Christians of Judea? Another argument for the Alexandrian destination of the Epistle is, that most of the quotations from the Old Testament follow the Septuagint version. But they do not quite invariably follow it; and if, as is now generally allowed, this Epistle was originally written in Greek (and not, as once fancied, in Hebrew), it is natural to conclude that the Greek writer, whether Paul or Barnabas, would involuntarily quòte the Greek of the Septuagint, as suggesting itself most readily to memory. To imagine that, at each quotation, he would recall the Hebrew words and then translate them into Greek of his own, seems very unnatural. In Paul's undoubted letters, the quotations seem to be always from the Septuagint, subject only to the inaccuracies of *memoriter* reference.

There are a few other personal and local references in the Epistle to the Hebrews, which must be mentioned as limiting, though not deciding, the question of authorship.

That it was written before the destruction of Jerusalem, is plain from the way in which the sacrifices and other services of the temple are mentioned as *still going on*. This is strangely disguised, indeed, in the Common Version, where several verbs of *present* time are translated as *past:* thus, "The priests went always into the first tabernacle" (ix. 6), is in the Greek "*go* always;" "he offered" (ix. 7) is properly "he *offers;*" and "they offered" (x. 1), "they *offer.*" So xiii. 11, where the present time is correctly preserved in the translation: "The bodies (of the sacrifices) are burnt without the camp."

The author of this letter writes in evident expectation of the speedy end of the Jewish age: "Ye see the day approaching." "Yet a little while, and he that shall come will come, and will not tarry" (x. 25, 37). These expressions bespeak a state of mind quite corresponding to that expressed by Paul in several of his acknowledged letters. Those who ascribe this to Barnabas or Luke, may indeed suppose that the Jewish war had already begun, and that the signs of the near fulfilment of Christ's prophecy were already visible in the state of Judea and Jerusalem. But Paul did not live to see so much.

The letter gives salutations from those "of Italy," whence we conclude it was written in Italy; and it says: "Our brother Timothy is set at liberty; with whom, if he come shortly, I will see you" (xiii. 23, 24). Can these intimations be reconciled with the supposition of Paul's authorship, or do they point elsewhere?

The imprisonment of Timothy here alluded to is not mentioned anywhere else explicitly; but, in both the apostle's letters to him, there are very strong allusions to his exposure to persecution for the sake of the Gospel. Those who assign the Epistle to the Hebrews to some other than Paul, imagine Timothy to have come to him during his final imprisonment (as urgently requested in the second letter), and to have been involved thereby (whether before or soon after Paul's martyrdom) in the persecution then raging against the Christians in Rome. They suppose him to have been, however, set at liberty soon after, and that Luke or Barnabas, writing to the Hebrew Christians, alludes to that circumstance. But, in the former of the letters to Timothy, written after the apostle's first imprisonment, there is an allusion (vi. 12) which is most naturally understood as implying that Timothy had already been brought before rulers and magistrates for the name of Christ, and that on such an occasion he had "confessed a good confession before many witnesses." Why may not this have taken place during Paul's first imprisonment, when Timothy was constantly with him, and his name was associated with Paul's in the letters written from Rome? What more likely than that Timothy also should have been placed under arrest? And why may not this letter to the Hebrews have been also written from Rome during that same imprisonment of Paul's, just after the temporary arrest, examination and liberation of Timothy? In his other letters of that date, to the Colossians, Philemon and the Philippians, Paul mentions his purpose, in case of the favourable issue of his trial, to visit those to whom he writes. The writer to the Hebrews, in like manner, says he means to come and see them (xiii. 19, 23). On the supposition, then, that Paul was the writer, he purposed going, not only into Macedonia and Asia, but also into Palestine; and there is no difficulty in the way of supposing that, on his release, he visited Jerusalem, as well as the other places usually conjectured in explanation of the facts implied in the Pastoral Epistles.*

From early times it has been questioned whether the literary *style* of the Epistle to the Hebrews can be fairly regarded as St. Paul's. There is, beyond doubt, a greater elegance and finish about it than usually characterizes his writings; while, on the other hand, there are a num-

* What seems a personal mark of time and place in ch. x. 34, is a false reading. "Ye had compassion of me in my bonds," should be, "Ye had compassion on the prisoners;"—*δεσμίοις*, not *δεσμοῖς μου*. The verse, thus read, is quite appropriate to the history of the Jerusalem church (as given in the book of Acts) in the "former days when they were first enlightened."

ber of expressions in it which might seem to identify its author with that of Paul's acknowledged writings, and which are, indeed, indirectly referred to him by those who ascribe the letter to the pen of his companion Luke. One passage, in particular, is not unnaturally compared by them to St. Luke's introductions to his Gospel and the Acts. It is ch. ii. 3, 4, where the writer says of the Gospel salvation, that it "began at the first to be spoken by the Lord, and was confirmed unto us by them that heard him; God also bearing witness, both with signs and wonders, and with divers miracles, and gifts of the Holy Spirit." Part of this is very like the conclusion of Mark's Gospel.

On the whole, we can add little to the judgment pronounced by Origen on this subject in the third century, who in his Homilies on the Epistle, preserved by Eusebius, says:

"That the style of the Epistle to the Hebrews has not the apostle's rudeness of speech, who has confessed himself rude in speech, that is in language (2 Cor. xi. 6). But this Epistle, as to the texture of style, is elegant Greek; as every one will allow who is able to judge of the differences of styles." * * * "The sentiments of the Epistle are admirable, and not inferior to the acknowledged writings of the apostle. This will be assented to by every one who reads the writings of the apostle with attention." * * * "If I was to speak my opinion, I should say the sentiments are the apostle's, but the language and composition are those of some one who committed to writing the apostle's sense, and, as it were, reduced into commentaries the things spoken by his master. If, therefore, any church receives this Epistle as Paul's, it is to be commended even on that account; for it is not without reason that the ancients have handed it down as Paul's; but who wrote this Epistle, God only knows certainly. But the account come down to us is various; some saying that Clement, who was bishop of Rome, wrote this Epistle; others, that it was Luke, who wrote the Gospel and the Acts." (Lardner, Vol. II. 467.)

Abstract of the Epistle to the Hebrews.

Ch. i. 1. The previous revelations of the Divine will through the Jewish prophets are now in the last days consummated through a Son of God,—the appointed heir of all (of Jews and Gentiles alike),—by whom, as representative of the Divine character, power and will, the progressive ages have been arranged;—who has now cleansed our sins,* and been placed on the right hand of Divine power, being made greater than the angels,† and inheriting a higher name than any of them. 5. Quotations are adduced from the Old Testament; few, if any, of them argumentatively convincing, yet to Jewish taste

* The Hebrews at once and without difficulty understood this *cleansing of sin* (according to its meaning in the Law of Moses) as the removal of all ritual or ceremonial uncleanness which would have disqualified for appearing in the temple. Gentiles (ritually unclean always) and Jews (frequently becoming so, and, whenever unclean, requiring the adoption of the purifying ceremonial) are all in a clean state, ceremonially considered, henceforth, through the abolition of the Jewish Law in Christ.

† What angels? The prophets just mentioned, some say, being the *messengers* of the former dispensations. For the word ἀγγἰλος is ambiguous, denoting messengers, whether human or superhuman, or even the unintelligent but personified powers of Nature; as in the Psalm—"He maketh his angels the winds, his ministers a flaming fire" (Ps. civ. 4). The later Jews, however, ascribed the inspiration of Moses and the prophets to the intervention of angels. Stephen (Acts vii. 53) says, they had received the Law "as ordinances of angels;" and Paul writes to the Galatians (iii. 19), that "it was ordained by angels, in the hand of a Mediator, Moses." So the writer to the Hebrews presently says (ii. 2), "the word was spoken by angels," meaning that the Law of Moses was. There is, indeed, no allusion to any such intervention in any part of the Hebrew Pentateuch; but in the Greek of the Septuagint translation (Deut. xxxiii. 2) there are these words: "His angels were with him on his right hand." The comparison designed in the Epistle before us is not, indeed, between the person of Moses, or any Hebrew prophet, and Jesus Christ, but between the *angel power*, the Divine *office and gifts* of the former and of the latter; and this vague, wide Jewish meaning of the term *angel* being borne in mind, the argument is intelligible and appropriate. *The angel of the Christian dispensation is incomparably superior to all those of the preceding ages*, for he is the beloved *Son of God* himself. This is the essence of the argument.

illustrative enough; the most appropriate of them having originally reference to Solomon.

Ch. ii. 1. The argument proceeds: If the word declared by those "angels" was steadfast, we must give the more earnest heed to the salvation now declared and attested by the Holy Spirit. 5. The world to come is not subjected to those angels, but to Jesus, to whom the writer applies the beautiful language of Psalm viii. respecting the subjection of the rest of the creation to mankind. Not yet, indeed (he says), are all things put under him; but they will be. 10. In bringing many sons to glory, God hath seen fit to complete* the Captain of their salvation by sufferings. The sanctifier and the sanctified are all brethren, children of one Father; and Jesus partook of the same flesh and blood as they, that through death he might destroy him that hath the power of death, and deliver those who were spending life in bondage through the fear of death. 16. His mission was not to help angels,† but to give the helping hand to the sons of Abraham, and be their faithful High-priest. Therefore he was made like unto his brethren; and having been tried by suffering, he can succour those who are similarly tried.

Ch. iii. 1. Christ is in higher honour than Moses. Both were alike faithful; but the one as a Servant in God's household, the other as a Son over that household. 6. Let us, as that household, hold fast our confidence and hope, taking warning by those to whom it was said: "To-day, if ye will hear my voice, harden not your hearts as your fathers did in the wilderness." 15. Those fathers in the wilderness had all been rescued from Egypt by Moses; yet they did not enter the promised land, simply for want of faith (trust) in God. Ch. iv. 1. The promise still remains (in a spiritual sense) of entering into His rest; and we who believe in Christ are

* To "make perfect" is the common version: τελειῶσαι. The term is used often in this Epistle to denote the *consummation* of spiritual privileges and blessings effected by the Gospel. τέλειος is elsewhere the *full-grown* man (Coloss. i. 28; 1 Cor. xiv. 20; Ephes. iv. 13).

† Literally, to "take by the hand." The Common Version loses this beautiful idea, and inserts a meaning which is quite irrelevant to the connection.

entering into it. 8. Joshua did not finally give the Jewish people rest; for David afterwards defines the time by saying, "*To-day*, hear His voice." So there is still a sabbath-rest in reserve for the true people of God. Let us strive to enter into that rest; for God's word and will are resistless!

14. Another motive to steadfastness is found in contemplating our great High-priest, Jesus the Son of God, who has passed through the heavens (as the Jewish High-priest passes through the veil into the Holy of Holies). He has a fellow-feeling for our infirmities, having been tried like us, yet without sin. Let us come boldly, therefore, to the throne of grace. Ch. v. 1. The office of every high-priest is to offer sacrifice for others and himself. No one may take upon himself such an office, unless called to it by God. Aaron was so called; and so was Christ, but on the basis of a higher and more ancient priesthood even than that of Aaron, namely, "after the order of Melchisedec."* 7. In the days of his flesh, Christ offered up prayers and supplications, with strong crying and tears; and God heard him for his piety. He is now made complete† and become the author of eternal salvation to all who obey him.

11. The writer has much more to say about this priesthood of Christ, but fears that his readers have become somewhat duller in understanding than formerly, and need to be fed on milk rather than on the solid food of full-grown‡ men. Ch. vi. 1. He will proceed, however, to the complete manly doctrine,§ assuming, as the foundation of Christian principles already laid, repentance from dead works, faith toward God,

* Of Melchisedec, the royal priest, see Vol. I. p. 168. If any one attempts to find a strictly logical argument here, he will be disappointed. The Psalm quoted (cx.) had original reference to a victorious king ruling in Zion (probably David), who is finely compared to Melchisedec, king and priest on that very spot in Abraham's time. To that mysterious personage, of whom we know nothing but what is contained in three verses of Genesis (xiv. 18—20), Jesus Christ is here compared in a strain of highly poetical allusion. And the argumentation is essentially sound, though not in form, when we take it as shewing that the Levitical priesthood was not the only one blessed by Divine favour.

† τελειωθεὶς, ver. 9. ‡ τελείων, ver. 14. § τελειότητα.

baptism, instruction, and laying on of hands, resurrection of the dead, and eternal judgment. 4. There is little hope of the restoration of those who have tasted the heavenly gift in Christ and then apostatized from it. 9. But he is persuaded better things of those to whom he writes, especially considering their kindness to the poor saints. 13. He recurs to the promise made to Abraham, and then resumes his very ingenious parallel between Melchisedec and Christ.

Ch. vii. 1. The name *Melchisedec* means *king of righteousness*. He was also *king of Salem*, which means *king of peace*. Of his father, mother, pedigree, birth and death, there is no account; but, like the Son of God, he remains "a priest for ever." 4. How great must have been his dignity, that Abraham paid a tenth of his spoils to him! And he gave his blessing to Abraham,—Abraham himself the possessor of the promises! Surely the one who blesses is greater than the one blessed! Then the priests of the tribe of Levi, who receive tithes according to the Law, are mortal; but Melchisedec is declared to be alive ("priest for ever")! And Levi himself, in the person of his ancestor Abraham, virtually paid tithe to this Melchisedec! 11. Now, if what was done under the Levitical priesthood had been final and complete,* what further need would there have been for another priest to arise, of the order of Melchisedec, instead of the order of Aaron? 12. Then this change of priesthood implies a change of the Law. Our Lord is not of the tribe of Levi, but of Judah, which had no part in the Mosaic priesthood. And this change is yet more clear when another priest arises like Melchisedec, not appointed under the Law of carnal commandments, but with the power of an endless life,—"a priest for ever after the order of Melchisedec." 18. The previous commandment is annulled, and a better hope is brought in. 20. Then, inasmuch as this new priesthood is established by an oath ("The Lord sware and will not repent"), it must be a better covenant of which Jesus is surety. 23. The Levitical priests, again, are *successive* on the deaths of their predecessors; but this one has an individual and permanent priesthood.

* τελείωσις.

27. They again, on statedly recurring days, offer up sacrifice; he once for all offered—himself. The Law, in short, ordains priests who have infirmity; but the word of this oath, spoken since the Law (Ps. cx. 4), appoints the Son who is complete* for ever.

Ch. viii. 1. The sum of what has been said is this: We have a High-priest at the right hand of Divine power, serving in the true heavenly tabernacle. As the others offer gifts, so does he. On earth he could not have been a priest (not being of the Levitical tribe); but he has a higher ministry as Mediator of a better covenant. 7. Had the first covenant been faultless, there would have been no occasion for a second. But the Jewish Scriptures themselves find fault, and anticipate a new covenant; therefore the old must be decaying and ready to vanish away.

Ch. ix. 1. The sanctuary and service of the first covenant are next briefly described; the holy place with its furniture; and, within the dividing veil, the holy of holies with its contents.† 6. In the outer sanctuary, or Holy place, the daily sacrifices and services are offered by the ordinary priests. 7. But, once a year, the high-priest enters the inner sanctuary, or Holy of Holies, carrying the blood of the sin-offerings, which have been presented for the annual expiation of the sins (pollutions) incurred by the holy place and altar, through the involuntary and unperceived uncleannesses of the people and the priest himself.‡ 8. This occasional and difficult access is an intimation "that the way into the holiest place is not yet fully manifested, while the outer tabernacle is still standing."

* τετελειωμένον.

† The golden altar of incense is described here as standing within the holy of holies (the inner apartment); while in Exod. xxx. 6, it is in the holy place (the first department). Those who are content to stake their faith on verbal inspiration, tremble at this discrepancy,—which is, however, the most natural thing in the world to the literary student. The Common Version translates "golden censer."

‡ For this ceremonial and its meaning, see Leviticus xvi. It was the Jewish atonement once a year for all the sins of ritual uncleanness not otherwise cleansed. See also Vol. I. pp. 218—223, for a brief account of the Jewish ceremonies as enjoined by the Law.

9. The gifts and sacrifices offered in it cannot complete the purpose of the worshiper, and were merely ordained "till the time of reformation." 11. But Christ, having come as "High-priest of the good things to come," carried his own blood into the holy place of a tabernacle not made with hands, and obtained eternal redemption for us from all the obligations of the Jewish Law; purging our consciences from dead works, that we may worship the living God. 15. From comparing the death of Christ to the Jewish sin-offering, the writer now digresses to speak of it as the confirmation also of a Divine Covenant.* He is the Mediator of the New Covenant; and he is the covenant-victim also, in whose blood that covenant is ratified. 18. The first covenant had been, in like manner, solemnized by blood, as recorded in the history of Moses. 22. And almost all things, under the Law, are purified with blood. 23. The patterns of the heavenly things having been thus purified, these heavenly things themselves had need also be purified, but with better sacrifices. 24. So Christ entered, not into the sanctuary made with human hands, but into heaven itself, to appear in the presence of God in our behalf. 25. Nor does he repeat this offering yearly, like the Jewish high-priest; but "once for all, on the completion of the ages, he has put away the sins altogether by the sacrifice of himself." For, (ch. x. 1) the Law of Moses, a mere foreshadowing of the good things to come, could never complete the aim of its worshipers. If it could, the sacrifices would have ceased to be offered;—if the votaries, once cleansed from sins, had been free from their recurrence ever after. 3. But that yearly custom of atonement itself confesses that its effects are not thorough. 4. Nor is it indeed possible that the blood of bulls and goats should remove the consciousness of sin. 5. The Jewish Psalmist† himself has beautifully said, that the Al-

* Not *Testament.* Our translators have made nonsense by this translation. The same word in Greek means both *covenant* and *testament*; here it is the former, and the latter idea is quite irrelevant. (See Vol. I. p. 9.)

† This quotation is from the Greek Septuagint, and contains an idea not in the Hebrew; as the English reader may see by turning to Psalm xl. 6, where "*mine ears thou hast opened,*" truly represents the Hebrew, and "*a body thou hast prepared me,*" represents the LXX.

mighty has no pleasure in such sacrifices, but only in obedience to His will,—"taking away the former, to establish the latter." 15. The Jewish prophets also announce a future covenant of virtuous obedience (the laws of God being in men's hearts and minds). These anticipations, therefore, are now fulfilled.

19. The writer exhorts those who have thus gained *free access** to the holy place of the Divine audience, "to draw near in full assurance of faith, with hearts sprinkled from the stain of an evil conscience;"—to be faithful and steadfast in their Christian profession, and mutually to encourage each other in all good works;—the more, as they see "the day approaching." 26. Wilful sin, after receiving the knowledge of Christian truth, is not to be wiped off by sacrifice. 32. He reminds them of the former days, soon after their "enlightenment," when they suffered cheerfully for Christ's gospel. 36. Let them have patience too: "yet a little while, and he that cometh will come, and not tarry." "By faith shall the righteous live."

Ch. xi. 1. This very important term, *Faith*, is now clearly defined, as "the substance (or groundwork) of things hoped for, the evidence (or conviction) of things not seen." Things of the mind and things of the future are thus the declared objects of religion. How clear this definition of a term so much debated! 2. The men of olden time earned their repute expressly as men of faith, acting from convictions of the spiritual and the future. 3. By faith we grasp the idea of the formation of the worlds (or, the successive ages of this world†) as caused by the Divine command. 4. Historical instances of its power are quoted from the Jewish records. Yet none of

* "Having, therefore, brethren, boldness (παῤῥησίαν, literally *free speech;* the margin of Common Version says, *liberty)* to enter into the holiest (the sanctuary), by the blood of Jesus, by a new and living way," &c. Let the careful reader notice, that this is the *result* of the higher priesthood and better sacrifice of Christ:—to give us constant access to the Divine presence, whereas that of the Jewish tabernacle or temple was continually interrupted by a sense of ceremonial uncleanness. Thus the spiritual Christianity emerges in its own light and beauty from this Jewish and ceremonial argument. Its terms are sacrificial and ceremonial, but its result is anti-ceremonial and anti-sacrificial.

† κατηρτίσθαι τοὺς αἰῶνας.

these men, thus celebrated for their Faith, received the fulness of Divine promise; something better being provided for us, that they should not attain their consummation without us.

Ch. xii. 1. In the presence, as it were, of such a cloud of witnesses, the writer exhorts his friends to pursue with perseverance the race set before them, looking to Jesus especially as "the leader and consummator of their faith, who, for the joy that was set before him, endured the cross, despising the shame, and is set down at the right hand of the throne of God." 4. Their trials have been as yet comparatively light; but they must endure chastening, as sons. 14. Let them follow peace and holiness. 18. They are not come to the awful Mount Sinai; but to the heavenly Jerusalem, where angels and the spirits of the good, where God and Jesus welcome them. 25. Let them not reject him who speaketh to them.

Ch. xiii. 1. Precepts of brotherly love, of personal purity and contentedness, and regard to their religious instructors, here ensue. 8. "Jesus Christ is the same yesterday, to-day and for ever." Let them not be carried away by strange and varying doctrines about meats and such matters. Meats have nothing to do with the Christian service of God; as the Jewish worshipers might not eat of the sin-offerings (though they did of the peace-offerings). Praise to God is the true sacrifice for them to offer. 18. The writer intreats their prayers that he may be the sooner restored to them. 20. Gives them his benediction in an admirable form of words. 23. Mentions the release of Timothy; gives salutations from the Italian brethren, and bids them adieu, saying: "Grace be with you all. Amen."

THE (SO-CALLED) CATHOLIC EPISTLES.

THE name *Catholic Epistles* has been, from very ancient times, applied to the seven remaining letters in the New Testament; that is, to all the Epistles except Paul's (reckoning the Hebrews as Paul's). The seven are, those ascribed to James, Peter, John and Jude. How they came to be called Catholic, and what was meant by giving them that name, are disputed points.

The word *Catholic* means *universal;* and it is generally said that these are called Catholic Epistles, as having been addressed not in a single copy to a particular church or person, like Paul's, but as a circular, in many copies, to Christians universally. (See Grotius on James's Ep.) But it is not the fact that these seven Epistles are all addressed to Christians in general. The second and third of John are addressed to individuals (the extreme reverse of Catholicity); the first of Peter is addressed to inhabitants of only one half of Asia Minor; and that of James to "the twelve tribes scattered abroad," which seems to mean Jewish Christians alone, wherever dispersed. These seven Epistles are not then distinctively Catholic, in this sense. So it has been thought that the term may have been originally given only to the first epistles of John and Peter, and perhaps that of James (which are the most *Catholic)*, when the others were little known and not generally acknowledged as apostolical; and that those others may have been afterwards added to the same part of the New Testament Scriptures, without a keen perception of the impropriety of extending the term Catholic to them.

Another explanation has been attempted, by supposing the term to have originally meant, not universally *addressed*, but universally *received*, and to have been applied only to 1 Peter and 1 John; which were indeed the only two of the seven universally received, according to Eusebius as already quoted in this volume (see pp. 146—149). Then, under this view as under the former, the term is supposed to have been afterwards most carelessly extended to the rest of the seven, the exclusion of which it seemed at first intended indirectly to mark.

It is somewhat confirmatory of the latter view, that

these seven Epistles were, by some writers of the sixth century, called the *Canonical* Epistles (as if uncanonizing all the others), the word being apparently confounded (together with the idea) with *Catholical*. (Lardner, VI. 466.)

Any way, however, the designation is inappropriate. These seven Epistles do not form a class resembling each other and differing from the rest. There is the same kind of variety among them as among Paul's letters, in regard to their being addressed to individual persons or to communities; the first of John, the second of Peter, and that of Jude, being only three out of the seven which do not carry with them *some* limitation of the circle of readers to whom they were originally addressed.

The doubtful authorship will be specifically alluded to in each case in which doubts exist.

THE EPISTLE OF JAMES.

There were two Jameses among our Lord's apostles; James the son of Zebedee, brother of John; and James the son of Alpheus, called also in the New Testament the Lord's brother, and in ecclesiastical history James the Less (or Younger) and James the Just. The former was early martyred, as related in Acts xii. 2, before the Gospel had spread much beyond Judea, and before the period of apostolic letter-writing. The latter was the James who was at the head of Christian affairs in the church at Jerusalem at the time of the "council of apostles," and on other occasions mentioned in the Acts (xii. 17, xv. 13, xxi. 18); and also alluded to by Paul in his Epistle to the Galatians. It is to the latter apostle that the Epistle before us is ascribed. To make James the

Lord's brother a different person from James the son of Alpheus, seems a very needless multiplication of persons; and the signs of their identity have been carefully traced in a previous part of this volume (pp. 284 and 290).

James is reputed, by ecclesiastical historians, to have been the first "bishop" of the church of Jerusalem, and to have resided there till his death. He is believed to have been martyred at Jerusalem by popular violence, when, after the death of Festus, there was for a while no Roman procurator in Judea. This would be about A.D. 62, during the time of Paul's first imprisonment at Rome. And it was a favourite idea with the old Christian fathers, that the political troubles which soon after befel the Jews, resulting in the destruction of their city, were sent upon them in retribution for the martyrdom of James the Just. Such is the testimony of Eusebius, quoting Hegesippus, Clement and Josephus, the last of whom is represented, however, as saying more than is now to be found in his works. (See Lardner, Vol. VI. pp. 480—488.)

The Epistle of James is classed by Eusebius among the *Antilegomena*, or books not universally received by the Christian church. But this is by no means conclusive against its being his genuine work. The positive testimony of Eusebius to the books universally accepted is decisive, indeed, in their favour; but the negative fact that certain others were not universally received is not decisive against them, especially if any other explanation can be given of the circumstances causing the ancient doubt. We must, in each instance, also take into careful consideration the internal evidence of the book itself, as to its fitness to be considered as the work of the alleged author. In the case of the Epistle of James, there is a strong outward testimony in the fact of its admission into the early Syriac version, from which the other disputed *Catholic* Epistles were excluded. Then, as regards internal evidence, there is nothing whatever in its contents inappropriate to the supposition of his having been its author. It is, in the judgment of most practical Christians, one of the most valuable parts of the New Testament. Its contents are altogether practical and devotional; they are truly admirable, and worthy of an apostle of Christ to have written. Nor are more specific marks of authorship wanting. Addressed "to the twelve tribes which are scattered abroad," it presents in this and in other incidental expressions, appropriate to the Jewish Christians, the strongest, while quite unostentatious, marks of such authorship as we ascribe to it. In ch. ii. 2, the writer, speaking of their assembly for worship, calls it their "synagogue." He speaks of Christianity repeatedly as their *Law*, "the perfect Law of liberty," "the royal Law" (i. 25, ii. 8, 9, iv. 11). The reproof to those who speak too confidently of "going into such a city and continuing there a year, buying and selling" (iv. 13—17), is full of living force when we remember that it is addressed to "Jews of the dispersion," whose locomotive and trading habits even yet verify the description. His caution against the use of oaths (v. 12), almost repeating the words of Christ in the Gospels, alludes to oaths of a peculiarly Jewish form. And the direction to anoint the sick (v. 14), seems, like an incident recorded in Mark's Gospel (vi. 13), to imply the adoption among them of a Jewish usage which makes its appearance nowhere else in the New Testament.*

* Michaelis says on this passage: "At the time when this Epistle was written, the practice of physic was attended with great superstition; and conscientious Jews were apprehensive that, if they sent for a heathen physician, he would either invoke some idol in the administration of his medicines or exercise magic arts. The author of this Epistle therefore advises those who are sick to send for the elders of the church, that they may pray

All these things are quite suitable to a letter from the head of the Christian church at Jerusalem to the dispersed Jewish Christians elsewhere.

One reason why this most excellent Epistle was not universally admitted into the canon of Scripture, seems to have been the doubt whether the James who wrote it was an apostle; for (as I have already hinted) a third James has been imagined as the "Lord's brother," but not an apostle; and some, both in ancient and modern times, holding this idea, have regarded this Epistle as his composition. Luther and some of the other Reformers repudiated it, with most unseemly expressions of detestation against its doctrine, that faith without works cannot save a man, thinking this inconsistent with Paul's doctrine of justification by faith, which they had totally misunderstood and perverted. Possibly the same feeling may have weighed with some in yet earlier times. But the two doctrines, when understood in the obvious and rational sense of the two writers, are perfectly consistent. If the modern *antinomian* abuse of St. Paul's doctrine can be supposed to have prevailed (as some fancy) in the apostolic days, it is conceivable that James may have had in view the correction, not indeed of Paul's doctrine, but of that irrational and immoral perversion.

The Epistle before us was evidently written before the destruction of Jerusalem, and in expectation of a great, however ill-defined, event, which the writer speaks of as "the coming of the Lord" (v. 7, 8, 9).

A peculiarity has been noticed in the Epistle to the Hebrews, viewed as a letter,—namely, the absence of an address or inscription at the beginning, while it ends with salutations like any regular letter. The reverse is

over the medicines and then administer them to the sick." (Introd. to N.T., Vol. IV. 313.)

the case with the Epistle of James: it begins with a regular inscription, but ends without salutation or customary conclusion.

Of the inscription—"James, a servant of God and of the Lord Jesus Christ, to the twelve tribes which are scattered abroad, greeting"—let it be observed that, strictly considered, it includes *all* the Jews out of Palestine, whether converted to Christianity or not. The writer thus seems to imply his conviction that the whole Jewish nation is concerned in the mission of Jesus as their Christ, and perhaps his hope also that they would yet, as a nation, accept it. He addresses them, indeed, purely from the Christian point of view, but avoids (perhaps purposely avoids) drawing the line between those who believe and those who reject the Gospel. This will explain the fact, that some parts seem more like warnings and denunciations for the unfaithful and disobedient, while, however, the Epistle in general implies that those to whom he writes possess Christian convictions, and he makes no clear mark of transition between his appeals to the one class and to the other. He would have them all, as true-born Israelites, see the Law perfected in the Gospel, as he himself rejoices to see it.

Most critics suppose the Epistle of James to have been written about A.D. 60 or 61. Michaelis is disposed to place it soon after the death of Stephen, during the life-time of James the son of Zebedee, though he ascribes it to James the Less.

Abstract of the Epistle of James.

Ch. i. 1. Inscription, as just quoted. 2. He bids them rejoice in trials of their faith, and trust to being made perfect*

* τέλειος and its derivatives are frequent in this Epistle, as in St. Paul's writings, for the *completed Law* and the *complete*, or full-grown, *man* in Christ (i. 4, 25; ii. 8; iii. 2; also ii. 22).

by patience in the endurance. 5. The earnest seeker after Divine wisdom will find it in answer to prayer. 9. The rich and poor should mutually rejoice in their equality of Christian privileges and hopes. 13. When tried and tempted, let no man say, "I am tempted by God." His own evil desires are the tempter, whereas all good gifts are from God, the Father of lights. 19. The children of God must be swift to hear, slow to speak, slow to wrath, pure from all defilement; doers of the word, and not merely hearers; able to command the tongue. Pure religion, in the sight of the Heavenly Father, consists of active benevolence and personal purity.

Ch. ii. 1. Respect of persons is deprecated, especially in their assemblies for worship. The poor are often richest in faith; the rich are often oppressive and exacting. But the Royal Law would be fulfilled, if each loved his neighbour as himself. He who wilfully offends against any one precept of duty, while keeping others, transgresses the Law as a whole. We shall be judged by a Law of liberty, under which mercy will exult over strict judgment. 14. The absurdity and emptiness of pretending to Christian *faith*, without exhibiting Christian *conduct*. The demons have "faith without works," and tremble therefore. Abraham's faith worked with his works, and was made complete thereby. Faith without works is dead, like the body without the spirit.

Ch. iii. 1. Rivalry and display among the teachers of the church are deprecated.* The importance of governing the tongue, that little but unruly member. He who can do this is a complete (full-grown) man. 13. Heavenly wisdom and earthly contrasted.

Ch. iv. 1. Even wars and fightings† have their source in

* "Whether the Jewish converts, to whom St. James wrote his Epistle, had places of worship apart from the synagogue, and in these places the abuses prevailed which St. James censures,—or whether they still met in the synagogue, and certain Christians abused the privilege of speaking, so as to create disorder,—is a question which has not yet been examined." (Michaelis, Vol. IV. p. 300.)

† Grotius (*in loco*) thought the writer referred particularly to dissensions among the Jews at Philadelphia, in the Perea, which had occurred in the reign of Claudius, as related by Josephus, Ant. xx. 1. But the allusion

the desire of sensual pleasures. 11. Evil-speaking is a defiance of the Divine Law. 13. The uncertainty of the future should rebuke the presumptuousness of too confident worldly schemes. He who knows what is right and does it not, sins.

Ch. v. 1. Riches will rust and be moth-eaten. Yet men are hoarding even in the last days! and even refusing the wages of their labourers! They are like those who condemned and killed the Just One! He does not resist them! 7. Ye then, brethren (the writer turns to those who would live worthily), "be patient unto the coming of the Lord," as the husbandman for the season which shall mature his labours. Take example by good men of old who patiently endured,—Job especially,—and endure ye likewise to the end. 12. Swear not; but let your yea be yea, and your nay be nay. 13. Let the afflicted pray and the happy sing praise to God. 14. Let the elders of the church pray with the sick and anoint him in the name of the Lord. 16. Let there be mutual confession of faults and prayer for one another: the effect of the prayer of a righteous man is very powerful, as seen in the instance of Elijah. 19. Any one who restores a sinner from his erring way will save that soul from death and cover his multitude of sins.

THE EPISTLES OF PETER.

THE FIRST of these Epistles is among the universally acknowledged books of the New Testament; the SECOND is among the disputed ones. Eusebius says: "One Epistle of Peter, called the first, is universally received. This the presbyters of ancient times have quoted in their writings as undoubtedly genuine. But that called his second, we have been informed, has not been [universally] received as a part of the New Testament. Nevertheless, appearing to many to be useful, it has been carefully studied with the other Scriptures." Jerome

may be general, and cannot be relied upon as a critical mark of time or place bespeaking the date of the letter.

says: "Peter wrote two Epistles called Catholic; the second of which is denied by many to be his, because of the difference of the style from the former." (See Lardner, VI. 562.)

The mind and character of Peter are impressed upon every reader of the Gospels and Acts; and we look with the greatest interest into the letters ascribed to his pen. Much obscurity attaches to the latter part of his history. He was the leading spirit in the affairs of the infant church at Jerusalem, and the honoured agent in first offering the Gospel to the Gentiles. He was at Jerusalem at the council of the apostles (Acts xv.); and was at Antioch shortly after, as we learn from Paul's letter to the Galatians (ii. 11—16). This brings us to about the year 50 A.D.; but from this time there is no distinct record of his actions. The little that is known of him, in connection with the history of Mark, has been already mentioned (pp. 270—274). A tradition which made him bishop of Antioch may be fairly taken as intimating that he was there for some time. Eusebius, quoting Origen, says: "Peter is supposed to have preached to the Jews of the dispersion in Pontus, Galatia, Bithynia, Cappadocia and Asia. And at length coming to Rome, he was crucified with his head downwards, himself having desired it might be in that manner." (Lardner, VI. 541.) The traditions which make him to have been bishop of Rome for many years, are quite inconsistent with the intire absence of all allusions to him in the Epistles written by Paul from Rome during the very time in question. Lardner thinks he did not come to Rome till after the death of Paul, and that he only survived a few years. His martyrdom there has the concurrent testimony of Christian antiquity, as having taken place by order of Nero;—Jerome expressly says, in the fourteenth year of his reign, which would be A.D. 68.

There is thus a considerable period of Peter's life, during which we have no direct testimony to shew where he was. Paul tells us that it was mutually agreed among the apostles, when they met at Jerusalem, that he and Barnabas should go unto the heathen, and Peter, James and John to the circumcision (Gal. ii. 9). We conclude, therefore, that the preaching of Peter was thenceforth chiefly devoted to the Jews in various countries. And his first Epistle being addressed to the Jewish Christians* in Pontus, Galatia, Cappadocia, Asia and Bithynia, makes credible the tradition above cited (which may possibly have arisen, indeed, from the inscription of this letter), that he did preach in those parts. It is also to be noticed that the Epistle is sent by the hands of "Silvanus, a faithful brother unto you, as I think." There seems no reason to doubt that this is the Silas of the book of Acts, who accompanied Paul on his second journey, and whom Paul calls Silvanus in his letters to the Thessalonians and Corinthians. That journey lay through some of the countries of Asia Minor here mentioned, and then through Macedonia and Achaia. In the history of the Acts, we lose sight of Silas at the end of that journey; and it seems likely enough that he joined Peter at Jerusalem at that time. How soon afterwards he was sent by Peter as the bearer of this letter into the parts already known to him as the companion of Paul, we cannot tell; nor whether the apostle Peter had intermediately visited them.

The letter seems, by the last verse but one, to date itself from Babylon, though the meaning of that verse is far from certain. The Common Version has it thus: "The *church that is* in Babylon, elect together with *you*, saluteth you; and *so doth* Marcus my son,"—where cer-

* The "*elect strangers, scattered*" through these parts, clearly means *Christian pilgrims* (or sojourners) of the *dispersed* Jewish race.

tain important words are marked in *italics* (as above) to shew that they are not in the original. There is, in fact, nothing said about a *church;* and (the grammatical forms being feminine) perhaps the most natural, certainly the most literal, translation is this: "She who is at Babylon, your fellow-chosen, saluteth you; and also Marcus my son." By this, some suppose Peter to mean his own wife, if not also a son of his own called Marcus. But the evangelist Mark is most naturally understood to be meant, whatever may be thought of the other relationship. Peter certainly was, or had been, a married man, as his wife's mother was cured of a fever by our Lord (Matt. viii. 14; Mark i. 30; Luke iv. 38); and Paul seems to imply, in his first letter to the Corinthians (ix. 5), that Peter's wife was at that time living. Tradition makes her to have suffered martyrdom at Rome before him. But so much doubt has been always felt as to Peter's residence in Babylon, that it was early imagined that he may have meant Rome "in a mystical sense" (as in the book of Revelation); and in some unimportant manuscripts, we read *Rome*, and also *Joppa*, instead of *Babylon*. Some have supposed the letter was written from a small place in Egypt called Babylon; and *Chalybon*, in Asia Minor, has also been conjectured. Yet there is, after all, no difficulty (beyond the mere want of positive testimony or tradition to that effect) in supposing that Peter may have visited Babylon, in Chaldea, at that time a fallen and ruined, but not uninhabited, place. There were Jews from Mesopotamia among those at Jerusalem on the great day of Pentecost (Acts ii. 9), who must have carried back with them the tidings of what they had seen and heard; and Peter may have preached through those parts and written from Babylon. It is ingeniously observed, moreover, as an evidence in favour of Babylon, rather than Rome, as the date of this Epistle, that the places to which it is addressed are enumerated in the order from east to west, as beginning with those nearest to the writer; whereas, if it had been written from Rome, the natural order of enumeration would have been the reverse, and the apostle would have begun with *Bithynia* and ended with *Pontus*. It is not, indeed, exactly true that he does begin with the nearest to Babylon (Cappadocia should have stood first, decidedly); but the order, as it stands, enumerates them in a kind of circle from north-east, round by the south, to north-west.

As to the time when the Epistle was written, all is mere conjecture. It alludes to persecutions as besetting them; says that the end of all things is at hand (iv. 7); and anticipates the "appearing of the Chief Shepherd" (v. 4); and some have suggested the time when St. Paul had been apprehended in Jerusalem and was imprisoned in Cæsarea, or already sent to Rome, as a probable date for this letter. Michaelis dates it about the year 60, and thinks the writer had seen Paul's letter to the Romans, from the resemblance of passages in it to passages in this. (Compare particularly Rom. xiii. 1—5, and 1 Pet. ii. 13, 14.) All is mere conjecture beyond the few facts (themselves not unmixed with conjecture) above stated. The Epistle is beyond doubt Peter's, written in anticipation of the yet undeveloped and unimaginable "end of the age." Its tone is devotional and practical, and quite sustains the estimate we form of his fervent and affectionate character.

Abstract of the First Epistle of Peter.

Ch. i. 1. The inscription is as already cited. 3. The apostle earnestly blesses God for the Gospel hopes, under whatever present trials. Prophets of old inquired after this salvation, and found it was still future. Even angels desire to look into it. 13. He exhorts them to worthy conduct, as children of a Heavenly Father, redeemed from vain conduct by the blood of Christ, and born again by the word of God.

Ch. ii. 1. Let them be built up with Christ, as their chief corner-stone, into a spiritual house, and be themselves its holy priesthood; kings and priests and a holy nation; the people of God,—once not His people, but now indeed His people, as a Jewish prophet had said (Hosea i. 9, 10). 11. He exhorts them, as "sojourners and pilgrims, to abstain from fleshly lusts which war against the soul,"—to submit to the requirements of civil government, and not use their liberty as a cloak of mischief, but as bondsmen of God. 18. On servants* he enjoins cheerful service, whether the master be good and gentle or froward, in imitation of the meekness of Christ.

Ch. iii. 1. Wives, he suggests, may, by their exemplary conduct in that relationship, recommend Christianity to some who do not yield to its reasonings,—their adornment being spiritual rather than external. Sara is quoted as the model to faithful women. 7. Husbands should evince towards their wives due considerateness and religious sympathy. 8. And all should live in mutual sympathy and kindness. 13. Such conduct will be, to a great extent, their protection against wrong. 14. But if they suffer for righteousness, there is the Gospel blessing upon them. Let them always be ready to defend their Christian profession against objectors; and if they suffer, it is better to do so, at God's will, for well-doing than for evil-doing,—as Christ had done before them. 18. He was put to death in the flesh, but quickened in the spirit ("by the which also he went and preached to the spirits in prison, who once were disobedient when the patience of God waited in the days of Noah while the ark was preparing, in which eight lives were saved on the water,"—a type of Christian baptism †), and he is now at the right hand of God, all

* *οἰκέται* is Peter's phrase; *δοῦλοι*, *slaves*, is Paul's in giving similar precepts. Was not the former more appropriate to the bondsmen of Jewish families, while the latter was the Gentile word and fact?

† This digression, or parenthesis, is the one difficulty of the Epistle; and some critics are disposed to regard it as an interpolation. But we must remember the Jewish taste for parallels drawn from the history or traditions

the heavenly angels and authorities being made subject unto him.

Ch. iv. 1. Christ having thus suffered for us in the flesh,* they should no longer live their fleshly life in lustful pleasures worthy only of Gentiles, who indeed think it strange that the Christians do not run into the same excesses; but they, too, must give an account to Him who will judge the quick and the dead.† "For this cause was the Gospel preached even to them that are dead, that though they might be judged according to men in the flesh, yet they might live according to God in the spirit." 7. "The end of all things is at hand;" let them be sober, watchful and devout, and above all things have fervent charity, which "will cover a multitude of sins."‡ 9. Hospitality is to be freely exercised. 10. Each man's gift to be devoted to the common good,—that of instruction in a manner worthy of the oracles of God,—that of administration, as the ability which God has given. 12. It is nothing strange that a fiery trial is coming upon them. They should rejoice, as partaking of Christ's sufferings and hoping to partake his glory. 15. Let none suffer as an evil-doer in any way; but as a Christian let no one be ashamed to suffer. 17. "For the time is come that judgment must begin at the house of God." Let them "commit the keeping of their souls to God in well-doing, as unto a faithful Creator."

Ch. v. 1. The elders are exhorted by their fellow-elder to feed the flock zealously, disinterestedly and meekly, till the Chief Shepherd shall appear. 5. The younger brethren are exhorted to due submission and humility. 8. Sobriety and

of the nation. And Peter has already (i. 11) spoken of the spirit anticipatory of Christ as having been in the Jewish prophets. Spiritually, and perhaps vaguely, we must endeavour to catch the thought here also, which in retrospect finds in the deluge a parallel for the alarming times now impending.

* The thought is identical with that of Paul in the beginning of the seventh chapter to the Romans.

† Both Christians and Heathens, perhaps; the spiritually alive and the spiritually dead. Or else, both those who are alive at his appearing and those who are dead. The next words may perhaps decide.

‡ The very same words are in James v. 20.

vigilance are needful, for their "slanderous adversary"* is looking out for his prey. They must resist him, knowing that the brotherhood are fulfilling the same sufferings elsewhere in the world. And may the God of grace establish them through sufferings! 12. Silvanus is the bearer of this letter. "She in Babylon, fellow-chosen with you, saluteth you, and so doth Marcus my son." Benediction concludes the letter.

THE SECOND EPISTLE OF PETER is of very doubtful authenticity, having been mentioned in that point of view in the 4th century by Eusebius, and wanting the attestations which are given by earlier writers to the undisputed books. Nor do its contents impress the careful reader in favour of its genuineness. It alludes (iii. 4) to the disappointment of the expectation of Christ's personal appearing, and thus seems to date itself after the destruction of Jerusalem, at any rate. It also alludes to Paul's letters (iii. 15, 16) as if collectively and generally known, in a manner much more suitable to the second century than to the time of Paul's life, or while his death was recent. It makes allusions to Old Testament events in a style which we might call an exaggerated imitation of the suspected parenthetical passage in the first Epistle. And it cites the later Jewish doctrine of fallen angels (unknown to the Old Testament), and speaks of other angels besides, in terms closely resembling some passages in the Epistle of Jude, and not calculated in either instance to make us appeal to internal evidence as settling the external doubts of authenticity. For the easier comparison of the two, we may place Jude's Epistle next after this (so-called) second of Peter,—an

* Is not this translation (which is Wakefield's) more appropriate to the sense of the passage, as it certainly is to the idiom of the original, *ὁ ἀντίδικος ὑμῶν διάβολος*, than the common version, "your adversary, the devil"? It describes the human persecutor, whether also implying diabolical suggestion or not.

arrangement which will also allow all the remaining writings of the New Testament, which are generally ascribed to John, to be considered together without interruption.

ABSTRACT OF THE SECOND EPISTLE OF PETER.

Ch. i. 1. The address is seemingly unlimited,—"to them that have obtained like precious faith with us." 3. In the name of their Christian blessings, the writer exhorts to Christian virtue; and so an entrance into the kingdom of Christ will be theirs. 12. He reminds them of things well known to them; but he would have them remember those things after his decease, which will shortly be, as Christ has shewn him. 16. He was himself an eye-witness of the majesty of Jesus when transfigured on the Mount. 19. The word of prophecy has become more sure by the Gospel events; it was as a lamp in the dark till daylight broke; for "no prophecy of the Scripture gives its own interpretation,"* when holy men speak it, not at their own suggestion, but at that of the Holy Spirit.

Ch. ii. 1. As there were false prophets formerly, so there will be now, secretly bringing in destructive divisions, and denying the Sovereign who redeemed them; impure and covetous men, whose destruction will not long be delayed. 4. As the angels that sinned were delivered over to chains and darkness,—as the old world in Noah's time was punished,—as Sodom and Gomorrha were in the days of Lot, those two righteous men being preserved,—so the Lord will again deliver the godly from their trial and reserve the ungodly for punishment; —especially those corrupt and licentious men who "despise government" and "speak evil of dignities,"—"whereas angels, though so much more powerful, do not bring any such railing accusation against those potentates before the Lord." 12. The utter corruption and wickedness of those false prophets is descanted upon in fearful terms indeed.

* Wakefield's translation. It is Rosenmüller's interpretation too. *πᾶσα προφητεία γραφῆς ἰδίας ἐπιλύσεως οὐ γίνεται.* The meaning seems plain in the Greek, but is made very obscure in the common English version. Prophecy is not self-interpretive; events are its interpreters. (See also Whately's ed. of *Paley's Evidences*, p. 218.)

Ch. iii. 1. This second Epistle, like the first, is intended to remind them of what prophets had foretold and apostles taught. 3. Scoffers will come in the last days, asking, "Where is the promised coming of Christ?" 5. They wilfully overlook the fact, that at the Divine word the heavens were first made and the earth stood out of the water, and again by the same command it was submerged in the deluge; and so they miss the solemn inference, that the same Divine power can destroy all by fire. 8. With God, one day is as a thousand years, and a thousand years as one day. He is not slack concerning His promise, though some think so; He is long-suffering rather, and gives time for all to repent. 10. "But the day of the Lord will come as a thief in the night; when the heavens shall pass away with a great noise, and the elements shall melt with fervent heat; the earth also, and the works that are therein, shall be burnt up." Let them live in this expectation, looking for "new heavens and a new earth wherein dwelleth righteousness." Let them keep free from spot and blemish, and count the long-suffering of the Lord as a means of salvation, "even as our beloved brother Paul has written."* Knowing these things, brethren, beware "that ye fall not from your steadfastness; but grow in the grace and knowledge of Jesus Christ, to whom be glory for ever."

THE EPISTLE OF JUDE.

THIS is another of the disputed books, which internal evidence does not tend to raise to apostolic rank in the Christian's estimation.

The Jude to whom it is ascribed, was, as stated in the introduction of the Epistle, the "brother of James;" whom we have identified with the apostle Thaddeus or Lebbeus,—and probably with Levi (pp. 283, 288-9),—being the son of Cleopas or Alpheus, and "the Lord's

* Most likely referring to his Epistles to the Thessalonians; in which, however, this idea of a fiery end of all things does not appear with any such distinctness as here (see 2 Thess. i. 8).

brother" (cousin, probably). Those who make James the Lord's brother a different person from James the son of Alpheus, also suppose two Judes as brothers to those two Jameses (quite unnecessarily); and some of them ascribe this Epistle to Jude the Lord's brother, not being an apostle. We know nothing of the history or character of the apostle Jude. The only personal notice of him preserved in the New Testament is, his having asked his Lord a question at the paschal table: "Lord, how is it that thou wilt manifest thyself unto us, and not unto the world?" (John xiv. 22).

This brief Epistle of Jude is, as already remarked, very like what is called the second of Peter. One would almost think they were from the same pen, whosesoever that may have been. If not, the one must have been an imitation of the other. Grotius ascribes the so-called 2 Peter to Simeon the successor of James as bishop or elder of the Jerusalem church, who lived into the reign of Trajan (A.D. 98 to 117); and he ascribes this Epistle of Jude to a later successor in that office, called Jude, who lived in the reign of Adrian (between A.D. 117 and 138). He observes, that Jude does not call himself an apostle;* and he supposes "brother of James" to have been inserted by ignorant but over-zealous transcribers, without authority; as also the words "Peter" and "apostle of Jesus Christ" in the opening of the other letter. This supposition seems to avoid the imputation of wilful forgery against any one; but then the expressions in 2 Peter i. 17, must be explained away; as Grotius himself, indeed, proposes to do. Then he supposes this so-called 2 Peter to have been originally two letters; the first of them ending with the second chapter, and being what the writer refers to in the third

* Nor indeed does James; nor John in any of his Epistles. This negative argument is not by any means conclusive by itself.

chapter as his "first epistle." He thinks both 2 *Peter* and *Jude* were written in reference to the disciples of Carpocrates, who were accused, whether justly or unjustly, of holding very immoral notions. (See Lardner, Vol. IX. 308—319; who, however, thinks they were misrepresented.) Some libertines or other, taking the guise of religion, are certainly pointed at in both the letters, in a way that betrays a horrible corruption of manners.

Abstract of the Epistle of Jude.

1. The inscription is: "Jude, the servant of Jesus Christ and brother of James, to them that are sanctified in God the Father, and preserved and called in Jesus Christ." 3. Being desirous of writing to them about the common salvation, he found no subject more urgent than to exhort them to strive earnestly for the Christian faith as at first delivered to the saints; because some deniers of it had insidiously* crept in among them. These were ungodly men, who turn the kindness of God into lasciviousness, and deny the only Sovereign† and our Lord Jesus Christ. He reminds them of what they know very well both in Jewish history and tradition: (5) the destruction of the unfaithful after they had been delivered from Egypt; (6) the angels who kept not their high estate, and are reserved in chains and darkness for judgment; (7) Sodom and Gomorrha destroyed for their filthy vices. 8. So these dreamers defile their bodies, "despise government, and speak evil of dignities."‡ "Yet Michael the archangel,§ when,

* So 2 Pet. ii. 1. † *δεσπότην* here and in 2 Pet. ii. 1.

‡ *κυριότητα ἀθετοῦσι, δόξας δὲ βλασφημοῦσιν.* In 2 Pet. the phrases are, *κυριότητος καταφρονοῦντας* and *δόξας βλασφημοῦντες*,—nearly identical and very remarkable, whether explained to mean a reckless disregard to civil authority, or, as some think, defiance of angelic powers. Many other verbal correspondences between the two writers, especially in the description of these corrupt intruders, are visible even in the English version.

§ A strange legend seems to have been founded upon the declaration in Deut. xxxiv. 6, that "no man knoweth of the sepulchre of Moses unto this contending with the devil, he disputed about the body of Moses, did not presume to bring against him a railing accusation, but said, The Lord rebuke thee !" 10. But these men speak evil of what they know not. (Their corruption is described, in terms very like those of 2 *Peter.*) 14. Enoch prophesied of them (in words quoted from an apocryphal book bearing his name). 17. The writer exhorts his friends to remember the words of Christ's apostles, who have said that scoffers would come in the last time, and (20) to build themselves up in their most holy faith, with prayer, keeping themselves in the love of God, and looking for the mercy of Christ to eternal life. 22. Let them compassionate and save those whom they can, but shrink from the very touch of pollution. A very fine doxology ends this Epistle: "Now unto Him that is able to keep you from falling," &c.

THE EPISTLES OF JOHN.

A BRIEF account of the life of the Apostle John was prefixed to the abstract of his Gospel. (See pp. 322—336.)

Of the three Epistles ascribed to him, the first and principal has been universally admitted to be genuine; and the second and third, though, according to Eusebius, not universally received before his time, are free from all reasonable doubt. Their being very short, and being also private letters addressed, the one to a Christian lady, and the other to a Christian named Gaius, will sufficiently explain how there might be many churches in the first century or two which had obtained copies of the first Epistle, but had not even heard of the others; while those who, like ourselves, possessed the three, could

day,"—to the effect that Satan wished to reveal the body of the Lawgiver in the hope of exciting the Jews to its idolatrous worship, and that Michael resisted his attempt. Josephus (Ant. iv. 8, 48) hints that Moses had some fear of a superstitious reverence arising towards him. "The Lord rebuke thee," is quoted from Zech. iii. 2.

never fail to recognize the same mind, feeling and verbal style of expression, in all of them. There is no rational doubt of their all being John's.

The times and places of their composition are merely conjectural, as are also the immediate destination of the first or *Catholic* Epistle, and the residences of the apostle's correspondents addressed in the other two.

The great question as to the time of the first Epistle is, whether it was written before the destruction of Jerusalem or after, as the apostle speaks very emphatically of its being "the last time." Grotius and Michaelis severally decide that it was written before that event; Mill, Whiston and Lardner place it after. There is in the Epistle no distinct allusion to the event as having happened; nor indeed is there anything implying distinctly that it had not. Much depends upon the view taken by each expositor, as to the "false prophets" or "antichrists" of whom the apostle speaks. Were these the false Christs predicted by our Lord as about to come before that event,—the Theudases and Judases who rashly promised temporal deliverance to the infatuated part of their nation? Or, were they the *doctrinal* antichrists, the *knowing* people of Paul's animadversion, the *Gnostics* of successive and rife growth during the next few centuries, the Carpocratians, Nicolaitans and other such?

I should scarcely presume to pronounce upon these intricate and obscure questions, even if their decision fell more strictly within the scope of my plan than it does. I shall be content to present in abstract the apostle John's own description of these men and their characteristics, as I have done in the case of those alluded to by Paul, and those described in the doubtful second Epistle of Peter and the doubtful Epistle of Jude. And, after this, we shall find both the Nicolaitans and a false prophet (either personal or emblematical) in the book of Revelation presenting very similar attributes. With all these heresies, false prophesyings, or antichristian principles in one view, as described by these various pens, it is the business of the ecclesiastical historian to decide whether they were identical or different, and what they really were.

THE FIRST EPISTLE OF JOHN is variously supposed to have been written from Ephesus or from Patmos. It bears no *address*, but is generally supposed to have been sent in the first instance to some of the churches in the province of *Asia*, where John had laboured. According to Augustine, it was anciently known as John's Epistle to the *Parthians*, and was believed to have been sent to the Jewish Christians beyond the Euphrates. But this idea finds no favour with the learned of the present day. There is, in this composition, neither the opening inscription nor the concluding benediction usual in ancient letters; yet it has the tone of a letter in other respects.

ABSTRACT OF THE FIRST EPISTLE OF JOHN.

Ch. i. 1. (The introduction, which identifies the author with that of the fourth Gospel, has been spoken of on pp. 332, 333.) The Word of Life, as manifested from the beginning, and seen, heard and handled by himself, the writer attests to those whom he addresses, in order that they may have fellowship with him and his fellow-apostles, that fellowship uniting them all with God and with Jesus Christ. 5. His message is, in brief: that God is light; and those who are in fellowship with Him must not walk in darkness; but if they walk in the light, "the blood of Jesus Christ cleanseth them from all sin."

Ch. ii. 1. He writes these things to his "dear children"* to keep them from sinning. Yet if any one sin, the way is

* *τεκνία μου*, not *little* children, but *dear* children,—a phrase appropriate to the writer as aged, rather than to the readers as all literally young.

open to the mercy-seat of God since Christ's propitiation, and he is our Advocate (Paraclete or Comforter) also. 3. The valid proof of a knowledge of God is obedience to His commands. All profession, short of this, is vain. He who says he abides in God, must walk as Christ did.* 7. This is no new commandment in everlasting morality; yet, in another sense, it is the new commandment of the Christian dispensation, inasmuch as the darkness is passing away and the true light now shines;—the commandment, namely, to love one another. (See John xiii. 34.) 12. To his "dear children," whether themselves fathers, young men or children in age, the apostle emphatically writes: "Love not the world, neither the things that are in the world. If any man love the world, the love of the Father is not in him." 17. The world is passing fast away. "It is the last time," and accordingly there are many antichrists, who "went out from us, but are not of us." Christian believers, by their anointing from the Holy One, know all these things. 22. The false teacher is "he who denieth that Jesus is the Christ. He is the antichrist, who denieth the Father and the Son. Whoso denieth the Son, the same hath not the Father." 24. Let them hold what they have been taught from the first. He writes thus much "in reference to those who would lead them astray." But they ought not to need teaching, after their Christian anointing. If they but abide in God, they will have confidence at His appearing. 29. As God is righteous, every one who practises righteousness is His child.

Ch. iii. 1. What love, to be called God's children! The world knows them not, as it knew not Him. Who can tell what the children of God will be, when they shall become like Him and see Him as He is! Such a hope should indeed purify them, as Christ was pure. 4. All sin is defiance of the Divine law. Christ, sinless himself, was manifested in order to take away our sins; therefore he who abides in Christ will not sin; and he who sins cannot really have seen or known Christ. 7. Let there be no sophistication or delusion on this

* *He* and *him* in the English translation are often obscure. The Greek has two pronouns; αὐτὸς is the Deity, ἐκεῖνος is Jesus Christ, in this case plainly, and I think wherever they are contrasted in this Epistle.

matter of Christian morality: the righteous and justified man is he who does what is right, like Christ himself. He who commits sin is the child of the devil, not of God. The contrast is clear and decisive. 10. And brotherly love is one chief branch of Christian righteousness. 13. No wonder if the world hates the brethren; among themselves the stronger brotherly love should prevail;—love in deed, not in tongue. He who keeps the Divine commandments abideth in God, and God in Him; and has the pledge of the Holy Spirit.

Ch. iv. 1. Not every professor of spiritual powers is to be trusted; they must "try the spirits, to see whether they are of God; because many false prophets are gone out into the world." The test is this: "Every spirit that confesses that Jesus Christ is come in the flesh* is of God. And every spiritual pretender that confesses not that Jesus Christ is come in the flesh is not of God, but is the spirit of antichrist." It is moreover a worldly spirit, and the world listens to it. He that is of God listens to us. 7. Let us love one another; for that is indeed a part of the divine life which a Christian should lead. God is Love. This is shewn in the mission of Christ. The children of God are bound, therefore, to love one another as brethren. Though God is invisible, He dwells in those who love one another, and His love is completed in them. 14. "We have seen and do testify, that the Father sent the Son to be the Saviour of the world. Whosoever shall confess that Jesus is the Son of God, God dwelleth in him and he in God." When this love is completed in the disciple, he will have "confidence† in the day of judgment." Thorough love excludes fear. Let us love God who first loved us! And the love of our brethren is essential to the real love of God.

Ch. v. 1. Whoever believes that Jesus is the Christ, is born

* Is the emphasis on the words *is come*, or on *in the flesh?* Are the false prophets those who said another was yet to come, or those who said the Christ was indeed come, but that he was not defiled by contact with mortal flesh, and that the man Jesus was a mere phantasm, not a corporeal being? Or does his having come in the flesh mean his lowly and suffering state, which was a stumbling-block to Jewish ideas of the Messiah?

† *παῤῥησίαν*, free speech, free access to the mercy-seat; as in Heb. iii. 6, iv. 16, x. 19, 35; also in this Epistle, ii. 28, iii. 21, v. 14.

of God; and if he truly loves his heavenly Father, he cannot but love his Christian brethren and keep the divine commands, which are not indeed grievous. 4. The children of this divine adoption can overcome the hostile influences of the world by their faith. Who but the Christian can conquer the world? "Who but he that believeth Jesus to be the Son of God? This is he who came by water and blood" (his baptism and his cross, the opening and the concluding testimonies to his divine mission), "even Jesus Christ; not by the water only, but by the water and the blood; and there is the Spirit too that beareth testimony, for the Spirit is truth. For there are three that bear testimony, the Spirit and the Water and the Blood, and these three agree to that one purport."* While human testimony might be accepted, this testimony of God must be decisive. And the purport of the testimony is, "that God hath given to us eternal life, and this life is in his Son." 14. "And this is the confidence (free access) which we have towards Him, that if we ask anything according to His will, He heareth us." 16. A Christian may intercede for an offending brother whose offence is not unto death (not capital?);† but not otherwise. The true child of God sins not, but guards himself, and the wicked one touches him not. "We know that we are of God, while the whole world lies in wickedness. The Son of God has given us discernment to know the true God; and we are in Him that is true, through His Son Jesus Christ. This is the true God. This is life everlasting. Dear children, keep yourselves from idols. Amen." So this Epistle ends.

* I have given this passage in full, according to the true text, omitting certain words which stand in the Authorized Version, but which are universally rejected by scholars as a comparatively modern forgery, and which make the passage into sheer nonsense and confusion, by obtruding upon it an idea utterly foreign to its whole scope and purpose. The spurious text (1 John v. 7) is almost a solitary blot upon the honesty of New Testament copyists and editors. It is one of the very few false readings that affect, or seem to affect, Christian belief. Perhaps it is the only corruption of the kind that cannot have been accidental.

† A very difficult passage. Is the sin contemplated *deadly* in a spiritual sense, or *capital* in the eye of human law? Is the intercession to be made with God, or with the human tribunal? Who shall know what sin is deadly, in the former aspect? when he may intercede, and when he may not? The latter sense seems the easier.

THE SECOND EPISTLE OF JOHN is thus addressed: "The elder to the elect lady and her children, whom I love in the truth." Some critics would translate, "To the elect Kyria," or rather would not translate the word *Kyria* (lady), but keep it as a proper name. Some, again, will have it that the elect lady is one of the churches of Asia, and that her "elect sister," whose children salute her in the last verse, is a sister church. A very forced interpretation, in my opinion. The letter is full of the same thoughts and phrases as the longer one just analyzed.

ABSTRACT OF THE SECOND EPISTLE OF JOHN.

1. Salutation and benediction to an elect, or Christian, lady. 4. The elder rejoices to have found some of her children walking in truth according to the divine command. The command to love one another is no new command, but "what ye have heard from the beginning." 7. Many deceivers and antichrists are come into the world, "who confess not that Jesus Christ is come in the flesh." He bids his friends beware of forfeiting the position they have gained, and warns them not to receive any such false teacher into the house, nor bid him God-speed. 12. He means to come soon and speak face to face, instead of writing more with paper and ink. "The children of thine elect sister greet thee. Amen."

THE THIRD EPISTLE OF JOHN is addressed by "the elder to the well-beloved Gaius, whom I love in the truth." That this Gaius (or Caius, one of the commonest Roman names) was either Paul's host at Corinth (Rom. xvi. 23; 1 Cor. i. 14), or the Gaius of Macedonia, mentioned (Acts xix. 29) as being with him at Ephesus, or the Gaius of Derbe (in Acts xx. 4), is mere fancy. We know not who he was, or where he lived. Michaelis seems disposed to think he was the Corinthian Gaius, and that Diotrephes was one of the ambitious spirits of the Corinthian church. But there is no trace of John's having ever laboured at Corinth. The Epistle repeats the very phrases of that addressed to the lady. Surely the three were written nearly at the same time.

Abstract of the Third Epistle of John.

1. Salutation to Gaius. The elder prays for his prosperity and health, even as his soul prospers. Rejoices to hear of his Christian faithfulness and hospitality to some brethren and strangers who have borne witness of his charity before the church, and whom he again commends to Gaius's kindness to put forward on their journey. For they "went forth for *his* name's sake,* receiving nothing from the Gentiles." 9. The elder has written to the church; "but Diotrephes, who loveth to have the pre-eminence, receiveth us not." When he comes he will remember this man's doings. 11. "Beloved, follow not that which is evil, but that which is good. He that doeth good is of God; but he that doeth evil hath not seen God." 12. Demetrius (one of those who bear the letter) is well reported of, and the elder attests the truth of his good repute. 13. There is much more to write; but not now with paper and ink, as he trusts shortly to see Gaius and speak face to face. "Peace be to thee. The friends salute thee. Do thou salute the friends by name."

THE APOCALYPSE, or REVELATION.

This most remarkable and obscure book has never been fully recognized by the Christian church as a genuine work of the apostle John. We have seen (pp. 137—151) the uncertain and conflicting testimonies of the early Fathers respecting it. Luther, in his original preface to

* ὑπὲρ τοῦ ὀνόματος, in behalf of *the* name. How truly expressive of genuine apostolic thought and feeling!

his German translation, declared that he held the book to be neither apostolical nor prophetical,—a judgment not reversed by him in his later editions, though he expressed himself less roughly on the subject. Michaelis (Vol. IV. p. 457) calls it "the most difficult and the most doubtful book in the whole New Testament;" and, after a laboured inquiry into its nature and contents, confesses that his "belief in the divine authority of the Apocalypse has received no more confirmation than it had before."

It seems quite impossible that any one who is able to read this book in the original, should for a moment ascribe it to the writer of John's Gospel and three Epistles. The acknowledged writings of John are in easy, neat and elegant Greek, though of the Hebraistic kind; whereas the style of the Revelation is rude and ungrammatical beyond anything in any other part of the New Testament. The concords of number, gender and case are strangely neglected; while the very sentences which display this Goth-like carelessness or ignorance of the language, are often fluent and eloquent in their order of thought. The writer of this book could not have risen to the literary style of the fourth Gospel; nor could the writer of that Gospel have fallen to the literary standard of the Revelation. The theory which ascribes the Revelation to the extreme old age of the apostle, would not by any means account for the difference.

But then the book itself does not claim to have been written by John the apostle. Its author merely calls himself a *servant* of Jesus Christ, where we might naturally have expected the son of Zebedee to have written *apostle*, or more likely *disciple whom he loved*. The common title of the book calls him "Saint John the *Divine*" (or the Theologian). According to Eusebius, quoting Papias, there was, besides the apostle John, a presbyter at Ephesus of the same name; and he seems to think the latter was the person "who saw the Apocalypse." At any rate, it cannot have been the apostle John who wrote it. There is nothing more palpably certain in literary criticism than this decision.

As to the interpretation of the book, the chief part of the difficulty is practically removed when we have decided that it is not the work of an apostle. For it would be with great reluctance that we could admit the apostle John to have written a book of minute anticipations relative to the coming fate of the church, which has proved to be founded on an utter mistake, however natural that mistake might, to a certain extent, be,* during the unfulfilled period of Christ's prophecy of the "end of the age." And this very reluctance, there can be no doubt, has been (in the minds of those who persist in ascribing the book to the apostle John), the origin of a number of most fanciful and violent interpretations, in defiance of the most natural and obvious sense of the words, which we now plainly see, by the events of history, to have implied an erroneous expectation.

If we read the book with a view simply to ascertain what the writer *meant and expected*, without asking ourselves at each step how and when it was, or will be, fulfilled, and thinking its fulfilment divinely certain, the conviction is irresistible that he speaks throughout of *things immediately impending*; things "*shortly to come to pass*," as he himself says, and in the human sense of *shortly*, not in that theological sense (so inappropriate here, while so reverent in its proper place) which declares that with God "a thousand years are as a single day."

* We have seen this mistake implied, in some degree, in Paul's earliest Epistles, but vanishing from his later ones. Besides these instances, it occurs chiefly in the doubtful Epistles ascribed to Peter and Jude. In the Apocalypse it grows to full luxuriance.

The supposed necessity of shewing that every vision has been fulfilled, or still remains to be fulfilled, has led learned and good men to strain their ingenuity to the utmost, and to propound the most widely varying fulfilments as having happened, in whole or in part, in the history of the world hitherto; while, on every new excitement of the religious or political atmosphere in our own day, we find fresh attempts made, with equal rashness, to read the coming future by the dim light of the yet unfulfilled visions of the Apocalypse.

"It is astonishing to us (says a recent American writer) that any intelligent person can peruse the Apocalypse and still suppose that it is occupied with remote events, events to transpire successively in distant ages and various lands. Immediateness, imminency, hazardous urgency, swiftness, alarms, —are written all over the book. A suspense, frightfully thrilling, fills it, as if the world were holding its breath in view of the universal crash that was coming with lightning velocity. Four words compose the key to the Apocalypse,— Rescue, Reward, Overthrow, Vengeance. The followers of Christ are now persecuted and slain by the tyrannical rulers of the earth. Let them be of good cheer; they shall speedily be delivered. Their tyrants shall be trampled down in 'blood flowing up to the horse-bridles,' and they shall reign in glory. 'Here is the faith and patience of the saints,' trusting that, if 'true unto death, they shall have a crown of life,' and 'shall not be hurt of the second death,' but shall soon rejoice over the triumphant establishment of the Messiah's kingdom, and the condign punishment of his enemies who are now 'making themselves drunk with the blood of the martyrs of Jesus.'" (*Christian Examiner*, Boston, July, 1854, p. 14.)

Even those who persist in the long-distant application, are forced to admit the vivid truth of the descriptions in a more immediate point of view. Thus Mr. Maurice, while cautiously reserving the customary interpretation, shews clearly the more immediate force of the descriptions. Speaking of ch. xviii., he says:

"You will find how many aspects of evil are disclosed to us there—sensual, commercial, spiritual. It reads, certainly, like a picture of the breaking up of a whole complicated system of society, that had been sustaining itself upon an unrighteous, anarchical, selfish, anti-christian principle. It is a prophecy, I doubt not,—a prophecy of which we shall find many fulfilments, and may yet find more perfect fulfilments; but it is also a most accurate history of that overthrow of all social order which affected the city of Rome itself, the great mercantile cities which Rome had adopted into its huge empire, and the city which was so holy in its own eyes, and which is so horrible in ours, whereof Rome was the destined scourge and destroyer."—(Lectures on Eccl. Hist. of 1st and 2nd Centuries, p. 159.)

If we place ourselves, in imagination, among the Christians of that generation which had been taught to expect in their own day the coming of Christ and the end of the age, and enter with any tolerable degree of imagination and sympathy into their wondering expectation as the time seemed to be drawing near, we may understand how the author of this book might, in the spirit of the old Jewish prophets, form the anticipations and see the visions here recorded. If we suppose the dreadful Jewish war to have actually begun, perhaps the siege of Jerusalem even to be going on, the crisis of the Jewish state evidently at hand, and the persecution of the Christians (seldom remitted from the time of Nero to that of Vespasian) now warranting their earnest supplication, How long, O Lord!—we may understand what the visions of the Apocalypse really signified in the mind that conceived them, and to those who heard or read them. Judging it by this criterion, we are not required to find the historical fulfilment of each or any part of the book; but simply to appreciate the expectations which it expresses. We have not now to ascribe the writer's proved mistakes to any apostolical representative of the Gospel; we have not to wonder at finding him more Jew than Christian in idea; and yet more relieved must we feel in not having to charge the vengeful spirit of many parts of the book upon John or any other apostle. Those vengeful passages might, indeed, if further argument were needed, satisfy us that the book could not have been written by the "Apostle of Love;" and to no other apostolic authorship has it ever been ascribed.

Let us proceed, then, to inquire what the unknown writer really says; and let us accept it as a vivid picture of what many believed and hoped, on the eve of the destruction of Jerusalem and of the coming of the Son of Man into his kingdom. Internal evidence is very strong for placing the date during the siege of Jerusalem.

Abstract of the Apocalypse.

Ch. i. 1. The book intitles itself: "A revelation of Jesus Christ, which God gave unto him, to shew unto his servants things which must shortly come to pass; and He sent and signified it by His angel* unto his servant John;† who hath declared this word of God and the testimony of Jesus Christ, according as he saw." Blessed they who read, hear and obey:—the time is at hand! 4. "John, to the seven churches in Asia," wishes grace from the Eternal God and the seven spirits before His throne, and from Jesus Christ, the faithful witness, the first-born from the dead, and the ruler of the kings of the earth. Everlasting glory to him for our redemption! Amen.

* Most easily understood to be Jesus Christ; but some suppose another intermediate angel, or messenger, between Jesus Christ and John, who in that case personates Jesus and speaks in his name continually.

† "His servant John;" it is not said, "his apostle," nor "that disciple whom he loved."

7. "Lo, he cometh in the clouds, and every eye shall see him, even they that pierced him, and all the kindreds of the earth shall wail because of him. Even so. Amen. I am Alpha and Omega (the beginning and the ending), saith the Lord God, who is and was and is to be,—the Almighty."

9. John proceeds to state that he, their brother in Christian hopes and trials, was in the island of Patmos on account of his Christian profession; and being in the spirit on the Lord's-day,* he heard a trumpet-like voice commissioning him to write in a book, and send to each of certain seven churches of the province of Asia the several messages following. 12. Looking round, he saw, in the midst of seven golden candlesticks, a majestic and dazzling vision of Christ, with seven stars in his right hand. He falls down as if dead before this celestial personage, who raises him and bids him not fear, saying, "I am the first and the last and the living, living for ever though I was dead, and possessing the keys of death and Hades." The seven candlesticks allegorically mean the churches to which he is to write, and the seven stars the angels† of those churches.

Ch. ii. 1. To the angel of the church at *Ephesus* he is to write in praise of his faithful zeal in opposing false apostles, and his patient endurance; reminding him, however, that he has relaxed from his earlier generosity and kindness,‡ and urging him to resume it, lest his candlestick be removed. He is to be especially commended for his antipathy to the Nicolai-

* "The Lord's-day" is found nowhere else in the New Testament for "the first day of the week," but is common in the Epistles of Ignatius. This seems to date the Apocalypse later than the Acts of the Apostles, at any rate, or to refer it to a hitherto unknown pen. We have the same word, *κυριακὸς*, once in Paul's first Epistle to the Corinthians (xi. 20) for the Lord's Supper, *κυριακὸν δεῖπνον*.

† Plainly the superintendents, presbyters or bishops, of the churches are thus called. Does this help to explain an obscure passage in Paul's first letter to the Corinthians (xi. 10), where it is said, "A woman ought to have a veil (the symbol of subjection) on her head, because of the angels"?

‡ So Grotius, and after him Rosenmüller, explain his "first love," *τὴν ἀγάπην σου τὴν πρώτην*. Many suppose Timothy to be the angel at Ephesus.

tans.* He that conquereth shall eat of the tree of life in God's paradise.

8. The message to the angel of the church at *Smyrna* praises their endurance of poverty and reproach at the hands of the Jews (that synagogue of Satan !). Some of them will suffer imprisonment. Let them be faithful even unto death. The conqueror shall not suffer harm from the second death.

12. The angel of *Pergamus* has been faithful to the name of Christ, though the throne of Satan is near his dwelling. But there are among that church some followers of Balaam. As that false prophet led the Israelites to idolatry and fornication, so, among the Pergamene Christians, there were some who adopted the hateful Nicolaitan † practices. The conqueror shall eat of the stored-up manna, and receive a white stone inscribed with a new name.

18. The church at *Thyatira* is commended, and its later works are pronounced better than its first. But there is a false prophetess, a Jezebel, seducing the servants of Christ into the same practices as the Balaamite prophets at Pergamus and Ephesus. She and her votaries shall be smitten with illness. Let those who have hitherto escaped this corruption persevere; and the conqueror shall rule over the nations and have the brightness of the morning star.

Ch. iii. 1. To the angel of the church of *Sardis* the message is one of deep reproof. If they do not forthwith repent, the judge will come upon them unawares. Yet there are a few names, even in Sardis, of those who have not defiled their garments, and who shall walk with Christ in white.

7. To the angel of *Philadelphia* it is written, that the opposing synagogue of Satan (who wrongly call themselves Jews !) shall come and fall at his feet, and this church shall be kept

* See afterwards at vers. 14, 15.

† It was observed by Wetstein, that *Balaam* in Hebrew means etymologically the same as *Nicolaus* in Greek, namely, *subduer of the people.* Nicolaitans may therefore mean Balaamites, such as are spoken of in 2 Pet. ii. 15, and Jude 11. Whether a Gnostic *sect* was known by that name thus early, let the learned decide. It is quite a gratuitous supposition to brand Nicolas the deacon (Acts vi. 5) with the disgrace of having originated an immoral sect.

safe in the coming trial; after which the conqueror shall become a pillar in the temple of God, inscribed with the names of God and of the New Jerusalem, and with the new name of Jesus.

14. The angel of the *Laodicean* church is reproached for indifference, worldliness and carelessness; he is neither hot nor cold, but lukewarm; says he is rich, and does not know that he is wretched and miserable and poor and blind and naked. The Lord rebukes and chastens those whom he loves. Let these repent. He knocks at the door, and will come in to those who open for him. The conqueror shall sit with him on his throne.

Ch. iv. 1. A second vision shews the elder "a door opened in heaven." The same voice that he had heard before says: "Come up hither, and I will shew thee what must come to pass after these things." Immediately he is "in the spirit," and sees the divine throne, much in the manner of Isaiah, Jeremiah and Ezekiel's visions. It is encompassed with twenty-four other thrones, on which the twenty-four elders* sit, clothed in white, with golden crowns on their heads. Seven lamps represent the seven administrative spirits of God. Four living creatures "full of eyes," and each having six wings, with the faces respectively of a lion, a calf, a man and an eagle,† adore before the throne continually.

Ch. v. 1. A book sealed with seven seals is produced, and proclamation is made, demanding who is worthy to open the book. 6. None could do it, except a little lamb that stood before the throne as if it had been slaughtered. It had seven horns and seven eyes, representing "the seven spirits of God sent forth into all the earth." It took the book from the right hand of Him upon the throne; and then the four creatures and the twenty-four elders sang blessings upon the name of the Lamb; myriads of angels responded; and all creation joined in praise of Him upon the throne and of the Lamb.

* Representing, apparently, the twenty-four courses of the Jewish priests (see 1 Chron. xxiv. 1—18), and perhaps also, as some think, the same number of elders in the Christian church at Jerusalem.

† Afterwards taken as symbols of the four evangelists. See p. 248.

Ch. vi. 1. The opening of the seven seals then takes place. On the *first* being broken, there comes forth a rider on a white horse, conquering and to conquer (doubtless the emblem of Christianity, if not of Christ personally).

3. On the *second* seal being broken, a rider on a bay horse comes forth, commissioned to take peace from the earth:—the messenger of War.

5. The *third* seal being broken, a rider appears on a black horse, representing Famine.

7. The *fourth* being opened, a pale horse, with a rider named Death, appears; and the grave goes with him. He is empowered to kill one-fourth of the earth's population.

9. On the opening of the *fifth* seal, the souls of Christian martyrs are seen under the altar, crying for vengeance. White robes are given to them, and they are told to rest awhile, till their number should be filled up by those who were still to be slain.

12. The Lamb opens the *sixth* seal, and there is a mighty shaking of sun, moon and stars; the heaven shrivels up as a roll of parchment; hills and islands are moved; men of all grades hide themselves in dens and mountains, and say to the hills and rocks, Fall on us!

Ch. vii. 1. The opening of the *seventh* seal is delayed. Four angels stand at the four corners of the earth restraining the four winds. Another angel hastens from the east with a warrant from the living God, crying out to the four not to hurt earth or sea till the servants of God shall have been sealed on their foreheads. 4. A hundred and forty-four thousand are so sealed, namely, twelve thousand of each tribe.* 9. A vast multitude from all nations, clothed in white, with palm branches in their hands, praise God and the Lamb. They are coming out of that great affliction, and are to be in the temple of God for ever.

Ch. viii. 1. The *seventh* seal is opened, amid silence in heaven

* In the twelve tribes here enumerated, Dan is omitted, Joseph (Ephraim) and Manasseh being both of them counted, and also Levi, who was omitted in the allotment of landed territory by Joshua. The number twelve seems inviolable, though the claims of Dan are not.

for half-an-hour. The seven angels have their trumpets given them. Another angel comes and stands by the altar with a golden censer, in which he offers much incense, that incense being "the prayers of the saints." Then he fills the censer with fire from the altar, and throws it upon the earth; and amid thunder, lightning and earthquake, the seven angels prepare to sound their trumpets.

7. The *first angel sounds* his trumpet; hail and fire destroy a third of the trees and all the grass.

8. The *second angel sounds;* and a third of the living creatures of the sea die, and a third of the vessels upon it are destroyed.

10. The *third angel sounds* his trumpet; and a third part of the water becomes wormwood, and many die from the bitterness of the waters.

12. The *fourth angel sounds;* and the third of the sun, moon and stars is smitten; whereupon a compassionate angel is heard lamenting for what still impends.

Ch. ix. 1. The *fifth angel sounds;* and a star falls from heaven to earth. The angel unlocks the bottomless pit; and amid the smoke, locusts come out to torment those who had not the seal of God on their foreheads. For five months these awful locusts harass their victims. They have a king over them, the angel of the bottomless pit, whose Hebrew name is *Abaddon*, and Greek *Apollyon* (Destroyer). This first woe is to be followed by two more.

13. The *sixth angel sounds* his trumpet; whereupon a voice from the horns of the golden altar commands him to "loose the four angels which are bound at the great river Euphrates."* They come forth commissioned for an hour, a day, a month and a year, to slay a third part of mankind. Their army is two

* The four that were temporarily restrained, ch. vii. 2. These plainly denote the Roman power, gathering its legions for the subjugation of Jerusalem and Judea. Some interpreters find four specific Roman commanders in these four angels. But this is not necessary. They are the angels of the four winds, which, as soon as they are loosed, will blow from all quarters upon the devoted land. For the beginning of the Roman preparations, see Tacitus, Hist. v. 1; and Josephus, Wars, iii. 4, § 2; also Milman's Hist. of the Jews, Vol. II. Book xiv., &c.

hundred millions. They do their commission; but the rest of mankind do not repent of their idolatry and wickedness. Ch. x. 1. Another mighty angel then descends, with a little book open in his hand; and setting his right foot upon the sea and his left upon the land, swears that there shall be no longer delay, but that so soon as the seventh angel shall sound his trumpet, "the mystery of God shall be finished, according to His glad-tidings to His prophets." 8. John receives from the angel the little open book, which he is directed to eat. He does so, and finds it sweet to the taste, but bitter afterwards. 11. The angel tells him he must prophesy further respecting many peoples and nations and tongues and kings. Ch. xi. 1. He gives him a measuring-rod, and bids him measure the temple, exclusive of the outer court, which is given to the Gentiles, who will tread the holy city under foot forty-two months.* Two witnesses meanwhile shall prophesy 1260 days in sackcloth: they are "the two olive-trees and the two candlesticks standing before the God of the earth."† But when they have finished their testimony, the beast from the bottomless pit will kill them, and their bodies will be exposed in the city of Jerusalem, "spiritually called Sodom and Egypt, where also our Lord was crucified." The Gentiles will exult over their death; but after three days and a half they will rise to life again, and ascend to heaven in a cloud; a great earthquake will destroy one-tenth of the city and 7000 men; and the survivors alarmed will give glory to God. This is the second woe; the third is close at hand.

15. The *seventh angel sounds;* and great voices in heaven proclaim that "the kingdoms of the world are become the

* So ch. xiii. 5; also in xii. 6, where 1260 days are equal to 3½ years of 360 days. It seems the reproduction of Daniel's "time and times and half time." See Vol. I. pp. 518 and 523. Daniel's very phrase is used in xii. 14, "a time and times and half a time."

† This imagery is plainly derived from Zech. iv. 3, 11, 14, where the two olive-trees are the king and priest of the restored Jewish people. Here they still symbolise the Jewish dispensation, though less distinctly. Some, however, take them to be the two Jewish high-priests, Ananus and Joshua (Josephus, Wars, iv. 5, § 2); some, less wisely, have taken them to be the two apostles and martyrs, James.

kingdoms of our Lord and of His Christ, and He shall reign for ever and ever." The twenty-four elders fall on their faces and thank God that He has taken to Him His great power, and that the time is come for judging the dead and recompensing His saints. The temple of God in heaven is laid open to view.

Ch. xii. 1. Another scene now opens. A woman, clothed with the sun, having the moon at her feet and twelve stars on her head, seems to represent Religion, or the Gospel, or the Church. A huge dragon is her antagonist. She brings forth a son, destined to "tend the Gentiles with an iron crook." The child is carried away to the throne of God; the woman retreats to the wilderness for 1260 days. 7. There is war in heaven between Michael and his angels and this dragon, who is the Devil and Satan. The latter and his angels are thrown down to the earth. Heaven rejoices; but woe for the inhabitants of the earth and sea, against whom the Devil now rages, conscious that his time is coming to an end. He pursues the woman, to whom wings are given to escape from him. He pours a torrent of water from his mouth to carry her away; but the earth drinks it up in her rescue. The dragon then "makes war upon the rest of her offspring who keep God's commands and have the testimony of Jesus Christ."

Ch. xiii. 1. The narrator is next standing on the sea-shore (in Patmos, we suppose), when he sees a wild beast coming up out of the sea, with seven heads and ten horns, a diadem on each horn, and a name of blasphemy upon each head. This wild beast is mixed up of leopard, bear and lion; and the dragon gives him his own power and throne and authority.* 3. One of his heads seems to receive a deadly wound,† but it is healed;

* The persecuting heathenism of Rome is evidently represented. The time denoted is variously guessed, from the persecuting part of Nero's reign to the time of Vespasian. The Neronian persecution began A.D. 64; the monster died in June, 68; Galba, Otho and Vitellius followed in quick succession, and Vespasian became emperor in 69.

† Some make this to be the death of Nero; others, the destruction of the Capitol by fire in the time of Vitellius; which latter event, Tacitus tells

and the beast, aided by the dragon, receives new homage every where. He is enabled to make war on the saints and overcome them, and has power, for forty-two months, over all but those whose names are in the Lamb's book of life. 10. But retribution shall come. Let the saints have patience! 11. Another beast comes up out of the earth, with two horns like a lamb, but with speech like a dragon. He wields the authority of the first beast,* performs wonders, and seduces men to the worship of the principal beast, putting a name or number on their right hands or foreheads, without which no one may buy and sell. This mysterious number seems to be 666.†

Ch. xiv. 1. The next vision, amid the sound of heavenly music, shews the Lamb standing on Mount Zion, with the 144,000 redeemed Israelites before mentioned (in vii. 4). They are "the first fruits to God and the Lamb," pure from all taint of idolatrous pollution. 6. Another angel flies forth with the Gospel, to offer it with all urgency to every nation, declaring that the hour of divine judgment is come. 8. Another angel follows, crying, "Babylon is fallen, is fallen" (evidently meaning, Roman paganism). 9. A third angel follows, proclaiming everlasting divine wrath against all who worship the beast and receive his mark. Let the saints be patient! 13. A voice from heaven proclaims, Blessed are the dead which die in the

us, caused the belief to gain ground in foreign nations that the end of the empire was at hand: "Nihil æque quam incendium Capitolii, ut finem imperio adesse crederent, impulerat." (Hist. iv. 54.)

* Vespasian's son and lieutenant Titus, some say. Others think Simon Magus, or Apollonius of Tyana, or the professors of magical arts in general, called the false prophet in xvi. 13.

† A various reading, known to Irenæus but disapproved by him, gives 616. Taken as 666, this enigma (for as such it is plainly designed) has exercised the ingenuity of interpreters in all ages. It is generally agreed that the name thus veiled in the number must be one which, if its letters be taken at their values as Greek numerals, will sum up to 666. The most ancient interpretations made the word to be *Latinus*, or else *Titan*. Grotius will have it *Ulpius*, the name of Trajan. Very strong Protestants have found the key in *Benedictus* (the ninth Pope of that name). Le Clerc too ingeniously suggested *Δίος εἰμι ἢ Ἥρας*, *I am Jove's or Juno's*, which seems like a combination of two alternative marks of ownership, instead of one. As curiosities, I set all these arithmetical solutions down, directing the

Lord henceforth! 14. Then a Son of Man appears upon a white cloud, with a sickle in his hand; and another angel, from the temple, bids him reap the ripe harvest of the earth. A third angel from the temple, armed with a sickle, is ordered by a fourth from the altar (who has power over fire) to gather the earth's vintage and cast it into the great wine-press of the wrath of God. All this is done accordingly.

Ch. xv. 1. Another vision shews seven angels having the last seven plagues to complete the wrath of God. Those who have successfully resisted the beast and his image and his mark, are singing the songs of Moses and of the Lamb to the One Almighty. The seven angels are seen coming out of the temple. One of the four living creatures gives them each a golden phial full of the wrath of the ever-living God. Ch. xvi. 1. A voice from the temple bids them go and pour their phials out upon the earth. The *first phial* produces ulcers upon those who worship the image of the beast. The *second* is poured upon the

attention of the scholar to an inner source of doubt arising from the two Greek forms of the letter S having different arithmetical values.

The number of the beast is χξς′ (χ=600, ξ=60, ς=6).

Latinus λατεινος	Titan τειταν	Ulpius ουλπιος	Benedictus βενεδικτος	διος ειμι η ηρας
λ = 30	τ = 300	ο = 70	β = 2	δ = 4
α 1	ε 5	υ 400	ε 5	ι 10
τ 300	ι 10	λ 30	ν 50	ο 70
ε 5	τ 300	π 80	ε 5	σ 200
ι 10	α 1	ι 10	δ 4	ε 5
ν 50	ν 50	ο 70	ι 10	ι 10
ο 70	666	ς 6	κ 20	μ 40
σ 200		666	τ 300	ι 10
666			ο 70	η 8
			σ 200	η 8
			666	ρ 100
				α 1
				σ 200
				666

One might feel tempted to seek the name of Vespasian or of Titus in this mystical number, if the above instances did not discourage further ingenuity. If we must choose an interpretation, however, we can hardly be wrong, as to the implied facts at any rate, in acquiescing in the old solution, *Latinus*. If we might adopt the reading of some MSS., χις, we could perhaps get *Titus* from it, thus: τιτς = 300+10+300+6=616.

sea and turns it into blood, destroying all life. The *third* is poured upon the rivers and springs, and they become blood. Then (5) the angel of the waters acknowledges the justice of this retribution upon those who had shed the blood of the saints; and an angel from the altar responds. The *fourth phial* is then poured upon the sun, causing it to scorch men; and they blaspheme instead of repenting. The *fifth phial* is poured upon the beast's throne and darkens his kingdom; and blaspheming increases. The *sixth* is poured upon the river Euphrates, drying it up so that the kings from the east can pass over. 13. Three unclean spirits, like frogs, come out of the mouths of the dragon, the beast and the false prophet,* and go to all the kings of the whole world to summon them for one final and desperate battle at *Armageddon* (mount of assembling). 17. Then the *seventh angel pours his phial* into the air, and Heaven shouts, It is done! Amid awful thunder, lightning, earthquake and hail, the great city breaks into three parts, and the other Gentile cities fall, and the great Babylon is remembered in wrath. But men blaspheme still.

Ch. xvii. 1. One of the seven angels calls the seer in spirit into the wilderness, and shews him this judgment under another emblem,—that of a woman sitting upon a scarlet beast with seven heads and ten horns, whose idolatrous abominations and persecution of the saints are described. Upon her head is the mysterious (or enigmatical) inscription, "Babylon the Great," &c. 8. The beast upon which she sits "was, but is not, and will appear again;" it is "about to ascend out of the bottomless deep and go to perdition." 9. The enigma is then expounded as follows: "The seven heads are seven mountains, on which the woman sits" (the seven hills of Rome). "They are also seven kings, of whom five have fallen, and one is, and the other is not yet come; and when he cometh he must continue but a short space. And the beast that was and is not is himself both an eighth and one of the seven, and is going to destruction."† 12. The ten horns are ten future

* The "other beast" of xiii. 11, lamb in appearance and dragon in speech.

† These are plainly Roman emperors; and one might think it an easy matter to count them up to eight, and so decide the very time when these

kings,* of transient power, to be derived from the beast, and used in his service in warring against the Lamb. The Lamb will overcome them, and they will then turn their power against the woman, Babylon.

Ch. xviii. 1. A powerful and glorious angel now proclaims, "Babylon the Great is fallen, is fallen!" 4. Another voice calls upon the people of God to come out of her, lest they partake her sins and punishment. In language recalling to mind that of the old Jewish prophets against the literal Babylon and Tyre and other doomed heathen cities, this voice denounces her and makes the heathen earth mourn for her, while heaven and apostles and prophets rejoice over her; and a mighty angel dashes a millstone into the sea, as an emblem of the utter destruction and oblivion that shall befal her. So shall the blood of the saints be avenged! Ch. xix. 1. All heaven praises God for this execution of vengeance. 4. The

curious visions were written. But the modes of reckoning vary; some proposing to include Julius Cæsar, while others begin with Augustus; and some counting, while others omit, the short reigns of Galba, Otho and Vitellius, which were scarcely heard of and probably never recognized in the remoter provinces. Let us put them down, however, and see what can be done. The emperors are, *Augustus*, B.C. 31; *Tiberius*, A.D. 14; *Caligula*, 37; *Claudius*, 41; *Nero*, 54; [Galba, June, 68; Otho, January, 69; Vitellius, April, 69;] *Vespasian*, July, 69; *Titus*, 79; *Domitian*, 81. By this list, the "five that have fallen" would end with Nero; the sixth, "which is" (omitting the three in parenthesis), would be Vespasian; the seventh, "who is not yet come," would be his son and lieutenant Titus; and the eighth, so oddly, yet appropriately, described as one "that was, but is not, and is going to destruction," would be his other son, Domitian, who, on Vespasian being proclaimed emperor by his troops in the East, was proclaimed Cæsar at Rome, and held the government of the city till his father's arrival, but was never afterwards, during Vespasian's lifetime, permitted to disgrace any public office whatever. This interpretation, which seems the most obvious, would date the book before us in the reign of Vespasian, when the siege of Jerusalem is impending, if it has not actually begun. (See Grotius on the passage.)

* *Ten* is probably to be taken as an indefinite or *round* number. And, on the view here taken of this curious book, we do not seek for a definite fulfilment of its predictions, but only endeavour to identify its historical facts and allusions. Commentators have found great difficulty in making out that the Roman empire was broken up into ten kingdoms, neither more nor fewer.

four-and-twenty elders and the four living creatures worship and praise God for it. 5. Heavenly voices proclaim the approaching marriage of the Lamb. His bride is ready, clothed in the righteous deeds of the saints. 10. The seer falls down and would have done homage to the angel that shewed him these things; but the angel forbade, saying, "I am thy fellow-servant and of thy brethren: worship God."

11. Heaven opens again, and the rider upon a white horse appears, as in ch. vi. His name is "Faithful and True," "The Word of God," "King of Kings and Lord of Lords." 17. An angel, standing in the sun, invites the birds of prey to banquet on the enemies of God. 19. The beast and the kings of the earth gather their armies together against the rider upon the white horse; the beast and the false prophet are seized and cast into the lake of burning brimstone; and the rider slays the rest with his sword which issues from his mouth, and the birds banquet on their carcases. Ch. xx. 1. An angel descends from heaven with the key of the bottomless pit and a chain, and binds the dragon, that old serpent, the Devil and Satan, and casts him into the pit for a thousand years.

4. Thrones are set out, and those who sit upon them are deputed to pass judgment. The souls of martyrs and of all who had refused to worship the beast and his image come to life, to reign with Christ the thousand years. This is the first resurrection. Happy he who shares in it! The second death will have no power over such. The rest of the dead are not to come to life till after the thousand years. 8. At that period Satan will be set loose again, and will seduce the nations, Gog and Magog* among the rest, to attack the camp of the saints and the beloved city; but they are destroyed by fire from heaven, and the Devil, their seducer, is finally cast into the fiery lake, to join the beast and the false prophet in torment for ever and ever. 11. Then all the dead are judged according to their works. Death and the grave are thrown into the lake of fire, with all who are not written in the book of life. This is the second death.

---

* See Ezekiel xxxviii. xxxix.; and Vol. I. p. 488.

Ch. xxi. 1. A more minute vision of the Millennium is now presented. Earth and heaven pass away, and a new earth and heaven arise. The New Jerusalem descends from heaven, and God will dwell with mankind in it. He who sits on the throne proclaims the blessedness of every one that conquereth, and devotes all the wicked to the "second death." 9. One of the seven angels of punishment carries the seer away in the spirit to a high mountain, where he sees the New Jerusalem, "the Lamb's wife," as it descends from heaven. A gorgeous description of it follows. Its extent, on measurement by the angel, proves to be 12,000 furlongs (about 1380 miles) square. 12. It has twelve gates, denoting the tribes of Israel; and its walls have twelve foundations (all of precious stones), denoting the twelve apostles of Christ. 22. There is no temple in this holy city, "for the Lord God Almighty and the Lamb are the temple of it;" nor are sun and moon needed to light it. 24. The nations shall walk in its light, and the kings of the earth shall bring glory and honour to it. Nothing that defiles shall enter it. Ch. xxii. 1. A pure river of living water, proceeding from the throne of God and the Lamb, flows along its streets; and between the street and the river, at intervals,* the tree of life grows, bearing fruit every month, and healing the nations by its leaves. 3. There the servants of God, with His name upon their foreheads, shall worship Him and behold His face, and reign for ever and ever.

6. The angel (Jesus apparently) asserts the truth of these visions, and their speedy fulfilment: "Behold, I come quickly; blessed is he that keepeth the sayings of the prophecy of this book." 8. John falls down at the angel's feet to do him homage (as once before), and is, as before, directed to worship God.

10. He must not seal up this prophecy, for the time is at hand. He that is unjust will now remain so, and he that is righteous will be righteous still. "Behold, I come quickly" (the angel pursues), "and my reward is with me, to give every man according as his work shall be. I am Alpha and Omega, the beginning and the end, the first and the last."

* *ἐντεῦθεν καὶ ἐντεῦθεν*, apparently for *ἔνθα καὶ ἔνθα*.

"Blessed they who do his commandments," the seer responds.

16. The angel resumes: "I, Jesus, have sent mine angel" (my messenger, John) "to testify unto you these things in the churches. I am the root and offspring of David and the bright morning star. And the spirit and the bride say, Come! And let him that heareth say, Come! And let him that is athirst come. And whosoever will, let him take the water of life freely." 18. Imprecations are uttered by the seer against any who should add to, or take from, the words of this prophecy; and the book concludes with the often-repeated intimation that its fulfilment is immediately at hand:

"He which testifieth these things saith, Surely I come quickly. Amen. Even so, come, Lord Jesus!

"The grace of our Lord Jesus Christ be with you all. Amen."

Postscript to First Edition.

To my Children.—As this book began with expressing my obligations to the wise and good man whose instructions, long years ago, chiefly fitted me to write it; I now end it with a few words to you, my dear children, who, I hope, are likely in due time, to be among its most careful readers. When I was little older than you now are, and was reading the Bible very diligently through, I sadly wanted just such a book; and that is the reason why I have written this for the use of those who are now young. That it may help you, and many other young persons, to understand the Scriptures, and teach you to value them, is the heartfelt prayer of

Your affectionate Father.

Wakefield, April 2, 1855.

INDEX OF SCRIPTURE PASSAGES

EXPLAINED OR ILLUSTRATED.

*** This Index does not include those passages which are noticed in the regular order of the Abstracts given of the books of Scripture. The order of the volumes themselves will be a sufficient key for finding all such passages.

i. and ii. refer to the volumes; the Arabic numerals to the pages; and n means note.

ALPHABETICAL INDEX

OF

SUBJECT MATTERS AND AUTHORS.

*** This Index is intended to aid in finding such matters as do not appear at once in the Tables of Contents prefixed to each volume; which Tables, however, being very full, will generally guide to the information specifically belonging to each of the books of Scripture in its place.

i. and ii. refer to the volumes; the Arabic numerals to the pages; and n means note.

CPSIA information can be obtained
at www.ICGtesting.com
Printed in the USA
LVHW110931160522
718424LV00013B/56

9 783375 002794